ROBERT LUDLUM'S EXPLOSIVE NEW BESTSELLER
"SEEMS TO LEAP RIGHT OUT OF THE HEADLINES!"

"Ludlum's premise is that J. Edgar Hoover didn't die a
natural death but was skillfully done in by a group of
high-minded and high-placed intellectuals calling themselves Inver Brass, who see a monstrous threat to the
country in the Number One G-Man's unethical use of his
scandal-ridden private files . . . THE CHANCELLOR MANU-
SCRIPT exerts a riveting appeal, as it seems to justify
our worst nightmares of what really goes on in the so-
called Intelligence Community in Washington."
—The New York Times Book Review

"A roaring ride on a roller coaster of suspense . . . Make
no mistake about it: Ludlum does this sort of thing better than anyone."
—Pittsburgh Press

"His most engrossing tale to date . . . Pure, adrenaline-
raising escapism."
—King Features

THE CHANCELLOR MANUSCRIPT
by
Robert Ludlum

Author of **The Scarlatti Inheritance** and
The Osterman Weekend

THE
CHANCELLOR
MANUSCRIPT

Robert Ludlum

BANTAM BOOKS · TORONTO · NEW YORK · LONDON

THE CHANCELLOR MANUSCRIPT
*A Bantam Book / published by arrangement with
The Dial Press*

PRINTING HISTORY
Dial edition published March 1977
2nd printing .... March 1977   3rd printing .... April 1977
                 4th printing .... May 1977
Literary Guild edition published May 1977
Bantam edition / February 1978
2nd printing .... February 1978   5th printing .... April 1978
3rd printing .... February 1978   6th printing ...... January 1979
4th printing .... February 1978   7th printing ...... October 1979
8th printing
9th printing

Lyrics from "Let It Snow, Let It Snow, Let It Snow," by Sammy Cahn and Jules Stein, used by permission of Edward Traubner.

Lines from "Buffalo Bill's" by e. e. cummings from COMPLETE POEMS 1913–1962 by e. e. cummings published by Harcourt Brace Jovanovich, Inc.

Cover photo by Terence F. Millar

Bantam Books are published by Bantam Books, Inc. Its trademark, consisting of the words "Bantam Books" and the portrayal of a bantam, is Registered in U.S. Patent and Trademark Office and in other countries. Marca Registrada. Bantam Books, Inc., 666 Fifth Avenue, New York, New York 10019.

PRINTED IN THE UNITED STATES OF AMERICA

FOR MARY—

The reasons increase each day.
Above all, there is Mary.

The
Chancellor
Manuscript

Prologue

June, 3, 1968

The dark-haired man stared at the wall in front of him. His chair, like the rest of the furniture, was pleasing to the eye but not made for comfort. The style was Early American, the theme Spartan, as if those about to be granted an audience with the occupant of the inner office should reflect on their awesome opportunity in stern surroundings.

The man was in his late twenties, his face angular, the features sharp, each pronounced and definite as if carved by a craftsman more aware of details than of the whole. It was a face in quiet conflict with itself, striking and yet unsettled. The eyes were engaging, deep set and very light blue, with an open, even questioning quality about them. They seemed at the moment to be the eyes of a blue-eyed animal, swift to level in any direction, steady, apprehensive.

The young man's name was Peter Chancellor, and the expression on his face was as rigid as his posture in the chair. His eyes were angry.

There was one other person in the outer office: a middle-aged secretary whose thin, colorless lips were set in constant tension, her gray hair stretched and spun into a bun that took on the appearance of a faded flaxen helmet. She was the Praetorian Guard, the attack dog who protected the sanctuary of the man behind the oak door beyond her desk.

Chancellor looked at his watch; the secretary glanced at him disapprovingly. Any indication of impatience was out of place in this office; the audience itself was everything.

It was quarter to six; all the other offices were closed. The small Midwest campus of Park Forest University was preparing for another late-spring evening, the controlled revelry heightened by the proximity of graduation day.

Park Forest strove to remain outside the unrest that had swept across the university campuses. In an ocean of turbulence it was an undisturbed sandbar. Insular, rich, at peace with itself, essentially without disruption. Or brilliance.

It was this fundamental lack of external concerns, so the story went, that brought the man behind the oak door to Park Forest. He sought inaccessibility, if not anonymity, which of course could never be granted. Munro St. Claire had been undersecretary of state for Roosevelt and Truman; ambassador-extraordinary for Eisenhower, Kennedy, and Johnson. He had flown about the globe with an open portfolio, bringing his Presidents' concerns and his own expertise to the world's troubled areas. That he had elected to spend a spring semester at Park Forest as visiting professor of government—while organizing the data that would form the basis of his memoirs—was a coup that had stunned the trustees of this wealthy but minor university. They had swallowed their disbelief and guaranteed St. Claire the isolation he could never have found in Cambridge, New Haven, or Berkeley.

So the story went.

And Peter Chancellor thought about the salient points of St. Claire's story to keep his mind off his own. But not entirely. At the moment, the salient points of his own immediate existence were as discouraging as one could imagine. Twenty-four months lost, thrown away into academic oblivion. Two years of his life!

His doctoral thesis had been rejected by the vote of eight to one by the honors college of Park Forest. The one dissenting vote was, naturally, that of his advisor and, as such, without influence on the others. Chancellor had been accused of frivolousness, of wanton disregard of historical fact, of slovenly research, and ultimately of irresponsibly inserting fiction in lieu of provable data. It was not at all ambiguous. Chancellor had failed; there was no appeal, for the failure was absolute.

From an exhilarating high he had sunk into a deep depression. Six weeks ago the *Foreign Service Journal* of Georgetown University had agreed to publish fourteen excerpts from the thesis. A total of some thirty pages. His advisor had managed it, sending a copy to academic friends in Georgetown, who thought the work was both enlightening and frightening. The *Journal* was on a par with *Foreign Affairs*, its readership among the country's most influential. Something was bound to result; somebody had to offer something.

But the *Journal*'s editors made one condition: Due to the nature of the thesis, the doctoral acceptance was mandatory before they would publish the manuscript. Without it they would not.

Now, of course, publishing any part was out of the question.

"The Origins of a Global Conflict" was the title. The conflict was World War II, the origins an imaginative interpretation of the men and the forces that collided during the catastrophic years from 1926 to 1939. It did no good to explain to the history committee of the honors college that the thesis was an interpretive analysis, not a legal document. He had committed a cardinal sin: He had attributed invented dialogue to historical figures. Such nonsense was unacceptable to the groves of academe at Park Forest.

But Chancellor knew there was another more serious flaw in the eyes of the committee. He had written his thesis in outrage and emotion, and outrage and emotion had no place in doctoral dissertations.

The premise that financial giants stood passively by while a band of psychopaths shaped post-Weimar Germany was ludicrous. As ludicrous as it was patently false. The multinational corporations could not feed the Nazi wolf pack fast enough; the stronger the pack, the more rapacious the appetites of the marketplace.

The German wolf pack's objectives and methods were conveniently obscured in the interests of an expanding economy. Obscured, hell! They were tolerated, ultimately *accepted*, along with the swiftly rising lines on profit-and-loss charts. Diseased Nazi Germany was given an economic clean bill of health by the financiers. And among the colossi of international finance who fed the Wehrmacht eagle were a number of the most honored industrial names in America.

There was the problem. He could not come out and identify those corporations because his proof was not conclusive. The people who had given him the information, and led him to other sources, would not allow their names to be used. They were frightened, tired old men, living on government and company pensions. Whatever had happened in the past was past; they would not risk losing the largess of their benefactors. Should Chancellor make public their private conversations, they would deny them. It was as simple as that.

But it *wasn't* as simple as that. It *had* happened. The story had *not* been told, and Peter wanted very much to tell it. True, he did not want to destroy old men who had merely carried out policies they had not understood, conceived by others so far up the corporate ladders they'd rarely met them. But to walk away from unrecorded history was wrong.

So Chancellor took the only option open to him: He had changed the names of the corporate giants, but in such a way as to leave no doubt as to their identities. Anyone who read a newspaper would know who they were.

This was his unforgivable error. He had raised provocative questions few wished to recognize as valid. Park Forest University was looked upon favorably when corporations and corporate foundations issued grants; it was not a dangerous campus. Why should that status be threatened—even remotely—by the work of a single doctoral candidate?

Christ! Two *years.* There were alternatives, of course. He could transfer his credits to another university and resubmit "Origins." But what then? Was it worth it? To face another form of rejection? One that lay in the shadows of his own doubts? For Peter was honest with himself. He had not written so unique or brilliant a work. He had merely found a period in recent history that infuriated him because of its parallels with the present. Nothing had changed; the lies of forty years ago still existed. But he did not want to walk away from it; he *would* not walk away. He would tell it. Somehow.

However, outrage was not a substitute for qualitative research. Concern for living sources was hardly an alternative for objective investigation. Reluctantly Peter acknowledged the validity of the committee's position. He was neither academic fish nor fowl; he was part fact, part fantasy.

Two years! Wasted!

The secretary's telephone hummed, it did not ring. The hum reminded Chancellor of the rumor that special communications had been installed so Washington could reach Munro St. Claire at any time of day or night. These installations, so the story went, were St. Claire's only departure from his self-imposed inaccessibility.

"Yes, Mr. Ambassador," said the secretary, "I'll send him in. . . . That's quite all right. If you need me, I can stay." Apparently she was not needed, and Peter had the impression that she was not happy about it. The Praetorian Guard was being dismissed. "You're scheduled to be at the dean's reception at six thirty," she continued. There was brief silence; then the woman replied. "Yes sir. I'll telephone your regrets. Good night, Mr St. Claire."

She glanced at Chancellor. "You may go in now," she said, her eyes questioning.

"Thank you." Peter rose from the uncomfortable straight-backed chair. "I don't know why I'm here either," he said.

Inside the oak-paneled office with the cathedral windows, Munro St. Claire got up from behind the antique table that served as his desk. He was an old man, thought Chancellor as he approached the extended right hand held over the table. Much older than he appeared at a distance, walking across the campus with a sure stride. Here in his office his tall slender body and aquiline head with the faded blond hair seemed to struggle to stay erect. Yet erect he stood, as if refusing to give in to infirmities. His eyes were large, but of no discernible color, intense in their steadiness, but not without humor. His thin lips were stretched into a smile beneath his well-groomed white moustache.

"Come in, come in, Mr. Chancellor. It's a pleasure to see you again."

"I don't think we've met."

"Good for you! Don't let me get away with that." St. Claire laughed and indicated a chair in front of the table.

"I didn't mean to contradict you, I just—" Chancellor stopped, realizing that no matter what he said, it would sound foolish. He sat down.

"Why not?" asked St. Claire. "Contradicting me would be minor compared to what you've done to a legion of contemporary scholars."

"I beg your pardon?"

"Your dissertation. I read it."

"I'm flattered."

"I was most impressed."

"Thank you, sir. Others weren't."

"Yes, I understand that. It was rejected by the honors college, I'm told."

"Yes."

"A damned shame. A lot of hard work went into it. And some very original thinking."

Who are you, Peter Chancellor? Have you any idea what you've done? Forgotten men have dredged up memories and whisper in fear. Georgetown is rife with rumor. An explosive document has been received from an obscure university in the Midwest. An insignificant graduate student has suddenly reminded us of that which no one cares to remember. Mr. Chancellor, Inver Brass cannot permit you to go on.

Peter saw that the old man's eyes were at once encouraging and yet noncommittal. There was nothing to be lost in being direct. "Are you implying that you might——?"

"Oh, no," interrupted St. Claire sharply, raising the palm of his right hand. "No, indeed. I wouldn't presume to question such a decision; it's hardly my place. And I suspect the rejection was based on certain applicable criteria. No, I wouldn't interfere. But I'd like to ask you several questions, perhaps offer some gratuitous advice."

Chancellor leaned forward. "What questions?"

St. Claire settled back in his chair. "First, yourself. I'm merely curious. I've spoken with your advisor, but that's secondhand. Your father's a newspaperman?"

Chancellor smiled. "He'd say *was*. He retires next January."

"Your mother's also a writer, isn't she?"

"Of sorts. Magazine articles, women's-page columns. She wrote short stories years ago."

"So the written word holds no terror for you."

"What do you mean?"

"A mechanic's son approaches a malfunctioning carburetor with less trepidation than the offspring of a ballet master. Generally speaking, of course."

"Generally speaking, I'd agree."

"Precisely." St. Claire nodded his head.

"Are you telling me my dissertation's a malfunctioning carburetor?"

St. Claire laughed. "Let's not get ahead of ourselves. You took your master's degree in journalism, obviously intending to be a newspaperman."

"Some form of communications, at any rate. I wasn't sure which."

"Yet you prevailed upon this university to accept you for a doctorate in history. So you changed your mind."

"Not really. It was never made up." Again Peter smiled, now with embarrassment. "My parents claim I'm a professional student. Not that they mind, particularly. A scholarship saw me through the master's. I served in Vietnam, so the government's paying my way here. I do some tutoring. To tell you the truth, I'm nearly thirty and I'm not sure what I want to do. But I don't suppose that's unique these days."

"Your graduate work would seem to indicate a preference for the academic life."

"If it did, it doesn't anymore."

St. Claire glanced at him. "Tell me about the dissertation itself. You make startling insinuations, rather frightening judgments. Essentially, you accuse many of the free world's leaders—and their institutions—of either closing their eyes to the menace of Hitler forty years ago, or worse: directly and indirectly financing the Third Reich."

"Not for ideological reasons. For economic advantage."

"Scylla and Charybdis?"

"I'll accept that. Right now, today, there's a repetition——"

"Despite the honors college," interrupted St. Claire quietly, "you must have done a fair amount of research. How much?"

What started you? That's what we have to know, because we know you will not let it go. Were you directed by men seeking vengeance after all these years? Or was it—far worse—an accident that primed your outrage? We can control sources; we can countermand them, show them to be false. We cannot control accidents. Or an outrage born of an accident. But you cannot go on, Mr. Chancellor. We must find a way to stop you.

Chancellor paused; the aged diplomat's question was unexpected. "Research? A lot more than the committee believes and a lot less than certain conclusions warrant. That's as honest as I can put it."

"It's honest. Will you give me specifics? There's very little documentation of sources."

Suddenly Peter felt uneasy. What had begun as a discussion was turning into an interrogation. "Why is it important? There's very little documentation because that's the way the people I spoke to wanted it."

"Then honor their wishes, by all means. Don't use names." The old man smiled; his charm was extraordinary.

We don't need names. Names can be uncovered easily, once areas are discerned. But it would be better not to pursue names. Much better. The whispers would start again. There is a better way.

"All right. I interviewed people who were active during the period from '23 to '39. They were in government—mainly the State Department—and in industry and banking. Also I spoke with about half a dozen former senior officers attached to the War College and the intelligence community. None, Mr. St. Claire, *none* would allow me to use his name."

"They provided you with so much material?"

"A great deal lay in what they would *not* discuss. And odd phrases, offhand remarks that were often non sequiturs, but just as often applicable. They're old men now, all —or nearly all—retired. Their minds wandered; so did their memories. They're kind of a sad collection; they're—" Chancellor stopped. He was not sure how to continue.

St. Claire did. "By and large, embittered minor executives and bureaucrats living on inadequate pensions. Such conditions breed angry, all too often distorted memories."

"I don't think that's fair. What I learned, what I wrote, is the truth. That's why anyone who reads the thesis will know which those companies were, how they operated."

St. Claire dismissed the statement as though he had not heard it. "How did you reach these people? What led you to them? How did you get appointments to see them?"

"My father started me off, and from those few came others. Sort of a natural progression; people remembered people."

"Your father?"

"In the early fifties he was a Washington correspondent for Scripps-Howard——"

"Yes." St. Claire interrupted softly. "So, through his efforts, you obtained an initial list."

"Yes. About a dozen names of men who had dealings in prewar Germany. In government and out. As I said, these led to others. And, of course, I read everything

Trevor-Roper and Shirer and the German apologists wrote. *That's* all documented."

"Did your father know what you were after?"

"A doctorate was enough." Chancellor grinned. "My father went to work with a year and a half of college. Money was tight."

"Then, shall we say, is he aware of what you found? Or thought you found."

"Not really. I figured my parents would read the thesis when it was finished. Now, I don't know if they'll want to; this is going to be a blow to the home front." Peter smiled weakly. "The aging, perpetual student comes to nothing."

"I thought you said *professional* student," corrected the diplomat.

"Is there a difference?"

"In approach, I think there is." St. Claire leaned forward in silence, his large eyes leveled at Peter. "I'd like to take the liberty of summarizing the immediate situation as I see it."

"Of course."

"Basically, you have the materials for a perfectly valid theoretical analysis. Interpretations of history, from doctrinaire to revisionist, are never-ending topics of debate and examination. Would you agree?"

"Naturally."

"Yes, of course. You wouldn't have chosen the subject in the first place if you didn't." St. Claire looked out the window as he spoke. "But an unorthodox interpretation of events—especially of a period in such recent history—based solely on the writings of others, would hardly justify the unorthodoxy, would it? I mean, certainly historians would have pounced on the material long before now if they had thought a case could be made. But it couldn't, really, so you went beyond the accepted sources and interviewed embittered old men and a handful of reluctant former intelligence specialists and came away with specific judgments."

"Yes, but——"

"Yes, *but*," broke in St. Claire, turning from the window. "By your own telling, these judgments were often based on 'offhand remarks' and 'non sequiturs.' And your sources refuse to be listed. In your own words your research did not justify numerous conclusions."

"But they did. The conclusions *are* justified."

"They'll never be accepted. Not by any recognized authority, academic or judicial. And quite rightly so, in my judgment."

"Then you're wrong, Mr. St. Claire. Because I'm *not* wrong. I don't care how many committees tell me I am. The facts are there, right below the surface, but nobody wants to talk about them. Even now, forty years later. Because it's happening all over again! A handful of companies are making millions all over the world by fueling military governments, calling them our *friends*, our 'first line of defense.' When their eyes are on profit-and-loss sheets, that's what they care about. . . . All right, maybe I can't come up with documentation, but I'm not going to throw away two years' work. I'm not going to stop because a committee tells me I'm academically unacceptable. Sorry, but *that's* unacceptable."

And that's what we had to know. At the last, would you cut your losses and walk away? Others thought you would, but I didn't. You knew you were right, and that's too great a temptation in the young. We must now render you impotent.

St. Claire looked down at Peter and held his eyes. "You're in the wrong arena. You sought acceptance from the wrong people. Seek it elsewhere. Where matters of truth and documentation are not important."

"I don't understand."

"Your dissertation is filled with some rather splendidly imagined fiction. Why not concentrate on that?"

"What?"

"Fiction. Write a novel. No one cares whether a novel is accurate, or has historical authenticity. It's simply not important." St. Claire once again leaned forward, his eyes steady on Chancellor. "Write fiction. You may still be ignored, but at least there's a chance of a hearing. To pursue your present course is futile. You'll waste another year, or two, or three. Ultimately, for what? So write a novel. Spend your outrage there, then go about your life."

Peter stared at the diplomat; he was at a loss, uncertain of his thoughts, so he merely repeated the single word. "Fiction?"

"Yes. I think we're back to that malfunctioning carburetor, although the analogy may be terrible." St. Claire settled back in his chair. "We agreed that words held no great fear for you; you've seen blank pages filled with them most of your life. Now, repair the work you've done with other words, a different approach that eliminates the necessity of academic sanction."

Peter exhaled softly; for several moments he had held his breath, numbed by St. Claire's analysis. "A *novel?* It never crossed my mind. . . ."

"I submit it may have unconsciously," interjected the diplomat. "You didn't hesitate to invent actions—and reactions—when it served you. And God knows you have the ingredients of a fascinating story. Farfetched, in my opinion, but not without merit for a Sunday afternoon in a hammock. Fix the carburetor; this is a different engine. One of less substance, perhaps, but conceivably quite enjoyable. And someone may listen to you. They won't in this arena. Nor, frankly, should they."

"A novel. I'll be damned."

Munro St. Claire smiled. His eyes were still strangely noncommittal.

The afternoon sun disappeared below the horizon; long shadows spread across the lawns. St. Claire stood at the window, gazing out on the quadrangle. There was an arrogance in the serenity of the scene; it was out of place in a world so locked in turbulence.

He could leave Park Forest now. His job was finished, the carefully orchestrated conclusion not perfect but sufficient unto the day.

Sufficient unto the limits of deceit.

He looked at his watch. An hour had passed since the bewildered Chancellor had left the office. The diplomat crossed back to his desk, sat down, and picked up the telephone. He dialed the area code 202 and then seven additional digits. Moments later there were two clicks over the line, followed by a whine. For any but those aware of the codes the sound would have simply signified a malfunctioning instrument.

St. Claire dialed five more digits. A single click was the result, and a voice answered.

"Inver Brass. Tape is rolling." In the voice was the flat *a* of Boston, but the rhythm was Middle-European.

"This is Bravo. Patch me through to Genesis."

"Genesis is in England. It's past midnight over there."

"I'm afraid I can't be concerned with that. Can you patch? Is there a sterile location?"

"If he's still at the embassy, there is, Bravo. Otherwise it's the Dorchester. No guarantees there."

"Try the embassy, please."

The line went dead as the Invor Brass switchboard linked up communications. Three minutes later another voice was heard; it was clear, with no distortions, as though it were down the street, not 4,000 miles away. The voice was clipped, agitated, but not without respect. Or a degree of fear.

"This is Genesis. I was just leaving. What happened?"

"It's done."

"Thank God!"

"The dissertation was rejected. I made it clear to the committee, quite privately of course, that it was radical nonsense. They'd be the laughingstock of the university community. They're sensitive; they should be. They're mediocre."

"I'm pleased." There was a pause from London. "What was his reaction?"

"What I expected. He's right and he knows it; therefore he's frustrated. He had no intention of stopping."

"Does he now?"

"I believe so. The idea's firmly planted. If need be, I'll follow up indirectly, put him in touch with people. But I may not have to. He's imaginative; more to the point, his outrage is genuine."

"You're convinced this is the best way?"

"Certainly. The alternative is for him to pursue the research and dredge up dormant issues. I wouldn't like that to happen in Cambridge of Berkeley, would you?"

"No. And perhaps no one will be interested in what he writes, much less publish it. I suppose we could bring that about."

St. Claire's eyes narrowed briefly. "My advice is not to interfere. We'd frustrate him further, drive him back. Let things happen naturally. If he does turn it into a novel, the best we can hope for is a minor printing of a rather amateurish work. He'll have said what he had to say, and it will turn out to be inconsequential fiction, with the usual disclaimers as to persons living or dead. Interference might raise questions; that's not in our interest."

"You're right, of course," said the man in London. "But then you usually are, Bravo."

"Thank you. And good-bye, Genesis. I'll be leaving here in a few days."

"Where are you going?"

"I'm not sure. Perhaps back to Vermont. Perhaps far away. I don't like what I see on the national landscape."

"All the more reason to stay in touch," said the voice in London.

"Perhaps. And then again, I may be too old."

"You can't disappear. You know that, don't you?"

"Yes. Good night, Genesis."

St. Claire replaced the telephone without waiting for a corresponding good-bye from London. He simply did not want to listen further.

He was swept by a sense of revulsion; it was not the first time, nor would it be the last. It was the function of Inver Brass to make decisions others could not make, to protect men and institutions from the moral indictments born of hindsight. What was right forty years ago was anathema today.

Frightened men had whispered to other frightened men that Peter Chancellor had to be stopped. It was wrong for this obscure doctoral candidate to ask questions that had no meaning forty years later. The times were different, the circumstances altogether dissimilar.

Yet there were certain gray areas. Accountability was not a limited doctrine. Ultimately, they were all accountable. Inver Brass was no exception. Therefore, Peter Chancellor had to be given the chance to vent his outrage, and in a way that removed him from consequence. Or catastrophe.

St. Claire rose from the table and surveyed the papers on top of it. He had removed most of his personal effects during the past weeks. There was very little of *him* in the office now; and that was as it should be.

Tomorrow he would be gone.

He walked to the door. Automatically he reached for the light switch, and then he realized no lights were on. He had been standing, pacing, sitting, and thinking in shadows.

The New York Times Book Review,
May 10, 1969, Page 3

Reichstag! is at once startling and perceptive, awkward and incredible. Peter Chancellor's first novel would have us believe that the early Nazi party was financed by nothing less than a cartel of international bankers and industrialists— American, British and French—apparently with the acknowledged, though unspoken, approval of their respective governments. Chancellor forces us to believe him as we read. His narrative is breathless; his characters leap from the page with a kind of raw power that illuminates their strengths and weaknesses in a manner that might be vitiated by more disciplined writing. Mr. Chancellor tells his tale in outrage, and far too melodramatically, but withal the book is a marvelous "read." And, finally, you begin to wonder: Could it have happened this way? . . .

The Washington Post Book World
April 22, 1970, Page 3

In *Sarajevo!* Chancellor does for the guns of August what he did for the Führer's *Blitzkrieg* last year.

The forces that collided in the July crisis of 1914, preceded by the June assassination of Ferdinand by the conspirator Gavrilo Princip, are abstracted, rearranged, and put back on a fast track by Mr. Chancellor, so that no one emerges on the side of the angels and all is a triumph of evil. Throughout, the author's protagonist—in this case a British infiltrator of a Serbo-Croat clandestine organization called, melodramatically, *The Unity of Death*—peels away the layers of deceit as they've been spread by the provocateurs of the Reichstag, the Foreign Office, and the Chamber of Deputies. The puppets are revealed; the strings lead back to the industrial vested interests on all sides.

As with so much else, these rarely discussed coincidences go on and on.

Mr. Chancellor has a conspiracy complex of a high order. He deals with it in a fascinating manner and with a high readability quotient. *Sarajevo!* should prove to be even more popular than *Reichstag!*

The Los Angeles Times Daily Review of Books
April 4, 1971, Page 20

Counterstrike! is Chancellor's best work to date, although for reasons that escape this reader, its serpentine plot is based on an extraordinary error of research that one does not expect of this author. It concerns the clandestine operations of the Central Intelligence Agency as they pertain to a spreading reign of terror imposed on a New England university city by a foreign power. Mr. Chancellor should know that all domestic involvements are specifically prohibited to the CIA in its 1947 charter.

This objection aside, *Counterstrike!* is a sure winner. Chancellor's previous books have shown that he can spin a yarn with such pace that you can't turn the pages fast enough, but now he's added a depth of character not mined previously.

Chancellor's extensive knowledge of counterespionage is, according to those who are supposed to know, on zero target. The CIA error notwithstanding.

He gets into the minds as well as the methods of all those involved in an absolutely frightening situation drawing an explicit parallel to the racial disturbances that led to a series of murders in Boston several years ago. Chancellor has arrived as a first-rate novelist who takes events, rearranges the facts, and presents startling new conclusions.

The plot is deviously simple: A man is chosen to perform a task for which he would seem to be ill equipped. He is given extensive CIA training, but nowhere in this training is there an attempt to strengthen his basic flaw. Soon we understand: That flaw is meant to bring about his death. Circles within circles of conspiracy. And once again, as with his previous books, we wonder: Is it true? Did this happen? Is this the way it was? . . .

Autumn. The Bucks County countryside was an ocean of yellow, green, and gold. Chancellor leaned against the hood of a silver Mark IV Continental, his arm casually around a woman's shoulder. His face was fuller now, the distinct features less in conflict with one another, softened yet still sharp. His eyes were focused on a white house that stood at the foot of a winding drive cut out of the gently sloping fields. The drive was bordered on each side by a high white fence.

The girl with Chancellor, holding the hand draped over her shoulder, was as engrossed by the sight in front of them as he was. She was tall; her brown hair fell softly, framing her delicate but curiously strong face. Her name was Catherine Lowell.

"It's everything you described," she said, gripping his hand tightly. "It's beautiful. Really very beautiful."

"To coin a phrase," said Chancellor, glancing down at her, "that's one hell of a relief."

She looked up at him. "You bought it, didn't you? You're not just 'interested,' you bought it!"

Peter nodded. "I had competition. A banker from Philadelphia was ready to put down a binder. I had to decide. If you don't like it, I'm sure he'll take it from me."

"Don't be silly, it's absolutely gorgeous!"

"You haven't seen the inside."

"I don't have to."

"Good. Because I'd rather show it to you on the way back. The owners'll be out by Thursday. They'd better be. On Friday afternoon I've got a large delivery from Washington. It's coming here."

"The transcripts?"

"Twelve cases from the Government Printing Office. Morgan had to send down a truck. The whole story of Nuremberg as recorded by the Allied tribunals. Do you want to guess what the title of the book's going to be?"

Catherine laughed. "I can see Tony Morgan now, pacing around his office like a disjointed cat in gray flannels. Suddenly he pounces on his desk and shouts, frightening everyone within earshot, which is most of the building: 'I've got it! We'll do something different! We'll use *Nuremberg* with an exclamation point!' "

Peter joined her laughter. "You're vilifying my sainted editor."

"Never. Without him we'd be moving into a five-flight walk-up, not a farm built for a country squire."

"And the squire's wife."

"And the squire's wife." Catherine squeezed his arm. "Speaking of trucks, shouldn't there be moving vans in the driveway?"

Chancellor smiled; it was an embarrassed smile. "Except for odd items, specifically listed, I had to buy it furnished. They're moving to the Caribbean. You can throw it all out if you like."

"My, aren't we grand?"

"Aren't we rich," replied Peter, not asking a question. "No comments, please. Come on, let's go. We've got about three hours on the turnpike, another two and a half after that. It'll be dark soon."

Catherine turned to him, her face tilted up, their lips nearly touching. "With every mile I'm going to get more and more nervous. I'll develop twitches and arrive a babbling idiot. I thought the ritual dance of meeting parents went out ten years ago."

"You didn't mention it when I met yours."

"Oh, for heaven's sake! They were so impressed just being in the same room with you, you didn't have to do anything but sit there and gloat!"

"Which I did not do. I like your parents. I think you'll like mine."

"Will they like me? That's the imponderable."

"Not for a second," said Peter, pulling her to him. "They'll love you. Just as I love you. Oh *God*, I love you!"

It's accurate, Genesis. This Peter Chancellor has the GPO reprinting everything relative to Nuremberg. The publisher has arranged transportation to an address in Pennsylvania.

It does not affect us, Banner. Venice and Christopher agree. We will take no action. That is the decision.

It's a mistake! He's going back to the German theme. Long after the errors were made. There's no association. Years before Nuremberg we saw clearly what we did not see at the beginning. There's no connection to us. Any of us, including you.

You can't be sure.

We are sure.

What does Bravo think?

Bravo's away. He has not been apprised, nor will he be.

Why not?

For reasons that don't concern you. They go back several years. Before you were called to Inver Brass.

It's wrong, Genesis.

And you're overwrought unnecessarily. You would never have been summoned if your anxieties had merit, Banner. You're an extraordinary man. We've never doubted that.

Nevertheless, it's dangerous.

The traffic on the Pennsylvania Turnpike seemed to move faster as the sky grew darker. Pockets of fog intruded abruptly, distorting the glare of onrushing headlights. A sudden cloudburst of slashing, diagonal rain splattered against the windshield too rapidly. The wipers were useless against it.

There was a growing mania on the highway, and Chancellor felt it. Vehicles raced by, throwing up sprays of water; drivers seemed to sense several storms converging on western Pennsylvania, and instincts born of experience propelled them home.

The voice on the Continental's radio was precise, commanding.

The highway department urges all motorists to stay off the roads in the Jamestown-Warren area. If you are currently en route, drive into the nearest service areas. We repeat: Storm warnings out of Lake Erie have now been confirmed. The storms have winds of hurricane force. . . .

"There's a turnoff about four miles up," said Peter, squinting at the windshield. "We'll take it. There's a restaurant two or three hundred yards out of the exit."

"How can you tell?"

"We just passed a Pittsfield sign; it used to be a mark for me. It meant I was an hour from home."

Chancellor never understood how it happened; it was a question that would burn into his mind for the rest of his life. The steep hill was an opaque blanket of torrential rain, which fell in successive, powerful gusts that literally caused the heavy car to sway on its axis, like a small boat in terrible seas.

And suddenly there were headlights blinding through the rear window, reflecting harshly off the mirror. White spots appeared in front of his eyes, obscuring even the torrents of rain against the glass. He saw only the glaring white light.

Then it was beside him! An enormous trailer truck was overtaking him on the dangerous incline of rushing water! Peter screamed at the driver through the closed window; the man was a maniac. Couldn't he see what he was doing? Couldn't he see the Mark IV in the storm? Was he out of his mind?

The unbelievable happened. The huge truck veered toward him! The impact came; the steel chassis of the carriage crashed into the Continental. Metal smashed against metal. The maniac was forcing him off the road! The man was drunk or panicked by the storm! Through the blanket of slashing rain Chancellor could see the outline of the driver high up in the perch of his seat. He was *oblivious* to the Mark IV! He did not know what he was doing!

A second crunching impact came with such force that Peter's window shattered. The Mark IV's wheels locked; the car whipped to the right, toward a vacuum of darkness that lay beyond the ridge of the embankment.

The hood rose up in the rain; then the car lurched over the shoulder of the highway, plunging downward.

Catherine's screams pierced the sounds of shattering glass and crushing steel as the Continental rolled over and over and over. Metal now screeched against metal as if each strip, each panel were fighting to survive the successive impacts of car against earth.

Peter lunged toward the source of the scream—toward Catherine—but he was locked in place by a shaft of steel. The automobile twisted, rolled, plunged down the embankment.

The screams stopped. Everything stopped.

1

The fifth limousine drove slowly through the dark, tree-lined streets of Georgetown. It stopped in front of marble steps that led up through sculptured foilage to a porticoed entrance sixty feet away. The entrance, like the rest of the house, had a quiet grandeur heightened by the muted lighting beyond the pillars that supported the balcony above it.

The four previous limousines had arrived three to six minutes apart; all were deliberately paced. They had been rented from five separate leasing agencies from Arlington to Baltimore.

Should an observer in that quiet street wish to learn the identities of the single passenger within each vehicle, he would not be able to do so. For none could be traced through the leasing arrangements, and all were unseen by the chauffeurs. A pane of opaque glass separated each driver from his charge, and none was permitted to leave his seat behind the wheel while his passenger entered or left the automobile. These chauffeurs had been selected with care.

Everything had been timed, orchestrated. Two limousines had been driven to private airfields, where for an hour they had been left locked and unattended in designated areas of the parking lots. At the end of that hour the drivers had returned, knowing their passengers would be there. The other three vehicles had been left in the same manner in three different locations: Washington's Union Station; the shopping complex in McLean, Virginia; and the country club in Chevy Chase, Maryland—to which the specific passenger did not belong.

Finally, should any observer in that quiet street in Georgetown try to interfere with the emerging passengers, a blond-haired man stood in the shadows on the balcony above the portico at the top of the marble staircase to prevent him. Around the man's neck was strapped a transistorized, high-impedence microphone through which he could relay commands to others on the block, using a language that was not English. In his hands was a rifle, a silencer attached to the barrel.

The fifth passenger got out of the limousine and walked up the marble steps. The automobile drove quietly away; it would not return. The blond-haired man on the balcony spoke softly into the microphone; the door beneath was opened.

The conference room was on the second floor. The walls were dark wood, the lighting indirect. Placed at the center of the east wall was an antique Franklin stove, and in spite of the fact that it was a balmy spring evening, a fire glowed from within the iron casement.

In the center of the room was a large circular table. Around it sat six men, their ages ranging from mid-fifties to eighties. Two fell into the first category: a graying, wavy-haired man with Hispanic features; and a man with very pale skin, Nordic face, and dark, straight hair combed smoothly back above his wide forehead. The latter sat to the left of the group's spokesman, the focal point of the table. The spokesman was in his late seventies; a fringe of hair extended around his balding head, and his features were tired—or ravaged. Across from the spokesman was a slender, aristocratic-looking man with thinning white hair and a perfectly groomed white mustache; he was also in the indeterminate seventies. On his right was a large Negro with an immense head and face that could have been chiseled from Ghanaian mahogany. On his left, the oldest and frailest man in the room; he was a Jew, a yarmulke on his hairless, gaunt skull.

All their voices were soft, their speech erudite, their eyes steady and penetrating. Each man had a quiet vitality born of extraordinary power.

And each was known by a single name that had specific significance to all at the table; no other name was ever used among them. In several cases the name had been held by the member for nearly forty years; in other cases it had been passed on, as predecessors died and successors were elected.

There were never more than six men. The spokesman

was known as Genesis—he was, in fact, the second man to hold the name. Previously, he had been known as Paris, the identity now held by the Hispanic man with the graying wavy hair.

Others were known as Christopher, Banner, Venice. And there was Bravo.

These were the men of Inver Brass.

In front of each was an identical manila folder, a single page of paper on top. Except for the name in the upper left-hand corner of the page, the remaining type-written words would have been meaningless to any but these men.

Genesis spoke. "Above all, at all costs, the files must be taken and destroyed. In this there can be no disagreement. We've finally established that they're stored in an upright vault, built into the steel wall of the walk-in closet, behind and to the left of the office desk."

"The closet lock is controlled by a switch in the center drawer," said Banner quietly. "The vault is protected by a series of electronic releases, the first of which must be triggered from his residence. Without the first release none of the others will activate. It would take ten sticks of dynamite to break in; the estimated time of operation for an acetylene torch is roughly four hours, with alarms sounding at the first touch of heat."

Across the table, his black face obscured in the dim light, Venice asked, "Has the location of this first release been confirmed?"

"Yes," answered Banner. "In the bedroom. It's in the shelf of the headboard."

"Who confirmed it?" asked Paris, the Hispanic member of Inver Brass.

"Varak," was Genesis's reply from the south end of the table.

Several heads nodded slowly. The elderly Jew, to the right of Banner, addressed him. "What of the rest?"

"The subject's medical records were obtained from La Jolla, California. As you know, Christopher, he refuses to be examined at Bethesda. The most recent cardioanalysis indicates minor hypochloremia, a low potassium condition in no way dangerous. The fact in itself, however, might be sufficient to warrant administering the required dosage of digitalis, but there's risk of exposure through autopsy."

"He's an old man." That statement was made by

Bravo, a man older than the subject in question. "Why would an autopsy be considered?"

"Because of who he is," said Paris, the Hispanic member, his voice evidence of his early years in Castile. "It might be unavoidable. And the country cannot tolerate the turmoil of another assassination. It would give too many dangerous men the excuse to move, to implement a series of horrors in the name of patriotism."

"I submit," interrupted Genesis, "that should these same dangerous men—and I refer without equivocation to Sixteen hundred Pennsylvania Avenue—should these men and the subject reach an accommodation, the horrors you speak of will be minuscule by comparison. The key, gentlemen, is in the subject's files. They're held out like raw meat to hungry jackals. Those files in the hands of Sixteen hundred would usher in government by coercion and blackmail. We all know what's taking place right now. We *must* act."

"Reluctantly I agree with Genesis," said Bravo. "Our information shows that Sixteen hundred has gone beyond the unattractive limits experienced in previous administrations. It's approaching the uncontrollable. There's hardly an agency or a department that has not been contaminated. But an Internal Revenue investigation, or a DIA surveillance report, pales beside those files. Both in nature and—far more seriously—in the stature of those they concern. I'm not sure we have an alternative."

Genesis turned to the younger member at his side. "Banner, would you summarize, please?"

"Yes, of course." The slender, fiftyish man nodded, paused, and placed his hands in front of him on the table. "There's very little to add. You've read the report. The subject's mental processes have disintegrated rapidly; one internist suspects arteriosclerosis, but there's no way to confirm the diagnosis. The La Jolla records are controlled by the subject. At the source. He screens the medical data. Psychiatrically, however, there's complete agreement: The maniac-depressive condition has advanced to the state of acute paranoia." The man stopped, his head turned slightly to Genesis but not excluding anyone else at the table. "Frankly that's all I have to know to cast my vote."

"Who reached this agreement?" asked the old Jew known as Christopher.

"Three psychiatrists, unknown to each other, retained

by remote and asked to submit independent reports. These were collectively interpreted by our own man. Acute paranoia was the only conceivable judgment."

"How did they go about their diagnosis?" Venice leaned forward, his large black hands folded as he asked the question.

"Infrared, telescopic motion-picture cameras were used over a thirty-day period in every possible situation. In restaurants, the Presbyterian Church, in arrivals and departures at all formal and private functions. Two lip-readers provided texts of everything said; the texts were identical. There are also extensive, I should say exhaustive, reports from our own sources within the bureau. There can be no dispute with the judgment. The man's mad."

"What of Sixteen hundred?" Bravo stared at the younger man.

"They're getting closer, making progress every week. They've gone so far as to suggest a formal, internal association, the objective obviously the files. The subject's wary; he's seen them all, and those at Sixteen hundred aren't the best. But he admires their arrogance, their *macho*, and they stroke him. That's the word that's used, incidentally. *Stroke*."

"How appropriate," replied Venice. "Is their progress substantive?"

"I'm afraid so. There's hard evidence that the subject has delivered several dossiers—or the most damaging information contained in them—to the Oval Office. Understandings are being reached both in the area of political contributions and the election itself. Two contenders for the opposition's presidential nomination have agreed to withdraw—one by exhausted finances, the other by an act of instability."

"Please explain that," instructed Genesis.

"A gross mistake by words or action that eliminates him from the presidential stakes but is not serious enough to threaten his congressional standing. In this case, a display of unreasonable behavior during the primaries. These things are well thought out."

"They're frightening," said Paris angrily.

"They stem from the subject," said Bravo. "May we touch once again on an autopsy. Can it be controlled?"

"It may not have to be," answered Banner, his hands now separated, the palms face down on the table. "We've flown in a man from Texas, an expert in cardiovascular research! He thinks he's dealing with a prominent family on Maryland's Eastern Shore. A patriarch going insane, capable of extraordinary damage, organic and psychiatric symptoms indistinguishable. There's a chemical derivative of digitalis that, when combined with an intravenous injection of air, may be untraceable."

"Who's overseeing this aspect?" Venice was unconvinced.

"Varak," said Genesis. "He's the source control of the entire project."

Once more there was a nodding of heads.

"Are there further questions?" asked Genesis.

Silence.

"Then, we vote," continued Genesis, removing a small pad from beneath the manila envelope. He tore six pages and passed five to his left. "The Roman numeral one signifies affirmative; two, negative. As is customary a tie vote is negative."

The men of Inver Brass made their marks, folded the papers, and returned them to Genesis. He spread them out.

"The vote is unanimous, gentlemen. The project is on." He turned to Banner. "Please bring in Mr. Varak."

The younger man got out of his chair and crossed to the door. He opened it, nodded his head to the figure standing outside in the hallway, and returned to the table.

Varak walked in, closing the door behind him. He was the same man who had stood guard on the dark balcony above the entrance at the top of the marble steps. The rifle was no longer in his hands, but the transistorized microphone was still strapped around his neck, and a thin wire led to his left ear. He was of indeterminate age, somewhere between thirty-five and forty-five—those years so well obscured by active men with strong, muscular bodies. His hair was light blond and cut short. His face was broad with high cheekbones that, together with his gently sloping eyes, were evidence of a slavic heritage. In contrast to his appearance, however, his speech was soft, the accent faintly Bostonian, the rhythm Middle European.

"Is there a decision?" he asked.

"Yes," replied Genesis. "Affirmative."

"You had no choice," said Varak.

"Have you projected a schedule?" Bravo leaned forward, his eyes steady, noncommittal.

"Yes. In three weeks. The night of May first; the body will be discovered in the morning."

"The news will break on the second of May, then." Genesis looked at the members of Inver Brass. "Prepare statements where you think they'll be solicited. Several of us should be out of the country."

"You're assuming the death will be reported in a normal fashion," said Varak, raising his soft voice slightly to imply the contrary. "Without controls I wouldn't guarantee that."

"Why?" asked Venice.

"I think Sixteen hundred will panic. That crowd would put the corpse on ice inside the President's clothes closet if they thought it would buy them time to get the files."

Varak's imagery gave rise to reluctant smiles around the table. Genesis spoke.

"Then, guarantee it, Mr. Varak. *We* will have the files."

"Very well. Is that all?"

"Yes."

"Thank you," said Genesis with a nod of his head. Varak left quickly. Genesis got out of his chair and picked up his single page of paper with the coded words typewritten on it. Then he reached down and gathered the six small notepad pages, all clearly marked with the Roman numeral *I*. "The meeting is adjourned, gentlemen. As usual, will each of you be responsible for his own disposal? If any notes were made, dispose of them as well."

One by one the men of Inver Brass approached the Franklin stove. The first member to reach it removed the cover with the tongs hung on the wall. He dropped the page of paper delicately into the well of burning coals. The others followed suit.

The last two men to perform the ritual were Genesis and Bravo. They stood away from the others. Genesis spoke quietly.

"Thank you for coming back."

"You told me four years ago I couldn't disappear," replied Munro St. Claire. "You were right."

"There's more, I'm afraid," Genesis said. "I'm not well. I have very little time."

"Oh, Lord———"

"Please. I'm the lucky one."

"What? How? . . ."

"The doctors said two or three months. Ten weeks ago. I insisted on knowing, of course. They're uncannily accurate; I can feel it. I assure you, there's no other feeling like it. It's an absolute, and there's a certain comfort in that."

"I'm sorry. More than I can say. Does Venice know?" St. Claire's eyes strayed to the large black man talking softly in the corner with Banner and Paris.

"No. I wanted nothing to interfere—or influence—our decision tonight." Genesis dropped the typewritten page into the yellow glow of the stove. Then he crumpled the six votes of Inver Brass into a ball and let it too drop into the flame.

"I don't know what to say," whispered St. Claire compassionately, watching Genesis's strangely peaceful eyes.

"I do," replied the dying man, smiling, "You're back now. Your resources are beyond those of Venice. Or any other man here tonight. Say that you'll see this through. In the event I'm removed from the premises, as it were."

St. Claire looked at the page in his hand. At the name in the upper left-hand corner. "He tried to destroy you once. He nearly succeeded. I'll see it through."

"Not that way," Genesis's voice was firm and disapproving. "There must be no rancor, no vengeance. That's not our way; it can *never* be our way."

"There are times when differing objectives are compatible. Even moral objectives. I'm merely recognizing the fact. The man's a menace."

Munro St. Claire looked once more at the page in his hand. At the name in the upper left-hand corner.

John Edgar Hoover.

He crushed the page in his hand and let it drop into the fire.

2

Peter Chancellor lay in the wet sand, the waves slapping gently over his body. He stared at the sky; the gray was receding, the blue emerging. Dawn had come to Malibu beach.

He pressed his elbows into the sand and sat up. His neck hurt, and within moments he would feel the pain in his temples. He had gotten drunk last night. And the night before, goddamn it.

His eyes strayed to his left leg below his undershorts. The thin scar that curved from his calf through his kneecap up into his lower thigh was a twisting white line surrounded by suntanned flesh. It was still sensitive to the touch, but the complicated surgery beneath had been successful. He could walk almost normally now, and the pain had been replaced by a numb stiffness.

His left shoulder was something else; the pain was never completely absent, just dulled at times. The doctors said he had torn most of the ligaments and crushed assorted tendons; it would take longer for them to heal.

Absently he raised his right hand and felt the slightly swollen rivulet of skin that extended from his hairline over his right ear and down to the base of his skull. His hair covered most of the scar now, the break in his forehead only noticeable at close range. During the past weeks more women had remarked about it than he cared to remember. The doctors told him that his head had been sliced as though by a razor blade through a soft melon; a quarter of an inch above or below would have killed him. There had been weeks when he devoutly wished it had. He knew the desire would pass. He did not want to die; he merely was not sure he wanted to live without Cathy.

Time would heal the injuries, inside and outside; he never doubted it. He just wished the process were faster. So the restless energy would return and the early hours of the day could be filled with work, not pounding temples and vague, uneasy concerns about the previous night's behavior.

But even if he remained sober, the concerns would still be there. He was out of his element; the tribes of Beverly Hills and Malibu confused him. In his agent's wisdom it was the positive thing for him to come to Los Angeles— Hollywood, why didn't he just say it, think it? Hollywood —to coauthor the screenplay of *Counterstrike!* The fact that he did not know the first thing about screenwriting apparently did not matter. The redoubtable Joshua Harris, the only agent he had ever known, told him it was a minor deficiency that would be compensated for by major money.

The logic had escaped Peter. But then so had his coauthor. The two men had met three times for a total of about forty-five minutes, of which, again perhaps, ten had been devoted to *Counterstrike!* And, of course, nothing had been written down. Not in his presence, at any rate.

Yet here he was in Malibu, staying in a hundred-thousand-dollar beach house, driving a Jaguar, and charging to the studio tabs from Newport Beach to Santa Barbara.

One did not have to get drunk to feel hints of guilt in a situation like that. Certainly not Mrs. Chancellor's little boy, who had been told early in life that you earn what you get just as surely as you are what you live.

On the other hand, *living* was what was uppermost in Joshua Harris's mind when he negotiated the contract. Peter had not been living at the house in Pennsylvania; he had been barely existing.

In the three months after his release from the hospital, he had done almost nothing on the Nuremberg book.

Nothing. When would there be something? Anything?

His head hurt now. His eyes watered with the pain, and his stomach sent up alarms. Peter got to his feet and walked unsteadily into the surf. A swim might help.

He ducked beneath the surface, then sprang up and looked back toward the house. What the hell was he doing on the beach in the first place? He'd brought a girl home last night. He was sure of it. Almost.

He limped painfully over the sand to the steps of the beach house. He paused at the railing, breathing hard, and looked up at the sky. The sun had broken through, burning away the mist. It was going to be another hot, humid day. He turned and saw that two residents were walking their dogs about a quarter mile away at the water's edge.

It would not do for him to be seen in wet undershorts on the beach. What remained of propriety ordered him back to the house.

Propriety and curiosity. And the vague feeling that something unpleasant had happened last night. He wondered what the girl would look like. Blond, he remembered, large-breasted. And how did they manage to drive from wherever it was in Beverly Hills to Malibu? The vague memory of the unpleasant incident was somehow related to the girl, but he could not remember how or why.

He gripped the railing and pulled himself up the steps

to the redwood deck. Redwood and white stucco and heavy
wooden beams—that was the beach house. It was an architect's version of Malibu Tudor.

The glass doors on the far right were partially open.
It was the bedroom entrance; on the table by the door was
a half-empty bottle of Pernod. The deck chair nearest the
bottle was overturned. A pair of strapless sandals lay toe to
heel beside it, in contradictory neatness.

Things were coming back to him. He had made love
to the girl with the dramatic breasts—inadequately, he recalled—and in disgust or self-defense had wandered out to
the porch and sat by himself, drinking Pernod without the
benefit of a glass.

Why had he done that? Where had the Pernod come
from? What the hell difference did it make to him whether
he performed acceptably or unacceptably with an accommodating body recruited from Beverly Hills? He could not
remember, so he held onto the railing and walked toward
the overturned chair and the open glass door.

There were dead flies floating in the Pernod; a live
one hesitantly circled the rim of the bottle. Chancellor
considered righting the fallen chair, but decided otherwise.
His head was in pain; not just the temples, but the winding
corridor of skin between his hairline and the base of his
skull. The pain was undulating, as though guided by an
unseen beam.

A warning signal. He had to move slowly.

He limped cautiously through the door. The room was
a mess. Clothes were strewn about the furniture, ashtrays
were overturned, their contents scattered about the floor; a
glass was smashed in front of the bedside table; the telephone was ripped out of its jack.

The girl was in the bed, lying on her side, her breasts
pressed together, stretching, swelling like two pointed
spheres. Her blond hair fell over her face, which was buried
in a pillow. The top sheet was draped across the lower half
of her body; one leg protruded, displaying the sun-darkened
flesh of her inner thigh. Looking at her, Peter could feel
the provocative stirring in his groin. He inhaled deeply for
a few moments, excited by the sight of the girl's breasts,
her exposed leg, her hidden face beneath the fallen blond
hair.

He was still drunk. He knew that, because he realized

he did not want to see the girl's face. He merely wanted to make love to an object; he did not want to acknowledge the existence of a person.

He took a step toward the bed and stopped. Fragments of glass were in his path; they explained the sandals outside. At least he'd had the presence of mind to wear them. And the telephone. He remembered yelling into the telephone.

The woman rolled onto her back. Her face was pretty in that innocuous California way. Pert, suntanned, the features too small and coordinated for character. Her large breasts separated, the sheet fell away, revealing her pubic hair and the swell of her thighs. Peter moved to the foot of the bed and pulled down his wet undershorts. He could feel sand on the tips of his fingers. He placed his right knee on the bed, careful to keep his left leg straight, and lowered himself on the sheets.

The woman opened her eyes. When she spoke, it was with a soft, modulated voice filled with sleep.

"Come on up, honey. You feeling better?"

Chancellor crawled beside her. She moved her hand to his half-swollen erection, cupping it gently.

"Do I owe you an apology?" he asked.

"Hell, no. Maybe to yourself, not me. You banged like a ram, but I don't think it did you any good. You just got mad and stormed out."

"I'm sorry." He reached for her left breast; the nipple was taut under the pressure of his fingers. The girl moaned and began pulling him in short swift movements. She was either a good performer or a highly developed sexual partner who needed very little priming.

"I still feel warm all over. You just didn't stop. You just went on and on and nothing happened for you. But *Jesus,* it did for me! . . . Fuck me, lamb. Come on, fuck me," she whispered.

Peter buried his face between her breasts. Her legs parted, inviting him into her. But the ache in his head increased; shafts of pain pulsed through his skull.

"I can't. I can't." He could barely talk.

"Don't you worry. Now, don't you worry about a thing," said the girl. She eased him back so his shoulders again touched the sheets. "You just hold on, honey. Hold on and let me do the work."

The moments blurred. He could feel himself waning,

then the swift movements of the girl's two hands and the
wet moisture of her lips, caressing, provoking. He was
becoming alive again. There was need.

Goddamn it. He had to be good for something.

He pulled her head into his groin. She moaned and
spread her legs; all was sweet wetness and soft flesh. He
grabbed her under her arms, pulling her parallel to him.
Her breath came in quick, loud, throated groans.

*He could not stop now. He could not allow the pain
to interfere. Goddamn it!*

"Oh, Pete, you're something. Oh, Christ, you're the
fucker of all *time*! Come on, lamb! Now! *Now!*"

The girl's whole body began to writhe. Her whispers
now bordered on shouts.

"Oh, *Jesus*! Jesus *Christ*! You're driving me crazy,
lover! You're the best there ever was! There was never
anyone like you! . . . Oh, *my*! Oh, my *God*!"

He exploded inside her, draining himself; his body
limp, the ache in his temples receding. At least he was good
for *something*. He had aroused her, made her want him.

And then he heard her voice, all professionalism.

"There, lamb. That wasn't so difficult, was it?"

He looked at her. Her expression was that of a well-
applauded performer. Her eyes were plastic death.

"I owe you," he said softly, coldly.

"No, you don't." She laughed. "I don't take money
from you. He pays me plenty."

Chancellor remembered everything. The party, the
argument, the drunken trip from Beverly Hills, his anger
on the telephone.

Aaron Sheffield, motion-picture producer, owner of
Counterstrike!

Sheffield had been at the party, his young wife in tow.
In fact, it was Sheffield who had called him, asking him
to come along. There was no reason not to accept, and
there was a very good reason to do so: His elusive coauthor
of the *Counterstrike!* screenplay was the host.

Not to worry. You wrote a winner, sweetheart.

But last night there was something to worry about.
They wanted to tell him in pleasant surroundings. More
than pleasant. Quite a bit more.

The studio had received several "very serious" calls
from Washington about the filming of *Counterstrike!* It
was pointed out that there was a major error in the book:

The Central Intelligence Agency did not operate domestically. It did not involve itself in operations within the borders of the United States. The CIA's 1947 charter had specifically prohibited this. Therefore, Aaron Sheffield had agreed to change that aspect of the script. Chancellor's CIA would become an elite corps of disaffected former intelligence specialists acting outside government channels.

What the hell, Aaron Sheffield had said. *It's better dramatically. We got two types of villains, and Washington's happy.*

But Chancellor was furious. He knew what he was talking about. He had spoken with truly disaffected men who had worked for the agency and was appalled at what they had been called upon to do. Appalled because it was illegal and appalled because there were no alternatives. A maniac named J. Edgar Hoover had severed all intelligence conduits between the FBI and the CIA. The men of the CIA themselves would have to go after the domestic information withheld from them. Who were they going to complain to? Mitchell? Nixon?

Most of whatever power *Counterstrike!* had was in the specific use of the agency. To eliminate it was to vitiate a great part of the book. Peter had objected strenuously, and the more angry he became, the more, it seemed, he drank. And the more he drank, the more provocative had the girl beside him become.

Sheffield had driven them home. Peter and the girl were in the backseat, her skirt above her waist, her blouse unbuttoned, her enormous breasts exposed in racing shadows driving him wild. Drunken wild.

And they'd gone inside together while Sheffield drove off. The girl had brought two bottles of Pernod, a gift from Aaron, and the games began in earnest. Wild games, drunken, naked games.

Until the shooting pains in his skull stopped him, providing a few moments of clarity. He had lurched for the telephone, thumbed insanely through his notes on the bedside table for Sheffield's number, and punched the buttons furiously.

He had roared at Sheffield, calling him every obscenity he could think of, screaming his objections—and his guilt —at having been manipulated. There'd be *no* changes in *Counterstrike!*

As he lay there on the bed, the blond girl beside him, Chancellor remembered Sheffield's words over the phone.

"Easy, kid. What difference does it make to you? You don't have script approval. We were just being polite. Get down from your sky-high perch. You're just a lousy little homemaker-fucker like the rest of us."

The blond girl beside Peter on the bed was Sheffield's wife.

Chancellor turned to her. The vacuous eyes were brighter, but still dead. The mouth opened, and an experienced tongue slid sensuously out and then back and forth, conveying an unmistakable message.

The well-applauded performer was ready to perform again.

Who gave a shit? He reached for her.

3

The man whose face was among the most recognized in the nation sat alone at table ten in the Mayflower Restaurant on Connecticut Avenue. The table was by a window, and the occupant kept glancing through the glass absently, but not without a certain vague hostility, at the passersby on the street.

He had arrived at precisely eleven thirty-five; he would finish his lunch and depart at twelve-forty. It had been an unbroken custom for over twenty years. The hour and five minutes was the custom, not the Mayflower. The Mayflower was a recent change, since the closing of Harvey's, several blocks away.

The face, with its enormous jaws, drawn-out mouth, and partially thyroid eyes, had disintegrated. The jaws were sagging jowls; creased, blemished flesh overlapped the slits that had been eyes; the touched-up strands of hair attested to the ferocious ego that was intrinsic to the aggressively negative expression.

His usual companion was not in evidence. Declining

health and two strokes prevented his elegantly dressed presence. The soft, pampered face—struggling for masculinity —had for decades been the flower to the bristled cactus. The man about to have lunch looked across the table as if he expected to see his attractive alter ego. That he saw no one seemed to trigger a periodic tremor in his fingers and a recurrent twitching of his mouth. He seemed enveloped in loneliness; his eyes darted about, alert to real and imagined ills surrounding him.

A favorite waiter was indisposed for the day; it was a personal affront. He let it be known.

Fruit salad with a dome of cottage cheese in the center was marked for table ten. It was processed from the open, stainless steel shelf in the kitchen to the service counter. The blond-haired second assistant chef, temporarily employed, marked off the various trays, appraising their appearance with a practiced eye. He stood over table ten's fruit salad, a clipboard in his hand, his gaze directed at the trays in front of it.

Underneath the clipboard a pair of thin silver tongs were held horizontally. In the tongs' teeth was a soft white capsule. The blond-haired man smiled at a harassed waiter coming through the dining-room door; at the same moment he plunged the silver tongs into the mound of cottage cheese beneath the clipboard, removed them, and moved on.

Seconds later he returned to the order for table ten, shook his head, and touched up the dome of cottage cheese with a fork.

Within the inserted capsule was a mild dose of lysergic acid diethylamide. The capsule would disintegrate and release the narcotic some seven to eight hours after the moment of ingestion.

The minor stress and the disorientation that resulted would be enough. There would be no traces in the bloodstream at the time of death.

The middle-aged woman sat in a windowless room. She listened to the voice coming out of the wall speakers, then repeated the words into the microphone of a tape machine. Her objective was to duplicate as closely as possible the now familiar voice from the speakers. Every slid-

ing tone, every nuance, the idiosyncratic short pauses that
followed the partially sibilant *s*'s.

The voice coming from the speakers was that of Helen
Gandy, for years the personal secretary of John Edgar
Hoover.

In the corner of the small studio stood two suitcases.
Both were fully packed. In four hours the woman and the
suitcases would be on a transatlantic flight bound for
Zurich. It was the first leg of a trip that would eventually
take her south to the Balearic Islands and a house on the
sea in Majorca. But first there was Zurich, where the Staats-
Banque would pay upon signature a negotiated sum into
Barclays, which would in turn transfer the amount in two
payments to an account at its branch in Palma. The first
payment would be made immediately, the second in eighteen months.

Varak had hired her. He believed that for every job
there was a correct, skilled applicant. The computerized
data banks at the National Security Council had been programed in secret, by Varak alone, until they produced the
applicant he sought.

She was a widow, a former radio actress. She and her
husband had been caught in the crosscurrents of the Red
Channels madness of 1954 and had never recovered. It was
a madness sanctioned and aided by the Federal Bureau of
Investigation. Her husband, considered by many to have
been a major talent, did not work for seven years. At the
end of that time, his heart had burst in anguish. He had
died in a subway station on his way to a clerical job at a
downtown bank. By now the woman had been finished professionally for eighteen years; the pain and the rejection
and the loneliness had robbed her of the ability to compete.

There was no competition now. She was not told why
she was doing what she was doing. Only that her brief
conversation had to result in a "yes" on the other end of
the line.

The recipient of the call was a man the woman
loathed with all her being. A basic accessory to the madness that had stolen her life.

It was shortly past nine in the evening, and the telephone truck was not an uncommon sight on Thirtieth
Street Place in northwest Washington. The short street was

a cul-de-sac, ending with the imposing gates of the Peruvian embassador's residence, the national shield prominently displayed on the stone pillars. Two thirds of the way down the block, on the left, was the faded red brick house belonging to the director of the Federal Bureau of Investigation. One or both residences were continuously upgrading communications facilities.

And every once in a while unmarked vans patrolled the area, antennas protruding from their roofs. It was said that John Edgar Hoover ordered such patrols to check out any unwanted electronic surveillance that might have been planted there by inimical foreign governments.

Frequently complaints were registered with the State Department by the Peruvian ambassador. It was embarrassing; there wasn't anything State could do about the situation. Hoover's private life was an extension of his professional barony.

Peru wasn't very important anyway.

The telephone truck drove down the street, made a U-turn, and retraced its route back to Thirtieth Street, where it turned right for fifty yards, then right again into a row of garages. At the end of the garage complex was a stone wall that bordered the rear grounds of 4936 Thirtieth Street Place, Hoover's residence. Above and beyond the garages were other houses with windows overlooking the Hoover property. The man in the telephone truck knew that in one of those windows was an agent from the bureau, one of a team assigned to twenty-four-hour surveillance. The teams were secret and were rotated every week.

The driver of the truck was also aware that whoever was in one of those windows beyond the garage would place a routine call to a special number at the telephone company. The inquiry would be simple, asked above a strange hum on the line: What was the problem that brought a repair truck into the area at that hour?

The operator would check her call sheet and reply with the truth as it had been given to her.

There was a short in a junction box. Suspect: an inquisitive squirrel invading rotted insulation. The damage was responsible for the noticeable buzz on the line. Didn't the caller hear it?

Yes, he heard it.

Varak had learned years ago, in his early days with the

National Security Council, never to give too simple an answer to questions raised by area surveillance. It would not be accepted, anymore than an overly complicated one would be accepted. There was always a middle ground.

The high-frequency radio phone in the truck hummed: a signal. An inquiring call had been made to the telephone company by an alert FBI man. The driver stopped the small van, once more turned around, and drove thirty-five yards back to the telephone pole. His sightlines to the residence were clear. He parked and waited, blueprints spread on the front seat as if he were studying them.

Agents often took late-night walks in the vicinity. All contingencies had to be covered.

The telephone truck was now eighty yards northwest of 4936 Thirtieth Street Place. The driver left his seat, crawled back into the rear of the van, and switched on his equipment. He had precisely forty-six minutes to wait. During that time he had to lock in on the flows of current being received in Hoover's residence. The heavier loads defined the circuits of the alarm system; the lesser ones were lights and radios and television sets. Defining the alarm system was crucial, but no less important was the knowledge that current was being used in the lower right area. It meant that electrical units were switched on in the maid's room. It was vital to know that. Annie Fields, Hoover's personal housekeeper for as long as anyone could remember, was there for the night.

The limousine made a right turn off Pennsylvania Avenue into Tenth Street and slowed down in front of the far west entrance to the FBI. The limousine was identical to the one that daily brought the director to his offices—even to the slightly dented chrome bumper Hoover had left as it was, a reminder to the chauffeur, James Crawford, of the man's carelessness. It was not, of course, the same car; that particular vehicle was guarded night and day. But no one, not even Crawford, could have told the difference.

The driver spoke the proper words into the dashboard microphone, and the huge steel doors of the entrance parted. The night guard saluted as the limousine passed through the concrete structure, with its three succeeding concrete doorways, into the small circular drive. A second Justice Department guard leaped out of the south entranceway, reached for the handle of the right rear door, and pulled it open.

Varak got out quickly and thanked the astonished guard. The driver and a third man—seated next to the driver—also stepped out and offered pleasant but subdued greetings.

"Where's the director?" asked the guard. "This is Mr. Hoover's private car."

"We're here on his instructions," said Varak calmly. "He wants us taken directly to Internal Security. They're to call him. IS has the number; it's on a scrambler. I'm afraid it's an emergency. Please hurry."

The guard looked at the three well-dressed, well-spoken men. His concern diminished; these men knew the highly classified gate codes that changed every night; beyond that, they carried instructions to call the director himself. On the scrambler phone at the Internal Security desk. That telephone number was *never* used.

The guard nodded, led the men inside to the security desk in the corridor, and returned to his post outside. Behind the wide steel panel with the myriad wires and small television screens, sat a senior agent dressed not unlike the three men who approached him. Varak took a laminated identification card from his pocket and spoke.

"Agents Longworth, Krepps, and Salter," he said, placing his ID on the couner. "You must be Parke."

"That's right," replied the agent, taking Varak's identification and reaching for the other two ID's as they were handed to him. "Have we met, Longworth?"

"Not in ten or twelve years. Quantico."

The agent looked briefly at the ID's, returned them to the counter, and squinted in recollection. "Yeah, I remember the name. Al Longworth. Long time." He extended his hand; Varak took it. "Where've you been?"

"La Jolla."

"Christ, you've got a friend!"

"That's why I'm here. These are my two best men in southern Cal. *He* called me last night." Varak leaned ever so slightly over the counter. "I've got bad news, Parke. It's not good at all," he said, barely above a whisper. "We may be getting near 'open territory.' "

The expression on the agent's face changed abruptly; the shock was obvious.

Among the senior officers at the bureau the phrase

open territory meant the unthinkable: The director was ill.
Seriously, perhaps fatally, ill.

"Oh, my God . . ." muttered Parke.

"He wants you to call him on the scrambler."

"Oh, Christ!" Under the circumstances it was obviously the last thing the agent wanted to do. "What does he want? What am I supposed to say, Longworth? Oh, Jesus!"

"He wants us taken up to Flags. Tell him we're here; verify his instructions and clear one of my men for the relays."

"The relays? What for?"

"Ask him."

Parke stared at Varak for a moment, then reached for the telephone.

Fifteen blocks south, in the cellar of a telephone-company complex, a man sat on a stool in front of a panel of interlocking wires. On his jacket was a plastic card with his photograph and, in large letters beneath it, the word *Inspector*. In his right ear was a plug attached to an amplifier on the floor; next to the amplifier was a small cassette recorder. Wires spiraled up to other wires in the panel.

The tiny bulb on the amplifier lighted up. The scrambler phone at the FBI security desk was in use. The man's eyes were riveted on a button in the cassette recorder; he listened with the ears of an experienced professional. Instantly he pushed the button; the tape rolled, and almost immediately he shut it off. He waited several moments and once again pushed the button, and once again the reels spun.

Fifteen blocks north Varak listened to Parke. The words had been lifted, edited, and refined from a number of tapes. As planned, the voice on the other end of the line would be louder than a normal voice; it would be the voice of a man wanting to not acknowledge illness, fighting to appear normal, and in so doing, speaking abnormally. It not only fit the subject psychiatrically, it had a further value. The volume lent authority, and the authority reduced the possibility that the deception would be spotted.

"Yes, what is it?" The gruff voice could be heard clearly.

"Mr. Hoover, this is senior agent Parke at Internal

Security. Agents Longworth, Krepps, and—" Parke stopped, forgetting the name, his expression bewildered.

"Salter," whispered Varak.

"Salter, sir. Longworth, Krepps, and Salter. They've arrived, and they said I was to call you to verify your instructions. They said they're to be taken upstairs to your offices, and one is to be cleared for the relays————"

"Those men," came the harsh, unrhythmic interruption, "are there at my personal orders. Do as they say. They are to be given complete cooperation, and nothing is to be said to anyone. Is that understood?"

"Yes, sir."

"What's your name again?"

"Senior Agent Lester Parke, sir."

There was a pause; Varak tensed his stomach muscles and held his breath. The pause was too long!

"I'll remember that," came the words finally. "Good night, Parke." A concluding click was heard on the line.

Varak breathed again. Even the use of the name worked; it had been lifted from a conversation the subject had had during which he had complained about the crime rate in Rock Creek Park.

"He sounds awful, doesn't he?" Parke replaced the telephone and reached underneath the counter for three night passes.

"He's a very courageous man," said Varak. "He asked for your name?"

"Yeah," replied the agent, inserting the passes into the automatic timer.

"If the worst happens, you might find yourself with a bonus," added Varak, turning his head away from his two companions.

"What?" Parke looked up.

"A personal bequest. Nothing official."

"I don't understand."

"You're not supposed to. But you heard the man; I heard him, too. Keep your own counsel, as the book says. You'll answer to me if you don't. . . . The director's the best friend I've ever had."

Parke stared at Varak. "La Jolla," he said.

"La Jolla," answered Varak.

A great deal more was conveyed than the name of a California seacoast town. Stories had circulated for years— the grand designs of a retired monarch, a mansion overlooking the Pacific, a clandestine government housing the secrets of a nation.

The sad-faced middle-aged woman watched the second hand of the clock on the wall in the small studio. Fifty-five seconds to go. The telephone was on the table, in front of the tape machine she had used to rehearse the words. Over and over again, a full week of rehearsals aimed for a single performance that would last no more than a minute.

Rehearsal. Peformance,

Terms of a nearly forgotten lexicon.

She was no fool. The strange, blond-haired man who had hired her had explained very little, but enough to let her know that what she was about to do was a *good* thing. Desired by far better men than the man she would talk to on the telephone in . . . forty seconds.

The woman reminisced as she watched the hand on the clock move slowly toward the mark. They had once said her husband was a fine talent; that's what everyone had said. He was on his way to becoming a star, a *real* star, not a photogenic accident. Everyone had said so.

And then other people came along and said he was on a list. A very important list that meant he was not a good citizen. And those on the list were given a label.

Subversive.

And the label was given legitimacy. Tight-lipped young men in dark suits began to show up in studios and producers' offices.

Federal Bureau of Investigation.

Then they went behind closed doors and held private conversations.

Subversive. It was a word associated with the man she was about to speak to.

She reached for the telephone.

"This is for you, my darling," she whispered. She was primed; the adrenalin was flowing as it used to flow. Then a calm swept over her. She was confident, a professional again. It would be the performance of her life.

John Edgar Hoover lay in bed, trying to focus on the television set across the room. He kept changing channels on the remote control; none of the pictures was clear. He was further aggravated by a strange hollowness in his

throat. He'd never experienced the feeling before; it was
as though a hole had been drilled in his neck, allowing too
much air into his upper chest. But there was no pain, just
an uncomfortable sensation that was somehow related to
the distortion in the sound now coming from the television set.

In and out. Louder, then softer.

And oddly enough, he felt hungry. He had never been
hungry at that hour; he had trained himself not to be.

It was all very annoying, the annoyance heightened
by the dull ring of his private telephone. No more than ten
people in Washington had the number; he was not feeling
up to a crisis. He reached for the phone and spoke angrily.

"Yes? What is it?"

"Mr. Hoover. I'm sorry to disturb you, but it's urgent."

"Miss Gandy?" What was wrong with his hearing?
Gandy's voice seemed to float, in and out, louder, then
softer. "What's the matter, Miss Gandy?"

"The President phoned from Camp David. He's en
route to the White House and would like you to see Mr.
Haldeman tonight."

"Tonight? Why?"

"He told me to tell you it was a matter of the utmost
importance, related to information the CIA has gathered
during the past forty-eight hours."

John Edgar Hoover could not help the scowl that
crossed his face. The Central Intelligence Agency was an
abomination, a band of sycophants led by the liberal ortho-
doxy. It was not to be trusted.

Neither was the present occupant of the White House,
but if he had data that rightfully belonged to the bureau
and it was sufficiently vital to send out a man—*that* man—
in the middle of the night to deliver it, there was no point
in refusing.

Hoover wished the hollowness in his throat would go
away. It was most irritating. And something else bothered
him.

"Miss Gandy, the President has this number. Why
didn't he call himself?"

"He understood you were having dinner out. He
knows you dislike being disturbed in a restaurant. I was to
coordinate the meeting."

Hoover squinted through his glasses at the bedside
clock. It was not the middle of the night; it was barely ten

fifteen. He should have realized that. He had left Tolson's at eight, claiming a sudden weariness. The President's intelligence was not very accurate, either. He was not at a restaurant, he had been with Clyde.

He was so tired he had gone to bed much earlier than usual. "I'll see Haldeman. Out here."

"I assumed that, sir. The President suggested that you might wish to dictate several memorandums, instructions to a number of field offices. I volunteered to drive out with Mr. Haldeman. The White House car is picking me up."

"That's very thoughtful, Miss Gandy. They must have something interesting."

"The President wants no one to know that Mr. Haldeman is coming to see you. He said it would be terribly embarrassing."

"Use the side entrance, Miss Gandy. You have a key. The alarms will be shut off. I'll notify surveillance."

"Very well, Mr. Hoover."

The middle-aged woman replaced the phone in front of the tape machine and sat back in the chair.

She had done it! She had really done it! She'd fallen into the rhythm, every tonal nuance, the imperceptible pauses, the slightly nasal inflections. Perfect!

The remarkable thing was that there had never been an instant of hesitation. It was as if the terrors of twenty years had been erased in a matter of moments.

She had one more call to make. Here she could use any voice she liked, the blander the better. She dialed.

"The White House," said the voice on the line.

"FBI, honey," said the middle-aged actress in a faintly southern accent. "This is just information for the logs, nothing urgent. At nine o'clock this evening the director received Mr. Haldeman's message. This is to confirm the receipt, that's all."

"Okay, it's confirmed. I'll list it. Muggy day, isn't it?"

"It's a beautiful night, though," replied the actress. "The most beautiful night ever."

"Someone's got a heavy date."

"I've got something better than that. Much better. Good night, White House."

"Good night, Bureau."

The woman got up from the chair and reached for her pocketbook. "We did it, my darling," she whispered. Her

last performance had been her finest. She was revenged.
She was free.

The driver in the telephone van studied the graph of
the electrical field scope closely. There were breaks in the
heavier circuits in the lower left and left central areas. It
meant that the alarm devices had been shut down in those
sections: the driveway entrance, the door in the stone wall,
and the path beyond it that led to the rear of the house.

Everything was on schedule. The driver looked at his
watch; it was nearly time to climb the telephone pole. He
checked the rest of his equipment. When he threw a switch,
the electrical current throughout Hoover's residence would
be interrupted. Lights, television sets, and radios would
fade and return in a quick series of disturbances. The dis-
ruptions would last for twenty seconds, no more. The
length of time was sufficient, the momentary distraction
enough.

But before that switch was thrown, there was a prior
job to be done. If a custom unchanged for years was repeated tonight, an obstacle would be removed efficiently.
He looked at his watch again.

Now.

He opened the rear doors of the van and jumped to
the pavement. He crossed rapidly to the pole, unhooked
one end of the long safety belt, and whipped it around the
wood, snapping the hook into his waist clamp. He lifted
his boots one at a time and kicked the spikes into place.

He looked around. There was no one. He slapped the
safety belt above him on the pole and began to climb. In
less than thirty seconds he was near the top.

The spill of the streetlight was too bright, too dangerous. It hung suspended from a short metal brace just above
him. He reached into his pocket and pulled out an air
pistol loaded with lead pellets. He scanned the ground, the
alley, the windows above the row of garages. He angled the
air gun up at the lighted glass sphere and pulled the trigger.

There was a spit, instantly followed by the quiet static
of exploding electric filaments. The light went out.

He waited silently; there was no sound. In the darkness he opened the flap of the equipment case and slid out a
metal cylinder eighteen inches long. It was the barrel of an
odd-looking rifle. From another compartment he withdrew
a heavy steel rod and attached it to the cylinder; at the end

was a curved brace. From a third pocket in the leather tool-case the driver extracted a twelve-inch infrared telescope that had been precision-tooled for the top of the cylinder; it was self-locking and once locked, accurate. Finally, the man reached into his jacket and pulled out the trigger-housing unit. He snapped it into the opening on the under-side of the barrel and tested the silent bolt action; all was ready, only the ammunition remained.

Cradling the odd rifle in his left arm, he slid his right hand into his pocket and took out a steel dart, the flared end dipped in luminous paint. He inserted it into the chamber and slid the bolt back into place. The hammer was cocked, the rifle ready to fire.

His watch read ten forty-four; if the longstanding habit was going to be observed this night, he'd know it shortly. Suspended thirty-five feet above the ground, the man rebraced himself and tightened the safety strap until his body was pressed against the pole. He raised the rifle and jammed the curved brace into his shoulder.

He looked through the luminous green circle that was the sight and moved it carefully until he had the rear door of the director's house clearly in view. In spite of the darkness, the picture was clear; the cross hairs of zero aim were focused directly on the steps of the entrance.

He waited. Minutes passed slowly. He stole a glance at the dial of his watch; it was ten fifty-three. He could not wait much longer; he had to return to the van to throw the switch.

Of all nights! Routine was not going to be observed!

Then he saw the porch light! The door opened; the driver felt a wave of relief.

Through his infrared scope the huge animal came into focus. It was Hoover's enormous bull mastiff, rumored to be among the most vicious of dogs. It was said the director enjoyed the comparisons between the faces of master and animal.

The custom of years was being carried out. Every evening between ten forty-five and eleven Hoover or Annie Fields let the dog out to wander in the enclosed grounds of the residence, its waste picked up in the morning.

The door closed, the porch light remained on. The man on the pole moved his weapon with his quarry. The cross hairs were now on the animal's enormous throat.

The driver squeezed the trigger; there was a slight

metallic click. Through the sight he could see the mastiff's eyes widen in shock; the huge jaws sprang open, but no sound came.

The animal fell to the ground, narcotized.

A nondescript gray automobile coasted to a stop a hundred feet past the driveway of 4936 Thirtieth Street Place. A tall man in a dark suit got out of the passenger door and looked up and down the block. Near the grounds of the Peruvian embassador's residence a woman walked a dalmatian. In the other direction, perhaps two hundred yards away, a couple were strolling up a path toward a lighted doorway.

Otherwise there was nothing.

The man looked at his watch and felt the small bulge in his coat pocket.

He had exactly half a minute, thirty seconds, and after that he would have precisely twenty seconds. He nodded to the driver and walked rapidly back toward the driveway, the crepe soles of his shoes noiseless on the pavement. He swung into the shadowed drive without breaking his stride, approached the door in the wall, and removed a small air pistol from his belt, shifting it to his left hand. The dart was in place; he hoped he would not have to use it.

He looked again at his watch. Eleven seconds; he would allow an additional three for safety. He checked the position of the key in his right hand.

Now.

He inserted the key, turned the lock, opened the door, and entered the grounds, leaving the door open six inches. The huge dog was on the grass, its jaws slack, its enormous head pressed against the earth. The driver of the telephone van had done his job efficiently. He would remove the dart on his way out; there would be no trace of the narcotic in the morning. He returned the dart gun to his pocket.

He walked rapidly to the door on the first floor, his mind ticking off the seconds. He could see the intermittent dimming of lights throughout the house. By his estimate nine seconds remained as he inserted the second key.

The lock would not turn! The tumblers jammed. He manipulated the key furiously.

Four seconds, three . . .

His fingers—his surgeon's fingers encased in surgical

gloves—delicately, swiftly maneuvered the jagged metal within the jagged orifice as if it were a scapel in flesh.

Two seconds, one . . .

It opened!

The tall man stepped inside, leaving this door, too, ajar.

He stood in the hallway and listened. The lights were steady again. There was the sound of a television set from the housekeeper's room at the other side of the house. Upstairs the sounds were fainter but discernible; it was the eleven o'clock news. The doctor wondered briefly what tomorrow's eleven o'clock news would be like. He wished he could be in Washington to hear it.

He crossed to the staircase and began to climb. At the top he stood in front of the door to the right of the staircase, in the center of the landing. The door that led to the man he had waited over two decades to see.

Waited in hatred. Deep hatred, never to be forgotten.

He turned the knob cautiously and opened the door. The director had dozed off, his enormous head angled down, the jowls falling over his thick neck. In his fat, feminine hands were the spectacles his vanity rarely allowed him to use to public.

The doctor went to the television set and turned it up so that the sound filled the room. He crossed back to the foot of the bed and stared down at the object of his loathing.

The director's head snapped down, then abruptly up. His face was contorted.

"What?"

"Put on your glasses," said the doctor above the noise of the television set.

"What's this? Miss Gandy? . . . Who are you? You're not——" Shaking, Hoover put on his glasses.

"Look closely. It's been twenty-two years."

The bulging eyes within the folds of flesh beyond the lenses focused. The sight they saw caused their possessor to gasp. "You! How——?"

"Twenty-two years," continued the doctor mechanically but loud enough to be heard above the sound of sirens and music from the television set. He reached into his pocket and took out a hypodermic needle. "I have a different name now. I practice in Paris, where my patients have heard the stories but don't concern themselves. *Le médecin américain* is considered one of the finest in the hospital——"

Suddenly the director swung his arm out toward the night table. The doctor lunged forward at the side of the bed, pinning the soft wrist against the mattress. Hoover began to scream; the doctor jammed his elbow into the jowls, cutting off all sound. He raised the naked, trembling arm.

With his teeth the doctor took off the rubber tip of the needle. He plunged the hypodermic into the rubbery flesh of the exposed armpit.

"This is for my wife and my son. Everything you stole from me."

The driver of the gray automobile turned in his seat, his eyes directed at the second-story windows of the house. The lights were extinguished for five seconds, then turned on again.

The unknown doctor had done his work; the release in the headboard had been found and activated. There were no seconds to be lost. The driver removed the microphone from the radio unit, pressed the button, and spoke.

"Phase One completed," he said tersely in a pronounced British accent.

The office stretched for nearly forty feet. The large mahogany desk at one end was slightly elevated, facing low, overstuffed leather chairs, forcing visitors to raise their eyes to its occupant. Beyond the desk, obscuring the wall beyond, was a row of flags, the Federal Bureau of Investigation's banner sharing the center position with the nation's.

Varak stood motionless in front of the desk, his eyes on the two telephones. One instrument had its receiver out of the cradle, the open line connected to a phone in the cellar of the building, to a man in the relay room where all alarms were controlled. The other phone was intact; it was an outside line that bypassed the bureau's switchboard. There was no number printed on the circular tab in the middle of the dial.

The center drawer of the desk was open. Beside it stood a second man, the spill of the desk lamp illuminating his right hand, which was angled, palm up, in the open space of the drawer. His fingers touched a small toggle switch recessed in the roof of the desk.

The telephone began to ring. Varak picked it up at the first hint of sound. He said one word quietly.

"Flags."

"Phase One completed," was the relayed reply over the line.

Varak nodded. The man in front of him snapped the unseen switch in his fingers.

Four stories below, in a concrete room, a third man watched a panel of dark squares built into the wall. He heard the whistle from the open telephone that lay within arm's reach on the steel table beside him.

Suddenly a bell shattered the stillness of the enclosure. A red light in the center of the panel shone brightly.

The man pushed the square beneath the bright red light.

Silence.

A uniformed guard burst through the corridor door, his eyes wild.

"We're testing," said the man in front of the panel, calmly replacing the telephone. "I told you that."

"*Christ!*" exploded the guard, inhaling deeply. "You nightcrawlers will give me a heart attack."

"Don't let us do that," said the man, smiling.

Varak watched Salter open the door of the closet beyond the flags and switch on the light inside. Both telephones were back in their cradles; there would be one more call. From Varak to Bravo.

Not Genesis. Genesis was dead.

The man was Bravo now. He would be told the job was done.

Several feet in front of the row of flags were two webbed metal baskets on wheels. They were a familiar sight in the bureau's hallways, through which scores like them moved mountains of paper from one office to another. In a few minutes they would be filled with hundreds, perhaps several thousand, dossiers and taken downstairs past a senior agent named Parke to a waiting limousine. The files of John Edgar Hoover would be consigned to a blast furnace.

And a growing Fourth Reich would be crippled.

"Varak! *Quick!*"

The shout came from the closet beyond the flags. Varak raced inside.

The steel vault was open, the locks on the cabinets sprung. The four drawers were pulled out.

The two drawers on the left were thick with papers, bulging. Files *A* through *L* were intact.

The two drawers on the right were empty. The metal dividers fell against each other, holding nothing.

Files *M* through *Z* were missing. One half of Hoover's cabinets of filth was gone.

4

Chancellor lay in the hot sun and read the *Los Angeles Times*. The headlines seemed almost unreal, as if the event were not really possible, rooted somehow in fantasy.

The man at last was dead. J. Edgar Hoover had died insignificantly in his bed, the way millions of old men die. Without drama, without consequence. Just the failure of the heart to keep pace with the years. But with that death a relief swept over the country; it was apparent even in the newspaper copy reporting the death.

The statements issued by Congress and the administration were, as could be expected, sanctimonious and dripping with obsequious praise, but even in these well-chosen words the tears of the crocodiles could be clearly seen. The relief was everywhere.

Chancellor folded the paper and shoved it into the sand to anchor it. He did not want to read any more.

Far more to the point, he did not want to write, either. Oh, Christ! When would he want to? Would he ever want to? If there were such a thing as a Sybaritic vegetable, he would be it.

What made it ironic was that he was getting rich. Joshua Harris had called from New York a half hour ago to report that another payment had been made by the studio on schedule.

Peter was making a great deal of money for doing absolutely nothing. Since the episode with Sheffield's wife he had not bothered to go to the studio or call anyone concerned with *Counterstrike!*

Not to worry. You wrote a winner, sweetheart.

So be it.

He raised his wrist and looked at his watch. It was almost eight thirty; the morning at Malibu had come quickly. The air was moist, the sun too bright, the sand already too hot. Slowly he got to his feet. He'd go inside and sit in an air-conditioned room and have a drink.

Why not? What was the old phrase? *I never drink before five in the afternoon. Thank God, it's five o'clock somewhere!*

Was it past five—in the morning—back East? No, he always got that mixed up; it was the other way around. Back East it was barely eleven thirty.

The sky was overcast, the air heavy and oppressive. A steady, humid drizzle threatened to become a downpour. The crowds in the Capitol Plaza were quiet; muted chants of war resisters behind barricades intruded on the hum of the throngs, threatening, as the drizzle threatened, to grow louder as the rain grew louder.

Here and there an umbrella snapped; ribbed circles of black cloth sprung open, stretching over passive faces. Eyes were dull, resentful; expressions lifeless. The day was angry. There was an undercurrent of fear, the final legacy, perhaps, of the man whose body was being transported in the enormous hearse that was twenty-five minutes late arriving. Suddenly it was there, efficiently swinging off the tree-lined drive onto the concrete grounds of the plaza.

Stefan Varak noted that the crowds seemed to move back, although none had been in the hearse's path. Further proof of the legacy, he thought.

Ranks of servicemen stood at attention at either side of the rotunda steps; uniforms were darkened with rain, eyes stared straight ahead. It was eleven twenty-five. The body of John Edgar Hoover was to lie in state throughout the day and night. It was an honor accorded to no civil servant before in the nation's history.

Or was it a desire on the nation's part to prove to itself and to the world that he was really dead—this man who had sprung giantlike out of the morass of corruption that had been the original Bureau of Investigation to fashion an efficient, extraordinary organization, only to disintegrate with the passing years, still believing in his own infallibility. If he had only stopped before the fever gripped him, thought Varak.

Eight servicemen had solemnly broken away from the ranks and were at the rear door of the hearse, four on either side. The heavy panel swung back; the flag-wrapped coffin slid out, dipping slightly as fingers gripped protruding steel handles and pulled it free of the vehicle. In a tortuously slow march the soldiers moved toward the steps through the thickening drizzle.

They began the agonizing climb up the thirty-five steps to the entrance of the rotunda. Lifeless eyes were focused forward, at nothing; faces were drenched with sweat and rain; veins close to bursting could be seen below the cuffs of the uniforms; collars were black from the rivulets of perspiration that rolled down straining necks.

The crowds seemed to suspend their collective breathing until the casket reached the top of the steps. The soldiers paused at attention; then they started again and carried their burden through the great bronze doors of the rotunda.

Varak turned to the cameraman at his side. Both stood on a small, raised platform. The metal initials below the thick lens of the camera were those of a television station in Seattle, Washington. The station was part of a West Coast pool; it had no personnel in the Capitol Plaza that morning.

"Are you getting everything?" asked Varak in French.

"Every group, every row, every face the zoom can reach," replied the Frenchman.

"Will the dim light—the rain—be a problem?"

"Not with this film. Nothing faster."

"Good. I'm going upstairs."

Varak, his NSC photo-identification prominent on his lapel, threaded his way through the crowds to an entrance and walked past the guards to the security desk. He spoke to the uniformed man on duty.

"Is the staircase from Documents sealed off yet?"

"I don't know, sir." The guard's eyes riveted on the page of instructions in front of him. "There's nothing here about closing it."

"Goddamn it, there should be," said Varak. "Make a note of it, please."

Varak walked away. There was no vital reason for that particular staircase to be closed, but by so ordering it, Varak had established his authority with the guard. If their communications equipment broke down, he would need access to a telephone, without seconds wasted for identification purposes. Those precious moments would not be lost now; the guard would remember.

He climbed the staircase, two steps at a time, and stood behind the crowd filling the House entrance to the rotunda. A perspiring congressman was trying to make his way through; he was drunk and twice stumbled. A younger man, obviously an aide, reached him, grabbed his left elbow and pulled him back out of the crowd. The congressman pivoted unsteadily and his shoulders slammed into the wall.

As Varak looked at the bewildered, sweating face, he remembered that the congressman had publicly accused the FBI of tapping his phone; he had embarrassed the director. Then abruptly the accusations had stopped. Suddenly, the evidence that had been promised did not materialize; the man had no more to say.

His is one of the missing files, Varak guessed as he walked down the corridor to a door. He nodded to the guard, who scrutinized the NSC identification and opened the door for him. Inside were the twisting, narrow steps that led to the dome of the rotunda.

Three minutes later Varak knelt beside a second cameraman 160 feet above the rotunda floor. They were on the upper walkway, closed for years to tourists. The quiet hum of the camera was barely heard; it was packed with triple insulation, the telescopic lens screwed in and locked with reinforced clamps. There was no way that camera or the man operating it could be seen from the floor. Several feet away were three cartons of film.

Below, in the rotunda, the bearers had placed the coffin on the catafalque. Beyond the ropes, crowded in with little dignity, were the leaders of the nation competing for solemn recognition. The honor guard took up its positions, each branch of the military represented. From somewhere far away in the great hall a telephone rang twice. Instinctively Varak reached into his pocket and pulled out the small radio unit that was his link to others. He held it to his ear, flipped on the switch, and listened. There was nothing and he breathed again.

A voice floated up; Edward Elson, the Senate chaplain and minister of the Presbyterian Church, delivered the opening prayer. He was followed by Warren Burger, who began his eulogy. Varak heard the words; the muscles of his jaw tensed.

". . . a man of quiet courage, who would not sacrifice principle to public clamor . . . who served his country and earned the admiration of all who believed in ordered liberty."

Whose principles? What is ordered liberty? mused Varak as he watched the scene far below. There was no time for such thoughts. He whispered to the cameraman; the language he spoke was Czech. "Is everything all right?"

"Yes, if I don't get cramps."

"Stretch out every now and then, but don't get up. I'll relieve you for thirty minutes every four hours. Use the room off the second walkway; I'll bring food."

"Through the night as well?"

"It's what you're being paid for. I want every face that walks through those bronze doors. Every goddamned face."

Beyond the echoing, bass-toned words that filled the dome he could hear another sound. Far in the distance, outside, behind barricades in the rain across the plaza, the war resisters had begun their own particular chant for the dead. Not for the body in the rotunda, but for thousands halfway across the world. A liturgical drama was being played out in bitter ecclesiastical irony.

"Every face," repeated Varak.

The spray of the fountain cascaded down into the waters of the circular pool in the gardens in front of the Presbyterian Church. Beyond the fountain the white marble tower rose in constricted splendor. To the right was the double-laned drive that passed under a stone portico, with doors on the left that led into the church. The effect was one of tollbooths, not a protected entrance into the house of God.

Varak had his cameras positioned, the two exhausted operators filled with coffee and Benzedrine. In a few hours it would all be over. Both would be far richer than they had been a few days ago; both would be flying home. One to Prague, one to Marseilles.

The limousines started arriving at nine forty-five; the funeral service was scheduled for eleven. The Czech was outside. The Frenchman was the one now cramped; he was on his knees—not in supplication—in a raised doorway to the far left of the altar. He and his camera were concealed by heavy drapes; the official-looking identification pinned to his breast pocket was stamped with the seal of the Department of Archives.

No one questioned it; no one knew what it meant

The mourners left their cars and filed inside; the cameras were rolling. The somber tones of the organ filled the church. An army chorus of twenty-five men in gold-ribbed black tunics marched like sleepwalkers into the chancel.

The service began. Unending words, delivered by those who loved and those who hated. Prayer and psalm, selection and recital. Somehow cold, too controlled, thought Varak. Not that he cared; the cameras were rolling.

And then he heard the familiar, sanctimonious voice of the President of the United States, its peculiar cadence fashioned to the occasion. A breathless, hollow echo.

"The trend of permissiveness, a *trend* which has *dangerously* eroded our national heritage as law-abiding people, is now being *reversed*. American people today are *tired* of a *disrespect* for law. America wants to come *back* to the *law* as a way of *life*. . . ."

Varak turned and walked out of the church.

There were better things to do. He crossed over the manicured lawn, past a row of spring flowers to a flagstone path that led to the fountain. He sat on the ledge, feeling the spray on his face. He pulled a road map from his pocket and studied it.

Their last stop was the Congressional Cemetery. They would arrive before the cortege and set up their cameras out of sight. They would photograph the final moments when the body of J. Edgar Hoover was consigned to the ground, his remains interred beneath the earth.

But not his presence. His presence would be felt for as long as the files were missing.

Files *M* through *Z*. Estimated number: 3,000. Three thousands dossiers that could shape the government, alter the laws and attitudes of the country.

Who had them? Who *was* it?

Whoever it was was recorded on film. It had to be so; there was no other conclusion. No stranger to Washington could have broken through the complex security and stolen them.

Somewhere in the tens of thousands of feet they had taken was a face. And a name that went with the face. He would find that face and that name, thought Varak angrily. He had to.

To fail was unthinkable.

5

The film rolled through the machine, projecting images on the wall. Magnified faces appeared one after another. Varak rubbed his eyes in weariness; he'd seen the film perhaps fifty times in the past three months.

M through *Z*. Fourteen letters. More than likely it was a face with a name that began with one of those letters. The man who had stolen the files would not have overlooked the possibility that his dossier was among them. But which man? The mathematical possibilities seemed infinite, compounded by the realization that code names were not ruled out. A man with a name that began with a *K* or a *G*—a Kleindienst or a Grey—could be known to the bureau as "Nelson" or "Stark." In point of fact, "Nelson" and "Stark" *were* Kleindienst and Grey.

The cellar of the Georgetown house had been converted into a studio with an adjacent office and sitting room. The films, the photographs, the cartons of paper—personnel and medical records, government dossiers, interviews, telephone and credit-card charges—it was all overwhelming. And there could be no staff to sort out and correlate. Only one man could have access to the materials. Anymore than one squared, then cubed, the possibilities of discovery.

It could *not* have begun with a stranger! In the beginning there had to be a friend, a close friend, an associate. It did not make sense otherwise; there were too many barriers for a stranger to surmount. No stranger could trigger the releases; no stranger could throw unseen switches and abort alarms in restricted rooms guarded day and night.

But which friends? Which associates? Thirteen weeks of going through an accumulation of voluminous records, dossiers, motion-picture film and photographs led him nowhere. Every unusual face, M through Z, every abnormal scrap of information in a dossier or an interview or a credit check had been cause for an exhaustive examination of the subject. And all had led nowhere.

Varak walked into the small, windowless office. It seemed that he never saw the sun anymore, or smelled fresh air. He looked over at the corkboard on the wall; the desk lamp was angled up at a photographic enlargement of Hoover's Last Will and Testament.

The sum total of the estate was written in the upper right-hand corner in the wide strokes of a felt-tipped marker. It was $551,500.

Included were the real estate on Thirtieth Street Place, bank accounts, stocks, bonds, and Civil Service benefits in the amount of $326,500. A family home in Georgetown had an estimated value of $100,000, and there was $125,000 worth of oil, gas, and mineral leases in Texas and Louisiana. Total: $551,500.

The chief beneficiary was his friend of nearly fifty years and second in command at the bureau, Clyde Tolson. Nearly everything was left to him; upon *his* death the estate was to be divided between the boys' clubs and the Damon Runyon Fund. A blank wall.

Minor bequests of $2,000, $3,000, and $5,000 were assigned respectively to his chauffeur, James Crawford; his housekeeper, Annie Fields; and the redoubtable Helen Gandy, his secretary. Three people who had spent their lives in his service were dismissed with penny candy. It said something unattractive, but still it was another blank wall.

And there were those who were not mentioned at all, eight survivors of the "close-knit" Hoover family. Four nieces and four nephews, including one nephew who had spent ten years in the bureau. Most had come to the gravesite.

None was mentioned in Hoover's will. Another blank wall behind which might be a room filled with rage and condemnation, but certainly it held no files.

So much for the Last Will and Testament of John Edgar Hoover, giant and myth. So much for everything else!

Damn!

Varak moved to the sitting room. Sitting room, bedroom, dining room, *cell*. Actually, Bravo had provided him with more than he needed. Bravo had also given him specific instructions in the event the diplomat died. Inver Brass was to be protected at all costs.

Strange, he never thought of Bravo as Munro St. Claire. He never thought of any of them by their rightful names. Bravo was simply Bravo.

His telephone rang; the outside line.

"Mr. Varak?" It was Bravo.

"Yes, sir?"

"I'm afraid it's begun. I'm in town. Stay where you are. I'll be there as soon as I can."

St. Claire settled back in the leather armchair and took several deep breaths. It was his way of approaching a crisis: in calm.

"Within the past twenty-four hours there have been two astonishing resignations," he said. "Lieutenant General Bruce MacAndrew at the Pentagon, and Paul Bromley at GSA. Do you know either of them?"

"Yes. MacAndrew. I don't know Bromley."

"What's your opinion of the general?"

"I'm high on him. He expresses opinions often at odds with a lot of people over there."

"Exactly. He's a moderating influence and yet very respected. But suddenly, just when he's at the top of his career, he chucks it all away."

"What makes you think his resignation has anything to do with the files?"

"Because Bromley's did. I've just come from seeing him. Paul Bromley's a sixty-five-year-old bureaucrat with the General Services Administration. He takes his job seriously."

"I do know him," interrupted Varak. "Or at least *of* him. A year or so ago he testified before a Senate hearing on cost overruns. He criticized the C-forty payments."

"For which he was soundly rebuked. He was reduced to auditing congressional cafeterias, or some such equally vital statistic. But the powers at GSA made a mistake a month ago. They filed an unsatisfactory-service report that precluded a grade raise. Bromley sued them. He based the suit on his C-forty testimony. . . . That's finished now. His resignation's effective immediately."

"Did he tell you why?"

"Yes. He received a telephone call." Bravo paused. He closed his eyes. "Bromley has a daughter. She's in her early thirties, married, lives outside Milwaukee. It's her second marriage, and apparently it's a good one. Her first was something else. She was still in her teens, her husband barely twenty. They were both into drugs, living in the streets. She sold herself to pay for narcotics. Bromley didn't see his daughter for nearly three years. Until a man came to his house one day and said she'd been arrested for the murder of her husband."

Varak did not have to be told the rest. A plea of temporary insanity had been entered by the girl's attorneys. It was followed by several years of rehabilitation and psychiatric care. There was a felony record, complete with the ugly details. Bromley's wife took their daughter to her parents' home in Wisconsin. Some sort of normality returned. The girl got her head back, met and married an engineer who worked for a concern in the Midwest, and started having babies.

Now, ten years later, a telephone call meant the past could surface. Loudly, publicly. It would not only destroy the daughter but stigmatize a family. Unless Paul Bromley dropped his lawsuit and resigned from the General Services Administration.

Varak leaned forward in the couch. "Does the current husband know?"

"In substance, yes; perhaps not every detail. Of course, he's not the only issue. They'd have to move, start over again. But it would be futile. They'd be found."

"Naturally," agreed Varak. "Did Bromley describe the voice on the telephone?"

"Yes. It was a whisper——"

"For effect," interjected Varak quietly. "It never fails."

"Or for disguise. He couldn't tell whether it was a man's voice or a woman's."

"I see. Was there anything unusual in the speech pattern?"

"No. Bromley looked for that. He's an accountant; the unusual attracts him. He said the oddest thing was the mechanical quality."

"Could the voice have been recorded? A tape?"

"No. It responded to his statements. They could not have been anticipated."

Varak sat back. "Why did he come to you?"

Bravo paused. When he spoke, there was a sadness in his voice, as if for some abstract reason he were holding himself responsible. "After Bromley's C-forty testimony, I wanted to meet him. This middle-level bureaucrat who was willing to take on the Pentagon. I asked him to dinner."

"Here?"

"No, of course not. We met at a country inn in Maryland." Bravo stopped.

"You still haven't told me why he got in touch with you."

"Because I told him to. I never thought for a minute he'd get away with interfering with the Pentagon. I told him to contact me if there were reprisals."

"Why are you convinced whoever called Bromley has the Hoover files? His daughter's problems are a matter of court record."

"Something the voice said. He told Bromley that he had all the 'raw meat' there was to have on him and his family. Do you know the significance of 'raw meat'?"

"Yes," replied Varak, his contempt apparent. "It was one of Hoover's favorite expressions. Still, there's an inconsistency. Bromley's name begins with *B*."

"Bromley explained that, although of course I didn't tell him about the files. At both the Pentagon and the bureau he had a code name: Viper."

"As though he were an enemy agent."

"Exactly."

"What about MacAndrew? Do we have anything?"

"I think so. We've been interested in him for a number of years. He was one of the few soldiers who believed utterly in the civilian control of the military. Frankly, one day he might have been a candidate for Inver Brass. We studied him; it was before you arrived. There was a lapse in his service record. The symbols indicated that the period in question—eight months in 1950—had been removed to G-Two, PSA."

"Psychiatric Systems Analyses," said Varak. "On his level that's usually reserved for defectors."

"Yes. We were stunned, naturally. We traced the G-Two abstract and found that it, too, had been removed. All that remained was the phrase 'Courier Delivered, FBI DS.' Domestic Security. I'm sure you can guess the rest."

"Yes," said Varak. "You got his FBI file, and there was nothing there. You cross-checked with Domestic Security. Still nothing. 'Raw meat.'"

"Precisely. Every paper, every insert, every addendum related to Security crossed Hoover's desk. And as we know, 'Security' took on the widest possible range. Sexual activities, drinking habits, marriage and family confidences, the most personal details of the subjects' lives—none were too remote or insignificant. Hoover pored over those dossiers like Croesus with his gold. Three Presidents wanted to replace him. None did."

Varak leaned forward. "The question is, what was in MacAndrew's service record? There's nothing to prevent us from asking him now."

"*Us?*"

"It can be arranged."

"Through an intermediary?"

"Yes. A blind. There'll be no connection."

"I'm sure of that," said Bravo. "But then what? Assuming you find some character flaw, sexual or otherwise, what have you got? MacAndrew wouldn't still have his maximum clearance if it were a permanent condition."

"It's more information. Somewhere the data will pinpoint the weakness in the chain. It'll break."

"That's what you've been counting on, isn't it?"

"Yes. It'll happen. Whoever stole the files has a first-rate mind, but it will happen."

Both men fell silent, Varak waiting for approval, Bravo deep in thought.

"That chain won't be broken easily," St. Claire said. "You're the best there is, and you're no closer now than you were three months ago. You say a 'first-rate mind,' but we don't know that. We don't know if we're dealing with a mind or minds. One man or many."

"If it's one," agreed Varak, "we're not even sure it's a man."

"But whoever it is, the first moves have been made."

"Then, let me put someone on MacAndrew."

"Wait . . ." Bravo clasped his hands beneath his chin. "An intermediary? A blind?"

"Yes. Untraceable."

"Bear with me for a moment. I haven't really thought it out; you can help. Basically, it's your strategy."

Varak glanced at St. Claire. The diplomat continued. "Am I correct in assuming that a blind, as you use the term with respect to interrogation or surveillance, is someone who finds out what you have to know without your being involved?"

"That's right. The blind has his or her own reasons for wanting the same information. The trick is to get it from him without his knowing what you're doing."

"The blind, then, is chosen with extreme care." It was a statement.

"More often than not, it's a question of finding someone with the same interests," answered Varak. "It can be difficult."

"But we could enlist the aid of an investigatory agency. I mean, it's within our capability to alert the authorities—or even a newspaper—to the possibility that Hoover's files survived his death."

"Certainly. The result would be to drive whoever has them further underground."

Bravo rose from the chair and paced aimlessly. "There's been almost no mention of those files in the newspapers. It's odd, because their existence was known. It's as though no one wants to talk about them."

"Out of print, out of mind, out of danger," said Varak.

"Yes, exactly. All Washington. Even the media. No one knows whether he's part of the files or not. So there's silence. And when men are silent, the triumph of evil follows. Burke was right about that. We can see it happening."

"On the other hand," countered the intelligence man, "breaking the silence isn't always the answer."

"That depends on who breaks it." Bravo stopped his pacing. "Tell me, under the harshest, most professional microscope could any of those involved in Hoover's death be unearthed?"

"None," was the firm reply.

"Where are they? I mean, specifically."

"Both telephone men are in Australia, the Kimberly bush; they'll never come back. They face indictments for homicide in the Marine Corps. The man who used the cover of 'Salter' is in Tel Aviv; nothing takes precedence over the Holy Land or the holy war. We feed him data on the Palestinian terrorists. He lives only for his cause, and we make it practical. The actress is in Majorca; she settled a debt and wants nothing more than what she's got. The Englishman who handled the car and the Phase One relay is back with MI-Six. He made money from the Russians as a double courier in East Berlin; he knows I have the facts that could lead to his execution. You know about the doctor in Paris, the least of our concerns. Each had a motive, none can be traced. They're thousands of miles away."

St. Claire stared at Varak. "You left out someone. What about the man in the alarm room? The one who used the cover of 'Krepps'?"

Varak returned Bravo's look. "I killed him. The decision was mine, and I'd make it again."

St. Claire nodded. "Then, what you're saying is that all personnel, all the *facts*, are submerged beyond discovery. Hoover's death could never be attributed to anything but natural causes."

"Precisely. Natural causes."

"So, if we used a blind, there would be no chance of that man discovering the truth. Hoover's assassination is beyond reach."

"Beyond reach."

Bravo began to pace again. "I've never asked you why there was no autopsy."

"Orders from the White House. Relayed very quietly, I understand."

"The White House?"

"They had a reason. I gave it to them."

St. Claire did not probe; he knew Varak had studied the White House structure and could surmise his strategy, which would be totally professional. "Beyond reach," repeated Bravo. "That's vitally important."

"To whom?"

"To a blind not restricted by fact. To a man interested only in a concept. A theory that did not have to be proven at every turn. Such a man could raise alarms, quite possibly provoke whoever had the files into revealing themselves."

"I don't follow you. Without traceable facts there's no motive for a blind. What could he hope to learn? What could we learn?"

"Perhaps a great deal. The key word is *fact*," St. Claire stared at the wall above Varak. It was strange, he reflected. He had not thought of Peter Chancellor in a long time. When he had thought of him—when he'd seen his name in a newspaper or a book supplement—it had always been with a bemused memory of a bewildered graduate student grappling for words six years ago. Chancellor had found the words since. A great many of them.

"I'm afraid I don't understand you," said Varak.

Bravo lowered his gaze. "Have you ever heard of a writer named Peter Chancellor?"

"*Counterstrike!*" said Varak. "I read it. It frightened a lot of people over at Langley."

"Still, it was fiction."

"It was too close. This Chancellor used a lot of wrong terms and incorrect procedures but on the bottom line, he described what happened."

"Because he wasn't restricted by fact. Chancellor approaches a concept, finds a basic situation, and extracts *selected* facts and rearranges them to suit the reality as he perceives it. He is not bound by cause and effect; he *creates* it. You say he frightened a lot of people over in Langley. I believe that; he has a wide readership. And he researches in depth. Suppose it was known that he was researching a book on Hoover, on his last days."

"On the *files*," added Varak, sitting forward. "Use Chancellor as the blind. Tell him the files disappeared. When he starts probing, he'll set off alarms, and we'll be there."

"Go to New York, Mr. Varak. Find out everything you can about him. The people around him, his life-style, his methods of work. Everything current. Chancellor has a conspiracy complex. We're going to program him with a conspiracy he'll find irresistible."

6

"Mr. Peter Chancellor?" asked the operator.

Peter lifted his hand above the covers and tried to focus on his wristwatch. It was nearly ten o'clock; the morning breezes were billowing the drapes through the open doors of the porch.

"Yes?"

"Long distance from New York, Mr. Anthony Morgan calling. One moment, please."

"Sure." There was a click and a hum on the line. It stopped.

"Hi, Mr. Chancellor?"

Peter would know that voice anywhere. It belonged to his editor's secretary. If she ever had a discouraging day, no one ever knew about it. "Hello, Radie? How are you?" Chancellor hoped she was better than he was.

"Fine. How's California these days?"

"Bright, humid, shiny, green. Take your choice."

The girl laughed. It was a pleasant laugh.

"We didn't wake you, did we? You're always up so early."

"No, Radie, I was in the surf," lied Chancellor for no reason.

"Hold on. Here's Mr. Morgan." There were two clicks.

"Hello, Peter?"

"How are you, Tony?"

"Christ, forget about me, how are *you?* Marie said you called last night. Sorry I wasn't home."

Chancellor remembered. "I apologize. I was drunk."

"She didn't mention that, but she said you were mad as hell."

"I was. I am. I was also drunk. Apologize to Marie for me."

"No need to. What you told her made her angry, too. I was greeted at the door with a lecture about protecting my authors. Now, what's this about *Counterstrike!?*"

Peter adjusted his head on the pillow and cleared his throat. He tried to rid his voice of bitterness. "At four thirty yesterday afternoon a studio messenger brought me the completed first draft of the screenplay. I didn't know we'd started."

"And?"

"It's been turned around. It's the opposite of what I wrote."

Morgan paused, then replied gently. "Wounded ego, Peter?"

"Good God, no. You know better than that. I didn't say it was badly written; a lot of it's pretty damned good. It's effective. I'd feel better if it wasn't. But it's a lie."

"Josh told me they were changing the agency's name——"

"They've changed everything!" interrupted Chancellor, his eyes blinking in pain with the rush of blood to his head. "The government people are all on the side of the angels. They don't have an impure thought in their heads! The manipulators are . . . 'them.' Weird exponents of violence and revolution and—so help me God—with 'faintly European accents.' Whatever the book said has been turned inside out. Why the hell did they buy it in the first place?"

"What does Josh say?"

"As I remember, and I do vaguely, I reached him around midnight my time. I guess it was about three this morning in New York."

"Stay around the house. I'll speak to Josh. One of us'll get back to you."

"All right." Peter was about to offer a last apology to Morgan's wife when he realized the editor was not finished. It was one of those silences between them that meant there was more to say.

"Peter?"

"Yes?"

"Suppose Josh can work things out. I mean with your studio contract."

"There's nothing to work out," interrupted Chancellor again. "They don't need me; they don't want me."

"They may want your name. They're paying for it."

"They can't have it. Not the way they're doing the film. I'm telling you, it's the opposite of what I said."

"Is it that important to you?"

"As literature—hell, no. As my own personal statement—hell, yes. Nobody else seems to be making it."

"I just wondered. I thought you might be ready to start the Nuremberg book."

Peter stared at the ceiling. "Not yet, Tony. Soon, not yet. I'll talk to you later."

He hung up the phone, the apology gone from his mind. He was thinking about Morgan's question and his own answer.

If only the pain would disappear. And the numbness. Both had lessened, but they were still there, and when he felt either or both, the memories returned. The shattering glass, the blinding light, the crunching metal. The screams. And his hatred of a man high up in a truck who had disappeared in the storm. Leaving one dead, one almost dead.

Chancellor swung his legs over the edge of the bed onto the floor. He stood up naked and looked around for his bathing suit. He was late for his morning swim; the dawn had turned into day. He felt guilty somehow, as if he had broken an important ritual. Worse, he understood that the ritual took the place of work.

He saw his bathing suit draped over a chair and started toward it. The telephone rang again. He reversed direction and answered it.

"It's Joshua, Peter. I've just spent an hour talking with Aaron Sheffield."

"He's a winner. Incidentally, sorry about last night."

"This morning," corrected the agent, not unkindly. "Don't worry about it. You were overwrought."

"I was drunk."

"That, too. Let's get to Sheffield."

"I suppose we have to. I gather you got the drift of what I told you last night."

"I'm sure most of Malibu Beach could repeat the better phrases word for word."

"What's his position? I won't budge."

"Legally that doesn't make any difference to him. You have no case. You have no script approval."

"I understand that. But I can talk. I can give interviews. I can demand that my name be removed. I might even try to get the courts to change the title. I'll bet a case can be made for that."

"It's unlikely."

"Josh, they've changed the whole meaning!"

"The courts might see the money you've been paid and not be impressed."

Chancellor blinked again and rubbed his eyes. He exhaled wearily. "I think you're saying they wouldn't be impressed. Period. I'm not Solzhenitsyn with the Siberian camps or Dickens on the death of children in the sweatshops. All right, what can I do?"

"Do you want it put plainly?"

"When you begin like that, the news isn't good."

"Some good can come out of it."

"Now I know it's terrible. Go ahead."

"Sheffield wants to avoid discord; so does the studio. They don't want you giving those interviews or going on talk shows. They know you can do that, and they don't want the embarrassment."

"I see. We reach the heart of the matter: gross receipts at the box office. Their essential pride, their manhood."

Harris was silent for a moment. When he continued, it was in a soft voice. "Peter, that kind of controversy wouldn't affect gross receipts one iota of a percentage point. If anything, it would hype them."

"Then, why are they concerned?"

"They really want to avoid embarrassment."

"They live in a perpetual state of embarrassment out here. They can't even recognize it. I don't believe that."

"They're willing to pay your contract in full, remove your name from the screen credits if you wish—not the title, of course—and deliver a bonus equal to fifty percent of the book purchase."

"Je*sus*. . . ." Chancellor was stunned. The figure Joshua Harris alluded to was in the range of a quarter million dollars. "For what?"

"For you to walk away and not make waves over the adaptation."

Peter stared at the billowing drapes in front of the glass doors. There was something very inconsistent, terribly wrong.

"Are you still there?" asked Harris.

"Wait a minute. You say controversy could only help the receipts. Yet Sheffield's willing to pay all that money to avoid controversy. He's got to lose. It doesn't make sense."

"I'm not his analyst. I just heard the money. Maybe he wants to keep his balls intact."

"No. I know Sheffield, believe me; I know the way

he operates. His balls are expendable." Suddenly, Chancellor understood. "Sheffield has a partner, Josh. And it's not the studio. It's the government. It's Washington! They're the ones who don't want the controversy. To quote from a far better writer than I'll ever be, they 'can't stand the light of day'! Goddamn it, that's *it*."

"It crossed my mind," admitted Harris.

"You tell Sheffield to shove his bonus. I'm not interested!"

Again, the agent paused. "I may as well tell you the rest. Sheffield's collected statements from all over Los Angeles and points north and south. The picture isn't pleasant. You're described as a wild alcoholic and something of a menace."

"Good for Sheffield! Controversy hypes the gross receipts. We'll sell twice as many books!"

"He says he has more," continued Harris. "He claims he has sworn affidavits from women who accuse you of rape and physical abuse. He has photographs—police photographs—that show the damage you've inflicted. One's a kid from Beverly Hills who's fourteen years old. He has friends who'll swear they removed narcotics from you when you passed out in their homes. He says you even attacked his wife, which is something he'd rather not make public but will if he has to. He says they've been cleaning up after you for weeks."

"They're lies! Josh, that's crazy! There's no truth in any of that!"

"That may be the problem. There's probably a few grains of truth. I don't mean the rape or the abuse or the narcotics; that stuff's easily manufactured. But you've been drinking, you haven't returned calls, there've been women. And I know Sheffield's wife. I don't rule her out, but I'm sure you weren't the cause of it."

Chancellor lurched from the bed. His head was spinning, the pain in his temples throbbed. "I don't know what to say! I don't believe this!"

"I know what to say; I know what to believe," said Joshua Harris. "They're not playing by any rules I've ever heard of."

Varak leaned forward in the velvet sofa and opened his briefcase on the coffee table. He withdrew two file folders, placed them in front of him, and moved the case to one side. The morning sun was streaming through the windows overlooking Central Park South, filling the elegant hotel suite with shafts of yellowish white light.

Across the room Munro St. Claire had poured himself a cup of coffee from a carafe on a silver tray. He sat opposite the intelligence man.

"Are you sure I can't get you a cup?" asked Bravo.

"No, thanks. I've gone through several pots this morning. Incidentally, I appreciate your flying up. It saves time."

"Every day is vital," replied St. Claire. "Every hour those files are missing is an hour we can't afford. What have you got?"

"Just about everything we need. My primary sources were Chancellor's editor, Anthony Morgan, and his literary agent, a man named Joshua Harris."

"They cooperated so easily?"

"It wasn't difficult. I convinced them it was standard procedure for a minimum-security clearance."

"Security clearance for what?"

Varak separated a page in the left file folder. "Before his accident Chancellor had the Government Printing Office send him the transcripts from the Nuremberg tribunals. He's writing a novel on the trials. He thinks Nuremberg was rife with judicial conspiracies. That thousands of Nazis went unaccountable, free to emigrate all over the world, transferring huge sums of money wherever they went."

"He's wrong. It was the exception, not the rule by any means," said Bravo.

"Regardless, some of those transcripts still have a security classification. He didn't get those, but he doesn't know that. I implied that he did, and my job was simply a routine follow-up. Nothing serious. Also, I said that I was a fan of Chancellor's. I enjoyed talking to people who knew him."

"Has he written this Nuremberg book?"

"He hasn't even started it."

"I wonder why."

Varak scanned another page as he spoke. "Chancellor was nearly killed in an automobile accident last fall. The woman with him was killed. According to the medical records, with another ten minutes of internal bleeding and pathogenic toxemia, he would have died. He was in the hospital for five months. He's been patched together;

eighty-five- to ninety-percent recovery is anticipated. That's the physical part." Varak paused and turned a page.

"Who was the woman?" asked Bravo quietly.

Varak shifted his attention to the folder on his right. "Her name was Catherine Lowell; they'd been living together for nearly a year and planned to get married. They were on their way to meet his parents in northwest Pennsylvania. Her death was a terrible shock to Chancellor. He went into a long period of depression. It's still with him to some degree, according to both his editor and agent."

"Morgan and Harris," added Bravo for his own clarification.

"Yes. They sweated out his recovery; first the physical injuries, then the depression. Both men admitted that during the past months there were times they thought he was finished as a writer."

"A reasonable assumption. He hasn't written anything."

"He's supposed to be now. He's in California coauthoring the screenplay of *Counterstrike!*, although nobody expects him to do very much. He has no experience in films."

"Then, why was he hired?"

"The value of his name, according to Harris. And the fact that the studio could have an advantage over others for his next book. Actually, that's the way Harris engineered the contract."

"Which means he wanted Chancellor involved since he wasn't working on anything."

"In Harris's opinion, his house in Pennsylvania, and his memories, were holding Chancellor back. It's why he wanted him in California." Varak turned several pages. "Here it is. Harris's words. He wanted his client to 'experience the perfectly normal Gargantuan excesses of a temporary Malibu resident.'"

Bravo smiled. "Are they having a positive effect?"

"There's progress. Not much, but some." Varak looked up from the paper. "That's something we can't allow."

"What do you mean?"

"Chancellor will be infinitely more valuable to us in a weakened psychological condition." The intelligence man gestured at both file folders. "The rest of this describes a fairly normal man before the accident. Whatever hostilities or excesses he had were transferred to his writing. He didn't display them in his life-style. If he returns to that normality, he'll be naturally cautious, he'll retreat when we don't want him to. I want to keep him off-balance, in a state of anxiety."

St. Claire sipped his coffee without comment. "Go on, please. Describe this life-style."

"There's not much, really. He has an apartment in a brownstone on East Seventy-first Street. He gets up early, usually before dawn, and works. He doesn't use a typewriter; he writes on yellow pads, Xeroxes the pages, and uses a typing service in Greenwich Village." Varak again looked up. "That could be an advantage to us in his research. We can intercept the originals and make our own copies."

"Suppose he works in Pennsylvania and has them driven in. Delivered by messenger."

"Then, we'll get inside the Village offices."

"Of course. Go on."

"There's very little left that's important. He has favorite restaurants where he's known. He skis, plays tennis—neither of which he may be able to do again. His friends, outside of Morgan and Harris, are generally found among other writers and newspapermen and, oddly enough, several lawyers in New York and Washington. That's about it." Varak closed the folder on his right. "Now, I'd like to bring up something."

"Yes?"

"Along the lines we've discussed, I think I know how to program Chancellor, but I need a backup. I'll use the Longworth cover: it's unbreakable. Longworth is in Hawaii and stays in hiding. We look enough alike—even to the duplication of the scar—and his FBI record can be traced. Still, we should have one more piece of bait Chancellor can't walk away from."

"Please clarify."

Varak paused, then said with conviction: "We have a crime but no conspiracy. None we can identify. He's got to follow his own speculations. We have none to give him. If we had, we wouldn't be using him in the first place."

"What are you proposing?" asked St. Claire, seeing the hesitation in Varak's eyes.

"I want to bring in a second member of Inver Brass.

In my opinion the only other man with your public stature. You call him Venice. Judge Daniel Sutherland. I want to be able to send Chancellor to him."

The diplomat was silent for several moments. "To lend weight to what you tell Chancellor? The irresistible confirmation?"

"Yes. To substantiate our story of the missing files. That's all I need. Sutherland's voice will be the bait Chancellor *has* to take."

"It's dangerous," said Bravo quietly. "No member of Inver Brass should ever be overt in any strategy."

"Time requires it. I ruled you out because of your previous relationship with Chancellor."

"I understand. The coincidence would raise questions. I'll talk with Venice. . . . Now, if you please, I want to return to something you said. Chancellor's psychological condition. If I understood you correctly——"

"You did," interrupted Varak quietly. "Chancellor cannot be allowed to recover. He can't be permitted to function at his previous rational level. He's got to draw attention to himself, to his research. If he remains volatile, he becomes a threat. If that threat is dangerous enough, whoever has those files will be compelled to eliminate it. When he does—or they do—we'll be there."

Bravo sat forward, his expression one of sudden concern. "I think that goes beyond the parameters we established."

"I wasn't aware we'd established any."

"They were intrinsic. There are limits to our use of Peter Chancellor. They don't include putting his life in jeopardy."

"I submit it's a logical extension of the strategy. Quite plainly put, the strategy may be useless without that factor. I think we'd willingly exchange Chancellor's life for those files. Don't you?"

St. Claire said nothing.

7

Chancellor stood by the doors overlooking the beach and parted the drapes again. The blond-haired man was still there. He'd been there for over an hour, walking back and forth in the hot afternoon sun, his shoes sinking into the warm sand, his shirt open at the collar, his jacket slung over his shoulder.

He was pacing up and down the short area of the beach fifty yards away, between the redwood porch and the water, every now and then glancing up at Peter's house. He was medium-sized, perhaps a shade under six feet, and muscular. His shoulders were broad and thick and stretched the cloth of his shirt.

Chancellor had first seen him around noon. He had stood motionless in the sand, staring up at the redwood porch; staring, Peter was sure, at him.

The sight of the man was no longer merely disconcerting, it was irritating. The first thought that came to Chancellor was that Aaron Sheffield had decided to put a watchdog on him. A great deal of money was now involved in *Counterstrike!* A great deal more had been offered under circumstances that raised disturbing questions.

Peter did not like watchdogs. Not this kind. He pulled back the drapes, slid open the door, and stepped out on the porch. The man stopped his pacing and again stood motionless in the sand.

They looked at each other and Peter's doubts vanished. The man was there for him, waiting for him. Peter's irritation turned into anger. He walked to the steps and down onto the beach. The man remained where he was, making no move toward him.

Goddamn you, thought Chancellor. There were very few people on this private area of Malibu; but if any were watching, the sight of the limping figure in slacks, naked above the waist, approaching a fully clothed man standing immobile in front of a beach house must have seemed odd. It *was* odd; the blond-haired stranger had a curious quality about him. He was pleasant-looking, a face clean-cut, even gentle in appearance. Yet there was something menacing about him. As he drew nearer, Chancellor realized what it was: the man's eyes were aware. They were not the eyes of a subordinate watchdog hired by an anxious studio executive.

"It's warm out here," began Peter bluntly. "I can't help asking myself why you're walking around in the heat. Especially since you keep looking up at my house."

"At your rented house, Mr. Chancellor."

"Then, I think you'd better explain," replied Peter, "since you know my name and, obviously, the conditions of my lease. It wouldn't be because those who hired you are paying the rent?"

"No."

"Score one for me. I didn't think so. Now, you've got a choice. Either you satisfy my curiosity, or I call the police."

"I want you to do more than that. You have sources in Washington. I want you to call one of them and check out my name in the personnel records of the Federal Bureau of Investigation."

"The *what*!" Peter was stunned. The man's words were spoken quietly, yet there was an undercurrent of urgency.

"I'm retired," added the man quickly. "I'm not here in any official capacity. But my name's in the bureau's personnel records. Check it out."

Chancellor stared at the man, apprehensive. "Why would I do that?"

"I've read your books."

"That's you, not me. It's no reason."

"I think it is. It's why I went to a lot of trouble to find you." The man hesitated, as if unsure of how to continue.

"Go on."

"In each of your books you show that certain events may not have happened the way people think they did. An event took place less than a year ago that falls into that category."

"What was it?"

"A man died. A very powerful man. They said he died of natural causes. He didn't. He was assassinated."

Peter stared at the stranger. "Go to the police."

"I can't. If you check me out, you'll understand."

"I'm a novelist. I write fiction. Why come to me?"

"I told you. I've read your books. I think that maybe the only way the story can be told is in a book. The kind you write."

"Novels." Peter did not ask a question.

"Yes."

"Fiction." Again it was a statement.

"Yes."

"But you say it isn't fiction. It's fact; you imply it's fact."

"That's what I believe. I'm not sure I can prove it."

"And you can't go to the police."

"No."

"Go to a newspaper. Find an investigative reporter. There are dozens of good ones."

"No newspaper would handle this. Take my word for it."

"Why the hell should I?"

"You might after you checked me out. My name is Alan Longworth. For twenty years I was a special agent for the FBI. I retired five months ago. My field office was in San Diego . . . and points north. I live now in Hawaii. On the island of Maui."

"Longworth? Alan Longworth? Should the name mean anything to me?"

"That's not remotely possible. Check me out. It's all I ask."

"Suppose I do. Then what?"

"I'll come by tomorrow morning. If you want to talk further, fine. If not, I'll leave." Again the blond-haired man hesitated, the urgency now in his eyes as he spoke softly. "I've traveled a long way to find you. I've taken risks I shouldn't have taken. I may have broken an agreement that could cost me my life. So I've got one more thing to ask you. I want your word on it."

"Or else what?"

"Don't check on me. Don't do anything; forget I came out here, forget we spoke."

"But you did come out here. We have spoken. It's a little late for conditions."

Longworth paused. "Haven't you ever been frightened?" he asked. "No, I don't imagine you have. Not this way. Strange, but you write about fear; you seem to understand it."

"You don't look like you frighten easily."

"I don't think I do. My record at the bureau might even confirm that."

"What's this condition?"

"Ask about me. Find out everything you can, say anything you want. But please don't say we met; don't repeat what I've told you."

"That's crazy. What am I supposed to say?"

"I'm sure you can think of something. You're a writer."

"That doesn't necessarily mean I'm a good liar."

"You travel a lot. You could say you heard about me in Hawaii. *Please*."

Peter shifted his feet in the hot sand. Common sense told him to walk away from this man; there was something unhealthy about the controlled, intense face and the too-alert eyes. But his instincts would not permit his common sense its right of decision. "Who's this man who died? The one you say was assassinated."

"I won't tell you that now. I will tomorrow if you want to talk further."

"Why not now?"

"You're a well-known writer. I'm sure a lot of people come up and tell you things that sound insane. You probably dismiss them quickly, as you should. I don't want you to dismiss me. I want you convinced that I have a certain reasonable stature of my own."

Peter listened. Longworth's words made sense. During the past three years—since *Reichstag!*—people had pulled him over into corners at cocktail parties or slid into chairs across from him at restaurants to impart weird information they *knew* was right up his *alley*. The world was filled with conspiracies. And would-be conspirators.

"Fair enough," said Chancellor. "Your name is Alan Longworth. You spent twenty years as a special agent; you retired five months ago, and you live in Hawaii."

"Maui."

"That would be listed in your file."

At the mention of the word *file*, Longworth drew back. "Yes, it would be. In my file."

"But then anyone might be able to learn the contents of a specific file. Give me something to identify you."

"I wondered if you'd ask."

"In my books I try to be convincing; it's just step-by-step logic, with no spaces. You want me to be convinced, so fill the space."

Longworth shifted his jacket from his right shoulder to his left, and with his right hand he undid the buttons of his shirt. He pulled his shirt open. Across his chest, descending below the belt, was an ugly, curving scar. "I don't think any of your blemishes can match this."

Peter reacted to the words with a brief rush of anger. There was no point pursuing the statement. If Longworth was who he said he was, he had taken the time to gather his facts together. Undoubtedly, they included a great deal about the life of Peter Chancellor.

"What time will you be by in the morning?"

"What time's convenient?"

"I get up early."

"I'll be here early."

"Eight o'clock."

"See you at eight." Longworth turned and began walking down the beach.

Peter stood where he was and watched him, aware that the pain in his leg had disappeared. It had been there all day, but it was gone now. He would call Joshua Harris in New York. It was around four thirty in the East; there was still time. There was a lawyer in Washington, a mutual friend, who could get the information on Alan Longworth. Josh once jokingly said that the attorney should demand royalties for *Counterstrike!*, so helpful had he been in Chancellor's research.

As Peter climbed up the porch steps, he found himself hurrying. It was a strangely gratifying sensation, and he could not really account for it.

An event took place less than a year ago. . . . A man died. A very powerful man. They said he died of natural causes. He didn't. He was assassinated. . . .

Peter rushed across the porch toward the glass doors and the telephone inside.

The morning sky was angry. Dark clouds hung over the ocean; the rain would come soon. Chancellor was dressed for it, had been dressed for over an hour; he wore a nylon jacket above his khaki trousers. It was seven forty-five—ten forty-five in New York. Joshua had promised to call by seven thirty—ten thirty back East. What was the delay? Longworth would be there by eight.

Peter poured himself another cup of coffee, his fifth of the morning.

The telephone rang.

"You picked a strange one, Peter," said Harris in New York.

"Why do you say that?"

"According to our friend in Washington, this Alan Longworth did what no one expected him to do. He retired at the wrong time."

"Did he have his twenty years?"

"Just barely."

"That's enough for a pension, isn't it?"

"Sure. If you supplement it with another salary. He hasn't, but that's not the point."

"What is?"

"Longworth had an exceptional record. Most important, he was singled out by Hoover himself for high-echelon advancement. Hoover personally attached a hand-written favorable recommendation to his file. You'd think he'd want to stay on."

"On the other hand, with that kind of record he could probably get a hell of a job on the outside. A lot of FBI men do. Maybe he's working for someone, and the bureau doesn't know it."

"Not likely. They keep extensive files on retired agents. And if he was, why does he live on Maui? There's not much activity there. At any rate, there's no listing of a current employer. He doesn't do anything."

Peter stared out the window; a light rain began to fall from the dark sky. "Do the other items check out?"

"Yes," answered Harris. "His field office was San Diego. Apparently, he was Hoover's personal liaison with La Jolla."

"La Jolla? What does that mean?"

"It was Hoover's favorite retreat. Longworth was in charge of all communications."

"What about the scar?"

"It's listed under identifying marks, but there's no explanation, and that's where we come to the strangest part of his file. His last medical records are missing, the last two annual checkups. It's very unusual."

"It's very incomplete," mused Peter out loud. "The whole thing."

"Exactly," agreed Joshua.

"When did he retire?"

"Last March. On the second."

Chancellor paused, struck by the date. Over the past several years, dates had come to have special meanings for him. He had trained himself to look for consistencies and inconsistencies where dates were concerned. What was it now? Why did the date bother him?

Through the kitchen windows he saw the figure of Alan Longworth walking across the beach in the rain toward the house. For some reason the sight triggered another image. Of himself. On the sand in bright sunlight. And a newspaper.

May second. J. Edgar Hoover had died on the second of May.

A man died. A very powerful man. They said he died of natural causes. He didn't. He was assassinated.

"Jesus Christ," said Peter quietly into the telephone.

They walked along the beach by the water through the drizzle. Longworth would not talk inside the house, nor within any enclosure that might contain electronic surveillance. He was too experienced for that.

"Did you check me out?" asked the blond-haired man.

"You knew I would," said Peter. "I just got off the phone."

"Are you satisfied?"

"That you are who you say you are, yes. That you had a good record, your abilities personally recognized by Hoover himself, and that you retired five months ago—yes to all that, too."

"I didn't mention any personal endorsements from Hoover."

"They're there."

"Of course they are. I worked directly for him."

"You were based in San Diego, as you said. You were his liaison to—or with—La Jolla."

Longworth smiled grimly, with no humor. "I spent more time in Washington than I ever spent in San Diego. Or La Jolla. You won't find that in my bureau record."

"Why not?"

"Because the director didn't want it known."

"Again, why not?"

"I told you. I worked for him. Personally."

"In what way?"

"With his files. His private files. I was a messenger. La Jolla meant a lot more than the name of a village on the Pacific coast."

"That's too cryptic for me."

The blond man stopped. "That's the way it's going to remain. Anything more you find out will have to come from someone else."

"Now you're arrogant. What makes you think I'll look?"

"Because you can't understand why I retired. Nobody could; it didn't make sense. I have a minimum pension with no additional income. Had I remained with the bureau, I might have become an assistant, even an associate, director."

Longworth started walking again. Peter kept pace, no pain whatsoever in his leg. "All right, why did you retire? Why don't you have a job?"

"The truth is that I didn't retire. I was transferred to another government post and given certain guarantees. My employer of record—a record you'll never find in any file—is the State Department. Foreign Service, Pacific operations. Six thousand miles from Washington. If I had stayed in Washington, I would have been killed."

"All right, hold it!" Chancellor stopped. "I've got a damned good idea what you're leading up to, and I'm getting sick of the bullshit. You're implying that J. Edgar Hoover was murdered. He's the 'powerful man' you meant."

"You pieced it together, then," said the agent.

"It's a pretty logical conclusion, and I don't believe it for a minute. It's ridiculous."

"I didn't say I could prove it."

"I would hope not. It's preposterous. He was an old man with a history of heart trouble."

"Maybe. Maybe not. I never knew anyone who ever saw his medical records. The originals were sent directly to him, and no copies were allowed. He had ways of enforcing those demands. No autopsy was permitted on his body."

"He was over seventy." Peter shook his head in disgust. "You've got one hell of an imagination."

"Isn't that what novels are all about? Don't you start with a concept? An idea?"

"Granted. But the kind I write have got to be at least credible. There's got to be some basic reality, or the appearance of it."

"If by reality you mean facts, there are several."

"Name them."

"The first is myself. Last March I was approached by a group of people who wouldn't be identified but who were influential enough to move the highest, most classified wheels at the State Department and effect a transfer that Hoover would never have permitted. Even I don't know how they did it. They were concerned with certain information Hoover had compiled. Dossiers on several thousand subjects."

"These were the same people who gave you the guarantees? For those services rendered you won't elaborate on?"

"Yes. I think—I can't be sure—but I think I know the identity of one of them. I'm willing to give it to you." Longworth stopped; he was, again, as he had been yesterday, uncertain. The urgency returned to his eyes.

"Go ahead," said Chancellor impatiently.

"I have your word that you'll never use my name with him?"

"Goddamn it, yes. To be honest with you, I have an idea we'll say good-bye in a few minutes and I won't even *think* of you."

"Have you ever heard of Daniel Sutherland?"

Peter's expression conveyed his astonishment. Daniel Sutherland was a giant, both figuratively and literally. A huge black man whose extraordinary accomplishments matched his enormous size. A man who had crawled his way out of the squalor of the Alabama fields a half century ago, and climbed to the highest circles of the nation's judicial system. He had twice refused presidential appointments to the Supreme Court, preferring the more active bench. "The judge?"

"Yes."

"Of course. Who hasn't? Why do you think he was one of the group who made contact with you?"

"I saw his name on a State Department tracer about me. I wasn't supposed to see it, but I did. Go to him. Ask him if there was a group of men concerned about the last two years of Hoover's life."

The request was irresistible. The stories about Sutherland were legend. Peter now took Alan Longworth far more seriously than he had only seconds ago.

"I may do that. What are the other facts?"

"There's only one that really counts. The rest are minor compared to it. Except perhaps one other man. A general named MacAndrew. General Bruce MacAndrew."

"Who's he?"

"Until recently, a man very high at the Pentagon. He had everything going for him; Chairman of the Joint Chiefs was probably his for a nod of the head. Suddenly, without any apparent reason he threw it all away. Uniform, career, Joint Chiefs, everything."

"Not unlike you in a way," ventured Chancellor. "On a somewhat grander scale, perhaps."

"Very unlike me," replied Longworth. "I have information about MacAndrew. Let's say it goes back to those services rendered. Something happened to him twenty-one, twenty-two years ago. No one apparently knows what— or if they do, they're not saying—but it was serious enough to have been removed from his service record. Eight months in 1950 or '51, that's all I remember. It could be tied in with that one single overriding fact—your basic fact, Chancellor—and that scares the hell out of me."

"What is it?"

"Hoover's private files. MacAndrew could be part of them. Over three thousand dossiers, a cross-section of the country. Government, industry, the universities, the military; from the most powerful to those lower down. You may hear otherwise, but I'm telling you the truth. Those files are missing, Chancellor. Since Hoover's death they've never been found. Someone's got them, and now that someone's using them."

Peter started at Longworth. "Hoover's files? That's insane."

"Think about it. That's my theory. Whoever has those files killed Hoover to get them. You've checked me out; I've given you two names to reach. I don't care what you say to MacAndrew, but you've given your word not to mention me to the judge. And I don't want anything from you. I just want you to think about it, that's all. Think about the possibilities."

Without indicating he had finished, without a nod or a gesture, Longworth turned and, as he had the day before, walked away across the beach. Stunned, Peter stood in the light rain and watched as the retired FBI man broke into a run toward the road.

8

Chancellor stood at the bar in the restaurant on East Fifty-sixth Street. It strove to be an uprooted English chophouse, and Peter liked it. The atmosphere was conducive to long lunches given to volubility.

He had called Tony Morgan and Joshua Harris and had asked them to meet him there. Then he'd taken the late afternoon flight out of Los Angeles. For the first time in months he slept in his own apartment—how sane it felt. He should have come back much sooner. His false California sanctuary had become a very real prison.

It was happening. Something inside his head had snapped, a barricade had been shattered, freeing stored-up energy. He had no idea whether anything Longworth told him made any sense at all. No, it was too preposterous! The fact of assassination was in and of itself beyond reason. But the premise was fascinating. And every story began with a premise. The possibilities were as provocative as anything he had approached. Would an extraordinary man named Sutherland concede there was even a remote chance Hoover had been killed? Could a long-missing insert in a military record of a general named MacAndrew be tied in with the concept?

A momentary flash of light shot through the windows that fronted the street, drawing his eyes to the outside. Then he smiled as he saw the figures of Anthony Morgan and Joshua Harris walking together toward the entrance.

The two men were arguing, but only those who knew them well would have understood that. To the casual observer they were two people talking quietly, oblivious to their surroundings and, conceivably, each other.

Tony Morgan was the physical embodiment of the Ivy League postgraduate turned New York publisher. He was slender and tall with shoulders slightly stooped from too many years of courteously feigning interest in the opinions of lesser mortals; his face was thin, the features clean, the brown eyes always a little distant but never vacant. Single-breasted charcoal suits and English style tweed jackets above inevitable gray flannel trousers were his uniforms. He and Brooks Brothers had gone together for most of his forty-one years, and neither saw any reason to change.

But clothes and appearances did not capture the mercurial essence of Anthony Morgan. That was found in his explosions of enthusiasm and his infectious proselytizing of a manuscript-in-progress or the discovery of an exciting new talent. Morgan was the complete publisher and an editor of rare perception.

And if Morgan the man was somehow sprung from within the cloistered walls of academic New England, Joshua Harris seemingly floated through the centuries from some elegant royal court of the 1700s. Generous of girth, Harris's posture was erect, his bearing imperial. His large body moved gracefully, each step taken with deliberateness as if he were part of a baronial procession. He too was in his early forties, the years further disguised by a black chin beard that lent a slightly sinister quality to an otherwise pleasant face.

Peter knew there were scores of editors and agents in New York of equal, perhaps more than equal, stature, and he realized that neither Morgan nor Harris was universally loved. He'd heard the criticisms: Tony's arrogance and often misplaced enthusiasms, Josh's relish for uncomfortable confrontations based frequently on unfounded charges of abuse. But the detractions did not matter to Chancellor. For him these men were the best. Because they cared.

Peter signed his bar check and made his way to the foyer. Josh walked through the front door held by Tony, who, quite naturally, allowed an intervening couple to enter in front of him. The greetings were too loud, too casual. Peter saw the concern in both men's eyes; each looked at him as though studying a disoriented brother.

The table was the usual table. In the corner, slightly separated from the others. The drinks were the usual drinks, and Chancellor was both amused and irritated to see Josh and Tony watch him closely when the whisky arrived.

"Call off the alert. I promise not to dance on the table."

"Really, Peter . . ." began Morgan.

"Come on, now . . ." completed Harris.

They cared. That was the important thing. And the moment passed, the recognition of the unspoken accepted. There was business to be discussed: Chancellor began.

"I met a man; don't ask me who, I won't tell you. Let's say I met him on the beach, and he told me the outlines of a story that I don't for a minute believe, but I think it could be the basis for one hell of a book."

"Before you go on," interrupted Harris, "did you make any agreement with him?"

"He doesn't want anything. I gave my word I'd never identify him." Peter stopped, his eyes on Joshua Harris. The literary agent had made the inquiries; he had placed the call to Washington. "As a matter of fact, you're the only one who could. By name. But you can't. I'll hold you to it."

"Go on," said Joshua Harris.

"Several years ago a few men in Washington became alarmed over what they considered a very dangerous situation. Maybe more than dangerous, maybe catastrophic. J. Edgar Hoover had compiled a couple of thousand dossiers on the most influential people in the country. In the House, the Senate, the Pentagon, the White House. Presidential and congressional advisors, leading authorities in a dozen different fields. The older Hoover got, the more concerned they became. Stories began to leak out of the bureau that Hoover was actually *using* those files to intimidate those who opposed him."

"Wait a minute, Peter," broke in Morgan. "That story —and variations of it—has been around for years. What's the point?"

Chancellor leveled his eyes on Morgan. "I'll jump.

Hoover died four months ago, and no autopsy was permitted. And those files were missing."

There was silence at the table. Morgan leaned forward, revolving his glass slowly, the ice cubes circling in the whisky. "That's quite a jump. Hoover was damned near eighty years old; he had a heart condition."

"Who says those files are missing?" asked Harris. "They could have been destroyed, shredded. Or buried."

"Of course, they could," agreed Peter.

"But you're implying that someone killed Hoover for them," said Morgan.

"I'm not implying, I'm stating it. As a fictional premise, not as fact. I didn't say I believed it, but I think I could make it believable."

Again there was silence. Morgan looked at Harris, and then at Peter. "It's a sensational idea," he said cautiously. "A powerful hypothesis. Perhaps too powerful, too current. You'd have to build a solid foundation, and I don't know if that's possible."

"This man on the beach," said Joshua. "This man neither of us will identify. Does he believe it?"

Chancellor stared at his drink. He realized that when he answered Harris, his voice was as tentative as his judgment. "I don't really know. I have an idea—and it's just an idea—that he thinks the killing was on a drawing board somewhere. That was enough for him. Enough for him to give me two sources to check out."

"Connected to Hoover?" asked Morgan.

"No, he didn't go so far as to claim that. He said it was only speculation. One name's related to that group in Washington who were nervous about the files, and Hoover's use of them. The other's pretty farfetched. It concerns lost information over twenty years old."

Morgan held Peter's attention. "They could be your foundation."

"Sure. But if there's any truth at all about that group, I'd have to fictionalize completely. He's that kind of man. The other I don't know anything about."

"Do you want to tell us who they are?" asked Joshua.

"Not yet. I just want your reaction to the idea. To a novel about Hoover's assassination. Killed by people who knew of those files and wanted them for their own purposes."

"It's sensational," repeated Morgan.

"It's going to cost you," said Harris, looking at the editor.

9

Congressman Walter Rawlins of the Roanoke Rawlinses, dynasty without substance, political manipulators of the Commonwealth of Virginia, sat in the library of his suburban Arlington home. It was past midnight; the single source of light was a brass stirrup lamp on the desk beneath enlarged photographs of various Rawlinses astride various horses in various stages of the hunt.

He was alone in the house. His wife had gone to Roanoke for the weekend, and it was the maid's day off, which meant night out; the black bitch couldn't wait for Thursday night to hustle her black ass. Rawlins grinned and raised a glass to his lips, taking several deep swallows of sour mash. It was goddamned sweet nigger ass, and he would have told her to stay except that he didn't trust the other bitch in the house. His wife had *said* she was taking the Cessna to Roanoke, but she could just as easily tell the pilot to turn around and head back to the field in McLean. His goddamned bitch wife could right now be down the street in a car, waiting for just the right moment to walk back into the house.

She'd love to catch him humping away on the nigger.

Rawlins blinked. Then he focused his eyes toward the desk, at the telephone on the desk. The goddamned thing was ringing. It was his office line, the private Washington tie. Goddamn!

The phone kept ringing. It would not stop. Goddamn! He hated to talk on the telephone after he had a little juice in him. He lurched out of the chair, holding onto his glass, and walked unsteadily to the desk.

"Yes? What is it?"

"Good evening."

The voice on the telephone was a whisper, high-pitched and flat. He couldn't tell whether it was a man or a woman.

"Who the hell is this? How did you get this number?"

"Neither question is relevant. What I'm about to say to you is, however."

"You're gonna' say nuthin' to me. I don't talk to —"

"*Newport News,* Rawlins!" The whispered voice spat out the words. "I wouldn't hang up if I were you."

Rawlins froze. He stared through the haze at the telephone in his hand. Slowly he brought it up to his ear, his breath suspended. "Who are you? What do you mean? Newport . . ." His voice trailed off; he could not finish the name.

"Three years ago, Congressman. I'm sure if you think very hard, you'll remember. The Newport News coronor estimated the time of death to be twelve thirty in the morning. Just about now as a matter of fact. The date was March twenty-second."

"Who the hell are you?" Rawlins felt sick to his stomach.

"I told you it's not important. No more important than that little black girl in Newport News. How old was she, Congressman? Fourteen? Was that it? It was grotesque, wasn't it? They said she was cut up, beaten rather badly."

"I don't know what you're talkin' about! It's got nuthin' to do with me!" Rawlins brought the glass swiftly to his mouth and drank. Most of the sour mash rolled down his chin. "I wasn't anywhere *near——*"

"Newport News?" interrupted the high-pitched whisper. "On the night of March twenty-second, 1969? I think you were. As a matter of fact, I have in front of me a detailed flight plan of a Cessna aircraft flying in and out of a private field ten miles north of Newport News. There's a description of the passenger: bloodstained clothes, drunk. Shall I read it to you?"

Rawlins dropped the glass. It shattered on the floor. "You . . . *stop . . . it!*"

"There's nothing to worry about. You see, you're chairing a committee in the House that interests me. It's just that I don't approve of your opposition to bill H.R.

three-seven-five. You're going to change that position, Rawlins. You're going to throw your full support behind that bill. . . ."

Phyllis Maxwell walked past the front desk in the Hay-Adams toward the Lafayette Room. There was the usual luncheon crowd waiting to be seated; it did not concern her. The Lafayette captain would spot her and usher her past the others to her table. She was fifteen minutes late; that was good. Her lunch date would be nervous, worried, wondering if she had forgotten; that was very good. He would be on the defensive.

She stopped by a full-length mirror, pleased with what she saw. Rather not bad, she thought. Not bad at all for a once plain, overweight girl named Paula Mingus from Chillicothe, Ohio, who was a good forty-seven. She was . . . well, elegant was appropriate. She was slender, the legs tapered, the breasts firm, the neck long—almost Grecian, really—nicely accentuated by the pearl choker. And it was a good face. Again the word *elegant* was quite applicable. Her eyes, of course, were striking; everyone remarked about them. Speckled, curious, the eyes of an experienced newspaperwoman. She used her eyes well, boring into whomever she interviewed, carrying the message: *I don't believe you for a second. You'll have to do better than that.*

She had pried a lot of truth from a lot of liars with her eyes. More than once she'd stunned Washington with a confirmed story many knew existed but never thought they would see in print. She had forced confirmations, often by remaining silent, letting her eyes do the work.

Of course, there were times when the eyes did more than doubt; they often promised. But she did not fool herself. Forty-seven was not twenty-seven, elegant or no. As the years went by, there were far more probes than promises. For a number of reasons.

Phyllis Maxwell was the name, not Paula Mingus of the Chillicothe Minguses; the first editor who let her have a byline had changed that a quarter century before. And she was good; she took her job seriously. She went after the hard news.

Like today. There was something rotten, deeply rotten, in the ongoing election campaign. Money was being gathered in staggering sums from reluctant contributors.

Threats undefined and assurances impossible to guarantee were being used as weapons.

"Miss Maxwell! So good of you to join us." It was the Lafayette captain.

"Thank you, Jacques."

"Right this way, Miss Maxwell. Your party is here."

He was. A cherub-faced, bland-looking young man with scrubbed skin and eager eyes sprang to obsequious attention at the booth. Another clean-cut liar; they were everywhere. *Stroke her.* Phyllis could hear the instructions.

"Sorry I'm late," she said.

"Who's late? I just got here." He smiled.

"Then, you were late, weren't you." It was a statement, accepted with a clumsy smile. "Never mind, Paul. Have a drink. You need one, and I won't snitch."

He did. Three. And he barely touched his eggs Benedict. Instead, he could not bear the waiting. "I'm telling you, Phyl, you're barking up the wrong tree! You don't want to saw yourself off the limb!"

"You're mixing your metaphors. You people do that a lot, Paul. Usually when you've got something to hide."

"We've got nothing to hide."

"Then let's get to business," she interrupted. Small talk irritated her; plunging in was one of her most effective techniques. "My information is as follows: Two airlines seeking new routes were told—not very subtly—that the CAB might look unfavorably, et cetera, et cetera, unless sizable contributions, et cetera. A major trucking firm was reached by the Teamsters. Contribute heavily or face a possible strike. The largest pharmaceutical company in the East was threatened with an investigative inquiry from the FDA two days after it was solicited. They paid up. There'll be no inquiry. Four banks. Four *leading* banks, Paul. Two in New York, one in Detroit, one in Los Angeles—all seeking mergers—were told their petitions might be tied up for years unless they reached sympathetic people. Contributions were made; favorable responses were received. Now, this is all documented. I've got names, dates, and figures. I intend to blow a very shrill whistle unless you've got answers that isolate—and I mean *isolate*—these eight examples from the rest of the campaign. You're not going to buy this or any other election. My God, you damn fools! You don't have to!"

The cherub paled. "You've got it all wrong! The radical posture expressed by the opposition would tear this nation apart. Weaken its very foundations, its fundamental liberties——"

"Oh, stop it, you ass!"

"Miss Maxwell?" It was Jacques. A telephone was in his hand. "A call for you. Shall I connect it?"

"Please."

The captain inserted plug into jack. He bowed and left.

"This is Phyllis Maxwell."

"I'm sorry to disturb your lunch."

"I beg your pardon. I can't hear you."

"I'll try to speak more clearly."

"Who is this?" The voice on the telephone was a whisper. Eerily flat and in an upper register. "Is this a joke?"

"Most emphatically not, Miss Mingus."

"Maxwell's my byline. The fact that you know my given name doesn't shock me. It's on my passport."

"Yes, I know," came the oddly horrible, whispered reply. "I've seen it registered at Immigration on the island of Saint Vincent. In the Grenadines, *Miss* Mingus."

The blood drained from Phyllis Maxwell's face; a terrible pain shot through her head. Her hand trembled. She thought she was going to be sick.

"Are you still there?" asked the horrible whisper.

"Who are you?" She could barely speak.

"Someone you can trust. Be assured of that."

Oh, *God*! The island! How was it possible? Who could *care* that much? What filthy mentality would take the trouble? . . . In defense of righteousness! But the righteous were wrong. It was freedom. From furtiveness and suspicion. Whom did they hurt?

Every year, for three weeks only, Phyllis Maxwell left Washington ostensibly for total seclusion at a retreat in Caracas. But Paula Mingus did not stay in Caracas; she —and others—flew to the Grenadines, to *their* island. And there they were themselves. Women who found the fullest expressions of love. With other women.

Paula Mingus was a lesbian. Phyllis Maxwell—in the interests of professionalism and at great, *great* cost to her well-being—did not acknowledge that word.

"You're obscene," she whispered to the terrible whisper.

"Most people would apply that word to you. You'd become your own dirty joke, your career destroyed. If the undeniable story were released."

"What do you want?"

"You must assure that very sincere young man with you that you will no longer pursue the topics you've obviously discussed by now. You will publish nothing."

Phyllis Maxwell replaced the telephone. Tears welled in her speckled, professional eyes. She was barely audible as she spoke.

"Is there nothing you won't do?"

"Phyl, I swear to you——"

"Oh, God! Steal the country!"

She got up and ran out of the restaurant.

Carroll Quinlan O'Brien, known as Quinn to his colleagues at the bureau, walked into his office and sat down behind his desk. It was nearly eight o'clock; the night force was well into its shift, which meant half the offices were empty.

But sixty-four percent of all violent crimes took place between the hours of seven thirty P.M. and six A.M., reflected O'Brien, and the country's major law-enforcement instrument was half-staffed during that time.

It was not a valid criticism. The bureau wasn't a field agency, it was a fact-finding house; and data was most obtainable when the rest of the country was awake. No, it was not a valid point to make, although vast reorganization was taking place; that's what everyone said.

They might start with Hoover's ridiculous term *Seat of Government*. S.O.G. It was just as definitive to say FBI and far less pretentious.

There was so much that was antediluvian, thought O'Brien. Confused organization charts. Contradictory and overlapping areas of assignment; strength where it was unnecessary, weakness where strength was mandatory. Dress codes, parameters of behavior—social, sexual, and meditative. Punishments meted out for inconsequential misbehavior, valid reprimands avoided by flattery and obsequiousness. Fear, fear, *fear*. It had run the bureau for as long as Quinn had been in Washington.

For four years he had kept his mouth shut. He and a few others who honestly believed they brought a touch of sanity to the upper levels of the Federal Bureau of Investigation. They were also in a position to keep their eyes out for the truly irregular, the conceivably dangerous. And let others know when they *had* to know.

He himself had funneled information to the intelligence community on a fairly regular basis when the director's fury over real or imagined insults prohibited liaison. He was reminded of the practice as his eyes fell on the small silver shamrock that hung on a chain around his pen set. It was a gift from Stefan Varak over at NSC. He had first met Varak two years before, when Hoover had refused to deliver profile data on Eastern-bloc UN personnel. The National Security Council needed that information. O'Brien had simply walked into Section I, made copies, and given them to Varak during their first dinner together. There'd been a great many dinners since. He had learned a lot from Varak.

Now Hoover was dead, and things were going to change. That's what everyone said. Quinn would believe it when he saw the directives. Then, perhaps, the decision of four years ago would make sense.

He had never fooled himself or his wife. His appointment to the FBI was a political cosmetic. He had been an assistant prosecutor in Sacramento when he'd been swept into the Vietnam War because of his reserve-officer status. He had not been assigned to legal work; he had been put into G2 for reasons vaguely related to criminal prosecution. A forty-plus lawyer suddenly transformed into an investigator for Army Intelligence. That was in 1964. Finally, unexpected combat in the northern sectors, capture, two years of survival under the most primitive conditions, and escape.

He had escaped in March of 1968 and had made his way through the torrential rains southwest across enemy lines, into UN territory. He had lost fifty pounds; his body was ravaged. And he had returned a hero.

It was a time when heroes were sought. They were needed desperately. Discontent had spread, myths were decaying. The FBI was not exempt, and Quinn's investigatory talents were noted; Hoover was impressed with heroes. So an offer had been made. And the hero had accepted.

His reasoning had been simple. If he could start

fairly high up the ladder and learn fast and well, there would be other fine opportunities within the Justice Department. Far more than in Sacramento. Now he was a forty-nine-year-old ex-hero who had learned very well indeed and had kept his mouth shut. He had learned *very* well, and that was what bothered him now.

Something was wrong. Something had not happened that should have happened. A vitally important element of Hoover's dictatorial reign had neither been revealed nor explained.

J. Edgar Hoover had had in his personal possession hundreds—perhaps thousands—of highly inflammatory dossiers. Files that contained devastating information about many of the nation's most influential and powerful men and women.

Since Hoover's death, however, nothing had been said about those files. There were neither demands to acknowledge their existence nor outcries for their destruction. It was as if no one wanted to be associated with bringing them to light. The fear of inclusion was too great; if nothing were said, perhaps they would fade into oblivion.

But that was not realistic; those files had to be somewhere. So Quinn had begun asking questions. He had started with the shredding rooms. Nothing had come down from Hoover's office in months. He had checked the microfilm and microdot laboratories. There had been no reductions of dossiers made within memory. Then he'd scrutinized the entry ledgers—anything related directly to Hoover in the areas of authorized deliveries or pickups. Nothing.

He'd found his first clue in the security logs. It was a late entry, authorized by scrambler, on the night of May 1, the night before Hoover's death. It had stunned him. Three field agents—Salter, Krepps, and a man named Longworth—had been admitted at eleven fifty-seven, but there had been no departmental clearance. Just authorization by way of the director's private scrambler. From Hoover's *home*.

It had not made sense. Quinn had then contacted the senior agent who had admitted the trio, Lester Parke. It hadn't been easy. Parke had retired a month after Hoover's death, drawing a minimum pension, but with enough money to buy a fair-sized condominium in Fort

Lauderdale. That hadn't made a hell of a lot of sense either.

Parke had clarified nothing. The senior agent had told Quinn that he had spoken with Hoover himself that night. Hoover, himself, had given specific and confidential instructions to admit the field agents. Anything else would have to come from them.

So Quinn had tried to find three field agents named Salter, Krepps, and Longworth. But "Salter" and "Krepps" were floating covers, names with biographies used by various agents at various times for clandestine operations. There was *no* record of the names having been assigned during the month of May; or if there was a record, Quinn was not cleared for it.

The information on Longworth had come in a little over an hour ago. It was so startling that Quinn had called his wife, telling her he would not be home for dinner.

Longworth had retired from the bureau two months before Hoover's death! He was now living in the Hawaiian Islands. Since this was the confirmed information, what was Longworth doing in Washington, at the west entry desk, on the night of May 1?

O'Brien knew he had found serious, unexplained discrepancies in official logs, and, he was convinced they were related to the files no one talked about. Tomorrow morning he would go to the attorney general.

His telephone rang, startling him. He reached for it. "O'Brien," he said, conveying his surprise; his telephone rarely rang after five in the evening.

"Han Chow!" The whisper seared over the line. "Remember the dead of Han Chow."

Carroll Quinlan O'Brien lost his breath. His eyes had gone blind; darkness and white light replaced familiar images. "What? Who's this?"

"They begged you. Do you remember how they begged you?"

"No! I don't know what you're talking about! Who is this?"

"Of course you know," continued the cold whisper. "The Cong commander threatened reprisals—executions—if anyone at Han Chow escaped. Very few were capable of trying. They agreed not to for the sake of the others. But not you, Major O'Brien. Not you."

"That's a lie! There were no agreements! None!"

"You know perfectly well there were. And you disregarded them. There were nine men in your compound. You were the healthiest. You told them you were going, and they begged you not to. The next morning, when you were gone, they were taken out in the fields and shot."

Oh, Christ! Oh, Holy Mary, Mother of God! It wasn't the way it was meant to be! They could hear the artillery through the rain in the distance. They'd never get another chance like that! So close! All he had to do was get through to the guns! To the American guns! Once he got through, he would pinpoint the Han Chow compound on a map, and it could be taken. The men—the dying men—would be freed! But the rain and the sickness and the night played horrible tricks on him. He never found the guns. And the men died.

"Are you remembering?" The whisper was soft now. "Eight men executed so the major could have a parade in Sacramento. Did you know Han Chow was taken less than two weeks later?"

Don't, O'Brien! Don't do it! If they're this close, Charlie will run and leave us! They won't move us. We'd slow them down! They won't kill us either! Unless you give them an excuse. Don't give it to them! Not now! That's an order, Major!

The words had been spoken in the darkness by a half-starved lieutenant colonel, the only other officer in the hut.

"You don't understand," he said into the telephone. "You've twisted everything. It's not the way it was!"

"Yes it is, Major," countered the whisper slowly. "A paper was found on a dead Viet Cong months later. On it was written the last testimony of a lieutenant colonel who knew what faced the prisoners of Han Chow. Eight men were shot because you disobeyed a direct order of your superior officer."

"Nothing was ever said. . . . Why?"

"The parades had taken place. That was enough."

Quinn O'Brien brought his hand up to his forehead. There was a hollowness in his chest. "Why are you telling me this?"

"Because you've involved yourself in matters that are no concern of yours. You will pursue them no further."

10

The immense figure of Daniel Sutherland stood at the far end of his chambers, in front of the bookshelves. He was in profile, tortoise-shell glasses on his enormous head, a heavy book in his massive black hands. He turned and spoke; his voice deep, resonant, and warmly pleasant.

"Precedents, Mr. Chancellor. The law is all too often governed by precedents, which in themselves are all too often imperfect." Sutherland smiled, closed the book, and replaced it carefully in the shelf. He walked to Peter, his hand extended. In spite of his age he moved with assurance, with dignity. "My son and granddaughter are avid readers of yours. They were most impressed that you were coming to see me. It's my loss that I haven't yet had the opportunity to read your books."

"I'm the one who's impressed, sir," replied Peter, meaning it, his hand enveloped. "Thank you for granting me an appointment. I won't take up much of your time."

Sutherland smiled, releasing Peter's hand, putting him immediately at ease. He indicated one chair among several around a conference table. "Please sit down."

"Thank you." Peter waited until the judge had selected his own chair three places away at the end of the table. They both sat.

"Now, what can I do for you?" Sutherland leaned back, the expression on his dark face was kind and not without a tinge of humor. "I admit to being fascinated. You told my secretary it was a personal matter, yet we've never met."

"It's difficult to know where to begin."

"At the risk of offending your writer's sense of cliché, why not at the beginning?"

"That's just it. I don't know the beginning. I'm not sure there is one. And if there is, you may feel strongly that I have no right to know about it."

"Then, I'll tell you, won't I?"

Peter nodded. "I met a man. I can't say who he is or where we met. He mentioned your name with respect to a small group of influential people here in Washington. He said this group had been formed several years ago for the express purpose of monitoring the activities of J. Edgar

Hoover. He said he believed you were the man responsible for this group's existence. I'd like to ask you if it's true."

Sutherland did not move. His large dark eyes, magnified by the lenses of his glasses, were expressionless. "Did this man mention any other names?"

"No, sir. Not related to the group. He said he didn't know of anyone else."

"May I ask how my name surfaced?"

"Are you saying it's true, then?"

"I'd appreciate your answering my question first."

Peter thought for a moment. As long as he did not name Longworth, he could answer the question. "He saw it on something he called a tracer. Apparently it meant that you were to receive specific information."

"About what?"

"About him, I imagine. Also about those people known to have been placed under negative surveillance by Hoover."

The judge breathed deeply. "The man you spoke with is named Longworth. A former field agent, Alan Longworth, currently listed as an employee of the State Department."

Chancellor tensed the muscles of his stomach in an effort to conceal his astonishment. "I couldn't comment on that," he said inadequately.

"You don't have to," replied Sutherland. "Did Mr. Longworth also tell you that he was the special agent in charge of this negative surveillance?"

"The man I spoke with made reference to that. But only a reference."

"Then, let me amplify." The judge shifted his position in the chair. "To answer your initial question. Yes, there was such a group of concerned individuals, and I stress the tense. *Was.* As to my participation, it was minor and limited to certain legal aspects of the issue."

"I don't understand, sir. What issue?"

"Mr. Hoover had a regrettable fecundity when it came to making unsubstantiated charges. Worse, he often cloaked them in innuendo, using provocative generalities against which there was little legal recourse. It was an unforgivable lapse of judgment, considering his position."

"So this group of concerned men—"

"And women, Mr. Chancellor," interrupted Sutherland.

"And women," continued Peter, "was formed to protect the victims of Hoover's attacks."

"Basically, yes. In his later years he could be vicious. He saw enemies everywhere. Good men would be let go, the reasons obscured. Later, often months later, the director's hand was revealed. We were trying to stem this tide of abuse."

"Would you tell me who else was in this group?"

"Of course not." Sutherland removed his glasses and held a stem delicately between the fingers of his hand. "Suffice it to say, they were people capable of raising strong objections, voices that could not be overlooked."

"This man you spoke of, this retired field agent——"

"I didn't say *retired*." Again Sutherland interrupted. "I said *former*."

Peter hesitated, accepting the rebuke. "You said this former field agent was in charge of surveillance?"

"Certain specific surveillances. Hoover was impressed with Longworth. He placed him in the position of coordinating the data on individuals with proven or potential antipathy to the bureau, or Hoover himself. The list was extensive."

"But he obviously stopped working for Hoover." Once more Chancellor paused. He was not sure how to ask the question. "You just said he was now employed by the State Department. If so, he was separated from the bureau under very unusual circumstances."

Sutherland replaced his glasses, letting his hand drop to his chin. "I know what you're asking. Tell me, what's the point of your visit this afternoon?"

"I'm trying to make up my mind whether there's a basis for a book on Hoover's last year. On his death, frankly."

The judge's hand dropped to his lap; he sat completely still, looking at Peter. "I'm not sure I understand. Why come to me?"

It was Peter's turn to smile. "The kind of novels I write require a certain credibility. They're fiction, of course, but I try to use as much recognizable fact as I can. Before I start a book, I talk to a great many people; I try to get a feeling for the conflicts."

"Obviously you're very successful with the approach. My son approves of your conclusions; he was very firm about that last night." Sutherland leaned forward, his forearms on the conference table. The trace of humor returned to his eyes. "And I approve of my son's judgment. He's a fine lawyer, albeit a little strident in the courtroom. You *do* respect confidences, don't you, Mr. Chancellor?"

"Of course."

"And identities. But of course again. You won't admit you talked to Alan Longworth."

"I would never use a person's name unless he gave me permission."

"Legally I'd suggest that you not." Sutherland smiled. "I feel as though I'm part of a creation."

"I wouldn't go that far."

"Neither would the Bible." Again, the judge leaned back in his chair. "Very well. It's past history now. And not particularly extraordinary; it's done every day in Washington. An inherent part of the checks and balances of our government, I sometimes think." Sutherland stopped and raised his right palm delicately toward Peter. "Should you use any part of what I tell you, you must do so with discretion remembering that the objective was a decent one."

"Yes, sir."

"Last March Alan Longworth was offered early retirement from one branch of the government, and under cover he was shifted to another. The shift took place in such a way as to remove him from the bureau's scrutiny altogether. The reasons were self-evident. When we learned that Longworth was the coordinator of this negative surveillance—a very apt phrase, by the way—we showed him the dangers of Hoover's abuses. He cooperated; for two months he pored over hundreds of names, recalling which were included and what the damaging information was. He traveled extensively, alerting those we thought should be warned. Until Hoover's death Longworth was our deterrent, our defensive weapon, as it were. He was very effective."

Peter was beginning to understand the strange, blond-haired man in Malibu. There had to be conflicting loyalties in the man; the agent must have been torn with guilt. It explained his odd behavior, the sudden accusations, the abrupt retreats.

"When Hoover died, this man's job was finished, then?"

"Yes. With Hoover's sudden, and I must say, unexpected death there was no further need for such a defensive operation. It ended with his funeral."

"What happened to him?"

"It's my understanding that he's been compensated handsomely. The State Department transferred him to what I believe is referred to as soft duty. He's living out his tenure in pleasant surroundings with a minimum work load."

Peter watched Sutherland closely. He had to ask the question; there was no reason not to now. "What would you say if I told you my informant questioned Hoover's death?"

"Death is death. How can it be questioned?"

"The way he died. By natural causes."

"Hoover was an old man. A sick man. I'd say Longworth—you won't use his name, but I will—might be suffering from intense psychological pressures. Remorse, guilt—it wouldn't be unusual. He had a personal relationship with Hoover. Perhaps he now feels he betrayed him."

"That's what I was thinking."

"Then, what troubles you?"

"Something this man I talked with said. He said Hoover's private files were never found. They disappeared with Hoover's death."

There was a flash of something—Chancellor did not know what; anger, perhaps—in the Negro's eyes. "They were destroyed. All of Hoover's personal papers were shredded and burned. We've been assured of that."

"By whom?"

"That information I can't possibly give you. We are satisfied; that much I can tell you."

"But what if they weren't destroyed?"

Daniel Sutherland returned Peter's gaze. "It would be an extraordinary complication. One I would not care to dwell on," he said firmly. Then the smile returned. "But it's hardly a possibility."

"Why not?"

"Because we'd know about it, wouldn't we?"

Peter was disturbed. For the first time Sutherland did not sound convincing.

He had to be careful, Peter reminded himself as he walked down the steps of the courthouse. He was not looking for concrete facts, merely credibility. That's what he was after. Supportive events ripped out of context and used to bridge the inevitable gap between reality and fantasy.

He could do it now. Daniel Sutherland had given him the answer to the basic enigma: Alan Longworth. The judge had explained the federal agent with perceptive simplicity. It was contained in the single word *remorse*. Longworth had turned against his mentor, the director who had awarded him the most confidential of assignments and written personal commendations on his service record. It was natural for Longworth to feel guilty, to want to strike back at those who had induced his betrayal. What better way than to question that death?

Knowing this freed Peter's imagination. It removed whatever obligation he might have felt toward Longworth. The concept could be accepted for what it was: a fascinating idea for a book. Nothing more was needed. It was a game, a goddamned game; and the writer in Chancellor was beginning to enjoy it.

He stepped off the curb and hailed a passing cab. "The Hay-Adams Hotel," he directed.

"I'm sorry, sir, it's an unlisted number," said the telephone operator in that peculiar condescension the Bell System reserved for such information.

"I see. Thank you." Peter hung up and leaned back on the pillows. He was not surprised; he had not been able to find MacAndrew's name in the Rockville, Maryland, directory. A Washington reporter he knew had told him the retired general lived in a rented house far out in the country, had lived there for several years.

But Chancellor was not a newspaperman's son for nothing. He sat up and opened the telephone book at his side. He found the name he was looking for and dialed nine and then the number.

"United States Army, Pentagon Operations," said the male voice on the other end of the line.

"Lieutenant General Bruce MacAndrew, please." Peter spoke the rank and name in clipped cadence.

"Just one minute, sir," came the reply, followed seconds later by the obvious. "There's no listing for General MacAndrew, sir."

"There was a month ago, soldier," said Chancellor authoritatively. "Let me have Directory."

"Yes, sir."

"Pentagon Directory. Good afternoon." The voice was female.

"There seems to be a foul-up somewhere. This is Colonel Chancellor. I've just returned from Command Saigon and I'm trying to reach General MacAndrew, Light General B. MacAndrew. I have a letter from the general dated twelve August. Arlington. Has he been transferred?"

The operator took less than half a minute to find the information. "No, Colonel. Not transferred. Retired."

Peter allowed himself the proper moment of silence. "I understand; his wounds were extensive. Do I find him at Walter Reed?"

"I have no idea, Colonel."

"Then, let me have his telephone number and address, please."

"I'm not sure I can—"

"Young lady," interrupted Peter. "I've just flown ten thousand miles. The general is a close friend; I'm very concerned. Do I make myself clear?"

"Yes, sir. There is no address listed. The number on the print sheet is area code . . ."

Chancellor wrote as the woman spoke. He thanked her, pressed down the telephone button, released it, and dialed.

"General MacAndrew's residence." The drawl on the line obviously belonged to a maid.

"May I speak with the general, please?"

"He's not here. He's expected back in an hour. May I take your name?"

Peter thought swiftly. There was no point in wasting time. "This is the Pentagon Messenger Service. We have a delivery for the general but the PMS address is unclear. What's the street number in Rockville?"

"RFD Twenty-three, the Old Mill Pike."

"Thank you."

He hung up and once again leaned back on the pillows, recalling Longworth's statements about MacAndrew. The agent had said the general had thrown away a brilliant career, including perhaps the chairmanship of the Joint Chiefs, for no apparent reason. Longworth had suggested there could be a connection between some missing information in MacAndrew's service record and the general's resignation.

A thought struck him. Why had Longworth even brought up MacAndrew? What was MacAndrew to him?

Chancellor sat up suddenly. Had Longworth, in wanting to strike back at those who had manipulated him, manipulated the general? Had the agent himself used damaging information about MacAndrew?

If so, Longworth was playing a serious game. One that went way beyond the bounds of remorse. It depended on the general: what kind of man was he?

He was of medium height, with broad shoulders and a stocky build; he was dressed in chinos and a white shirt, open at the collar. His face was the face of a professional soldier; the skin was taut, the wrinkles deeply etched, the eyes noncommittal. He stood in the doorway of the old house on the back country road, a middle-aged man somewhat startled by a stranger whose features seemed vaguely familiar.

Peter was used to the reaction. His occasional appearances on television talk shows produced it. People rarely knew who he was but were sure they'd seen him somewhere.

"General MacAndrew?"

"Yes?"

"We haven't met," he said, extending his hand. "My name's Peter Chancellor. I'm a writer. I'd like to talk to you."

Was it fear he saw in the general's eyes? "Of course I've seen you. On television, your photograph. I read one of your books, I think. Come in, Mr. Chancellor. Forgive my astonishment, but I—well—as you said, we've never met."

Peter stepped into the hallway. "A mutual friend gave me your address. But your telephone's unlisted."

"A mutual friend? Who's that?"

Chancellor watched the general's eyes. "Longworth. Alan Longworth."

There was no reaction whatsoever.

"Longworth? I don't think I know him. But obviously I must. Was he in one of my commands?"

"No, General. I think he's a blackmailer."

"I beg your pardon?"

It *was* fear. The eyes darted briefly toward the staircase, then toward Peter.

"May we talk?"

"I think we'd better. It's either that, or I throw you out on your ass." MacAndrew turned and gestured through an archway. "In my study," he said curtly.

The room was small, with dark leather chairs, a solid pine desk, and mementos of the general's career on the walls. "Sit down," said MacAndrew, indicating a chair in front of the desk. It was an order. The general remained standing.

"I may have been unfair," said Peter.

"You were something," replied MacAndrew. "Now, what's this all about?"

"Why did you retire?"

"None of your damned business."

"Maybe you're right; maybe it's not mine. But it's somebody's besides yours."

"What the hell are you talking about?"

"I heard of you through a man named Longworth. He suggested that you were forced to resign. That something happened a number of years ago, the information removed from your military record. He implied that this information became part of a collection of missing files. Dossiers that contained suppressed facts that could destroy the subjects in question. He led me to believe that you were threatened with exposure. Told to get out of the Army."

For a long moment MacAndrew stood silently, frozen into position, his eyes a curious mixture of hatred and fright. When he spoke, his voice was flat. "Did this Longworth say what the information was?"

"He claimed not to know. The only conclusion I can draw is that it was of such a damaging nature that you had to follow instructions. If I may say so, your reaction would seem to bear out that assumption."

"You prick bastard." The contempt was absolute. "You don't know what you're talking about."

Peter met his eyes. "Whatever's troubling you is none of my business, and perhaps I shouldn't have come here. I was curious; curiosity's a writer's disease. But I don't want to know your problem; believe me, I don't want that burden. I only wanted to know why your name was given to me, and now I think I do. You're a substitute. You make a pretty scary example."

MacAndrew's look grew less hostile.

"Substitute for what?"

"For someone under the gun. If those files really were missing, in the hands of a fanatic, and this fanatic wanted to use the information against another person— well, you're what that other person would be like."

"I don't follow you. Why would my name be given to you?"

"Because Longworth wants me to believe something to the degree that I'll write a book about it."

"But why me?"

"Because something did happen years ago, and Longworth had access to the information. I know that now. You see, General, I think he used both of us. He gave me your name, and before he gave it to me, he threatened to expose you. He wanted a victim. I think——"

It was as far as Chancellor got. With the speed born of a hundred combat assaults MacAndrew sprang across the space between them. His hands were curved into claws that dug into the cloth of Peter's jacket, pressing down, then pulling up, yanking Chancellor to his feet.

"*Where is he?*"

"Hey! For Christ's sake——"

"Longworth! Where is he? Tell me, you prick bastard!"

"You crazy son of a bitch. Let me *go!*" Peter was larger than the soldier but no match for MacAndrew's strength. "Goddamn it, be careful of my head!"

It was a silly thing to say, but it was all that came to mind. The soldier pinned him against the wall, the hard face with the furious eyes inches from his.

"I asked you a question. Now, you answer me! Where can I find Longworth?"

"I don't know! I met him in California."

"Where in California?"

"He doesn't live there. He lives in Hawaii. Damn it, let go of me!"

"When you tell me what I want to know!" MacAndrew pulled Chancellor forward, then slammed him back into the wall. "Is he in Honolulu?"

"No!" Peter's head ached beyond endurance, the pain spreading across his right temple, shooting down to the back of his neck. "He's in Maui. For Christ's sake, you've got to let *go* of me! You don't understand——"

"The hell I don't! Thirty-five years down the chute. When I'm needed. *Needed.* Can you understand that!" It was not a question.

"Yes. . . ." Peter grabbed the soldier's wrists with all the strength he had left. The pain was awful. He spoke slowly. "I asked you to listen to me. I don't care what happened; it's not my business. But I *do* care that Long- worth used you to get to me. No book's worth it. I'm sorry."

"*Sorry?* It's a little late for that!" The soldier ex- ploded again, smashing Peter back into the wall. "This happened because of a goddamned book?"

"Please! You can't——"

There was a crash beyond the door. From the living room. It was followed by a terrible moaning—half chant, half mad, a toneless singsong. MacAndrew froze, his eyes on the door. He released Peter, throwing him into the desk as he reached for the doorknob. He pulled the door open and disappeared into the living room.

Chancellor supported himself on the edge of the desk. The room was spinning. He inhaled deeply, re- peatedly, to regain his focus, to lessen the pain in his head.

He heard it again. The moaning, crazy singsong. It grew louder; he could distinguish the words.

". . . *outside is frightful but the fire is so delightful and since we've no place to go,* . . . *Let it snow! Let it snow! Let it snow! . . .*"

Peter limped unsteadily to the study door. He looked into the living room—and wished he hadn't.

MacAndrew was on the floor, cradling a woman in his arms. She wore a torn, disheveled negligee that barely covered a faded nightgown, itself old and worn. All around were fragments of shattered glass. The tulip stem of a smashed wine goblet rolled silently on a small rug.

MacAndrew was suddenly aware of his presence. "Now you know what the damaging information is."

". . . *since we've no place to go, Let it snow! Let it snow! . . .*"

Peter did know. It explained the old house way out in the country, the unlisted telephone, and the absence of an address at the Pentagon Directory. General Bruce MacAndrew lived in isolation because his wife was mad.

"I see," said Chancellor quietly. "But I don't understand. Is this why?"

"Yes." The soldier hesitated, then looked back at his wife, lifting her face to his. "There was an accident; the doctors said she had to be sent away. I wouldn't do that."

Peter understood. High-ranking generals in the Pentagon were not permitted certain tragedies. Other varieties, yes. Death and mutilation on the battlefield, for instance. But not this, not a tormented wife. Wives were to remain deep in the shadows of a soldier's life, interference denied.

". . . when we finally kiss good night, how I'll hate going out in the storm . . ."

MacAndrew's wife was staring at Peter. Her eyes grew wide, her thin, pale lips parted, and she screamed. The scream was followed by another. And another. She twisted her neck and arched her back, the screams wilder, uncontrollable.

MacAndrew held her tightly in his arms and stared up at Chancellor. Peter backed further into the study.

"No!" roared the general. "Come back out! Go to the light! Get by the light; put your face above the shade. In the *light*, goddamn you!"

Simply, blindly, Peter did as he was told. He edged his way toward a lamp on a low table and let the spill wash up into his face.

"It's all right, Mal. It's all right. Everything's all right." MacAndrew swayed back and forth on the floor, his cheek hard against his wife's face, calming her. Her screams subsided.

They were replaced with sobs. Deep and painful.

"Now, get out of here," he said to Chancellor.

11

Old Mill Pike swung west out of Rockville before turning south into the Maryland highway that led to Washington. The highway was nearly twenty miles from MacAndrew's house, the old road to it cut out of the countryside, twisting and turning around massive boulders and rock-dotted hills. It was not rich country. But it was remote, isolated.

How MacAndrew must have searched for such a location! thought Chancellor. The setting sun was directly in front of him now, filling the windshield with blinding light. He pulled down the visor; it didn't help much. His thoughts returned to the scene he had just left.

Why had the disturbed woman reacted so hysterically to the sight of him? He had been in shadow when she'd first seen him. She calmed down when he followed Mac-Andrew's command to go into the light. Could he have resembled someone so completely? Impossible. The windows of the old house were small, and the trees outside were full and tall, blocking the late afternoon sun. The general's wife could not have seen him that clearly. So perhaps it wasn't his face. Yet what else could it have been? And what nightmares had he evoked?

Longworth was despicable, yet he had made his point. What better way than to offer the pathetic figure of Mac-Andrew as the object of the most ruthless type of extortion? Taking Longworth's premise that Hoover's private files survived and could be used viciously, the general was the perfect subject. The man in Chancellor was outraged, the writer primed. The concept was valid; there was a novel in the premise. He had a beginning based in recent events, Daniel Sutherland had provided the facts. And an example of what might have been; he himself had observed it.

He felt his energy flowing. He wanted to write again.

A silver car pulled alongside; Peter slowed down, allowing it to pass in the blinding yellow sunlight. The driver must know the road, thought Chancellor. Only someone familiar with the curves would pass, especially with the sun filling the windshield.

The silver car, however, did not pass. It stayed parallel; and if Peter's eyes were not playing tricks on him, it narrowed the space between them. Chancellor looked across the diminishing gulf. Perhaps the driver was trying to signal him.

He was not—*she* was not. The driver was a woman. Her dark hair, crowned by a wide-brimmed hat, fell over her shoulders. She wore sunglasses, and her mouth was a splash of red lipstick emphasizing her pale white skin. An orange scarf billowed out from the top of her jacket. She stared straight ahead as if oblivious to the automobile beside her.

Peter pressed his horn repeatedly; the cars were inches from each other. The woman did not respond. A sharp downhill curve to the right appeared in the road. If he braked, he knew he would slide into the silver car. He held the wheel firmly to negotiate the turn, his eyes switching back and forth from the road to the automobile perilously close to him. He could see more clearly; the sunlight was blocked by trees.

It was an S curve; he swung the wheel to the left, his foot cautiously on the brake. The blinding light returned to the windshield; on his right he could barely make out the gully that lay beyond the road's shoulder. He remembered seeing it when he'd driven out an hour before.

The impact came! The silver car collided with the side of his. It was trying to force him off the road. The woman was trying to send him into the gully! She was trying to kill him!

It was Pennsylvania all over again! The silver car was a Mark IV Continental. The same make of car he had driven that terrible night in the storm. With Cathy.

There was a flat stretch of road at the bottom of the hill. He stabbed the accelerator with his foot; sending his car forward in a burst of speed.

The Continental kept pace; his rented Chevrolet was no match for it. They reached the foot of the hill, the flat road now the course. Chancellor's panic prohibited clear thought and he knew it. He should simply stop the car . . . *stop the goddamned car* . . . but he could not. He had to get away from the horrible silver apparition.

His breath came erratically as he held the pedal against the floorboard. He drew slightly ahead of the Continental, but the silver mass of steel surged forward, its gleaming grill pounding the side of his door.

The dark-haired woman stared straight ahead impassively as if unaware of the terrible game she played.

"Stop it! What are you doing?" Peter screamed through the open window. She acknowledged nothing.

But the Mark IV dropped back again. Had his screams gotten through? He gripped the wheel with all his strength; perspiration covered his hands and rolled down his forehead, adding to the blindness of the sunlight.

He was jolted; his head snapped back, then crashed forward into the windshield. The impact came from behind. Through the rearview mirror he could see the glistening hood of the Continental. It crashed again and again into the trunk of the Chevrolet. He swung to the left side of the road; the Mark IV did the same. The pounding continued. Peter weaved back and forth. If he stopped now, the larger, heavier car would plow into him.

There was nothing else he could do. He spun the wheel violently to the right; the Chevrolet lurched off the road. A final crash propelled the rented car into a lateral spin; it swerved, the tail swinging to the forward left side, causing it to smash sideways into a barbed-wire fence.

But he was off the road!

He slammed his foot back onto the accelerator. *He had to get away.* The car bolted into the field.

The sickening thud of a collision came. Peter ducked, hovering over the wheel, his whole body lifted off the seat. The motor raced thunderously, but the Chevrolet had stopped.

He had crashed into a large rock in the field. Involuntarily, his neck arched back on the seat; blood ran down his nostrils profusely, mingling with the perspiration on his face.

Through the open window he saw the silver Continental racing away to the west down the flat stretch of road in the sunlight. It was the last thing he saw before his eyes closed.

He could not tell how long he'd been there, slumped in his own darkness. In the distance he heard the sound of a siren. Then soon a uniformed figure was outside the window. An arm reached in and turned off the ignition.

"Can you respond?" the patrolman asked.

Peter nodded. "Yes. I'm all right."

"You're a mess."

"It's just a nosebleed," replied Chancellor, fumbling for a handkerchief.

"Do you want me to radio for an ambulance?"

"No. Help me out. I'll walk around."

The officer did. Peter limped into the field, blotting his face, finding his sanity again.

"What happened, mister? I'll need your license and registration."

"It's a rented car," said Chancellor, taking his wallet from his pocket, withdrawing his license. "How come you're here?"

"Headquarters got a call from the owner of the property. Over there. That farmhouse." The patrolman gestured toward a house in the distance.

"They just called? They didn't come out?"

"It was a woman. Her husband's not home. She heard the crash and the racing motor. The circumstances were suspicious, so headquarters told her to stay inside."

Chancellor shook his head, bewildered. "The driver was a woman, too."

"What driver?"

Peter told him. The officer listened; he pulled a notebook from his pocket and wrote it all down.

When Chancellor had finished, the patrolman studied his notes. "What are you doing in Rockville?"

Peter did not want to mention MacAndrew. "I'm a writer. I often take long drives when I'm working. It clears the head."

The officer looked up from his notebook. "Wait here. I'll radio in."

Five minutes later, the man returned from the patrol car, shaking his head. "Jesus! What they let on the road these days! They got her, Mr. Chancellor. Everything you said checked out."

"What do you mean?"

"Crazy bitch was spotted outside of Gaithersburg. She played chicken with a goddamned mail truck! Can you beat that? With a mail truck! They got her in the drunk tank. Her husband's been called."

"Who is she?"

"Wife of some Lincoln-Mercury dealer in Pikesville. Got a record of drunken driving; her license was revoked a couple of months ago. She'll get off with probation and a fine. Her husband's a wheel."

The irony was not lost on Peter. Ten miles back a broken man, a career soldier with no future, cradled a tormented woman in his arms. Ten or twenty miles ahead an automobile salesman was racing down the highway, the fix already begun.

"I'd better get to a phone and call the rental agency about the car," said Chancellor.

"No sweat," replied the patrolman, reaching into the Chevrolet. "I'll take the keys. Give them my name, and I'll meet the tow truck. Tell them to ask for Donnelly. Officer Donnelly in Rockville."

"That's very nice of you."

"Come on, I'll drive you into Washington."

"Can you do that?"

"Headquarters cleared it. The accident took place within our municipal limits."

Peter looked at the patrolman. "How did you know I was staying in Washington?"

For an instant the officer's eyes went blank. "You're pretty shook up. You mentioned it a few minutes ago."

The silver Continental came to a stop beyond the bend in the road. The wail of the siren diminished in the distance. Soon it would fade, and the man in uniform would do his job. A man hired to impersonate a nonexistent police officer named Donnelly, to provide Peter Chancellor with erroneous information. It was part of the plan—as was the silver Continental, the sight of which would have to terrify the novelist, evoking memories of the night he had nearly been killed.

Everything had to be orchestrated swiftly, thoroughly; each thread of truth, half-truth, and lie woven quickly throughout the net so that Chancellor would not be capable of distinguishing one from the other. All had to be accomplished within a matter of days.

Chancellor's mind was the key. His life was expendable. The files were everything.

The driver removed the wide-brimmed hat and the sunglasses. Hands swiftly unscrewed the top of a cold-cream jar; Kleenex was pulled from a box on the seat, dipped into the cream, and scrubbed over the mouth until the lipstick faded. The scarf and the jacket were taken off and thrown to the floor of the car. Finally Varak removed the dark brown shoulder-length wig. And it, too, was deposited on the floor of the car. He checked his watch; it was ten minutes past six.

Word had reached Bravo. The high-pitched whisper

might have made contact with another subject of Hoover's private files. There was a congressman named Walter Rawlins, chairman of the powerful House Subcommittee on Reapportionment. Within the past week his behavior on the Hill had shocked his colleagues. Rawlins was a closet racist whose intransigence on several bills—one especially—had collapsed without explanation. He had absented himself during a number of crucial meetings, voting sessions he had sworn to attend.

If Rawlins had been reached, another name would be fed to Peter Chancellor.

As Peter approached the bank of elevators, he saw his image in a lobby mirror. He was, as Officer Donnelly had so aptly put it, a mess. His jacket was torn, his shoes filthy, his face streaked with dirt and dried blood. He was not exactly the picture of respectability the Hay-Adams was used to; he had the impression the desk clerks wanted him out of the lobby just as rapidly as possible, which was all right with him. He wanted a hot shower and a cold drink.

He saw a woman approaching as he waited for the elevator. It was the newspaperwoman Phyllis Maxwell, her face familiar from scores of televised press conferences.

"Mr. Chancellor? Peter Chancellor?"

"Yes. Miss Maxwell, isn't it?"

"I'm flattered," she said.

"So am I," he replied.

"What in heaven's name happened? Were you mugged?"

Peter smiled. "No, not mugged. Just in a minor accident."

"You're a mess."

"There seems to be general agreement about that. I'm going to my room to clean up."

The elevator arrived; its doors opened. Phyllis Maxwell spoke quickly. "Afterward would you agree to an interview?"

"Good lord, why?"

"I'm a newspaperwoman."

"I'm not news."

"Of course you are. You're a best-selling author, probably in Washington to research another book like *Counterstrike!* I find you limping across the Hay-Adams lobby, looking as though a truck had run over you. That's potential news."

"The limp's not new, and the accident was minor." Peter smiled. "If I were working on something, I wouldn't talk about it."

"Even if you did and you didn't want it public, I wouldn't print it."

Peter knew she was telling the truth. He'd heard his father call her one of the best correspondents in Washington. Which meant she was a *student* of Washington; she might tell him things he wanted to know. "Okay," he said. "Give me an hour, will you?"

"Fine. In the lounge?"

Chancellor nodded. "Okay. See you in an hour." He entered the elevator, feeling foolish. He was about to suggest that she could wait upstairs in his suite. Phyllis Maxwell was a striking woman.

He showered for nearly twenty minutes, far longer than usual. It was part of his recovery process when he was agitated or depressed. He'd learned little tricks over the past months, small indulgences that helped restore whatever equilibrium he had temporarily lost. He lay down naked on the bed and stared at the ceiling, breathing deeply.

The time passed; his calm was restored. He dressed in a brown leisure suit and went downstairs.

She was at a small table in the corner. The lounge was so · dimly lit he could barely see her, but the flickering candles picked up the features of her handsome face. If not the youngest, Phyllis Maxwell was the best-looking woman there.

The opening conversation was relaxed and comfortable. Peter ordered a round of drinks, and then a second. They talked about their respective careers from Erie, Pennsylvania, and Chillicothe, Ohio, to New York and Washington. Peter ordered a third drink.

"I shouldn't," said Phyllis firmly, but not firmly enough. "I can't remember when I've had three drinks at one sitting. It gets in the way of my imprecise shorthand. But then I can't remember interviewing a most attractive . . . young novelist before." Her voice slipped into a low register. Somewhat nervously, thought Chancellor.

"Not that attractive and, God knows, not so young."

"The point is, neither am I. My days of irreverent youth took place when you were learning algebra."

"That's downright condescending, as well as false. Look around you, lady. There's no one here in your league."

"Thank God it's dark, or I'd have to describe you as a charming liar." The drinks came; the waitress left. Phyllis took out a small notepad. "You don't want to discuss whatever you're working on. That's all right. Tell me what you think of today's fiction. Has entertainment returned to the modern novel?"

Peter looked across the table at the speckled, anxious eyes. The candlelight made them appear larger and softened the lines on her face. "I didn't know you wrote for the comics section. Or am I categorized?"

"Are you offended? I think it's an interesting subject. What does a well-paid, well-received storyteller think? God knows you make your theories clear. They're hardly comic."

Chancellor grinned. Phyllis Maxwell was succinct; she was no doubt devastating to any storyteller who took himself too seriously. Peter answered carefully, eager to get to another subject. She jotted down notes as he talked. She was an expert interviewer, as he had expected.

Their drinks were finished. Peter nodded at the glasses. "Another?"

"No thanks! I just misspelled *the*."

"Do you use *the* in shorthand?"

"Another reason I should refuse."

"Where are you having dinner?"

Phyllis hesitated. "I have an engagement."

"I don't believe you."

"Why not?"

"You haven't looked at your watch. Organized women check their watches if they have dinner engagements."

"Not all women are alike, young man."

Peter reached across the table, covering her wrist. "What time's your dinner date?"

At his touch she stiffened. Then quickly resumed the game. "That's not fair."

"Come on, what time?"

She smiled, blinking her eyes. "Eight thirty?"

"Forget it," he said, removing his hand. "He's given

up and left. It's ten past nine. You'll have to have dinner with me."

"You're incorrigible."

"We'll eat here, okay?"

Again she hesitated. "All right."

"Would you rather go someplace else?"

"No, this is fine."

Peter grinned. "We may not be able to tell the difference." He signaled the waitress, indicating a refill. "I know, I know. I'm incorrigible," he said. "May I ask *you* a couple of questions? You know Washington as well as anyone I can think of."

"Where's your notebook?" She put hers away in her purse.

"I've got a running tape in my head."

"That's not reassuring. What do you want to know?"

"Tell me about J. Edgar Hoover."

At the sound of the name, Phyllis's eyes made sharp, angry contact with his. And yet there was more than anger, thought Chancellor.

"He was a monster. I speak ill of the dead without the slightest compunction."

"All bad?"

"Within recent memory, yes. I've been in Washington sixteen years. I can't remember a year when he didn't destroy someone of extraordinary value."

"You put it strongly."

"I feel strongly. I despised him. I saw what he did. If ever there was an example of terror by fiat, he personified it. The story hasn't been told. I don't think it ever will be."

"Why not?"

"The bureau will protect him. He was the monarch. The heirs apparent won't let the image be tarnished. They fear infected bloodlines, and they damned well should."

"How can they stop it?"

Phyllis coughed a derisive laugh. "Not can, did. The furnaces, dear; little dark-suited robots went through the whole damn building burning anything and everything remotely harmful to their deceased progenitor. They're after canonization; it's their best protection. Then it's business as usual."

"Are you sure about that?"

"The word—and I grant you it's hearsay—is that Clyde showed up at Eddie's house before the body was cold. They say he and a few courtiers went from room to room with portable shredders."

"That Tolson?"

"The Tulip himself. What he didn't burn, he banked."

"Are there witnesses?"

"I suppose so." Phyllis stopped. The waitress was at the table; she removed the empty glasses, replacing them with new drinks.

Peter looked up at the girl. "Should we reserve a table in the dining room?"

"I'll take care of it, sir," replied the waitress, backing away.

"The name is——"

"I know, sir. Maxwell." The waitress left.

"I'm impressed," said Chancellor, smiling, seeing the satisfaction in Phyllis's eyes. "Go on. Were there witnesses?"

Instead of answering, she leaned forward. The open space at the top of her blouse swelled as her breasts rose. Peter was drawn to them; she seemed oblivious to his interest.

"You're working on a book about Hoover, aren't you?"

"Not the man himself. Not his story as such, although it's a vital part. I have to know as much as I can learn. Tell me what you know. Then I'll explain, I promise."

She began in the lounge and continued at dinner. It was an angry narrative, the anger heightened by her professionalism. Phyllis would not print what she could not document, and the documentation was impossible, regardless of the existing truth.

She spoke of senators and congressmen and cabinet members made to toe the Hoover line or face the Hoover wrath. She described powerful men weeping, remaining silent when silence was abhorrent to them. She detailed Hoover's actions following the assassinations of both Kennedys and Martin Luther King. His behavior had been obscene, his joy apparent, his responsibility denied.

"The press is convinced he withheld damaging information from the Warren Commission. God knows how devastating it was; it might have altered the judgments at Dallas. And Los Angeles, *and* Memphis. We'll never know."

She outlined Hoover's use of electronic and telephone

surveillance; it was worthy of the gestapo. No one had been sacrosanct; enemies and potential enemies had been held at bay. Tapes had been spliced and edited; guilt had come by remote association, innuendo, hearsay, and manufactured evidence.

As she talked, Peter sensed a fury beyond mere contempt. She drank wine during the meal; she drank brandy afterward. When she was finished, she was silent for several moments, then forced a smile. Her anger had burned up much of the alcohol; she was in control of herself, but she was not quite sober.

"Now, you promised. And I promised not to print it. What are you working on? Another *Counterstrike!*?"

"There's a parallel, I suppose. It's a novel based on the theory that Hoover was assassinated."

"Fascinating. But not credible. Who would dare?"

"Someone who had access to his private files. That's why I asked you if there were any witnesses to the burning or shredding of Hoover's papers. Anyone who actually saw them destroyed."

Phyllis was transfixed, her eyes riveted on him. "And if they weren't destroyed? . . ."

"That's the assumption I'll work under. Fictionally."

"What do you mean?" Her voice was flat, abruptly cold.

"That whoever—fictionally—killed Hoover now has those files and is capable of extortion just as Hoover was. Not only capable, but actively operating. Reaching influential people, forcing them to do what he wants them to do. Hoover was obsessed with sex, so that'll be a primary weapon. It's always effective. Simple, very powerful blackmail."

Phyllis moved back in her chair, her hands flat on the table. Peter could hardly hear her. "With a whisper over the telephone, Mr. Chancellor? Tell me, is this some kind of terrible joke."

"Is it a what?"

She stared at him, her eyes wide, filled with an odd dread. "No, it couldn't be," she continued in that same cold, distant tone. "I was here in the lobby; it was my choice to be here. I saw you; you didn't see me. . . ."

"Phyllis, what's the matter?"

"Oh, dear God, I'm losing my *mind*. . . ."

He reached across the table for her hand. It was cold,

trembling. "Hey, come on." He smiled reassuringly. "I think the last brandy was doctored against you."

Her eyes blinked. "Do you really find me attractive?"

"Of course I do."

"May we go up to your room?"

He looked at her, trying to understand. "You don't have to suggest that."

"You don't want me, do you?" There was no question in her words, not as she spoke them.

"I think I want you very much. I——"

She suddenly leaned forward, gripping his hand almost viciously, cutting him off. "Take me upstairs," she said.

She stood above him, naked, beside the bed. Her firm breasts denied her years. Her hips swelled invitingly below her slim waist; her thighs were tapered, somehow Grecian. He reached for her hand, inviting her to the bed.

She sat down gracefully but hesitantly. He released her hand and touched her breast. She trembled and held her breath; then suddenly, unexpectedly, she turned and slid her hand over his stomach, to his groin.

Without words she rolled her naked body over his and pressed her face against his cheek. He could feel the moisture of her tears. She rolled again, now beside him, now spreading her legs, now pulling him on top of her.

"Be quick! Be *quick!*"

It was the strangest act of sex Peter had ever experienced. For the next several minutes—blurred, perplexing, without explanation—he made love to an accommodating but totally unresponsive body. He was making love to dead flesh.

It was over and he gently pivoted, swinging his legs away, his stomach off hers, his chest above her firm but unexcited breasts. He looked down at her, feeling at once compassion and bewilderment. Her neck was arched, her face pressed sideways into the pillow. Her eyes were shut tight, the tears streaming down her cheeks. Muffled sobs came from her throat.

He reached down and touched her hair, running his fingers through the strands. She trembled and pressed her face further into the pillow. Her voice was strained. "I think I'm going to be sick."

"I'm sorry. Can I get you a glass of water?"

"No!" She turned her tear-stained face toward him. Without opening her eyes, she screamed, and the scream filled the room. "But you can *tell them*! You can *tell them now*!"

"It was the brandy," he whispered. It was all he could think of to say.

12

Chancellor heard the birds first. He opened his eyes and focused on the skylight he had built in the ceiling between the heavy beams of his bedroom. Light was filtering through the tall trees.

He was home. It seemed as if he had been away for years. And it was a very special morning. It was the first morning of his life that he wanted to work in his own home.

He got out of bed, put on his bathrobe, and went downstairs. Everything was as he had left it, but infinitely neater. He was glad he had kept the previous owner's furniture; it was comfortable and profuse with wood and looked lived in.

He walked across the room to the door leading into the kitchen. It was spotless, everything in its place. He was grateful to Mrs. Alcott, the stern-faced but cheerful housekeeper he had inherited with the house.

He brewed coffee and took it to his office. It had been the previous owner's study, on the west side of the house with enormous windows in the garden-side walls, light oak paneling everywhere else.

The Nuremberg cartons were stacked neatly in the corner by the door, next to his Xerox machine. That certainly was not how he had left them; he'd opened them indiscriminately, scattering the contents over the floor. He wondered who had gone to the trouble to repack them. Again Mrs. Alcott come to mind. Or had Josh and Tony driven down, trying to put another part of his life together?

The cartons would stay in the corner. Nuremberg could wait. He had something else to do. He walked over to the long hatch table beneath the far window. His equipment was there, all the equipment he needed. Two yellow pads were on the left by the telephone, his sharpened pencils in the pewter tankard beside them. He carried his tools to the large coffee table in front of his leather couch and sat down. There was no hesitation. His thoughts came as rapidly as he could write.

To: *Anthony Morgan, Editor.*

Outline: *Hoover Manuscript—Book Untitled.*

In the prologue a well-known military figure —a sympathetic man, a thinker in the George Marshall tradition—has returned from a tour in Southeast Asia. He is about to confound Washington's military establishment with evidence of grossly inflated success estimates and, more important, proof of incompetence and corruption in the command ranks. Wholesale slaughter has been the result of ineptness and mendacity in Saigon. Those few colleagues who know what he is about to do have pleaded with him not to do it; they claim his timing is disastrous. He replies that the way the war is being prosecuted is a disaster.

The soldier is approached by a stranger, who delivers a message to him, referring to an event that took place years ago; an incident born of temporary derangement, under extreme stress, but nevertheless an act of such impropriety— even indecency—that its revelation would discredit the soldier and destroy his reputation, his career, his wife, and his family.

The stranger demands that the soldier destroy the Saigon report, make no charges, remain silent. In essence, he is to let the military status quo continue—and thus, intrinsically, the slaughter. Failure to do so will result in the exposure of the damaging information. He is given twenty-four hours to decide.

The soldier's frustration is climaxed by the longest casualty list forwarded from Saigon in months. The moment of decision comes. He is tormented, but ultimately he cannot disobey the stranger's command.

In his living room he takes a file of papers

from his briefcase (the incriminating evidence he brought back from Southeast Asia), crumples the pages and burns them in the fireplace.

There is a change of scene. We see the stranger walk into an enormous vault in the Federal Bureau of Investigation. He goes to a cabinet, opens it, and replaces the soldier's file. He closes the drawer and locks it.

Printed in the center of the drawer's index tab is:

A–L — Property of the Director

Peter sat back on the couch and scanned what he had written. He wondered if MacAndrew would recognize himself. From what he had learned about him the fictionalized portrait was applicable. The general's influence would be sorely missed at the Pentagon. But not *by* the Pentagon.

In the opening chapter four or five influential, very different people—in government and out—are shown in the grip of various stages of extortion. The blackmailers are concerned only with silencing dissent. Leaders of legitimate organizations representing the disaffected, the underprivileged, and the minorities are attacked. Accusations based on remote association, innuendo, hearsay, and manufactured evidence are hurled at the dissenters, crippling their effectiveness. The country is on its way to becoming a police state.

Peter stopped, struck by the words. *Remote association, innuendo, hearsay, and manufactured evidence.* They were Phyllis Maxwell's words.

He went back to his writing.

The main character will be different from the usual suspense novel hero. I see him as an attractive middle-forties lawyer with a wife and two or three children. His name is *Alexander Meredith*. He is a late bloomer, just beginning to recognize his capacities. He has come to Washington for an interim appointment with the Justice Department. His field is criminal law. He's a detail man with broad knowledge.

He has been hired to evaluate the procedures used by certain departments of the Federal Bureau of Investigation—a job created by the alarming increase of questionable methods used by the bureau's field offices. Unsubstantiated charges have been made public; illegal searches and seizures have multiplied. Prosecutors at Justice are concerned that legitimate cases will be thrown out of court due to constitutional violations.

Meredith has been at the Washington job for a year, and what began as a relatively routine professional assignment has exploded into a series of staggering revelations.

Within the Federal Bureau of Investigation there is an ongoing covert operation designed to gather inflammatory information on a wide spectrum of public and private figures. Meredith makes the connection between several newspaper stories about influential men doing the astonishingly unexpected, and names he has unearthed at the bureau. These are, of course, the victims described in the first chapter. Two are startling. The first is a Supreme Court justice—a man Hoover is known to loathe—who suddenly resigns from the bench. The second is a black civil rights leader publicly condemned by Hoover, who is found dead, a suicide.

Alarmed, Meredith begins a search for concrete evidence of the illegal practices carried out within the FBI. He ingratiates himself with executive personnel close to Hoover. He feigns sympathies he does not have. He digs deeper and deeper, and what he discovers frightens him even more.

At the highest level of the bureau there is a small corps of fanatics blindly devoted to Hoover. They implement policies and carry out orders issued by the director with the full knowledge that many are grossly illegal. Meredith finds that there is one man, assigned to the field office in La Jolla, California, who acts as Hoover's gunslinger. He consistently appears on the scene when the unexpected action of a national figure takes place. His description will match that of the *stranger* in the prologue.

Chancellor put down the pencil and finished his coffee. He thought about Alan Longworth, Hoover's "gunslinger" in reality. Longworth remained an enigma. Assuming the premise that it was remorse over his betrayal of Hoover that had brought the agent to Malibu, why would he jeopardize his current situation in Hawaii? Why had he broken an agreement that could cost him his life? Why, ultimately, had he sent Peter to Daniel Sutherland, who instantly identified the former FBI man?

Was Longworth's guilt so pervasive that there was nothing left of self-interest? Was his need for revenge so intense that nothing else mattered? Apparently, that was the case. He had not hesitated to destroy MacAndrew in the process. And because Longworth had done that, Chancellor felt no compunction at including a portrait of the man in his novel.

Meredith gathers in his evidence; it is appalling. J. Edgar Hoover has compiled several thousand dossiers on the nation's most influential people. They contain all manner of rumors, half-truths, and lies. Also, since few humans are saints, the files are rife with documented facts of the most damaging nature. Sexual appetites and aberrations are dwelled upon at length, the public exposure of which would destroy hundreds of men and women who otherwise conduct themselves responsibly, often brilliantly.

The existence of these files constitutes a threat to the country. What's terrifying is that Hoover is actually *using* them. He is systematically making contact with scores of subjects he believes are in opposition to policies he favors, threatening to expose their private weaknesses if they do not retreat from their positions.

Meredith knows that the most alarming question of all must be answered: Is Hoover acting alone or has he allies? For if he has made a pact with his ideological counterparts in the intelligence community, the Congress, or the White House, the republic may well be near a state of collapse.

Meredith decides to take his evidence to an assistant attorney general. From that moment on, his life becomes virtually unbearable. The assistant A.G. is a decent man, although frightened. He is, however, the weapon; members of his staff have leaked portions of Alex's report back to the bureau. The assistant attorney general removes it, and in his one courageous move, delivers it secretly to the office of a senator.

Peter leaned back on the couch and stretched. He had a prototype for his senator. Less than a year ago the man had been his party's leading contender for the presidential nomination. He had held millions transfixed with the fiery integrity of his eyes. The incumbent President was no match for the senator's clarity of thought, the depth of his vision, and his ability to communicate. His reasoned, calm exposition of the issues had evoked a sweeping acceptance across the land. And then something had happened to him. In a brief few minutes during a snowy winter morning the contest had been aborted. An intemperate speech had suicidally been delivered by an exhausted campaigner; the senator was effectively disqualified.

Chancellor leaned forward and took a fresh pencil from the tankard.

A pattern of psychological harassment is implemented against Meredith. His every move is watched; he is placed under continuous surveillance. Telephone calls—some obscene, some threats of physical abuse—are made to his wife. His children are questioned about their father by FBI agents during and after school hours. Automobiles wait outside the Meredith house at night; flashlights shine into darkened windows. Every day becomes a nightmare; the nights themselves are still worse.

The point is to cast doubt upon Meredith's credibility by discrediting his life. He goes to the authorities; he tries to confront the men at the bureau as well as those following him; he approaches his congressman. All efforts to escape his own personal trial by terror fail. He is driven to the brink of resignation. Even the assistant attorney general will have no more to do with him. The man has been warned. Hoover's insidious controls are everywhere.

You'll note that I have used Hoover's name.
As they say, I speak ill of the dead without the
slightest compunction— —

It was not "they" who said that, thought Chancellor,
pausing for a second. It was Phyllis Maxwell who said it.

——and, Mean Person, I intend to use it in the
book. I see no reason to even faintly disguise the
identity or cloak it in some nonsense like J.
Edwin Haverford, praetor of the Federated
Branch of Intelligence. I want to call him what
he was: a dangerous megalomaniac who should
have been forced from office twenty years ago.
A monster——

Phyllis Maxwell again. When he thought about it, the
newspaperwoman had painted such a memorable—and
grotesque—portrait that she was as much a springboard
as Longworth had been. Her fury was contagious.

——whose tactics were more in tune with the
policies of the Third Reich than those of a
democratic society. I want people to be outraged
by *J. Edgar Hoover's* manipulations. (So you'd
better show this to the legal department—Steve
will probably have apoplexy and start some kind
of estate search to see if there are relatives
around who might sue.)
    The preceding material will require six
chapters, or roughly one third of the book. At
this juncture, the focus will shift from Meredith
to the victims of Hoover's extortions. Primarily
to the senator who is revealed to have been a
target of Hoover's.
    Since these victims are men of considerable
influence in the government, it's credible that
two of them would make contact. Here it will be
the senator and an outspoken member of the
cabinet who has opposed the President and is
forced to resign. I envision a scene in which two
strong figures admit to being helpless under
Hoover's assault. They are worthwhile giants
brought to bay by an aging jackal.
    However, a positive result comes from their
meeting. They recognize the obvious: If Hoover

can silence them, he can silence others. So they
gather together a small group of men——

Peter lifted the pencil from the paper. He remembered Daniel Sutherland's words about the Washington
group: "And women, Mr. Chancellor." But what kind of
women would be recruited? Or selected? He smiled to himself. Why not a newspaperwoman? A character patterned
after Phyllis Maxwell. However, unlike her; in the book
the woman had to be a victim before becoming a member
of the group. That was vital,

——and women for the purpose of mounting a
defense against Hoover's insidious attacks. They
have a starting point: Hoover's gunslinger. They
go to the intelligence community and are covertly
given every scrap of information that can be unearthed about the man. Dossiers, service records,
bank statements, credit references—everything
available.

Chancellor stopped writing. There it was again, the
enigma named Longworth. Sutherland said that they had
appealed to the agent's conscience and had rewarded him
with a soft job in Maui, his safety guaranteed. All that was,
perhaps, credible, but what had Hoover been doing in the
meantime? Had he just sat on his ass and said, "Sure,
Alan, my boy. Your twenty years are up and you deserve
your pension, and you have my best wishes for a pleasant
retirement"?
      Not likely. The Hoover that had been described to
him would have had Longworth killed before cutting him
loose.
      There had to be another explanation.

The gunslinger is reached by the senator's
group. Through a combination of pressures he is
recruited, and a medical deception is mounted.
The man complains of prolonged abdominal
pains and is sent to Walter Reed Hospital. The
"report" is forwarded to Hoover: The agent is
riddled with duodenal cancer. It has spread beyond surgery; his life expectancy is no more than
a few months at best.

Hoover has no alternative. He releases the man, believing the agent is going home to die.

Thus, the anti-Hoover Nucleus is formed. The "retired" field agent is isolated and put to work. It will be established that he not only had access to the files but, being less a saint than an opportunist, pored over the dossiers with an appetite worthy of a KGB bureaucrat in the middle of a purge.

He provides the anti-Hoover group with hundreds of names and biographies. Names and facts trigger other names and additional facts. A master list of potential victims is prepared.

Its scope is frightening. Included are not only powerful men in the three branches of government but leaders of industry, labor, the academic world, and the news media.

The Nucleus—the name of the Washington group—must act immediately.

Confidential appointments are arranged. The agent is sent to scores of subjects, warning them of Hoover's dossiers.

Their strategy will be described in rapid scenes. I won't dwell on the specific information. It would be too confusing to introduce a whole new set of characters.

Speaking of the characters, I'll get to them shortly. I want to carry out the plot line first.

Peter took a new pencil.

The turning point comes with two events: The first is when Alexander Meredith is contacted by the Nucleus. The second is the decision on the part of two or three of the Nucleus to assassinate Hoover.

This decision will be arrived at gradually, for these men are not killers. They come to regard assassination as an acceptable solution, and that is their unacceptable flaw. When Meredith learns of this, knowing that it is the decision of superior minds, all his values are put to a final test. For him murder cannot be a solution. He now struggles against opposing forces: the fanatics of the Bureau and those of the Nucleus.

His attempts to stop the assassination and

expose the illegalities of the bureau supply the momentum to carry the book to its conclusion.

Fictionally, the most difficult aspect of the narrative will be precisely what horrifies Alex Meredith: the decision on the part of two or three extraordinary people to accept murder as the solution.

The blocks of logic here will have to be built carefully, so that no other solution appears to be at hand. I think the acceptance of assassination will come with two events "rearranged" from recent history: the withdrawal of the most qualified man from the presidential race, and the resignation of an innovative justice of the Supreme Court.

The Nucleus recognizes both of these catastrophes as the work of J. Edgar Hoover. Irreparable damage is being done to the body politic.

The pencil broke, its point shattered under the force of his pressure. He was getting angry again, and the rage should be used later, when he was writing the novel itself. Now was the time to think.

History had provided a peaceful solution. A madman's death and the destruction of his recorded poisons had allowed the Nucleus—if Sutherland was right—to disband. The alert was over.

These were the facts. But he was not dealing with historical reality. What would such a group of concerned, decent people do if faced with the collapse of the checks and balances so vital to the open form of government? Would such a group consider execution? Assassination?

In one sense they would have no alternative. Yet in taking that action, they would be plunging themselves down to the same level as the murdered man. Therefore, not all would subscribe to such a solution, and no such solution would be openly proposed.

But two, or perhaps three, might consider it the only decision that could be made. And here would be the Nucleus's flaw. Murder is murder, its definition altered only by specific conditions of war. Those who employ murder as a solution are ultimately no better than their targets. The Nucleus would harbor two or three members who would become committed killers.

As Peter conceived it fictionally.

In the Nucleus are two men, and perhaps a woman (the dramatic possibilities here are interesting), of stature, dedicated to the principles espoused by the rest of the group. What we see, however, is a gradual change in their perspectives. It is born of frustration and anguish, a genuine detestation of Hoover's progress and the Nucleus's apparent ineffectiveness. It is brought to a head by the manipulation of a presidential election and the repressive shaping of the court. They have been pushed to the wall; no alternatives remain. There is only assassination.

But that would remove only half the cancer, the other half being Hoover's files. They must be taken. They cannot be allowed to fall into the hands of his successor after his death.

These rebels within the Nucleus conceive of a plan of execution and theft. I think it should be written in a crosscut documentary style, the suspense heightened by the ingeniousness of the plan itself and the realization that at any moment an error of timing or reaction could blow it all apart.

This is as far as I want to go with the plot line at the moment.

Peter stretched his arms, wincing as a sharp pain shot through the muscles of his left shoulder. He did not give it an instant's thought. His concentration was on the page in front of him. Now it would begin. The people.

He started with shadows, formless shapes slowly coming into focus. And then names. As was his custom, he would sketch out his cast of characters, restricting each to a couple of pages, knowing that each in turn would lead to his or her own friends and enemies, known and unknown. Characters gave birth to other characters; it was often as simple as that.

In addition to those he had already considered—the soldier in the prologue, Alexander Meredith, Hoover's gunslinger, the senator, and the cabinet member—he would flesh out the group—the Nucleus—first. There would be several from outside the government: a scholar, a lawyer, perhaps. And unquestionably a judge, but not a Negro judge—that he could not do. There was only one Daniel

Sutherland. And the women: They would have to be thought about carefully. The temptation to invent too close a fictional counterpart of Phyllis Maxwell had to be resisted. But some aspects of her would go into the book.

He leaned forward and began.

There is a man in his seventies, an attorney named . . .

He could not tell how long he had been writing. Time was blurred, his concentration absolute. The sun was at quarter point in the sky, its rays streaming through the north window.

He looked at the pages next to the yellow pad; he had sketched no fewer than nine characters. His energy was flowing; he was grateful beyond words because the words were there at last.

The telephone rang, disorienting him. He walked across the room to answer it.

"Hello?"

"Is this here a writer by the name of Chancellor? A Peter Chancellor?" The man on the line spoke with a thick southern accent.

"Yes. This is Peter Chancellor."

"What are you trying to *do* to me? You got no right——"

"Who is this?"

"You know goddamned well who ah am."

"I'm afraid I don't."

"Fun-*nee*. Your friend Longworth come to see me in Washington."

"*Alan* Longworth?"

"You got it. And you're huntin' in the wrong fields! You want to start a Nigra' version of 1861 all over again, you go right ahead. But you better know what you're doin'."

"I haven't the vaguest idea what you're talking about. Now, who the hell is this?"

"Congressman Walter Rawlins. Today's Wednesday. I'll be in New York on Sunday. We're goin' to meet."

"Are we?"

"Yes. Before we both get our goddamned heads shot off."

13

He had done something he'd never done before: He had started writing the book before Morgan approved the outline. He could not help himself. The words kept leaping from head to paper.

With a twinge of guilt Peter admitted to himself that it did not matter. The story was everything. Through the story, a monster named Hoover was being revealed. It was important to Chancellor—somehow more important than anything he had ever tried to do before—that the Hoover myth be shown for what it was. Just as quickly as possible, so that it would never happen again.

But the work had to be interrupted for a day. He had agreed to meet with Rawlins. He did not want to meet with him; he had told Rawlins that whatever Alan Longworth had said to him, whatever threats he had made, Longworth was no friend of his. Peter wanted nothing further to do with him.

Still, Longworth had been in Washington four days ago when Rawlins telephoned. He was not back in the Hawaiian Islands. The enigma had reappeared. Why?

Chancellor decided to stay the night in his New York apartment. He had promised to have dinner with Joshua Harris.

He drove north on the old road parallel to the banks of the Delaware, through the town of Lambertville, and swung west up the long hill into Route 202. If he hit a minimum of country traffic, he'd reach the turnpike in forty-five minutes; from Exit 14 it was another half hour into New York.

There was almost no traffic. A few hay and milk trucks came cautiously out of dirt roads onto the highway, and speeding cars overtook him intermittently: salesmen who had covered the day's territory, racing to the next motel. If he cared to, he could outrun just about anything on the road, he thought, fingering the thick steering wheel. His car was a Mercedes 450 SEL.

Fear had determined his selection of a car. He chose the heaviest he could find. As it happened, the car immediately available was a dark blue. That was fine; anything as long as it was not . . .

Silver?

Silver! He could not believe what he saw!

Behind him! In the wide convex mirror outside the window, the image magnified by the curvature, the shining grill immense! It was a silver automobile! The silver Continental!

His eyes were playing tricks on him. They had to be! He was almost afraid to look at the driver; he didn't have to. The silver car pulled alongside him, the driver in his direct line of sight.

It was the woman! The same woman! *Two hundred miles away!* The wide hat, the long dark hair, the sunglasses, the pale white skin punctuated by bright red lips above an orange scarf. It was insane!

He jammed his foot on the accelerator; the Mercedes lunged forward. Nothing on the road could keep up with him!

But the Continental did. Effortlessly. *Effortlessly!* And the macabre driver was staring straight ahead. As if nothing were unreal, nothing out of the ordinary. Straight ahead. At nothing!

Peter glanced at the speedometer. The needle wavered over a hundred. It was a dual highway; cars on the other side were blurs. Cars. *Trucks!* There were two trucks up ahead! They followed one another around a long curve in the road. Chancellor moved his foot off the accelerator; he would wait till he was closer.

Now! He pressed the brake pedal; the Continental shot ahead, pulling to the right side of the highway to block him.

Again, *now*! He stabbed the accelerator, turning the wheel counterclockwise, swinging to the left side of the road, the engine thundering as he sped past the terrible silver thing and the insane woman who drove it.

He raced past the two trucks in the curve, stunning the drivers, the Mercedes's wheels half in the center island of autumn grass, the tires screaming.

Ringos. The sign on the road said *Ringos!*

There was a Ringo years ago, at a place where death had occurred, a gunslinger firing in a burst of fury.

Gunfight at the O.K. Corral.

Why did he think of such things? Why did his head ache so?

Buffalo Bill's
defunct . . . .
        Jesus
he was a handsome man

. . . e. e. cummings. Why did he think of e. e. cummings?
What the hell was *happening*?

His head was splitting.

In the distance, perhaps a mile away, he could see an
amber circle of light suspended in the air. For a moment
he did not know what it was.

It was a traffic light at a highway intersection. Three
cars up ahead were slowing down, one on the left, two on
the right. He could not pass. They were half a mile away
now. He slowed the Mercedes.

Oh, *God*! It was there again!

The Continental was approaching rapidly, its grill
growing larger in the rearview mirror. But the traffic light
was directly ahead; both cars would have to stop.

He had to control himself, control the pain in his
head, and do what he had to do! The madness had to stop!

He pulled to the right side of the road behind the two
automobiles and waited to see what the Continental would
do. It swung into the left lane behind the single car but
stopped directly alongside his Mercedes.

Chancellor snapped up the handle and leaped out. He
raced over to the Continental and grabbed the door handle,
pulling with all his strength.

The door was locked. He pounded on the window.

"*Who are you?* What are you *doing*?"

The impassive face—a macabre mask of a face—
stared straight ahead behind the glass. There was no
acknowledgment whatsoever.

Peter shook the handle and smashed his hand against
the window. "You can't do this to me!"

The drivers in the other cars peered out their windows.
The light had turned green, but no one drove away.

Chancellor ran around the hood to the driver's window, yanking the handle, hitting the glass.

"You crazy bitch! Who are you? What do you want?"

The terrible pale face, concealed by the hair and the
glasses and the hat, turned and stared up at him. It *was* a
mask, horrible and totally impassive. White powder and
set, tight lips outlined in fiery red lipstick. He was studying

some obscene giant insect made up to look like a ghastly clown.

"Goddamn it, answer me! *Answer me!*"

Nothing. Nothing but that terrible stare from the mask of that terrible face.

The cars ahead started to move. Peter heard the gunning of engines. He held onto the door, mesmerized by the macabre sight behind the window; he pounded the glass again.

"*Who——?*"

The Continental's motor roared. His hand loosened its grip, and the Mark IV lurched forward, speeding through the intersection and up the highway.

Peter tried to read the license. There was none.

"You crazy bastard! I'll break your head open. Motherfucker!"

The words, roared in anger, were not his words. The first of the two trucks he had insanely passed in the curve of the highway had come to a stop twenty yards away. Above the step to the driver's cabin, a door opened and a barrel-chested trucker climbed out, a lug wrench in his hand.

"You son of a bitch! You damned near ran me off the road!"

Peter limped to the Mercedes. He threw himself into the seat and slammed the door, his fingers slapping down the lock. The trucker was within feet now, the wrench held high.

The Mercedes's motor was still running. Chancellor reached for the gearshift and pulled it back, his foot hard on the accelerator, his hand on the wheel. The 450 SEL exploded in a burst of power; Peter gripped and swung the wheel to prevent the car from jumping the curb. He straightened it out and sped up the road.

It was a nightmare. A goddamned *nightmare!*

He sat alone in the living room of his apartment for over an hour. The lamp on top of the piano was the only source of light; sounds of the New York night came through the partially opened window. He wanted the air, and the sounds were reassuring. He was still perspiring, and the room was cool.

He had to control his panic. He had to think. Someone was trying to drive him out of his mind. He had to fight back; he had to trace the terrible mask of a face. He had to go back—to a country road in Maryland where the terrible face had first appeared.

What was the name of the patrolman in Rockville? Connelly? Donovan? He'd given it to the rental agency at Dulles Airport; he would call them and find out. Then he would call the patrolman and ask——

The telephone rang. He winced and got up from the chair. The caller had to be the congressman from Virginia. No one else knew he was in town. Rawlins had said he'd telephone during the evening and they would set up a time and a place to meet.

"Hello?"

"Peter?"

It was Joshua Harris. Chancellor had forgotten completely about him. "Hey, I'm sorry, old friend. I had some problems. I just got in."

"What's the matter?" Alarm was apparent in Harris's voice.

"I—" No, he would not tell Joshua. Not now. Everything was too confused. "Nothing serious. Car repairs. It took longer than I thought. Where are you?"

"I was about to leave for the restaurant. The Richelieu, remember?"

Yes, he remembered. But he could not sit through the leisurely pace of a meal at an elegant restaurant. He'd go out of his mind, wanting and not wanting to confide in his literary agent.

"Would you mind if we postponed for a day if it fits your schedule? To tell you the truth, I worked from four thirty this morning till four this afternoon. Then the drive. . . . I'm whacked out."

"The Hoover book's coming along, then?"

"Better and faster than I ever thought possible."

"That's fine, Peter. I'm happy for you. Strange, Tony didn't tell me."

Chancellor interrupted quietly. "He doesn't know. It's the longest outline I've ever turned in; it'll take him days to read it."

Why didn't he just say he'd started the damned book?

"You'll bring me a copy, of course," Harris said. "I don't always trust you two, left alone with all those words."

"Tomorrow night, I promise."

"Tomorrow night, then. I'll switch the reservation. Good night, Peter."

"Good night." Chancellor hung up and walked to the window overlooking Seventy-first Street. It was a quiet, tree-lined block, the sort of block that people associated with another time in the city.

As he looked out the window, he was aware of an image coming into focus. He knew it was not real, but he was incapable of stopping it. It was the macabre face in the Continental. He was looking at that terrible mask of a face! It was in the glass, staring out at him, unseen eyes behind the enormous dark glasses, the bright red lipstick painted with precision in a sea of caked white powder.

Peter shut his eyes and brought his hand up to his forehead. What had he been about to do before Josh called? It had something to do with that horrible image in the glass. And the telephone. He was going to use the telephone.

The telephone rang. But it had just rung a few moments ago. It could not be ringing again.

It was ringing. Oh, Christ! He had to lie down; his temple ached, and he was not sure— *Answer the telephone.* He limped across the room.

"Chancellor?"

"Yes."

"Rawlins. How good are you in the morning?"

"Is that supposed to be a funny joke?"

"Huh?"

"I work in the morning."

"That don't concern me. You know a place here in New York called the Cloisters?"

"Yes." Peter held his breath. Was that, too, a horrible joke? The Cloisters had been a favorite of Cathy's. How many summer Sundays had they walked over its lawns? But Rawlins could not know that. Or could he?

"Be there at five thirty tomorrow morning. Use the west entrance; the gate will be open. There's a path about four hundred feet north that leads to an open courtyard. I'll see you there." The phone went dead.

The Southerner had chosen a strange location, a stranger hour. They were the choices of a frightened man. Alan Longworth had once more triggered the fear; he would have to be stopped, this "retired" agent, this gunslinger filled with remorse.

But it was no time to think about Longworth. Peter knew he had to rest. Four thirty would come quickly.

He walked into the bedroom, kicked off his shoes, and unbuttoned his shirt. He sat nearly at the edge of the bed. Involuntarily, his body slowly fell backward, his head sinking into the pillow.

And the dreams came. The nightmares.

The grass was moist with dew, the early light breaking in the eastern sky. Relics and statuary were everywhere, and gnarled trees that seemed transported through the centuries. The only thing missing was the music of a lute or gentle voices singing madrigals.

Chancellor found the path. It was bordered by flowers and led up a small hill toward stone walls that turned out to be a rebuilt garth of a thirteenth-century French monastery. He approached it and stood in front of an ancient archway. Inside the courtyard were marble benches and miniature trees in artistic isolation. It was eerily still. He waited.

The minutes went by; the early morning light grew faintly brighter, enough to pick up the glistening white of the marble. Peter looked at his wristwatch. It was ten minutes to six. Rawlins was twenty minutes late.

Or had the congressman decided not to come after all? Was the fear so great?

"*Chancellor.*"

Peter turned, startled by the whisper. It came from a cluster of bushes about thirty feet away, foliage that surrounded a wide pedestal on the grass. On top of the stand was the sculptured head of a medieval saint. Coming out of the shadows was the figure of a man.

"Rawlins? How long have you been there?"

" 'Bout three quarters of an hour." Rawlins walked toward Peter. No handshake was offered.

"Why did you wait so long to come out?" Peter asked. "I've been here since five thirty."

"Five thirty-three," said the Southerner. "I waited to see if you were alone."

"I am. Let's talk."

"Let's *walk.*" They started down the path that led away from the pedestal. "Something wrong with your leg?" asked Rawlins.

"It's an old football injury. Or a war wound. Take

your choice. I don't want to walk. I want to hear what you have to say. I didn't ask for this meeting, and I've got work to do."

Rawlins's face reddened. "There's a bench over there."

"There were benches inside the courtyard."

"And maybe microphones."

"You're crazy. So's Longworth."

The congressman did not reply until they reached the white wrought-iron bench. "Longworth's your partner, ain't he? In this here extortion." Rawlins sat down as he spoke. The dim light washed over his face; the bravado of seconds ago was fading.

"No," answered Peter. "I have no partner and I'm not an extortionist."

"But you're writin' a book."

"That's how I make my living. I write novels."

"Sure. That's why the Central Intelligence boys had a lot of soiled underwear in a 'round-the-clock laundry. I heard about that one. Thing called *Counterstrike!*"

"I think you're exaggerating. What did you want to tell me?"

"Leave it alone, Chancellor." The congressman spoke in a flat voice. "The information you got ain't worth a thimble of piss. Oh hell, you can ruin me, but I'll save my butt legally; I can do that. Then you gotta answer for what follows."

"What information? Whatever Longworth told you is a lie. I have no information about you."

"Don't bullshit me. I don't deny I got problems. I know what people like you think of me. I use the word *nigger* in private more than you'd like to hear; I got a fondness for pretty black ass when I'm juiced up—'though, goddamn it, I suppose that could be in my favor; I'm married to a bitch whore who can blow the whistle on me anytime and take just about everything I got north of Roanoke. I may live with all that, boy, but I do my job on that Hill! And I ain't no killer! Do you understand?"

"Sure. Just your normal, everyday plantation family. Very quaint and lovable. You've said enough. I'm leaving."

"No, you're not!" Rawlins was on his feet, blocking Peter's path. "Please. Listen to me. I'm a lot of things, but you can't label me a redneck. No one with the brains to get naked out of the rain is any longer. 'Cause the numbers and the motives ain't what they used to be. The whole world's changin', and to be blind to that is to invite a goddamned bloodbath. Nobody wins; everybody loses."

"Motives?" Chancellor studied the southerner's face. It was devoid of artifice. "What are you driving at?"

"I never blocked responsible change. But I fight like a trapped cat when that change is irresponsible. To turn over million-dollar decisions to folks who ain't qualified, who *don't* have the brains to get out of the rain, that only sets *everybody* back."

Peter was fascinated, as he always was when the image and the substance clashed. "What has this got to do with whatever it is you think I've got?"

"I was *set up* in Newport News! I was fed a barrel of sour mash and taken down dark alleys I never saw. I may have humped that little girl, but I didn't kill her! I wouldn't know how to do what *they* did to her! But I know who did it. And those black bastards know I know. They're worse than scum; they're nigger Nazis, killin' their own, hidin' behind——"

There was a spit of air behind them, somewhere in the distance. And then the unbelievable—the *inconceivable*—happened. Chancellor stared in terror, unable to move.

Rawlins's mouth had sprung open. A circle of red had formed above his right eyebrow. Blood spewed out, gushing at first, then rolling down in rivulets over the ashen skin and unblinking eye. Still, the body *stood*, frozen in death. And then, slowly, as if in some horrible ballet, Rawlins's legs gave way and his corpse fell over, collapsing in the wet grass.

A muted expulsion of breath came from Peter's throat; a scream had been born, but no sound came, his shock beyond any cry of terror.

There was another spit; the air waves shattered above him. And another; there was a *ping*, and the earth exploded beneath him. A bullet had ricocheted off the bench! Whatever remained of his instincts propelled him off his feet; he dove to his left, rolling on the grass and lunging out of the target area. There were more spits, more furious explosions of grass and dirt. A fragment of stone whipped past his ear; inches closer and he would have been blinded or killed. Suddenly his forehead scraped a hard surface, the palm of his hand stinging as it pressed against jagged rock.

He had lurched into a monument of some kind, a medallion of stone surrounded by bushes.

He spun over on his back. He was hidden, but all around were the sickening thumps of bullets.

Then there were shouts, half crazed, hysterical. They came from over *there*, and *there*, and *there*! Moving, racing, fading. And finally one voice, one roar, hard and guttural, commanding obedience.

"Get out of here!"

A powerful hand gripped the front of his jacket, bunching his shirt and the skin beneath in its grasp, pulling him up from the stone shield. A second hand held a large automatic, a thick cylinder on its barrel. It was leveled in the direction the shots were coming from; bursts of fire and smoke spat out of its bore.

Peter was beyond speech, beyond protest. Above him was the blond-haired Longworth. The despised Alan Longworth was saving his life!

He crashed through the bushes, his body low, diving through sharp nettles to the grass beyond. He scratched the earth with his feet and hands, propelling himself forward. The air was gone from his lungs, but only escape mattered. He raced down through the gardens.

14

He walked the streets like a man who wanders in deep sleep. Time and place were lost; disorientation had swept over him. His first thought was to find help, find the police, find *someone* who could impose order on the chaos he had barely lived through. But there was no one. He approached several pedestrians; they looked at his odd appearance and shook him off, hurrying away. He stumbled into the street; horns blew, automobiles skirted around him angrily. There were no police to be seen, no patrol cars in this quiet section of the city.

His temples throbbed, his left shoulder ached, his

forehead felt as though it had been scraped with a file. He looked at the palm of his right hand; the skin was red; specks of blood had been forced to the surface.

Slowly, after he had walked for miles, Chancellor began to find part of his mind. It was a strange realization, a stranger process. Knowing and not knowing, aware of his very dangerous mental state. He vaguely understood that his defenses were not capable of repelling the assaults on his mind, so he tried to force the images from his consciousness. He was a man desperately trying to regain control. He had decisions to make.

He looked at his watch, feeling like a lost traveler in a foreign land who was told that if he had not reached a certain destination by a specific time, he had taken a wrong turn. He had taken a great many wrong turns. He looked up at the street sign; he'd never heard of the name.

The sun told him it was morning. He was grateful for that. He had wandered the streets for four hours.

Four hours. Oh my God, I need help.

His car! The Mercedes was back at the Cloisters, parked on the street in front of the west entrance. He put his hand in his trousers pocket and pulled out his money clip. He had enough for a taxi.

"Here's the west gate, Mac," said the driver with the florid face. "I don't see no Mercedes. What time did you leave it?"

"Early this morning."

"Didn't you look at the sign?" The driver pointed out the window. "This is a busy street."

He had parked in a towaway zone.

"It was dark," said Peter defensively. He gave the driver his address in Manhattan.

The cab turned left onto Seventy-first Street from Lexington Avenue; Chancellor stared in astonishment. His Mercedes was parked in front of the brownstone, directly in front of the steps to his apartment. It stood there in eerie splendor, the dark blue glistening in the sunlight. There was no other automobile like it on the block.

For an insane moment Peter wondered how it had been moved from across the street, where he had parked it the night before. Cathy must have moved it. She often did that because of the sidestreet parking regulations. Cars had to be removed by eight o'clock.

Cathy? Oh, Jesus, what was wrong with him?

He waited on the curb until the taxi disappeared. He approached the Mercedes, looking at it carefully, as if inspecting an object he had not seen in years. It had been washed and polished, the interior vacuumed, the dashboard cleaned, the metal parts gleaming.

He took out his key case; the climb up the steps seemed interminable. There was a typewritten note on the outside door, stapled to the wood.

Things got out of control. It won't happen again,
And you will not see me again.

Longworth

Chancellor ripped the note from the door. Then he looked carefully at the paper. The *o*'s of the script were slightly raised; the paper was a thick bond, cut off at the top.

The note had been typed on his typewriter. The paper was his stationery, his name removed.

"His name is Alan Longworth. Josh found out about him." Peter leaned against the window, staring down at the Mercedes in the street.

Anthony Morgan sat in a leather armchair across the room, his long slender frame uncharacteristically rigid.

"You look like hell. Did you do much drinking last night?"

"No. I didn't sleep well. What sleep I had was filled with nightmares. That's another story——"

"But not booze," interrupted Morgan.

"I told you, no!"

"And Josh is in Boston?"

"Yes. The office said he was taking the four o'clock shuttle back. We're supposed to have dinner tonight."

Morgan got out of the chair; apparently convinced, he spoke emphatically. "Then for Christ's sake, why haven't you called the police? What the hell do you think you're doing? You saw a man killed. A congressman was murdered in front of you!"

"I know, I know. You want to hear something worse? I blanked out. I walked around for damned near four hours in a fog. I don't even know where I was."

"Have you heard anything on the radio? The news must have hit by now."

"I haven't turned it on."

Tony walked to the bookcase radio and tuned in a news station, keeping the volume low. Then he went to his writer, forcing Chancellor to turn from the window. "Listen to me. There's no one I'd rather have you call than me. Except right now, the police. I want to know why you haven't!"

Chancellor groped for words. "I don't know. I'm not sure I can tell you."

"All right, all right," said Morgan gently.

"I'm not talking about hysteria. I'm learning to live with that. It's something else." He displayed his injured palm. "I drove my car to Fort Tryon. Look at my hand. My fingerprints, maybe specks of blood, should be on the steering wheel. The grass was wet and there was mud. Look at my shoes, my jacket. Traces should be in the car. But the car was washed clean; it looks like it just came out of the showroom. I don't even know how it got back here. And the note on the door. It was typed with my typewriter, on my stationery. And for hours after the . . . madness, the insanity, I can't account for myself!"

"Peter, stop it!" Morgan grabbed Chancellor's shoulders, raising his voice. "This isn't fiction. You're not one of your characters! This is real. It happened." He lowered his voice. "I'm calling the police."

Two detectives from the twenty-second precinct interrupted Peter's story with sporadic questions. The older man was in his fifties, with wavy gray hair, the younger about Chancellor's age, and black. They were both alert, experienced professionals and made an effort to put Peter at ease.

When Chancellor finished, the older man went to use the telephone, the younger talked about *Sarajevo!* He had liked it very much.

It was only when the older man rejoined them that Chancellor realized the black had prevented him from listening to the phone conversation. Peter admired the professionalism. He would remember it.

"Mr. Chancellor," began the gray-haired detective cautiously, "there seems to be a problem. When Mr. Morgan called us, we dispatched a team to Fort Tryon. To save time, we included forensic; to make sure the area wasn't tampered with, we called the Bronx precinct and had them post street patrolmen. There's no evidence of gunfire at the scene. There's no disturbance of the grounds."

Peter stared at the man in disbelief. "That's crazy. That's wrong! I was there!"

"Our men are very thorough."

"They weren't thorough enough! You think I'd make up a story like that?!"

"It's a pretty good one," said the black, smiling. "Maybe you're trying out some material."

"Hey, wait just a minute!" Morgan stepped forward. "Peter wouldn't do that."

"It would be a foolish thing to do," said the older man, nodding without agreeing. "It's against the law to falsely report a crime. Any crime, to say nothing of homicide."

"You *are* crazy . . ." Peter's voice trailed off. "You really don't believe me. You get your little report over the telephone, take it as gospel, and conclude I'm a lunatic. What kind of police officers *are* you?"

"Very good ones," said the black.

"I don't think so. I don't think so at all, goddamn it!" Chancellor limped to the phone. "There's a way to settle this; it's been five, six hours now." He dialed and within seconds spoke. "Washington Information? I want the office number of Congressman Walter Rawlins, House of Representatives."

He called out the number as the operator gave it to him; Tony Morgan nodded. The detectives watched without comment.

He dialed again. The wait was interminable; his pulse raced. In spite of his own undeniable knowledge he had to prove himself to the two professionals.

A woman's voice came on the line, subdued and obviously southern. He asked for the congressman.

And when he heard her words, the ache returned to his temples and his eyes momentarily lost focus.

"It's simply terrible, sir. The bereaved family released the news just minutes ago. The congressman passed away last night. He died of a coronary in his sleep."

"No. *No!*"

"We all feel that way, sir. The funeral arrangements will be announced——"

"No! That's a lie! Don't tell me that! It's a lie! Five, six hours ago—in New York! A *lie!*"

Peter felt the restraining arms around his shoulders, hands on hands, taking the telephone from him, pulling him back. He kicked out, shoving his elbows viciously into the policeman behind him. His right hand was free; he grabbed the head nearest him, lashed out his hand, and wrenched the hair half out of the skull. He yanked the head up; the man had fallen to his knees.

Tony Morgan's face was in front of his, wincing in pain, but he made no move to protect himself.

Morgan. Morgan, his *friend*. What was he doing?

Peter slumped; he was still. Arms lowered him to the floor.

"There won't be any charges," said Morgan, coming into the bedroom, carrying drinks. "They were very understanding."

"Which means I'm a lunatic," added Chancellor from the bed, an icebag on his forehead.

"Hell, no. You're exhausted. You've been working much too hard. The doctors advised you against that——"

"For God's sake, Tony, not with me!" Peter sat up. "Everything I said was true!"

"Okay. Here's your drink."

Chancellor took the glass but did not drink. He placed it on the bedside table. "No you don't, old friend." He pointed to a chair. "Sit down. I want to get some things very clear."

"All right." Morgan ambled to the chair and fell into it. He stretched his long legs out in front of him; the casualness did not fool Peter. The editor's eyes betrayed his concern.

"Calmly, rationally," continued Chancellor. "I think I know what happened. And it won't happen again, which explains Longworth's note. He wants me to believe that; otherwise he's convinced I'll howl like a banshee."

"When have you had time to do any thinking?"

"Those four hours in the streets. I didn't realize it, but the pieces were falling together. And when you and the police were having your conference downstairs, I saw the pattern."

Morgan looked up from his glass. "Don't talk like a writer. 'Patterns,' 'pieces falling together.' That's bullshit."

"No, it's not. Because Longworth is forced to think like a writer. He has to think as I do, don't you see?"

"No, but go ahead."

"Longworth has to be stopped; he knows I know it. He got me started with scraps of information and one pathetic example of what might have happened if Hoover's files still existed. Remember, he knew those files; he retained a hell of a lot of damaging information. Then to make sure I was really hooked, he provided one more example: a southern congressman with problems, mixed up with the rape of a black girl and a killing he didn't commit. Longworth put the forces in motion and me in the middle. But when he got everything going, he realized he'd gone too far. The trap was murder; he hadn't figured on that. When he found out, he saved my life."

"Thus saving the book?"

"Yes."

"*No!*" Morgan got to his feet. "You're talking like a kid around a campfire. And why not? It's your job; all storytellers are kids around campfires. But for heaven's sake, don't confuse it with what *is*."

Chancellor studied Morgan's face. The realization was painfully obvious. "You don't believe me, do you?"

"You want the truth?"

"Since when have we changed the rules?"

"All right." Tony drained his glass. "I think you did go to the Cloisters. How you got in I don't know; you probably climbed a wall. I know how much you love the early morning, and the Cloisters at dawn must be something else. . . . I think you heard about Rawlins's death——"

"How could I? His office said the news was just released!"

"Forgive me. You heard that, I didn't."

"Oh, Christ!"

"Peter, I'm not trying to hurt you. A year ago no one knew whether you'd live or die; you were that close to death. You suffered a terrible loss; Cathy was everything to you, we all knew it. . . . Six months ago we thought— *I* honestly believed—you were finished as a writer. It had gone out of you; the desire had died; the kid around the fire was killed on the Pennsylvania Turnpike. Even when you got out of the hospital, there were entire days—weeks —when you didn't say a word. *Nothing.* Then the drinking began. And then less than three weeks ago your personal volcano erupts. You fly in from the Coast more excited than I've ever seen you, filled with energy, wanting to go back to work with a vengeance. And I mean vengeance. . . . Don't *you* see?"

"See what?"

"The mind's funny. It can't take going from zero miles an hour to Mach one so quickly. Something's bound to snap. You yourself said you didn't know where you were for nearly four hours."

Chancellor did not move. He watched Morgan, conflicting thoughts going through his head. He was angry with the editor for not believing him, yet he was strangely relieved. Perhaps it was better this way. Morgan was protective by nature; the events of the past year had magnified that natural instinct. If he believed Peter, there was no question in Peter's mind what the editor would do. Morgan would stop the book.

"Okay, Tony. Let's forget it. It's over. I'm not entirely well. I can't pretend that I am. I don't know."

"I do," replied Morgan gently. "Let's have a drink."

Munro St. Claire studied Varak as he came through the door of the diplomat's library in Georgetown. The agent's right arm was in a sling, and there was a strip of gauze on the left side of his neck. Varak closed the door and approached the desk where Bravo sat, the ambassador's expression grim.

"What happened?"

"It's taken care of. His Cessna was at the Westchester airport. I flew him to Arlington and contacted a doctor we use at NSC. His wife had no choice, nor did she want any. Rawlins didn't have assassin insurance. Besides, she's a dirty book. I read her several episodes."

"What about the others?" asked Bravo.

"There were three; one was killed. Once Chancellor was out, I stopped firing and concealed myself on the far side of the area. Rawlins was dead; what more did they want? They fled, taking their colleague's body with them. I threaded the zone, picked up shells, replaced grass; there were no signs of any disturbance."

Bravo rose from the chair, his wrath apparent. "What you've done is beyond anything we sanctioned! You made decisions you knew I would not condone, took action that cost the lives of two men, and nearly killed Chancellor."

"One of those men was a killer himself," replied Varak simply. "And Rawlins was marked. It was only a question of time. As to Chancellor, I nearly lost my own life saving him. I think I paid for my error of judgment."

"Error of judgment? Who gave you the right?"

"You did. You all did."

"There were intrinsic prohibitions! You understood that."

"I understood there are hundreds of missing files that could be used to take this country right into a police state! Please remember that."

"And I ask you to remember this is not Czechoslovakia. Not Lidice in 1942. You are not a thirteen-year-old boy crawling over corpses, killing anyone who might be your enemy. You were not brought here thirty years ago to be turned into your own Sturm und Drang."

"I was brought here because my father worked for the Allies! My family was massacred because he worked for you." Varak's eyes clouded. Off guard, he couldn't hold back the tears when he thought of the sunny morning of June 10, 1942. A morning of death everywhere, of succeeding nights hiding in the mines, of subsequent days and nights when, aged thirteen, he made X marks on a mine shaft, each symbol representing another dead German. A child had turned killer of consequence. Until the British brought him out.

"You were given everything," said Bravo, lowering his voice. "Obligations were acknowledged, nothing was spared. The finest schools, all the advantages——"

"And the memories, Bravo. Don't forget those."

"And the memories," agreed Munro St. Claire.

"You misunderstand me," said Varak quickly. "I'm not looking for sympathy. What I'm saying to you is that I do remember." Varak took a step closer to the edge of the desk. "I've spent eighteen years paying for the privilege of that memory. Paid willingly. I'm the best in NSC, I'll seek out the Nazi in any form he is revived in and go after him. And if you think there's any difference between what those files represent and the objectives of the Third Reich, you're very much mistaken."

Varak stopped. The blood had risen to his face; he was close to shouting, but of course that was out of the question. Munro St. Claire watched the agent in silence, his own anger subsiding.

"You're very persuasive. I'll convene Inver Brass. It must be kept apprised."

"No. Don't call a meeting. Not yet."

"A meeting's already scheduled for this month. We have to choose a new Genesis. I'm too told; so are Venice and Christopher. That leaves Banner and Paris. It's an awesome——"

"Please." Varak pressed his fingers on the edge of the desk. "Don't call that meeting."

St. Claire narrowed his eyes. "Why not?"

"Chancellor's begun the book. The first part of the manuscript was delivered the day before yesterday. I broke into the office of the typing firm. I've read it."

"And?"

"Your theory may be more accurate than you thought. Chancellor's conceived of several things that never occurred to me. And Inver Brass is in the book."

15

The cold snap came, turning autumn into winter. The election was over, the results as predictable as the frost that covered the Pennsylvania countryside. Mendacity and Madison Avenue had prevailed over vascillating amateurs. Nobody won anything of value, least of all the republic.

Peter had not paid much attention to politics. Once the players were fielded, there wasn't much that interested him. Instead, he was consumed by the novel. Each morning was his personal adventure. He had refined the plot; the characters had sprung to life.

He was into the seventh chapter, the point where decent men were gradually reaching an indecent decision: murder. The assassination of J. Edgar Hoover.

Before the actual writing of a chapter he always outlined it; then he put the outline aside, barely if ever refer-

ring to it. It was a technique suggested by Anthony Morgan
years ago:

*Know where you're going, give yourself a direction so
you're not floundering, but don't restrict the natural inclina-
tion to wander.*

It was strange about Tony, thought Chancellor as he
bent over the table. They had talked several times since
the incredible madness at the Cloisters several weeks before, but Morgan had never mentioned it. It was as though
it had not happened.

Still Morgan had read the first hundred pages of the
novel. He said it was the best writing Peter had ever done.
That was all that mattered. The book was everything.

Chapter 7 — Outline

A rainy afternoon in a Washington hotel suite.
The senator sits in front of a window watching
the rain splattering against the glass. He is thinking back thirty years ago, to his days in college
when the incident had taken place that when revealed three decades later would take him out
of the presidential race. It was the indiscretion
Hoover's messenger had confronted him with.
He couldn't recall how or when it had happened.
His emotions had run high and wild and indiscreet. But there it was: his youthful signature
on the card of an organization later revealed to
be part of the Communist apparatus. Innocuous,
of course; defensible, certainly—laughable, actually. But not in terms of the presidency. It was
enough to disqualify him. It would not have been,
of course, had his present political philosophy
been in tune with the director of the Federal
Bureau of Investigation's.

The senator's thoughts are interrupted by
the arrival of the newspaperwoman, the columnist silenced by Hoover, now part of the Nucleus.
The senator rises and offers her a drink.

The woman replies that if she could accept,
she would not be there in the first place. She
explains she is an alcoholic; she has not had a
drink in over five years, but prior to that she was
often drunk for days at a time. It was Hoover's
hook into her. During one such binge, photographs were taken.

"Committing unnatural acts with various unsavory gentlemen is the easiest way to describe them. But for the life of me, I don't remember. Good God, how could I?"

Hoover has the photographs. Her dissent has been effectively muted.

The third member of the Nucleus arrives. This third person is the former cabinet member described in the first chapter, whose indiscretion is the fact that he's a closet homosexual.

He brings alarming news. Hoover has made a temporary pact with the White House. Every viable candidate in the opposition will be reached and eliminated. Where facts do not exist, conjecture under the FBI imprimatur will be used. The bureau's name is sufficient to wreak havoc among politicians. By the time defenses are mounted, the damage has been done.

The opposition will field its weakest candidate; the election of the incumbent is assured. Inherent in this agreement is that Hoover has no less damaging weapons to use against the White House. In essence, the director will soon control the pressure points of the country; he'll be running it.

"He's gone too far. The corpses are piling up too fast, too dead. He has to be removed, I don't care how. Even if it means killing him."

The senator is appalled at the cabinet officer's words. He knows what it is to feel Hoover's knife, but there are legitimate ways to fight him. He takes Meredith's report from his briefcase.

The decision is made to reach the messenger, the man who operates with Hoover's private files. Whatever's required will be used to recruit him; above all, the files must be taken.

"First the files. If they can be used the way Hoover uses them, they can be turned around. They can be used for good! Then the execution. There is no other way." The cabinet officer will not waver.

The senator will not listen further; he refuses to acknowledge the statement. He leaves, saying only that he is going to arrange a meeting with Meredith.

Peter stopped. There was enough to start with; he could begin the actual writing.

He picked up his pencil and began.

He was oblivious to time, lost in the accumulated pages. He leaned back on the couch and looked up at the windows, mildly astonished to see tiny flakes of snow drifting downward. He had to remind himself that it was late in December. Where had the months gone?

Mrs. Alcott had brought him the newspaper an hour ago and he felt like taking a break. It was ten thirty; he had been writing since quarter to five. He reached for the paper on the edge of the coffee table and snapped it open.

The headlines were the usual headlines. The Paris negotiations were stalled—whatever that meant. People were dying; he knew what *that* meant.

Suddenly Peter stared at the one-column head in the lower right-hand corner of the front page. A sharp pain shot through his temples.

GEN. BRUCE MACANDREW APPARENT
MURDER VICTIM
Body Washed Up on Waikiki Beach

Waikiki! Oh, my God! Hawaii!

The story was macabre. MacAndrew's body had two bullet holes in it, the first piercing his throat, the second entering his skull below the left eye. Death had been instantaneous and had occurred some ten to twelve days before.

Apparently no one knew the general had been in Hawaii. Hotels and airlines showed no reservations in his name. Interrogations within the island's military establishment produced no information; he had not contacted anyone.

Reading further, Peter was startled again by a paragraph head near the bottom of the page.

Wife Died Five Weeks Ago

The information was scarce. She had simply died "after a prolonged illness that restricted her activities in recent years." If the reporter knew anything more, he had charitably omitted it.

The story then took a strange twist. If the reporter had been charitable to Mrs. MacAndrew, he impugned the general in terms worthy of the Hoover novel.

The Hawaii police are reportedly looking into rumors that a former high-ranking American Army officer was involved with criminal elements operating out of the Malay Peninsula through Honolulu. There are many retired military men and their families in the Hawaiian Islands. Whether or not these rumors are in any way related to the homicide victim could not be established.

Then why include the information? thought Peter angrily, remembering the pathetic sight of the soldier cradling his wife. He flipped the pages to find the continuation of the article. There was a brief biography devoted to MacAndrew's military record, culminating in mention of the general's sudden and unexpected resignation and his differences with the Joint Chiefs, speculations as to the extramilitary cost of his wife's illness, and the subtle insinuation that the maverick general had been subjected to extreme psychological pressures. The connection between these "pressures" and the previously mentioned "rumors" was for the reader to draw, and no reader could help doing so.

The last part of the article took another turn, surprising Peter. He had not realized MacAndrew had a grown daughter. From the description in the paper she was an angry, independent woman.

Reached at her New York apartment, the general's daughter, Alison MacAndrew, 31, an illustrator for the Welton Greene Agency, an advertising firm at 950 Third Avenue, responded angrily to the speculations surrounding her father's death. "They drove him out of the Army, and now they're trying to destroy his reputation. I've been on the phone with the authorities in Hawaii for the past twelve hours. They've concluded my father was killed fighting off an attack by armed muggers. His wallet, wristwatch, signet ring, and money were stolen."

Asked if she could explain why there were

no records of airline or hotel reservations, Miss MacAndrew replied, "That's not unusual. He and my mother generally traveled under another name. If the Army people in Hawaii knew he was vacationing there, they would have hounded him."

Peter understood what she was saying. If MacAndrew traveled anywhere with his mentally ill wife, he would of course use an assumed name to protect her. But MacAndrew's wife was dead. And Chancellor knew the general had not gone to Hawaii for a vacation. He had gone to find a man named Longworth.

And Longworth had killed him.

Peter let the newspaper drop from his hands. Revulsion swept over him, part fury, part guilt. What had he done? What had he let happen? A decent man killed! For what?

A book.

In his messianic drive to assuage his own guilt Longworth had killed again. *Again*. For he was responsible for Rawlins's death at the Cloisters as surely as if he had pulled the trigger that took the congressman's life. And now half a world away, there was another death, another murder.

Chancellor got up unsteadily from the couch and walked aimlessly about the room, the protected sanctuary where fiction took place, life and death only products of the imagination. But outside that room life and death were real. And they touched him because they were a part of his fiction; the marks on paper had sprung from the motives that drove other lives, brought about other deaths. *Real* life and *real* death.

What was happening? A nightmare, more realistic and grotesque than anything he might have dreamed, was being played out in front of a backdrop of fiction. A *nightmare*.

He stopped at the telephone as if somebody had commanded him to remain still. Thoughts of MacAndrew triggered images of a silver Mark IV Continental and a mask of a face behind the wheel.

Suddenly, Peter remembered what he had been about to do months ago, before the telephone call from Walter Rawlins that culminated in the madness in Fort Tryon. He had been about to telephone the Rockville, Maryland, police! He had never done so; he had never made that call!

He had protected himself by forgetting. He remembered now. Even the name of the patrolman. It was Donnelly.

He dialed information for the Rockville area code. Thirty seconds later he was speaking with a desk sergeant named Manero. He described the incident on the back road, gave the date, and identified Officer Donnelly.

Manero hesitated. "Are you sure you want Rockville, sir?"

"Of course I am."

"What color was the patrol car, sir?"

"Color? I don't know. Black and white, or blue and white. What difference does it make?"

"There's no Officer Donnelly in Rockville, sir. Our vehicles are green with white stripes."

"Then, it was green! The patrolman said his name was Donnelly. He drove me back to Washington."

"Drove you into— Just one minute, sir."

There was the click of a hold button. Chancellor stared out the window at the wind-blown flakes of snow and wondered whether he was losing his mind. Manero came back on the line.

"Sir, I've got the police blotter for the week of the tenth. There's no record of any accident involving a Chevrolet and a Lincoln Continental."

"It was a silver Mark Four! Donnelly told me it was picked up! A woman driver in dark glasses hit a mail truck."

"I repeat, sir. There's no Officer Donnelly——"

"Goddamn it, there is!" Peter could not help shouting. Perspiration broke out on his forehead; the pain in his temples increased. His memory raced back. "I remember! He said she was a drunk! With a record of violations, that was it. She was the wife of a Lincoln-Mercury dealer in—in Pikesville!"

"Just a minute!" The desk sergeant raised his voice. "Is this some kind of joke? My in-laws live in Pikesville. There's no Lincoln dealer there. Who the hell could afford one? And there's no police officer named Donnelly in this station. Now, get off the line. You're interfering with official business!"

The phone went dead. Chancellor stood immobile, not believing the words he'd heard. They were trying to tell him he had lived a fantasy!

The car rental agency at Dulles Airport! He had telephoned from the Hay-Adams and spoken to the manager. The manager had assured him that everything would be taken care of: the agency would simply bill his account. He dialed.

"Yes, of course, I remember our conversation, Mr. Chancellor. I enjoyed your last book very——"

"Did you get the car back?"

"Yes, we did."

"Then someone had to take a tow truck out to Rockville. Did he see a police officer named Donnelly? Can you find out for me?"

"It won't be necessary. The next morning the car was back in our parking depot. You said you thought there might be damage, but there wasn't. I remember the dispatcher saying that it was about the cleanest automobile ever returned."

Peter tried to control himself. "Did whoever brought back the car have to sign anything?"

"Yes, of course."

"Who was it?"

"If you'll hold on, I can find out."

"I'll hold." Peter gripped the phone with all his strength; the muscles in his forearms ached. His mind went blank. Outside, the snowflakes fell.

"Mr. Chancellor?"

"Yes?"

"There was a mistake, I'm afraid. According to the depot, the signature on the invoice was yours. Obviously there was a misunderstanding. Because the car was leased to you, the man who returned it probably thought——"

"There was no mistake," interrupted Peter quietly.

"I beg your pardon?"

"Thank you," he said, hanging up the telephone.

It was suddenly clear. Everything. The terrible mask of a face. The silver Continental. A clean, repaired Chevrolet in a Washington parking depot. A spotless Mercedes in front of his New York apartment. A note on the door.

It was Longworth. It was all Longworth. The grotesque, powdered face, the long dark hair, the black glasses . . . and memories of a horrible night of death a year ago in a rainstorm. Longworth had done his research; he was trying to drive him mad. But *why*?

Chancellor walked back to the couch; he had to sit down and let the pain in his temples pass. His eyes fell on the newspaper, and he knew what he had to do.

Alison MacAndrew.

16

He found her name in the New York telephone directory he kept in Pennsylvania, but the number had been disconnected. Which was to say a new, unlisted number had been assigned.

He called the Welton Greene Agency; a secretary told him Miss MacAndrew would be away from the office for several days. No explanation was offered, none sought.

Still, he had the address. It was an apartment building on East Fifty-fourth Street. He knew the one; it was on the river. There was nothing else to do. He had to see this woman, talk with her.

He threw a few clothes into the Mercedes, put his manuscript into his briefcase, and drove into the city.

She opened the door, her large brown eyes conveying both intelligence and curiosity. Curiosity tinged, perhaps, with anger, in spite of the sadness in her face. She was tall and seemed to have her father's reserve, but her features were her mother's. Fragile, etched in definition, the bone structure elegant, even aloof. Her light brown hair was casually shaped. She wore beige slacks and a yellow blouse, open at the neck. There were dark circles under her eyes; the effects of grief were evident but not for display.

"Mr. Chancellor?" she asked directly, no hand extended.

"Yes," he nodded. "Thank you for seeing me."

"You were very persuasive on the lobby phone. Come in, please."

He walked inside the small apartment. The living room was modern and functional, given to swift, sharp lines of glass and chrome. It was a designer's room, icelike and cool, yet somehow made comfortable by the owner's presence. Beyond her quality of directness Alison Mac-Andrew had a warmth about her she could not conceal. She gestured toward an armchair; he sat down. She sat on the couch opposite him.

"I'd offer you a drink, but I'm not sure I want you to stay that long."

"I understand."

"Still, I'm impressed. Even a bit awestruck, I guess."

"Good heavens, why?"

"Through my father, I 'discovered' your books several years ago. You've got a fan, Mr. Chancellor."

"I hope for my publisher's sake there are two or three others. But that's not important. It's not why I'm here."

"My father was one," said Alison. "He had your three books; he told me you were very good. He read *Counterstrike!* twice. He said it was frightening and quite possibly true."

Peter was startled. The general hadn't conveyed any such feeling. No admiration beyond vague—very vague—recognition. "I didn't know that. He didn't say anything."

"He wasn't given to flattery."

"We talked about other things. Things much more important to him."

"So you said on the phone. A man gave you his name and implied my father was forced out of the Army. Why? How? I think it's ridiculous. Not that there weren't any number who wanted him out, but they couldn't force him."

"What about your mother?"

"What about her?"

"She was ill."

"She was ill," agreed the girl.

"The Army wanted your father to send her away. He wouldn't do it."

"That was his choice. It's a moot point whether she would have received more professional care if he had. God knows he chose the most difficult way for him. He loved her, that was the important thing."

Chancellor watched her closely. The hard patina, the clipped, precise words were only part of the surface. Beneath, he felt there was a vulnerability she was doing her utmost to hide. He could not help himself; he had to probe. "You sound as if you didn't. Love her, that is."

Anger flashed briefly in her eyes. "My mother became

. . . ill when I was six years old. I never really knew her. I never knew the woman my father married, the one he remembered so vividly. Does that explain anything to you?"

Peter was silent for a moment. "I'm sorry. I'm a damned fool. Of course it does."

"Not a damned fool. A writer. I lived with a writer for nearly three years. You play with people; you can't help it."

"I don't mean to," he protested.

"I said you couldn't help it."

"Would I know your friend?"

"You might. He writes for television; he lives in California now." She offered no name. Instead, she reached for a pack of cigarettes and a lighter on the table next to her. "Why do you think my father was forced out of the Army?"

Chancellor was confused. "I just told you. Your mother."

She replaced the lighter on the table, her eyes locked with his. "What?"

"The Army wanted him to send her away. To an institution. He refused."

"And you think that's why?"

"Yes, I do."

"Then, you're wrong. As I'm sure you've gathered, I disliked many things about the Army, but its attitude toward my mother wasn't one of them. For over twenty years the men around my father were very sympathetic, those above him and below. They helped him whenever they could. You look astonished."

Peter was. The general had spelled it out. *Now you know what the damaging information is . . . doctors said she had to be sent away . . . I wouldn't do that.* Those were his words! "I guess I am." He leaned forward. "Then, why did your father resign? Do you know?"

She inhaled on her cigarette. Her eyes strayed, seeing things Peter could not see. "He said he was finished, that he didn't care anymore. When he told me that, I realized a part of him had given up. I think I knew the rest of him would go soon. Not the way it happened, of course, but somehow. And even that. Shot in a holdup—I've thought about it. It fits so well. A last protest. At the end, proving something to himself."

"What do you mean?"

Alison brought her eyes back to him. "To put it in its simplest terms, my father lost his will to fight. At that moment, when he said the words to me, he was the saddest man I ever saw."

At first Peter did not reply. He was disturbed. "Are those the words he used? That he 'didn't care anymore'?"

"Essentially, yes He was sick of it all. Pentagon infighting is very cruel. There's never any letup. Get the hardware, always more hardware. My father used to say it was understandable. The men who run the Army now were once young officers In a war that really mattered, where hardware had won it. If we had lost that war, there would have been nothing."

"When you say a war that 'really mattered,' do you mean——?"

"I mean, Mr. Chancellor," interrupted the girl, "that for five years my father opposed our policy in Southeast Asia. He fought it every chance he could get. It was a very lonely position. I think the word is *pariah*."

"Good lord. . . ." Peter's mind spun back involuntarily to the Hoover novel. To the prologue. The general he had invented was the pariah Alison MacAndrew had just described.

"My father wasn't political; his judgment had nothing to do with politics. It was purely military. He knew the war couldn't be won in any conventional way, and to use the unconventional was unthinkable. We couldn't win it because there was no real commitment among those we supported. There were more lies coming out of Siagon than in all the court martials in military history—that's what he said. He considered the whole thing an enormous waste of life."

Chancellor sat back on the couch. He had to clear his head. He was hearing words he had written. Fiction. "I knew the general was opposed to certain aspects. I never thought he dwelt on the corruption, the lies."

"It was almost all he dwelt on. And he was vehement about it. He was in the process of cataloguing hundreds of contradictory reports, logistical misrepresentations, body counts. He once told me that if the body counts were only fifty percent accurate, we would have won the war in '68."

"What did you say?" asked Peter incredulously. These were *his words*.

"What's the matter?" asked Alison.

"Nothing. Go ahead."

"There's nothing more to tell. He was barred from attending conferences he knew he should be a part of, ignored in staff meetings. The more he fought, the more they disregarded him. Finally he saw it was all futile."

"What about the reports he was cataloguing? The misrepresentations? The lies out of Siagon?"

Alison looked away. "They were the last things we talked about," she said quietly. "I'm afraid it wasn't my finest hour. I was angry. I called him names I now deeply regret. I didn't realize how beaten he was."

"What about the reports?"

Alison raised her head and looked at him. "I think they became a symbol for him. They represented months, maybe years, of further agony, turning against men he'd served with. He wasn't up to it anymore. He couldn't face it. He quit."

Peter again leaned forward. Consciously, he spoke with a hard edge in his voice. "That doesn't sound like the professional I spoke with."

"I know it doesn't. That's why I yelled at him. You see, I could argue with him. We were more than father and daughter. We were friends. Equals in a way. I had to grow up fast; he didn't have anyone else to talk to."

The moment was filled with anguish. Chancellor let it pass. "A few minutes ago you said I was wrong. Now it's my turn. The last thing your father wanted to do was resign. And he didn't go to Hawaii for a vacation. He went there to find the man who forced him out of the Army?"

"What?"

"Something happened to your father years ago. Something he didn't want anyone to know about. This man found out and threatened him. I liked your father very much. I liked what he stood for, and I feel guilty as hell. That's as honestly as I can put it. And I want to tell you about it."

Alison MacAndrew sat motionless, her large eyes level with his. "Would you care for that drink now?" she asked.

He told her the story, everything he could remember. From the blond-haired stranger on the beach at Malibu to the astonishing phone call that morning to the Rockville police. He omitted only the killing at Fort Tryon; if there was a connection, he did not want to burden her with it.

In the telling he felt cheap; the commercial novelist in search of a grand conspiracy. He fully expected her to be outraged, to damn him for being the means to her father's death. In a very real sense he wanted her condemnation, so deep was his own guilt.

Instead, she seemed to understand the depth of his feelings. Remarkably, she tried to lessen his guilt, telling him that if what he told her was true, he was no villain; he was a victim. But regardless of what he believed, she would not accept the theory that there was an incident in her father's past so damaging that threats of exposure could force him to resign.

"It doesn't make sense. If anything like that existed, it would have been used against him years ago."

"In the newspaper, you said he was driven out."

"Yes, but not that way. By wearing him down, ignoring his decisions. That was the method. I saw it."

Chancellor remembered his prologue; he was almost afraid to ask the question. "What about his report on the corruption in Siagon?"

"What about it?"

"Isn't it possible they tried to stop him?"

"I'm sure they did. But it wasn't the first time he'd done something like that. His field reports were always very critical. He loved the Army; he wanted it to be the best it could be. He would never have made it public, if that's what you're driving at."

"It was."

"Never. He wouldn't do that."

Peter did not understand, nor did he press for an explanation. But he had to ask the obvious. "Why did he go to Hawaii?"

She looked at him. "I know what you think. I can't refute you, but I know what he told me. He said he wanted to get away, go on a long trip. There was nothing to prevent him. Mother was gone."

It was no answer; the question remained suspended. And so they talked. For hours, it seemed. Finally, she said it. The next afternoon her father's body was arriving in New York, flown in on a commercial jetliner from Hawaii. An army escort would meet the plane at Kennedy Airport, the coffin be transferred to a military aircraft and taken to Virginia. The funeral was the day after in Arlington. She was not sure she could face the ordeal.

"Isn't anyone going to be with you?"

"No."

"Will you let me?"

"There's no reason——"

"I think there is," said Peter firmly.

They stood together on the enormous field of concrete that was the cargo area. Two Army officers remained at attention several yards to their left. The wind was strong, swirling odd pieces of paper and leaves from faraway trees into the air in circles. The huge DC-10 taxied to a stop. Shortly, the large panel underneath the giant fuselage slid back; an electric freight dolly approached and was centered beneath. Seconds later the coffin was lowered.

And Alison's face was suddenly ashen, her body rigid. The trembling began at her lips, then reached her hands; her brown eyes stared, unblinking; tears started to roll down her cheeks. Peter put his arm around her shoulders.

She held back as long as she could—far longer, in far greater pain, than made sense. Chancellor could feel the spasms that shot through her arms; he held her tighter. Finally she could take no more. She turned and fell against him, her head buried in his coat, the sobs muffled, the agony complete.

"I'm sorry. . . . I'm so sorry," she whispered. "I promised myself I wouldn't."

He held her close and spoke softly. "Hey, come on. It's allowed."

17

Peter had made up his mind, but she changed it for him. He was going to abandon the book; he had been manipulated, and the price of that manipulation was symbolized for him by the dead MacAndrew. He had implied as much to Alison the night before.

"Say you're right," she had said to him. "I don't think you are, but say it's true. Isn't that all the more reason to go on?"

It was.

He sat across the aisle from her on the air force plane. She wanted to be alone; he sensed that and understood. Below them, in the cargo area of the aircraft, was the body of her father. She had a great deal to think about, and he could not help her. Alison was a private person; he understood that, too.

And she was unpredictable as well. He had learned that when he picked her up in the taxi earlier in the afternoon. He told her he had phoned the Hay-Adams in Washington and made reservations for them.

"Don't be silly. There's plenty of room in the Rockville house. We'll stay there. I think we should."

Why should they? He did not pursue the question.

Chancellor opened his briefcase and took out the leather notebook that traveled with him wherever he went. It had been a gift from Joshua Harris two years before. There was a row of sharpened pencils in the inside pocket of the cover. He removed one and wrote on the attached pad.

Chapter 8 — Outline

Before he began he thought about Alison's remark the night before.

. . . *say it's true. Isn't that all the more reason to go on?*

He looked at the words he had just writen: *Chapter 8 — Outline.* The coincidence was disquieting. This was the chapter in which Meredith is driven to the point of madness because of a terrible secret of his own.

Alex leaves his office at the Federal Bureau of Investigation earlier than usual. He knows he's being followed, so he tries to lose himself in the crowds, walking up short streets and alleys, through several buildings, going in one entrance, emerging from another. He dashes onto a bus; it takes him to within a block of the apartment where the assistant attorney general lives. They have agreed to meet.

At the apartment house the doorman hands him a note from the assistant attorney general. He will not see Alex. He does not want any further association. If Meredith persists, the man will be forced to report his odd behavior to others. In his judgment, Alex is unbalanced, paranoid over imagined abuses.

Meredith is stunned, the lawyer in him furious. The evidence *is* there. The assistant attorney general has been reached as so many others have been reached. Hoover's forces have succeeded in blocking Meredith's every move. The raw power of the FBI is all-pervasive.

Outside the apartment house he sees the bureau vehicle that has picked up his trail. There is a driver and a man beside him; they stare at Alex silently. It is part of the strategy of fear aroused when a man knows he is being watched, especially at night. It fits Hoover's methods.

Meredith takes a cab to the garage where his car is parked. We see him speeding down Memorial Parkway, weaving in and out of traffic, aware of the FBI car behind him.

On impulse he changes direction, taking an unfamiliar exit off the highway into the Virginia countryside. The husband and father in him has rebelled. He will not lead those following him back to his house again, back to his wife and his children. His fear is turning into fury.

There is a chase through the back roads. The speed, the rushing scenery, the screeching tires around sharp curves, all contribute to Alex's growing panic. He is a man alone racing in a maze for survival. We understand that the disorientation produced by the events of the past weeks is heightened by the madness of the chase. Meredith is beginning to crack.

In the growing darkness Alex miscalculates a sudden curve. He slams on the brakes; the car swerves, jumps the road and plunges through the fence into the field.

Bruised, his forehead bleeding from the impact with the windshield, Meredith climbs out of the car. He sees the FBI vehicle back on the road. He races toward it, screaming. His state of mind demands violence, physical confrontation.

He does not get it in the way that he seeks it. Instead, the two FBI men get out of the car and swiftly subdue him. They feign professional procedures by searching him for a weapon.

The driver speaks coldly. "Don't press us, Meredith. We don't have much use for people like you. Men who put on a uniform and work for the other side."

Alex collapses. It is the secret that is buried in his past. Years ago, during the Korean War, as a young lieutenant barely in his twenties, Meredith had been captured and broken by his captors. He was not alone; there were hundreds. Men driven mad by physical and psychological tortures unknown in modern warfare. The Army understood; the Geneva covenants had been violated. The broken men were assured that all records of their nightmare would be expunged. They had served honorably; they had faced things for which the Army had never prepared them. Each could pick up his life without punishment.

Now Alex realizes that the darkest moment of his life is known by men who will use it ruthlessly against him, and even against his wife and children.

The FBI agents release him. He wanders down the country road in the twilight.

Peter closed the notebook and looked over at Alison. She was staring straight ahead, her eyes wide, unblinking. The two-man military escort sat in the front of the plane, where their attentions could not fall on private grief.

She felt his gaze on her and turned to him, forcing a smile. "You working?"

"I was. Not now."

"I'm glad you were. It makes me feel better. Less like I was interrupting you."

"That's hardly the case. You made me go on, remember?"

"We'll be there soon," she said mechanically.

"No more than ten or fifteen minutes, I think."

"Yes." She went back to her thoughts, looking out the window at the bright blue sky beyond.

The aircraft began its descent into Andrews Field.

They taxied to a stop, disembarked, and were instructed to wait in the officers' lounge at terminal six.

The only person in the lounge was a young army chaplain, obviously ordered to be in attendance. He was both relieved and somewhat startled to find his presence superfluous.

"It's kind of you to be here," said Alison with authority, "but my father died several days ago. The shock's worn off."

The minister shook hands solemnly and left. Alison turned to Peter. "They've scheduled the service for ten tomorrow morning at Arlington. I've requested the minimum; just the officers' cortege within the grounds. It's nearly six. Why don't we have an early dinner somewhere and get out to the house?"

"Fine. Shall I rent a car?"

"No need to. They'll have one for us."

"That means a driver, doesn't it?"

"Yes." Alison frowned again. "You're right. That's a complication. Do you have your license with you?"

"Of course."

"You can sign for the vehicle. Do you mind?"

"Not at all."

"It'll be simpler without a third person," she said. "Army drivers are notorious scouts for superior officers. Even if we didn't ask him in, I'm sure his orders would be to remain on the premises until relieved."

Alison's words could be taken on several levels. "What do you mean?" he asked.

Alison saw his caution. "If something did happen to my father years ago, something he considered so terrible it could change his life, then there might be a clue to what it was in the Rockville house. He kept mementos from his posts. Photographs, roster sheets, things that were important to him. I think we should go through them all."

"I see. Better done by two than three," added Peter, curiously satisfied that this was what Alison meant. "Perhaps you'd rather look by yourself. I can stand by and take notes for you."

She searched his eyes in that strange noncommittal way that reminded him of her father. But there was warmth in her voice. "You're very considerate. It's a quality I admire. I'm not. I wish I were, but I don't think it went, as they say, with the territory."

"I've got an idea," he said. "I have one solid talent: I can cook a hell of a meal. You're anxious to get to Rockville. So am I. Why don't we stop at a supermarket and I'll pick up some things? Like steaks and potatoes and Scotch."

She smiled. "We'd save a lot of time."

"Done."

They took the eastern roads north and west into the Maryland countryside, stopping at a store in Randolph Hills for groceries and whisky.

It was growing dark. The December sun was below the hills; elongated shadows shot across the windshield of the army car, creating odd shapes that came and went swiftly. As he swung off the highway into the twisting back road that led to the general's house, he reached the flat stretch of farmland and saw the outlines of the barbed-wire fence and the field beyond, where three months before he'd thought he would lose his life.

The road turned sharply. He held his foot on the accelerator, afraid to lessen the pressure. He had to get away. The ache was at his right temple now, spreading downward, curving in his neck, throbbing at the base of his skull. Faster!

"Peter! For God's sake!"

The tires screeched; he held the wheel firmly as they rounded the turn and came out of it. He braked the car, reducing speed.

"Is anything the matter?" she asked.

"No," he lied. "I'm sorry. I just wasn't thinking." He could feel her looking at him; he had not fooled her for an instant. "That's not true," he continued. "I was remembering when I was here before, when I saw your father and mother."

"I was thinking about my last visit, too," she said. "It was this past summer. I came down for a few days. I was supposed to stay a week, but it didn't work out that way. I upped and left with a number of choice words I wish to God I'd never said."

"Was that when he told you he was resigning?"

"Had resigned. I think that bothered me as much as

anything. We'd always discussed important things. And then the most important decision of his life arose, and I was cut off. I said terrible things."

"He made an extraordinary decision without explaining it to you. Your reaction was natural."

They fell silent; neither said anything of consequence for the final ten miles. The night had come quickly; the moon had risen.

"There it is. The white mailbox," said Alison.

Chancellor slowed down and turned into the concealed driveway, hidden by the profuse foliage on either side and the low-hanging branches of the trees beyond. Had it not been for the mailbox, the entrance could have easily been missed.

The house stood in eerie isolation, ordinary and alone and still. Moonlight filtered through the trees, speckling the front with shadows. The windows were smaller than Peter remembered, the roof lower. Alison got out of the car and walked slowly up the narrow path to the door. Chancellor followed, carrying the groceries and the whisky from the store in Randolph Hills. She unlocked the door.

They both smelled it at once. It was not overpowering, or even unpleasant, but it pervaded the area. A musk-like odor, faintly aromatic, a dying fragrance escaping closed quarters into the night air. Alison squinted her eyes in the moonlight, her head angled in thought. Peter watched her; for a moment she seemed to shiver.

"It's Mother's," she said.

"Perfume?"

"Yes. But she died over a month ago."

Chancellor remembered her words in the car. "You said you were here last summer. Didn't you come down ——"

"For the funeral?"

"Yes."

"No. Because I didn't know she'd died. My father called me when everything was over. There was no announcement, no service to speak of. It was a private burial, just he and the woman he remembered as no one else remembered her." Alison walked into the dark hallway and turned on the light. "Come on, we'll put the bags in the kitchen."

They walked through the small dining room to a

swinging door that led to the kitchen. Alison switched on the lights, revealing oddly old-fashioned counters and cabinets in contrast to a modern refrigerator. It was as if a 1930s kitchen had been intruded upon by a futuristic appliance. Peter was struck by his memory of the house. Except for the general's study, what he had seen of it was old-fashioned, as if deliberately decorated for a different era.

Alison seemed to read his thoughts. "My father reconstructed wherever possible the types of surroundings she associated with her childhood."

"It's an extraordinary love story." It was all he could say.

"It was an extraordinary sacrifice," she said.

"You resented her, didn't you?"

She did not flinch from the question. "Yes, I did. He was an exceptional man. He happened to be my father, but that was irrelevant. He was a man of ideas. I read once that an idea was a greater monument than a cathedral, and I believe that. But his cathedral—or cathedrals —never got built. His commitments were always sidetracked. He was never allowed the time to see them through. He had *her* in his footlocker."

Chancellor did not let her angry eyes waver from his. "You said the men around him were sympathetic. They helped him in every way they could."

"Of course they did. He wasn't the only one with a whacked-out woman. It's pretty standard, according to the West Point underground. But he was different. He had something original to say. And when they didn't want to hear it, they killed him with kindness. 'Poor Mac! Look what he has to live with!' "

"You were his daughter, not his wife."

"I *was* his wife! In everything but the bed! And sometimes I wondered whether that—It doesn't matter. I got out." She gripped the edge of the counter. "I'm sorry. I don't know you that well. I don't know anyone that well." She bent over the counter, trembling.

Peter resisted the instinct to hold her. "Do you think you're the only girl in the world who's felt that way? I don't think so, Alison."

"It's cold." She pushed herself partially up; still he did not touch her. "I can feel the cold. The furnace must have gone off." She stood erect and wiped away the tears with the back of her hand. "Do you know anything about furnaces?"

"Gas or oil?"

"I don't know."

"I'll find out. Is that the door to the basement?" He pointed to a door in the right wall.

"Yes."

He found the light switch and walked down the narrow stairs, pausing at the bottom. The furnace was in the center of a low-ceilinged room; an oil tank was against the left wall. It *was* cold; a damp chill permeated the basement as though an outside door had been left open.

But the outside door was bolted. He checked the oil-tank gauge; it registered half full, but could very well be inaccurate. Why else would the furnace be off? Mac-Andrew was not the sort of man to leave a house in the country without heat in the winter. He tapped the side of the tank. Hollow above, full lower down. The gauge was accurate.

He lifted the plate of the firing mechanism and saw the cause of the problem. The pilot light had gone out. Under normal circumstances it would take a strong gust of wind to extinguish it. Or a blockage in the line. But the furnace had been checked recently. There was a small strip of plastic adhesive dating the last inspection. It was six weeks old.

Peter read the instructions. They were nearly identical to those of his parents' furnace.

Press red button for sixty seconds. Hold match beneath . . .

He heard a sudden, sharp clattering; the sound caused him to gasp. The muscles of his stomach tensed; he angled his head, frozen by the *rat-tat-tat* somewhere behind him. It stopped.

Then started again! He spun around and moved toward the stairs. He looked up.

On the top of the basement wall a window was open. It was at ground level; the wind outside was hammering against it.

That was the explanation. Wind from the window had extinguished the pilot light. Chancellor walked to the wall, suddenly afraid again.

The pane of glass had been shattered. He could feel

the crunching of glass beneath his feet. Someone had broken into MacAndrew's home!

It happened too quickly. For an instant, he could not send commands from his mind to his body.

Screams came from upstairs. Again and again! Alison!

He raced up the narrow steps to the kitchen. Alison was not there, but her screams continued, animallike and terrified.

"Alison! Alison!"

He ran into the dining room.

"*Alison!*"

The screaming subsided abruptly, replaced by low moans and sobs. They came from across the house, through the hallway and the living room. From Mac-Andrew's study!

Peter raced through the rooms, kicking one chair out of the way, sending another crashing to the floor. He burst through the study door.

Alison was on her knees, holding a faded, blood-stained nightgown in her hands. All around her were smashed bottles of perfume, the odor overpowering now and sickening.

And on the wall, painted in blood-red enamel, were the words:

MAC THE KNIFE. KILLER OF CHASŎNG.

18

The paint on the walls was soft to the touch but not wet. The blood on the tattered nightgown was moist. The general's study had been searched thoroughly by professionals. The desk had been pried apart, the leather upholstery carefully slit. The boxed windowsills and weight sashes had been separated and exposed, the bookcase emptied of its contents, the bindings precisely cut.

Peter led Alison back into the kitchen, where he

poured two glasses of straight Scotch. He returned to the basement, started the furnace, and plugged the broken window with rags. Upstairs in the living room he discovered that the fireplace worked; more than a dozen logs were in a large wicker bin to the right of the screen. He built a fire and sat with Alison on the couch in front of it. The horror was fading, but the questions remained.

"What's Chasŏng?" he asked.

"I don't know. I think it's a place in Korea, but I'm not sure."

"When we find out, we may learn what it was that happened. What it was they were looking for."

"Anything could have happened. It was war, and—" She stopped, watching the flames.

"And he was a soldier who sent other soldiers into combat. It might be as simple as that. Someone who lost a son or a brother; someone out for vengeance. I've heard of such things."

"But why him? There were hundreds like him. And he was known for leading his men, not staying behind. No one ever questioned any of his commands. Not that way."

"Someone did," said Peter. "Someone very sick."

She looked at him for several moments, not answering. "You know what you're saying, don't you? Whether sick or not, whatever the person knows, or thinks he knows, it's true."

"I haven't thought it out that far. I'm not sure it follows."

"It has to. My father wouldn't have turned his back on everything he believed in if it were anything else." She shuddered. "What could he have *done*?"

"It had something to do with your mother."

"Impossible."

"Is it? I saw that nightgown the afternoon I was here. She was wearing it then. She'd fallen down. There was broken glass around her."

"She was always breaking things. She could be very destructive. The gown is a last cruel joke. I suppose it signifies my father's impotence. That wasn't a secret."

"Where was your mother during the Korean War?"

"In Tokyo. We both were."

"That was in fifty or fifty-one?"

"Around then, yes. I was very young."

"About six years old?"

"Yes."

Peter sipped his Scotch. "Is that when your mother became ill?"

"Yes."

"Your father said there was an accident. Do you remember what happened?"

"I *know* what happened. She drowned. I mean, really drowned. They brought her back with electric shock, but the loss of oxygen was too prolonged. It was enough to cause the brain damage."

"How did it happen?"

"She was caught in the undertow at Funabashi Beach. She was swept out. The lifeguards couldn't reach her in time."

They were both silent for a while. Chancellor finished his Scotch, got up from the sofa, and poked the fire. "Shall I fix us something to eat? Then afterward we can——"

"I'm *not* going back in there!" she said harshly, staring at the fire, interrupting him. Then she looked up. "Forgive me. You're the last person I should yell at."

"I'm the only one here," he answered. "If you feel like yelling——"

"I know," she broke in, "it's allowed."

"I think it is."

"Are there no limits to your tolerance?" She asked the question softly, gentle humor in her eyes. He could feel her warmth. And vulnerability.

"I don't think I'm particularly tolerant. It's not a word often associated with me."

"I may test that judgment." Alison rose from the sofa and approached him, putting her hands on his shoulders. With the fingers of her right hand she delicately outlined his left cheek, his eyes, and, finally, his lips. "I'm not a writer. I draw pictures; they're my words. And I'm not capable of drawing what I think, or feel, right now. So I ask your tolerance, Peter. Will you give it to me?"

She leaned into him, her fingers still on his lips, and pressed her mouth against his, removing her fingers only when her lips widened.

He could feel the trembling in her body as she thrust herself against him. Her needs were born of exhaustion and sudden, overwhelming loneliness, thought Peter. She desperately wanted the expression of love, for a love had been taken away. Something—anything, perhaps—had to replace it, if only for a while, for a moment.

Oh, *God*, he understood! And because he understood he wanted her. It was in a way a confirmation of his own agonies. They had been born of the same exhaustion, the same manner of loneliness and guilt. It suddenly occurred to him that for months he'd had no one to talk to, no one had been permitted near him.

"I don't want to go upstairs," she whispered, her breath coming rapidly against his mouth, her fingers digging into his back as she clung to him.

"We won't," he answered softly, reaching for the buttons of her blouse.

She turned partially away from him and brought her right hand to her throat. In one gesture she tore her blouse away; with a second she opened his shirt. Their flesh met.

He was aroused in a way he had not been for months. Since Cathy. He led her to the couch and gently unhooked her brassiere. It fell away, revealing her soft, sloping breasts, the nipples taut, awakened. She pulled his head down, and as his mouth roamed over her skin, she reached for the buckle of his belt. They lay down and the comfort was splendid.

Alison fell into a deep sleep, and Peter knew it was pointless to try to get her upstairs into a bed. Instead, he brought down blankets and pillows. The fire had subsided. He lifted Alison's head, placing the softest pillow beneath her, and draped a blanket over her naked body. She did not move.

He arranged two blankets on the floor in front of the fireplace, only feet from the couch, and lay down. He had understood a number of things during the past few hours, but not the state of his own exhaustion. He was asleep immediately.

He awoke with a start, unsure for a moment where he was, jolted by the sound of a log settling into its cradle of embers. There was dim light coming from the small front windows; it was early morning. He looked over at Alison on the couch. She was still asleep, the deep breathing had not changed. He lifted his wrist to see his watch. It was twenty to six. He had slept nearly seven hours.

He got up, put on his trousers, and wandered into

the kitchen. The groceries were still there unopened, and he put them away. Rummaging in the old-fashioned cabinets, he found a coffeepot. It was a percolator, in keeping with the decor; it must have been made forty years ago. There was coffee in the refrigerator, and Peter tried to remember how to manipulate the pot and the grounds. He did the best he could and left the percolator over a small flame on the stove.

He walked back into the living room. Quietly, he put on the rest of his clothes, returned to the hall, and let himself out the front door. Then two suitcases and his brief case weren't going to do them any good in the army staff car parked in the small driveway.

It was cold and damp. The Maryland winter could not make up its mind whether to produce snow or stay on the edge of freezing mist. As a result the dampness was penetrating. Peter opened the car door and reached into the back seat for their luggage.

His eyes were abruptly riveted in shock; he was unable to control the gasp that emerged from his throat. The sight was appalling, grotesque.

And it explained the blood on the walls of MacAndrew's study and on the nightgown.

On his suitcase, which lay flat on the seat above Alison's on the floor, were the severed hind legs of an animal carcass, its ugly tendons extended beyond its blood-soaked fur. And on the leather, finger-painted in blood, was the word:

Chasŏng

Peter's shock was replaced by a shudder of fear and revulsion. He backed out of the car, darting his eyes into the thick foliage and toward the road beyond. He walked cautiously around the automobile. He knelt down and picked up a rock, not sure why he did so, yet strangely, only slightly comforted by the primitive weapon.

There was the snap of a branch! A twig had been broken somewhere. *There,* or *there,* or—*footsteps.*

Someone was running. Suddenly *running!* On gravel.

Peter did not know whether his fear was suspended by the sound or by the fact that the racing footsteps were running away, but he ran as fast as he could after them. Then the footsteps were muted; the racing feet were now on a hard surface, not gravel. The road!

He crashed through the foliage, branches snapping back into his face, roots and trunks impeding his progress. He reached the road, fifty yards away a figure was running in the dim, early light toward an automobile. Vapor mingled with the morning mist; the car's engine was being gunned. The right door was opened by an unseen hand from inside the car; the figure leaped in, and the automobile sped away into the semidarkness.

Peter stood in the road, perspiration rolling down his forehead. He let the rock drop and wiped his face.

The words came back to him, spoken by an angry woman over candlelight at the Hay-Adams in Washington.

Terror by fiat.

It was what he was witnessing now. Someone wanted to frighten Alison MacAndrew out of her mind. But *why*? Her father was dead. What was to be gained by terrifying the daughter?

He decided to keep part of the horror away from Alison. He *wanted* to keep it from her. Everything had happened too quickly, but he knew a void was being filled for him. Alison had come into his life.

He wondered if it would last. That question was suddenly very important to him. He turned and walked back to the car, removed the blood-soaked animal legs, and threw them into the woods. He took out the two suitcases and his briefcase and carried them back into the house. He was thankful that Alison was still asleep.

He left Alison's suitcase in the hallway, picked up his own with his briefcase, and carried the two pieces into the kitchen. He remembered from somewhere that cold water removed blood more easily than hot. He turned on the tap, found paper towels, and for fifteen minutes rubbed the stained leather clean. What markings were left he scraped with the blade of a bread knife, roughing the surface until the outline of the letters disappeared.

And then, for reasons he could not explain to himself, he opened the briefcase, removed his notebook, and placed it on the table in the old-fashioned kitchen. The percolator bubbled. He poured a cup of coffee and returned to the table. He opened the notebook and stared at the yellow page half filled with words. It was not merely a compulsion of the morning; it was somehow fitting that he should try to examine his thoughts and put them down through another's mind. For he had just lived through an experience he had attributed to a character he had created. He had been followed in darkness.

The FBI agents release Meredith. He wanders down the country road in the twilight.

There is a lapse of time.

Meredith has returned home. He tells his wife he was in an accident on Memorial Parkway, the car towed away for repairs. She does not believe him.

"Truth is not spoken here anymore," she screams. "I can't stand it any longer! What's happening to us?"

Alex knows what's happened to them. Hoover's strategy of fear is too effective. The tensions have become unbearable; even their very strong marriage is in danger of coming apart. He is beaten. He accepts his wife's ultimatum: They will leave Washington. He will leave the Justice Department and go back to private practice, a part of him dead. The most professional part. Hoover has won.

Another space. It is past midnight. Alex's family are in bed. He has remained downstairs in his living room, a single table lamp on, the light dim, shadows everywhere. He has been drinking heavily. Mingled with his fear is the realization that everything he has believed in is meaningless.

In his drunken state he passes a window. Frightened, he parts the drapes and peers outside. He sees an FBI car parked down the block. Men are watching his house.

His mind snaps. The alcohol, the fear, the depression, and the anxiety combine to produce hysteria. He rushes to the front door and goes outside. He does not yell or scream; instead he imposes a grotesque silence on himself, a *conspiratorial* silence. In his drunkenness he wants to reach his tormentors and surrender, to throw himself at their mercy, to become one of them. His panic is identical to his psychological collapse in wartime years ago.

He runs down the block. The car is gone;

he hears voices in the darkness, but he can see no one. He races around the streets after the unseen voices, a part of him wondering if he's gone mad, another part desperately wanting only to surrender, to give up to the victors and plead for their forgiveness.

He doesn't know how long he's been running, but the night air, the heavy breathing, and the physical strain reduce the effects of the alcohol. He begins to take hold of himself. He starts back toward his house, unsure of the streets. He must have run several miles.

As he walks, he spots the FBI car. It is around a corner, in shadows. There's no one inside; the men who have followed him, watched him, abused him, are walking too, in the dark, quiet streets.

He hears footsteps in the darkness. Behind him, in front of him, to the right, to the left. They fall into the rhythm of his heartbeat, becoming louder, until they're like kettledrums; menacing, deafening.

He recognizes a street sign; he knows where he is. He begins to run again; the footsteps keep pace, producing the panic once more. He races in the middle of the street, turning corners, running like a maniac.

He sees his house. He is suddenly alarmed further, filled with a new fear that is overpowering. He had left the front door open. And there is a strange automobile parked in front of the curb.

He runs faster toward the strange car, prepared to kill if need be.

But the man inside the automobile arrived only minutes ago. He has been there waiting, thinking that perhaps Alex had taken a dog for a walk, carelessly leaving the door open.

"At five-thirty tomorrow afternoon, go to the Carteret Hotel. Room 1201. Take the elevator to the top floor, then walk down the stairs to the twelfth floor. We'll have men watching. If you're followed, we'll throw them off."

"What is all this? Who are you?"

"A man wants to meet with you. He's a senator."

"Peter, where are you?" It was Alison, her startled voice carried from the living room. The sound brought him back to the other world, the real one.

"In the kitchen," he called out, his eyes on his suitcase; the leather was still damp, the scraping obvious. "I'll be right there," he said.

"Don't bother," Alison replied, her relief obvious. "There should be coffee in the 'fridge, and the pot's in the upper right cabinet."

"I found them," he answered, picking up the suitcase, turning it around, and placing it in the corner. "The coffee didn't turn out so well. I'll try again."

He went quickly to the table, brought the pot back to the sink, and began dismantling the antiquated mechanism. He threw the used grounds into an empty grocery bag and turned on the faucet.

Seconds later Alison came through the door, a blanket wrapped around her. Their eyes met, the message —the communication—clear. At the sight of her Peter ached; the ache was pleasant and warm.

"You've come into my life," she said softly. "I wonder if you'll stay."

"I wondered the same about you. In my life."

"We'll see, won't we?"

19

Varak came through the door of Bravo's study without the usual knock."

"It's more than one man," he said. "Or if it's one man, he's commanding others. They've made their first overt move. Chancellor thinks it's directed to the girl. It's not, of course; it's meant for him."

"They want to stop him, then." Bravo did not ask a question.

"And if he won't be stopped," added Varak, "throw him off the scent. Decoy him."

"Please explain."

"I've run the tapes. You can hear them if you like. And see them—both audio and video. They tore apart MacAndrew's study, searching for something . . . or giving the illusion of searching. I tend to favor the latter. The decoy was in the name. *Chasŏng.* They want him to think it's a key."

"Chasŏng?" said Bravo, reflecting. "That goes back a long time, if I'm not mistaken. I remember Truman exploding over it. The Battle of Chasŏng, Korea."

"Yes. Five minutes ago I got a computer readout from G-Two archives. Chasŏng was our worst defeat north of the thirty-eighth parallel. It was an unauthorized attack——"

"For minor real estate," interrupted St. Claire. "A few meaningless hills. It was the first in a series of debacles that eventually led to MacArthur's dismissal."

"The printout doesn't put it quite that way, of course."

"Of course. So?"

"MacAndrew was a colonel then. He was one of the commanders."

Bravo reflected. "Does Chasŏng correspond in time with the missing data in MacAndrew's service record?"

"Approximately. If it's the decoy, it would have to. Whoever has Hoover's files can't know precisely what MacAndrew told Chancellor. A panicked man under the stress of being discovered will often base his cover in accurate chronology and false information."

" 'While the bank was being robbed ten days ago, I was at the movies.' "

"Exactly."

"Lifted to this level, it becomes quite cerebral, doesn't it?"

"The chess tournament's begun. I think you should hear and see the tapes."

"Very well."

The two men walked quickly out of Bravo's study to the brass-grilled elevator at the rear of the front hall. A minute later St. Claire and Varak walked into the small studio in the basement complex. The equipment was set to run.

"We'll start at the beginning. It's the videotape." Varak switched on the video projector. The blank lead-in tape produced a white square on the wall. "The camera was too obvious to place inside the house. Incidentally, it's tripped electronically. Please remember that."

The image of MacAndrew's house was thrown on the wall. But the light was not that of early evening, the time when Chancellor and the girl had arrived. Instead, there was bright sunlight.

The agent snapped a switch. The tape stopped; a still picture remained on the wall. "Yes," said Varak. "The camera was tripped. It's very sensitive. The timer tells us it was three o'clock in the afternoon. Someone has entered the house, obviously from the rear, out of camera range." He snapped the switch again; the tape continued. Then it stopped again. The projector shut off automatically. Again, St. Claire looked quizzically at Varak.

"They're in the house now. The trip's deactivated. We go to audio." The agent pressed a button on his audio tape machine.

There were the sounds of footsteps, a door being opened, the squeak of a hinge, more footsteps, the opening of a second door. "There are two men," said Varak. "Or possibly one man and a heavy woman. According to the decibel count, each weighs over a hundred and fifty pounds." There was an indistinguishable series of rustling sounds and then a strange, eerie bleat. It came again, now more pronounced and, in its way, quite terrible. Varak spoke. "It's an animal. Sheep family, I think. But perhaps a pig. I'll refine it later."

The next minutes were taken up with harsh, swift sounds. Paper cut, leather and fabric sliced, drawers opened. Finally there was the smashing of glass, interspersed with the strident squeals of the unknown animal, squeals that suddenly erupted into a screech.

"The animal is being killed." Varak spoke simply.

"Good God!" said St. Claire.

Then from the speakers came a human voice. Two words.

Let's go.

The tape stopped. Varak turned off the machine. "We'll pick up approximately three hours later. With the arrival of Chancellor and MacAndrew's daughter. There's a twenty-second video still of the house; that's the intruders leaving—again out of range, so we have no picture of them." The agent paused as if unsure of how to explain something. "I've edited out a particular section, and with your permission I'll destroy it. It's irrelevant. It merely establishes the fact that Chancellor and the girl have formed a relationship. Temporary, probably."

"I understand and I thank you," said Bravo.

The house once again appeared briefly on the wall. It was night now. A car was seen driving up to the stone path leading to the front door. Alison emerged and stood for a moment looking at the house. She proceeded up the path. Chancellor came into view carrying grocery bags. They paused on the small porch, talked briefly, and then the girl opened her purse and searched for a key. Taking it out, she opened the door.

The two seemed startled at something. A further discussion ensued, more animated than before, and then they went inside. With the closing of the door the videotape stopped. Without speaking, Varak reached over and pressed the audio button.

Come on, we'll put the bags in the kitchen. The girl. Footsteps, the rustling of paper, the metallic squeak of a hinge, and then a prolonged silence followed. The woman finally spoke again.

My father reconstructed wherever possible the types of surroundings she associated with her childhood.

Chancellor: *It's an extraordinary love story.*

It was an extraordinary sacrifice. The girl.

You resented her, didn't you. Chancellor.

Yes, I did. He was an exceptional man. . . .

Suddenly Varak reached over and snapped the switch. "That's the key. The *mother*. I'd stake everything I know on it. Chasŏng's a decoy. For the next half hour, listen very, *very* carefully. The writer in Chancellor honed in on her instinctively, but she dissuaded him. Not intentionally, because I don't think she knows."

"I shall listen most carefully, Mr. Varak."

They both did. Several times Bravo was forced to dart his eyes away, at nothing, in response to the unexpected: at the girl's scream from inside her father's study, at the sobs and the tears that followed, at Chancellor's compassion and sharp interrogation. The writer's imagination would not be stopped. His original premise was right, St. Claire reflected. In less than nine weeks Chancellor had made extraordinary progress. Neither he nor Varak knew how or why, but the murder of Walter Rawlins was related to the files somehow, and now there was this maverick general, his outspoken daughter, and a decoy called Chasŏng. Above all, the overt move had been made. Men had come out of the dark, the sounds of their actions recorded.

St. Claire did not know where Chancellor was taking them. Only that Hoover's files were closer.

The images appeared once again on the wall: Chancellor coming out of the house, opening the car door, and recoiling. Then cautiously walking around the car, picking up a rook, running into the foliage, returning, throwing two indistinguishable objects out of the car, removing the suitcases, and going back into the house.

Sound then: running water and scraping.

"An hour ago I stopped the tape and studied the picture. He's removing the name Chasŏng from the suitcase," Varak explained. "He doesn't want the girl to see it."

Silence ensued. The microphones picked up the scratching of a pencil against paper. Varak jumped the tape to the sound of recorded voices.

Peter, where are you?

In the kitchen. . . .

A discussion about making coffee, rapid footsteps, obscure movement.

You've come into my life. I wonder if you'll stay. Spoken softly by Alison MacAndrew.

I wondered the same about you. In my life.

We'll see, won't we?

It was over. Varak turned off the machine and stood up. Bravo remained in the chair, his aristocratic fingers joined together under his chin.

"That scratching we heard," he said. "Can we presume he was writing?"

"I think so. It fits his habits."

"Remarkable, isn't it? In the midst of it all, he turned to his novel."

"Unusual, perhaps. I don't know how remarkable. If we're doing things right, his novel is becoming very real to him."

Bravo disengaged his fingers and placed his hands on the arms of the chair. "Which brings us to that novel and your interpretation of it. As inconceivable as I find it, do you still believe our quarry is a member of Inver Brass?"

"First, let me ask a question. When I asked you to

call a meeting the night before last, did you give the members the information I thought advisable? That Chancellor had met the girl?"

"I would have told you if I hadn't."

"I knew you disapproved."

"My disapproval was based on my conviction. That same conviction led me to follow your instructions, if only to prove you wrong." Bravo's speech was clipped, bordering on the disagreeable. "Now, what's your answer? Are you still convinced a member of Inver Brass has those files?"

"I'll know within a day or two."

"Which is no answer."

"It's the best I can do. Frankly I think I'm right; everything points to it."

St. Claire sat up. "Because I told them about Chancellor and the girl and gave them MacAndrew's name?"

"Not just the name," replied Varak. "The fact that eight months is missing from his service record."

"Inconclusive! Whoever has Hoover's files knows it."

"Precisely. That decoy—the diversionary Chasŏng—occurred during those eight months. I think we can assume that whatever happened at Chasŏng, whatever military decisions MacAndrew made or refused to make, could not have been sufficiently damaging to cause him to resign. If they had, there were enough men at the Pentagon who would have forced him out long ago."

"A disagreeable incident, perhaps," Bravo agreed, "but not a disastrous one. A part of the file, but not the vital part."

"A cover for it," agreed Varak. "Something else happened, possibly related, possibly not. Assuming there's a primary connection—which we must assume—it's that something else that can lead us to whoever has Hoover's files."

"Then, what you're telling me is"—St. Claire's eyes strayed—"that given the twenty-four-hour period between Inver Brass's meeting and Chancellor's arrival at MacAndrew's house, the decoy was culled from the files. The other night was the first Inver Brass had heard of Chancellor, to say nothing of MacAndrew."

"The first Inver Brass—as a *group*—had heard of Chancellor. But not whoever has the files. He knew because Chancellor made contact with two of the victims.

MacAndrew and Rawlins. I don't think there's any question that they were victims."

"All right, I'll accept that." Bravo got out of the chair. "So then, it boils down to one specific piece of information: Peter Chancellor had made contact with the general's daughter. They were on their way to the Rockville house. And rather than have the encounter lead to a blank wall, the Chasŏng ruse is planted. To send Chancellor off in another direction."

"That's it," said Varak firmly. "Otherwise, why use Chasŏng at *all*?"

"Still," said St. Claire, "why does it have to be a member of Inver Brass?"

"Because no one else knew that Chancellor had made contact with the girl. I can assure you of that. Except for our taps his phones are sterile; there is no surveillance on him but our own. Yet, within twelve hours of Inver Brass's meeting MacAndrew's house is broken into and an elaborate deception is mounted for Chancellor. Those twelve hours were enough to examine MacAndrew's dossier and come up with the Chasŏng decoy."

St. Claire nodded sadly. "You're very convincing."

"The facts are convincing. I wish they weren't."

"God knows, so do I. A member of Inver Brass! The most honored men in the nation. You speak of probability. That's one I would have considered nonexistent."

"Chancellor didn't. For him it was defined at the outset. You said it yourself when we began: He's not restricted by fact or conditioning. Incidentally, he calls *his* Inver Brass the Nucleus."

St. Claire stared at the wall where minutes before the images had been projected. "The reality and the fantasy. It's extraordinary." He let the words trail off.

"It's what we wanted," said Varak. "What we hoped for."

"Yes, of course. You'll know for certain within a day or two, you say?"

"I'll guarantee it if you'll call another meeting. After MacAndrew's funeral. I want two more names fed to Inver Brass."

"Oh? Who?"

"The first is a newspaper columnist, Phyllis Maxwell. She's——"

"I know who she is. Why?"

"I'm not sure—she hasn't surfaced before. But Chancellor's met her, and he's written a character into his novel that bears a striking resemblance to her."

"I see. Who's the other?"

Varak hesitated. It was obvious he expected resistance. "Paul Bromley. The man from General Services Administration."

"No!" The diplomat reacted emphatically. "I won't permit it. Bromley has my word! For one thing, it doesn't make sense. Bromley begins with *B*. We're after names from *M* to *Z*!"

"Remember, Bromley's code name is Viper," replied Varak. "It's been in continuous use at the Pentagon, G-Two, and the bureau for over twenty months. He's been out of sight since August; he's virtually disappeared. He's dangerous to a lot of people in Washington, but no one's heard from him. Viper's the forgotten man, and thus he's ideal for our purposes."

Bravo paced slowly. "The man's suffered so much. You're asking a lot."

"Minor compared to our objective. From what I know about Bromley, I believe he'd be the first to agree."

St. Claire closed his eyes, thinking of the anguish Bromley had lived through. The aging, irascible accountant who had had the courage to take on the Pentagon by himself. His reward was an addicted daughter, who, missing for three years, had returned as an unbalanced killer; and now that his world was stable again, the nightmare promised to return. He was to be used as bait.

But in his field, in the dark corners of his exotic profession, Stefan Varak was brilliant. And he was right.

"Go to work," St. Claire said. "I'll convene Inver Brass tonight."

The drum rolls were soft. Muted intrusions of thunder carried on the December wind. The grave was in the north section of Arlington Cemetery. The honor guard stood on the west flank. The rigid phalanx carried the Army's unspoken command: *The coffin will be taken this far, and no further. It will then be lowered beneath the earth. We are here in military splendor to demand respect. It shall be rendered. But silently. There will be no signs of private grief, for these are not seemly. This is Army ground. We are men. Dead men.*

It was frightening, thought Chancellor, standing several feet behind Alison, who was seated in a single, plain black chair at the foot of the cordoned-off area. One did not touch, one did not relate. To anything except the ritual.

We are put to rest by the numbers. Count off!

Around the square gravesite, beyond the chains, stood the senior officers of the Pentagon. A dozen or so had come up to Alison, speaking softly, holding her hands. She was the Greek chorus that told Peter who the players were in relation to her father. And he kept his eyes alert. It was entirely possible that someone at that gravesite held the secret of Chasŏng. He could only study the faces and allow his imagination free rein.

There was one man, roughly the same age as MacAndrew, who caught Peter's attention. He was a major, and he was dark-complexioned. Mediterranean heritage, Chancellor thought. He stood silently throughout the brief service, talking to no one. When the coffin was carried from the hearse across the lawn to the grave, the man's eyes remained front; he did not acknowledge the presence of the deceased.

It was only during the chaplain's eulogy that the major showed any sign of emotion. It was brief—barely a flash—in his eyes, at the corners of his mouth. The expression was one of hatred.

Peter kept looking at him. For a moment the major seemed aware that he was being watched, and for an instant he locked eyes with Chancellor. The hatred flashed again and disappeared. He looked away.

When the service was over and the flag given to the daughter of the buried soldier, the officers came up one by one to say the expected words.

But the dark-complexioned major turned and walked away without saying anything. Peter watched him. He reached the slope of a small hill beyond the serrated ranks of graves and stopped. Slowly he turned and looked back, an isolated figure standing above the headstones.

Chancellor had the instinctive feeling that the major wanted a last look at MacAndrew's grave, as though to convince himself that the object of his loathing was really dead. It was a bleakly curious moment.

"I could feel your eyes behind me," said Alison as they settled back in the limousine that would take them out of Arlington Cemetery into Washington. "I glanced at you once. You were studying the crowd. And I know you heard every word said to me. Did you find anyone—or anything—interesting?"

"Yes," replied Peter. "A major. An Italian-looking fellow, or Spanish. He didn't come up to you. He was the only one of the officers who didn't."

Alison looked out the window at the passing rows of graves. She kept her voice low so as not to be heard by the army chauffeur and the escort. "Yes, I saw him."

"Then, you had to see the way he acted. It was strange."

"It was normal. For him. He wears his resentments like decorations. They're *part* of his decorations."

"Who is he?"

"His name is Pablo Ramirez. He's from San Juan, one of the first appointments to West Point from the territory. I guess you'd call him the token Hispanic, before anyone knew what the term meant."

"Did he know your father?"

"Yes. They served together. Ramirez was two years behind him at the Point."

Peter touched her arm. "Did they serve together in Korea?"

"You mean Chasŏng?"

"Yes."

"I don't know. Korea, yes. Also in North Africa in World War Two, and several years ago in Vietnam. But I don't know about Chasŏng."

"I'd like to find out. Why did he resent your father?"

"I'm not sure he did. Any more than he resented anyone else. I said *resentments*. Plural."

"Why?"

"He's still a major. Most of his contemporaries are light colonels, full birds, or brigadiers."

"Is his resentment justified? Did he get passed over because he's Puerto Rican?"

"Oh, I suppose, partially. It's a pretty closed society in those regions. And I've heard the jokes: 'Be careful if you take Ramirez to a fleet cocktail party. They'll put a jacket on him.' In the navy the P.R.'s are houseboys. That sort of thing."

"That sort of thing justifies a lot of resentment."

"I'm sure it does, but it's not the whole picture.

Ramirez was given a great many opportunities—more than most—perhaps because he *was* a member of a minority. He hasn't done much with them."

Peter glanced out the window, vaguely troubled. The look he had seen in Ramirez's eyes was specific hatred, directed at specific objects. MacAndrew's coffin. MacAndrew's grave. MacAndrew.

"What did your father think of him?" he asked.

"About what I just told you. He was a lightweight, hotheaded and too emotional. Not at all reliable. Dad refused to second two field promotions for him. Beyond that, he didn't say much."

"What did he mean, 'not at all reliable'?"

Alison frowned. "I'd have to think. It was in the areas of recap and recon, I believe."

"That's nice. I haven't the vaguest idea what you're talking about."

She laughed. "Sorry. They're written reports to field headquarters. Combat summaries and reconnaissance."

"That doesn't help much, but I think I know what you mean. Your father was saying that Ramirez was a liar. Either emotionally or by design."

"I guess so. He's not important, Peter." Alison placed her hand on his. "It's over. Finished, past, *over*. Thank you, thank you more than I can ever say."

"We're not 'over,' " he said.

She held his eyes. "I hope not." Then she smiled. "A hotel's a beautiful idea. We'll luxuriate for a whole day and not think about anything. I'm sick of thinking. Then tomorrow I'll go see the lawyer and take care of things. I don't want you to feel you have to stay. I'll be back in New York in a few days."

Chancellor was startled; he wondered if she'd forgotten. So abruptly, so completely. He held her hand, not wanting her to pull away. "But there's the house in Maryland. Men broke in and——"

"Oh, God! Let it go! He's dead. They made their point, whatever it was."

"We'll talk about it later," he said.

"All right."

Peter understood. Alison had faced the agony of her father's death and the further anguish of examining that death. At the burial she had confronted the men who had tried to destroy him. The service at Arlington was a symbol for her: The Gordian knot had been severed; she was free to find her own world. And now he was asking her to go back.

He had to. Because it wasn't over. He knew it and so did she.

Chancellor knew something else, too. Alison had said that Ramirez was not important.

He was.

20

Once again the limousines arrived at the Georgetown house at different times, from different points of origin. Once again silent drivers had met their passengers sight unseen. Inver Brass convened.

It had been an unspoken agreement for many weeks between the elders—Bravo, Venice, and Christopher— that the choice of a new Genesis was between the two remaining younger men: Banner and Paris.

Beyond doubt, each was qualified, each brilliant, each extraordinary in several fields.

Banner had come to Inver Brass six years ago. He had been the youngest president in the history of a major eastern university, but he had left to assume chairmanship of the international Roxton Foundation. His name was Frederick Wells, and his expertise was in global finance. And yet, in spite of the worldwide impact of his decisions, Wells had never lost sight of the fundamental human need for dignity, respect, and the freedoms of choice and expression. Wells believed deeply in human beings, with all their flaws, and those who sought to repress human beings or shape them or dominate them felt his wrath.

As John Edgar Hoover had unknowingly felt it.

Paris was the newest recruit; he had joined Inver Brass barely four years before. He was a scholar. His ancestral roots were in Castile, but his own were fervently planted in America, where his family had fled to escape the Falangists. His name was Carlos Montelán. Presently, he occupied the Maynard Chair of International Relations at Harvard and was considered the country's most perceptive analyst of twentieth-century geopolitical thought. For a dozen years succeeding administrations had tried to recruit Montelán into the State Department, but he had demurred. He was a scholar, not an activist. He knew the intrinsic dangers that existed when theoreticians moved into the swift world of pragmatic negotiations.

Yet Montelán never stopped probing, never ceased his questioning of men and their motives—whether personal or related to a larger cause. And when he found one or both without merit, or destructive, he did not hesitate to make an active decision.

As he had not hesitated in the case of John Edgar Hoover.

Bravo had put off the selection of either contender, in spite of Christopher's urging. Christopher was Jacob Dreyfus, a banker, and last of the Jewish patriarchs, whose house rivaled the Baruchs' and the Lehmans'. Christopher was eighty and knew his time was short; it was important to him that Inver Brass install its leader. A house without a man to give it direction was no house at all. And for Jacob Dreyfus there was no "house" in this beloved land as vital as the one he had helped found— Inver Brass.

He had said as much to Bravo, and Munro St. Claire knew that no one said it better than Jacob. St. Claire had been there at the beginning, too, as had Daniel Sutherland, the black giant whose extraordinary intellect had carried him from the fields of Alabama to the highest judicial circles in the country. But neither Bravo nor Venice could summon the words that defined Inver Brass as well as Christopher could.

As Jacob Dreyfus expressed it, Inver Brass had been born in chaos, at a time when the nation was being torn apart, on the edge of self-destruction. The market had collapsed, business had ground to a halt; factories had been closed, storefronts boarded up, farms allowed to fall into disuse as cattle died and machinery rusted. The inevitable explosions of violence had begun to take place.

In Washington inept leaders had been incapable of action. So in the last months of 1929 Inver Brass had been formed. The first Genesis had been a Scotsman, an investment banker who'd followed the advice of Baruch and Dreyfus and had gotten out of the market. It had been he who had given the group its name, after a small marshland lake in the Highlands that was not on any map. For Inver Brass had to exist in secrecy. It operated outside the government bureaucracy because it had to operate swiftly, without encumbrances.

Massive sums of money had been transferred to countless distressed areas where violence—born of need—had erupted. Throughout the country the sharp edges of that violence had been dulled by the wealth of Inver Brass; the fires had been dampened, contained within acceptable limits.

But mistakes had been made, corrected as soon as they'd been understood. Some had gone beyond repair. The Depression had been worldwide; infusions of capital had been required beyond the nation's shores.

There was Germany. The economic devastations of the Versailles Treaty, the inadequacy of the Locarno pacts, the impracticality of the Dawes Plan—they were all misunderstood, the men of Inver Brass had thought. And that had been their most calamitous mistake. One that thirty-five years later a graduate student named Peter Chancellor began to perceive as the one thing it was *not*. A conspiracy of global politics.

He had to be stopped, this young man Chancellor. Inver Brass was in the shadows of his imagination, and he did not know it.

But the mistake had led the men of Inver Brass into new territory. They had entered the realm of national policy. At first it was to try to rectify the errors they had made. But later it was because they could contribute. Inver Brass had the wisdom and the resources. It could act and react swiftly, without interference, answerable to no one but its collective conscience.

Munro St. Claire and Daniel Sutherland had listened to Jacob's impassioned plea for the quick appointment of a new Genesis. Neither replied with any passion at all. Each had agreed without conviction, essentially saying nothing. St. Claire knew that Sutherland could not know what he knew: There was the possibility Inver Brass harbored a traitor. So Sutherland's doubts had to lie elsewhere. St. Claire thought he knew what those doubts were: The days of Inver Brass were coming to a close. Perhaps they would end with the elders, and maybe it was better that way. Time mandates change; they were from another era.

St. Claire's doubts were much more specific. It was why he could not permit the elevation of a new Genesis. Not from either contender. For if there was a traitor in Inver Brass, it was either Banner or Paris.

They sat around the circular table, the empty Genesis chair a reminder of their essential impermanence. There was no need for a fire in the Franklin stove. No papers would have to be burned; none were on the table, nor would there be any. No coded reports had been delivered, for there were no decisions to make, only information to be imparted and comments to be heard.

A trap was to be set. First, developments had to be described in such a way that St. Claire could observe the reaction of each man at that table. And then two names would be given: Phyllis Maxwell, journalist; Paul Bromley —code: Viper—vanished critic of the Pentagon. Vanished, but easily traced by any man at that table.

"Our meeting will be short this evening," said Bravo. "The purpose is to bring you up to date and hear anything you might have to say regarding the new developments."

"I trust that includes a comment on past decisions," said Paris.

"It includes anything you like."

"Good," continued Paris. "Since the other evening, I've picked up two books by Peter Chancellor. I'm not sure why you chose him. True, he has a quick mind and a flair for prose, but he's hardly a writer of lasting distinction."

"We weren't looking for literary merit."

"Neither am I. And I don't discount the popular novel. I merely refer to this specific writer. Is he as capable as perhaps a dozen others? Why him?"

"Because we knew him," interjected Christopher. "We don't know a dozen others."

"I beg your pardon?" Paris leaned forward.

"Christopher's point is well taken," said Bravo. "We know a great deal about Chancellor. Six years ago we had reason to learn. You both know the history of Inver Brass; we've concealed nothing from you. Our contributions, our errors. In the late sixties Chancellor was writing . . ." Bravo paused and addressed Paris—"an analytical dissertation on the Weimar collapse and the emergence of militant Germany. He came very close to identifying Inver Brass. He had to be stopped."

There was silence around the table. St. Claire knew that the Negro and, more profoundly, the Jew were thinking about those days. Each in his own anguish.

"That dissertation," clarified Banner, staring at Paris, "became the novel *Reichstag!*"

"Wasn't that dangerous?" asked Paris.

"It was fair," replied Venice.

"It was also fiction," added Christopher disagreeably.

"That answers my question," said Paris. "It was a matter of familiarity as much as anything. Better a known entity with its limitations than an unknown one with greater promise."

"Why do you persist in discrediting Chancellor?" asked Venice. "We're after Hoover's files, not literary distinction."

"Subjective comparisons," answered the scholar. "He's the type of writer that annoys me. I know something about the events of Sarajevo and the conditions prevalent at the time. I read his book. He bases his conclusions on intentionally misinterpreted facts and on exaggerated associations. Yet I'm sure thousands of readers accept what he writes as authentic history."

Bravo leaned back in his chair. "I read that book too, and know something about the events leading up to Sarajevo. Would you say that Chancellor's inclusion of the industrial conspiracy was in error?"

"Of course not. It's been established."

"Then, regardless of how he arrived at it, he was correct."

Paris smiled. "If you'll forgive me, I'm relieved that you don't teach history. But as I said, my question is answered. What are the new developments?"

"The developments constitute authentic progress; they can be termed nothing else." Bravo proceeded to describe Chancellor's driving with Alison to Kennedy Airport, their meeting with the military escort, and the arrival of the plane bearing the general's coffin. As Varak had suggested, St. Claire spoke slowly, watching for any reaction that would indicate someone at the table anticipated his words because the events were known to him. It would be in the eyes, Varak had said. A brief, clouded response that was recognition. Certain chemical changes could not be concealed; the eyes were the microscope.

St. Claire found no such reactions. No such responses. Only total absorption from each member at the table.

He proceeded to describe what had been heard on the tape, what had been seen on film.

"Without Varak's preparations we wouldn't have learned of the extraordinary action taken against Chancellor. And it *was* against Chancellor, not MacAndrew's daughter. We believe it's an attempt to throw him off course; to convince him . MacAndrew's resignation was the result of command decisions made years ago in Korea, at a place called Chasŏng."

Paris's eyes widened; he reacted visibly. Then he spoke. "The killers of Chasŏng. . . ."

A sharp pain shot through St. Claire's chest; he lost his breath, unable for a moment to find it. He struggled for control as he looked sharply at Carlos Montelán.

The words Paris spoke were chilling to him. There was no way Paris could have known them! Nowhere on the tapes had the phrase been employed, and St. Claire had not used it!

"What does that mean?" asked Venice, shifting his large frame in the chair.

"As any military historian will tell you, it was an epithet used to characterize the officers at the Battle of Chasŏng," said Paris. "It was suicidal madness. Troops revolted up and down the lines; many were shot by their own officers. It was a disastrous strategy, in some ways the political turning point of the war. If MacAndrew was there, it's quite possible a long-dormant victim may have surfaced. It *could* be his motive for resigning."

St. Claire watched Paris closely, relieved by the academic's explanation.

"Could it be related to his death in Hawaii?" asked Christopher, his gnarled hands trembling as he spoke.

"No," replied Bravo slowly. "MacAndrew was shot by Longworth."

"You mean Varak?" asked an incredulous Wells.

"No," said Bravo. "The real Longworth. In Hawaii."

It was as though a loud whip had been cracked. Eyes were riveted on St. Claire.

"How? *Why?*" Anger was in Venice's voice. Daniel Sutherland was outraged.

"It was unpredictable and therefore uncontrollable.

As you know, Varak used Longworth's name with Chancellor. It was a source he could check, a springboard. Chancellor gave the name to MacAndrew, told him that Longworth had access to the files. After his wife died, the general flew halfway across the world to find Longworth. He found him."

"Then MacAndrew presumed that only Longworth knew what happened at Chasŏng," said Frederick Wells thoughtfully. "That the information was in Hoover's files and nowhere else."

"And *that* leads us nowhere. Except back to the files." Once again Christopher spoke disagreeably.

"It does help," added Banner, looking at Bravo. "It confirms what you say. Chasŏng is a diversion."

"Why?" asked Venice.

Wells turned to the judge. "Because there was no reason for it. Why was it used at all?"

"I agree." St. Claire leaned forward, his composure regained. The first part of Varak's trap had produced nothing. It was the moment for the second, the two names. "As I told you the other night, Chancellor is well into his novel. Varak managed to get his hands on the manuscript. There are two rather startling developments. I should say, two people have surfaced, neither of whom were considered previously. We don't know why. One is a thinly disguised character in the book, the other a man in Chancellor's notes—a man he is trying to find. The first is the newspaper columnist, Phyllis Maxwell. The second, an accountant named Bromley, Paul Bromley. He used to be with General Services. Do any of you have any particular information on either of these people?"

None did. But the names were planted, the second trap set. If there was substance in Varak's conclusions, St. Claire wondered which of them would be caught. Banner or Paris? Frederick Wells or Carlos Montelán.

The conversation trailed off. Bravo indicated that Inver Brass's meeting was over. He pushed back his chair but was stopped by Wells's voice.

"Is Varak outside in the hallway?"

"Yes, of course," answered the diplomat. "He's made arrangements for your departures, as usual."

"I'd like to ask him a question. I'll address it first to all of you. There were microphones inside the Rockville house. You describe the sounds of men breaking in and ransacking MacAndrew's study but no words to accompany these sounds. Outside, a camera is triggered but shows nothing because the intruders were out of visual range. It's almost as if they knew about the equipment."

"What's your question?" asked Montelán, a sharp edge to his voice. "I'm not sure I like the implication."

Banner looked at Paris. It was unmistakable, thought St. Claire. Lines were drawn. Lines? Lions, perhaps. The young standing up against the aging and each other, growling for leadership of the pride.

"I find it curious. The files were taken in such a way—at such a time—as to indicate the thieves anticipated Hoover's death. Months of intensive investigation led nowhere; one of the best intelligence specialists in this country reports that he's made no progress. Bravo conceives of the idea of using this writer Chancellor to probe. Our intelligence specialist expedites the plan; the writer is programmed and begins his work. As expected, he creates a disturbance. Those who have Hoover's files are alarmed and make their move against him. A move, I submit, that should have been sufficient for them to be trapped. But we have no one on film, no voices on a tape."

Montelán leaned forward in his chair. "Are you suggesting——?"

"I'm suggesting," interrupted Banner, "that although our specialist is known for his thoroughness, there was a conspicuous absence of it yesterday."

"Too much!" Christopher exploded. His gaunt features were pinched, his bony fingers trembled. "Have you any idea who Varak *is*? What he's *seen* in his life? What *drives* him?"

"I know he's filled with hatred," replied Banner softly. "And that frightens me."

There was silence at the table. The essential truth of Frederick Wells's statement had its effect. It was possible that Stefan Varak had operated on a different level from them, motivated by a hatred unknown to anyone in that room.

St. Claire remembered Varak's words: *I'll seek out the Nazi in any form he is revived in and go after him. If you think there's any difference between what those files represent and the objectives of the Third Reich, you're very much mistaken.*

Once the Nazi was found and destroyed, what better way to control his disciples than to control the files?

Bravo pushed his chair back and rose from the table. He went to a cabinet in the wall, unlocked it, and took out a short-barreled, .38-caliber pistol. He closed the cabinet, returned to his chair, and sat down. The weapon was in his hand, out of sight.

"Will you ask Mr. Varak to come in, please?"

Stefan Varak stood behind the empty Genesis chair studying the members of Inver Brass. St. Claire watched him closely, until Varak's eyes met his.

"Mr. Varak, we have a question to ask you. We would appreciate a concise answer. Proceed, if you will, Banner."

Wells did so. "Mr. Varak, through Chancellor you anticipated an event that could have led us to Hoover's files," he concluded. "One identification, visually or by a voice print. You set the trap, which presumes you understood its importance. Yet your acknowledged thoroughness, your professionalism, was not in evidence. I ask myself why. It would have been a simple matter to have positioned two, three, six cameras, if necessary. Had you done so, the hunt might have been over now, the files in our possession. Why, Mr. Varak? Or why not?"

The blood rushed to Varak's blond head; he was flushed with anger. All the signs he had taught Bravo to look for were apparent in the teacher. Did anger, like fear, produce the uncontrollable chemical changes Varak had spoken of? St. Claire moved the pistol on his lap and inserted his finger over the trigger.

And then the moment passed. Varak imposed self-control. "It's a fair question," he said calmly. "I'll answer it as concisely as I can. As you know, I work alone except in rare instances where I employ others who can never trace my identity. A case in point was a taxi driver in New York. He picked up Chancellor and the girl and drove them to the airport; their conversation was taped. The driver reached me in Washington and played it over the telephone. It was the first I heard about their staying in Rockville. I had very little time to get my equipment, drive out to the house, and install it. I was fortunate to mount even one camera with the proper infrared film. That's my answer."

Again the silence as the members of Inver Brass

studied Varak. Beneath the table St. Claire removed his finger from the trigger. He had spent a lifetime learning to discern the truth when he heard it. In his judgment he had just heard the truth.

He hoped to God he was right.

21

Habit caused Peter to wake up at four thirty in the morning. Custom willed him to get out of bed, go to his briefcase on a bedroom chair, and remove his leather notebook.

They were in a suite at the Hay-Adams, and it was Alison's introduction to his odd hours of work.

She heard him and bolted upright in the bed.

"Is there a fire?"

"I'm sorry. I didn't think you'd hear me."

"I know I can't see you. It's dark out. What happened?"

"Nothing happened. It's morning. It's when I like to work. Go back to sleep. I'll be in the next room."

Alison fell back into the pillow, shaking her head. Peter smiled and carried his notebook into the sitting room. To the coffee table and the couch.

Three hours later he had finished the eighth chapter. He had not referred to the outline; it was not necessary. He knew the emotions he was defining for Alexander Meredith. He had been gripped with fear; he had panicked. He knew what it was to be the object of a violent chase; he had heard racing footsteps in the darkness.

Alison awoke shortly before eight. He joined her and they made love. Slowly, enfolded in each other, each awakened response more lovely, more exciting than the last, until they were caught in the desperate rhythm of their combined hunger, neither allowing the other to lessen the intensity.

And they fell asleep in each other's arms, the comfort each sought found in the other.

They awoke at ten thirty, had breakfast in the room, and began thinking about the rest of the day. Peter had promised her a day of "luxuriating"; he wanted to provide it. She deserved it. As he watched her across the breakfast table, he was struck by something that he should have noticed before. In spite of the strain and the sadness Alison had a quality of quiet humor within her; it was never far away.

Cathy had had that quality.

Peter reached across the table for her hand. She took it smiling, her eyes searching his with kindness.

The telephone rang. It was her father's lawyer. There were various papers to sign and government forms to be filled out and legal rights to be understood. The general's will was simple, but the army's death procedures were not. Would Alison please be at his office at two o'clock? If there were no complications, she'd be finished by five.

Chancellor promised that they would luxuriate tomorrow. Actually they would start at one minute after five.

Because the next day, Peter thought to himself, he would bring up the subject of the Rockville house.

Alison left at one thirty for the lawyer's office. Chancellor returned to his leather notebook.

Chapter 9 — Outline

The chapter's objective is the meeting of Alex Meredith and the senator. It will take place in the hotel room after a harrowing chase during which Alex *must* elude those following him. In meeting the senator, Alex becomes aware that there is a group of powerful men willing to fight Hoover. He is not alone. It is the beginning of his journey back to sanity.

He accepts the dangers that will face him now, for there are people he can turn to; his dependence on them is established immediately. His relief is given added impact by the senator's revelation of the identities of his two closest associates: the former cabinet officer and the newspaperwoman. They, too, want to meet with Meredith.

There is a plan. Alex does not know what it is, but the fact that one exists is enough. He is committed without fully understanding his own commitment.

The hours passed; the words were compulsively there. He had reached the point where the senator explains the conversion of Hoover's messenger. Chancellor read the words, which he'd use virtually intact in the actual chapter, with satisfaction.

"For reasons of survival Alan Long has seen the error of his ways. His past is no more immune to scrutiny than anyone else's. An isolated fact can be twisted here, taken out of context there. It's only the source that matters, the damning imprimatur—like the letters *F-B-I*. Long is about to retire from the bureau because of a terminal illness. A report has been sent to the director to that effect. In truth, however, Long is going to work for us. Although one could not exactly say he's been washed in the blood of the lamb, he *is* less inclined toward the archangel of darkness. He's afraid. And fear is a weapon he knows well."

It was not a bad day's work, thought Peter, looking at his watch. It was nearly four thirty. The late afternoon sun created blocks of shadows on the buildings outside the hotel window. The December wind was harsh; every now and then a leaf spiraled up beyond the glass.

Alison would be back soon. He would take her to a small restaurant he knew in Georgetown, where they would have a quiet dinner and look at each other and touch each other. There would be the laughter in her eyes, and in her voice, and he would be grateful for her nearness. And they would come back to the hotel and make love. So wondrously. With meaning. There had been no meaning in his bed for so long.

Peter got up from the couch and stretched, revolving his neck. It was habit; when the pain came to his temples, it helped to move his head in circles. Yet there was no pain now. In spite of the stress of the past forty-eight hours, there had been only a few brief moments when he'd felt the alarms. Alison MacAndrew had come into his life. It was really as simple as that.

The telephone rang. He smiled, reacting like an adolescent. It had to be Alison; no one else knew he was there. He picked up the phone, expecting her to tell him with her own particular brand of laughter that all the cabs in Washington were avoiding her; she was marooned in a concrete zoo and the animals were snarling.

It was a woman's voice, but it was not Alison's. Only the hard, strained tones of a frightened human being.

"What in God's name have you *done*? How could you put me in your book? Who gave you the *right*?"

It was Phyllis Maxwell.

It was the beginning of the madness.

He left a note for Alison, a second message at the desk in case she overlooked the note. He had no time to explain; there was an emergency, and he had to leave for an hour or so. He'd call her at the first opportunity. And he loved her.

Phyllis Maxwell. It was insane! What she had said was crazy. And Peter had to give a lot of rapid explanations. Yes. There was a character in his book that some might—only might—think was possibly—only possibly— reminiscent of her! But it could just as easily be reminiscent of half a dozen others!

No! He hadn't set out to destroy her. Or anyone or anything! Except the reputation of J. Edgar Hoover, and for that there would be no apologies! For Christ's sake, *no*! He worked alone! Whatever research he did, whatever sources he used, none of it had anything to do with her!

Or . . . Paula Mingus . . . whoever the hell *she* was.

There was no reasoning with the voice on the other end of the line—one moment faint and inaudible, the next shrill and hysterical. Phyllis Maxwell was losing her mind. And somehow he was responsible.

He tried speaking rationally; it was useless. He tried shouting at her; it was chaos. Finally, he extracted her promise to meet him.

She would not come to the Hay-Adams. She had been with him at the Hay-Adams. Didn't he remember that? Was it so repulsive?

Jesus Christ! Stop it!

She would not meet him anywhere of his choosing. She did not trust him; for God's sake, how could she? And she would not meet any place where they might be seen together. There was a house on Thirty-fifth Street Northwest, near the corner of Wisconsin, behind Dumbarton Oaks. It belonged to friends who were out of the country;

she had a key. She was not sure of the number; it didn't matter, there was a white porch with a stained-glass window over the door. She'd be there in a half hour.

She hung up with the words: "You were working with them all along, weren't you? You must be very proud of yourself."

A taxi swerved up to the curb. Chancellor jumped in, gave the address to the driver, and tried to collect his thoughts.

Someone had read his manuscript; that much was clear. But who? How? It was the *how* that frightened him because it meant that whoever it was had gone to extraordinary lengths to get it. He knew the precautions the typing service took; they were a part of the service, one of its strongest recommendations. The typing service had to be ruled out.

Morgan! Neither by design nor permission, but by accident! Tony had the aristocrat's carelessness. His peripatetic mind crashed about, overseeing dozens of projects simultaneously. It was entirely possible that Morgan had absently left the manuscript on someone's desk. Or, God forbid, the men's room.

The taxi reached the intersection of Pennsylvania Avenue and Twentieth Street. There was an empty telephone booth on the corner. Peter looked at his watch; it was ten minutes to five. Tony would still be in the office.

"Pull up to that telephone, will you please?" he said. "I have to make a call. I won't be long."

"Take your time, mister. The meter's running."

Peter closed the door of the glass booth and dialed Morgan's private number.

"It's Peter, Tony. I've got to ask you a question."

"Where the hell *are* you? I spoke to Mrs. Alcott this morning, and she said you were in town. I called the apartment, but all I got was the machine."

"I'm in Washington. I haven't time to explain. Listen to me. Someone's read the Hoover manuscript. Whoever it was has done a terrible thing, made an awful mistake ——"

"Hey, *wait* a minute," broke in Morgan. "That's impossible. First things first. What terrible thing? What mistake?"

"Told someone she—he—was in the book."

"He or she?"

"What *difference* does it make? The point is someone read it and is using the information to scare the hell out of somebody else!"

"Was it a mistake? Is there such a character?"

"Not really. It could be half a dozen different people, but that doesn't matter." There was no time for Morgan's questions.

"I only meant that several of your characters are loosely based on people down there. That general, for one."

"Oh, God . . ." In the convoluted process of inventing a character he had taken one aspect of Phyllis Maxwell's life—her career as a newspaperwoman—and built another person. *Another* person, not *her*! Not Phyllis. The person he created was the victim of extortion; that wasn't Phyllis! It was fiction! But the voice on the Hay-Adams telephone was not a product of fiction. "Have you let anyone else read the manuscript?"

"Of course not. Do you think I want people to know how unpublishable you are before my editorial hand goes to work?"

It was the usual joke between them, but Chancellor did not laugh. "Then, where's your copy?"

"Where? As a matter of fact it's in the drawer of my bedside table, and we haven't been robbed in over six months. I think it's a record."

"When did you last look?"

Morgan paused, suddenly serious, obviously recognizing the depth of Peter's concern. "The other night. And the drawer's locked."

"Did you make a Xerox for Joshua?"

"No, he'll get one when the editing's finished. Could anyone have read your copy?"

"No. It's in my suitcase." Chancellor stopped. *The suitcase.* His briefcase was in the car with the suitcases! The night in Rockville! The early morning, the racing footsteps; the horrible, severed legs of an animal; the bloodstained suitcase. It could have happened then. "Never mind, Tony. I'll call you in a day or so."

"What are you doing in Washington?"

"I'm not sure. I came down to learn something. Now I don't know. . . ." He hung up before Morgan could speak.

*   *   *

He saw the white porch and the dim light shining through the stained-glass window above the front door. The block was lined with old homes, once stately, now beyond their time.

"That's the house," he said to the driver. "Thanks a lot, and keep the change."

The driver hesitated. "Hey, mister," he said. "I could be wrong, and it's none of my business. Maybe you expected it, maybe it's why you telephoned. But I think you were followed out here."

"What? Where's the car?" Peter spun around and looked out the rear window of the taxi.

"Don't bother looking. He waited until we slowed down; then he made a left turn at the corner back there. He slowed down pretty good himself. To see where you stopped, maybe."

"Are you sure?"

"Like I said, I could be wrong. Headlights at night, they're all just a little bit different. You play games."

"I know what you mean." Peter thought for a moment. "Do you want to wait here for me? I'll pay."

"Hey, no thanks. This trip took me way the hell out. My old lady's gonna' be groaning as it is. Wisconsin's just down the way. Plenty of cabs heading back into town."

Chancellor got out and closed the door. The cab sped off down the street; Peter turned toward the house. Except for the dim light in the hall there were no other lamps turned on. Yet it was almost an hour since he'd talked to Phyllis Maxwell. She should be here by now. He wondered if she was in a sane enough frame of mind to follow her own instructions. He started up the path to the porch.

He reached the top step and heard the metallic click of a lock. In front of him the door opened, but no one came into view.

"Phyllis?"

"Come in quickly," was the whispered reply.

She was standing against the wall to the left of the door, her back pressed against the faded wallpaper. In the dim light she looked much older than she had over the candles in the Hay-Adams dining room. Her face was pale with fear. Lines of strain were pronounced at the edges of her mouth. Her eyes were penetrating but devoid of the flair he remembered; there was no curiosity in them now, only dread. He closed the door.

"You don't have to be afraid of me. You never did. I mean that, Phyllis."

"Oh, young man, you're the worst kind," she said, her whisper filled with sadness and contempt. "You kill sweetly."

"That's utter nonsense. I want to talk to you. And not standing where I can't see you."

"There'll be no lights turned on!"

"At least now I can hear you." Suddenly, Peter's thoughts were on the cab driver's alarming information. There was a car outside on the streets. Watching, waiting. "All right, no lights. May we sit down?"

Her answer was a glare followed by a sudden movement away from the wall. He walked behind her through an archway into a dark living room. In the wash of hall light he could see overstuffed chairs and a large sofa. She went directly to the chair opposite the sofa, the rustle of her skirt the only sound. He took off his topcoat, throwing it on the arm of the couch, and sat down across from her. Her face caught the light from the hallway better than if she'd been sitting next to him.

"I'm going to tell you something," he began. "If I tell it awkwardly, it's because I've never had to explain anything like this before; maybe I've never analyzed what is dubiously called the creative process." He shrugged, denigrating the term. "I was awfully impressed with you," he said.

"You're too kind."

"Please. You know what I mean. My father's been a newspaperman all his life. When we met, I'm sure I was more impressed than you were. The fact that you wanted to interview me struck me as kind of foolish. You gave me a lift when it didn't hurt, and it had nothing to do with my books. You're part of something very important, with a significance I don't have. I was *damned* impressed, and it was a terrific evening. I drank too much and so did you, but what of it?"

"Kill sweetly, young man," she whispered.

Peter held his breath, controlling himself. "I went to bed with a great lady. If that's my crime, I'm guilty."

"Go on." Phyllis closed her eyes.

"I asked you a lot of questions about Hoover that

night. You gave me answers, told me things I didn't know. Your vehemence was electric. Your morality had been deeply offended, and you showed me an anger in person that I'd never read in anything you'd written."

"What are you driving at?"

"It's part of my awkward explanation. I was in Washington getting background; a few days later I started work. Your anger was very much on my mind. Beyond that, it was a woman's anger. An articulate, successful woman. So it was a logical step to invent a variation of that woman, someone possessing the same characteristics. That's what I did. That's my explanation. You gave me the idea for the character, but you're *not her.* She's only an invention."

"Did you also invent a general who was buried yesterday at Arlington?"

Chancellor sat motionless, stunned. Her dead eyes stared at him through the dim spill of light. "No, I didn't invent him," he answered quietly. "Who told you about him?"

"Surely you know. A horrible, flat, high-pitched whisper over the telephone. It's frighteningly effective for something so basic. Surely you know." Phyllis spaced her words out, as if afraid to hear herself say them.

"I don't know," replied Peter, indeed not knowing but beginning to perceive the spreading of a terrible pattern. He struggled to remain calm, to sound reasonable, but he knew his anger showed. "I think this has all gone far enough. Whispers over a telephone. Words painted on walls! Houses broken into. Animals cut up! Enough!" He got up and turned around. "It's going to stop." He saw what he was looking for: a large lamp on a table. Deliberately he went to it, put his hand beneath the shade, and pulled the chain. The light went on. "There's not going to be any more hiding, no more dark rooms. Someone's trying to drive you crazy, drive Alison crazy, drive me out of my goddamned mind! I've *had* it. I'm not going to let——"

It was as far as he got. A pane in one of the front windows exploded. Simultaneously there was a harsh splitting of wood; a bullet imbedded itself somewhere in a molding. Then another pane shattered; glass fragments shot through the air, cracks of plaster sliced the wall like the jagged edges of black lightning.

Instinctively, Peter lashed out his hand, sending the lamp spiraling off the table onto the floor. It landed on the side of its shade, the bulb still lit, eerily projecting light across the room on the floor.

"Get down!" screamed Phyllis.

Chancellor realized as he dove to the floor that there were bullets, but there were no gunshots! And terrifying images came back to him.

Dawn at the Cloisters! A man killed in front of his eyes; a circle of blood abruptly, without warning, formed on a white forehead. A body in spastic contortion before it fell. *There had been no gunshots then!* Only sickening spits that had disturbed the stillness and filled it with death.

Move! For Christ's sake, *move!* In his panic he had lunged toward Phyllis, pulling her to the floor with him.

Another pane of glass exploded, another bullet cracked the plaster. Then another, this one ricocheting off stone somewhere, smashing the glass of a photograph on the wall.

Move! There is death!

He had to get the light. They were targets with it on. He pushed Phyllis away, holding her down, hearing her moans of fear. He darted his eyes to his right, then his left. Stone! There had to be a fireplace! It was directly behind him and he saw what he wanted. A poker leaning against the brick. He lurched for it.

Glass erupted; twin cracks appeared on the walls, partly obscured by shadows. Phyllis screamed, and for an instant Peter thought she might be heard, but then he remembered the house was on the corner, the nearest house at least a hundred feet away. The night was cold; windows and doors were shut. Her screams would bring no help.

He crawled toward the lamp, raised the poker, and smashed it down on the shade as if killing a deadly animal.

There was still the light in the hallway! It took on the intensity of a searchlight, the spill probing corners, washing the room with a brightness he would never have thought possible. He lunged up, racing to the archway, and heaved the poker toward the fixture in the ceiling. It spun through the air like a whirling crossbar and crashed into the teardrops of glass. All went dark.

He dove back onto the floor and crawled toward Phyllis. "Where's the phone?" he whispered.

He could feel her trembling; she could not answer.

"The phone? *Where is it?*"

She understood him. In the dark shadows produced by faraway street lamps he could see her eyes grasping what he said. She was barely audible between her sobs. "Not here. A jack in here, no phone."

"*What?*" What was she trying to tell him? A jack? No telephone?

One more explosion of glass filled the room, the bullet cracking inches over their heads, snapping into the wall above them. Suddenly from outside there was a loud gunshot in counterpoint to the muted firing, and a guttural shout, muffled quickly. It was followed by the sounds of screeching tires and metal against metal. Another roar of a furious voice. A car door opened and closed.

"Kitchen," whispered Phyllis, pointing in the darkness to her right.

"The telephone's in the kitchen? *Where?*"

"Through there."

"Stay down!" Peter crawled like a panicked insect over the floor, through an archway to a doorway. He felt kitchen tiles beneath him. The phone! Where was it? He tried to adjust his eyes to the new darkness.

He scraped his hands along the walls in panic. Kitchen telephones were usually on the wall, cords spiraling below. . . . He found it! His hand shot up; he tore the instrument from its cradle and brought it to his ear, his free hand reaching up for the dial. The last circle. *0.*

The phone was dead.

There was a deafening crash. Glass shattered on the opposite side of the pitch black kitchen. The top of the outside door had been smashed; a brick bounced off the wall. A brick had been thrown through the glass.

A brick! The fireplace! He'd seen it at the corner of the slate, to the right of the grate. He was sure of it. It was the answer! The only one left.

He propelled himself on all fours—half crawling, half lunging—back into the darkness of the living room. Phyllis was crouched next to the sofa, frozen in shock.

There it was! Now, if only the owners of the house had meant it when they'd put it there.

Some people called it a New England fire lighter; in the Midwest it was known as a Lake Erie starter. A round porous stone at the end of a brass rod soaking in a pot of kerosene. Held under logs, it acted as kindling.

He reached for the pot and took off the metal lid. There was liquid inside. Kerosene!

A fusillade of gun spits erupted. Bullets cracked the air, some breaking new glass, others having a clear path through previously shattered windowpanes. The walls and ceiling absorbed them; he could hear the *pings* as the deadly missiles ricocheted off metallic objects, deflected in their flights.

Perspiration rolled down Peter's face. He was sure he had his answer, but he did not know how to construct it. And then the words came back to him, rooted in his own fiction. He had *invented* the answer before.

> *Dobric tore off his shirt and plunged it into the vat of gasoline. The harvest was finished; there were stacks of hay in the field. The nearest would go up in flames, and the wind would carry the fire. Soon the grasslands would be ablaze, and platoons of soldiers would be diverted from their search. . . .*

Sarajevo! An incident like that had happened after the assassination of the Archduke Ferdinand.

Peter tore off his jacket and shirt. He lurched over the floor to the table where the lamp had been. He yanked the tablecloth off and returned to the fireplace. He spread his shirt on the floor, placed the tablecloth over it, and poured the kerosene over both, saving only a little. He sprang toward the couch and pulled off a sectional cushion; he poured the remaining kerosene on it.

There were more sickening spits from outside, more shattering of glass; Chancellor thought he would vomit in fear. The pain in his temples had returned with such force he could barely focus his eyes. He closed them for an instant, wanting to scream but knowing he could not.

He placed the empty iron pot in the center of the tablecloth and proceeded to wrap the tablecloth and the shirt around it. He tied the sleeves together until the pot was securely bedded inside, one sleeve extended. He reached into his trouser pocket and took out a book of matches.

He was ready. He crawled toward the windows on the left, to the wall, pulling the pot behind him, pushing the cushion in front. Slowly he rose to his feet, out of sight, one hand clutching the extended sleeve, the soaked cushion on the floor. He manipulated the book of matches awkwardly between both hands, tore off a match, and struck it. He dropped the flame on the saturated fabric; it exploded in a burst of fire.

In two motions he swung the sleeve behind him, then brought it forward with all his strength, letting go at the last instant. The flaming pot crashed through the remaining glass, whirling out over the lawn like the fireball it was. The outside rush of air intensified the flames; dripping liquid caught fire, leaving a wake of jagged, leaping yellow.

Peter heard footsteps, then incomprehensible shouts. And more footsteps, these coming from the side of the house. Men were trying to put out the fireball. It was the moment for his second weapon. He struck another match, holding the flame in his left hand. With his right he picked up the cushion and brought the lighted match to it.

Again a burst of fire, singeing the hairs on his arm. He raced to the far right window and propelled the flaming cushion through the glass. It landed where he hoped it would: At the base of the white porch.

The old wood and the windy kerosene fire were compatible. The porch began to burn.

Again there were shouts, words screamed in some unknown tongue. What was it? What language? He'd never heard it before.

A last barrage of muted gunshots was leveled at the windows, fired aimlessly into the house. He heard the racing of a powerful engine. Car doors were opened and closed, tires screeched, spinning on the street. The car sped away.

Peter ran back to Phyllis. He pulled her to her feet, holding her close, feeling the trembling body in his arms.

"It's over. It's all over. It's all right. We have to get outside. Through the back door. This place is going to go up like—like a haystack."

"Oh, God! Oh, my God. . . ." She buried her face in his naked chest; her tears would not stop.

"Come on, let's go! We'll wait outside for the police. Someone'll see the fire and call them. Come on!"

Slowly Phyllis looked up at him, a strange, pathetic panic in her eyes, seen clearly in the reflection of the spreading flames outside the windows. "No," she said in the harsh whisper she had used before. "No. Not the police!"

"For Christ's sake! People tried to *kill* us! You'd better goddamned well believe we're going to see the police!"

She pushed him away. An odd passivity seemed to grip her; she was trying, he thought, to find a moment of sanity. "You have no shirt———"

"I've got a jacket. And a coat. Come on."

"Yes, I see. . . . My purse. Can you get my purse? It's in the hall."

Chancellor looked over at the hallway. Smoke was streaming in through the cracks in the front door; the porch was blazing, but no fire had yet penetrated the house.

"Sure." He released her and reached down for his jacket by the fireplace.

"It's on the staircase, I think. Or perhaps I left it in the closet. I'm not sure."

"It's okay. I'll get it. You go on outside. Through the kitchen."

Phyllis turned and started out. Peter put on his jacket and went quickly toward the hall, picking his topcoat off the couch on his way.

It was over. There would be conversations with the police, with the authorities, with anyone who wanted to listen. But tonight was the end of it. There would be no book at this cost.

The purse was not on the stairs. He walked halfway up to the landing; it was nowhere in sight. The smoke was thicker now. He had to hurry; the front door had caught fire. He ran down the steps and turned left at the bottom of the staircase, looking for the closet. It was in the far right corner of the hall. He walked over quickly and opened the door. There were coats, two fedoras, and various scarves on the hooks and hangers, but no purse.

He had to get out. The smoke was becoming impenetrable. He began to cough, and his eyes were tearing. He raced back through the living room, through the arch to the dining room, into the kitchen, and out the open door.

In the distance he could hear the wail of sirens.

"Phyllis?"

He ran along the side of the house to the front. She was not there. He continued around to the other side, down the driveway to the backyard again.

"Phyllis! *Phyllis!*"

She was nowhere. And then he knew. There was no purse on the staircase or in the closet. She had fled.

The sirens were louder, no more than a few blocks away. The old house was going quickly. The whole front section was on fire, the flames spreading rapidly inside.

Peter was not sure why, but he knew he could not talk to the police alone. Not now, not yet.

He raced away into the night.

22

The pain in his temples made him want to drop to the ground and smash his head on the cement curb, but he knew it would not help.

Instead, he kept walking, his eyes on the traffic heading into downtown Washington. He was looking for a taxi.

He should have remained at the burning house on Thirty-fifth Street and told the incredible story to the police. And yet a part of him told him that to do so without Phyllis would raise questions to which he was not sure there were answers. Answers that excluded the destruction of Phyllis Maxwell. The shadows of responsibility fell across his thoughts; there were things he did not know, and *had* to know. He owed her that much. Perhaps no more, but at least that.

At last there was a cab; the lighted yellow rooftop sign was like a beacon. He stepped off the curb and waived his arms. The taxi slowed down; the driver peered cautiously out the window before he stopped.

"The Hay-Adams Hotel, please," said Chancellor.

"Good lord! What *happened*?" asked Alison, stunned as she opened the door.

"There's a bottle of pills in my suitcase. In the back flap. Get them quickly, please."

"Peter, my darling! What *is* it?" Alison held him as he leaned against the door. "I'll call a doctor."

"No! Do as I say. I know exactly what it is. Just the pills. Quickly." He could feel himself falling. He grabbed her arms, and with her help he stumbled into the bedroom. He lay back and gestured toward the suitcase, still on the luggage rack in the corner. She raced to it.

He did what he rarely did: He took two tablets.

She ran into the bathroom, emerging seconds later with a glass of water. She sat next to him, holding his head as he drank.

"Please, Peter. A doctor!"

He shook his head. "No," he replied weakly, trying to smile a semblance of reassurance. "He couldn't do anything. It'll pass in a few minutes." The darkness was closing in, his eyelids terribly heavy. He could not allow the dark to fall until he had calmed her. And prepared her for what might happen when the darkness was complete. "I may sleep for a while. Not long, it's never long. I may talk, even yell a little. Don't worry. It doesn't mean anything. Just rambling, just nonsense."

The dark filled his mind; his personal night had fallen. There was nothingness, and he floated, suspended in calm, gentle breezes.

He opened his eyes, not knowing how long he had been in bed. Looking down at him was Alison's lovely face, her eyes made more beautiful by the tears that filled them.

"Hey," he said, reaching up to touch her moist cheek. "It's all right."

She took his hand, holding it against her lips. "Her name was Cathy, wasn't it?"

He had done what he'd hoped he would not do, said what he had not wanted to say. There was nothing for it. He nodded. "Yes."

"She died, didn't she?"

"Yes."

"Oh darling. So much hurt, so much love——"

"I'm sorry."

"Don't be."

"It can't be very nice for you."

She reached down and touched his eyes, and then his cheek and lips. "It was a gift," she said. "A beautiful gift."

"I don't understand."

"After you spoke her name, you called for me."

He told Alison what had happened at the house on Thirty-fifth Street. He minimized the physical danger, calling the erratic gunfire a strategy of fear, designed to terrify, not to injure or to kill.

It was clear she did not believe him, but she was a soldier's daughter. In one form or another she had heard such false reassurances before. She accepted the watered-down explanation without comment, letting her eyes convey her disbelief.

When he finished, he stood by the window looking down at the Christmas decorations on Sixteenth Street; across the street muted church bells played in an agonizing cadence. Christmas was only days away; he had not thought about it. He wasn't really thinking about it now. His only thoughts were on what he had to do: Go to the Federal Bureau of Investigation, to the source of the madness, and let it put the madness to a stop. But private property had been destroyed, lethal weapons fired. Phyllis Maxwell had to go with him.

"I've got to reach her," he said softly. "I've got to make her understand she has to come with me."

"I'll get the number for you." Alison took the phone book from the bedside table. Peter continued to stare out the window. "It's not here. She's not listed."

Chancellor remembered. Alison's father had not been listed, either. He wondered if he could unearth the number as easily as he had MacAndrew's. It would be a variation of the same ploy, a newsman's ruse. An old reporter friend, in town for the night, anxious to make contact.

But the ploy did not work; the man at the city desk had probably used it too often himself. The paper would not give out Maxwell's number.

"Let me try," said Alison. "There's a press officer on duty at all times in the Pentagon. Bad news and casualties don't have business hours. Filtered-down rank still has its privileges. I'll know somebody, or someone'll know me."

The Pentagon had two numbers for Phyllis Maxwell. One was her private phone, the other the switchboard of the apartment house in which she lived.

There was no answer on her private line. The apartment switchboard gave out no information on its tenants;

it would only take messages. But because the caller was not absolutely sure of the correct address, the operator gave it.

"I want to go with you," Alison said.

"I don't think you should," Peter replied. "She mentioned your father, not by name, but she spoke of a burial yesterday at Arlington. She's frightened out of her mind. All I want to do is convince her to come with me. If she saw you, it might stop her."

"All right." Alison nodded. The soldier's daughter understood. "But I worry about you. Suppose you have another attack?"

"I won't." He paused for a moment and then reached out, pulling her to him. "There's something else," he said, looking down into her eyes. "I don't want to involve you. It's over, finished. You said it yourself, remember? I didn't agree with you then. I do now."

"Thank you for that. I guess what I'm saying is that whatever he did, it's done and can't be changed. He stood for something. I don't want that damaged."

"I have something important in mind too, and that won't be changed, either. Or damaged. Us." He kissed her lightly. "When tonight's over, we can start living our own lives. I find that prospect very exciting."

She smiled and returned his kiss. "I was shameless. I caught you at a weak moment and seduced you. I should be branded." And then her smile waned; she held his eyes, the vulnerability in her own. "Everything's happened so fast. I don't require commitments, Peter."

"I do," he answered.

"If you'll take a seat inside the lobby, sir, I'll be with you shortly," said the doorman at Phyllis Maxwell's apartment house. The man did not hesitate for an instant; it was almost as though he expected him.

Peter sat down in a green plastic chair and waited. The doorman simply stood outside, rocking back and forth on his heels, his gloved hands clasped behind his uniformed overcoat.

It was very odd.

Five minutes went by. The doorman made no move to come inside the lobby. Was it possible he'd forgotten? Chancellor got out of the chair and looked around. He had spoken to an operator; where was the apartment switchboard?

There was a small glass panel at the rear of the lobby, sandwiched between rows of mailboxes and a bank of elevators. He walked over to it and peered inside. The operator was talking into a mouthpiece attached to her single-eared headset. She spoke rapidly, with emphasis; the conversation was between friends, not switchboard and inquirer. Peter tapped on the glass; the operator suspended her conversation and slid the panel open.

"Yes, sir?"

"I'm trying to reach Phyllis Maxwell. Will you ring her apartment and let me speak with her, please? It's urgent."

The operator's reaction was as odd as the doorman's. Different, but nevertheless strange. She hesitated, embarrassed.

"I don't believe Miss Maxwell is in," she said.

"You won't know until you ring her, will you?"

"Have you checked with the doorman?"

"What the hell *is* this?" Peter understood. These people were following instructions. "Ring her apartment!"

As he could have predicted, there was no answer on the switchboard telephone and no point in wasting any more time. He walked rapidly back outside and confronted the doorman.

"Let's cut the crap, shall we? You've got something to tell me. What is it?"

"It's touchy."

"What is?"

"She described you, said your name was Chancellor. If you'd arrived, say, an hour ago, I was to tell you to come back at eleven o'clock. That Miss Maxwell had called in saying she'd be back then."

Peter looked at his watch. "All right. It's almost eleven. What happens then?"

"Just a little while longer, okay?"

"Not okay. Now. Or you can say whatever it is to me and the police."

"Okay, okay. What the hell, it's only a few minutes." The doorman reached into his inside overcoat pocket and took out an envelope. He gave it to Chancellor.

Peter looked at the man, then the envelope. His

name was written on it. Moving back inside to the light, he ripped open the envelope and took out the letter.

> My dear Peter:
> I'm sorry I ran, but I knew you would follow me. You saved my life—and to some degree my sanity—and you deserve an explanation. I'm afraid it will be limited.
> By the time you read this, I'll be on a plane. Don't try to trace me. It would be impossible. For several years I've had a false passport, knowing that someday I might have to use it. Apparently the time is now.
> This afternoon, after that horrible call telling me I was a character in your novel, I informed my paper that I might be taking an extended leave for reasons of health. In truth, my editor did not argue very much. My work hasn't been particularly outstanding in recent months.
> The decision to leave is not sudden. I've considered it for quite a while. Tonight simply made it irreversible. Whatever my transgressions, they do not warrant the loss of my life. Mine, yours, or anyone's. Nor should they compromise the responsibilities I have professionally.
> This last has been accomplished. My work *is* compromised. Truths are suppressed when they should be told. The loss of life was avoided —for how long, who knows?—because of you. I cannot continue any longer.
> Thank you for my life. And my deepest apologies for my thinking you were part of something you were not.
> A part of me says, for God's sake, give up your book! It is balanced by another voice that says you *can't*!
> You will not hear from me again, my dear young, young man. But you will always have a part of my love. And my gratitude.
>
> Phyllis

Peter reread the letter, trying to grasp the meaning behind the words. Phyllis had chosen her phrases with a deliberateness born of extraordinary fear. But of what? What were her "transgressions"? What could she have done—or not done—that would cause her to throw away a lifetime of accomplishment? It was insane!

It was *all* insane. Everything! And the insanity was going to stop! He started for the door. From somewhere he heard a prolonged buzzing. It stopped as he had his hand on the glass bar of the door. And then he heard the words, accompanied by the sliding of a glass panel.

"Mr. *Chancellor*?" The operator was calling him, her head halfway through the switchboard opening. "There's a call for you."

Phyllis? Perhaps she'd changed her mind! He ran across the lobby and took the phone.

It was not Phyllis Maxwell. It was Alison.

"Something dreadful's happened. You had a telephone call from a man in Indianapolis. He was out of his mind. He was at the airport, catching a plane for Washington——"

"Who was it?"

"A man named Bromley. He said he was going to kill you."

Carroll Quinlan O'Brien took the security logs from the guard and thanked him. The Pennsylvania Avenue doors were closed; the list of names of those who had entered and exited would be processed and sent down to the main desk. At all times every person in the FBI complex was accounted for; at no time was anyone permitted to leave without surrendering his pass.

It was a security-logs entry that had started it all four months before, O'Brien thought. Started his rapid decline in the eyes of the bureau. Four months ago he had found three names on the May 1 P.M. logs: Salter, Krepps, and Longworth. Two names were unassigned field covers, the third belonged to a retired agent living on the island of Maui in the Pacific. These three unknown men had gained entrance that night. The next morning Hoover was dead, and all traces of the director's files had vanished. The dossiers themselves had become a quickly forgotten legacy from hell that no one cared to exhume or examine.

So Quinn O'Brien had asked questions, keeping his voice down, seeking counsel from those he knew would listen because they cared. Men like him within the bureau whose sensibilities had been offended during the past years —theirs more than his, mostly. At least over a longer time.

He had arrived only four and a half years before, the war hero from Sacramento, the cosmetic from Army G2, the forty-year-old lawyer who had escaped from a Viet Cong prison camp and had later been given parades in California. Washington had summoned him, the President had decorated him, Hoover had employed him. It was good public relations. He lent a much-needed air of dignity to the bureau. It was supposed to be good for Quinn, too. He could have had a future at the Justice Department.

Could have had. No longer. Because he had asked questions. A whisper over a telephone had ordered him to stop. A flat, terrible, high-pitched whisper that told him they knew. *They* had a deposition written by a captured lieutenant colonel who faced execution with seven other men because of the actions of one Major Carroll Quinlan O'Brien. The major had disobeyed a direct order. Eight American soldiers had been executed as a result.

Of course, it was only one half of the story. There was another half. It told of this same major looking after the sick and the wounded of the compound with far greater concern than the executed lieutenant colonel. It told how this major had taken others' work details, how he had stolen food and medicine from the guards to help sustain the men, how in the last analysis he had made his escape as much for the other prisoners as for himself.

He was a lawyer, not a soldier. It was the lawyer's logic that had guided him, not a soldier's strategy. Nor a soldier's willingness to accept the unbearable cruelties of war—and therein, he realized, was the weakness of his argument. Did he do what he did for the combined concerns of all? Or did he do what he did for himself alone?

O'Brien was not sure there was a clear-cut answer. It was the question itself that could destroy him. An exposed "war hero" was the most despicable of citizens. People had been fooled; they were embarrassed—that was the part that made them furious.

These were the things the terrible whisper had made clear. And all because he had asked questions. Three unknown men without accountability had gained entrance the night before Hoover's death. And the next morning Hoover's files had disappeared.

If O'Brien needed proof of his continuing decline within the bureau, he had only to look at his own assignment sheet. He had been removed from several committees; he no longer received classified reports dealing with the newly reestablished liaisons with NSA and CIA. And he was suddenly drawing continuous night-duty assignments. Night duty! It was the Washington equivalent of the Omaha field office. It forced an agent to reevaluate a lot of things, primarily his own future.

It also forced O'Brien to wonder who within the bureau was after him. Whoever it was knew something about three unidentified men using improper covers to infiltrate the building the night before Hoover died. And whoever it was perhaps knew a great deal more about hundreds and hundreds of dossiers that had been Hoover's private files.

One other consideration was forced on Quinn O'Brien. It was not one he relished thinking about. Since that whispered voice on the telephone four months ago the will to resist, to fight, had gone out of him. It was entirely possible that his decline at the bureau was due to himself. To his own performance.

The ring of the telephone interrupted his thoughts, bringing him back to the minor realities of night duty. He looked at the lighted button; it was an inside call from one of the two entrance desks.

"This is the Tenth Street desk. We've got a problem. There's a man down here who insists on seeing someone in authority, whoever's in charge. We told him to come back in the morning, but he refuses."

"Is he drunk? Or a nut?"

"Can't say that he's either. As a matter of fact, I *know* who he is. I read a book he wrote. A thing called *Counterstrike!* His name's Chancellor. Peter Chancellor."

"I've heard of him. What's he want?"

"He won't say. Only that it's an emergency."

"What do you think?"

"I think he'll stay here all night until somebody sees him. I figure that's you, Quinn."

"All right. Check him for weapons, assign an escort, and send him up."

23

Peter walked into the office, nodding his thanks to the uniformed guard, who closed the door and left. Behind the desk in front of the window a stocky man with reddish brown hair got to his feet and extended his hand. Chancellor approached and took it; the grip was strange. It was cold, physically cold, and abrupt.

"I'm Senior Agent O'Brien, Mr. Chancellor. I'm sure I don't have to tell you that your coming here at this hour is highly irregular."

"The circumstances are irregular."

"You sure you don't want the police? Our jurisdiction is limited."

"I want you."

"Whatever it is can't wait until morning?" asked O'Brien, still standing.

"No."

"I see. Sit down, please." The agent gestured to one of the two chairs in front of the desk.

Peter hesitated. "I'd prefer to stand, at least for now. To tell you the truth, I'm very nervous."

"Suit yourself." OBrien returned to his chair. "At least take your overcoat off.-That is, if you intend to be here long."

"I may be here for the rest of the night," said Chancellor, removing his coat and draping it over a chair.

"I wouldn't count on it," said O'Brien, watching him.

"I'll let you decide. Is that fair?"

"I'm an attorney, Mr. Chancellor. Elliptical responses, especially when phrased as questions, are pointless and irritating. They also bore me."

Peter stopped and looked at the man. "An attorney? I thought you said you were an agent. A senior agent."

"I did. Most of us are lawyers. Or accountants."

"I forgot."

"Now I've reminded you. But I can't imagine it's pertinent."

"No, it isn't," replied Chancellor, forcing his concentration back to the issue. "I've got a story to tell you, Mr. O'Brien. When I'm finished, I'll go with you to whoever you think should hear it, and repeat it. But I have to start at the beginning; it won't make sense otherwise. Before I do, I'd like to ask you to make a telephone call."

"Wait a minute," interrupted the agent. "You came here voluntarily and refused our suggestion that you return in the morning for a formal appointment. I won't accept any preconditions, and I won't make any phone calls."

"I've a good reason for asking you to."

"If it's a precondition, I'm not interested. Come back in the morning."

"I *can't*. Among other reasons, there's a man flying in from Indianapolis who says he's going to kill me."

"Go to the police."

"Is that all you can say? That, and 'Come back in the morning'?"

The agent leaned back in his chair; his eyes conveyed his growing suspicion. "You wrote a book called *Counterstrike!*, didn't you?"

"Yes, but that's not——"

"I remember now," interrupted O'Brien. "It came out last year. A lot of people thought it was true; a lot of other people were upset. You said the CIA was operating domestically."

"I happen to think it's true."

"I see," continued the agent warily. "Last year it was the agency. Is it the FBI this year? You come off the street in the middle of the night trying to provoke us into doing something you can write about?"

Peter gripped the back of the chair. "I won't deny it started with a book. With the *idea* of a book. But it's gone way beyond that. People have been killed. Tonight *I* was nearly killed; so was the person with me. It's all connected."

"I repeat emphatically. Go to the police."

"I want *you* to call the police."

"Why?"

"So you'll believe me. Because it concerns people here at the Federal Bureau of Investigation. I think you're the only ones who can stop it."

O'Brien leaned forward, still wary, but aroused. "Stop what?"

Chancellor hesitated. He had to appear rational to this suspicious man. If the agent thought he was a lunatic— even half a lunatic—he'd throw him to the police. Peter did not reject the police; they were protection and he welcomed them. But the solution did not lie with the police. It lay within the bureau. He spoke as calmly as he could.

"Stop the killing, that's first, of course. Then stop the terror tactics, the extortion, the blackmail. People are being destroyed."

"By whom?"

"By others who think they have information that could irreparably damage the FBI."

O'Brien remained motionless. "What's the nature of this 'irreparable damage'?"

"It's found in the theory that Hoover was assassinated."

O'Brien stiffened. "I see. And this phone call to the police. What's that about?"

"An old house on Thirty-fifth Street Northwest, near Wisconsin, behind Dumbarton Oaks. It was burning when I left several hours ago. I set it on fire."

The agent's eyes widened, his voice urgent. "That's quite an admission. As a lawyer I think you should——"

"If the police look," continued Peter, overriding O'Brien's urgency, "they'll find shells on the front lawn, bullet holes in the walls and woodwork as well as the furniture, and the upper half of the kitchen door smashed. Also, the telephone wires were cut."

The FBI man stared at Chancellor. "What the hell are you saying?"

"It was an ambush."

"Weapons were fired in the middle of a residential neighborhood?"

"The gunshots were muffled by silencers. No one heard anything. There were periods of quiet—probably for passing cars. That's why I thought of the fire. The flames would be spotted by someone."

"You left the scene?"

"I ran away. Now I'm sorry I did."

"Why did you?"

Again Peter hesitated. "I was confused. Frightened."

"The person with you?"

"That's part of it, I imagine." Chancellor paused, seeing the obvious question in the agent's eyes. For a hundred reasons he could not protect her. As Phyllis herself had put it, whatever her transgressions, they did not warrant the loss of life. "Her name is Phyllis Maxwell."

"The newspaperwoman?"

"Yes. She ran first. I tried to find her. I couldn't."

"You said this all happened several hours ago. Do you know where she is now?"

"Yes. On a plane." Peter reached into his jacket pocket and took out Phyllis's letter. Reluctantly, but knowing he had to, he handed it to O'Brien.

As O'Brien read, Peter had the distinct impression that something was happening to the FBI man. For a moment the color seemed to drain from his face. At one point he raised his eyes and stared at Peter; the look he conveyed Chancellor knew well, but he did not understand it coming from this stranger. It was a look of fear.

When he was finished, the agent put the letter face down, reached for a booklet on his desk, opened it to a specific page, and picked up his telephone. He pressed a button and dialed.

"This is the FBI, one of the night-duty officers, emergency code, seven-five-sparrow. There was a fire at a house on Thirty-fifth Northwest. Near Wisconsin. Do you have anyone on the scene? . . . Can you patch me through to the officer in charge? Thank you." O'Brien looked up at Peter. He spoke curtly; it was not a request but an order. "Sit down."

Chancellor did so, vaguely realizing that in spite of the agent's commanding tone, the strange fear he had seen in O'Brien's eyes was now in his voice.

"Sergeant, this is the FBI." The agent shifted the phone to his right hand. Bewildered, Peter saw that the palm of O'Brien's left hand, the hand that had been holding the telephone, was moist with sweat. "You've received my clearance. I want to ask you a couple of questions. Is there any evidence as to how the fire was started, and are there any signs of gunshots? Cartridge shells in front or bullet holes inside?"

The agent listened, his eyes riveted on the desk, staring at nothing, really, but staring intently. Chancellor watched him, mesmerized. O'Brien's forehead broke out in small beads of perspiration. Absently, his breath suspended, the FBI man raised his left hand and wiped the sweat away. When finally he spoke, he was barely audible.

"Thank you, Sergeant. No, it's not our basket. We don't know anything, just following up an anonymous lead. It's got nothing to do with us."

O'Brien hung up. He was profoundly disturbed; there was a sudden sadness in his eyes.

"As near as can be determined," O'Brien said, "the fire was deliberately set. Remnants of fabric soaked with kerosene were found. There were shells on the lawn, windows shot out; there's every reason to expect bullets impacted throughout the interior—what's left of it. Everything will be sent to the laboratories."

Peter sat forward. Something was wrong. "Why did you tell the sergeant you didn't know anything?"

The agent swallowed. "Because I want to hear what you have to say. You've told me it concerns the bureau; some crazy theory about Hoover being murdered. That's enough for me. I'm a career man. I want to hear it first. I can always pick up the phone and call that precinct back."

O'Brien gave his explanation in a flat, quiet voice. It was reasonable, thought Chancellor. Everything he had learned about the bureau pointed to the fact that the bottom line was public relations. Avoid embarrassment at all costs. Protect the Seat of Government. Phyllis Maxwell's words came back to him.

The story hasn't been told. I don't think it ever will be. . . . The bureau will protect him. . . . The heirs apparent won't let the image be tarnished. They fear infected bloodlines, and they damned well should.

Yes, reflected Chancellor. O'Brien fitted the mold. His burden was the heaviest because he was the first to hear the extraordinary news. Something was very rotten in the bureau, and this agent would have to carry the message of that rot to his superiors. His dilemma was understandable: Messengers were often held accountable for their reports of catastrophe; the bloodlines could be infected after all. It was no wonder that this career man perspired.

But nothing in his imagination prepared Peter for what followed.

"To go back to the beginning," said Chancellor. "I was on the West Coast four, five months ago, living in Malibu. It was late afternoon; a man was on the beach staring up at my house. I went out and asked him why. He knew me; he said his name was Longworth."

O'Brien bolted forward in his chair, his eyes locked with Peter's. His lips formed the name, but only a shadow of sound emerged. "Longworth!"

"Yes, Longworth. You know who he is, then."

"Go on," the agent whispered.

Peter sensed the cause of O'Brien's shock. Alan Longworth had betrayed Hoover, defected from the bureau. Somehow the word had gotten out. But Hoover was dead, the defector half a world away—the stain removed. Now Senior Agent O'Brien had to bear the news that the vanished Longworth had surfaced. In a strange way Chancellor felt sorry for this middle-aged career man.

"Longworth said he wanted to talk to me because he'd read my books. He had a story to tell, and he thought I was the one to write it. I told him I wasn't looking for anything. Then he made that extraordinary statement about Hoover's death, linking it to some private files of Hoover's that were missing. He told me to check out his name; I have sources to do that, and he knew it. I know it sounds crazy, but I bit. God knows I didn't believe it; Hoover was an old man with a history of heart disease. But the concept fascinated me. And the fact that this Longworth would go to the trouble of———"

O'Brien got out of his chair. He stood behind the desk looking down at Peter, his eyes burning. "Longworth. The files. Who sent you to me? Who *are* you? Who the hell am I to *you*?"

"What?"

"You expect me to believe this? You walk off the street in the middle of the night and tell this to me! For Christ's sake, what do you want from me? What more do you want?"

"I don't know what you're talking about," said Chancellor, stunned. "I never saw you before in my life."

"Salter and Krepps! Go on, say it! *Salter and Krepps!* They were there, too!"

"Who are Salter and Krepps? Where were they?"

O'Brien turned away. He was breathing rapidly. "You know where they were. Unassigned field covers. Longworth in the Hawaiian Islands."

"He lives in Maui," agreed Peter. "They paid him off that way. I don't know the other two names; he never mentioned them. Were they working with Longworth?"

O'Brien stood motionless, his body rigid. Slowly he turned back to Chancellor, his eyes narrowed. "Working with Longworth?" he asked, barely above a whisper. "What do you mean, 'working with Longworth'?"

"Just that. Longworth was transferred from the bureau. His cover was an assignment with the State Department. But it was never true. It was only an accommodation. I've learned that much. What amazes me is that you people even know about Longworth."

The senior agent continued to stare in silence. His frightened eyes widened. "You're clean . . ."

"What?"

"You're *clean.* You walk in off the goddamned streets and you're clean!"

"What do you mean, I'm clean?"

"Because you wouldn't have told me what you just did. You'd be crazy to. A deep-cover accommodation that's false. With *State.* . . . Oh, Christ." O'Brien was like a man in a trance, aware of his state of suspension but incapable of shaking it. He braced himself against the desk, the fingers of both hands pressed into the wood. He closed his eyes.

Peter was alarmed. "Maybe you'd better take me to someone else."

"No. Wait a minute. Please."

"I don't think so." Peter got out of the chair. "As you said, this isn't your 'basket.' I want to talk to one of the other night-duty officers."

"There aren't any others."

"You said on the phone——"

"I know what I said! Try to understand. You *have* to talk to me. You've got to tell me everything you know. Every detail!"

Never, thought Peter. There'd be no mention of Alison; she was not going to be touched. Nor was he yet sure he wanted to talk further with this strangely disturbed man. "I want others to hear what I have to say."

O'Brien blinked several times. The trance was broken; he walked swiftly to a shelf on the other side of the room, pulled out a cassette recorder, and returned to the desk. He sat down and opened a bottom drawer. When his hand emerged, it held a small plastic box in which there was a cassette tape.

"The seal's unbroken; the tape is unused. I'll play it through if you like." The agent snapped the box open, removed the cassette, and inserted it. "You have my word. Others will hear what you have to say."

"A tape won't do."

"You've got to trust me," said O'Brien. "Whatever you think of my behavior these past few minutes, you've got to trust me. You can only tell your story on tape. And don't identify yourself. Describe yourself as a writer, that's all. Use all the other names involved except those associated with you personally or professionally. If that becomes impossible, if those people are intrinsic to the events, hold up your hand; I'll stop the tape, and we'll talk about it. Have you got that?"

"*No.*" Chancellor balked. "Now *you* just wait a minute. This isn't what I came here for."

"You came here to put a stop to it! That's what you told me. Stop the killing, stop the terror, stop the blackmail. Well, I want the same thing! You're not the only one who's been pushed to the fucking wall! Or this Maxwell woman or *any* of you. Christ, I've got a wife and family!"

Peter recoiled, stung by O'Brien's words. "What did you say?"

Self-consciously, the FBI man lowered his voice. "I have a family. It's not important, forget it."

"I think it's very important," said Peter. "I don't think I can ever tell you how important it is to me right now."

"Don't bother," interrupted O'Brien. He was abruptly the complete professional. "Because I'm doing the telling. Remember what I said: Don't identify yourself, but use the names of everyone else who approached you or you were sent to—people *not* known to you previously. Give the other names to me later, but not on the tape. I don't want you traced. Speak slowly; think about what you're saying. If you have any doubts, just look at me; I'll know. I'm going to start now. Give me a moment to identify myself and the circumstances."

O'Brien depressed two buttons on the small recorder and spoke in a clipped, hard voice.

"This tape is being prepared by Senior Agent C. Quinlan O'Brien, Eye-dent clearance seventeen-twelve, on the night of December eighteenth at approximately twenty-three hundred hours. The man you will hear was escorted to the night-duty office. I have removed his name from the security logs and informed the desk agent to report to me any and all inquiries, under the aforementioned seventeen-twelve in-house clearance." O'Brien paused, picked up a pencil, and scribbled a note to himself on a pad. "I consider the information on this tape to be of the highest priority of classification and for reasons of security can accept no interference. I fully understand the irregularity of the methods I employ and—for personal reasons—fully assume responsibility."

The agent stopped the machine and looked at Peter. "Ready? Start last summer. At Malibu and your meeting with Longworth." He pressed the buttons; the tape rolled.

Through the mists of disbelief Chancellor began, speaking slowly, trying to follow the instructions of this man he suddenly, strangely knew so well. This man who was somehow a part of his own invention. C. Quinlan O'Brien. *Alexander Meredith.* Attorney. *Attorney.* The bureau. *The bureau.* A wife and family. . . . *A wife and family . . .*

Frightened men.

O'Brien was visibly shaken as the story unfolded, both stunned and disturbed by the incidents Peter described. Whenever he mentioned Hoover's private files, the agent tensed and his hands shook.

When Peter came to Phyllis's description of the horrible, flat, high-pitched whisper over the telephone, O'Brien could not conceal his reaction. He gasped, his neck arched back, his eyes closed.

Peter stopped; the tape continued rolling. There was silence. O'Brien opened his eyes, staring at the ceiling. Slowly he turned to Chancellor.

"Go on," he said.

"There isn't much more. You read her letter."

"Yes. Yes, I read the letter. Describe what happened. The gunshots, the fire. Why you ran away."

Peter did. And then it was over. He had said it all. Or nearly all. He had not mentioned Alison.

O'Brien stopped the tape, rewound it for a few seconds, and played the last words back for clarity. Satisfied, he shut off the machine.

"All right. You've put down what you wanted to. Now, tell me the rest."

"What?"

"I asked you to trust me, but you haven't told it all. You were writing in Pennsylvania; suddenly you came to Washington. Why? According to you, your research was completed. You ran away from a burning house on Thirty-fifth Street nearly five hours ago. You got here two hours ago. Where were you for three hours? With whom? Fill in the gaps, Chancellor. They're important."

"No. That's not part of our bargain."

"What bargain? Protection?" Angrily, O'Brien got to his feet. "You damned fool, how can I offer protection if I don't know whom to protect? And don't kid yourself, protection *is* the bargain. Besides, it would take me—or anyone who really wanted to—roughly an hour to trace every move you made since you left Pennsylvania."

The agent's logic was undeniable. Chancellor had the feeling that he was an ill equipped amateur facing a hardened professional. "I don't want her part of this. I want your word on that. She's been through enough."

"So have we all," replied O'Brien. "Did she receive a telephone call?"

"No. But you did, didn't you?"

"I'm asking the questions." The agent sat down again. "Tell me about her."

Peter told the dark, sad story of Lieutenant General Bruce MacAndrew, his wife, and the daughter who was forced to grow up so early in her life. He described the isolated house on the back-country road in Maryland. And the words sprayed in blood-red paint on a wall: *Mac the Knife. Killer of Chasŏng.*

Quinn O'Brien closed his eyes and said softly, "Han Chow."

"Is that Korea?"

"Different war. Same method of extortion: military records that never reached the Pentagon. Of if they did, were removed. And now someone else has them."

Peter held his breath. "Are you talking about Hoover's files?"

O'Brien stared at him without replying. Chancellor felt torn apart; the insanity was complete.

"They were shredded," whispered Peter, unsure of his own mind. "They were destroyed! What the hell are you trying to tell me? This is a book! None of it's real! You have to protect your goddamned bureau! But not *this*! Not the *files*!"

O'Brien stood up, raising the palms of his hands. It was a reassuring gesture, a father calming an hysterical child. "Take it easy. I didn't say anything about Hoover's files. You've been through a lot tonight, and you're making assumptions. For a second I did, too. But it's wrong. Two isolated incidents involving military records hardly constitute a pattern. Those files were destroyed. We know that."

"What's Han Chow?"

"Not pertinent."

"A minute ago you thought it was."

"A minute ago a lot of thoughts went through my head. But things are clear now. You're right. Someone's using you. And me and probably a couple of dozen others to tear the bureau apart. Someone who knows us, knows the working structure. Very possibly it's one of us. It wouldn't be the first time."

Peter studied the FBI man. Since Hoover's death there had been rumors, many reported in the newspapers, that factions within the bureau were fighting among themselves. And Quinn's intelligence and sincerity were convincing.

"I'm sorry," he said. "You scared hell out of me."

"You've got every right to be scared. Much more than I do. Nobody's fired a gun at me." O'Brien smiled reassuringly. "But that's all over with. I'll find men to stay with you around the clock."

Chancellor returned the smile weakly. "Whoever they are, I hope they're the best you've got. I don't mind telling you, I've never been so frightened in my life."

The smile disappeared from O'Brien's face. "Whoever they are, they won't be from the bureau."

"Oh? Why not?"

"I don't know who to trust."

"Then, apparently you know there are people you can't trust. Anyone in particular?"

"More than one. There's a pack of extremists here. We know some of them, not all. They're loosely called the Hoover Group. When Hoover died, they thought they'd take over. They didn't and they're angry. Some are as paranoid as Hoover was."

Again Chancellor was struck by O'Brien's words; it was confirmation of Peter's original thinking. Everything that had happened—from Malibu to Rockville to the old house on Thirty-fifth Street—was the result of violent infighting within the FBI. And Longworth had reappeared.

"We have a bargain," he said. "I want protection. For the girl and myself."

"You'll have it."

"From where? Who?"

"You mentioned Judge Sutherland. A couple of years ago he was instrumental in repairing a severed connection between the bureau and the rest of the intelligence community. Hoover had cut off the flow of information to the CIA and the NSC."

"I know that," interrupted Chancellor quietly. "I wrote a book about it."

"That was *Counterstrike!*, wasn't it? I guess I'd better read it."

"I'll send you a copy. You send protection. I repeat; Who? Where from?"

"There's a man named Varak. Sutherland's man. He owes me."

O'Brien collapsed in the chair. His head fell back, his breathing fast and erratic as if he could not let sufficient air into the lungs. He brought his face forward into his hands; he could feel the trembling in his fingers.

He had not been sure he could carry it off. A number of times during the past two hours he thought he was going to fall apart.

It was the writer's panic that had gotten him through the last minutes. The realization that Chancellor had to be controlled; he could not be allowed to learn the truth.

Hoover's files were not destroyed, as Quinn *knew* they had not been. That much seemed certain. And now someone else knew it, too. How many? How many phone calls had been made? How many others had been reached by that terrible high-pitched whisper. A dead general, a murdered congressman, a vanished newspaperwoman—how many more?

Things were not the same as they had been two hours ago. Peter Chancellor's revelation meant there was work to do quickly, and to his great relief, O'Brien began to think he was again capable of doing it.

He picked up the phone and dialed the National Security Council. But Stefan Varak could not be traced.

Where was Varak? What kind of assignment would cut the NSC agent off from the bureau? Especially from *him*? Varak and he were friends. Two years ago Quinn had taken an enormous risk for Varak. He had provided him with profile data Hoover had restricted; it could have cost him his career.

Now he needed Varak. Of all the men in the intelli-

gence community Varak was the best. His range of expertise and the sheer numbers and depth of his contacts were
extraordinary. He was the man Quinn wanted to hear
Chancellor's tape first. Varak would know what to do.

In the meantime the writer had temporary protection.
His name had been removed from the security logs, all
inquiries directed to O'Brien. There were a couple of men
at CIA Quinn had fed print information to during Hoover's
embargo. When O'Brien told them the subject to be
guarded was the author of *Counterstrike!*, they damned
near refused. But, of course, they did not refuse. Reasonable men in the most unreasonable of professions had to
help each other. Otherwise unreasonable men would assume control, and that way lay disaster.

Perhaps they had. Perhaps disaster had already come.

24

The FBI escort made his delivery to the Hay-Adams lobby.
Chancellor was the package. He was signed for by a nod
and a corresponding "Okay. . . . Good night," spoken
politely by the man from the Central Intelligence Agency.

In the elevator Peter tried to make conversation with
this stranger who had volunteered to protect him. "My
name's Chancellor," he said foolishly.

"I know," replied the man. "I read your book. You
did quite a job on us."

It was not the most reassuring of greetings. "It wasn't
meant that way. I have several friends in the CIA."

"Want to bet?"

Not reassuring at all. "There's a man named Bromley
flying in from Indianapolis."

"We know. He's sixty-five years old and in poor
health. He had a weapon on him at the Indie airport. He
has a permit, so it's supposed to be returned to him at the
National terminal, but it won't be. It'll be lost."

"He could pick up another."

"Not likely. O'Brien put a man on him."

They reached the floor; the elevator door opened. The CIA man blocked Peter's exit with his arm and walked out first, his right hand in his overcoat pocket. He glanced up and down the corridor, turned, and nodded to Chancellor.

"What about the morning?" asked Peter, coming out of the elevator. "Bromley could walk into any gun store——"

"With an Indianapolis permit? No retailer would sell him a firearm."

"Some would. There are ways."

"There are better ways to prevent it."

They were at the door of the suite. The CIA man removed his right hand from his coat pocket; he held a small automatic. With his left he undid the two middle buttons of his overcoat and shoved the weapon out of sight. Peter knocked.

He could hear Alison's racing footsteps. She opened the door and moved to embrace him, stopping at the sight of the stranger. "Alison, this is— I'm sorry, I don't know your name."

"Tonight I don't have one," the CIA man said, nodding to Alison. "Good evening, Miss MacAndrew."

"Hello?" Alison was understandably bewildered. "Please come in."

"No, thank you." The agent looked at Chancellor. "I'll be right out here in the corridor at all times. My relief comes on at eight in the morning, which means I'll have to wake you up so you know who he is."

"I'll be up."

"Fine. Good night."

"Wait a minute. . . ." An idea struck Peter. "If Bromley shows up, and you're sure he's not armed, maybe I should talk to him. I don't know him. I don't know why he's after me."

"That's up to you. Let's play it as it comes." He closed the door.

"You were gone so long!" Alison threw her arms around him, her face next to his. "I nearly went out of my mind!"

He held her gently. "That's finished with. Nobody's going out of his mind. Not any more."

"You told them everything?"

"Yes." He moved her back so he could look at her face. "Everything. About your father, too. I had to. The man I talked with knew I was holding back. He made it clear that they could trace every move we made. They wouldn't have to go very far; just across the river to the Pentagon."

She nodded and took his arm, leading him away from the door into the sitting room. "How do you feel?"

"Fine. Relieved. How about a drink?"

"My man's been working. I'll make them," she said, heading for the bar stocked by the hotel's room service. Peter fell into an armchair, his body limp, his feet stretched out. "I've been meaning to ask you," said Alison, pouring whisky and opening the ice bucket. "Do you always have a bar set up for you wherever you go? You don't drink that much."

"A few months ago I drank that much." Chancellor laughed; it was good to remember, knowing things had changed, he thought. "To answer your question, it's an indulgence that came with the first large advance. I remembered all those movies. Writers in hotel rooms always had fancy bars and wore smoking jackets. I don't have a smoking jacket."

It was Alison's turn to laugh. She brought his drink to him and sat in the chair opposite his. "I'll buy you one for Christmas."

"Next Christmas," he said, holding her eyes. "This Christmas give me a plain gold ring. It'll go on the third finger of my left hand. Just as yours will."

Alison drank from her glass and glanced away. "I meant what I said a few hours ago. I don't require any commitments."

Chancellor looked at her, alarmed. He put his drink down and went to her. He knelt by her side and touched her face. "What am I supposed to say? 'Thank you, Miss MacAndrew, it's been a nice interlude'? I won't say it, and I can't think it. I don't think you can, either."

She stared at him, her eyes vulnerable. "There's a great deal you don't know about me."

Peter smiled. "What? You're the daughter of the regiment? The whore of battalion twelve? Virgin you're not, but the other doesn't fit, either. You're not the type. You're too damned independent."

"You make judgments too quickly."

"Good! I'm glad you think so. I'm very decisive, a

quality that's been noticeably absent for a long time . . .
before I met you."

"You were recovering from a very painful experience.
I was here. And in trouble of my own."

"Thank you, Madame Freud. But you see, I *am* recovered, and I *am* decisive. Try this decision out. I realize
marriage isn't in fashion this year, it's so middle class."
He moved closer to her. "But you see, I meant what I said
before, too. I do require a commitment. I believe in marriage, and I want to live with you for the rest of my life."

Her eyes filled with tears. She shook her head and
held his face. "Oh, Peter. Where were you for so many
years?"

"In a different life."

"So was I. What's that silly poem? 'Come live with me
and be my love. . . .' "

"Marlowe. Not so silly."

"And I'll come live with you, Peter. And be your love.
For as long as it makes sense for both of us. But I won't
marry you."

He moved back, again alarmed. "I want more than
that."

"I can't give you any more. I'm sorry."

"I know you can! I feel it! So completely, so much
like—" He stopped.

"Like her? Like your Cathy?"

"Yes! I can't bury that."

"I'd never want you to bury it. Maybe we can have
something just as beautiful. But not marriage."

"Why?"

Tears rolled down her cheeks. "Because marriage
means— I won't have children, Peter."

She was saying something obliquely, and Chancellor
knew it. He was just not sure what it was. "You're jumping
ahead. I hadn't thought one way or the other about—"
Suddenly it was clear to him. "It's your mother. Her madness."

Alison closed her eyes, her face streaked with tears.
"My darling, try to understand."

Peter did not move; he remained at her side and
forced her to look at him. "Listen to me. I understand
something else, too. You never believed what they told
you, what your father told you. That your mother's illness

came about because she nearly drowned. You never accepted that. Why not?"

The look in her eyes was pathetic. "I couldn't be sure. I'm not sure why. That's the awful, awful thing."

"Why couldn't you be sure? Why would your father lie to you?"

"I don't know! I knew him so well, every inflection of his voice, every gesture. He must have told me the story fifty times, always compulsively, as if he wanted me to love her as he once loved her. But there was always something false, something missing. Finally I understood. She was simply a crazy woman. She had grown insane naturally. *Naturally*. And he never wanted me to know. Do you understand now?"

Chancellor reached for her hand. "He could have been hiding something else from you."

"What? Why would——?"

The telephone rang. Peter looked at his watch. It was past three in the morning. Who the hell would call him now? It had to be O'Brien. He picked up the phone.

"You think you've stopped me, but you haven't!" The voice on the line was strident, the breathing heavy.

"Bromley?"

"You animal. You rotten, filthy scum!" Age was in the voice now. The hysterical voice belonged to an old man.

"Bromley, who *are* you? What have I ever done to you? I've never met you before in my life!"

"That wasn't necessary, was it? You don't have to know a person to destroy him. Or her. Destroy a child! And her children!"

Phyllis Maxwell had used the same word! *Destroy*. Did Bromley mean Phyllis? Was he talking about *her*? It couldn't be; she had no children.

"I swear I don't know what you're talking about. Somebody's lied to you. They've lied to others."

"No one lied. They read it to me! You dug out the court transcripts, the confidential transcripts, the psychiatric reports. You wrote it all down, every filthy thing! You used our names, where we live, where *she* lives!"

"None of that's true! I haven't used any court transcripts or psychiatric reports! There's nothing like that in the manuscript! I haven't the vaguest idea what it all means!"

"Scum. Liar." The old man drew out his words in

hatred. "Do you think I'm a fool? Do you think they didn't give me proof? I've been responsible for printing thousands of audits." The voice exploded. "They gave me a number and I *checked* that number and I *called* that number! Bedford Printers! I spoke with the typographer. He read me what you'd written! What he'd set in type a week ago!"

Peter was stunned. Bedford was the printing house his publisher used for its books. "That's impossible! The manuscript's not with Bedford. It couldn't be. It's nowhere near finished!"

There was a momentary silence. Chancellor could only hope he was getting through to the old man. But Bromley's next words told him he was not.

"You go to such lengths to lie! The publication date is set for April. Your publication date's always April."

"Not this year."

"Your book's printed. And I don't care anymore. You weren't satisfied destroying me. Now you go after *her*. But I'll stop you, Chancellor. You can't hide from me. I'll find you, and I'll kill you. Because I don't care. My life is over."

Peter thought quickly. "Listen to me! What's happened to you has happened to others. Let me ask you. Did someone call you, whisper over the telephone? A high-pitched whisper——?"

The phone went dead. Chancellor looked at it and then turned to Alison, her face still damp with tears. "He's insane."

"It's the season for it."

"I won't listen to that," he said, reaching into his pocket for the page of notepaper with O'Brien's number on it. He dialed. "It's Chancellor. Bromley called me. He's desperate. He thinks my book's coming out in April. Like Phyllis Maxwell, he's convinced there's damaging information in it."

"Is there?" asked O'Brien.

"No. I've never heard of him before in my life."

"I'm surprised. He's the GSA accountant who took on the Defense Department over the C-forty cargo plane. He said there was collusion in the overruns."

"I remember. . . ." Peter's mind raced back, picturing the newspaper stories. "There were Senate hearings. He was a pretty lonely guy, if I recall. The super-patriots painted him pale red and into a corner."

"That's the one. His code name over here was Viper."

"It would be. What happened to him?"

"They removed him from 'sensitive' audits—that's what they called it. Then some damned fool at GSA tried to make points with the administration and withheld a rating. He instituted a civil suit."

"And?"

"We don't know. The suit was dropped and he disappeared."

"But we do know, don't we?" said Chancellor. "He received a telephone call with a high-pitched whisper on the other end of the line. And he just received another. With enough scraps of accurate information to convince him he was hearing the truth."

"Easy. He can't touch you. Whatever he thinks you did to him——"

"Not him," interrupted Peter. "He talked about 'her,' 'a child,' 'her children.' "

O'Brien paused. Chancellor knew what the FBI man was thinking: *I've got a wife and family.*

Alexander Meredith.

"I'll try to find out," said the agent finally. "He's checked into a hotel downtown. I've got him under surveillance."

"Does your man know why? Couldn't he be——?"

"Of course not," interrupted Quinn. "Code Viper was enough. The fact that a weapon was picked up on him in Indianapolis was more than enough. He's immobilized. Get some sleep."

"O'Brien?"

"What?"

"Tell me something. Why him? Why a sick old man?"

Again the agent paused before answering. When he spoke, a cold pain formed in Peter's stomach. "Old men move around freely. Very few people stop them or suspect them; not much importance is accorded them. My guess is that an old man who's desperate could be programed into a killer."

"Because he doesn't care anymore?"

"That's part of it, I imagine. Don't worry. He won't get near you."

Chancellor hung up. He needed sleep. There were many things to think about, but he was incapable of thinking. The strain of the night had caught up with him; the pills had worn off.

He could sense Alison watching him, waiting for him to say something. He turned and their eyes met. Deliberately, he walked over to her, with each step more sure of himself. He spoke calmly, with deep concern.

"I'll accept whatever conditions you want to make, whatever way of living you choose, as long as we can be together. I don't ever want to lose you. But there's one condition I insist on. I'm not going to let you torment yourself over something that may not exist. I think something happened to your mother to drive her mad. I've never heard of a person normal one minute and mentally wasted the next unless he or she was pushed. I want to find out what happened. It may be painful, but I think you've got to know. Will you accept my condition?" Peter held his breath.

Alison nodded. A half smile appeared on her face. "Maybe we both have to know."

"Good." Peter resumed breathing. "Now the decision's made, I don't want to talk about it for a while. We don't have to; we've got all the time in the world. As a matter of fact, I don't want to talk about anything vaguely unpleasant for days."

Alison remained in the chair, looking up at him. "Is your novel unpleasant?"

"The blackest. Why?"

"Are you going to stop writing it?"

He paused. It was odd, but once he'd made the decision, actually *gone* to the bureau and told his story, the pressure had been lifted, and his mind was clearer. The professional in him was emerging again. "It'll be a different book. I'll take out people, put in new ones, change the circumstances. But I'll keep a lot, too."

"Can you do that?"

"It'll happen. The premise is still strong. I'll find a way. I'll go slowly for a while; it'll come to me."

Alison smiled. "I'm glad."

"That's the last decision for the night. Anyway, I want to go back to the first one."

"Which is?"

He smiled. "You. Come live with me and be my love."

He heard rapid tapping through the mists of sleep. Alison stirred beside him, burying her head deeper into her pillow. He slid out of the bed and grabbed his trousers from the chair where he had draped them. Naked, he walked into the sitting room, closing the bedroom door behind him. Awkwardly pulling on his trousers, he hopped toward the foyer.

"Who is it?" he asked.

"It's eight o'clock," said the voice of the CIA man beyond the door.

Peter remembered. At eight o'clock the guard changed; it was time for identifications, his and the new sentry's.

And it was all he could do to conceal his shock. He blinked and stifled a yawn and rubbed his eyes to further hide his astonishment. The new man was the CIA "domestic" who had given Peter material for *Counterstrike!* Given it freely. In anger. Deeply concerned over the illegalities the agency was forced to perpetrate.

"Names aren't necessary," said the agent initially assigned to Chancellor. "He'll take over for me."

Peter nodded. "Okay. No names, no handshakes. I wouldn't want you to catch anything."

"What you've got jumps," said the second man quietly, with an offensive tone worthy of his companion. He turned to the first agent. "He stays in the hotel, right?"

"That's what we've agreed to. No outside work."

Both men turned, dismissing him, and walked toward the elevators. Peter went inside and closed the door. He listened for the faint sounds of the elevator. When they came, he waited an additional ten seconds before he opened the door.

The CIA man slid past Chancellor into the small foyer of the suite. Peter closed the door. "Christ!" said the agent. "I nearly had a cardiac arrest when I got the call last night."

"You? I damned near fell over when I saw you standing there!"

"You carried it off. Sorry. I couldn't take the chance of phoning you."

"How did it happen?"

"O'Brien. He's one of our contacts at the bureau. When Hoover shut down communications, O'Brien and several others worked with us, got us information we had to have. It wouldn't make sense for him to call anyone else; they'd probably refuse him. He knew we wouldn't."

"You owed him," said Chancellor.

"More than you can realize. O'Brien and his friends put their necks as well as their careers on the line for us. If they'd ever been found out, Hoover would have gone berserk. He'd have made sure they were sent to some choice prisons for ten to twenty years apiece."

Peter winced. "He could do that, couldn't he?"

"Could and did. There are several unadvertised carcasses rotting away in Mississippi cells even now. It was his last Siberia. O'Brien's owed; we can't forget that."

"But Hoover's dead."

"Maybe somebody's trying to bring him back. Isn't that what this is all about? Why else would O'Brien call us in?"

Chancellor wondered. It was as valid a possibility as he had heard. O'Brien spoke of the Hoover group—some known, others not, none to be trusted. Did they have Hoover's files? Were they trying to regain control of the bureau? If so, men like Quinn O'Brien had to be destroyed for that control to be taken. "You could be right," he said.

The man nodded. "It starts all over again. Not that it's ever really stopped. When I heard your name last night, I wondered what had taken you so long."

"What does that mean?" Peter was confused.

"The information I gave you. You used it pretty exclusively against us. Why? There were a lot of people at fault, not just us."

"I'll say now what I said two years ago. The agency used the failings of other people as an excuse. Too damned quickly and with too much enthusiasm. I thought we'd agreed. I thought that's why you gave me the information."

The man shook his head. "I guess I thought you'd spread the guilt around a little more. Then I figured you were saving it for another book. That *is* what this is all about, isn't it? You're writing a book about the bureau."

Chancellor was stunned. "Where did you hear that?"

"I didn't hear it, I read it. In this morning's paper. Phyllis Maxwell's column."

25

She had done it. The column was short, ominous in its brevity as well as its content, and centered on the editorial page with a black border around it. It would be read widely, raising startling questions and no less startling alarms. Chancellor could picture the distraught Phyllis Maxwell at the airport, clinging to her sanity, reaching the inevitable decision and calling her newspaper's night desk. No editor would cut the copy; she had a sure reputation for documenting her facts. But beyond this, it was a last gesture, a final testament, and recognizable as such. She owed it to her profession, and that profession would not turn its back on her.

Washington, December 19—Information from an unimpeachable source reveals that the Federal Bureau of Investigation will soon be confronted with extraordinary charges of malfeasance, extortion, suppression of criminal evidence, and illegal surveillance of citizens in flagrant violation of their constitutional rights. These allegations will be made in a forthcoming novel by Peter Chancellor, author of *Counterstrike!* and *Sarajevo!* Although the work has been written as fiction, Chancellor has developed his material from fact. He has traced victims and observed their paralyses. Due only to his own sense of morality has he withheld identities and fictionalized the events. This book is long overdue. Throughout this magnificent city with its symbols everywhere of a people's unique struggle for freedom, men and women are afraid. For themselves, their loved ones, their very thoughts, and often their sanity. They live with their fears because a giant squid has reached its tentacles into every corner, spreading its terror. The head of this monster is somewhere within the FBI.

This reporter has been touched by these tactics. Therefore, in conscience, I will be absent from these pages for an indeterminate period of time. It is my hope to return one day, but it will only be when I can dispatch my responsibilities in a manner to which you, the reader, are entitled.

A final word. Too many good and powerful men in the government have been compromised by the working methods of the Federal Bureau of Investigation. These assaults must stop. Perhaps Mr. Chancellor's fiction will bring about that reality. If so, a part of our system will be cleansed.

It was a bombshell; its crater was smoldering, defined by the black border. Peter looked at his watch; it was twenty minutes past eight. He was surprised O'Brien had not called him. Surely he'd seen the paper; surely there was chaos at the FBI. Perhaps the agent was being exceptionally careful. A telephone was suddenly an instrument of danger.

And then, as if his thoughts had willed it, the phone rang and O'Brien was there.

"I knew they were waking you at eight," said Quinn. "Have you seen the paper?"

"Yes. I wondered when you'd call."

"I'm in a phone booth. Obviously. I didn't want to call from home. I got off at four this morning and drove around just thinking for a while, then managed a couple of hours' sleep. Did you expect her to do this?"

"It's the last thing I expected. But I can understand. Maybe it was the only thing she thought she could do."

"It's an unnecessary complication, that's what it is. They'll be looking for her. God help her if she's found. One side will want her life, the other her testimony."

Peter thought for a moment. "She wouldn't have done what she did if she believed she'd be found. She meant what she said in her letter: She planned this for a long time."

"Which means a dead skip. I know something about dead skips. All too often they end up more dead than skipped. But that's her problem; we've got enough of our own."

"Your compassion is touching. Did you reach your man Varak?"

"I've put out an emergency defector code for him. He'll have to respond. It's his specialty."

"What do we do until then?"

"Stay where you are. We'll move you later. Varak will know where."

"*I* know where," said Peter angrily. O'Brien was treating them like fugitives. "My house in Pennsylvania. We'll go there. You just get us——"

"No," interrupted the FBI man firmly. "For the time being you stay away from that house and your apartment. You go where I tell you to go. I want you alive, Chancellor. You're very important to me."

The words had their effect; memories of gunfire returned. "All right. We sit and wait."

"Does anyone in New York or Pennsylvania know where you are?"

"Not specifically. They know I'm in Washington."

"Would they know where to look?"

"Probably this hotel. I stay here a lot."

"You're no longer registered there," said O'Brien. "You checked out late last night; the manager made that clear to the front desk."

It was a chilling piece of news. That it could be effected so easily, that it was even necessary in the agent's judgment, caused Peter to swallow involuntarily. Then he remembered. "I called room service. I gave my name and room number. I signed the bill."

"Goddamn it!" O'Brien exploded. "I didn't consider that."

"I'm glad you're not perfect."

"Less so than I want to think about. It's the kind of mistake Varak wouldn't make. We'll handle it, though. It's only for a few hours. You simply want to be incognito."

"What's my new name?"

"Peters. Charles Peters. It's not very original, but it doesn't matter. I'll be the only one calling you. Now, as soon as you can, telephone anyone in New York who knows you're in Washington. Tell them you and Miss Mac-Andrew have decided to take a couple of days off. You're driving down through Virginia, the Fredericksburg route, toward the Shenandoah. Have you got that?"

"I've got it, but I don't know what I've got. Why?"

"There are a limited number of hotels and motels where you could stay overnight. I want to see who shows up."

Chancellor felt a knot in his stomach. For a moment he was speechless. "What the hell are you saying?" he whispered. "You think Tony Morgan or Joshua Harris are a part of this? You're out of your mind!"

"I told you," replied O'Brien. "I drove around last night just thinking. Everything that's happened to you has happened because of this book you're writing. Most of the places you've been—not all, but most—have been known by those men because you told them."

"I won't listen to this! They're my friends!"

"They may have no choice," said O'Brien. "I know the recruitment methods better than you do. And I'm not saying they *are* involved, I'm only saying they could be. I guess what I'm telling you is not to trust anyone. Not for the moment; not until we learn more." O'Brien lowered his voice. "Perhaps not even me. I say I'm ready to be tested, and I think I am. But I haven't been tested yet. I can only give you my word that I'll try like hell. I'll be in touch."

Quinn hung up abruptly, as if he could not bring himself to talk a second longer. The fact that he was able to express his own self-doubt was remarkable. He was a brave man because he was so obviously frightened, accepting his fear in a loneliness that Chancellor did not have to know.

Peter sat down to breakfast. Only vaguely aware that he was eating, he went through juice, eggs, bacon, and toast. His thoughts were on what O'Brien had said to him: *I guess what I'm telling you is not to trust anyone.*

There was the echo of unreality about it. A once-removed quality too couched in melodrama to be part of life. Abnormal, false.

Fiction.

Without his thinking about it, his eyes strayed beyond the coffeepot to his notebook on the table in front of the couch. He got out of the chair, carrying his coffee, and sat down on the couch. He opened the notebook, staring at the words he had written yesterday before the madness had begun. The madness that had led him to Quinn O'Brien.

The compulsion was there. He recognized it for what it was: a need to translate the madness he had experienced into a reality he could communicate. Because he *had* experienced it. He had always imagined what it would be like to be hunted, to be trapped, to be frightened and confused and face death—to strain every fiber and brain cell in a search for escape and survival. He had never before lived those feelings, until now. The changes in the book could come later, but for now he'd follow the story line he had developed and complete the chapter tomorrow. He had to put it down, this new, firsthand madness.

Chapter 10 — Outline

Meredith has joined the Nucleus. He is to develop undeniable evidence that within the FBI there is a group of *specific* men who are involved in grossly illegal activities. Not words on paper but voices on tape.

The method will be entrapment, and Alex is tutored by Alan Long. The converted Hoover gunslinger tells Meredith that the only approach is to feign total capitulation to the fanatics inside the bureau. He has the motive: He cannot take the harassment any longer.

The trap will be in the form of a miniaturized tape machine, placed in his handkerchief pocket, activated by touch.

There is a series of short, emotional confrontations in which Alex is seen abjectly "surrendering" to the Hoover forces. It is not difficult for him to be convincing, for he is reflecting a state of mind he has experienced.

There is a scene at night in which Meredith overhears—in detail—a plan to "eliminate" an FBI informant who has threatened to expose the bureau's involvement in the killing of five black radicals in Chicago. The massacre was the direct result of FBI provocation. The informant is marked for death; the method will be an untraceable weapon in a crowded subway.

Alex has activated the miniaturized equipment. He has the voices on tape. The evidence is now undeniable: conspiracy to commit murder.

The enormity of the charge is enough to drive Hoover from office. It will lead to the uncovering of additional abuses, for it is only one incident in a network of conspiracies. Hoover is finished.

Alex is seen leaving, but the Hoover men sense his duplicity.

Meredith races out of the bureau to his car. He has been given an address in McLean, Virginia, to reach in emergencies. There has never been an emergency like this; he has in his pocket the evidence that will destroy the Man and the men who would turn the country into their own personal police state.

As he drives out of the parking lot, he spots a car behind him he believes to be an FBI vehicle.

A wild chase ensues through the streets of Washington. At a traffic light the man beside the driver of the FBI automobile rolls down the window shouting *"There!"* He then leaps out for Meredith's door. Alex jumps the light, careening down the street, pressing his horn, dodging other cars.

He recalls a tactic: lose an automobile, lose surveillance. He stops in front of a government building, leaves the motor running, gets out, and races up the steps inside.

Only a uniformed guard is there. Meredith flashes his FBI identification and runs across the marble floor past banks of elevators, pressing the buttons, looking for another exit. He sees a pair of glass doors leading to an open-air corridor that connects the building to another. He races out; from behind a pillar a man emerges. It is one of the two men following him. He holds a gun in his hand. Alex touches the recorder, activating it.

"It's an old trick, Meredith. You're not very good at it."

"You're executioners! You're Hoover's executioners!" screams Alex in panic.

The screams are enough to cause the man to lose his concentration; screams can be heard. In that brief instant Meredith does what he never believed he'd be capable of doing. He rushes at the man with the gun.

A violent struggle takes place; two shots are fired.

The first wounds Alex in the shoulder. The second kills the FBI fanatic.

Meredith stumbles through the corridor holding his wound. The second FBI man is seen running toward the glass doors at the other end.

He gets through to the other building and out on the street. He hails a taxi, falls back into the seat and gives the driver the address in McLean.

He reaches McLean, barely conscious. He struggles up the path to the door and holds his hand on the bell. The former cabinet officer answers; it is his residence.

"I'm shot. In my pocket. The recorder. Everything's on it."

He falls into unconsciousness.

He awakes in a darkened room; he is on a couch, bandages across his chest and shoulder. He hears voices beyond the closed door; he gets up and edges his way along the wall to the door and opens it an inch. Beyond, around a dining room table, sits the cabinet officer, the news-paperwoman, and Alan Long. The senator is not there.

Alex's tape recorder is by the ex-member of the President's cabinet. He is speaking to Long.

"Did you know about these . . . execution squads?"

"There've been rumors," replies Long cautiously. "I was never involved."

"You wouldn't be trying to save your own neck?"

"What's there to save?" asks Long. "If anyone found out what I've done—what I'm doing—I'm dead."

"Which brings us back to these squads," says the woman. "What did you hear?"

"Nothing specific," answers Long. "No proof. Hoover departmentalizes everything. Everybody. He does it all secretly; no one really knows what the man in the next office does. That way everyone stays in line."

"Gestapo!" says the woman.

"What *did* you hear?" The cabinet officer.

"Only that there were final solutions if everything fell apart on a project."

The woman stares at Long, then briefly closes her eyes. "Final—Oh, my God."

"If we ever needed a last, overwhelming justification," says the balding man, "I think we have it. Hoover will be killed two weeks from Monday, the files taken."

"No!" Alex has yanked the door open with such force that it crashes into the wall. "You can't do it! You have everything you need. Bring him to trial! Let him face the judgment of the courts! Of the country!"

"You don't understand," says the cabinet officer. "There's not a court in the land, not a judge, not a member of the House or of the Senate, not the President or any of his cabinet, who can bring him to trial. It's beyond that."

"No, it isn't! There are laws!"

"There are the files," says the newspaper-woman softly. "People would be reached . . . by others who have to survive."

Meredith sees the eyes staring at him. The eyes are cold, without sympathy.

"Then, you're no better than he is," says Alex, knowing that if he ever gets out of that house, he will be hunted again.

Chancellor let the pencil drop. He was suddenly aware of Alison in the doorway. She stood in her blue bathrobe, looking down at him. He was grateful for the warmth in her eyes and the smile on her lips.

"Do you know I've been standing here for nearly three minutes and you didn't see me."

"I'm sorry."

"Don't be. I was fascinated. You were so far away."

"I was in McLean, Virginia."

"That's not so far."

"It better be." Peter got up from the couch and took her in his arms. "You're adorable and I love you and let's go to bed."

"I just got out of bed. Let me have some coffee; it'll wake me up."

"Why wake up?"

"So I can enjoy you. Is that too lascivious?" She kissed him.

"The coffee's cold," he said. "I'll order more."

"That's okay. I don't mind."

"I want to mail something anyway."

"What?"

"The work I've done during the past couple of days. I should get it up to the typists."

"Now?"

Peter nodded. "I should reread it, have it Xeroxed, send it by messenger. But I don't want to look at it for a while. I just want to get rid of it. I've got some manila envelopes in my briefcase." He walked to the phone across the room, remembering O'Brien's instructions. "Operator? This is Mr. Peters in five-eleven. I'd like room service, but I'd also like to mail something special delivery. May I give it to the waiter to bring to the desk?"

"Certainly, Mr. Peters." There seemed to be a smile in the operator's voice.

They lay naked in each other's arms, warmed by the moment and the desire each felt growing again.

The afternoon sun was reflected from unseen windows outside. From somewhere down in the streets the faint strains of a Christmas carol drifted up from a storefront down the block. It occurred to Peter that most of the day was gone.

The telephone rang. Chancellor reached for it.

"Mr. Peters?" It was the operator; he recognized the voice.

"Yes?"

"Mr. Peters, I know this is very improper. I realize you don't want it known you're registered, and I can assure you I didn't say anything to the contrary—"

"What is it?" interrupted Peter, his heart racing.

"There's a man on the line. He says it's an emergency and that he has to talk to a Mr. Chancellor. He sounds quite ill, sir."

"Who is it?"

"He says his name is Longworth. Alan Longworth."

The pain in Peter's temples made him shut his eyes.

26

"Get out of my life, Longworth! It's over! I've gone to the bureau and told them everything!"

"You damned fool. You don't know what you've done."

It was Longworth's voice, yet it was more guttural than Peter remembered, more pronounced in its Middle-European accent.

"I know exactly what I've done, and I know what you're trying to do. You and your friends want control of the FBI. You think it's yours by some kind of right or inheritance. Well, it isn't. And now they'll stop you."

"You're wrong, all wrong. It's we who want to stop it. Always *we*." Longworth coughed; it was a horrible sound. "I can't talk on the phone. We must meet."

Again there was the strange echo of an accent. "Why? So you can set up a firing squad like you did on Thirty-fifth Street?"

"I was there. I tried to stop it."

"I don't believe you."

"Listen to me." Longworth went into another spasm of coughing. "There were silencers. Everywhere. Weapons with silencers, as there were in Fort Tryon."

"I remember. I'll never forget."

"But one shot last night was *not* fired through a silencer! Can you remember that?"

Longworth's words triggered a memory. There *had* been a shot, a loud explosion in counterpoint to the spits. And one shout of anger. He hadn't thought of it then; there had been far too much going on. But now it seemed clear. A gunman had forgotten to employ a silencer.

"Do you remember?" continued Longworth. "You must."

"Yes. What's your point?"

"It was I! There was that *tone* again. And the proper grammar. Most men in panic would say: It was *me*.

"You?"

"Yes. I followed you. I'm always near you. When those men appeared, I wasn't prepared for what happened. I did what I could. Frankly, I don't know how you got out alive. . . ." Longworth coughed again.

Chancellor had never heard a death rattle, but in his imagination he was hearing one now. And if he was, Longworth was telling the truth. "I have a question," he said. "Maybe an accusation, I don't know. You say you're always near me. I know you ride in a silver Continental, that'll come later——"

"*Quickly!*"

"If you're always near me, it means you've been waiting for someone to reach me."

"Yes."

"Who?"

"Not on the telephone! Especially not now."

"I've been *bait!*"

"You were never to be hurt," said Longworth.

"But I was, wasn't I? I was damned near killed. You say you weren't prepared. In New York and down here. Why not?"

Longworth paused. "Because what happened was contrary to everything we knew, everything we projected."

"Inconceivable?" asked Peter sarcastically.

"Yes. That such chances would be taken— There's no more time. I'm very weak, calls can be traced. You must come to see me for your own safety. For the girl's safety."

"There's a CIA man in the corridor. He'll stay here. I'll come with the police!"

"You do and they'll kill you on sight. The girl will be next."

Chancellor knew it was true. It was in Longworth's voice. A dying man's voice. "What happened? Where are you?"

"I escaped. Listen to me; do as I tell you. I'll give you three telephone numbers. Do you have a pencil?"

Peter turned. "There's a pencil and paper——" He did not have to finish. Alison got out of bed and brought them rapidly to him. "Go ahead."

Longworth gave three telephone numbers, repeating each. "Take coins with you. In precisely thirty minutes call each of these numbers from a telephone booth. From one you'll recognize something you've written. You'll know where to find me. You'll understand. There'll be questions."

"Questions? Something I've *written?* I've written three books!"

"It is a short paragraph, but I believe you thought

deeply about it when you wrote it. Expect to be followed. Take the man in the corridor with you. You've got thirty minutes. Lose those who follow you. The agent in the corridor will know what to do."

"*No*," said Peter firmly. "He stays here. With Mac-Andrew's daughter. Unless he's replaced by another man."

"There's no time!"

"Then you'll just have to trust that I know what I'm doing."

"You don't."

"We'll see. I'll call in thirty minutes." Chancellor hung up the telephone and stared at it.

Alison touched his arm. "Who stays with me and where are you going?"

"The CIA man. I'm going out."

"Why."

"Because I have to."

"That's no answer. I thought you said it was over!"

"I was wrong. But it will be soon, I promise you that." He got out of bed and began dressing.

"What are you going to do? You can't just leave without telling me." Her voice was shrill.

Chancellor turned, buttoning his shirt. "Longworth's hurt, I think pretty seriously."

"Why do you *care*? Look what he's done to you! What he's done to us."

"You don't understand. It's the way I want him, the only way I can force him to go with me." From his suitcase Peter pulled out a dark brown sweater and put it on.

"Go where?"

"To O'Brien. I don't give a damn what Longworth says, I trust him. Quinn won't tell me everything, but he knows what's going on. I heard him on that tape. He's risking his career, maybe his life. This whole goddamned thing started inside the bureau, and that's where it's going to end. Longworth's the key. I'm going to deliver him to O'Brien. Let O'Brien unravel it."

Alison put her hands on his arms. Her grip was firm. "Why deliver him? Why not call O'Brien now? Let *him* find him."

"It wouldn't work; Longworth's an expert—I've seen that. He'll take precautions. If he even suspected what I intended to do, he'd run." Chancellor left unspoken the thought that Longworth might die before O'Brien could get the answers, the identities, from him. If that happened, the insanity would continue.

"Why did he give you three telephone numbers?"

"He'll be at one of them. It's part of the precautions; he's not taking chances."

"When you talked to him, you mentioned your books——"

"More of the same," interrupted Peter, going to the closet for his jacket. "He's going to quote something he says I'll recognize. It'll tell me specifically where he is. It's another reason O'Brien would be useless right now."

"*Peter!*" Alison confronted him, her eyes concerned and angry. "He wanted that man in the hallway to go with you, didn't he?"

"It doesn't make any difference what he wants." Chancellor walked into the sitting room. He went to the coffee table, tore off several pages of blank paper from his notebook, and picked up a pencil. Alison followed.

"Take him with you," she said.

"No," he answered simply. "There's no time."

"For what?"

He turned and faced her. "To talk anymore. I have to go."

She would not let him. "You told him you were going to call the police, bring them with you. Why won't you?"

It was the question he'd hoped she would not ask. The answer was found in threats of death, threats he knew were based in truth. "For the same reason I can't call O'Brien. Longworth would run. I have to find him, take him, and deliver him. I can't let him get away." He held her by the shoulders. "I'll be fine. Trust me. I know what I'm doing."

He kissed her, went to the foyer without looking back, and stepped outside into the corridor. The agency man snapped his head up, startled.

"I have to go out," Peter said.

"No way," replied the CIA man. "That's not part of the rules."

"There are no rules. For instance, you and I have an agreement. Two years ago I needed information, and you gave it to me. I swore to you I'd never say where I got it. But I'm changing that. If you don't help me, I'll go back inside that room, pick up the phone, call the agency, and reveal every source I had for *Counterstrike!* Do I make myself clear?"

"You rotten son of a bitch——"

"You'd better believe it." Chancellor did not raise his voice. "Now, there are men watching this hotel who are going to try to follow me. If I can get out without their seeing me, I've got a fair chance. I want that chance, and you're going to tell me how to get it; you'd better be good. If I'm caught, so are you. But you're not going to leave this hallway. Because if you do, if anything happens to that girl, you're hung."

The agency man said nothing. Instead, he pressed the wall button; the elevator on the right arrived first, but there were passengers in it. He let it go by. The second elevator came from the lobby; it was empty. The CIA man stepped inside, pressed the stop button, and picked up the emergency telephone. When maintenance got on the phone, he identified himself as a building inspector, but he made light of it, joking with the man on the line. He needed help, he said. Would his new friend please send up a repairman right away? He had loused up the panel box and did not have his tools. He hung up and turned to Chancellor.

"Have you got money?"

"Some."

"Let me have twenty dollars."

Peter gave it to him. "What are you going to do?"

"Get you out of here."

In less than a minute the door of the elevator on the left opened, and the repairman came out. He wore overalls and a large tool belt. The agency man greeted him, flashed his CIA identification, and asked him to step into the car. They talked so quietly Chancellor could not hear them, but he could see the agent hand the man the twenty dollars. He came out and motioned Peter inside.

"Do what he says. He thinks it's an agency training exercise."

Chancellor walked into the elevator. The repairman was taking off his overalls. Peter watched him, astonished. Underneath the work clothes the repairman wore a soiled undershirt and a pair of white shorts with blue and red polka dots, not unlike a Wonder bread wrapper.

"I can't give you the tool belt, you understand. That's personal property."

"I understand," said Chancellor. He put on the overalls and the repairman's cap.

They took the elevator directly to the basement. The repairman led Chancellor around a corner and up a short flight of cement steps into a locker room.

Two hotel employees were dressed and ready to leave. The repairman talked quietly with them.

"Come on, mister," said the man on the right. "You've practically got a union card."

"What do you know?" said his companion. "The super spies play games."

The basement door opened into an alley, which in turn led to the street. The alley was narrow and lined with garbage cans. Peter could see the figure of a man in a raincoat at the street entrance, silhouetted against the dull yellowish twilight beyond. The streets would be dark soon. He would use the darkness and the crowds, thought Chancellor. But first he had to get past the man in the raincoat. The man wasn't there by coincidence.

He walked between the two hotel employees, and nodded at the figure ahead; the two men understood. They entered the game, enjoying it. Each began talking at once, directing their conversation at Peter as they walked past the man in the entrance.

"You!" said the man in the raincoat.

Chancellor froze. A hand was clamped on his shoulder. He shrugged it off angrily. The man spun Peter around, ripping the repairman's cap off his head.

Chancellor rushed at the man, body checking him back into the alleyway. The two hotel employees looked at each other, suddenly concerned.

"You guys play rough," said the man on the left.

"I don't think they're playing," said his companion, moving away.

Peter heard no more. He ran, dodging the pedestrians on the sidewalk. He reached the corner; the light was red and traffic filled the street. He turned to his right, aware of a racing figure behind him, and started running again down the block. He dashed into the street, glancing off the fender of a car, and reached the other side. There was a crowd in front of a store window; beyond the glass a marionette show depicted Santa Claus and his elves. Chancellor forced his way between bodies like a man possessed. He looked back over the heads of the crowd.

The man in the raincoat was on the other side of the street, but he was making no move to cross over. Instead, he held a rectangular case against his face, angled from cheek to mouth. He was talking into a radio.

Peter edged his way along the side of the building, away from the crowd. Before he realized it, he was in front of another window, this one a jeweler's. Suddenly the glass splintered; it was like no other sound he had ever heard.

An alarm went off, filling the air with a deafening bell. People turned to stare at him. Petrified, he looked at the window. Only inches from him was a small circle in the glass. A bullet hole! *An unseen hand was firing at him!*

The crowds on the sidewalk began yelling. He raced to the corner; a man ran after him.

"Stop! I'm a police officer!"

Peter lunged into the crowd; if the policeman had his pistol leveled, he dared not fire it. He tugged and pulled and crashed his way to the curb, where he started racing along the edge of the street. The intersection was jammed, the rush-hour traffic at a standstill.

There was an empty taxi up the block, halfway toward the next corner. Chancellor ran toward it, hoping no one would reach it first. It was more than a means of travel, it was sanctuary.

"I'm off duty, buddy. No more fares."

"Your light's on!"

"A mistake. Now it's off." The driver looked at him, shaking his head in disgust.

Peter was suddenly aware that the repairman's overalls had split; he looked disheveled, maybe worse. Without thinking, he began taking them off in the middle of the street.

"A pret-ty girl . . . is like . . . a mel-odie. . . ."

A drunk on the curb was watching him, clapping in the rhythm of the strip. The traffic moved; the taxi drove forward. Chancellor stepped out of the overalls and hurled them at the drunk on the curb.

The cars in the street jerked to a stop. Peter leaped between bumpers and trunks and ran into the crowds. He looked at his watch. It was twenty-seven minutes since he had talked to Longworth. He had to get to a telephone.

In the next block, diagonally across the street, he could see the reflection of colored lights off the glass of a booth. It was no longer twilight, it was evening. Above, the Washington sky was dark.

He threaded his way through the traffic in the street. The booth was occupied. A teen-aged girl in dungarees and a red flannel shirt was talking animatedly. Peter looked at his watch; twenty-nine minutes had passed. Longworth had said to call in precisely thirty minutes. How crucial was it? Would a minute or two make any difference?

Chancellor knocked on the glass. The girl shot him a hostile glance. He pushed the door and shouted. "I'm a police officer! I need that phone!" It was the only thing that came to mind.

It was enough. The girl dropped the phone. "Sure." She started to slide out; then she thrust her head down toward the dangling instrument. "I'll call ya', Jennie!" She ran out into the crowds.

Peter replaced the phone, took out the paper with the numbers written on it, inserted a coin, and dialed.

"Manfriedie's," announced the voice on the line. There was music in the background; it was a restaurant.

"Peter Chancellor. I was told to call this number." It was going to be one of the decoys, Peter was sure of it.

"There was a strange occurrence in Munich in the year 1923. It was a portent of things to come, but no one recognized it. What was it, describe it, name the book of yours in which it appeared."

"It took place in the Marienplatz. Thousands of men held a rally. They were dressed in identical uniforms, and each carried a shovel. They called themselves the Army of Shovelers. The *Schutzstaffel*. It was the beginning of the Nazi. The book was *Reichstag!*"

There was a brief silence, then the voice came back again. "Disregard the next telephone number given you. Use the same exchange, but the last four digits are now five, one, seven, seven. Fifty-one, seventy-seven. Have you got that?"

"Yes. Five, one, seven, seven. Same exchange."

The man hung up. Peter dialed the new number.

"Arts and Industries," said a woman's voice.

"My name is Chancellor. Do you have a question for me?"

"Yes, I do," answered the woman pleasantly. "There was an organization in Serbia, established during the second decade of the century and headed by a man——"

"Let me save you time," interrupted Peter. "The organization was called the Unity of Death. It was formed in 1911, and its leader was known as Apis. His real name was Dragutin and he was the director of Serbia's military intelligence. The book was *Sarajevo!*"

"Very good, Mr. Chancellor." The woman sounded as though she were in a classroom, appreciating a well-prepared student. "Now, here's a new telephone number for you."

She gave it to him; he dialed it. Again the exchange was the same.

"History and Technology, Laboratories Division." The speaker was male. Peter identified himself and was told to wait a moment. Another voice came on the line, this time a woman's, the accent foreign.

"I should like you to tell me what moves a man to separate himself from all he has known and accepted, and to risk becoming a pariah in the eyes of his peers. For to refuse that risk, to continue as he has, is to die within himself."

Chancellor stared at the white casing of the telephone. Those were his words, from *Counterstrike!* One short paragraph among thousands, but for Peter it was the key to the entire book. If Longworth had the capacity to discern that, there was, perhaps, more to the man than he had considered.

"The knowledge that the administration of justice and fairness no longer mattered to the country's leaders. The people must be shown this, the leaders confronted." Chancellor felt foolish; he quoted himself.

"Thank you, Mr. Chancellor," said the woman with the accent. "Please analyze your reply and the telephone calls you have just made. The combination will tell you what you want to know."

Peter was bewildered. "It tells me nothing! I've got to reach Longworth! Now, you tell me where he is!"

"I don't know any Mr. Longworth; I'm only reading what was given me over the phone by an old friend."

There was a click and then the whine of a dial tone. Peter slammed his hand on the phone. It was crazy! Three unconnected phone calls involving books he'd written over— Unconnected? No, not actually. The exchanges were identical. That meant the locations— Where was the telephone book?

It was on a chain on the right side of the booth. He found Manfriedie's Restaurant. The address was on Twelfth Street Northwest. The second call was taken by a woman who said the words *Arts and Industries*. The third was *History and Technology*. Where was the connection?

It was suddenly very obvious. They were buildings in the Smithsonian complex! Manfriedie's was near the Mall. Near the Smithsonian! Probably the only restaurant in the area.

But where in the Smithsonian? It was immense.

Analyze your reply.

The knowledge that the administration of justice and fairness . . .

Administration!

The administration building at the Smithsonian! One of Washington's landmarks.

That was it! Longworth was there!

Peter let the telephone book swing back into place. He turned and yanked the door open.

He stopped. In front of him stood the man in the raincoat. In the darkness, illuminated by the flashing colors of the Christmas lights, Chancellor saw the gun in the man's hand. On its barrel was the perforated tube of a silencer. The weapon was pointed at his stomach.

27

There was no time for thought. So Peter screamed. As loudly and as maniacally as he could.

He swung his left hand down toward the obscene perforated cylinder. There were two vibrations, shots; a piece of cement exploded. Only yards away a man and a woman cried out hysterically. The woman grabbed her stomach, collapsing on the sidewalk, writhing; the man reeled, holding his face, blood rolling through his fingers.

There was chaos. The man in the raincoat pulled the

trigger again. Chancellor heard the spit, his hand felt the white heat of the cylinder, and glass shattered behind him. Peter would not let go of the deadly thing; he kicked at the man's legs, brought his knees up into the man's groin, and pushed him backward into the street. The traffic was moving; the man crashed into the fender of an onrushing car, the impact hurling him back onto the curb.

Peter's hand was burned, the skin blistered, but his fingers were still gripped around the cylinder, stuck to it. The gun was his.

With the strength born of panic the man in the raincoat staggered up; a knife was in his hand, the long blade whipping out from its recess. He lunged at Chancellor.

Peter fell against the booth, avoiding the knife. He pulled the cylinder from his left hand; the blistered skin of his palm came partially off with it. He pointed the barrel at the man in the raincoat.

He could not pull the trigger! He could not fire the gun!

The man slashed the knife up in a backhand lunge, the blade meant to sever Chancellor's throat. Peter lurched away, the blade's point entering his sweater. He brought his right foot up, catching the man in the chest and hammering him backward. The man fell on his shoulder. For an instant he lay stunned.

Sirens wailed in the distance now. Shrill whistles blew as the police converged. Chancellor followed his physical instincts. Holding the pistol in his hand, he sprang at his stunned attacker and brought the barrel down on the man's head.

Then he ran through the hysterical crowds to the intersection, out into the street, against the traffic. He kept running.

He turned into a narrow side street; the cacophony of sirens and screams receded behind him. The street was darker than those of the shopping district; it housed small offices in old two- and three-story brick buildings.

Peter fell into the shadows of a doorway. His chest and legs and temples were in pain. His breath was so spent he thought he would vomit; so he went limp and let air fill his lungs.

Somehow he would have to get to the Smithsonian. To Alan Longworth. He did not want to think about it, not for a few minutes. He had to find a moment of quiet, a void where the pounding in his head would cease because there would be no——

Oh, Jesus! At the entrance of the narrow street, in the dim spill of the streetlights, two men were stopping pedestrians, asking questions. They had followed him. His scent was no less than that left by a fugitive tracked down by bloodhounds.

Chancellor crept out of the shadows into other shadows on the sidewalk. He could not run; he would be seen too easily. He spun around behind the iron grillwork of a railing that rose above a stone staircase, and looked back between the fluting. The men were talking to each other now, the man on the right holding a walkie-talkie next to his ear.

There was the sound of a horn. A car was turning into the street, and the two men were in its path. They moved to their left to let the automobile go by; they were blocked from sight. If they were blocked, so was he! But it would only be for seconds—two or three at most.

Chancellor stepped out from behind the grillwork and started running to his right down the sidewalk. If he could pace himself somehow with the approaching car, he could stretch out the time he would be out of sight; three or four more seconds would be enough. He listened for the engine behind him. The maneuver worked! He was at the corner. He ducked behind the edge of the building and pressed his back against the stone. He inched his face forward and looked around into the narrow street. The two men were moving cautiously from doorway to doorway, their caution itself bewildering Peter. Then he understood. In his panic he had forgotten, but the weight in his jacket pocket reminded him: He had the gun. The gun he could not fire.

Strollers looked at him; a couple hurried past; a mother and child crossed to the curb edge of the sidewalk to avoid him. Chancellor raised his eyes to the street sign. New Hampshire Avenue; diagonally across was the intersection of T Street. He had been in the shopping district north of Lafayette Square; he had run between fifteen and twenty blocks, perhaps more if he took into account the various cutoffs and alleyways. He had to double back somehow and head southeast toward the Mall.

The two men were no more than fifty yards away. To his right, a half block north of where he was, the traffic light turned green. Chancellor started to run again. He reached the corner, crossed the street, turned left, and stopped. A policeman stood beneath the traffic signal; he was looking at Peter.

It was, thought Chancellor, perhaps the only opportunity he'd have. He could go up to the police officer, identify himself, and say that men were hunting him. The officer could call in and learn of the chaos twenty blocks away, hear for himself how a gun had been fired and shoppers wounded. He could say all this to the officer and plead for assistance.

But even as he considered the idea, he realized that there would be questions, and forms to fill out, and statements to be made. Longworth would wait only so long. And there were men with radios and weapons looking for him; back at the hotel Alison was alone, with only one man to protect her. The madness would not be stopped by going to the police. It would only be prolonged.

The light changed. Peter walked rapidly across the intersection, past the police officer, and into T Street. He stepped into a doorway, into the shadows, and looked back. A block and a half south a black limousine heading north had pulled to a stop at the corner of the narrow street and New Hampshire Avenue. Directly in front of the car was a streetlamp. He could see the two men approaching the car; a rear window slid down.

A taxi headed south on New Hampshire. The light was red; the cab stopped. Chancellor raced to it from the doorway. In the backseat was an elderly, well-dressed man. Peter opened the door.

"*Hey!*" yelled the driver. "I've got a fare!"

Chancellor addressed the passenger. He tried to sound reasonable, a man doing his best to remain calm in a crisis. "Please forgive me, but there's an emegency. I have to get downtown. My—my wife is very ill. I've just heard——"

"Come in, come in," said the elderly man without hesitation. "I'm only going as far as Dupont Circle. Is that convenient? I can——"

"That's fine, sir. I'm very grateful." Peter stepped in as the light changed. He slammed the door; the taxi bolted forward.

Whether it was the door slam or the driver's loud voice, Chancellor would never know, but as they passed the limousine on the other side of New Hampshire, he could see that the two men spotted him. Peter looked out the rear window. The man on the right had his walkie-talkie against his face.

They reached Dupont Circle; the elderly man got out. Chancellor instructed the driver to go south on Connecticut Avenue. The traffic was heavier, guaranteed to become worse as they headed into the center of Washington. It was both an asset and a liability. The congested streets allowed him to look in all directions carefully to see if anyone had picked up his trail. Conversely, the heavy traffic allowed others to find him, to catch up with him on foot if necessary.

They reached K Street; to the right was Seventeenth. Peter tried to visualize a Washington map, the main intersecting thoroughfares south of the Ellipse.

Constitution Avenue! He could have the driver turn left on Constitution and head for the Smithsonian through the Mall's entrance. Was there an entrance in that stretch of block?

There had to be. In the chapter outline that morning, he had envisioned Alexander Meredith driving—racing— out of the Mall. Had he written that? Or was it only——?

Chancellor saw it through the rear window. A gray car had swung out of the traffic and sped forward in the left-turn lane. It drew parallel to the taxi; suddenly a beam of light shot through the window, crisscrossing with the shafts of headlights behind. Peter edged forward, keeping his face obscured by the car frame, and looked out. Across the short distance a man next to the driver had the window rolled down. His flashlight was aimed at the cab's identification on the door panel. Chancellor heard him speak.

"There! That's it!"

It was madness within madness. In his imagination that morning two men had careened through the Washington streets after Alexander Meredith. An automobile had pulled alongside Meredith's car; a window had been rolled down, and a voice had exclaimed:

"There!"

The man got out of his car. He jumped across the narrow space between the two vehicles, his hand thrust forward, gripping the handle of the taxi door. The traffic light changed, and Chancellor yelled at the driver.

"Go down Seventeenth! Hurry!"

The cab lurched forward, the driver only vaguely aware there was a problem he wanted none of. Behind them horns blared. Peter looked out the window. The man was still in the street—confused, angry, blocking traffic.

The taxi sped south on Seventeenth Street, past the Executive Office Building to New York Avenue and the Corcoran Gallery. A traffic light was red; the cab stopped. There were lights still on in the gallery; he had read something in the newspaper about a new exhibition from a museum in Brussels.

The traffic light was taking too long! The gray car would be beside them any moment. Peter reached into his pocket for his money clip. There were a number of singles and two ten-dollar bills. He removed them all and leaned forward.

"I want you to do something for me. I have to go inside the Corcoran Gallery, but I want you to wait for me outside the door with your motor running and roof light off. If I'm delayed more than ten minutes, forget it, you're paid."

The driver saw the tens and took them. "I thought your wife was sick. Who the hell was that back there? He tried to open the door——"

"It doesn't matter," interrupted Chancellor. "The light's changing; please do as I say."

"It's your money. You got ten minutes."

"Ten minutes," agreed Peter. He climbed out. Above the short flight of steps the glass doors were closed; beyond them a uniformed guard stood casually beside a small desk. Chancellor walked swiftly up the steps and opened the door. The guard glanced at him but made no move to interfere.

"May I see your invitation, sir?"

"For the exhibition?"

"Yes, sir."

"I'm embarrassed, officer," said Peter quickly, reaching for his wallet. "I'm from *The New York Times*. I'm supposed to cover the exhibition for next Sunday's paper. I was in a traffic accident a few minutes ago, and I can't find . . ."

He hoped to God he had it in his wallet. A year ago he'd written several pieces for the *Times Magazine;* the editors had given him a temporary press pass.

He found it between credit cards. He held it out for the guard, his thumb covering the expiration date. His hand trembled; he wondered if the guard noticed.

"Okay, okay," said the guard. "Take it easy. Just sign the register."

Chancellor leaned over the desk, picked up the chained ball-point pen and scribbled his name. "Where's the exhibition?"

"Take one of the elevators on the right to the second floor."

He walked rapidly to the bank of elevators and pressed the buttons. He looked back at the guard; the man was paying no attention. An elevator door opened, but Peter had no intention of taking it. He wanted the sound to cover his steps as he ran to an exit on the other side of the building.

There was another sound. Behind him the glass doors opened. Chancellor saw the figure of the man from the gray car. The decision was made for him. He went swiftly into the empty elevator, his hand pressing the first buttons he could reach on the panel. The door closed; the elevator started up.

He walked out into a milling crowd and the pools of light that shot down from the ceiling. Waiters in red jackets carrying silver trays mingled among the guests. Paintings and sculpture were everywhere, illuminated by spotlights. The guests were the diplomatic corps and those who traveled with that crowd, including members of the Washington press. He recognized several.

Peter stopped a waiter for champagne. He drank it quickly so he could hold the empty glass up, partially concealing his face, and look around.

"You're Peter Chancellor! I'd know you anywhere!" The greeter was a Brunhilde, her Valkyrie helmet a flowery hat set squarely above her Wagnerian face. "When's your new novel being published?"

"I'm not working on anything right now."

"Why are you in Washington?"

Peter looked at the wall. "I'm partial to Flemish art."

Brunhilde had a small spiral pad in her left hand, a pencil in her right. She wrote as she talked. "Invited by the Belgian Embassy . . . a connoisseur of Flemish art."

"I didn't say that," protested Chancellor. "I'm not."

Through the crowd he saw the elevator door slide

open. Out walked the man who moments ago had rushed through the glass doors downstairs in the lobby.

Brunhilde was saying something; he had not been listening. "I'd much rather you were having an affair with an embassy wife. Anybody's wife."

"Is there a staircase up here?"

"What?"

"A *staircase*. An exit!" Chancellor took her elbow and maneuvered her ample body between himself and the man's line of sight.

"I *thought* I recognized you!" The thin, high-pitched woman's voice belonged to a blond-haired columnist Peter vaguely recognized. "You're Paul Chancellor, the writer."

"Close enough. Do you know where an exit is? I have to get downstairs in a hurry."

"Use the elevator," said the columnist. "Look, there's one now." She stepped back to gesture.

The movement attracted the man's attention. He started toward Peter. Chancellor backed away.

The man made his way through the crowd. In the far corner of the room, beyond an hors d'oevres table, a waiter came through a swinging door. Chancellor dropped his glass and grabbed the arms of the two astonished newspaperwomen, propelling them toward the door.

The man was only yards behind them, the swinging door just beyond the table. Peter lurched to the side, still holding on to the columnists. As the man broke free of the crowd, Chancellor spun the women around and pushed them as hard as he could toward the onrushing figure. The man yelled; the obese woman's pencil pierced his lower lip. Blood trickled from his mouth. Peter swung his hands under the wide table filled with food and two huge punch bowls and heaved it up, sending the mass of silver, glass, liquid, and food crashing to the floor.

Shouts became screams; someone blew a whistle. Chancellor raced through the swinging door into a pantry.

On the left wall he saw a red Exit sign. He grabbed a serving cart, rolling it behind him with such force a wheel came off. Bowls of salad crashed in front of the swinging door. He ran to the exit and body checked it open. He looked behind him; there was chaos at the pantry entrance and no sign of the man chasing him.

The staircase was empty. He took the steps three at

a time to the landing and swung himself around by the railing.

His feet slammed to a stop, his left knee smashed into the iron post. Below him, in front of the lobby door, stood the man he had last seen on Connecticut Avenue. The man who had jumped out of the car. He was not part of a novel now; he was real. As the gun in his hand was real.

The madness! The insane thought came to Peter that he must have a tape recorder in his handkerchief pocket. Involuntarily, he raised his left arm to press the cloth. To start the recorder. A nonexistent recorder! What was *happening* to him?

"What do you want with me? Why are you following me?" he whispered, not sure what was fact anymore.

"We just want to talk to you. Make sure you understand——"

"No!" His mind exploded. He sprang from the landing, conscious only of empty space. Somewhere deep in the sound waves of that space he heard the sickening spit of a bullet, but he was not affected; his disbelief was complete.

Suddenly his hands clamped on skin and hair. The thrust of his flying body made contact; he slammed the man's head into the metal door.

The real man with the real gun collapsed, his hair and face covered with blood. Peter rose and stood for an instant in shock, trying to separate fantasy and reality.

He had to run. There was nothing left but running. He crashed open the door and started across the marble floor. The guard was at the entrance to the street, his hand on his holster, a walkie-talkie next to his ear.

As Peter approached, the guard spoke. "Some trouble up there, huh?"

"Yes. Couple of drunks, I think."

"Did the two guys find you? They told me you're with the bureau."

Peter stopped, gripping the entrance door in his hand. "*What?*"

"Your backup? The other two guys. They came in right after you. They showed me their IDs. They're with the FBI, too."

Chancellor did not wait to hear more. The madness was now complete. The FBI! He ran down the short flight of steps, his eyes blurred, his breath gone.

"You've still got time on the meter, mister."

Not eight feet away from him at the curb was the taxi. He ran to the door and got inside.

"Drive down to Ellipse road! For God's sake, hurry! Go around to the Smithsonian Park. I'll tell you where to let me off."

The cab accelerated. "It's still your money."

Peter spun around and looked out the rear window at the Corcoran. A man came running down the steps onto the sidewalk, one hand on his face, the other holding a walkie-talkie. It was the man from the second floor reception, the man whose lip had been pierced by the obese columnist's pencil. He had seen the taxi. Others would be waiting. Somewhere.

They entered the curve around the Ellipse. To the south was the Washington Monument, floodlights washing the alabaster needle. "Slow down," instructed Peter, "near the edge of the grass. But don't stop. I'm going to jump out, but I don't want . . ." Peter's voice faded; he did not know how to say it.

The driver helped him. "But you don't want whoever might be watching my cab to see you jump, is that it?"

"Yes."

"You in trouble?"

"Yes."

"Is it the cops?"

"Jesus, no! It's . . . personal."

"You sound okay to me. You were fair with me; I'm fair with you." The driver slowed down. "About fifty yards ahead, at the farthest point in the curve before it swings straight, jump. Then I'll go like a bat outta' hell for a couple of blocks. Nobody'll see you. Got it?"

"Yes. I've got it. Thanks."

"*Now!*"

The cab had slowed. Chancellor opened the door and jumped over the edge of the curb, the force of his leap and the curve of the road propelling him onto the grass.

The driver held the horn down in one continuous blast. Other automobiles swung to the right, allowing the taxi to pass. The sound was the sound of emergency; someone was in trouble.

Peter watched the scene from his concealed position in the grass. One automobile did not stop or hesitate or swing to the right as the others did in front of and behind the screaming cab. It was not affected by the sound of panic. Instead, it fell in line with the taxi and raced after it.

It was the black limousine he had seen on New Hampshire Avenue.

Peter lay motionless for a moment. Tires screeched in the distance. From across the Ellipse road, in the direction of Continental Hall, another automobile was careening into the circular drive. Looking for him? He got to his feet and started running over dirt and grass.

He felt concrete beneath him; he was in the street. Buildings were in front of him, cars alongside him, driving slowly. He kept running, knowing that beyond the dark buildings and the scattered trees stood the Smithsonian.

He fell suddenly and rolled over on the pavement. Behind him he heard the unmistakable sounds of racing footsteps. They'd found him!

He scrambled to his feet, lurching forward, the over-anxious sprinter jumping the gun. He kept racing where instinct directed him, and suddenly he saw it! Its parapets were silhouetted against the sky! The outlines of the Smithsonian! He ran as fast as he could across an unending lawn, jumping over low, sagging chains that bordered paths, until he stood, breathless, in front of the enormous building.

He was there, but where was Longworth?

For an instant he thought he heard sounds behind him. He turned; there was no one.

Suddenly, two tiny specks of light flashed from somewhere in the darkness, beyond the steps that led to the road in front of the entrance. They came from ground level, to the left of the statue that stood at the top of the steps. They flashed agin, as if aimed at him! He walked rapidly toward the source of the light. Nearer, nearer; thirty feet, twenty feet. He was walking toward a dark corner of the massive museum; there was shrubbery in front of the stone.

"Chancellor! Get down!"

Peter threw himself to the ground. Two flashes came from the darkness: muted pistol shots.

Behind him he heard a body fall. In the dull gray of the night he saw the gun in the slain figure's hand. It had been aimed at him.

"Drag him back here!" It was a whispered command from the darkness.

All thought dulled, Chancellor did as he was told. He pulled the body over the grass into the shadows, and then he crawled to Alan Longworth.

The man was dying. His back was against the Smithsonian stone. In his right hand was the gun that had saved Peter's life; his left hand held his stomach. His fingers were covered with blood.

"I haven't got time to thank you," said Chancellor, barely able to hear himself. "Maybe I shouldn't. He was one of your men."

"I haven't got any men," replied the blond-haired killer.

"We'll talk about that later You're coming with me. *Now*." Angrily, Peter struggled to his feet.

"I'm not going anywhere, Chancellor. If I stay still and keep things in place, I've got a few minutes. Not if I move."

There was that strange, guttural sound in Longworth's voice again. "Then, I'll go find someone!" said Peter, his answer now mixed with fear. He could not let Longworth die. Not *now*. "I'll get an ambulance!"

"An ambulance won't help. Take my word for it. But you have to be told. You have to understand."

"I understand everything. A group of fanatics is trying to tear the FBI apart so that they can take control. And you're one of them."

"That's not true. It goes beyond the bureau. We're trying to stop them; I've tried. And now you're the only one who can. You're closest to the core; no one else has your advantage."

"Why?"

Longworth seemed to ignore the question. He took a deep breath. "The missing files. Hoover's private dossiers——"

"There *are* no missing files!" broke in Peter, furiously. "There are only men like you and the man you just killed. You made a mistake, Longworth. He was following me, chasing me. He used his identification; he's FBI! He's one of you!"

Longworth stared at the body of the man he had killed. "So the maniacs found out about the files. I imagine it was unavoidable. They can be used by the one who has them. They're the perfect foils; they'll be blamed for everything."

Chancellor was not listening. The only thing that mattered was to deliver Longworth to Quinn O'Brien. "I'm not interested in any more of your observations."

"You say you love that girl," said Longworth, breathing hard. "If you do, you'll listen to me."

"You bastard! You leave her out of this!"

"Her mother, her father. . . . It's them. Something happened to the mother."

Peter knelt closer. "What do you know about her mother?"

"Not enough. But you can learn. Bear with me. To begin with, my name isn't Longworth."

Chancellor stared in disbelief, yet he knew he was hearing the truth. Circles within circles. Reality and fantasy, but which was which? The moon came out of the gray night sky. For the first time he was able to see Longworth's face clearly. The dying man had no eyebrows, no lashes. There was only raw scraped flesh around the sockets and blisters everywhere. He had been beaten, tortured.

28

"My name is Stefan Varak. I'm a code specialist for the National Security Council, but I also perform certain functions for a group of——"

"*Varak?*" It took several seconds for the name to register, but when it did, the shock made Peter grow cold. "You're the man O'Brien's looking for!"

"Quinn O'Brien?" asked Varak, wincing in pain.

"Yes. He's the man I talked to, the one I told the story to. He's been trying to reach you!"

"I was in no position to receive messages. You were lucky. Quinn's one of the quickest and cleanest men over there. Trust him." Varak coughed, pain visible in his face. "If the maniacs have surfaced, O'Brien will stop them."

"What have you got to tell me? What do you know about MacAndrew's wife?"

Varak held up his bloody hand. "I have to explain. As quickly as possible. You've got to understand. . . . From the beginning you were programed. Part truth, part lie. We had to get you involved, get you started, force the enemy to react, show themselves." Varak was gripped by a spasm.

Chancellor waited till it passed; then he asked: "Part lie, part truth. Which was which?"

"I told you. The files. They disappeared."

"There was no assassination, then?"

"Inconceivable." Varak stared at Peter, his breath coming fast. "The men who fought Hoover were honorable. They protected Hoover's victims by the law, not outside of it."

"But the files were taken."

"Yes. That part's true. Dossiers with the letters *M* through *Z*. Remember that." Again a spasm took hold of Varak. Peter held his shoulders; it was all he could think of to do. The shivering ran its course; Varak continued. "And now I must elaborate. I use your words."

His words? Varak's eyes were glazed; the accent was there once more. "My words? What do you mean?"

"In your fourth chapter——"

"My what?"

"Your manuscript."

"You've read it?"

"Yes."

"How?"

"It doesn't matter. There's no time. . . . Your Nucleus. You concentrate on three people. A senator, a newspaperwoman, a cabinet member. . . ." Varak's eyes lost control; his voice faded.

"What about them?" pressed Chancellor, not understanding.

"Use the files for good. . . ." The dying man inhaled suddenly. "You said that."

Peter remembered. The *files*. In the manuscript he had given the words to the former cabinet officer. *If they can be used the way Hoover uses them, they can be turned around. They can be used for good!* It was the false reasoning that would lead to tragedy.

"What if I did? What are you talking about?"

"It's what happened. . . ." Varak's eyes came briefly into focus, his concentration all-consuming. "One man turned into a killer. A killer who hires killers."

"*What?*"

"Five men. One of four . . . not Bravo. Never Bravo. . . ."

"What did you say? Who's Bravo?"

"A splendid temptation. To use the files for good."

"*Splendid?* . . . There's nothing splendid. It's extortion!"

"That's the tragedy."

Oh, *Christ!* His words! "What five men? What do you mean?"

"Venice you know. . . . Bravo, too, but *not* Bravo! *Never* Bravo!" Varak struggled with his bloodied right hand; he inched it away from the wound in his stomach to his jacket pocket. He withdrew a piece of paper, white paper soiled with blood. "One of four men. I thought it was Banner or Paris. Now I'm not sure." He pushed the paper into Chancellor's palm. "Code names. Venice, Christopher, Banner, Paris. It's one of them. Not Bravo."

" 'Venice' . . . 'Bravo' . . . who are they?"

"The group. Your Nucleus." Varak pulled his hand down to his wound. "One of them knows."

"Knows what?"

"The meaning of *Chasŏng.* The mother."

"MacAndrew? His *wife?*"

"Not him. *Her!* He's the decoy."

"Decoy? You've got to be clearer."

"The slaughter. The meaning behind the slaughter of Chasŏng!"

Peter looked at the bloodstained paper in his hand. Names were written on it. "One of these men?" he asked the dying man, unsure what he meant by his own question.

"Yes."

"Why?"

"You and the daughter. *You!* It was to throw you off. To make you think it was the answer. It isn't."

"*What* answer?"

"Chasŏng. Something *beyond* it."

"*Stop* it! What are you saying?"

"Not Bravo. . . ." Varak's eyes swam in their sockets.

"Who *is* Bravo? Is he one of them?"

"No. *Never* Bravo."

"Varak, what *happened*? Why are you so certain about Chasŏng?"

"There are others who'll help. . . ."

"What about *Chasŏng*?"

"Thirty-fifth Street. The house. They took me and taped my eyes, my face. I never saw them. They needed a hostage. They know what I've done. . . . I didn't see them, but I heard them. They spoke a language I didn't know, which means they knew I didn't know it. But they used the name *Chasŏng*. Each time . . . fanatically. It has another meaning. Find what it was behind the killing at Chasŏng. It will lead you to the files."

Varak fell forward. Chancellor grabbed him, pulling him back. "There's got to be more!"

"There's very little." Varak's whisper faded. Peter had to put his ear next to the agent's lips to hear him. "They drove me through a town; they thought I was unconscious. I heard automobiles. I crashed through the door with the tapes on my face. They fired at me but drove away. I had to get you alone. I could not talk on the telephone. I was right. The two false numbers I gave you were called. If I had told you on the phone what I'm telling you now, you'd have been killed. Protect the girl. Find the meaning behind the slaughter of Chasŏng."

Chancellor felt panic swell inside him; his head was about to explode. Varak was nearly dead. He'd be gone in moments! In seconds! "You said there were others! Who can I go to? Who'll *help*?"

"O'Brien," whispered Varak. Then he stared at Peter, a strange smile on his bloodless lips. "Look to your manuscript. There's a senator. He might have been— Go to him. He's not afraid."

Varak's eyes closed. He was dead.

And Chancellor's mind was filled with white light and thunder. The detonations shook the earth; there was no sanity left. A senator. . . . He had crossed a line no one should cross. He let Varak's head fall back into the stone and slowly got to his feet, backing away, filled with a terror so personal, so absolute, he could not think.

But he could run. And so, blindly, he ran.

He was near water. The reflections of light shimmered on the surface like thousands of miniature candles flickering in an unfelt wind. How long he had been running he could not tell. As his mind began to clear, he thought for a moment he was back in New York, at dawn, within the sculptured confines of Fort Tryon, where a blond-haired man named Longworth had just saved his life.

But his name was not Longworth. It was Varak, and he was dead.

Peter closed his eyes. The void he had sought for so long swept over him. He slowly lowered himself to the ground; his knees touched the grass, and he trembled.

He heard the sound of an engine approaching. Gravel crunched beneath wheels. He opened his eyes and looked around.

A motor scooter parked, its single headlight angled diagonally down. A police officer got off. He shot the beam of his flashlight over at Peter.

"You all right, mister?"

"Yes. Yes, I'm all right."

The officer approached. Chancellor rose unsteadily, noting that behind the beam of the light, the man's hand had unsnapped his pistol holder. "What are you doing down here?"

"I'm—I'm not sure. To tell you the truth, I had a little too much to drink, so I went for a walk. I do that; it's better than getting into a car."

"It certainly is," replied the officer. "You're not thinking about doing anything foolish though, are you?"

"What? What do you mean?"

"Like taking a swim, not figuring to come out?"

"What?"

The officer was standing in front of him, scrutinizing him carefully. "You're pretty messed up."

"I fell. I told you, I had——"

"I know. Booze. Funny, I don't smell any."

"Vodka."

"You depressed? Family problems? In trouble? You want to see a priest or a rabbi? Or a lawyer?"

Peter understood. "I see. You think I want to drown myself."

"It's happened. We've pulled bodies out of the Basin."

"We're at the Tidal Basin?" asked Chancellor.

"Southwest point." The officer gestured to his right. "That's Ohio Drive over there. Across the water's the Jefferson Memorial."

Peter looked at his watch, at the radium dial. It was a little after nine thirty. He had lost nearly two hours; he'd drawn a blank for *two hours*. And there were things to do. The first was to mollify a concerned policeman. He struggled for the words.

"Look, I'm fine, officer. I really am. As a matter of fact I've got to get to a telephone. Is there a booth around here?"

The officer reached down and snapped his holster shut. "Over on Ohio, about a hundred yards south, maybe less. You can probably get a cab there, too. But if you're stopped again, watch out. Other cops may be rougher than I am."

"Thanks for the warning." Peter smiled. "And thanks for your concern."

"Part of the job. Take care, now."

Chancellor nodded and started across the lawn toward Ohio Drive. Someone had tapped into his hotel phone; he could call Alison, but he could not say anything. Instead, he must reach Quinn O'Brien.

"Where the hell *are* you? My orders were for you to stay in that hotel! Goddamn you———"

"The maniacs tried to kill me," broke in Chancellor quickly, remembering Varak's description.

"The *maniacs*?" It was as if O'Brien had been struck. "Where did you hear that term?"

"That's what we're going to talk about. That and other things. I just got out of the Corcoran Gallery."

"The *Corcoran*. . . . *You* were there?"

"Yes."

"Oh, my God!" O'Brien sounded frightened.

"I'm down at ———"

"Shut *up!*" yelled the FBI man suddenly. "Don't say another thing! Wait a minute . . . stay on the line." Peter could hear O'Brien's breathing; the agent was thinking. "Our conversation last night. Think carefully. You told me you placed three phone calls to New York from telephone booths. You used your credit card."

"But I———"

"I said shut up! Think. They were placed before and after the fire on Thirty-fifth Street."

"I———"

"Listen to me! There was one call in particular— I

think it was after, I'm not sure. Get to the booth you made that call from. Now, do you understand me? Don't answer right away. Filter it."

Peter tried to understand what O'Brien was telling him. There had not been three phone calls, there had only been one. He had called Tony Morgan before the insanity on Thirty-fifth Street. He had made no calls after.

Filter it. Eliminate. That was it! The agent referred to that one call, that one booth. "I understand," he said.

"Good. It was after, wasn't it? After Thirty-fifth Street."

"Yes," said Chancellor, knowing it was a lie.

"Somewhere on Wisconsin, I think."

"Yes." Again, the deception.

"Good. Get there. I'll call every ten minutes. Pick out a phrase I'd remember from our talk and say it when you answer. Have you got that?"

"Yes."

Peter hung up the phone and went out of the booth. He continued walking south toward the bridge lights extending over the Potomac, looking for a cab. As he walked, he tried to remember the exact location of the phone booth where he had called Morgan. It was near George Washington University.

A cab came. They found the phone booth easily. There were crowds again, and colored lights and Christmas carols coming from unseen speakers. He asked the driver to wait; the only money he had was two fifty-dollar bills from his wallet. He would need to change them, and he would need the taxi.

He knew exactly what he was going to do.

Find the meaning of Chasŏng.

He closed the door of the booth and took the phone out of its cradle, making sure his finger held the lip down. The ring barely started when he released the tab and spoke.

" 'I may be here for the rest of the night. . . . I'll let you decide. . . .' " It was one of the first things he had said to the agent when they met.

"Good enough," said O'Brien. "I'm ten blocks away on Twentieth Street. I may have been followed, so we can't meet. Now, tell me what happened. Where did you hear the term *maniacs*?"

"Why? Is it special?"

"Don't joke. You don't have time."

"I'm not joking. I'm being careful. If I see anyone paying attention to me, or see a car stop, I'm going to run. I think you're clean, O'Brien; that's what I was told. But I want to make sure. Now, you tell *me* what the term means. Who are the maniacs?"

O'Brien exhaled audibly. "Five or six special agents who worked secretly, closely with Hoover. They were in his confidence. They want the old regime back; they want to control the bureau. I implied as much to you last night. Still, I didn't use the word *maniacs*."

"But they're not part of this, are they? They don't have the missing files."

O'Brien fell silent, his shock evident to Peter over the phone. "You know, then?"

"Yes. You said those files were destroyed; that there was no pattern, but you lied. There is a pattern; they *weren't* destroyed. Whoever has them thinks I'm close to learning who he is . . . who they are. It was the whole idea behind everything. I was the snare. It nearly worked, but the man who programed me was killed in his own trap. Now, you tell me what you know, and tell it straight!"

O'Brien replied calmly, his urgency controlled. "I think the maniacs *do* have those files. They operated with them; they had access. That's why I couldn't talk to you from my office; they've tapped my line. They had to. Now, for Christ's sake, tell me what happened."

"Fair enough. I found your man Varak."

"What?"

"I knew him as Longworth."

"*Longworth*? May first . . . the security logs! He has the *files*!" O'Brien involuntarily shouted into the phone.

"That doesn't make *sense!*" said Peter, bewildered. "He's dead. He threw his life away to find those files." Chancellor told the agent everything that had happened from Varak's phone call through Varak's death and the dying man's conviction that O'Brien would stop the maniacs. But he did not mention Chasŏng. For the time being, that was private.

"Varak gone," O'Brien said softly. "I can't believe it. He was one of the ones we counted on. There aren't many left."

"The guy from CIA—we knew each other. He said a number of you people work together. All over Washington. That you had to."

"We do. The hell of it is, there's no one to go to for legal advice. There's not an A.G. at Justice I'd trust."

"There may be someone. A senator. Varak told me. But not yet. Not now. . . . You're good at giving orders, O'Brien. How are you at taking them?"

"Not good. They have to make sense."

"Are those files sense enough?"

"A stupid question."

"Then, do two things for me. Get Alison MacAndrew out of the Hay-Adams, stay with her, and take her someplace where she'll be safe. They want me. They'll use her to get me."

"All right, I can do that. What's the other?"

"I need the address of a major named Pablo Ramirez. He's stationed at the Pentagon."

"Wait a minute."

Suddenly Peter was alarmed. Over the telephone he could hear the rustling of paper. *Paper!* He put his hand up to the cradle of the telephone, about to break the connection and run. "O'Brien! I thought you said you were ten blocks away. In a phone booth!"

"I am. I'm looking in the phone book."

"Oh, *Christ*. . . ." Chancellor swallowed.

"Here it is. Ramirez, P. He lives in Bethesda." The agent read the address; Peter memorized it. "Is that all?"

"No. I'm going to want to see Alison later tonight, or in the morning. How do I find out where you are, where you've taken her? Do you have any ideas?"

Silence. Five seconds later O'Brien spoke. "Do you know Quantico?"

"The marine base?"

"Yes, but not the camp. There's a motel on the bay. It's called the Pines. I'll take her there."

"I'll rent a car."

"Don't do that. Rental agencies are too easily covered. There's a machine that can scan every one in the city. They'd pick you up. That goes for cab companies, too; no one withholds destinations. They'd know where you went."

"What the hell am I going to do? Walk?"

"There are trains to Quantico every hour or so. That's your best bet."

"All right. I'll see you later."

"Wait a minute." O'Brien's tone was urgent, but again

controlled. "You're holding back again, Chancellor. It's MacAndrew."

Peter's head snapped back; he stared at the crowds through the glass booth. "You're making assumptions."

"You're making a fool of yourself. It doesn't take any powers of deduction. Ramirez works at the Pentagon; so did MacAndrew."

"Don't push it, O'Brien. *Please.*"

"Why shouldn't I? You haven't told me the most important thing Varak said; why he had to see you."

"I *did*. He explained his strategy. How I was programed."

"He wouldn't waste his time, not when he was dying. He learned something, and he told you what it was."

Chancellor shook his head; perspiration rolled down his brow. O'Brien could not be told the significance of Chasŏng—until Peter found out what it was. For the deeper he went, the more Peter was convinced that Alison's survival was at stake.

"Give me till tomorrow morning," he said.

"Why?"

"Because I love her."

Paul Bromley stared into the cracked mirror on top of the dresser with knobs missing from the middle drawers. What he saw saddened him: the pallid face of a sick old man. The stubble of his gray beard was obvious; he had not shaved in over forty-eight hours. The wide space between the dirty starched collar and his throat was further evidence of his illness. He had very little time left. But it would be enough. It had to be.

He turned away from the mirror and walked over to the bed. The spread was filthy. His eyes swept over the walls and ceiling. There were cracks everywhere and peeling paint.

They thought they had him trapped, but their arrogance was misplaced. He was owed favors. A lifetime in Washington overseeing vast expenditures left many people in his debt. Everything was a trade-off: You can do this if you give me that. Most of the time it worked very well. By and large, he was proud of his Washington record; he had done many fine things.

He had done several things he was not very proud of, too. One in particular for a scoundrel who had provided him with the data he needed to go after the thieves at Defense. That was the debt he was going to call in. If the man refused, a phone call would be made to the *Washington Post*. The man would not refuse.

Bromley picked up his jacket from the bed, put it on, and went out the door into the filthy hallway, then down a flight of steps to the lobby. The FBI agent who had been assigned to him stood awkwardly in the corner, a clean-cut manikin amongst the human debris. At least the man did not have to wait in the upstairs hallway. The hotel's only exit was its front door—testimony to the trust placed in its clientele.

Bromley walked to the pay telephone on the wall, inserted the coin, and dialed.

"Hello?" The voice was nasal and unattractive.

"This is Paul Bromley."

"Who?"

"Three years ago. Detroit. The project."

There was a pause before the voice replied. "What do you want?"

"What I'm owed. Unless you'd rather I call friends at the *Post*. They almost got you three years ago. They could do it now. I've also prepared a letter. It will be mailed if I don't return home."

Again there was a pause. "Spell it out."

"You send a car for me. I'll tell you where. And when you do, send one of your thugs with it. There's a federal man here watching me. I want him temporarily side-tracked. It's the sort of thing you do very well."

Bromley waited on the sidewalk outside the Hay-Adams. He would wait all night if need be. And when daylight came, he could hide in the church doorway across the avenue. Sooner or later Chancellor would emerge. When he did, Bromley would kill him.

The gun in his pocket had cost him five hundred dollars. He doubted it was worth more than twenty. But he had only asked his Detroit contact for help, not for charity.

Bromley kept raising his eyes to the right front windows on the fifth floor of the hotel. They were Chancellor's rooms. Expensive rooms. Last night he had asked a then-unsuspecting switchboard operator the number of the suite before he had called the writer. The despicable novelist lived well.

He would not live long.

Bromley heard the sound of a car racing south on Sixteenth Street. It pulled into the hotel driveway. A red-haired man got out, spoke to the doorman, and went inside the lobby.

The accountant recognized the unmarked automobile. He had routinely approved scores of such purchases whenever the rubber stamp was requested. It was the FBI; without doubt, it had come for Chancellor!

Bromley went back across the street and walked up the driveway, staying in the shadows by the wall of the building, to the right of the entrance next to the FBI car. The doorman had walked down the path to whistle for a cab. A couple followed him to the curb, since the driveway was blocked.

Everything was perfect! Chancellor would die!

Moments later a woman came out with the red-haired man. But there was no Chancellor!

He had to be there!

"Are you sure?" the woman asked, concerned.

"He'll take the train down later tonight," said the red-haired man. "Or in the morning. Don't worry."

A train.

Bromley pulled up the collar of his overcoat and began the long walk to Union Station.

29

In a taxi headed for Ramirez's house, Peter took out the page of bloodstained paper with the dead Varak's handwriting on it. Once again he was awed by the names. Awed and frightened, for they were extraordinary men—each renowned, each brilliant, each immensely powerful. And one of them had Hoover's files.

For God's sake, why? Peter looked at each name; each evoked an image.

The lean, sharp-featured Frederick Wells—code name: Banner. University president, dispenser of millions through the huge Roxton Foundation, one of the brightest architects of the Kennedy years. A man who was known never to compromise on principle, even when his stand incurred the wrath of all Washington.

Daniel Sutherland—Venice—perhaps the most honored black in the country. Honored not only for his accomplishments, but for the wisdom of his judicial decisions. Peter had felt the judge's compassion in his brief half-hour conversation with him months ago. It was in his eyes.

Jacob Dreyfus—Christopher. Dreyfus's face was less clear than the others in Peter's mind. The banker shunned public attention, but he could never be ignored by the financial community, which meant the financial press. His influence often formed the basis of national monetary policy; the Federal Reserve rarely made decisions without consulting him. His charity was known throughout the world, his generosity limitless.

Carlos Montelán—Paris—was the tutor of presidents, a force at the Department of State, an academic giant whose analyses of global politics were discriminating and audacious. Montelán was a naturalized American; his family was Spanish, intellectual Castilians who had fought a compromising church and Franco alike. He was an archenemy of oppression in any form.

One of these four exceptional men had betrayed the beliefs he professed to hold. Was it Varak's "splendid temptation?" The commission of dreadful acts for an idealistic reason? It was impossible to accept. From lesser men perhaps. Not these.

Unless one of the four was not what he appeared to be. And that was the most frightening thing of all. That a man could be raised to such height concealing such fundamental corruption.

Chasŏng.

Varak knew he was dying, and so he had selected his words carefully. He had at first narrowed his options down to Wells and Montelán—Banner and Paris—and then reversed himself and expanded the possibilties to include Sutherland and Dreyfus—Venice and Christopher. His change of mind had been related to a language he did not know and the fanatic repetition of the name Chasŏng. But why these? What had led Varak to single out an unfamiliar language and a repeated cry? What had been his reasoning? He had not had time to explain.

The meaning behind the slaughter of Chasŏng. The slaughter! Peter remembered Ramircz's expression of cold loathing at MacAndrew's burial. Ramirez hated MacAndrew. But was it connected to Chasŏng? Or just the passions of jealousy that found no comfort in a rival's death? That was possible, but there was something too specific in Ramirez's eyes.

He would know soon; the taxi had crossed into Bethesda. And if the connection *was* there, to which of the four extraordinary men would Chasŏng lead? And how?

Peter folded Varak's scrap of paper and shoved it into his jacket pocket. There was a fifth man, unidentified —code name: Bravo. Who was he? And had Varak mistakenly protected him? Could the unknown Bravo have the files? Suddenly Peter remembered something else. *Venice you know. . . . Bravo, too. . . .* How would he know such a man, Peter wondered. Who *was* Bravo?

There were too many questions, too few answers. Only one stood out: Alison MacAndrew. She was his answer to so much.

The house was small and made of brick. The neighborhood was one of those middle-class developments that had proliferated in the Washington area—plots of equal size, frontages identical. Chancellor told the driver the truth: He had no idea how long he'd be. He did not even know if Ramirez was home. Or if he was married, or had children. It was possible he had made the trip to Bethesda for nothing, but if he had called first, Major Ramirez doubtless would have refused to see him.

The door opened. To Peter's relief Pablo Ramirez stood in the frame, his expression quizzical.

"Major Ramirez?"

"Yes. Have we met?"

"No, but we were both at Arlington Cemetery the other morning. My name's——"

"You were with the girl," interrupted the major. "His daughter. You're the writer."

"Yes. My name's Peter Chancellor. I'd like to talk with you."

"What about?"

"MacAndrew."

Ramirez paused before replying, studying Peter's face.

He spoke quietly, with the slightest trace of an accent, but to Chancellor's surprise there was no hostility in his voice. "I really haven't anything to say about the general. He's dead. Leave him in peace."

"That wasn't what you had in mind at the burial. If the dead could be killed twice, your looks would have done just that."

"I apologize."

"Is that all you'll say?"

"I believe it's sufficient. Now, if you don't mind, I have work to do."

Ramirez stepped back, his hand on the doorknob. Peter spoke quickly.

"Chasŏng. The *slaughter* at Chasŏng."

The major stopped, his body rigid. The connection *was* there. "That goes back a long time. The 'slaughter,' as you call it, was thoroughly investigated by the Inspector General. The heavy losses were attributed to unexpected and overwhelming Chincom firepower."

"And perhaps overzealousness in command," added Peter swiftly. "For instance, in the command of Mac the Knife, killer of Chasŏng."

The major remained immobile, his eyes clouded in that odd, noncommittal way peculiar to the military.

"I think you'd better come inside, Mr. Chancellor."

Peter had a sense of déjà vu. Once again he had stepped up to a stranger's door—that stranger an Army officer—and demanded an audience through the use of information he was not supposed to have. There was even a similarity between Ramirez's and MacAndrew's studies. The walls were lined with photographs and mementos of a career. Chancellor glanced at the open study door, his mind wandering back for a moment to the isolated house in the countryside. Ramirez misinterpreted his look.

"There's no one else here," he said curtly—as curtly as MacAndrew had spoken months before. "I'm a bachelor."

"I didn't know that. I know very little about you, Major. Except that you went to West Point around the same time MacAndrew did. Also that you served with him in North Africa and later in Korea."

"I'm sure you've learned other things. You couldn't know even that much without having been told more."

"Such as?"

Ramirez sat down in the armchair opposite Peter. "That I'm discontented, if not a certified malcontent. A troublemaker from Puerto Rico who feels he's been passed over because of his race."

"I heard a tasteless Navy joke I didn't like."

"Oh, the fleet cocktail party? The one where they put a busboy's jacket on me?" A mechanical smile appeared on the major's face. Chancellor nodded. "That's not bad. I made that one up myself."

"What?"

"I work in a very specialized, extremely sensitive department of the Pentagon. But it has nothing to do with orthodox intelligence. For lack of a better phrase, we call it minority relations."

"Major, what are you saying? . . ."

"I'm not a major. My permanent rank is brigadier general. I will undoubtedly receive my second star in June. You see, a major—especially one of my age—can go into many areas and have better communication with the men than can a colonel or a general."

"You have to go to those extremes?" asked Peter.

"Today's military faces an extraordinary problem. Nobody likes to put it into words, but no one can bury it, either. The ranks are being filled with unemployables, the outcasts. Do you know what can be the result when that happens?"

"Sure. The quality of the services diminishes."

"That's the first stage. We get the My Lais, and we get spaced-out troops trading in narcotics like C-rations. Then there's another step, and it's not far down the road. By simple attrition, the lack of quality recruitment, *and* a superiority of numbers, the quality of leadership deteriorates. Historically, that's frightening. Forget Genghis Khan and even the later-day Cossacks; their environments were barbarian. There's a more recent example. The criminals took over the German army, and the Nazi Wehrmacht was the result. Do you begin to understand?"

Peter shook his head slowly. The soldier's evaluations seemed exaggerated; there were too many controls. "I can't buy some kind of black terrorist junta."

"Neither can we. Statistics—base demographics, actually—confirm what we've suspected for a long time. The average black drawn to the military is more highly and properly motivated than his white counterpart. Those that aren't motivated run with the wild packs anyway. It's a very democratic filtering system: Garbage attracts garbage. And they *are* minorities: Spanish Harlem, Slovak Chicago, Chicano Los Angeles. The words are *unemployment, poverty,* and *ignorance.*"

"And you're the Army's solution?"

"I'm a beginning. We try to reach them, upgrade them, make them better than they are. Educational programs, lessening of resentments, instilling self-respect. All the concepts the liberals think we're incapable of practicing."

There was something missing, something that did not make sense. "This is all very enlightening," Peter said, "but what's it got to do with General MacAndrew? With what I saw at Arlington?"

"What's your reason for going back to Chasŏng?" countered the brigadier.

Peter looked away, at the photographs and decorations that were so reminiscent of MacAndrew's study. "I won't tell you how, but the name Chasŏng came up after MacAndrew resigned. I think it had something to do with his resignation."

"Highly unlikely."

"Then I saw you at Arlington," continued Chancellor, ignoring Ramirez's comment. "I'm not sure why, but I thought there might be a connection. I was right; there was. A few minutes ago you were closing the door in my face; I mention Chasŏng and you ask me in."

"I was curious," said the soldier. "It was a highly inflammatory issue."

"But before we talk about it," said Peter, again ignoring the interruption, "you make damned sure I hear about this sensitive department you work in. You're preparing me for something. What is it? Why did you hate MacAndrew?"

"All right." The brigadier shifted his position in the chair. Peter knew he was stalling, allowing himself a brief moment to consider how much to hide. Part truth, part lie. Peter had described many characters doing the same thing. "We all funtion best in those areas we feel deeply about. Although I'm no malcontent, I am discontented. I have been, throughout my career. I've been an angry man. And in many ways MacAndrew represented the reason for my anger. He was an elitist, a racist. Strangely enough, he was a fine commander because he truly believed he was superior and thought of everyone else as inferior. All the faults of middle command were the result of inferior human beings given responsibilties beyond their capabilities. He would study roster sheets and equate last names with ethnic origins; too often those associations formed the basis of his decisions."

Ramirez stopped. Peter remained silent for a moment, too disturbed to speak. The soldier's explanation had both the ring of truth and the ring of falsehood to it. It *was* part truth, part lie. "You knew him very well, then," he finally said.

"Well enough to understand the insidiousness."

"Did you know his wife?"

There it was again. The rigidity in Ramirez's bearing. It passed as rapidly as it appeared.

"She was a sad case. Unfortunate, unstable. A vacuous woman with too many servants, too little to do, and too much to drink. She went off the deep end."

"I didn't know she was an alcoholic."

"Terms are unimportant."

"Was there an accident? A near drowning?"

"She was involved in a number of 'accidents.' A few rather unsavory, I understand. But in my opinion the larger accident was inactivity. I really know very little about her."

Again Peter sensed the lie in Ramirez's words. This major-brigadier knew a great deal about Alison's mother, but he was determined to say nothing. So be it, Chancellor thought. *Not him. Her! He's the decoy.* Varak's words. "There's nothing more?" Peter asked.

"No. Now, I've been honest with you. What have you heard about Chasŏng?"

"That there was an unnecessary slaughter and maiming of thousands of men."

"Chasŏng is only one of many battles represented in scores of veterans' hospitals. To repeat, it was investigated."

Chancellor sat forward. "Okay, General, I'll be honest with you. I don't think it was investigated anywhere near thoroughly enough. Or if it was, the results were shoved under a rug so fast the dust flew. There are a lot of things I don't know, but the picture's getting clearer. You hated MacAndrew; you freeze at the name Chasŏng; you give me a sermon, saying what a great guy you are; and then you freeze again when MacAndrew's wife is mentioned, telling me that you don't know much about her. A lie—you're filled with lies and evasions. I'll tell you what I think. I think Chasŏng is tied in with MacAndrew, his resignation, his murder, a gap in his service record, and missing files from the Federal Bureau of Investigation. And somewhere in this mess is MacAndrew's wife. How much more there is, I haven't the vaguest idea, but you'd better tell me. Because I'm going to find out. There's a woman involved, and I love her, and I won't let any of you go on any longer. Cut the bullshit, Ramirez! Tell me the truth!"

The brigadier reacted as though suddenly pinned down by gunfire. His body tensed; his whisper was strained. "The gap in his service record. How did you know? You didn't mention it. You had no right— You tricked me." He began to shout. "You had no right to do that! You can't understand! We *did*. We *tried*!"

"What happened at Chasŏng?"

Ramirez closed his eyes. "Only what you think. The slaughter was unnecessary. The command decisions faulty. . . . It was so long ago. Let it *be*!"

Chancellor got up from the chair and looked down at the brigadier. "No. Because I'm beginning to understand. I think Chasŏng was the biggest military cover-up in this country's history. And somewhere, somehow, it's in those files. I think after all these years, MacAndrew couldn't live with it anymore. At long last he was going to talk about it. So you all got together and went after him because you couldn't live with *that*!"

Ramirez opened his eyes. "That's not true. For God's sake, leave it alone!"

"Not true?" said Peter quietly. "I'm not sure you'd know the truth. You're so guilty, you're running standing still. Your righteousness is very suspect, General. I liked you better at Arlington; your anger was genuine then. You're hiding something—maybe from yourself, I don't know. But I know I'm going to find out what Chasŏng means."

"Then, may God have mercy on your soul," whispered Brigadier General Pablo Ramirez.

Chancellor hurried through Union Station toward the Amtrak gate. It was past two in the morning; the cavernous domed enclosure was nearly deserted. There was a scattering of old men slumped on the long benches, gathering warmth, escaping the December chill of the Washington night. One old man seemed to sit up and take notice as Peter rushed past toward the gate. A lonely dream of what never could be had been disturbed, perhaps.

He had to hurry. The train to Quantico was the last until six. He wanted to reach Alison; he had to talk with her, make her remember. Too, he also had to sleep; there was so much to do that to go on without rest would diminish whatever capabilities he had left. A plan was coming into focus. The beginnings of it were found in Ramirez's offhand remark: *Chasong . . . is represented in scores of veterans' hospitals.*

Peter walked to the center of a deserted car and slid into the seat by the window, noting his reflection in the spotted glass. Although the image was dark and filmy, there was no mistaking the haggard, drawn expression on his face. From somewhere outside on the platform a mechanical voice blared through a loudspeaker. Chancellor closed his eyes and sank into weariness as the wheels gathered speed, the rhythm quickly hypnotic.

He heard muted footsteps behind him in the aisle, heard them over the sounds of rolling metal against metal. He presumed it was the conductor, so he kept his eyes shut, expecting to be asked for his ticket.

No request came. The footsteps had stopped. Peter opened his eyes and turned in the seat.

It all happened so fast. The sick, pale, maniacal face behind him, the muffled report, the explosion of fabric beside him.

The seat had been blown apart! The man not three feet away had tried to kill him! Chancellor spun out of the seat, his body arcing in the air, his hands lunging downward for the bony white fingers that held the weapon. The old man tried to get up, tried to force the barrel of the gun into Peter's stomach. Chancellor crashed the thin wrist against the metal arm of the seat; the weapon fell into the aisle, and Peter spun again, throwing himself between the seats, covering the gun, reaching under his body until it was in his grasp. He lurched to his feet; the old man started to run toward the end of the car. Chancellor sprang after him, grabbing him with one hand. He forced him to stop, pressing him against the rim of an aisle seat.

"Bromley!"

"Child killer!"

"You're a goddamned lunatic!" Peter turned, pinning

Bromley fiercely against the seat in the deserted car. Where was the conductor? The conductor could stop the train and summon the police! Then Chancellor balked; did he want the police?

"How could he have done it?" The old man was whimpering, the words spoken bitterly between his tears. "How could he have told you?"

"What are you talking about!?"

"Only one man knew. St. Claire . . . Munro St. Claire. I thought he had such greatness, such honor." Bromley broke down and wept uncontrollably.

Peter released him, unable to control his own shock. *Munro St. Claire.* A name out of the past, but always a part of the present. The man responsible for all that had happened since the days of rejection and indecision at Park Forest.

All?

Oh, my God. . . .

Venice you know. . . . Bravo, too but not Bravo! Never Bravo! Stefan Varak.

Such greatness, such honor. Paul Bromley.

The fifth man. Bravo.

Munro St. Claire.

Clouds swirled in Chancellor's mind; the pain returned to his temples. He watched, helpless, unable to move, unable to stop him, as the old man rushed to the metal door between the cars and pulled it back. And then there was the crash of another door and a terrible rush of wind above the amplified sounds of the wheels hammering against the tracks below.

There was a scream of anguish, or of courage—whatever, it was of death. Bromley had hurled himself into the night.

And there was no peace for Peter Chancellor.

Munro St. Claire.

Bravo.

30

The Quantico cab turned off the bay highway and drove through the stone gateposts of the Pines Motel and Restaurant. It was isolated from any other structure in that section of the bay area. There were no buildings on either side—only tall brick walls—and the motel itself appeared to be directly on the water.

Peter got out and paid the driver in the bright light of the motel's entrance. There were floodlights everywhere. The cab sped away; Chancellor turned and started toward the large colonial doors.

"Stop where you are! Don't move your hands!"

Chancellor froze; the biting commands had come from the darkness beyond the floodlights, to the left of the entranceway.

"What do you want?"

"Turn this way," ordered the man in shadows. "Slowly! It *is* you. I wasn't sure."

"Who are you?"

"Not one of the maniacs. Go on inside and ask for Mr. Morgan."

"*Morgan?*"

"Mr. Anthony Morgan. You'll be taken to the room."

The insanity again. *Anthony Morgan!* Numbly, he followed the incomprehensible instructions and walked into the lobby. He approached the front desk; a tall, muscular clerk sprang to attention behind the counter. Bewildered, Chancellor asked for Mr. Anthony Morgan.

The clerk nodded. There was more than intelligence behind the man's clear eyes; there was conspiracy. He tapped a bell on the counter. Seconds later a uniformed bellhop arrived; he, too, was tall and powerfully built.

"Take this gentleman to room seven, please."

Peter followed the uniformed man down a carpeted hallway. A window at the far end of the corridor overlooked the waters of the bay. Chancellor thought he saw iron grillwork beyond the glass. They reached a door with the number seven on it; the bellhop rapped lightly.

"Yes?" said the voice behind the door.

"Needle one," said the tall bellhop softly.

"Four," replied the voice behind the door.

"Eleven."

"Thirteen."

"Ten."

"Terminate," said the unseen man. A bolt slid back; the door opened. O'Brien was silhouetted in the dim light of a comfortable sitting room. He nodded to the bellhop and motioned Chancellor inside. Peter saw him put a pistol back in its holster.

"Where is she?" Peter asked instantly.

"Shhh." The FBI man closed the door, a finger against his lips. "She dozed off about twenty minutes ago. She hasn't been able to sleep; she's worried sick."

"Where is she?"

"In the bedroom. Don't worry, there's a set of electronically tripped windows on the water side, with grill-work and bulletproof glass. No one can touch her. Let her be; we'll talk."

"I want to see her!"

O'Brien nodded. "Sure. Go ahead. Just be quiet."

Chancellor opened the door a crack. A lamp was on. Alison lay on the bed, a blanket draped over her. Her head was angled back; her strong, lovely face caught the light. She was breathing deeply. She'd been asleep for twenty minutes. He would let her rest only a little while longer. What he had to do would be best done when Alison was close to exhaustion.

He closed the door. "There's a breakfast alcove back here," O'Brien said.

The sitting room was larger than Peter realized. At the east end, beyond a slatted room divider, was a round table by a window overlooking the water. Peter could now clearly see the grillwork behind the glass. The area contained a small kitchenette. There was coffee on the stove; O'Brien took two cups from a shelf and poured.

Peter sat down. "Not exactly a regular motel, is it?"

O'Brien smiled. "It's a good restaurant, though. Very popular with the social set."

"A proprietary? CIA?"

"Yes to the first. No to the second. It belongs to Naval Intelligence."

"Those men outside. The clerk, the bellboy. Who are they?"

"Varak told you. There aren't many of us, but we know who we are. We help each other." O'Brien drank from his cup. "Sorry to throw you with Morgan's name. I had a reason."

"What was it?"

"You and the girl will be out of here in the morning, but Morgan will still be registered. If anyone picks up your trail and it leads them here, the name Morgan in the registry will mean something. They'll come to room seven. We'll know who they are."

"I thought you knew who the maniacs were." Peter drank his coffee, watching O'Brien carefully.

"Only some of them," replied the agent. "You ready to talk?"

"In a minute." The pain in his head was subsiding, but it was not gone. He needed a few moments; he wanted to think clearly. "Thanks for taking care of her."

"You're welcome. I have a niece about her age—my brother's daughter. They're very much alike. Strong, good faces. Not just pretty, you know?"

"I know." The pain was nearly gone. "What were all those numbers about at the door?"

The FBI man smiled. "Corny but effective. Not much different from what you read in spy novels: progressions and timing, mainly. That's what you writers don't seem to know about."

"What are they?"

"A basic code with a number. As the respondent I add a number, and the contact is trained to associate that number with another figure—plus or minus. He has to reply pretty damned quickly."

"What happens if he doesn't?"

"You saw my gun out. I've never used it that way, but I wouldn't have hesitated. I would have shot him through the door."

Chancellor put the coffee cup down on the table. "We'll talk now."

"Good. What happened?"

"Bromley followed me on the train. He tried to kill me. I was lucky, but he wasn't. He ran from me and threw himself off the train."

"Bromley? It's impossible!"

Peter reached into his pocket and pulled out the revolver he had recovered on the train. "This was fired through a seat in the middle of the third or fourth car on the two o'clock train from Washington. I didn't fire it."

O'Brien got out of the chair and walked to a telephone in the alcove. He spoke as he dialed. "The man we placed with Bromley was on official assignment. We can check him out right away." The agent became the executive. "Security. Surveillance, D.C. area, Duty Officer O'Brien . . . Yes, Chet, it's me. Thanks. Clear me, please. . . . This is O'Brien. There's a special agent covering a subject named Bromley. The Olympic Hotel, downtown area. Raise him, please. Right away." O'Brien held his hand over the mouth-piece and turned to Chancellor. "Did you go back to the hotel? Did you tell anybody—Ramirez, *anyone*—that you were taking the train?"

"No."

"Taxi drivers?"

"I've taken one cab since nine thirty. He drove me to Bethesda and waited for me. He didn't know I would be going back to Union Station."

"Jesus, it doesn't— Yes, yes, what is it? You can't?" The agent's eyes squinted as he spoke into the phone. "There's no response at all? Send a backup squad down to the Olympic immediately. Get clearance from the D.C. police, and let them help. That man may be in trouble. I'll check with you later." O'Brien hung up; he was be-wildered and showed it.

"What do you think happened?" asked Peter.

"I don't know. Only two people knew. The girl and myself." The agent stared at Chancellor.

"Now *wait* a minute. If you're——"

"I'm not," broke in O'Brien. "She's been with me every moment. She hasn't used the telephone; she'd have had to go through the switchboard here."

"What about the men outside? The ones who are so good with progressions."

"No way. I waited until the last train before I told anyone you might show up. And even then I never men-tioned your means of travel. Don't mistake me, I'd trust them with our lives. It was just easier, less responsibility spread around." The agent walked slowly back to the table; then he suddenly brought his hand to his forehead. "Mother of Christ, it could have been me! Outside the Hay-Adams, when we were getting into the car. She was upset; I told her then. He could have been waiting in the drive by the wall. In the shadows."

"What are you talking about?"

O'Brien sat down in weary disgust. "Bromley knew where you were; he could have been waiting for you outside the hotel, hoping to get you in close range. If he was, he could have overheard me. I think I have to apologize for nearly getting you killed."

"That's an apology I find hard to accept."

"I don't blame you. What about this Ramirez? Why did you go see him?"

The transition from Bromley to Ramirez was too rapid for Peter. It took him several moments to clear the image of the sick old man from his mind. But he had made his decision. He would tell the FBI man everything. He reached into his pocket and withdrew the bloodstained scrap of paper with the names written on it.

"Varak was right. He said the key was Chasŏng?"

"That's what you held back on the phone, wasn't it?" O'Brien asked. "Because of MacAndrew and his daughter. Ramirez was at Chasŏng?"

Chancellor nodded. "I'm sure of it. They're all hiding something. I think it's a massive cover-up. Even after twenty-two years they're frightened out of their minds. But that 's only the beginning. Whatever's behind Chasŏng will lead to one of these four men." Chancellor handed O'Brien the scrap of paper. "Whoever he is, he has Hoover's private files."

The agent read the names; the blood drained from his face. "My God! Have you any idea who these people are?"

"Of course. There's a fifth man, but Varak didn't want him identified. He thought a great deal of him and didn't want him hurt. Varak was convinced the fifth man was used, that he was not involved."

"I wonder who he is."

"I know who he is."

"You're full of surprises."

"I found out through Bromley, but he didn't know he told me. You see, I knew the man. Years ago. He resolved a personal quandry I was in. I owe him a great deal. If you insist, I'll give you his name, but I'd rather see him first myself."

O'Brien considered. "All right. Fair enough. But only if you'll let me have a support option."

"Speak English."

"Write out the name and give it to an attorney who will hand it over to me after a reasonably short period of time."

"Why?"

"In case this fifth man kills you."

Chancellor studied the agent's eyes. O'Brien meant precisely what he said. "Fair enough."

"Let's talk about Ramirez. Tell me everything he said; describe every reaction you recall. What was his relationship to MacAndrew? To Chasŏng? How did you know it? What took you to him in the first place?"

"Something I saw at Arlington Cemetery and something Varak said. I put the two together; call it an educated guess . . . or perhaps it fit something I might have written. I don't know. I just didn't think I could be too far wrong. I wasn't."

It took Chancellor less than ten minutes to tell it all. During his narrative Peter could see Quinn O'Brien making mental notes, just as he had done the night before in Washington. "Let's leave Ramirez on a burner and go back to Varak for a minute. He built his connection between Chasŏng and one of those four men on the list because specific information was leaked that couldn't have come from any other source but one of them. Is that right?"

"Yes. He worked for them. He fed them the information."

"And the fact that a language was spoken that he didn't know."

"Apparently he knew several."

"Six or seven, I imagine," agreed O'Brien.

"His point was that the men who took him at the Thirty-fifth Street house had to know he wouldn't be able to understand what they said. They had to know *him*. Again, one of those four men. They all knew him, knew his background."

"Another link in the connection. Could he at least identify the root of the language? Like Oriental or Middle Eastern?"

"He didn't say. He only said that when the name Chasŏng was used, it was spoken fanatically, repeated fanatically."

"What he might have meant was that Chasŏng has become a kind of cult."

"A cult?"

"Let's go back to Ramirez. He confirmed the slaughter, admitted the command foul-up?"

"Yes."

"But he'd already told you Chasŏng was investigated by the Inspector General, that the losses were attributed to unexpected enemy forces who were superior in numbers and firepower."

"He was lying."

"About the I.G. investigation? I doubt that." O'Brien got up and poured more coffee.

"About the findings, then," said Peter.

"I doubt that, too. You could research them too easily."

"What are you driving it?"

"The sequence. I'm a lawyer, remember?" The agent put the pot back on the stove and returned to the table. "Ramirez told you about the I.G. investigation without any hesitation. He just assumed you'd accept the findings if you checked them out. Then moments later he reverses himself. He's suddenly not sure you're going to accept them; and that concerns him. He actually pleads with you to leave it alone. You had to give him a reason to change his mind. It had to be something you said."

"I accused him. I told him it was a cover-up."

"But accused him of what? What were they covering up? You didn't say because you don't know. Hell, charges like that are the reason the I.G. steps in to begin with. He wasn't afraid of those. It was something else. Think."

Chancellor tried. "I told him he hated MacAndrew; that he froze at the name Chasŏng, that it was tied in with MacAndrew's resignation, with a gap in his service record, with the missing files. That he—Ramirez, I mean—was filled with lies and evasions. That he and the others had gotten together because they were frightened to death——"

"Of Chasŏng," completed Quinn O'Brien. "Now go back. What specifically did you say about Chasŏng?"

"That it involved MacAndrew! It was why he resigned, because he was going to expose it. That the information, the cover-up, was in the missing FBI files. It was why he was murdered."

"That's everything? That's *everything* you said?"

"Christ, I'm *trying*."

"Calm down." He put his hand on Peter's arm. "Sometimes the most relevant evidence is right in front of us and we don't see it. We dig so hard for details, we miss the obvious."

The obvious. Words—it was always words. The uncanny way they could provoke a thought, give rise to an image, prod a memory—the memory of a brief flash of recognition in a frightened general's eyes. Of a dying man's statement: *Not him. Her! He's the decoy.* Peter looked through the thin, delicately woven slats of the room divider. His eyes were focused on the door of Alison's room. He turned to O'Brien.

"Oh God, that's it," he said quietly.

"What?"

"MacAndrew's wife."

31

Senior Agent Carroll Quinlan O'Brien agreed to leave. He understood. Things were going to be said behind that door that were terribly private.

Also, he had work to do. There were four celebrated men to learn about and a remote stretch of hills in Korea that two decades ago had been a killing ground. Wheels had to start turning, knowledge had to be unearthed.

Peter entered the bedroom, unsure of how he would begin, sure only that he had to. At the sound Alison stirred, moving her head from one side to the other. She opened her eyes as if startled, and for an instant she stared at the ceiling.

"Hello," said Chancellor gently.

Alison gasped and sat up. "Peter! You're here!"

He walked swiftly to the bed and sat on the edge, embracing her. "Everything's all right," he said, and then he thought of her father and mother. How many times had Alison heard her father say those words to the madwoman who was her mother?

"I was frightened." Alison held his face with both her hands. Her wide brown eyes searched his for evidence of pain. Her whole face was alive and concerned. She was the most intensely beautiful woman he had ever known, and much of that beauty came from within her.

"There's nothing to be frightened about," he said, knowing the lie was preposterous, sensing she knew it, too. "It's almost over. I've just got to ask you some questions."

"Questions?" Slowly she took her hands from his face. "About your mother."

Alison blinked. For a moment he felt her resentment. It was always there when her mother was mentioned.

"I've told you what I can. She became ill when I was very young."

"Yet she remained in the same house with you. You had to know her even in her illness."

Alison leaned against the headboard. She was not relaxing, however; she was wary, as if afraid of the conversation. "That's not entirely right. There was always someone caring for her, and I learned early to keep my distance. And there were the boarding schools from the time I was ten. Whenever my father was sent to a new post, the first thing he did was to find me a school. For two years when we were in Germany, I went to school in Switzerland. When he was in London, I was at the Gateshead Academy for Girls; that's in the north country, near Scotland. So you see, I wasn't in the same house very often."

"Tell me about your mother. Not after she became ill, but before."

"How can I? I was a child."

"What you know about her. Your grandparents, her home, where she lived. How she met your father."

"Is this necessary?" She reached for a pack of cigarettes on the bedside table.

Chancellor looked at her, his eyes steady. "I agreed to your condition last night. You said you'd accept mine. Remember?" He took the matches from her and lighted her cigarette, the flame between them.

She returned his look and nodded. "I remember. All right. My mother, as she was before I knew her. She was born in Tulsa, Oklahoma. Her father was a bishop in the Church of Heavenly Christ. It's a Baptist denomination, very rich, very strict. As a matter of fact both her parents were missionaries. She traveled almost as much as I did when she was young. Remote places. India, Burma, Ceylon, the Po Hai Gulf."

"Where was she educated?"

"Missionary schools mainly. That was part of the up-bringing. All God's children were the same in Jesus' eyes. It was also fake. You went to school with them—probably because it helped the teachers—but damned if you could eat with them or play with them."

"I don't understand something." Peter leaned side-ways, across her covered legs, his elbow resting on the bed, his head in his hand.

"What?"

"That kitchen in Rockville. The nineteen-thirties' de-cor. Even the goddamned coffee pot. You said your father had it designed to remind her of her childhood."

"The happier moments, I said. Or should have said. As a child my mother was happiest when she was back in Tulsa. When her parents returned for spiritual R and R. It wasn't often enough. She hated the Far East, hated the traveling."

"Strange she should wind up marrying an army man."

"Ironic, perhaps—not so strange. Her father was a bishop; her husband became a general. They were strong, decisive men and very persuasive." Alison avoided his eyes; he did not try to reengage them.

"When did she meet your father?"

Alison drew on her cigarette. "Let me think. God knows he told me often enough, but there were always variations. As if he constantly, purposely, exaggerated or romanticized."

"Or left something out?"

She had been looking across the room at the wall. She shifted her eyes quickly to him. "Yes. That, too. Anyway, they met during the Second World War, right here in Washington. Dad was recalled after the North African campaign. He was being transferred to the Pacific, which meant briefing and training in D.C. and Benning. He met her at one of those army receptions."

"What was the daughter of a Baptist bishop doing at an army reception in wartime Washington?"

"She worked for the army as a translator. Nothing dramatic—pamphlets, manuals. 'I am an American pilot who has parachuted into your beautiful country, and I am your ally'—that sort of thing. She could read and write several Far Eastern languages. She could even work her way through basic Mandarin."

Chancellor sat up. "Chinese?"

"Yes."

"She was in China?"

"I told you. The provinces of the Po Hai Gulf. She spent four years there, I think. Her father operated—if that's the word—between Tientsin and Tsingtao."

Peter looked away, trying to conceal his sudden apprehension. A dissonant chord had been struck, its abrasive sound disturbing. He let the moment pass as quickly as possible and turned back to Alison. "Did you know your grandparents?"

"No. I vaguely recall Dad's mother, but his father——"

"Your mother's parents."

"No." Alison reached over and crushed out her cigarette. "They died proselytizing."

"Where?"

Alison held her extinguished cigarette against the glass of the ashtray and replied softly without looking at Peter. "In China."

They were silent for several moments. Alison sat back against the headboard. Chancellor remained motionless and held her gaze. "I think we both know what we're saying. Do you want to talk about it?"

"About what?"

"Tokyo. Twenty-two years ago. Your mother's accident."

"I don't remember."

"I think you do."

"I was so young."

"Not that young. You said you were five or six, but you shaved a couple of points. You were nine. Newspapermen are usually accurate in matters of age; it's easy to check. That article on your father gave your right age——"

"*Please*——"

"Alison, I love you. I want to help you, help us. At first only I had to be stopped. Now you're involved because you're part of the truth. Chasŏng is part of it."

"What truth are you talking about?"

"Hoover's files. They were stolen."

"No! That's in your book. That's not real!"

"It's been real from the beginning. Before he died, they were taken. They're being used right now. And the new owners are tied in with Chasŏng. That's all we know. Your mother's tied in, and your father protected that connection throughout her life. Now we've got to find out what it was. It's the only thing that will lead us to the man who has those files. And we've got to find him."

"But that doesn't make sense! She was a sick woman, getting worse. She wasn't important!"

"She was to somebody. She still is. For God's sake, stop running away from it! You couldn't lie to me, so you skimmed over it, then you circled it, and finally you said it: *China*. The Po Hai provinces are *China*. Your mother's parents died in *China*. At Chasŏng we were fighting *China!*"

"What does it mean?"

"I don't know! I may be so far off base, but I can't help thinking. *Nineteen fifty* . . . Tokyo. Korea. The Chinese Nationalists thrown out of the mainland; they wandered pretty freely, I would think. And if they did, they could be infiltrated. Orientals can tell one another apart; Westerners can't. Was it possible your mother was reached? The wife of one of the top commanders in Korea reached and somehow compromised—because she had parents in China. Until something snapped. What happened twenty-two years ago?"

The words came painfully to Alison. "It started several months before, I think. When we first got to Tokyo. She just gradually began to slip away."

"What do you mean, 'slip away'?"

"I'd say something to her and she'd simply stare at me, not hearing. Then she'd turn without answering and walk out of the room, singing bits and pieces of tunes."

"I heard one in the Rockville house. She was singing an old tune. 'Let It Snow.' "

"That sort of thing came later. She'd get attached to a song, and it would last for months. Over and over again."

"Was your mother an alcoholic?"

"She drank, but I don't think so. At least, not then."

"You remember her quite well," said Peter softly.

Alison looked at him. "More than my father knew, and less than you think."

He accepted the rebuke. "Go on," he said gently. "She began slipping away. Did anybody know? Was anything done for her?"

Alison reached nervously for another cigarette. "I suppose I was the reason something was done. You see, there was no one to talk to. The servants were all Japanese.

What few visitors we had were army wives; you don't talk to army wives about your mother."

"You were alone, then. A child."

"I was alone. I didn't know how to cope. Then the telephone calls started coming late at night. She'd get dressed and go out, sometimes with that dazed look in her eyes, and I didn't know if she'd ever come back. One night my father called from Korea. She was always home when he called; he would write her the day and the time. But that night she wasn't, so I told him everything. I guess I just blurted it out. A few days later he flew back to Tokyo."

"How did he react?"

"I don't remember. I was so happy to see him. I just knew everything would be all right."

"Was it?"

"It was stabilized for a while; that's the word I'd use now. An army doctor began coming to the house. Then he brought others, and they'd take her away for several hours every few days. The phone calls stopped, and she stopped going out at night."

"Why do you say 'stabilized for a while'? Did things come unglued?"

Tears formed in her eyes. "There was no warning. She just suddenly went. It happened late one bright, sunny day; I'd just come home from school. She was screaming. She'd chased the servants out of the house; she was raving, smashing things. Then she stared at me. I've never seen such a look. As though she loved me one moment, then hated me, then was terrified by me." Alison brought her hand to her mouth; it was trembling. She stared down at the blanket, her eyes frightened. She whispered the rest. "Then mother came at me. It was horrible. She had a kitchen knife in her hand. She grabbed me by the throat; she tried to plunge the knife into my stomach. She kept trying to stab me. I held her wrist and screamed and screamed. She wanted to kill me! Oh, *God*! She wanted to *kill me!*"

Alison fell forward on her side, her whole body convulsed, her face ashen. Peter reached for her and held her, rocking her back and forth.

He could not let her stop now. "Please, try to remember. When you came in the house, when you saw her, what was she screaming? What was she saying?"

Alison pushed herself away from him and leaned back

on the headrest, her eyes shut tight, her face wet with tears. But the crying had stopped. "I don't know."

"*Remember!*"

"I *can't!* I didn't *understand* her!" Her eyes opened; she stared at him. They both understood.

"Because she was speaking a foreign language." He said the words firmly, not asking a question. "She was screaming in Chinese. Your mother, who spent four years in the Po Hai provinces, who was fluent in Mandarin, was screaming at you in Chinese."

Alison nodded. "Yes."

The real question was not answered; Chancellor understood that. Why would mother attack daughter? For a few seconds Peter let his mind wander, recalling vaguely the hundreds of pages he had written in which irrational conflicts led to terrible acts of violence. He was no psychologist; he had to think in simpler terms. Schizophrenic infanticide, Medea complex—these were not the areas to probe even if he were capable. The answer lay elsewhere. In more obvious descriptions. . . . Descriptions? A madwoman in a rage, unbalanced, unfocused. *Unfocused.* Late afternoon. Bright sunshine. Most houses in Japan were light and airy. Sun streaming through the windows. A child walks through the door. Peter reached for the child's hand.

"Try very hard to remember what you were wearing."

"It's not hard. We wore the same thing every day. Dresses were considered immodest. We wore light, loosefitting little slacks and jackets. It was the school uniform."

Peter looked away. A *uniform.* He turned back.

"Was your hair long or short?"

"During those days?"

"During that day. When your mother saw you coming through the door that afternoon."

"I was wearing a cap. We all wore caps, and we usually kept our hair short."

That was it! thought Peter. An unbalanced woman in a rage, sun streaming through the windows, perhaps through the door; a figure comes in wearing a *uniform.*

He reached for Alison's other hand. "She never saw you."

"What?"

"Your mother never saw you. That's what Chasŏng's all about. It explains the broken glass, the old nightgown underneath the words on the wall in your father's study, the look in Ramirez's eyes when your mother was mentioned."

"What do you mean, she never saw me? I was there!"

"But she didn't see *you*. She saw a uniform. That's *all* she saw."

Alison brought her hand to her mouth, curiosity and fear intermingled. "A uniform? Ramirez? You went to see Ramirez?"

"There's a lot I can't tell you because I don't know myself, but we're getting nearer. Officers were rotated back and forth from the Korean combat zones to the command centers in Tokyo. That's common knowledge. You say your mother went out frequently at night. There's a pattern, Alison."

"You're saying she was a whore. That she whored to get information!"

"I'm saying it's possible she was forced into acts that tore her apart. Husband and father. On the one hand, her husband, a brilliant commander at the front; on the other, an adored father held captive in China. What could she do?"

Alison raised her eyes to the ceiling. Again she understood; it was a conflict with which she could identify. "I don't want to go on. I don't want to know any more."

"We have to. What happened after the attack?"

"I ran outside. One of the servants was there; he had called the police from the house nearest ours. He took me there, and I waited . . . waited while the Japanese family stared at me as if I were diseased. Then an MP came and took me to the base. I stayed with a colonel's wife for several days until my father came back."

"Then what? Did you see your mother?"

"About a week or so later, I think. It's hard to remember precisely. When she came home, a nurse was with her. She was never without a nurse or a companion ever again."

"How was she?"

"Withdrawn."

"Permanently damaged?"

"That's difficult to say. It was more than a breakdown; that's obvious to me now. But she might have recovered sufficiently to function then."

"Then?"

"When she came home from the hospital the first time. With the nurse. Not after the second time."

"Tell me about it. The second time."

Alison blinked. The memory was obviously as painful to her as the violent image of her mother's attack. "Arrangements had been made for me to go back to the States, to Dad's parents. As I said, Mother was quiet, withdrawn. Three nurses were on eight-hour shifts; she was never alone. My father was needed back in Korea. He left, believing everything was under control. Other officers' wives would come to the house to see Mother, take us both out for picnics, take her shopping for an afternoon—that sort of thing. Everyone was very kind. Too kind. really. You see, mentally ill people are like alcoholics. If they're gripped by an obsession, if they want to break away, they'll suddenly pretend normality; they'll smile and laugh and lie convincingly. Then when you least expect it, they're gone. That's what I think happened."

"You think? You don't know?"

"No. They told me that she'd been pulled out of the surf. That she'd been underwater so long, they thought she was dead. I was a child, and it was an explanation I could accept. It made sense; Mother was taken out for the day to Funabashi Beach. It was a Sunday, but I had a cold, so I stayed home. Then sometime in the afternoon the phone started ringing. Was my mother there? Had she come back? The first few calls were from the women who had taken her to Funabashi, but they didn't want me to know that. They pretended to be other people, so as not to alarm me, I guess. Two Army officers drove out to the house. They were nervous and agitated, but they didn't want me to know it, either. I went to my room; I knew something was wrong, and all I could think of was that I wanted my father."

The tears came again. Peter held both her hands; he spoke gently. "Go on."

"It was awful. At night, quite late, I heard screams. Then shouts and people running outside. Then there were the sounds of automobiles and sirens and tires screeching in the streets. I got out of bed and went to the door and opened it. My room was on the landing above the hall. Downstairs the house seemed to be filling up with Americans—Army mostly, but civilians, too. There probably weren't more than ten men, but everyone was walking around rapidly, talking into the telephone, using hand radios. Then the front door opened, and she was brought inside. On a stretcher. She was under a sheet, but there were bloodstains on the cloth. And her face—it was white. Her eyes were wide, staring blankly as if she were dead. At the corners of her mouth were trickles of blood that rolled down over her chin onto her neck. As the stretcher passed beneath a light, she suddenly lurched up screaming, her head wrenching back and forth, her body writhing but held in place by the straps. I cried out and ran down the stairs, but a major—a handsome black major, I'll never forget—stopped me and picked me up and held me, telling me that everything was going to be all right. He didn't want me to go to her, not then. And he was right—she was in hysterics; she wouldn't have known me. They lowered the stretcher to the floor, unstrapped her, and held her down. A doctor tore some cloth. He had a hypodermic needle in his hand; he administered it, and within seconds she was quiet. I was crying. I tried to ask questions, but nobody would listen to me. The major carried me back to my room and put me to bed. He stayed with me for a long time, trying to reassure me, telling me there'd been an accident and my mother would be all right. But I knew she wouldn't be, not ever again. I was taken to the base and stayed there until Dad came back for the next to last time before we were flown home to America. His tour of duty had only a few months left."

Chancellor pulled her to him. "The only thing that's clear is that the accident didn't have anything to do with being caught in an undertow and pulled out to sea. For one thing, she was brought to the house, not to a hospital. It was an elaborate hoax that you pretended to believe but never did. You don't believe it now. Why did you pretend all these years?"

Alison whispered. "It was easier, I think."

"Because you thought she tried to kill you? Because she screamed at you in Chinese, and you didn't want to think about that? You didn't want to consider the alternatives."

Alison's lips trembled. "Yes."

"But now you've got to face it—you understand that, don't you? You can't run away from it anymore. It's what's in Hoover's files. Your mother worked for the Chinese. She was responsible for the slaughter at Chasŏng."

"Oh, *God*. . . ."

"She didn't do anything *willingly*. Maybe not even

knowingly. Months ago, when I was with your father, and your mother came downstairs, she saw me and began screaming. I started to back away into the study, but your father yelled at me and told me to get by a lamp. He wanted her to see my face, my features. She stared at me, then calmed down and just sobbed. I think your father wanted her to realize I wasn't an Oriental. I think the accident that Sunday afternoon was no accident at all. I believe she was caught and tortured by the people who had been using her, forcing her to work for them. It's possible your mother was a much braver woman than anyone's given her credit for. She may have finally stood up to them and taken the consequences. That's not congenital madness, Alison. That's a person who's been *driven* out of her mind."

He stayed with her for nearly an hour, until exhaustion made her finally close her eyes. It was past five; the sky outside the window was growing brighter. It would be morning soon. In a few hours Quinn O'Brien would move them to some other place of safety. Peter knew that he, too, had to sleep.

But before he could allow himself sleep, he had to know if what he believed was true. It had to be confirmed, and one man could do that. Ramirez.

He let himself out the bedroom door and walked to the telephone. He rummaged through his pockets until he found the scrap of paper on which he'd written Ramirez's number. No doubt O'Brien's man would be listening at the switchboard, but it did not matter. Nothing mattered anymore but the truth.

He dialed The phone was answered almost immediately.

"Yes, what is it?" The voice was slurred with sleep. Or was it alcohol?

"Ramirez?"

"Who's this?"

"Chancellor. I've got the answer now, and you're going to confirm it for me. If you hesitate, if you lie, I'm going right to my publisher. He'll know what to do."

"I told you to stay out of it!" The words spilled over each other; the soldier was drunk.

"MacAndrew's wife. There was a Chinese connection, wasn't there? Twenty-two years ago she was carrying information to the Chinese. She was responsible for Chasŏng!"

"No! Yes. You don't understand. Let it alone!"

"I want the truth!"

Ramirez was momentarily silent. "They're both dead."

"Ramirez!"

"They had her on drugs. She was totally dependent; she couldn't go two days without a needle. We found out. We helped her. We did our best for her. Things were going badly. It made sense . . . to do what we did. Everyone agreed!"

Peter's eyes narrowed. The dissonant chord was there again, louder and more jarring than before. "You *helped* her because it made sense? Things were going badly, so it made some sort of goddamned *sense*?"

"Everyone agreed." The soldier's voice was nearly inaudible.

"Oh, my God! You didn't help her, you *maintained* her! You *kept* her on drugs so you could transmit the information you wanted to get through."

"Things were going badly. The Yalu was——"

"Wait a minute! Are you telling me MacAndrew was a part of this? He let his wife be used this way?"

"MacAndrew never knew."

Chancellor felt sick. "Yet in spite of everything you did to her, Chasŏng still happened," he said. "And all these years MacAndrew thought his wife was responsible. Drugged, tortured, nearly beaten to death, made a traitor by an enemy that held her parents captive. You bastards!"

Ramirez screamed into the telephone. "He was a bastard, too! Don't you ever forget it! He was a *killer*!"

32

He was a bastard, too! Don't you ever forget it! He was a killer! He was a bastard, too! . . . a killer! The drunken words rang in Chancellor's ears. He watched the swiftly passing countryside, Alison in the back seat of the government car with him, and tried to understand.

He was a bastard, too! It did not make sense. Mac-

Andrew and his wife were victims. They had been manipulated by *both* antagonists—the woman destroyed, the general living out his life with a terrible fear of exposure.

He was a bastard, too! . . . *a killer!* If Ramirez meant that MacAndrew had become irrational, a commander who did not care about the cost of destroying an enemy that had destroyed his wife, *bastard* was hardly the right term. Mac the Knife had hurled hundreds, perhaps thousands, to their death in a futile attempt at vengeance. Reason had deserted him; vengeance was everything.

If these were the things that caused Ramirez to judge MacAndrew a bastard, so be it. But what bothered Peter, and it bothered him deeply, was the unclear picture of this new MacAndrew, this *bastard*, this killer. It conflicted with the man Chancellor had met, the soldier who truly hated war because he knew it so well. Or had Alison's father merely lapsed momentarily—a matter of months in a lifetime—into a madness of his own.

So now the secret of Chasŏng was known. But where did it lead them? How could MacAndrew's betrayed, manipulated wife lead to one of the four men on Varak's list? Varak was convinced that whatever was behind Chasŏng would take them directly to the man who had Hoover's files. But how?

Perhaps Varak was wrong. The secret was known, and it led nowhere.

The government car reached an intersection. A lone gas station stood on the right; a single automobile was parked by a pump. The driver beside O'Brien turned the wheel, and they drove up to it. He nodded to O'Brien and got out of the car; the FBI man slid over behind the wheel. The driver walked to the parked automobile. He greeted the man inside and climbed in the front seat.

"They'll stay with us until we reach Saint Michael's," said Quinn from behind the wheel.

A minute later they were on the road again, the car behind them following at a discreet distance.

"Where's Saint Michael's?" asked Alison.

"South of Annapolis, on the Chesapeake. We can use a house there. It's sterile. Do you want to talk now? The radio's off; there are no tapes. We're alone."

Peter knew what Quinn meant. "Was a tape made of what was said between Ramirez and me?"

"No. Only a shorthand transcript. One copy; it's in my pocket."

"I haven't had time to explain everything to Alison, but she knows some of it." He turned to her. "Your mother was strung out on narcotics—probably heroin—by the Chinese. She became dependent; that was the 'slipping away' you described. She was used to gather bits and pieces of information. Troop movements, combat strength, supply routes—a hundred things she might overhear from the officers she met at night. Besides the drugs, her mother and father were being held in a Chinese prison. The combination was overpowering."

"How horrible. . . ." Alison looked out the window.

"I doubt that she was the only one," said Peter. "I'm sure there were others."

"I know damned well there were," added O'Brien.

"I'm afraid that doesn't help," Alison said. "Did my father know? It must have killed him——"

"Your father knew only what the Army wanted him to know. It was only part of the truth, the Chinese part. He was never told the rest of it."

Alison turned from the window. "What rest of it?"

Peter took her hand. "There was another connection. The Army's. She was manipulated to transmit selected, misleading intelligence back to the Chinese."

Alison stiffened, her eyes boring in on his. "How?"

"There are a number of ways to do it. Keep her spaced out on narcotics or administer chemicals that heighten the withdrawal pains. Probably that was it; the agony would drive her right back to her original connection. With the information the Army wanted carried."

Alison pulled her hand away in anger. She closed her eyes, breathing deeply, in an agony of her own. Chancellor did not touch her; the moment was hers alone.

She turned back to Peter. "Make them pay," she said.

"We know what Chasŏng means now," said Quinn O'Brien from the front seat. "But where does it take us?"

"To one of four men," Varak believed." Chancellor saw O'Brien's head jerk up, his eyes looking at Peter in the rearview mirror. "I've told her there are four men," he explained. "I haven't used names."

"Why not?" asked Alison.

"For your own protection, Miss MacAndrew," answered the FBI man. "I'm working on those. I'm not sure what to look for."

"Something to do with China," Peter said. "Anything Chinese."

"You mentioned that you wanted to reach a fifth man. How soon?"

"Before the day's over."

Quinn was silent behind the wheel. Several moments went by before he spoke.

"You agreed to leave the name with a lawyer."

"I don't need a lawyer. I'll leave it with Morgan in New York. Get me to a phone. There should be one on a road around here somewhere."

O'Brien frowned. "You're not experienced making these kind of contacts. I don't want you taking unnecessary risks. You don't know what you're doing."

"You'd be surprised how many secret meetings I've invented. You just get me an unmarked car and give me a few hours. And don't go back on your word. I'll know if you have me followed. Believe that."

"I'm forced to. Mother of God. A *writer*."

"Goddamn it, where are you?" Tony shouted the question, his next words only slightly less strident. "The hotel said you'd checked out, and the night manager told me you were on your way to the Shenandoah Valley! And your doctor phoned, asking me if I expected you in New York. Would you please explain——?"

"There isn't time. Except that he wasn't the hotel's night manager, he was an FBI man. And I doubt my doctor called you. It was someone else looking for me."

"What are you *doing*?"

"Trying to find the man who has Hoover's files."

"Stop that! We had this out a couple of months ago. You're crossing the line again; you're not someone in one of your goddamned books!"

"But the files *are* missing. They've been missing from the beginning; that's what it's all about. I'll come back to New York, I promise, but first I want you to call someone for me. I want you to tell him to meet me in a car at the precise location and time I give you. He's in Washington and probably very difficult to get through to. But you'll be able to do it if you say your name is Varak. Stefan Varak. Write that down; you mustn't use your own name."

"And I suppose," said Morgan sarcastically, "that I should place the call from a pay phone."

"Exactly. On the street, not in the building."

"Come on. This is——"

"The man you're calling it Munro St. Claire."

The name had its effect; Morgan was stunned. "You're not joking, are you." It was not a question.

"I'm not joking. When you get St. Claire on the line, tell him you're a contact from me. Tell him Varak is dead. He may know it by now, but he may not. Have you got a pencil?"

"Yes."

"Write this down. St. Claire uses the name Bravo. . . ."

Peter waited in the unmarked car on the back road that led to the edge of the Chesapeake; it was a dead end that stopped at the water. The banks were marshland, the wild reeds tall and swaying in the December winds. It was shortly past two in the afternoon; the sky was overcast, the air cold, and the dampness penetrating.

Alison and O'Brien were several miles north in the sterile house in Saint Michael's. The FBI man had agreed to give him three hours—until five o'clock—before he telephoned Morgan for Bravo's identity. If Chancellor had not returned by then, Quinn made it clear that Peter was to be presumed dead and appropriate measures would be taken.

Chancellor remembered Varak's words. There was a senator. A man who was not afraid, who among all men in Washington could be sought out for help. For Peter it had been another part of the madness. He had invented a senator for his Nucleus. The parallel was once again too close; the fictional character had its basis in a living man.

He gave the senator's name to Quinn in case he did not return.

In the distance a black limousine had rounded a bend in the road and was approaching slowly. He opened the door of the car and got out. The limousine came to a stop twenty feet away. The chauffeur's window was lowered.

"Mr. Peter Chancellor?" asked the man.

"Yes," answered Peter, alarmed. There was no one in the rear seat of the car. "Where's Ambassador St. Claire?"

"If you'll get in, sir, I'll take you to him."

"That wasn't part of my instructions!"

"It has to be this way."

"No, it doesn't!"

"The ambassador told me to tell you it was for your own protection. He asked me to remind you of a conversation four and a half years ago. He did not mislead you then."

Peter's breathing stopped for a moment. Munro St. Claire had *not* misled him four and a half years before. He had given him his life. Chancellor nodded and got into the limousine.

The enormous Victorian house stood on the waterfront. A long dock protruded into the bay at the center point of the large front lawn. The house itself was four stories high. On the first level was a wide screened-in porch that ran along the side of the building that faced the Chesapeake.

The chauffeur preceded Chancellor up the steps to the entrance. He unlocked the door and motioned Peter inside.

"Turn to the right, through the archway, and into the sitting room. The ambassador is waiting for you."

Chancellor stepped into the hall; he was alone. He walked through an archway into a high-ceilinged room and adjusted his eyes. At the far end a lone figure stood in front of a pair of glass French doors overlooking the porch and the waters of the Chesapeake. His back was to Chancellor; he was looking out at the everchanging surface of the bay.

"Welcome," said Munro St. Claire, turning to face Peter. "This house belonged to a man named Genesis. He was Bravo's friend."

"I've heard of Banner and Paris, Venice and Christopher. And, of course, Bravo. I haven't heard of Genesis."

St. Claire had obviously been testing. He controlled his astonishment, but it was there. "There would be no reason for you to. He's dead. I find it incredible that Varak gave you my name."

"He didn't. As a matter of fact, he refused to. A man named Bromley did, but he didn't know he did. His code name at the Bureau was Viper. The *B* becomes *V* and thus one of the missing files. Part truth, part lie. That's how I was programed."

St. Claire narrowed his eyes as he moved away from

the glass doors toward Chancellor. " 'Part truth, part lie'; Varak said that?"

"Yes. He died in front of me. But not before he told me everything."

"Everything?"

"From the beginning. From Malibu to Washington. How I was provoked into getting involved; how I was the snare for provoking others into showing themselves. He didn't say so directly, but it really didn't matter whether I lived or died, did it? How could you do it?"

"Sit down."

"I'd prefer standing."

"Very well. Are we two gladiators circling each other?"

"Perhaps."

"If so, you've lost the battle. My chauffeur is watching us from the porch."

Chancellor turned toward the windows. The chauffeur stood motionless, a gun in his hand. "You think I've come to kill you?" Peter asked.

"I don't know what to think. I only know that nothing can stand in the way of retrieving those files. I'd willingly *give* my life if that could be accomplished."

"Letters *M* through *Z*. The man who has them whispers over the telephone, threatens his victims. And he's one of four men: Banner, Paris, Venice, or Christopher. Or perhaps he's Bravo; that's possible. I guess. He's reached Phyllis Maxwell, Paul Bromley, and Lieutenant General Bruce MacAndrew. The general was about to expose a twenty-two-year-old cover-up that he couldn't live with anymore when he was forced out. How many others this man has reached, no one knows. But if he's not found, if the files aren't found—and destroyed—he'll control the pressure points of the government."

Peter made the statements flatly, but they had their effect. "You know things that could cost you your life," said St. Claire.

"Since I've nearly lost it several times, thanks to you, that doesn't surprise me. It just frightens me. I want it to stop."

"I wish I could stop it. I wish to God it was over and the files brought back. I wish with all my heart that I was convinced it would end that way."

"There's a way to bring it about. To insure it, as a matter of fact."

"How?"

"Make public the names of your group. Acknowledge Hoover's missing files. Force the issue."

"You're out of your mind."

"Why?"

"The issue is far more complex than you seem to understand." St. Claire moved to an armchair. He placed his hands on the rim of the back, his long fingers extended delicately over the fabric. His hands trembled. "You say Bromley gave you my name," he said. "How?"

"He tracked me down on a train and tried to kill me. He had been told that my manuscript was finished, that it included information about his family. I gather that information could only have come from you. He used your name; suddenly everything was clear. From the beginning, the very beginning. All the way back to Park Forest. I owed you a debt, and you took your payment. The debt's canceled."

St. Claire looked up. "Your debt to me? It was never owed. But I submit you have a debt to your country."

"I'll accept that. I just want to know how I'm paying." Peter raised his voice. "Make public the names of your group! Tell the country—since debts are owed—that Hoover's private files are missing!"

"*Please!*" St. Claire held up one hand. "Try to understand. We came together under extraordinary circumstances——"

"To stop a maniac," interrupted Chancellor.

Bravo nodded. "To *try* to stop a maniac. In doing so, we exceeded the limits of authority in a number of areas. We bent the machinery of government because we thought it was justified. We could be ruined, everything we stand for destroyed; we understood that. Our only motive was fairness, our only protection anonymity."

"Change the rules! One of you already has!"

"Then, he must be found. But the others can't be made to pay!"

"I'm not getting through to you. The debt's canceled, Mr. St. Claire. You've *used* me. I've been manipulated, kept off balance until I was damned near out of my mind. For what? So *you*, the Pentagon, the Federal Bureau of Investigation—for all I know, the White House, the Justice

Department, the Congress . . . half the goddamned government—can go on lying? Telling people those files were destroyed when they weren't? I'm not asking; I'm demanding! Either you go public, or I will!"

St. Claire could control his trembling but not conceal it. The long, thin fingers were pressed into the chair. "Tell me about Varak," he said softly. "I'm entitled to that; he was a friend."

Chancellor told him, omitting Varak's conclusion that Chasŏng was the key. Alison was too intrinsic to that key, he did not trust St. Claire with her name.

"He died," said Peter, "convinced it wasn't you, but one of the other four. 'Never Bravo.' He said that over and over."

"And what about you? Are you convinced?"

"Not yet, but you can convince me. Go public."

"I see." St. Claire turned from the chair and looked out at the waters of the Chesapeake. "Varak told you you were programed with part truth, part lie. Did he explain that?"

"Of course. The missing files were the truth; the assassination was the lie. I never believed it anyway. It was only a concept for a book. . . . We've talked long enough. I want your answer. Will you go public with the story, or will I?"

St. Claire turned around slowly. Gone was the anxiety of seconds ago; it was replaced by a gaze so cold Peter was frightened. "Don't threaten me. You're in no position to do that."

"You can't be sure. You don't know what precautions I've taken."

"Do you think you're a character in one of your novels? Don't be foolish." Bravo glanced at the window. The chauffeur was watching them closely, the gun held steady in his hand. "You're not important, and neither am I."

Chancellor felt on the edge of panic. "There's a man in New York who knows I've come to see you. If anything happened to me, he'd identify you. As a matter of fact you spoke with him."

"I listened to him," replied St. Claire. "I didn't agree to anything. You drove your car to a dead-end road on the banks of the Chesapeake. I am listed in the State Department logs as being in conference at this moment with an undersecretary who will swear I was there. But an alibi isn't necessary. We could kill you anytime. Tonight, to-morrow, next week, next month. But no one wants to do that. It was never part of the plan. . . . Four and a half years ago I steered you into the world of fiction. Go back to that world; leave this one to others."

Peter was stunned. Their roles had reversed. St. Claire's fears had evaporated, as though the news an out-raged young man had brought him were no longer vital. It didn't make sense. What caused the change? His eyes strayed to the window. The chauffeur seemed to sense the tension inside; he had moved closer to the glass. St. Claire saw Peter's concern and smiled.

"I said you could go back. That man's there only for my protection. I didn't know the state of your mind."

"You still don't. How can you be sure that I won't leave here and tell the story?"

"Because we both know that isn't the right way. Too many people could lose their lives; neither of us wants that to happen."

"I should tell you I know who Banner, Paris, Venice, and Christopher are! Varak wrote out their names for me!"

"I presumed he had. And you must do what you have to."

"Goddamn it, I *will* tell the story! The killing's going to stop! The lying's going to stop!"

"In my judgment," said St. Claire icily, "if you do, Alison MacAndrew will be dead before the day is over."

Peter tensed, then took a step toward Bravo.

There was a crash of glass as a single window pane was smashed; the chauffeur's gun protruded through the open space.

"Go home, Mr. Chancellor. Do what you have to do."

Peter turned and ran out of the room.

Munro St. Claire opened the glass doors and stepped out onto the porch. The air was cold, the winds off the bay growing stronger. The sky was dark now. Soon it would rain.

It was remarkable, St. Claire reflected. Even in death Varak orchestrated events. He understood that only one option remained: Peter Chancellor had to take Varak's place. The writer was now the provocateur. He had no choice but to go after Banner, Paris, Venice, and Christopher.

Chancellor said he had been manipulated. What he did not know was that the manipulation had not stopped. It was a question now of watching the novelist very closely, keeping track of his every move, until he led them to the one who had the files.

There would be a final tragedy, and like the assassination of John Edgar Hoover, it could not be avoided. Two men would die. The betrayer of Inver Brass and, unquestionably, Peter Chancellor.

At the last Stefan Varak had been a professional. With Chancellor's death all avenues would be closed. And Inver Brass disbanded, forever unknown.

33

"You still won't tell me who he is?" asked O'Brien, across from Peter at the kitchen table. Each had a half empty glass of whisky in front of him.

"No. Varak was right. He doesn't have the files."

"How can you be sure?"

"Because he would never have let me come back alive."

"Okay, then. I won't probe. I think you're crazy, but I won't probe."

Chancellor smiled. "It wouldn't do you any good. What have you found out about our four candidates? Is there a China connection? Anything remotely possible?"

"Yes. Two possibilities. Two mostly negative. One of the possibilities is pretty dramatic. I'd say a probable."

"Who is it?"

"Jacob Dreyfus. Christopher."

"How?"

"Money. He arranged heavy financial backing for several multinationals operating out of Taiwan."

"Openly?"

"Yes. His public posture was to help create a viable Formosan economy. There was a lot of resistance; most of the banks thought Taiwan would fall, but Dreyfus was a tiger. Apparently he got assurance from Eisenhower and Kennedy. He rallied the institutions and single-handedly brought in new industry."

Peter's doubts were aroused; it was too obvious. A man like Dreyfus would not be obvious. "There was nothing secret? No undercover deals or anything?"

"Not that we can find. Why are they necessary? Money means involvement. That's what we're looking for."

"If money's the bottom line, we are. I'm not convinced it is. Who's the other possibility?"

"Frederick Wells—Banner."

"What's his relationship to the Nationalists?"

"To China, not necessarily the Chinese government. He's a Sinophile. His hobby is early Oriental history. He has one of the most extensive Chinese art collections in the world. They're lent to museums all the time."

"An art collection? What's that got to do with anything?"

"I don't know. We're looking for a connection. It's a connection."

Chancellor frowned. Actually Wells might be a more logical contender than Dreyfus, he considered. A man steeped in the culture of a nation was more apt to be caught up in the mystique of that culture than someone who dealt merely in money. Was it possible that beneath Frederick Well's pragmatism there was an Oriental mystic in conflict with the Western shell? Or was it preposterous?

Anything was possible. Nothing could be overlooked.

"You said the other two were *mostly* negative. What did you mean?"

"Neither could be construed as having any tangible Chinese sympathies per se. Still, Sutherland—Venice— ruled against the government in a suit brought by three New York journalists who'd been refused passports to the mainland by the State Department. Essentially he contended that as long as Peking was willing to let them in, it was an abridgment of the First Amendment to prohibit them."

"That sounds logical."

"It was. There was no appeal."

"What about Montelán?"

"Paris has been an active anti-Nationalist for a long time. He tagged Chiang Kai-shek as a corrupt warlord years ago. He was outspoken in his support for Red China's admission to the UN."

"So were a lot of people."

"That's what I mean by mostly negative. Both Venice and Paris took positions that might have been unpopular, but they weren't very unusual."

"Unless there were other reasons for those positions."

"Unless anything. I'm going by probabilities at this point. I think we should concentrate on Dreyfus and Wells."

"They can be first, but I'm going to reach all four. Confront each one." Peter finished his whisky.

O'Brien leaned back in his chair. "Would you mind repeating that?"

Peter got out of the chair and carried his glass to the counter, where there was a bottle of Scotch. They'd had one drink; Chancellor hesitated, then poured a second. "How many men can you count on? Like those at the motel in Quantico and the ones who followed us here."

"I asked you to repeat what you just said."

"Don't fight me," said Peter. "Help me, but don't fight me. I'm the connecting link between all four men. Each knows how I've been manipulated. One knows—or will *think* he knows—that I've zeroed in on him."

"And then?"

Chancellor poured his drink. "He'll try to kill me."

"That crossed my mind," said O'Brien. "You think I'm going to be responsible? Forget it."

"You can't stop me. You can only help me."

"The hell I can't stop you! I can formalize a dozen charges against you that will put you in isolation!"

"Then what? *You* can't confront them."

"Why not?"

Chancellor walked back to the table and sat down. "Because you've been reached. Han Chow, remember?"

O'Brien remained motionless, returning Peter's stare. "What do you know about Han Chow?"

"Nothing, Quinn. And I don't want to know. But I can guess. The first night we talked, when I mentioned Longworth's name, when I told you what happened to Phyllis Maxwell . . . when I said the word Chasōng. Your face, your eyes; you were frightened. You said the name

Han Chow as if it was killing you. You looked at me the way you're looking now; you started to accuse me of things I couldn't understand. You may not want to believe this, but I invented you before I met you."

"What kind of crap is that?" O'Brien asked, his voice strained.

Peter drank self-consciously. He took his eyes away from Quinn's and looked at the glass. "You were my cleansing process. My good guy who has to face his vulnerabilities and surmount them."

"I don't understand you."

"Every story about corruption has to have a foil. The person on the side of the angels. I think the difference between a fair novel and a cartoon is that no one in a novel begins as a hero. If he becomes one, it's only because he forces himself to overcome his own fear. I'm not good enough to write a tragedy, so you can't call that fear a tragic flaw. But you can call it a weakness. Han Chow was your weakness, wasn't it? You're part of the files."

Quinn swallowed involuntarily, his eyes still on Chancellor. "Do you want to hear about it?"

"No. I mean that. But I do want to know why you were reached. It had to be before I came to see you."

O'Brien's words were clipped, as if he were afraid of them. "The night before Hoover died, the names of three men were recorded in the security logs at the bureau. Longworth, Krepps, and Salter."

"Longworth was *Varak!*" interrupted Peter harshly.

"Or was he?" replied Quinn. "*You* told me Varak died trying to get the files back. A man doesn't kill himself trying to find what he's already got. It was someone else."

"Go on."

"There was no way the real Longworth could have been there. Krepps and Salter were unassigned covers. I couldn't establish any identities. Three unknown men, in other words, were cleared for admittance into Hoover's office that night. I began asking questions. I got a phone call——"

"A high-pitched whisper?" asked Peter.

"A whisper. Very courteous, very precise. I was told to stop. Han Chow was the lever."

Chancellor leaned forward. Two nights ago O'Brien had been the interrogator; now it was his turn. The amateur was leading the professional. Because the professional was frightened.

"What's an unassigned cover?"

"An identity prepared in advance for emergencies. Biographical data. Parents, schools, friends, occupation, service records—that sort of thing."

"In ten minutes a man has a personal history."

"Let's say a couple of hours. He's got to memorize a number of things."

"What led you to the security logs in the first place?"

"The files," said O'Brien. "A few of us wondered what had happened to them; we talked about it. Quietly, just among ourselves."

"But why the security logs?"

"I'm not sure. Process of elimination, I guess. I checked the shredding rooms, the furnaces, computerized inputs—there were no loads to speak of. I even made inquiries about the cartons of personal effects taken from Flags."

"Flags?"

"Hoover's office. He didn't like the name. It was never used in his presence."

"Were there a lot of cartons?"

"Nowhere near enough to contain the files. To me that meant they'd been removed. And that scared the hell out of me. Remember, I'd seen them in use."

"Alexander Meredith. . . . I've been here before."

"Who's this Meredith?"

"Someone you should meet. Only he doesn't exist."

"Your book?"

"Yes. Go on."

"Since physical removal was a possibility, I began researching the logs. Everyone knew Hoover was dying; there'd even been a code name for his death: 'open territory.' The meaning, I think, is clear. After the director, who?"

"Or what?"

"Right. I pored over the records, going back several months before he died, concentrating on the night entries because dollies filled with cartons from Flags would be a little awkward to remove during the day. There was nothing out of order—everything and everyone checked out—until I noticed the logs for the night of May first. That's where I found the three names. Two of them were meaningless, without identities." Quinn paused and sipped his whisky.

"What was your theory then? When you realized there were no identities."

"Then, and in part now." O'Brien lit a cigarette. "I think Hoover died a day before they said he did." The agent inhaled deeply.

"That's quite a statement."

"It's logical."

"How?"

"The unassigned covers. Whoever appropriated them had to be familiar with clandestine operations, had to be able to come up with authentic IDs. The agent at the desk that night, a man named Parke, won't discuss what happened. He claims only that the three men were cleared personally on Hoover's scrambler. That checks out; it was used. But I don't think he talked with Hoover. He talked with someone else at Hoover's house. It was enough for him. That phone was sacred."

"So he talked with someone at Hoover's house. So what?"

"Someone whose authority he wouldn't question. Someone who found Hoover dead and wanted those files removed before it was known that Hoover had died and everything was shut up tight. I think the files were taken the night of May first."

"Any ideas?"

"Up until two hours ago, yes. I thought it was Hoover's second-in-command, Tolson, and the maniacs. But thanks to you, that's no longer realistic."

"Thanks to me?"

"Yes. You damned near killed a man at the Corcoran Gallery. He was found in a stairwell—one of the maniacs. He was confronted in the hospital and given a choice: Name the others in a deposition and resign, or face prosecution, loss of pension, and one hell of a long jail sentence. He chose the first, naturally. Two hours ago I got word from one of our people. All the maniacs have resigned. They wouldn't do that if they had the files."

Chancellor watched O'Brien closely. "Which leads us back to our four candidates. Banner, Paris, Venice, and Christopher."

"And Bravo," added O'Brien. "I want you to use him. Follow your own advice: Make him force the issue. If he's the man you think he is—or Varak thought he was—he won't refuse. Go back to him."

Chancellor shook his head slowly. "You're missing the point. He's tired; he can't do it anymore. Varak knew that. It's why he came to me. It's you and me, O'Brien. Don't look for anyone else."

"Then, we'll force the issue! We'll name them!"

"Why? Whatever we said would be denied. I'd be dismissed as a hack writer promoting a book, and far worse, you have to live with Han Chow." Peter pushed his drink away. "And it wouldn't stop there. Bravo was very clear about that. Sooner or later there'd be a couple of accidents. We have to face that. We're expendable."

"Goddamn it, they can't deny the missing files!"

Chancellor watched the angry, frustrated agent. Alex Meredith lived in Quinn O'Brien. Peter decided to tell him.

"I'm afraid they might deny it very successfully. Because only half the files are missing. Letters *M* through *Z*. The rest were recovered."

O'Brien was stunned. "Recovered? By whom?"

"Varak didn't know."

Quinn crushed out his cigarette. "Or wouldn't say!"

"*Peter! Quinn!*"

It was Alison shouting from the living room. O'Brien reached the door first. All was dark. Alison stood by the window, her hand on the drapes.

"What is it?" asked Chancellor, going to her. "What's wrong?"

"Up the road," she answered flatly. "The rise between the gates. I saw someone, I know I did. He stood there, just watching the house. Then he moved back."

Quinn walked rapidly to a panel in the wall partially concealed by the drapes. There were two rows of convex white disks barely distinguishable in the shadows. They looked like two columns of blankly staring eyes. "None of the photoelectric cells was tripped," he said as if he were discussing a sameness in the weather.

Peter wondered what precisely made a "sterile" house, outside of the radio sets, the heavy glass, and the grillwork everywhere. "Are there electronic beams all around the place? I assume that's what those lights are."

"Yes. All around, infrared and crisscrossed. And there are auxiliary generators underground if the electricity goes off; they're tested every week."

"This place is like the motel in Quantico, then?"

"Same architect designed it, same construction firm built it. Everything is steel, even the doors."

"The front door's wood," interrupted Chancellor.

"Paneling," replied Quinn calmly.

"Could it have been a neighbor out for a walk?" asked Alison.

"Possible, but not likely. The houses here are on three-acre lots. The homes on both sides are owned by State personnel, diplomatic level, very high up. They've been alerted to stay away."

"Just like that?"

"It's nothing unusual. This place is used to house defectors during periods of debriefing."

"There he is!" Alison held the drape back.

Silhouetted in the distance, between the stone gateposts, was the figure of a man in an overcoat. He was on the rise in the road, outlined against the night sky. "He's just standing there," said Peter.

"Not making any move to go through the gate," added Quinn. "He knows they're tripped. And he wants us to know he knows it."

"Look," whispered Alison. "He's moving now!"

The figure took a step forward and raised his right arm. As though it were a ritualistic gesture, he brought it slowly down in front of him, cutting the air. Instantly there was a hum from the panel. A white disk turned bright red.

The man moved to his left and disappeared into the darkness.

"What was that all about?" O'Brien asked, more of himself than of the others.

"You just said it," answered Chancellor. "He wants us to know he knows the posts are wired."

"That's not so impressive. Most of these houses have alarm systems."

A second hum abruptly shot out of the panel; another white disk turned red.

Then in rapid succession hum followed hum, red light followed red light. The cacophony was all-encompassing, the alarms actually painful to the ears. Within thirty seconds every disk was bright red, every hum activated. The room was washed in magenta.

O'Brien stared at the panel. "They know each vector point! Every damned one!" He ran across the room to a cabinet in the wall. It contained a radio set. O'Brien pressed a button and spoke; there was no mistaking his urgency. "This is Saint Michael's One, come in, please! Repeat, Saint Michael's One, emergency!"

The only response was continuous static.

"Come in, please! This is Saint Michael's One. Emergency!"

Nothing. Only the static, which seemed to grow louder. Peter glanced about the room, adjusting his eyes to the red spill and the shadows. "The phone!" he said.

"Don't bother." O'Brien stepped back from the radio. "They wouldn't leave it; they'd cut the wires. It's dead."

It was.

"What about the radio?" asked Alison, trying to speak calmly. "Why can't you get through?"

Quinn looked at them. "They've jammed the frequency, which means they had to know which one it was. It's changed daily."

"Then, try another frequency!" said Chancellor.

"It's no use. Somewhere outside, within fifty to a hundred yards, there's a computerized scanner. By the time I raised anybody, before I could get our message across, they'd jam that, too."

"Goddamn you, try!"

"No," replied O'Brien, looking back up at the panel. "That's exactly what they want us to do. They want us to panic; they're counting on it."

"Why shouldn't we panic? What difference does it make? You said nobody could trace us here. Well, someone did trace us, and the radio's useless! I'm not about to trust your steel constructions and your two-inch glass! They're no match for a couple of blow-torches and a sledgehammer! For Christ's sake, do something!"

"I'm doing nothing, which is what they don't expect. In two or three minutes I'm going back on that frequency and deliver a second message." Quinn looked over at Alison. "Go upstairs and check the windows front and rear. Call down if you see anything. Chancellor, get back in the dining room. Do the same."

Peter held his place. "What are you going to do?"

"I haven't got time to explain." He walked to the front window and peered out. Peter joined him. Between the gateposts, once more silhouetted against the night sky, stood the figure. He stood motionless for ten or fifteen seconds, and then he seemed to raise both his hands in front of him.

And now a searchlight of several thousand candle-power shot out, slicing through the darkness.

"In the front!" Alison yelled from upstairs. "There's a——"

"We see it!" roared O'Brien. He turned to Chancellor. "Check the rear of the house!"

Peter ran across the room toward the small archway that led to the dining room. A second blinding beam of light hit the much smaller network of windows in the dining room's rear wall. He looked away, closing his eyes; the light made his forehead ache. "There's another back here!" he yelled.

"And on *this* side!" shouted O'Brien, his voice coming from an alcove at the far end of the living room. "Check the kitchen! On the north side!"

Peter raced into the kitchen. As Quinn had antic-ipated, there was a fourth beam shooting through the grilled windows at the north end of the house. Peter shielded his eyes again. It was a nightmare! Wherever they looked outside, they were blinded by the hot white light. They were being attacked by blinding white light!

"*Chancellor!*" screamed O'Brien from somewhere out-side the kitchen. "Go upstairs! Get Alison and stay away from the windows! Get in the center of the house. *Move!*"

Peter could not think, he could only obey. He reached the staircase, grabbed the railing, and swung himself around. As he started up the steps, he heard O'Brien's voice. In spite of the madness it was controlled, precise. He was back at the radio.

"If I'm getting through, emergency is canceled. Saint Michael's One, repeat. Emergency is canceled. We've raised Chesapeake on the alternate equipment. They're on their way. They'll be here in three or four minutes. Repeat. Stay out of the area. Emergency canceled."

"What are you doing?" Chancellor screamed.

"Goddamn it, get upstairs! Get the girl and stay in the center of the house!"

"Whose side are you *on*?"

"Those ghouls are trying to trick us! They're drawing us to the windows, then blinding us!"

"What are you saying? . . ."

"It's our only hope!" roared the agent. "Now get to Alison and do as I tell you!" He turned back to the radio and again depressed the microphone button.

Peter did not wait to hear O'Brien's words; he saw only that the agent had crouched below the cabinet, behind a chair, as near to the floor as possible, his hand extended up to the radio. Chancellor raced up the steps. "Alison!"

"In here! In the front room."

Peter dashed through the upper hall into the bedroom. Alison was at the window, hypnotized by the sight below. "Someone's running!"

"Get away from there!" He pulled her out of the room and into the hall.

The first thing he heard was a metallic sound—an object striking the glass, or the grillwork of the bedroom window. And then it happened.

The explosion was thunderous, the force of the vibrations hurling them to the floor. The thick glass of the bedroom window blew out in all directions, fragments imbedded themselves in the walls and the floor; pieces of grillwork rang as they struck solid objects.

The entire house shook; plaster cracked as beams were twisted. And Peter realized, as he held Alison in his arms, that there must have been two or three explosions, so closely timed as to be indistinguishable.

No. There had been *four* explosions, one at each side of the house, from each source of blinding light. O'Brien had been right. The strategy had been based on luring them to the windows and then throwing explosives. If they were in front of the windows, the sharp fragments of glass would be imbedded all over their bodies. Veins and arteries would be severed, heads sliced as his had been sliced so many months ago on the Pennsylvania Turnpike. The similarities were too painful. Even the plaster dust brought back images of the dirt and mud inside the reeling automobile; the woman in his arms another woman.

"Chancellor! Are you all right? Answer me!"

It was Quinn, his voice strident, in pain, from somewhere downstairs. Peter could hear automobiles racing away in the distance.

"Yes."

"They're gone." O'Brien's voice was weaker now. "We've got to get out of here! Now!"

Peter crawled to the edge of the staircase and reached for the hallway light switch. He snapped it on. O'Brien was bent over the bottom step, his hand gripped on the railing. He looked up at Chancellor.

His face was covered with blood.

Chancellor drove; Alison cradled O'Brien in her arms in the back seat of the unmarked car. The FBI man had fragments of glass embedded in his right arm and shoulder and numerous lacerations about his face and neck, but the wounds were not severe, merely painful.

"I think we should take you home," said Peter, his breath still coming rapidly, accelerated by fear, "to your wife and your own doctor."

"Do as I tell you," replied Quinn, suppressing the effects of his pain. "My wife thinks I'm in Philadelphia; my doctor would ask questions. There's another man we use."

"I think questions are in order right now!"

"No one would listen to the answers."

"You can't do this," said Alison, wiping O'Brien's face with a handkerchief. "Peter's right."

"No, he's not," O'Brien winced. "We're closer to those files than we've ever been. We have to find them. Take them. It's the only answer. For us."

"Why?" asked Peter.

"The Saint Michael's house is restricted territory. A four-million-dollar piece of real estate that's out of reach."

"You reached it," interrupted Chancellor.

"Strangely enough, I didn't." Quinn inhaled audibly. The pain passed, and he continued. "If the State Department or the bureau ever found out how I lied or what I divulged, I'd spend twenty years in a federal prison. I've violated every oath I took."

Peter felt a rush of affection for him. "What happened?" he asked.

"I used Varak's name with the State Department. He was a defector specialist, and I knew the clearance procedures to obtain the use of a sterile house. The bureau's been involved with defectors before. I said it was a joint operation between my office and NSC. Varak's name insured acceptance. My office could be questioned. Not Varak."

Chancellor swung the car around a long curve to the right. Even in death Varak was part of everything. "Wasn't it dangerous using Varak? He was dead. His body had to be found."

"But his prints were burned off years ago. I'd guess that even his dental work was done under an assumed name. With the number of homicides in this city and the procedures the police have to follow, it could be a week before his identity is known."

"What's your point? You used Varak's name to gain access to the Saint Michael's house. So what? Why are we closer to the files?"

"You'd never make a lawyer. Whoever attacked us tonight had to know two specific things. One: the clearing process at State that made the house available. And two: that Varak was dead. Those four men you're going to see. Banner, Paris, Venice, or Christopher. One of them knew both."

Peter gripped the wheel. He remembered the words he had heard only hours ago.

I am listed in the State Department logs as being in conference at this moment . . .

Munro St. Claire, ambassador-extraordinary with access to the secrets of the nation, knew Varak was dead.

"Or Bravo," said Chancellor angrily. "The fifth man."

34

There were no further sterile locations available to O'Brien. His resources had come to an end. Even the most sympathetic of his associates would not help him. Saint Michael's One had been destroyed; a four-million-dollar piece of government property had been blown up.

There might have been explanations for that disaster, explanations that could have conceivably been in O'Brien's favor. But there was no explanation in the intelligence community that covered the shocking revelation of a certain killing.

Varak's corpse had been found on the scene, his body riddled with bullets. *Outside* the sterile house. Treason had to be considered.

Peter understood, but his understanding was of no consequence. Varak's body had been found by the men following him, chasing him over the lawns of the Smithsonian, and it had been brought to Saint Michael's to add an insidious complication.

No consequence. Who would listen?

The word was out. A senior agent, Carroll Quinlan O'Brien, had disappeared. The urgent request for Saint Michael's One had been relayed to the State Department from O'Brien's office at the bureau. The clearance procedures included Varak's name and the statement that the request was a joint operation between the FBI and NSC. The statement was false, and O'Brien was nowhere to be found.

And a secret debriefing center had been destroyed.

Phone calls made by O'Brien from booths along the highways and the back roads revealed a government net closing in with alarming swiftness. Quinn's wife was frantic. Men had come to see her, saying terrible things—men who only days ago had been their friends. O'Brien could only try to reassure her. Quickly. He could say nothing of substance. Undoubtedly their telephone was tapped. Besides, he and Peter and Alison had to get out of each area where a call was placed. Phone booths could be traced.

Chancellor called Tony Morgan in New York. The editor was frightened: Government people had been in touch with him. And with Joshua Harris. They had made startling accusations. Peter had given false statements to a night-duty officer at the Federal Bureau of Investigation that had resulted in the deaths of Justice Department personnel. Further, he had assaulted an FBI agent in the Corcoran Gallery. The man was in critical condition; if he died, the charge would be murder. Beyond these charges there was evidence linking him to the destruction of highly classified government property, the value of which was four million dollars.

"Lies!" Peter cried. "The man I assaulted tried to kill me! He was a maniac; he was forced to resign. Did they tell you that?"

"No. Who told *you*? An agent named O'Brien?"

"Yes!"

"Don't believe him. O'Brien's an embittered career man, an incompetent. The government people made that clear. He was being eased out when you came along."

"He saved my life!"

"Maybe he just wanted you to think so. Come back, Peter. We'll get you the best lawyers. There are legitimate explanations, the government people realize that. My God, you've been under a terrible strain; last year you were barely alive. Your head was sliced half off; no one knows the extent of the damage."

"That's bullshit and you know it!"

"I don't know it. I'm trying to find reasons." Morgan's voice cracked. He cared.

"Tony, listen to me. I haven't much time. Don't you see what they're doing? They can't admit the truth. They'll try to correct the situation, but they can't admit that the situation exists! Hoover's files are missing!"

"Get away from the *campfire*! You're *killing* yourself!" Morgan's explosion came from deep within him.

Chancellor understood. Now Tony was being used, manipulated, too. "Did you mention the files?"

"Yes. . . ." Morgan could barely speak.

"Did they deny that the files were missing?"

"Of course. They were never missing because they were destroyed. Hoover himself gave the instructions."

The lying was total. Phyllis Maxwell's words came back to Peter. *They fear infected bloodlines.* Were they Phyllis's? Or had he invented them? He was not sure any longer. Fact and fantasy had converged and they were one. The only certainty was Quinn O'Brien's judgment:

The files had to be found and produced. There was no other way. Until then, the three of them were fugitives.

"You've been lied to, Tony. I wish to God it weren't so, but it is." He replaced the phone and ran from the booth to the car.

They found an almost deserted motel on the beach at Ocean City. Winter, two days before Christmas; there was a dearth of reservations. A doctor ministered to Quinn, taking the money but no other interest. A transient had fallen through a glass door. It was explanation enough.

On Christmas Eve the rogue agent came close to

breaking. Quinn's wife and children were less than two hours away, but they might as well have been on the other side of the world behind fences of barbed wire, crisscrossed by searchlights. He could give them no words of comfort, not even words of hope. There was only the separation and the knowledge of the pain it was causing. Peter watched as O'Brien struggled with his fear and his guilt and his loneliness, knowing that one day his words and his emotions would be put in the mind of another. On paper. Peter was watching a man of reluctant courage whose panic was consuming him and whose heart was breaking, and it both touched and outraged him.

One professional. Two amateurs. Three fugitives. It was up to them now. There wasn't anyone else. Alison could no longer be excluded; she was needed. Together they had to solve the riddle, or the destruction would continue. They would be destroyed themselves in the process. The unfairness of it all was appalling.

It was a painful Christmas. The three of them shared what the motel manager called his Upper South Suite. It was a second-floor complex with windows facing the side of the building as well as the beach. The entrance was below them in plain sight. There was a bedroom and a sitting room with a sofa bed, along with a small kitchenette. The decor was Middle Plastic.

They waited, knowing the wait was necessary. The radio and the television set were kept on to pick up any sudden breaks in the news, any hints that one hundred miles away in Washington someone had decided to acknowledge their disappearance. They bought newspapers from the metal machine in the lobby and read thoroughly. One article caught their attention.

Saint Michael's, Md.—An explosion caused by a malfunctioning gas furnace wrought considerable damage to a suburban home in this exclusive section of the Chesapeake. Fortunately there was no one in residence at the time. The owners, Mr. and Mrs. Chancellor O'Brien, are abroad. They are being contacted. . . .

"What does it mean?" asked Peter.

"They want us to know they have proof we were there," replied Quinn. "Subtle, aren't they?"

"How could they know?"

"Easy. Fingerprints. You were in the service; mine are in any number of records."

"But they don't know about Alison." Chancellor felt a surge of relief. It was quickly blunted.

"I'm afraid they do," said O'Brien. "That's why they used the 'Mr. and Mrs.' "

"I don't care!" Alison was angry. "I *want* them to know. They think they can threaten whomever they please! They won't threaten me. I've got a great deal to say!"

"They'll tell you they do, too," said Quinn softly, walking to the window overlooking the beach and the ocean. "My guess is they'll give you a choice—for reasons of national security. Keep silent about everything you've seen and heard, or face the disclosure of your mother's activities twenty-two years ago. Activities recently come to light that cost upwards of a thousand American lives in a single day. Inevitably this will raise questions regarding your father."

"Mac the Knife?" said Peter coldly. "Killer of Chasŏng?"

O'Brien turned from the window. "That's too ambiguous. Traitor of Chasŏng would be more like it. Whose drug-addict wife whored for an enemy twenty-two years ago and killed American soldiers."

"They wouldn't dare!" cried Alison.

"It's pretty farfetched," added Chancellor. "They'd be in dangerous territory. It could snap back in their faces."

"Revelations of this kind," said O'Brien with a quiet conviction Peter recognized as being intensely personal, "are always the most dramatic. They go on page one. Later, whatever explanations there are don't seem to be so important. The damage has been done; it's not easily undone."

"I don't believe that," countered Alison nervously. "I don't want to believe it."

"Take my word for it. It's the story of Hoover's files."

"Then, let's get the files," said Peter, folding the newspaper. "We'll start with Jacob Dreyfus."

"He's Christopher, isn't he?" asked Alison.

"Yes."

"It's appropriate," she said, turning her head to look at O'Brien. "I can't believe there's no one we can turn to."

"There's a senator," interrupted Peter. "We can go to him."

"But even he'll want more than the case I built," said Quinn. "Perhaps not two days ago, but now he will."

"What do you mean?" Chancellor was alarmed. The other evening O'Brien had been so sure of himself. The files were missing; Quinn had the evidence. Things were desperate now.

"I mean we can't go to him."

"Why not?"

"Saint Michael's happened. Destruction of government property, violations of security procedures. He's bound by oath to report it if we make contact. If he doesn't, it's obstruction of justice."

"Shit! Words."

"Law. He may offer to help; if Varak was right, he probably will. But it'll be after the fact. He'll insist we surrender ourselves. Legally that's the only position he can take."

"And if we do, that's where they want us! It's no good!"

Alison touched his arm. "Who are 'they,' Peter?"

Chancellor paused. The answer to her question was as appalling as the circumstances in which they found themselves. "Everyone. The man who has the files wants to kill us; we know that now. The people who know the files are missing refuse to acknowledge it and want us quiet. They're willing to sacrifice us to get that silence. Yet, they want the same thing we do." Peter walked slowly across the room past O'Brien to the window. He looked out at the ocean. "You know, Bravo said something to me. He said that four and a half years ago he steered me into a world I hadn't considered. He told me to go back to that world, leave the real one to others. To him and people like him." He turned from the window. "But they're not good enough. I don't know if we are, but I know they're not."

Jacob Dreyfus rose from the breakfast table, not a little annoyed. The butler said the White House was on the line. The damned fool was probably calling to wish him Merry Christmas. *Merry Christmas!* It would not have occurred to the President to call on the first day of Chanukah. That was on the twenty-fifth day of Kislev, and not exactly a date commemorating the birth of Christ.

The word was that the man was drinking heavily. It was not surprising. There had been no administration in the history of the republic like this one. The venality was unsurpassed, the lust for power the essential evil. Of course, the man drank heavily. It was his balm of Gilead.

Jacob considered not taking the call, but respect for the office demanded that he do so.

"Good morning, Mr. Pres——"

"I'm not the President," a voice said. "I'm someone else. Just as you are someone else, Christopher."

The blood drained from Jacob's face. It was suddenly difficult to breathe. His gaunt legs were weak; he thought he might fall to the floor. The secret of a lifetime was known. It was beyond belief. "Who's this?"

"A man who's been working for you. My name is Peter Chancellor, and I've done my job too well. I've learned things I'm sure you never intended me to learn. And because of that we have to meet. Today. Early this afternoon."

"This afternoon? . . ." Dreyfus felt faint. Peter Chancellor, the writer? How in the name of God could the writer have done this? "I don't make appointments on such short notice."

"You'll make this one," said Chancellor.

The writer was nervous; Jacob could sense it. "I don't take orders. Nor have I ever heard of a Christopher. You used a clever ruse in reaching me. However, I enjoy your little entertainments. If you'd care to lunch with me one day next week."

"This afternoon. No lunch."

"You don't listen——"

"I don't have to. It's possible my 'little entertainments' aren't important anymore. Maybe I'm interested in other things. Perhaps you and I can reach an understanding."

"I can't imagine there being an understanding between us."

"There won't be if you talk to the others. Any of them."

"The others?"

"Banner, Paris, Venice, or Bravo. Don't talk to them."

Jacob's body trembled. "What are you saying?"

"I'm saying they don't understand you. I think I do. That's the writer's job—to try to understand people. That's why you people used me, isn't it? I believe I understand you. The other's can't."

"What are you talking about?" Dreyfus could not control his hands.

"Let's call it a splendid temptation. Anyone familiar with Chasŏng would grasp the logic. But the others, they'd kill you for it."

"Chasŏng? Kill me?" Jacob's eyes blurred. A terrible error had been made! "Where do you want to meet?"

"There's a stretch of beach north of Ocean City in Maryland; any cab driver can find it. So take a cab, and come alone. Get a pencil, Christopher. I'll give you the directions. Be there by one thirty."

Perspiration poured down Peter's forehead. He leaned against the glass panel of the telephone booth. He had done it; he had actually *done* it. An idea born of fiction worked in fact!

The strategy was to present Christopher—as he would present the others—with options. If Christopher had the files, he could draw only one conclusion: He had been found out. If so, he would agree to meet for the sole purpose of killing the man who had unearthed him. It was doubtful in that case he would come alone.

If Christopher did not have the files, there were two alternatives: Dismiss the caller, refusing to meet. Or agree to meet on the dreadful possibility that one or all of the others had betrayed their cause. In this case he would come alone.

Only the middle option—dismissal—exonerated the candidate. And Christopher had not chosen it. Peter wondered if any of them would choose it.

Alison tapped on the door. For a second he simply looked at her through the glass, struck once again by her lovely face, and the intelligent eyes that conveyed love in the midst of anxiety.

He pulled the door open. "One down."

"How did it go?"

"It depends on how you look at it. He'll be here."

The love and the anxiety remained in Alison's eyes. But now there was an added element.

Fear.

35

Frederick Wells looked up from the Christmas breakfast table, astonished. He was not at all sure he had heard the maid's words accurately through the shouts of the children.

"Be quiet!" he ordered; the table was silent. "What did you say?"

"The White House is on the telephone, sir," replied the maid.

The squeals that accompanied the statement served only to remind Wells that he had married too late in life. At least, too late to have young children. If the truth were known, he did not really like children; they were fundamentally uninteresting.

He rose from the table, his eyes briefly locking with his wife's. She seemed to be reading his thoughts.

Why in heaven's name would the White House be calling? Short of blatantly insulting the President and his corps of incompetents, Frederick Wells had made his position clear. He did not approve of the man in the White House.

Was it possible the President was using the pretext of Christmas greetings to offer olive branches to his enemies? The man had an embarrassment of embarrassments.

Wells closed the door of his study and walked to his desk, his eyes falling on the row of Yüan and Ming vases locked behind the glass in the case. They were exquisite; he never tired of looking at them. They reminded him that there was peace and beauty in the midst of ugliness.

He picked up the phone.

"Mr. Frederick Wells?"

Sixty seconds later his personal world had collapsed. The writer had done it! How was immaterial, the fact was everything!

Inver Brass could protect itself. Instant dissolution, nonexistent records. . . . If need be, a second justifiable assassination, removing Peter Chancellor from this world.

But what about *him?* Banner had all the weapons save one. And that remaining weapon was exposure. Exposure of a name over which he had absolutely no control. To Wells, exposure was tantamount to destruction.

A lifetime wasted!

Still he could fight. This time on a country road west of Baltimore. An accommodation had to be reached. For everyone's good.

His eyes fell once again on the Chinese vases behind the glass. They did nothing for him.

Carlos Montelán sat back in the church pew and watched with a certain detached hostility as the priest went through the incantations of the Christmas mass. He would not kneel; there were limits to the hypocrisy he indulged in for his wife and family.

Boston was not Madrid, but the memories were too sharp still. The Spanish church had been a sworn companion of the political winds, concentrating on its own survival without compassion for its brutalized flocks.

Montelán felt the vibration an instant before he heard the hum. The worshippers in the immediate vicinity were startled; several turned toward him, their faces angry. The Lord's house was being intruded upon by an alien caller, but the recipient of the call was a great man, an advisor to Presidents. The Lord's house was not immune to the emergencies of this man's world.

Carlos thrust his hand inside his jacket, shutting off the sound. His wife and children turned; he nodded to them, got out of the pew, and walked up the marble aisle past flickering candles. He went outside, found a telephone booth, and called his service.

The White House was trying to find him, but he was not to return the call. It had to be made on a special telephone. He was to leave a number where he could be reached.

The conspiracies of *idiotas*! thought Montelán. He gave the number of the telephone booth.

The telephone rang, its strident bell echoing harshly within the booth. Swiftly Carlos removed the instrument and brought it to his face.

The words had the effect of sharp knives entering his stomach; the pain was ice cold. The writer had found him out! Everything he had done, everything he had agreed to, was exploded in the accusations of Peter Chancellor.

The agreement, his pact, had been necessary! It was the final preservation of Inver Brass's integrity! There could be no other way!

The writer had to be made to understand! Yes, of

course, he'd meet with him. A golf course, east of Annapolis, the tenth green? Yes, he'd find it. The hour did not matter; he would be there shortly past midnight.

His hand trembling, Montelán hung up the phone. For several moments he stood in the cold, staring at the instrument. He wondered briefly whether he should pick it up again and call Jacob Dreyfus.

No, he could not do that. Christopher was a very old man. A coronary was not out of the question.

Daniel Sutherland drank his sherry and listened to his son, Aaron, hold forth with his two sisters and their husbands. The couples had flown in from Cleveland for Christmas; the children were in the sun-room with their grandmother and Aaron's wife, wrapping presents. Aaron, as usual, held his audience mesmerized.

The judge watched his son with profoundly mixed emotions. Love was paramount, of course, but close to it was disapproval. The newspapers called Aaron a firebrand, the brilliant attorney of the legitimate black left. Still, Daniel wished he weren't so fiery, so sure that only he had the answers to the problems of race.

There was such hatred in his son's eyes, and hatred was not the way; there was no essential strength in it. One day his son would learn that. And one day he would also learn that his ill-conceived loathing of all whites was not only fruitless but often misplaced.

His name said something about that. It had been given him by the dearest friend Daniel had ever had. Jacob Dreyfus.

His name must be Aaron, Jacob had said. *The older brother of Moses, the first priest of the Hebrews. It is a beautiful name, Daniel. And he is a beautiful son.*

The telephone rang.

Aaron's wife, Abby, came through the door. As always Daniel looked at her lovingly, and not without a certain awe. Alberta Wright Sutherland was, perhaps, the finest black actress in the country. Tall, erect, with a magnificent presence that could, when necessary, subdue her own husband. Her audience, unfortunately, was limited by her taste. She would not accept roles that exploited either her sex or her race.

"I'll try to deliver the line with a straight face, all right?" she said.

"All right, my dear."

"The White House is on the telephone."

"It's bewildering, to say the least," said Daniel, getting out of the chair. "I'll take it in the dining room."

It *was* bewildering. His last four appellate decisions had infuriated the administration, its disapproval expressed in print.

"This is Judge Sutherland."

"You're also Venice," said the flat, hard voice on the phone.

The writer had done it! The commitment of a lifetime was suddenly, awesomely, suspended. If it was destroyed, there was nothing, for nothing was worth the loss. The deceivers would inherit the earth.

Daniel listened carefully, weighing each word the writer spoke, each inflection.

There might be a way. It was a desperate strategy, one he was not sure he could survive, much less execute. But it had to be attempted.

Deception.

"Tomorrow morning, Mr. Chancellor. At sunrise. The inlet east of Deal Island, the trawler moorings. I'll find it. I'll find you."

Sutherland's eyes were focused absently over the telephone, through the hallway arch into the distant living room. His daughter-in-law came into view. She stood erect and proud.

She had been a superb Medea, Daniel recalled. He remembered her final words in the last act, a cry to the heavens.

Here are my babes, bloodied and slain for the love of a god named Jason!

Sutherland wondered why those words came back to him. Then he knew.

They had been in the corner of his mind only seconds ago.

36

The winter wind came in gusts off the water, bending the wild grass on the dunes. The sun kept breaking through the fast-moving clouds above, intensely bright when it did so but carrying no warmth in its rays. It was early afternoon on Christmas day, and it was cold on the beach.

Chancellor looked down at his footprints. He had been pacing back and forth between the boundaries prescribed by Quinn O'Brien. From within that ten-yard space he had a clean sightline to the clump of foliage above the dunes to the left of the planked path that led from the road. O'Brien was stationed there, concealed from any view but Peter's.

According to O'Brien the tactic was basic. He would wait in the cluster of wild bushes as Jacob Dreyfus arrived. He would make sure that Dreyfus dismissed the cab as he'd been instructed to do; in the event Christopher betrayed them—either by not dismissing the cab or by having his own men in nearby vehicles—Quinn would signal Peter, and they would race to a concealed area above an adjacent beach, where Alison waited in the unmarked car.

This aspect of self-protection Quinn called "up front." The more immediate and less controllable protection was up to Peter. In his jacket pocket was the short-barreled .38-caliber revolver he had taken from Paul Bromley on the train. The gun that had been meant to kill him. He was to use it if he had to.

Peter heard a short, piercing whistle: the first signal. The taxi was in sight.

He could not tell how many minutes passed before the gaunt figure came into view. Each second was interminable; the pounding in his chest unbearable. He watched the small, frail Dreyfus unsteadily inch his way over the planks toward the open beach. He was so much *older* than Peter had pictured him, older and infinitely more fragile. The wind off the ocean buffeted him; sand whipped against him, causing him to bow and twist his head; his cane kept slipping on the planks.

He came to the end of the boarded path to the beach and poked his cane into the sand before stepping off. Chancellor could sense the question in the eyes behind the thick glasses. The wracked body did not want to make the rest of the journey; could not the younger man come to him?

But Quinn had been adamant. Position was everything; rapid escape had to be considered. Peter held his place, and Dreyfus painfully continued over the wind-swept beach.

Dreyfus fell. Chancellor started across the sand but was stopped by the waving arms of O'Brien beyond. The FBI agent was firm, his message clear.

Dreyfus was within thirty feet, his face seen clearly now. Somehow the banker understood; his expression turned to one of determination. Using his cane, he struggled to his feet. Unsteadily, blinking against the wind and the sand, he walked up to Chancellor; no hand was offered.

"We meet," said Dreyfus simply. "I have things to say to you, and you have things to say to me. Which of us shall begin?"

"Did you follow my instructions?" asked Peter, as he had been instructed to ask.

"Of course I did. We have information to exchange; we both want to know what the other knows. Why add complications? You're wanted, you know."

"Yes. For the wrong reasons."

"The people hunting you don't think so. However, that's irrelevant. If you're not guilty, your innocence can be established."

"The only thing I'm guilty of is being a goddamned fool! Besides, we're not here to discuss me."

"We're here to discuss certain events that affect both of us." Dreyfus brought his hand up to shield his face from a sudden guest of wind. "We must reach an understanding."

"I don't have to reach anything with you! I've been manipulated, lied to, shot at. Four men were killed—four that I know about. Three I watched die. God knows how many people have been driven out of their minds by a whisper over the telephone! You know who they are. I know several." Peter looked away briefly at the water, then turned back to Dreyfus. "I've written it all down. It's not what you expected me to write, but I wrote it. Now, you either reach an understanding with me, or I let the world know who you really are."

Dreyfus stared at him in silence for several moments, the sound of the wind the only intrusion between them. His eyes were devoid of fear. "And who do you think I am? *What* do you think I am?"

"You're Jacob Dreyfus, known as Christopher."

"I concede that. I don't know how you unearthed it, but it's a name I carry with pride."

"Maybe you deserved it until you turned on them."

"Turned on whom?"

"The others. Banner, Paris, Venice, Bravo. You betrayed them."

"Betrayed them? Betrayed Paris? Venice? You don't know what you're talking about."

"Chasŏng! Chasŏng's in Hoover's files, and you've got them!"

Jacob Dreyfus stood motionless, his skull-like face a mirror of shock. "Almighty God, you believe that?"

"You've worked with the State Department!"

"On many occasions."

"You could easily trace a sterile location if you knew where to look!"

"Perhaps. If I knew what it was."

"You knew Varak was dead!"

"Varak dead? That can't be!"

"You're lying!"

"You're a madman. And dangerous. Whatever you've written down must be destroyed. You don't know what you've done. Over forty years of service to the country, countless millions spent. You must understand. I must *make* you understand!"

The unbelievable was happening! Dreyfus reached into his overcoat, his bony hand trembling. Peter knew he was reaching for a gun.

"Don't do that! For Christ's sake, *don't!*"

"I have no choice."

Behind Dreyfus, on the mountain of sand in the cluster of wild bushes, Chancellor could see the figure of O'Brien suddenly stand up. He was seeing what Peter saw: The old man was going to take out a gun. He had come alone, but he had come armed. At the last he was prepared to kill.

Chancellor gripped the weapon in his own pocket, his finger on the trigger. He could not squeeze it! He could not *pull* the trigger!

A shot was heard above the wind. Dreyfus's head snapped back, his throat a mass of blood and shattered bone. His body arched, then fell on its side in the sand. Beyond, O'Brien lowered the gun and raced over the dunes.

Christopher was dead, killed on a deserted stretch of windswept beach.

And then Peter saw what was in his hand.

It was a folded page of paper. Not a gun. A letter.

He knelt down, overwhelmed by a sense of revulsion, and removed the paper. He stood up, his breathing erratic, the pain in his temple robbing him of thought. O'Brien was beside him; the FBI man took the paper and unfolded it. Chancellor stared at it, and together they read it. It was a Xeroxed copy of a handwritten letter. The addressee was a single name: Paris.

> I.B. must be dissolved. Venice and Bravo agree with this conclusion. I can see it in their eyes, although we have not discussed it among ourselves. We are consumed with memories. But we are old and have very little time left. What concerns me deeply is that the end may come for one or all of us without the proper means for dissolution. Or worse, that our faculties will desert us, and our old tongues will rattle. This can never be allowed. Therefore, I beg you, should age destroy reason, do for one or all of us what we cannot do for ourselves. Under separate cover the tablets have been sent to you by messenger. Place them in old men's mouths and pray for us.
>
> If this is impossible for you, show this letter to Varak. He will understand and carry out what must be done.
>
> Lastly, to Banner, whose weakness is his commitment to his own extraordinary capabilities. He will be tempted to carry on I.B. This also cannot be allowed. Our time is past. If he insists, Varak again will know what to do.
>
> The above is our covenant.
>
> Christopher

"He said he didn't know what a sterile location was," said Peter weakly.

"He didn't know Varak was dead," added O'Brien softly, rereading the letter. "He wasn't the one."

Chancellor turned away and wandered aimlesssly toward the water. He fell to his knees in the lapping waves and vomited.

They buried the body of Jacob Dreyfus in the sand beneath the dunes. The question of responsibility was not considered; time was needed. Desperately. Responsibility would come later.

Frederick Wells would not be met on an expanse of abandoned beach. Instead, the man known as Banner was to walk into a field south of a stretch of road off Route 40 west of Baltimore. O'Brien had used the location for an informer drop less than six months before. He knew it well.

It was a curving section of the highway removed from all-night diners and filling stations; it was bordered by fields that looked like marshland in the darkness.

Peter waited in the field several hundred feet beyond the embankment where Wells was to park his car. He looked up at headlights racing down the highway, flickering and magnified in the rain that drenched the field and sent chills throughout his body. O'Brien had concealed himself halfway down the embankment, his weapon drawn, waiting. Again, Chancellor had his instructions: At the first sign of the unexpected he was to immobilize Frederick Wells with his gun. Fire it, if need be.

For added precaution O'Brien had a flashlight. Should Wells bring others with him, Quinn would switch on the light, covering the lens with his fingers, and wave it in circles. It was the signal for Peter to run across the field and up to the road, where Alison waited in the car.

There were two blasts of an impatient horn from the road. An automobile slowed down and pulled over on the shoulder; the car behind swung around it, accelerating in anger.

The automobile stopped by the embankment, and a lone figure climbed out. It was Frederick Wells; he walked to the railing overlooking the field and peered through the rain.

The beam of light shot down briefly from the far end of the embankment. It was O'Brien's first signal. Wells was alone; there were no overt signs of a weapon. Peter did not move; it was up to Banner to come to him.

Wells climbed over the railing and made his way down the incline. Chancellor crouched in the wet grass and withdrew the .38.

"Take your hands out of your pockets!" he shouted as he'd been instructed to shout. "Walk forward slowly with your hands at your sides."

Wells stopped and stood motionless in the rain, then did as he was told. His bare hands held out at his sides, he walked into the darkness of the field. When he was within five feet, Peter rose from the ground.

"Stop right here!"

Wells gasped, his eyes wide. "Chancellor?" He took several deep breaths, blinking as the rain pounded down on his face, saying nothing until his breathing was steady —an Oriental exercise to suspend thought, to restore calm.

"Listen to me, Chancellor," Wells said at last. "You're beyond your depth. You've made friends with the wrong people. I can only appeal to whatever feeling you have for this country to give me their names. I know one, of course. Give me the rest."

Peter was stunned. Wells had taken the initiative. "What are you talking about?"

"The files! Files M through Z! They have them, and they're using you. I don't know what they've promised you—what *he's* promised you. If it's your life, I'll guarantee it far better than he could. The girl's, too."

Chancellor stared at the shadowed, wet face of Frederick Wells. "You think somebody sent me. You think I'm a messenger. I never mentioned the files to you over the phone."

"Did you think you had to? For God's sake, stop it! Destroying Inver Brass is no answer! Don't let them do it!"

"Inver Brass?" Peter's mind raced back to the handwritten letter in a dead man's hand, the covenant between Christopher and Paris. *I.B. must be dissolved. . . . I.B.* . . . Inver Brass.

"You can't become a part of it, Chancellor! Don't you see what he's done? He programed you too well; you learned much too quickly. You were closing in on *him*! He can't kill you now; he knows we'd know he did it. So he tells you things, reveals Inver Brass, feeds you lies so you'll set us against one another!"

"Who?"

"The man who has the files. Varak!"

"Oh, *Christ*. . . ." Peter's stomach knotted.

It was not Frederick Wells.

"I have the answer." Wells was speaking in his sharp, nasal voice; Peter barely listened, so futile did everything suddenly seem. "It will extricate you and get the files back. They *must* be taken! You tell Varak there's no way he can connect Inver Brass with the events of last May. There are no records, no transactions that can be traced. Varak was the killer, not Inver Brass. He did his job too well; there are no links. But I can and will raise disturbing questions about his every move from the tenth of April through the night of May first. I'll do it in a way that will leave no doubt; he'll be exposed. And we remain unknown. Carry that message back."

It was all too much for Peter. Truths, half-truths, and lies piled on abstractions; dates woven into a fabric of accusations. "You think Varak betrayed the others?"

"I know it! It's why you must work with me. The country needs me now. Varak has those files!"

The rain came down in torrents. "Get out of here," Peter said.

"Not until I have your word."

"*Get out of here!*"

"You don't *understand*!" Wells could not tolerate the dismissal. His arrogance gave way to desperation. "The country needs me! I must lead Inver Brass. The others are old, weak! Their time is finished. I'm the one! I must have those files. I'm *in them*!"

Chancellor raised the revolver. "Get out of here before I kill you."

"You want that excuse, don't you? That's what you *really* want!" Banner's words were rushed, his voice again strident, now panicked. "Varak told you it was *me*, didn't he? I had nothing to do with it! It was *him*! I asked him to intercede with Bravo, that's all I asked him to do! He was closest to St. Claire; everyone knew that. He was sworn to protect us all, each one of us. . . . You were going back to Nuremberg! We couldn't allow you to do that! Varak understood!"

"Nuremberg. . . ." Peter felt the rain on his skin. It had been raining the night his silver Continental was hit, the night Cathy had died. There was a highway in the distance now, as there was then; and an embankment. And the rain.

"But good *God*! I never wanted him to kill you! Or the girl! That was *his* decision; he was never afraid to act."

Varak. Longworth. The horrible mask of a face behind the wheel. A driver at night oblivious to the storm, staring straight ahead as he killed.

Varak, the professional, who used vehicles as weapons.

The pain in his temple was unendurable. Peter raised the gun, pointing it at Banner's head. He squeezed the trigger.

Banner's life was saved by the inexperience of an amateur. The safety catch prevented the hammer from exploding the shell.

Frederick Wells ran through the rain toward the road.

East of Annapolis, several miles beyond the Severn River, were the rolling hills of the Chanticlaire. It was a patrician golf club formed in the thirties by the proper aristocrats, thus given to exclusivity, and by extension, it was a gathering place for executives of the Central Intelligence Agency, an organization prone to the old school tie.

It was also used as an information drop between agents of the FBI and the CIA during those times when J. Edgar Hoover stopped the flow of data from the former to the latter. O'Brien knew it well; it was to be the meeting ground for Carlos Montelán. Paris was to be there no sooner than midnight, no later than twelve thirty. On the tenth tee; the instructions were clear.

Quinn took the wheel; he knew the back roads from Route 40 to the Chanticlaire. Alison and Peter sat in the back. Chancellor did his best to dry off, his mind still numbed by the shock of Banner's revelation.

"He killed her," said Peter, drained, absently watching the headlights in the diminishing rain. "Varak killed Cathy. What kind of man was he?"

Alison gripped his hand. O'Brien spoke from behind the wheel.

"I can't answer that. But I don't think he thought in terms of life and death. In certain situations he thought only of eliminating problems."

"He wasn't human."

"He was a specialist."

"Which is the coldest thing I've ever heard."

O'Brien found an out-of-the-way country inn. They went inside for warmth and coffee.

"Inver Brass," said Quinn at the table in the dimly lit dining room. "What is it?"

"Frederick Wells assumed I knew," replied Peter. "Just as he assumed Varak had sent me to him."

"You're sure he wasn't feeding you false information? Trying to throw you off?"

"I'm sure. His panic was genuine. He's in the files. Whatever's there could ruin him."

"Inver Brass," repeated O'Brien quietly. "The *inver* is Scottish, the *brass* could be anything. What does the combination mean?"

"I think you're overcomplicating things," said Peter. "It's the name they've given their nucleus."

"Their what?"

"Sorry. *My* 'Nucleus.'"

"Your book?" asked Alison.

"Yes."

"I'd better read that damned manuscript," said O'Brien.

"Is there any way," asked Chancellor, "that we can trace Varak's movements from April tenth through May second of this year?"

"Not now there isn't," O'Brien answered.

"We know Hoover died May second," continued Peter. "So the implication——"

"The implication won't stand scrutiny," interrupted Quinn. "Hoover died of heart failure. That's been established."

"By whom?"

"Medical records. They were fragmentary but complete enough."

"So we're back at the beginning," concluded Peter wearily.

"No, we're not," said Quinn, looking at his watch. "We've eliminated two candidates. It's time for the third."

It was the most secure contact location the FBI man had engineered, and for that reason he was particularly cautious. They arrived at the Chanticlaire an hour before Montelán was due to appear; the agent explored the area thoroughly. When he had finished, he told Peter to walk out to the tenth tee while Alison remained in the car at the far end of the drive near the gates and he concealed himself in the grass off the fairway.

The ground was wet, but the rain had stopped. The moon struggled to penetrate the passing clouds, its light progressively getting brighter. Chancellor waited in the shadows of an overhanging tree.

He heard the sound of a car driving through the open gate and looked at the radium dial of his wristwatch. It was five minutes past midnight; Montelán was anxious. Yet no more filled with anxiety than he was, reflected Peter. He felt the handle of the gun in his jacket pocket.

In less than a minute he saw the figure of Carlos Montelán walking rapidly around the corner of the clubhouse. The Spaniard was walking too fast, Peter thought. A frightened man was a cautious man; the figure coming toward him was not cautious.

"Mr. Chancellor?" Paris began calling fifty yards from the tee. He stopped and put his left hand into his overcoat pocket. Peter took out his .38 and leveled it in front of him, watching in silence.

Montelán pulled his hand from his pocket. Chancellor lowered the gun. Paris held a flashlight; he turned it on, shooting the beam in several directions. The shaft of light hit Peter.

"Turn off the light!" yelled Chancellor, crouching.

"As you wish." The shaft of light disappeared.

Remembering O'Brien's instructions, Peter ran several yards away from his former position, keeping his eyes on Montelán. The Spaniard made no extraneous moves; he had no weapon. Chancellor stood up, knowing he could be seen in the moonlight.

"I'm over here," he said.

Montelán turned, adjusting his eyes. "Sorry about the light. I won't do that again." He approached Peter. "I had no trouble coming here. Your directions were excellent."

In the pale yellow light Peter could see Montelán's face. It was strong, the features Latin, the dark eyes searching. Peter realized there was no fear in the man. In spite of the fact that he had been told to meet a stranger, known to him by name only, on an isolated golf course in the middle of the night—a stranger he had to at least con-

sider might do him violence—Paris behaved as though
their meeting were merely a mutually desirable business
conference.

"This is a gun in my hand," said Chancellor, raising
the barrel.

Montelán squinted. "Why?"

"After what you've done to me—what Inver Brass has
done to me—can you even ask?"

"I don't know what's been done to you."

"You're lying."

"Let me put it this way. I know that you were given
misinformation on the premise that you might write a
novel based on that false information. It was hoped this
might alarm certain individuals who are part of a conspiracy and force them to reveal themselves. In all candor
I've doubted the wisdom of the exercise since I first heard
of it."

"That's all you've learned?"

"I gather there's been some unpleasantness, but we
were given assurance that no harm would come to you."

"Who are the 'certain individuals'? What's the 'conspiracy'?"

Paris paused for a moment as if resolving a conflict
within himself. "If no one's told you, perhaps it's time
someone did. There *is* a conspiracy. A very real and
dangerous one. An entire section of J. Edgar Hoover's
private files is missing. They've disappeared."

"How do you know that?"

Again Montelán fell briefly silent, then having made
the decision, continued. "I can't give you specifics, but
since you mentioned the name and—more to the point—
referred to the others in your telephone call this morning,
I must assume you've learned more than was intended for
you to learn. It doesn't matter; it's coming to an end.
Inver Brass managed to get hold of the remaining files."

"How?"

"I can't tell you that."

"Can't or won't?"

"A little of both, perhaps."

"That's not good enough!"

"Do you know a man named Varak?" asked Paris
softly, as if Chancellor had not shouted.

"Yes."

"Ask him. He may tell you, he may not."

Peter studied the Spaniard's face in the moonlight. Montelán was not lying. He did not know of Varak's death. Chancellor felt a hollowness in his throat; a third contender had been eliminated. Questions remained, but the most vital issue was resolved. Paris did not have the files.

"What did you mean when you said it didn't matter what I'd learned? That it was 'coming to an end'?"

"The days of Inver Brass are over."

"What exactly is Inver Brass?"

"I presumed you knew."

"Don't presume anything!"

Again the Spaniard paused before he spoke. "A group of men dedicated to the well-being of this nation."

"A nucleus," said Peter.

"I imagine it could be called that," replied Montelán. "It's made up of outstanding men, men of extraordinary character and great love for their country."

"Are you one of them?"

"I was privileged to be asked."

"This is the group that was formed to warn Hoover's victims?"

"It has had many functions."

"How many weeks ago were you asked to join? Or was it months?"

For the first time Paris seemed bewildered. "Weeks? Months? I've been a member for four years."

"Four years?!" There was the dissonant chord again. As far as Peter knew, the group—St. Claire's nucleus, this Inver Brass—had been formed to combat Hoover's final and most vicious tactic: the exploitation of fear through his private files. It was a late-in-the-day defense born of necessity. A year, a year and a half, two years at the most, had been the span of its existence. Yet Paris spoke of four years. . . .

And Jacob Dreyfus had used the phrase "forty years of service"; then he'd followed it with a reference to "countless millions spent." At the time, during those moments of panic on the beach, Chancellor had thought Dreyfus had somehow been referring to himself. But now . . . *forty years . . . countless millions.*

Frederick Well's biting words suddenly came back to Peter. *The country needs me. I must lead Inver Brass. The others are old, weak! Their time is finished. I'm the one!*

Four years . . . *forty* years! Countless *millions*.

And finally Peter remembered Dreyfus's letter to Montelán. The covenant between Christopher and Paris. *We are consumed with memories. . . .*

Memories of what?

"Who are you people?" he asked, staring at Montelán.

"Beyond what I've said, I'll say no more. You were right, Mr. Chancellor. I presumed. In any event, I'm not here to discuss such matters. I came to try to convince you not to interfere any longer. Your inclusion was an error of judgment by a brilliant but frustrated man. There was no great harm as long as you remained in the background, poking among the ruins, but should you surface and be asked questions publicly, that would be disaster."

"You're frightened," said Chancellor, surprised. "You pretend to be very cool, but underneath you're frightened out of your wits."

"I most certainly am. For you as well as for all of us."

"Does 'us' mean Inver Brass?"

"And many others. There's a rift in this country between the people and its leaders. There is corruption at the highest levels of government; it goes beyond mere power politics. The Constitution has been seriously assaulted, our way of life threatened. I'm not being melodramatic; I'm telling you the truth. Perhaps a person not born here, who has seen it happen before, understands more clearly what these things mean."

"What's the answer? Or is there one?"

"There certainly is. The rigid, dispassionate application of the legal process. I repeat, dispassionate. The people must be awakened to the real dangers of abuse. Clearly, reasonably, not propelled by emotional accusations and demands for recrimination. The system will work if it's given the chance; the process has begun. It's *no* time for explosive disclosures. It's a time for intensive examination. And reflection."

"I see," said Peter slowly. "And it's not the time for the exposure of Inver Brass, is it?"

"No," said Montelán firmly.

"Perhaps it will never be."

"Perhaps. I told you. Its time has passed."

"Is that why you have your covenant with Jacob Dreyfus? With Christopher?"

It was as though Paris had been slapped harshly

across the face. "I wondered," he said softly. "I nearly called him but thought better of it. So you reached him."

"I reached him."

"I'm sure he spoke as I have. His devotion to this country is infinite. He understands."

"I don't. I don't understand any of you people."

"Because your knowledge is limited. And you'll learn no more from me. I can only beg you again to go away. If you continue, I think you'll be killed."

"That's been suggested. One last question: What happened at Chasŏng?"

"Chasŏng? The Battle of Chasŏng?"

"Yes."

"A terrible waste. Thousands lost over an inconsequential stretch of barren territory. Megalomania superseded civilian authority. It's on the record."

Peter realized he still held the gun in his hand. It was meaningless; he put it back in his pocket.

"Go back to Boston," he said.

"You'll consider carefully everything I've said?"

"Yes." But he knew he would have to go on.

For Daniel Sutherland, O'Brien had chosen an inlet east of Deal Island on the Chesapeake. The rendezvous was a commercial marina where fishing boats were moored, primarily oyster craft that would by necessity stay in shore for another week or two. The beds were poor; the ocean was not hospitable at this point in December.

The waves lapped incessantly against the pilings beneath the docks. The creaking of the boats at their moorings kept up a steady, snapping tattoo as the gulls cawed in the sky above in the early light.

Venice. The last of the candidates, thought Peter as he sat on an oily railing of a trawler at the end of the dock. The last, that is, unless Bravo was the one. That Peter would go back to Munro St. Claire seemed certain. The possibility that Sutherland was the betrayer of Inver Brass, the whispering killer who had the files, was remote. But then nothing was as it seemed to be. Anything was conceivable.

Sutherland had told him that the committee formed to combat Hoover's viciousness had been disbanded. Too, Sutherland had maintained that the files had been destroyed. As a member of Inver Brass he knew both were lies.

But why would Sutherland want the files? Why would he kill? Why would he belie the law he championed?

Peter could barely distinguish the entrance to the dock, beyond the hoist pulleys and the engine winches. They formed a strange, silhouetted archway, sharp black lines against a background of gray. He looked across the short span of water to his right where he knew O'Brien lay concealed on the deck of a scow. He turned his head to the left, trying to make out the automobile sandwiched between dry-docked oyster boats pulled out of the water for repairs. Alison was in the car. In her hand was a book of matches, a single match torn off, ready to strike. It was to be struck and held in the window, its flame shielded from the front, should there be anyone but the judge in Sutherland's automobile.

Suddenly, Peter heard the low tones of a powerful engine approaching in the distance. Moments later dual headlight beams shot through the fenced entrance into the shipyard, reflecting off the dry-docked hulls. The automobile continued on, turning right down a wide space between the boats toward the water's edge.

The headlights were shut off, leaving a lingering residue of light in Chancellor's eyes. He crouched below the gunwale of the trawler and kept watching the base of the dock. Lapping waves slapped against pilings in erratic rhythms; the creaking of boats continued ceaselessly.

A car door opened and closed, and moments later Sutherland's immense figure emerged from the darkness and filled a large area under the arch of steel and the taut metal coils of the winches. He walked out on the dock toward Peter, his footsteps heavy and cautious but without hesitation.

He reached the end of the dock and stood motionless, looking across the bay, a giant black man at dawn by the water's edge. Daniel Sutherland looked as if he were the last man on earth, contemplating the end of the universe. Or waiting for a barge to dock and men to order a huge buck to start unloading.

Peter stood up, pushing himself away from the trawler's railing, his hand in his pocket, gripping the gun. "Good morning, Judge. Or should I call you Venice?"

Sutherland turned and looked toward the trawler's ship where Chancellor stood on the narrow walkway. He said nothing.

"I said good morning," continued Chancellor softly, even courteously, unable to shut out the respect he felt for this man who had achieved so much in a lifetime.

"I heard you," replied Sutherland in his resonant voice, itself a weapon. "You called me Venice."

"That's the name you're known by. That's the name Inver Brass gave you."

"You're only half right. It's a name I gave myself."

"When? Forty years ago?"

Sutherland did not at first reply. He seemed to absorb Peter's statement with equal degrees of ire and astonishment, equally controlled. "When's not important. Neither's the name."

"I think both are. Does Venice mean what I think it means?"

"Yes. The Moor."

"Othello was a killer."

"This Moor is not."

"That's what I'm here to find out. You lied to me."

"I misled you for your own good. You should never have been involved at the start."

"I'm sick of hearing that. Why was I, then?"

"Because other solutions had failed. You seemed worth a try. We faced a national catastrophe."

"Hoover's missing files?"

Sutherland paused, his large dark eyes locked with Chancellor's. "You've learned then," he said. "It's true. Those files had to be found and destroyed, but all attempts to locate them had failed. Bravo was desperate and sought desperate measures. You were one of them."

"Then, why did you tell me the files had been destroyed?"

"I was asked to confirm certain aspects of the story given you. However, I didn't want you to take yourself too seriously. You're a novelist, not an historian. To allow you greater latitude would have placed you in danger. I couldn't permit that."

"Bait me in, but not all the way in, was that it?"

"It will do."

"No, it won't. There's more. You were protecting a

group of men who call themselves Inver Brass. You're one of them. You told me a few concerned men and women got together to fight Hoover and then disbanded after his death. You lied about that, too. This group goes back forty years."

"You've let your imagination run away with you." The judge was breathing harder.

"No, I haven't. I've spoken to the others."

"You've *what!*" Gone was the control, the sense of judicial propriety that underscored his every phrase. Sutherland's head trembled in the early light. "What in the name of God have you done?"

"I listened to the words of a dying man. And I think you know who that man was."

"Oh, God! *Longworth!*" The black giant froze.

"You *knew!*" The shock caused Peter to lose his breath. His muscles tensed, his foot slipped; he steadied himself. It *was* Sutherland. None of the others had made the connection. Sutherland had! He would not have made it, *could* not have made it, without following Varak, without tapping the Hay-Adams's switchboard!

"I know it now," said the judge in a flat, ominous monotone. "You found him in Hawaii, you brought him back and broke him. You may have touched off a chain of events that could drive the fanatics over the edge! Send them screaming into the streets with their charges of conspiracy and worse! What Longworth did was necessary. It was *right!*"

"What the hell are you talking about? Longworth was Varak, and you damned well know it! He found *me!* He saved my life, and I watched him die."

Sutherland seemed to lose his equilibrium. His breathing stopped, his immense body wavered as if he might fall. He spoke softly, in deep pain. "So Varak was the one. I had considered it but didn't want to believe it. He worked with others; I thought it was one of them. Not Varak. The wounds of his childhood never healed; he couldn't resist the temptation. He had to have all the weapons."

"Are you telling me he took the files? It won't wash. He didn't have them."

"He delivered them to someone else."

"He what?" Chancellor took a step forward, stunned by Sutherland's words.

"His hatred ran too deep. His sense of justice was twisted; all he wanted was revenge. The files could give him that."

"Whatever you're saying, it's wrong! Varak gave his life to find those files! You're lying! He told me the truth! He said it was one of four men!"

"It is. . . ." Sutherland looked away across the water. The awful silence was broken by the sounds of the boat basin. "Almighty God," he said, turning back to Peter. "If he had only come to me. I might have convinced him there was a better way. If he'd only come to me——"

"Why should he? You weren't above suspicion. I've spoken to the others; you're still not. You're one of the four!"

"You arrogant young *fool*!" thundered Daniel Sutherland, his voice echoing throughout the bay. Then he spoke quietly, with enormous intensity. "You say I lie. You say you've spoken to the others. Well, let me tell you, you've been lied to far more expeditiously by someone else."

"What does that mean?"

"It means that I know who has those files! I've known for weeks! It is, indeed, one of four men, but it's not *I*. This discovery was not so difficult. What will be difficult is getting them back! Convincing a man who's gone mad to seek help. You and Varak may have made that impossible!"

Peter stared at the black giant. "You've never said anything to anyone——"

"I couldn't!" interrupted the judge. "The situation had to be contained; the risks were too great. He hires killers. He has a thousand hostages in those files." Sutherland took a step toward Chancellor. "Did you tell anyone you were coming here? Did you watch to see if you were followed?"

Chancellor shook his head. "I travel with my own protection. No one followed me."

"You travel with what?"

"I'm not alone," said Peter quietly.

"Others are *with* you?"

"It's all right," said Chancellor, frightened by the old man's sudden dread. "He's *with* us."

"*O'Brien?*"

"Yes."

"Oh, my God!"

There was a sudden loud splash of water. It could not be mistaken for an anxious fish. There was a human being beneath the dock. In darkness. Peter ran to the edge.

Two rapid explosions of gunfire came from behind him. From the direction of Quinn's boat! Chancellor dove to the wood, flattening himself against the planks. The whole area erupted; shots came from the surface of the water, from the railings of other boats. Spits cracked in the air; bullets fired from weapons equipped with silencers. Peter rolled to his left, instinctively seeking the cover of adjacent pilings. Wood splintered in front of his face; he covered his eyes, opening them in time to see a flash of gunfire from an opposing dock. He brought his own gun up and pulled the trigger in panic.

There was a scream, followed by the sounds of a falling body, crashing into unseen objects and rolling over the dock into water.

Chancellor heard a grunt to his left. He turned. A man in a black wet suit was climbing over the edge of the pier. Peter aimed and fired; the man-monster arched his back, then fell forward in a last attempt to reach out at him.

Alison! He had to get to her! He lunged backward and came in startled contact with human flesh. It was Sutherland's body! The face was covered with blood, the overcoat stained throughout the upper section; splotches of deep red were everywhere.

The black giant was *dead*.

"Chancellor!" O'Brien was yelling at him, his voice penetrating the explosions and the spits of gunfire. For what purpose? To kill him? Who was O'Brien? *What* was O'Brien?

He would not answer; he would not become a target. Survival forced him to move. He lurched over the slain Daniel Sutherland toward the mass of steel machinery at the foot of the dock. He scrambled on all fours, diving, twisting, zigzagging as fast as he could over the filthy planks.

There was the ping of a ricocheting bullet. He had been *seen*! He had no choice; he rose partially off the ground, his legs aching in fear, and sped toward the black iron objects. He was in front of them; he plunged between the arch of cascading coils, twisting to his right behind a shield of steel.

"Chancellor! *Chancellor!*" Still O'Brien's shouts punctuated the gunfire. Still Peter would not heed him. For there was only one explanation. The man he had pitied, admired, given his life to, had led him into the trap!

There was a sudden fusillade, followed by an explosion. Flames leaped up from the stern of a trawler two docks away. Then a second detonation; another boat erupted in fire. There were shouts, orders; men ran over the docks and jumped from railings into the water. The gunfire seemed to diminish in the confusion. Then there was a single loud report, and a third boat burst into flames. Another shot followed; a man screamed. He screamed *words*.

The words were unintelligible. All but one: Chasŏng. *Chasŏng!*

A man was hit, his last words a roar of defiance before death; no other motive could cause the fanatic sound. It was the language Varak had not understood! Chancellor now heard it for himself; it was like no other he had ever heard.

The noise abated. Two men in wet suits climbed over the end of the short pier where Daniel Sutherland lay dead. Across the water on the opposing dock three shots came in rapid succession; a ricocheting bullet glanced harshly off a gearbox above Peter and imbedded itself in the wood beside him. A figure raced toward the shore, jumping between the boats, over railings, onto decks, around wheelhouses. More shots; Chancellor ducked beneath the shield of steel. The figure of the racing man reached the muddy shore and dove beyond a beached rowboat. He stayed there only seconds, then rose and ran into the darkness.

It was *O'Brien!* Peter watched in disbelief as he disappeared into the woods that bordered the boat basin.

The gunfire stopped. From the water beyond the docks came the sound of a motor launch. Chancellor could not wait any longer. He crawled out of his sanctuary, got to his feet, and raced between the boats toward the automobile.

Alison lay prostrate on the ground next to the car. Her eyes were glazed, her body trembled. Peter sank down beside her and held her in his arms.

"I never thought I'd see you alive!" she whispered, her fingers digging into him, her moist cheek against his.

"Come on. Quickly!" He pulled her to her feet. He yanked the car door open and pushed Alison inside.

There was a commotion on the dock. The motor launch he had heard in the distance had pulled alongside. There was an argument; men turned, several started toward the shore.

It was the moment to move. In seconds it would be too late. He looked through the windshield and turned the ignition key. The motor groaned but did not start.

The morning dampness! The car had not run in hours!

He heard shouts from the base of the dock. Alison heard them, too; she grabbed for his gun from the seat where he had dropped it. Automatically, with the swiftness born of experience, she cracked out the magazine.

"You've only got two shells left! Do you have others?"

"Bullets? No!" Peter turned the key again, pressing the accelerator.

The figure of a man in a wet suit loomed between the hulls of the beached trawlers. He started toward them.

"Watch your eyes!" shouted Alison.

She fired the weapon, the explosion thunderous inside the car. The side window blew open. The motor started.

Chancellor yanked the gearshift into drive and plunged his foot on the accelerator. The car lurched forward wildly. He swung the wheel to his right; the car skidded sideways, throwing up sprays of mud and dust. He straightened the wheel out and sped toward the exit turn.

They could hear shots behind them; the back window exploded.

Chancellor pushed Alison to the floor of the car as he whipped the steering wheel to the left. She would not stay down but lunged up, firing the second and last bullet. Briefly the gunshots behind them stopped.

Then they resumed, the bullets wild, without effect. Peter reached the entrance of the boat basin and raced down the road cut out of the forest toward the highway.

They were alone. An hour before there had been three fugitives; now there were two.

They had given their trust to Quinn O'Brien; he had betrayed them.

Whom would they turn to now?

They had only each other. Houses and office buildings were watched. Friends, acquaintances, placed under surveillance. Telephones were tapped, their car known. The highways and back roads would soon be patrolled.

Peter began to feel a remarkable change within himself. He wondered for a moment whether it was real or merely another aspect of his imagination; whatever, he decided he was grateful for it.

The fear—the sense of utter helplessness—was replaced by anger.

He gripped the wheel and drove on, the scream of death he had heard only minutes before echoing in his ears.

Chasŏng!

After everything was said, it was still the key.

37

The average citizen was not aware of their flight. No radio broadcasts described them; no photographs appeared on television or in the newspapers. And yet they ran, for ultimately there would be no protection; laws had been broken, men had been killed. To turn themselves in would lead to a dozen traps. The unknown men were everywhere among the authorities.

Hoover's private files were their only vindication, their only hope of survival.

Death had brought them nearer to the answer. Varak had said it was one of four men. Peter had added a fifth. Now Sutherland was dead and Dreyfus was dead and that left three. Banner, Paris, and Bravo.

Frederick Wells, Carlos Montelán, Munro St. Claire.

You've been lied to far more expeditiously by someone else.

But there was the key. *Chasŏng.* It was not a lie. One of the three remaining members of Inver Brass was somehow deeply, irrevocably associated with the waste at Chasŏng twenty-two years ago. Whoever he was had the files.

Peter recalled Ramirez's words. *Chasŏng is . . . represented in scores of veterans' hospitals.*

There was only a remote chance that something might be learned from the survivors. Their memories would be vague, but it was the only step he could think of. Perhaps the last one.

His thoughts turned to Alison. She had developed an anger matching his own, and in that anger was a remarkable sense of inventive determination. The general's daughter had resources, and she used them; her father had accumulated favors during a lifetime of service. She approached only those she knew were far removed from the centers of Pentagon influence and control. Men she had not spoken with in years received telephone calls asking for help—tactful assistance to be rendered privately, without questions.

And so that no complete picture be traced to a single source, the requests were divided.

An Air Force colonel attached to NASA Ordnance met them across the Delaware line in Laurel and gave them his car. O'Brien's automobile was hidden in the woods near the banks of the Nanticoke River.

An artillery captain at Fort Benning made reservations for them in his name at a Holiday Inn outside of Arundel Village.

A lieutenant commander in the Third Naval District, once a skipper on an LCI at Omaha Beach, drove to Arundel and brought three thousand dollars to their room. He accepted—without question—a note from Chancellor addressed to Joshua Harris instructing the literary agent to pay the borrowed sum.

The last thing they needed was the hardest to get: the casualty records of Chasŏng. Specifically, the whereabouts of the permanently disabled survivors. If there was a single focal point that might be under round-the-clock surveillance, it was Chasŏng. They had to work on the assumption that unseen men were watching, waiting for an interest to be shown.

It was nearly eight in the evening. The lieutenant commander had left minutes ago, the three thousand dollars dropped casually on the night table. Peter reclined wearily on the bed, leaning against the headboard. Alison was across the room at the desk. In front of her were her notes. Dozens of names, most crossed out for one reason or another. She smiled.

"Are you always so nonchalant about money?"

"Are you always so handy with a gun?" he replied.

"I've been around weapons most of my life. It doesn't mean I approve of them."

"I've been around money for about three and a half years. I approve of it very much."

"My father used to take me out to the pistol and rifle ranges several times a month. When nobody was around, of course. Did you know I could dismantle a carbine and a regulation .45 blindfolded by the time I was thirteen? God, how he must have wished I were a boy!"

"God, how he must have been out of his mind," said Chancellor, imitating her cadence. "What are we going to do about the casualty lists? Can you pull another string?"

"Maybe. There's a doctor at Walter Reed. Phil Brown. He was a medic in Korea when my father found him. He flew helicopter runs to the front lines and treated the wounded when the doctors said no thank you. Later, Dad got him started in the right direction, including medical school, courtesy of the Army. He was from a poor family; it wouldn't have been possible otherwise."

"That was a long time ago."

"Yes, but they stayed in touch. We stayed in touch. It's worth a try. I can't come up with anyone else."

"Can you get him here? I don't want to talk on the phone."

"I can ask," said Alison.

Within the hour a slender forty-three-year-old army doctor walked through the door and embraced Alison. There was a good-natured quality about the man, thought Chancellor; he liked him, although he had an idea that when Alison had said they'd "stayed in touch," she meant precisely that. They were good friends; they had once been better friends.

"Phil, it's so good to see you!"

"I'm sorry I didn't make Mac's burial," said the doctor, holding Alison by the shoulders. "I figured you'd understand. All those sanctimonious words from all those bastards who wanted his stars impounded."

"You haven't lost your directness, Charlie Brown."

The major kissed her on the forehead. "I haven't heard that name in years." He turned to Peter. "She's a

Peanuts freak, you know. We used to wait up for the Sunday papers——"

"This is Peter Chancellor, Phil," interrupted Alison.

The doctor focused on Peter and offered his hand. "You've upgraded your friends, Ali. I'm impressed. I enjoy your books, Peter. May I call you Peter?"

"Only if I can call you Charlie."

"Not in the office. They'd think I was an intellectual; that's frowned upon. . . . Now, what's this all about? Ali sounded like a fugitive from a narc raid."

"Right to the first," said Alison. "Far worse than the second. May I tell him, Peter?"

Chancellor looked at the major, at the abrupt concern in his eyes, at the strength veiled in pleasantness. "I think you can tell him everything."

"I think you'd better," said Brown. "This girl means a lot to me. Her father was an important part of my life."

They told him. Everything. Alison began; Peter filled in. The telling was cathartic; there was someone they could trust at last. Alison started to explain the events in Tokyo twenty-two years before. She stopped when she got to her mother's attack on her; further words would not come.

The doctor knelt in front of her. "Listen to me," he said professionally. "I want to hear it all. I'm sorry, but you have to tell it."

He did not touch her, but in his voice was the soft, firm command.

When she had finished, Brown nodded to Peter and got up to make himself a drink. Chancellor went to Alison and held her as the doctor poured himself a drink.

"The bastards," said Brown, revolving the glass in his hands. "Hallucinogens—that's what they plateaued her on. They may have strung her out on a morphine derivative or cocaine, but the hallucinogens provoke visual displacement; that's the prime symptom. Both sides were into heavy experiments in those days. The *bastards!*"

"What difference does it make which narcotics were used?" asked Chancellor, his arm around Alison.

"Maybe none at all," answered Brown. "But there could be. Those experiments were very restricted, very secret. Somewhere there are records—God knows where —but they exist. They could tell us the strategy, give us names and dates, tell us how wide the net spread."

"I'd rather talk to the men who were at Chasŏng," Peter said. "A few of the survivors, the higher the rank the better. Those in the VA hospitals. But there's no time to chase all over the country looking for them."

"You think you'll find the answer there?"

"Yes. Chasŏng's become a cult. I heard a dying man scream the name as if his own death were a willing sacrifice. There was no mistaking it."

"All right." Brown nodded in agreement. "Then why couldn't the sacrifice be based in revenge? Retribution for the activities of Mac's wife, her mother?" The doctor looked at Alison, his expression apologetic. "Actions she had no control over, but whoever's looking for revenge wouldn't know that."

"That's the point," interrupted Peter. "The kind of people involved in this are followers, willing to die—rank and file—not command personnel. They wouldn't know anything about her mother. You just said it. Ramirez confirmed it. Those experiments were restricted, very secret. Only a few people knew. There's no connection."

"*You* found it. With Ramirez."

"I was *expected* to find it, expected to settle for it. But something else happened at Chasŏng. Varak sensed it, but he couldn't put a label on it, so he called it a decoy."

"A decoy?"

"Yes. Same pond, wrong duck. 'Mac the Knife' had nothing to do with his wife's manipulation. The torn nightgown on the floor of the study in Rockville, the smashed glasses, the perfume—they were all signposts pointing in the wrong direction. Pointing toward a wreck of a woman destroyed by the enemy, and I was supposed to leap at it. I did, too, but I was wrong. It's something else."

"How do you know all this? How can you be so sure?"

"Because, goddamn it, I've invented this sort of thing myself. In books."

"In *books*? Come on, Peter, this is real."

"I could answer that, but you'd tie me up and take me in for observation. Just get me as many names as you can of the Chasŏng survivors."

Major Philip Brown, M.D., looked at the memorandum that resulted from the morning's conference. He was pleased with himself. The memo had just the right portentous ring to it without raising alarms that might be too shrill.

It was the sort of paper he could use to gain access to those thousands of microfilmed records that specified the location and brief medical histories of the disabled men residing in veterans' hospitals throughout the country.

Essentially the memorandum theorized that in a number of older disabled soldiers certain internal tissues were deteriorating at a somewhat faster pace than the normal aging process allowed for. These men had served in Korea, in and around Chagang Province. It was quite possible that a virus had infected their bloodstreams, and though it had appeared dormant, it was in fact molecularly active. The memo theorized that it was the *Hynobius*, a microscopic antigen carried by insects indigenous to Chagang Province. Further study was recommended as priorities allowed.

It was effective nonsense. The major had no idea if a *Hynobius* antigen existed. He reasoned that if he invented it, there could be no one to dispute him.

Memorandum in hand, Brown walked into the microfilm depository. He did not use the name Chasŏng with the staff sergeant in charge. Instead, he let the sergeant arrive at the selections. The enlisted man took his detective work seriously; he went back into the metal stacks and returned with the microfilms.

Three hours and twenty-five minutes later, Brown stared at the last projection on the screen. His tunic had been removed long ago, draped over a chair. His tie had been loosened, his collar unbuttoned. He sat back stunned.

In the hundreds of feet of microfilm there was not one mention of Chasŏng.

Not one.

It was as though Chasŏng had never existed. Nothing had ever happened there according to the microfilm depository of the Walter Reed Hospital.

He stood up and carried the rolls back to the sergeant. Brown knew he had to be cautious, but whatever the risk, it had to be taken. He had reached a dead end.

"I've extracted a lot of what we need," he said, "but I think there's more. *Hynobius* in the Ss sub-groupings turned up in the mobile labs around P'yŏng-yang. A number of these records refer to a Chasŏng district or province. I wondered if you had an index on it."

There was an immediate response from the sergeant, a speck of recognition in his eyes. "Chasŏng? Yes sir, I know the name. I saw it recently. I'm trying to think where."

Brown's pulse accelerated. "It could be important, Sergeant. It's just another line in the spectrograph, but it could be the one we need. The *Hynobius* is a bitch. Try to remember, please."

The sergeant got out of his chair and came to the counter, still frowning. "I think it was an entry on another shift, the insert in the far right column. That's always a little unusual, so it sort of stands out."

"Why is it unusual?"

"That column's for removals. The films are signed out. Generally people use the equipment here like you did."

"Can you pinpoint the time?"

"Couldn't have been more than a day or so ago. Let me look." The clerk pulled a metalbound ledger from a shelf. "Here it is. Yesterday afternoon. Twelve strips were signed out. All Chasŏng. At least signing them out makes sense."

"Why is that?"

"It'd take someone two days in here to go through all that material. I'm surprised it was even collated the way it was."

"What way was that?"

"Coded indexes. National-security classification. You need the master schedule to locate the films. Even though you're a doctor, you couldn't see them."

"Why not?"

"Your rank isn't high enough, sir."

"Who did sign them out?"

"A Brigadier General Ramirez."

Brown turned his TR-6 into the drive of the enormous data-processing center in McLean, Virginia. There was a guardhouse on the left. Across the roadway was a barrier with the inevitable Authorized Government Personnel Only sign affixed to the metal strips.

It hadn't taken much pressure to convince the staff sergeant at the depository that if men died because a general named Ramirez had removed the means of tracing the *Hynobius,* the sergeant could well be responsible.

Besides, Brown was perfectly willing to take full responsibility—rank and medical—and sign for the microfilm identification numbers under his own name. The sergeant was not giving him the film, only the numbers; Reed Security would clear him for the duplicates in McLean.

The doctor reasoned that he had a personal score to settle with Ramirez. The brigadier had destroyed General MacAndrew, and MacAndrew had given Phil Brown, farm boy from Gandy, Nebraska, a very decent chance in life. If Ramirez didn't like it, he could always file charges.

Somehow Brown didn't think the brigadier would do that.

Breaching the security desk at Walter Reed was not very difficult. It was a question of using the memorandum to browbeat a nonmedical security officer into giving him a general clearance for McLean.

Brown showed his clearance to the civilian behind the entrance desk at McLean. The man punched the buttons of a computer; small green numbers appeared on the miniature screen, and the doctor was directed to the proper floor.

The main point, reflected Brown as he walked through the doors into Section M, Data Processing, was that since he had the serial numbers for the material signed out by Ramirez, he needed nothing else. Each strip of microfilm had its own individual identification. The medical clearance was accepted; the obstacles fell, and ten minutes later he sat in front of a very complicated machine that, weirdly enough, looked like a shiny new version of an old-time Moviola.

And ten minutes after that he realized the staff sergeant at the depository was wrong when he said it would take someone two days to go through these records. It would take less than an hour. Brown was not sure what he had found, but whatever it was, it caused him to stare in disbelief at the information flashed on the small screen in front of him.

Of the hundreds of men who had engaged in the Battle of Chasŏng, only thirty-seven had survived. If that were not startling enough, the disposition of the thirty-seven was appalling. It was in contradiction to every accepted psychological practice. Men severely maimed or crippled in the same combat operation were rarely separated. Since they would spend the rest of their lives in institutions, their comrades were often all they had left, families and friends visiting them less and less frequently until they were only uncomfortable, unseemly shadows in far distant wards.

Yet the thirty-seven survivors of Chasŏng had been meticulously isolated from one another. Specifically, thirty-one had been separated, in thirty-one different hospitals from San Diego to Bangor, Maine.

The remaining six were together, but their close association was next to meaningless. They were in a maximum-security psychiatric ward ten miles west of Richmond. Brown knew the place. The patients were certifiably insane—all dangerous, most homicidal.

Still, they were together. It was not a pleasant prospect, but if Chancellor believed he could learn something, here were the names of six survivors of Chasŏng. From the writer's point of view the circumstances might be advantageous. As long as communication was possible, these men whose mental capacities had been destroyed at Chasŏng might be capable of revealing a great deal. Unconsciously perhaps, but without the inhibiting strictures imposed by rational thought. The causes of insanity rarely left the minds of the insane.

Something he could not define bothered the doctor, but he was too stunned to analyze it. His mind was too packed with the inexplicable to think anymore.

Too, he wanted to get out of the data-processing center into the cold fresh air.

They were not entering a hospital, Peter felt. They were going inside a prison. A sanitized version of a concentration camp.

"Remember, your name is Conley, and you're an M.N. subgroup specialist," said Brown. "I'll do the talking."

They walked down the long white corridor lined with white metal doors on both sides. There were small, thick observation windows in the walls beside the doors, behind which Chancellor could see the inmates. Grown men lay curled up on bare floors, many soiled by their own wastes. Others paced like animals, when, suddenly catching sight of strangers in the corridor, they thrust contorted faces against the glass. Still others stood at their windows, staring blankly at the sunlight outside, lost in silent fantasies.

"You never get used to it," said the psychiatrist accompanying them. "Human beings reduced to the lowest primates. Yet they were once men. We must never forget that."

It took Peter a moment or two to realize the man was speaking to him. At the same time he knew his face reflected the impact of the emotions he was experiencing: equal parts compassion, curiosity, revulsion.

"We'll want to talk to the Chasŏng survivors," said Brown, relieving Chancellor of the need to reply. "Will you arrange that, please?"

The staff doctor seemed surprised but did not object. "I was told you wanted blood samples."

"Those, too, of course. But we'd also like to talk to them."

"Two can't talk, and three usually don't. The first are catatonic, the others are schizophrenic. Have been for years."

"That's five," said Brown. "What about the sixth? Would he remember anything?"

"Nothing you'd want to hear. He's homicidal. And anything can set off his rage—a gesture of your hand or the light from a bulb. He'll be the one in the jacket."

Chancellor felt ill; the pain shot through his temples. They'd made the trip for nothing, for nothing could be learned. He heard Brown ask a question, his tone reflecting an equal sense of dispair.

"Where are they? Let's make it quick."

"They're all together in one of the south-wing labs. They're prepped for you. Right this way."

They reached the end of the hallway and turned into another, wider corridor. It was lined with separate enclosed cubicles, some with benches against the walls, others with examination tables in the center. Each cubicle was fronted by an observation window made of the same thick glass as in the hallway they had just left. The psychiatrist led them to the last cubicle and gestured through the window.

Chancellor stared through the glass, his breath suspended, his eyes wide. Inside were six men in green buttonless fatigues. Two sat immobile on benches, their eyes distant. Three were sprawled on the floor, moving their bodies in horrible, tortured motions—giant insects imitating one another. One stood in the corner, his neck and shoulders twitching, his face a series of unending contortions, his trapped arms straining against the tight fabric that bound his upper body.

But what caused Peter's sudden and profound terror was not merely the sight of the pathetic half-humans beyond the glass but the sight of their skin.

All were blacks.

"That's *it*," he heard Brown whisper. "The letter *n*."

"What?" asked Chancellor, barely able to be heard, so intense was his fear.

"It was there. Everywhere," said the major quietly. "It didn't register because I was looking for other things. The small letter *n* after the names. Hundreds of names. Negro. All the troops at Chasŏng were black. All Negroes."

"Genocide," said Peter softly, the fear total, the sickness complete.

38

They raced north on the highway in silence, each with his own thoughts, each consumed with a horror neither had ever before experienced. Yet both knew precisely what had to be done; the man they had to confront had been identified: Brigadier General Pablo Ramirez.

"I *want* that son of a bitch," Brown had said as soon as they left the hospital.

"Nothing makes sense," answered Peter, knowing it was no reply. "Sutherland was black. He was the only connection. But he's dead."

Silence.

"I'll make the call," said Brown finally. "You can't; he'd never see you. And there are too many ways for a general to be suddenly transferred halfway around the world."

They drove into one of those Colonial-style restaurants that seem to breed in the Virginia countryside. There was a telephone booth at the end of a dimly lit hallway. Chancellor waited by the open door; the doctor went inside and dialed the Pentagon.

"Major Brown?" asked the irritated Ramirez over the phone. "What's so urgent you can't discuss it with my secretary?"

"It's more than urgent, General. And you *are* a general according to the microfilm depository at Walter Reed. I'd say it's an emergency."

A momentary silence conveyed the brigadier's shock. "What are you talking about?" he asked, barely audible.

"A medical accident, I think, sir. I'm a doctor assigned to trace a viral strain that had its origins in Korea. We isolated the districts; one of them was Chasŏng. All the casualty records were removed under your name."

"Chasŏng has a national-security classification," said the brigadier quickly.

"Not medically, General," interrupted Brown. "We have controlled priority. I received clearance to check the duplicates at data processing. . . ." He let his voice trail off, suspended, as if he had more to say but did not know how to say it.

Ramirez couldn't stand the tension. "What are you driving at?"

"That's it, sir. I don't know, but as one military man to another, I'm scared to death. Hundreds of men killed at Chasŏng; hundreds missing with no postwar resolutions. All Negro troops. Thirty-seven survivors; except for six insane men, thirty-one in thirty-one separate hospitals. All black, all isolated. That's against every accepted practice. I don't care if it *is* twenty-two years ago, if all this comes out——"

"Who else knows about these records?" broke in Ramirez.

"At this juncture no one but me. I called you because your name——"

"Keep it that way!" said the brigadier curtly. "That's an order. It's seventeen-thirty hours. Come to my house in Bethesda. Be there at nineteen hundred." Ramirez gave him the address and hung up.

Brown stepped out of the booth. "We're here; we've got time. Let's get something to eat."

They ate mechanically, with a minimum of conversation.

The coffee came; Brown leaned forward. "How do you explain O'Brien?" he asked.

"I can't. Any more than I can explain a man like Varak. They take lives, they risk their own lives, and for what? They live in a world I can't understand." Chancellor paused, remembering. "Maybe O'Brien explained it himself. Something he said when I asked him about Varak. He said there were times when life and death weren't the issues; times when all that mattered was the elimination of a problem."

"That's incredible."

"It's inhuman."

"It still doesn't explain O'Brien."

"Something else might. He was part of the files. He told me he thought he was ready to be tested, but he wasn't sure. We know the answer now."

Peter's eyes were drawn to a slight movement at the window overlooking the porch of the restaurant. The front lights had been switched on, the day having turned into early evening. Suddenly he froze. His hand stayed where it was, the glass at his lips, his eyes riveted on the window, on the figure of a man on the porch.

For an instant he wondered if he were going mad, if his mind had cracked under the strain of the swiftly disintegrating line between the real and the unreal. Then he knew he was seeing someone he had seen before. Outside another window, standing on another porch. A man with a gun!

The *same man*. Through the window, on the walk-around porch of the old Victorian house on Chesapeake Bay: Munro St. Claire's chauffeur. He was waiting for them, checking to make sure they were still there!

"We've been followed," he said to Brown.

"What?"

"There's a man on the porch. He's looking inside. Keep your eyes on me! . . . He's walking away now."

"Are you sure?"

"Positive. He's St. Claire's man. Which means if he's followed us here, he's been following us the whole time. He knows Alison's in Arundel!" Peter got to his feet, doing his best to conceal his fear. "I'm going to call."

Alison answered.

"Thank God you're there," he said. "Now listen to me, and do as I tell you. That lieutenant commander from the Third District, the one who gave us the money. Get hold of him and ask him to come out and stay with you. Tell him to bring a gun. Until he gets there call the hotel's security and say I telephoned and insisted you be taken to the dining room. There are crowds there; stay in the dining room until he arrives. Now, do as I say."

"Of course I will," said Alison, sensing his panic. "Now tell me why."

"We've been followed. I don't know for how long."

"I understand. Are you all right?"

"Yes. Which means, I think, they're following us to see where we lead them. Not to harm us."

"Are you leading them somewhere?"

"Yes. But I don't want to. I don't have time to talk, just do as I tell you. I love you." He hung up and walked back to the table.

"Is she there?" Brown asked. "Everything all right?"

"Yes. Someone's coming to stay with her. Another friend of the general's."

"He had a lot of them. I feel better. As you surmised, I'm fond of that girl."

"I surmised."

"You're a lucky man. She passed on me."

"I'm surprised."

"I wasn't. She didn't want anything permanent with a uniform. She pictured it on you even when— What are we going to do?"

The abrupt shift would have amused Peter any other time. "How strong are you?"

"That's a hell of a question. What do you mean?"

"Can you fight?"

"I'd rather not. You're not challenging me, so you must mean our friend outside."

"There could be more than one."

"Then, I like the prospects less. What did you have in mind?"

"I don't want them following us to Ramirez."

"Neither do I," Brown said. "Let's find out if it's a 'them' or a 'him.' "

It was a "him." The man stood leaning against a sedan at the far end of the parking lot, under the branches of a tree, his eyes focused on the front entrance. Chancellor and Brown had come out a side door; St. Claire's man did not see them.

"Okay," Brown whispered. "There's only one. I'll go back inside and walk out the front. You'll see me swing the car around. Good luck."

"I hope you know what you're doing."

"It's better than fighting. We could lose. Just hold on tight. I only need a second."

Peter remained in the shadows by the side door until he saw St. Claire's man push away from the hood of the sedan and walk quickly around to the tree side, out of sight. The chauffeur had spotted Brown coming out of the front entrance. Why didn't the man get into his car? It was curious.

Several seconds passed. Brown sauntered casually across the parking lot toward the Triumph under the restaurant's floodlights.

Peter moved. Crouched, he made his way along the border of the paved area, hidden by the parked cars, toward St. Claire's man. The ground beyond the border consisted of unkempt shrubbery and uncut grass. When Chancellor was within thirty feet of the chauffeur, he stepped over the curb and into the foliage. As quietly as he could, he crept nearer, counting on the sounds of the Triumph's engine to cover whatever noise he made.

In the parking lot Brown backed his car out of its slot and pointed it toward the exit; then he suddenly yanked the gears into reverse and gunned the motor furiously. The Triumph lurched backward toward the tree.

Chancellor was within fifteen feet of St. Claire's chauffeur, hidden by darkness and the shrubbery. The man was confused, astonishment seen clearly on his face. He ducked beneath the windows of the sedan; he had no other choice. Brown had slammed on the brakes of the Triumph within inches of the sedan's front bumper and climbed out. The chauffeur stepped back, his concentration totally on Brown.

Chancellor sprang out of the shadows, his hands outstretched toward St. Claire's man. The chauffeur heard the sounds from the darkness to his right. He whipped around, reacting instantly to the attack. Peter grabbed his coat, swinging him around against the metal of the sedan. The chauffeur's foot lashed out, striking Chancellor's kneecap. A sharp punch caught Peter in the throat. An elbow crashed into his chest, the pain excruciating; a knee hammered into his groin with the swift, harsh impact of a piston.

In the sudden, stinging agony Chancellor found himself pitched into a frenzy. He could feel outrage welling up inside him. There was only the violence, the brute force he hated remaining to him.

Peter clenched his right fist; he kept his left hand open, a claw soaring in to grab flesh. He threw his weight against the thrashing man, crashing him into the steel of the sedan, his fist pummeling the chauffeur's stomach and below, hammering the man's testicles. His open hand found the chauffeur's face; he dug his fingers into the man's eyes, his thumb ripping up into a nostril. He yanked with all his strength, sending the skull sideways, smashing it into the roof of the automobile. Blood poured out of the chauffeur's mouth, eye sockets, and nostrils. Still he would not stop; his fury matched Chancellor's.

Peter yanked the man's head again, twisting away from the chauffeur's knees. He crashed the skull again into the metal; his hands were slippery, covered with blood. He smashed the chauffeur against the window with such force that the glass shattered.

"For Christ's sake!" screamed Brown. "Just hold him!"

But Chancellor could not control himself. His rage had found an outlet, brutal and satisfying. He was avenging so much!

He ripped at the chauffeur's neck, his hand sliding around to the throat. He pushed suddenly upward, catching the man's chin, sending the head back once more into steel as he brought his own knee up into the dark trousers of the chauffeur's uniform and slammed his upper leg with surging impact into the man's groin.

The chauffeur screamed and began to go limp.

"Shit!" exploded Brown.

"What is it?" gasped Chancellor, no breath left in his lungs.

"The goddamned needle broke!"

In his hand the doctor held a hypodermic; he had plunged it into the chauffeur's shoulder. Suddenly the man fell forward against Peter. Brown stepped back and spoke again.

"Son of a bitch. . . . Enough got through."

A crowd had gathered on the restaurant porch. Someone had heard the chauffeur's scream and had gone back for help.

"Let's get out of here!" Brown said, grabbing Chancellor's arm.

At first Peter did not respond; his mind was filled with mist and light. He could not think.

Brown seemed to understand. He pulled Chancellor away from the sedan, propelling him to the door of the Triumph. He opened it and shoved Chancellor inside; then he ran around the hood and climbed in behind the wheel.

They raced out of the parking lot, into the darkness of the highway, and drove in silence for several minutes. Brown reached behind him into the well of the backseat and pulled up his medical bag.

"There's a bottle of alcohol and some surgical gauze," he said. "Clean yourself up."

Still dazed, Chancellor did as he was told.

The major spoke again. "What the hell were you? A Green Beret?"

"Nothing."

"I beg to differ. You were something! I'd never have believed it. You just don't seem the type."

"I'm not."

"Well, if I ever raise my voice to you, I apologize in advance. I'll also run like hell. You're the best street fighter I've seen."

Peter looked at Brown. "Don't talk like that," he said simply.

They fell quiet again. The major slowed as they approached an intersection, then swung the Triumph to the left, into the road that would take them to Bethesda.

Chancellor touched the doctor's arm. "Wait a minute." The obscure question that had bothered him when Brown walked out of the restaurant had formed in his mind. *Why hadn't the chauffeur gotten into his car?*

Peter's memory raced back in time nearly two and a half years, when he was researching *Counterstrike!* To the disaffected men he had spoken with and the technology they had described.

"What's the matter?" asked Brown.

"If we've been followed, how come we never realized it? God knows we were watching."

"What are you talking about?"

"Pull over!" interrupted Chancellor, alarm in his voice. "Do you have a flashlight?"

"Sure. In the glove compartment." Brown pulled off the road onto the shoulder.

Peter took the flashlight, jumped out of the car, and ran back to the trunk, lowering himself to the ground. He switched on the light and crawled under the chassis.

"I've got them!" he yelled. "Get me your tool kit. The lug wrench!"

Brown got it for him. Chancellor stayed beneath the car, working furiously with the iron instrument. Crunching, prying sounds came from the rear axle area, then Peter slid out, holding two small metallic objects in his left hand.

"Transmitters," he said. "A primary and a backup! That's why we never saw anyone. They could stay three to five miles behind and still follow us. Wherever we went, whomever we met, they just waited for the right moment." He paused for a second, his face grim. "But I found them. They're cut off. Let's go to Bethesda."

"I've changed my mind. I think I should go with you," said Brown as they drove down Ramirez's tree-lined street.

"No," replied Peter. "Let me off at the next corner. I'll walk back."

"Has it occurred to you he might try to kill you? He's expecting me. I wear the same uniform he does."

"That's why he won't kill me. I'll tell him the truth. I'll make it clear that you're waiting for me. A fellow officer. If I don't come out, you'll go somewhere else, and Chasŏng will blow up in their faces."

They approached the corner; Brown slowed the Triumph. "That might work with a rational person. It may not with Ramirez. If Chasŏng's what we think it is——"

"*Know* it *was*," broke in Chancellor.

"All right, say it's true. He may not want to face the consequences. He's Army, don't forget that. He may decide to take you out, then go with you."

"Kill himself?" asked Peter incredulously.

"The incidence of military suicide," said the doctor, stopping the car, "isn't discussed much, but it's sky high. Some say it goes with the terrain. I didn't ask you before. Do you have a gun?"

"No. I had one; ran out of bullets. Never tried to get more."

Brown reached into his medical bag, rummaged inside a flap, and pulled out a small revolver. "Here, take this. We're issued these because we carry drugs. Good luck. I'll be waiting."

Chancellor reached the flagstone path. Ramirez was at the window, staring outside, his face reflecting his astonishment at seeing Peter. Astonishment, but not shock, not panic. He let the curtain fall back and disappeared. Chancellor walked down the path and up the steps; he rang the bell.

The door opened. The brigadier's Latin eyes looked harshly at Peter.

"Good evening, General. Major Brown sends his regrets. The Chasŏng records disturbed him so much he didn't want to talk to you. But he's waiting for me down the block."

"I thought so," replied Ramirez noncommittally. "The doctor has a short memory, or he thinks others do. The enlisted man, the medic from Korea MacAndrew made a doctor. The one who had an affair with his daughter." He looked past Chancellor, raised his hand, and chopped the night air twice.

It was a signal.

From behind him in the street, Peter heard an engine start. He turned. The headlights of a military police car were switched on. It pulled out swiftly, gathering speed, and raced to the corner, stopping barely in sight, near the spill of a streetlight, the brakes screeching. Two soldiers jumped out and ran toward a third figure. He, in turn, started to run but was not quick enough.

Chancellor watched as Major Philip Brown was taken, no match for the military police. He was led back to the army car and thrown inside.

"No one's waiting for you now," said Ramirez. Peter turned in fury, his hand going for the gun.

Then he stopped. Leveled at his chest was a .45 automatic.

"You can't do this!"

"I think I can," said Ramirez. "The doctor will be held in isolation, allowed no visitors, no calls, no outside communication whatsoever. That's standard for officers who violate national-security. Come inside, Mr. Chancellor."

39

They were in Ramirez's study. The brigadier's eyes grew wide, his lips parted, and slowly he lowered the gun.

Look to the fiction, always the fiction, thought Peter. *In fiction lies reality, the devices of the imagination more powerful than any weapon.*

"Where is this letter?" asked the general.

Chancellor had lied to Ramirez, telling him he had written a letter detailing the cover-up and the racial character of Chasŏng. It had been mailed to New York, copies to be sent to major newspapers, the Senate Armed Services Committee, and the secretary of the Army if the general did not cooperate.

"Out of my control," replied Peter. "Out of yours, too. You couldn't intercept it. Unless I show up in New York by noontime tomorrow, it'll be opened. The story of Chasŏng will be read by a very aggressive editor."

"He'd trade your life for it," said Ramirez cautiously. The threat was hollow; his voice lacked conviction.

"I don't think so. He'd weigh the priorities. I think he'd take the risk."

"There are other priorities! They go way beyond us!"

"I'm sure you've convinced yourself of that."

"It's true! An accident of command, a coincidence that could not occur again in a thousand years must not be given a label it doesn't deserve!"

"I see." Chancellor looked down at the gun. The brigadier hesitated, then placed the weapon on the table beside him. He did not move from the table, however. The gun was within a swift hand's reach. Peter acknowledged the gesture with a nod. "I see," he repeated. "That's the official explanation. An accident. A coincidence. All the troops at Chasŏng just happened to be black. Over six hundred men killed, God knows how many hundreds missing —all black."

"That's the way it was."

"That's the way it *wasn't!*" contradicted Chancellor. "There were no segregated battalions then."

Ramirez's expression was contemptuous. "Who told you that?"

"Truman gave the order in '48. All branches of the service were integrated."

"With all deliberate speed," said the general in a flat monotone. "The services were no faster than anyone else."

"Are you saying you were caught by your own delay? Your resistance to a presidential order resulted in a whole-sale slaughter of black troops? Is that it?"

"Yes." The brigadier took a step forward. "Resistance to an impossible policy! But Christ, you can see how it would be twisted by the radicals of this country! Beyond the country!"

"I can understand that." Peter saw a flicker of hope in Ramirez's eyes. The soldier had reached out for an elusive lifeline, and for a brief moment he believed he had it in his grasp. Chancellor altered the tone of his voice just enough to take advantage of the brigadier's false hope. "Let's leave the casualties for a minute. What about MacAndrew? Where does he fit in with Chasŏng?"

"You know the answer to that. When you called, I said things I should never have told you."

It was all so pat. The lie was deep, thought Peter. There were two fears of exposure, one more terrifying to Ramirez than the other, so the lesser—the transmitting of erroneous intelligence to an enemy—was put forward to avoid the more damaging. What was that other fear?

"MacAndrew's wife?"

The general nodded, guilt accepted in humility. "We did what we believed was right at the time. The objective was to save American lives."

"She was used to send back false information," said Peter.

"Yes. She was the perfect conduit. The Chinese oper-ated extensively in Japan; some Japanese fanatics helped them. For many it came down to Oriental against white."

"I never heard that before."

"It was never given much coverage. It was a con-stant thorn in MacArthur's side; it was played down."

"What kind of information did you feed MacAndrew's wife?"

"The usual. Troop movements, supply routes, con-centration of ordnance, and tactical options. Mainly troop movements and tactics, of course."

"She was the one who relayed the tactical information about Chasŏng?"

Ramirez paused; his eyes strayed to the floor. There was something artificial in the brigadier's reaction, something rehearsed. "Yes," he said reluctantly.

"But that information wasn't false. It wasn't inaccurate. It resulted in a massacre."

"No one knows how it happened," continued Ramirez. "To understand, you must realize how these reverse conduits operate. How compromised people like MacAndrew's wife are used. They're not given blanket lies; outright misinformation would be rejected, the conduit suspect. They're provided with variations of the truth, subtle alterations of the possible. 'The Sixth Engineer Battalion will enter Combat Sector Baker on three July.' Only it's not the Sixth Engineers, it's the Sixth Tank Artillery, and it reaches Combat Baker on July five, outflanking the positioned enemy. With the Chasŏng operation the variation given MacAndrew's wife was not, in fact, the variation at all. It was the actual strategy. Somehow the orders were fouled up in G-Two command. She carried back information that resulted in wholesale slaughter." The soldier leveled his eyes with Peter's and stood erect. "Now you know the truth."

"Do I?"

"You have the word of a general officer."

"I wonder if it's any good."

"Don't press me, Chancellor. I've told you more than you have any right to know. To make you see the anguish that would result if the tragedy of Chasŏng were made public. Facts would be misinterpreted, the memory of fine people dragged through filth."

"Wait a minute," interrupted Peter. In his sanctimonious rendering of the obvious, Ramirez had *said* it. *The memory of.* . . . Alison's *memories.* Her mother's parents held prisoners in the Po Hai Gulf; that was the first Chinese connection, but that wasn't it! It was something Alison said that happened *after* the night her mother had been carried on the stretcher. Something about her father. . . . Her father had flown back to Tokyo for the next to last time. That was it: the *next* to last time! Between his wife's final collapse and his return to the States, MacAndrew had gone back to Korea! The Battle of Chasŏng took place *then.* Weeks after Alison's mother was hospitalized. She couldn't have relayed information, accurate or otherwise.

"What's the matter?" asked the brigadier.

"You. Goddamn it, *you*! The *dates*! It couldn't have happened! What did you say a few minutes ago? Some battalion or other is expected on the third of July but doesn't get there until the fifth, and anyway it's a different battalion. What did you call it? Some bullshit phrase . . . 'subtle alteration of the possible.' Wasn't that it? Well, General, you just blew it! The massacre at Chasŏng took place weeks after MacAndrew's wife was hospitalized! She couldn't have carried that information to anyone! Now, you son of a bitch, you tell me what happened! Because if you don't, there won't be any waiting until tomorrow. That letter I sent to New York will be read tonight!"

Ramirez's eyes bore into his; his mouth twitched. "*No!*" he roared. "You won't! You can't! I won't let you!"

He was reaching for the gun!

Chancellor rushed forward, throwing himself at the general. His shoulder crashed into Ramirez's back, propelling the soldier into the wall. Ramirez gripped the gun by its barrel; he swung it up viciously. The handle of the gun caught Chancellor at the temple. Searing shafts of pain caused a thousand white spots to converge in front of him.

His left hand was dug into Ramirez's tunic, the fabric clutched against the soldier's chest. His right hand lashed out in thrust and counterthrust, trying to grab and hold the heavy weapon.

He felt the handle! He brought his knee up into the general's stomach, smashing him against the wall. He had the handle of the gun, and he would not let go! Ramirez kept punching hysterically at Peter's kidney. Chancellor thought he might collapse, so intense was the pain.

His finger was near the trigger! In the slashing movements of both their arms, Peter felt the rim of the trigger enclosure.

But he could not let it fire! An explosion would bring neighbors! The police! If that happened, nothing could be learned!

Chancellor took a half step back, then crashed his left leg up, pulling the soldier's tunic down with all his strength. His knee smashed into Ramirez's face, sending his head back. The general expelled a chestful of air; the gun left his hand; his fingers straightened in agony. The weapon flew across the room, crashing into the marble pen set on top of the desk. Peter released the tunic. Ramirez collapsed, unconscious, blood pouring out of his nostrils.

It took Peter a minute to find his thoughts again. He knelt in front of the soldier and waited until his breathing was steadier, until the white spots faded and the pain in his temples began to subside. Then he picked up the gun.

There was a bottle of Evian water on a silver tray in a bookshelf. He opened the bottle and poured the water into his palm, splashing it over his face. It helped. He was finding his sanity again.

He poured what was left in the bottle on the soldier's unconscious face. The water mingled with blood on the floor from the general's nosebleed, producing a sickening pink.

Slowly Ramirez regained consciousness. Peter yanked a loose cushion from an easy chair and threw it over to him. The general blotted his face and neck with the pillow and stood up, supporting himself against the wall.

"Sit down," ordered Peter, waving the barrel of the gun toward the leather armchair.

Ramirez sank into the chair. He let his head fall back. "Slut. *Whore*," he whispered.

"That's progress," said Chancellor softly. "A few nights ago she was unfortunate,' 'unstable.' "

"That's what she was."

"What she was or what you turned her into?"

"The material has to be there to work with," replied the general. "She sold out."

"She had a mother and father in China."

"I have two brothers who emigrated to Cuba. You think the *Fidelistas* haven't tried to reach *me*? Right now they're rotting in prison. But I won't be compromised!"

"You're stronger than she was. You've been trained not to be compromised."

"She was the wife of an American combat officer! His Army was *her* Army."

"Then, she wasn't up to it, was she? Instead of helping her you *used* her. You filled her full of lethal junk and sent her right back into a fight she couldn't win. Brown said it best. You *bastards*!"

"The strategy was optimum!"

"Cut that army bullshit! Who gave you the right?"

"No one! *I* saw the tactic. *I* created the strategy. *I* was the source control!" Ramirez blanched. He had gone too far.

"*You?*" Alison's words came back to Peter; he had

asked her after the funeral what MacAndrew had thought of Ramirez. *A lightweight, hotheaded and too emotional. Not at all reliable. Dad refused to second two field promotions for him.*

"There were many such operations. Others were involved, naturally." Ramirez retreated.

"No, they weren't! Not with this one!" broke in Chancellor. "It was all yours! What better way to get at the man who pegged you for what you were. A hothead! A liar! Who refused to let them give you a rank you weren't qualified for! You got revenge through his wife!"

"I *got* the rank! He couldn't stop me; that *whore* couldn't stop me!"

"Of course not! You immobilized him through her! How did you begin? By sleeping with her?"

"It wasn't difficult. She was a slut!"

"And you had the candy! Oh, you're a thoroughbred! And when you got your goddamned rank, you didn't have the stomach for it because you knew how you'd gotten it. You invited reasons how to hide it because you knew you weren't qualified for it. You don't pretend to be a major so you can talk to the men. You don't give a damn for anybody! You're afraid of the rank! You're a fraud!"

Ramirez sprang up from the chair, his face on fire. Chancellor caught him in the stomach with his foot; the general fell back into the chair.

"You filthy liar!" screamed the soldier.

"Hits a nerve, doesn't it." It was not a question. Suddenly Peter stopped. *Whore?* It didn't make sense. An enormous contradiction was apparent. "Wait a minute. You couldn't have compromised MacAndrew that way. He would have killed you! He never knew his wife was a reverse conduit because you couldn't tell him! Any of you. He had to be told something else; he had to believe something else. He never knew!"

"He knew his wife was a whore! He knew that!"

A sharp image sprang to Peter's mind. A strong but broken man cradling a madwoman on the floor of an isolated house. Cradling her lovingly, telling her that everything would be all right. It was too great an inconsistency. Regardless of the personal anguish a whoring wife would have been ripped out of MacAndrew's life.

"I don't believe you," said Chancellor.

"He saw for himself! He *had* to know!"

"He saw *something* for himself. He was *told* something. Or maybe it was just hinted at. You people are terrific at indicating something but never coming out and saying it. I don't think MacAndrew thought his wife was a whore. I don't think he'd put up with that for a minute!"

"All the symptoms were there! The slut's mentality."

Symptoms. Peter stared down at Ramirez. He was getting closer, he could sense it. *Symptoms.* According to Alison her mother had begun to "slip away" several months before the explosion came. Alison's father did not know why, so he ascribed it to a progressive deterioration of her faculties, using an accident at a beach to pin the final breakdown on. Used it so often he came to believe it himself.

In the recesses of his mind such a man would continue to love, continue to protect, because his wife was not to blame. No matter what she did. Conflicting forces—parents in the hands of an enemy, a husband fighting that enemy every day—had driven that woman out of her mind.

And all the while trusted friends hinted at promiscuous behavior in order to cover their own actions.

What those colleagues did not understand was that MacAndrew was a far better man than they could imagine. Far better and far more compassionate. Whatever the manifestations of an illness it was the illness that was to be despised, not the actions of the human being afflicted.

And this maggot with his bloody face perspiring in the chair, this "source control" who had held out the lethal candy until he'd slept with the wife of the man he hated, could only repeat the words *whore* and *slut*.

Those words were the screen that concealed the truth. "What's a 'slut's mentality,' General?"

Ramirez's eyes were wary; he suspected a trap. "She hung around the Ginza," he said. "In the off-limit bars. She picked up men."

"Those bars were in the southwest district of the Ginza, weren't they? I've been in Tokyo; those bars were still there in '67."

"A number of them, yes."

"They trafficked in narcotics."

"It's possible. More to the point, they sold sex."

"What did they sell it for, General?"

"What it's always sold for."

"Money?"

"Naturally. And kicks."

"No! Not naturally! MacAndrew's wife didn't *need* money. *Or* kicks. She was looking for drugs! You strung her out, and she tried to find junk by herself! Without going to the Chinese! That's what you found out! And by her doing that your whole strategy would blow up in your faces! Just one arrest, one Tokyo bust investigated by an outside agency, and you were finished! *Exposed!* You had the most to hide, you motherfucker! But others were involved, too. What did you say a few minutes ago? 'There were many such operations.' You were all running for cover, trying to protect yourselves!" Again Peter stopped, the realization there. "Which means you had to *control* what happened——"

"It happened!" screamed Ramirez, interrupting. "We weren't responsible! She was found down an alley in the Ginza! We didn't put her there! She was found. She would have died!"

The images and the phrases wove swiftly in and out of Chancellor's mind. Alison's words came back like the echoes of kettle drums. Her mother had been taken on a Sunday afternoon to Funabashi Beach. *The phone started ringing. Was my mother there? . . . Two Army officers drove out to the house. They were nervous and agitated. . . .*

Was my mother there? Was my mother there?

At night, quite late, I heard screams. . . . Downstairs . . . men . . . walking around rapidly, using hand radios. Then the front door opened, and she was brought inside. On a stretcher. . . . Her face—it was white. Her eyes were wide, staring blankly . . . blood rolled down over her chin onto her neck. As the stretcher passed beneath a light, she suddenly lurched up screaming . . . her body writhing but held in place by the straps.

Christ! thought Peter. Alison's next words!

I cried out and ran down the stars, but a . . . black major . . . stopped me and picked me up and held me.

A black major!

The black soldier had to be at the bottom of the stairs, near the light! *He* was what Alison's mother had seen!

Chancellor remembered other words. A command barked at him by a man in agony twenty-two years later in the late afternoon, still protecting a loved one who'd been driven out of her mind by an event so horrible she could never forget it.

Get by the light; put your face above the shade. It was not to show that his features were Western and not Oriental. It wasn't that at all! It was to show he was not *a black!*

Alison's mother had *not* been tortured by Chinese agents sending back a message to Army Intelligence. She had been raped! At an off-limits bar in the filthiest district of the Ginza, where she'd come for a connection, she had been dragged down an alley and raped!

"Oh, my *God*," whispered Peter in revulsion. "That's what you told him. That's what you kept hammering at; that's what you used. She was raped by blacks. She was trying to find a connection in a bar, and she got raped."

"It was the truth!"

"In one of those places it could have been anybody! *Anybody!* But it wasn't, so you *used* it! You blamed the blacks! Oh, *Christ!*" It was all Chancellor could do to restrain himself. He wanted to kill or maim, so complete was his abhorrence of this man. "You don't have to spell out the rest. It's goddamned clear! It's the information missing in MacAndrew's record. It's what's in Hoover's files! After his wife had been put in the hospital, you made sure he was sent back to Korea. But not to his *own* outfit! To another! To a black command! And somehow you relayed the battle plans—the *actual* strategy—back to the Chinese! It was so obvious! An officer's wife is raped, driven insane, by blacks, so he subjects black troops to murderous gunfire, willing to die with them if he has to, but above all, vengeance! A trap set by men in his own Army! Hundreds of men killed, hundreds missing, so the truth of what you did to his wife and probably dozens like her would never be known! Your experiments hidden! That's what you held over him: rape and genocide! The first he wouldn't talk about, the second he didn't understand. But he saw the connection between them! It must have paralyzed him!"

"Lies!" Ramirez's head moved back and forth convulsively. "That's not what happened. You've built a terrible lie!"

Peter stood over the brigadier in the last extremity of loathing. "You *look* like a man who's heard a lie," he said sarcastically. "No, General, you've just heard the truth. You've been running from it for twenty-two years."

Ramirez's head moved faster, the denial more emphatic.

"There's no proof!"

"There are questions. They lead to other questions. That's how it works. People in high places betray the rest of us who put them there. *Bastards!*" Chancellor thrust his left hand down and grabbed Ramirez by the shirt, pulling him forward, the gun inches from the general's eyes. "I don't want to talk to you anymore. You disgust me! I think I could pull this trigger and kill you, and that scares the hell out of me. So you do exactly what I tell you, or you won't live to do anything else. You go over to the telephone on your desk and you call wherever you had that major taken and you tell them to release him. Now!"

"No!"

In a single, swift movement Peter whipped the barrel of the Colt automatic across Ramirez's face. The skin broke; a trickle of blood rolled down the soldier's cheek. Chancellor felt nothing. There was something frightening in that absence of feeling. "Make that call."

Slowly Ramirez got to his feet, his eyes on the weapon, his hand touching the blood on his face. He picked up the phone and dialed.

"This is General Ramirez. I called for a special detail to be at my residence at eighteen-hundred for an arrest. The prisoner is a Major Brown. Release him."

Ramirez listened as the voice on the line spoke. Peter pressed the barrel of the automatic into the brigadier's temple.

"Do as I tell you," said Ramirez. "Return the major to his vehicle." He replaced the telephone, his hand still on the instrument. "He'll be here soon. The MP depot's ten minutes away."

"I just told you I didn't want to talk to you anymore, but I've changed my mind. We're going to wait for Brown, and you're going to tell me everything you know about Hoover's files."

"I know nothing."

"The hell you don't. You people are into this thing like it was a pocket of quicksand. You're choking in it. You removed eight months' worth of material from Mac-Andrew's service record."

"That's all we did."

"Eight months! And the dates corresponded to the events leading up to Chasŏng. All the incriminating material. Then the massacre where MacAndrew sent waves of black troops into suicidal gunfire. Everything but the truth! You knew where that material ended up!"

"Not at first." The general could barely be heard. "At first it was standard procedure. All compromising information about candidates for the Joint Chiefs is removed and placed in G-Two archives. Someone thought it was dangerous; it was routed to PSA."

"What's that?"

"Psychiatric Systems Analyses. Until recently certain people at the bureau had access. PSA deals with defectors, potential blackmail of high-ranking officers, espionage. Lots of things."

"Then, you knew it was in Hoover's files!"

"We found out."

"How?"

"A man named Longworth. He was a retired FBI agent living in Hawaii. He came back—for only a day, maybe two, I don't remember—and warned Hoover that he was going to be killed. For his files. Hoover went out of his mind. He combed through them, looking for anything that might lead to the identity of the killers. He came across Chasŏng, and we got a phone call. We swore we were not involved; we offered guarantees, protection, *anything*. Hoover just wanted us to know what he knew. Then, of course, he was killed."

Peter dropped the gun. The crash of metal against wood was loud and abrasive, but he did not hear it. He heard only the echo of the brigadier's last words.

Then, of course, he was killed. . . . Then, of course, he was killed. . . . Then, of course, he was killed.

Spoken as if the incredible information were neither electrifying nor even shocking, neither appalling nor even, perhaps, out of the ordinary. Instead, as though it were routine, common knowledge—data recorded and accepted and so entered into the books.

But it was not *real*. Other things were real, but not that. Not the assassination. That was the fantasy, the fiction that had propelled him into the nightmare, but it was the one thing that had never happened!

"What did you say?"

"Nothing you didn't know," said Ramirez, staring at the gun on the floor next to his shoes.

"Hoover died of heart failure. The medical examiner called it a cardiovascular disease. That's how he died! He was an old *man!*" Chancellor spoke without breathing.

The brigadier looked up into Peter's eyes. "Are you playing games? There was no autopsy. You know why and so do I."

"You tell me. Don't assume I know anything. Why wasn't there an autopsy?"

"Orders from Sixteen hundred."

"Who?"

"The White House."

"Why?"

"They killed him. If they didn't, they think they did. They think someone there did it. Or had it done. They give oblique orders over there, very ambiguous. You're either on the team or you're not; you learn how to read what's said. He had to be killed. What's the difference who did it?"

"Because of the files?"

"Partly. But they're records; they can be burned, destroyed. It was the dispatch units. They'd gone too far."

"Dispatch units? What are you talking about?"

"For God's sake, Chancellor! You know what I'm talking about, or you wouldn't be here! You wouldn't have done what you did!"

Peter grabbed Ramirez by the cloth of his shirt. "What are dispatch units? What were Hoover's dispatch units?"

The general's eyes were flat. It was as if he did not care any longer. "Assassination teams," he said. "Men assigned to engineer situations in which specific people were killed. Either by provoking violence resulting in local police or national-guard action, or by hiring psychopaths, known killers or potential killers, to do the work and cutting them down when it was done. It was all once removed, divided secretly inside the bureau. No one knows how far it went. How far it was going. What assassinations could be attributed to Hoover. Or who would be called an enemy next."

Slowly, staring in disbelief as the throbbing in his temples increased, Chancellor released the brigadier. Blinding white spots converged again in front of his eyes.

Dispatch units! *Execution squads!*

His own words came back to him. He saw the page and read it in his mind's eye with terrible pain.

"Did you know about these . . . execution squads?"

"There've been rumors."

"What did you hear?"

"Nothing specific. No proof. . . . Hoover departmentalizes everything. Everybody He does it all secretly. . . . That way everyone stays in line."

"Gestapo!"

"What did you hear?"

"Only that there were final solutions. . . ."

"Final—Oh, my God."

"If we ever needed a last, overwhelming justification, I think we have it. Hoover will be killed two weeks from Monday, the files taken."

It was all true. It had been true from the beginning. God in heaven, it was never fiction! it was fact!

J. Edgar Hoover had not died the natural death of a sick old man. He had been assassinated.

And with sudden clarity Peter knew who had called for that assassination. It had not been the White House. Instead, it had been a group of men above reproach who made decisions of such impact that they were often the unseen, unelected force that ran the nation.

"You can't do it! You have everything you need. Bring him to trial! Let him face the judgment of the courts! Of the country!"

"You don't understand. . . . There's not a court in the land, not a judge, not a member of the House or of the Senate, not the President or any of his cabinet, who can bring him to trial. It's beyond that."

"No, it isn't! There are laws!"

"There are the files. . . . People would be reached . . . by others who have to survive." . . .

"Then, you're no better than he is."

All true.

Inver Brass had demanded the death of J. Edgar Hoover, and the order had been carried out.

It happened so fast Chancellor could only react with a twisting, lurching movement of his body. He felt hands on his chest, then Ramirez's shoulder against his ribs. He fell, turning sideways to avoid a second blow, but he was too late.

The brigadier had fallen to one knee, his right hand shooting out for the gun on the floor. He grabbed it, twisting it firmly in his grip, his fingers expertly around the handle, his thumb flicking upward instinctively to check the safety. He raised it.

Peter understood that if he had to die at this moment, he had to die trying to avoid that death. He sprang off his feet, hurling himself at the general.

Again he was too late. The thunderous explosion filled the room. Blood and tissue slapped against the nearby wall. The smoke from the barrel billowed in an acrid cloud.

Below him the soldier was dead. Brigadier General Ramirez, source control of Chasŏng, had blown off most of his head.

40

The gunshot—the explosion—was so shattering it had to have been heard blocks away. Someone would have called the police. He could not be seen leaving the house. He had to get out the back way *quickly*, into the darkness, into the shadows.

He ran in blind panic through a narrow hallway into a small kitchen. He lurched across the tiled floor to the back door, opened it cautiously, and let himself out, spinning around the door frame, pressing his back against the wall.

The house that faced him was separated from Ramirez's by a tall hedge; he could see a driveway beyond the garage. Peter leaped off the small back porch onto the lawn and ran toward the hedge, shouldering his way through the thick branches until he was on the other side. He raced down the driveway into the street, turned left and kept running. Brown's Triumph was in the next block, back on Ramirez's street. At the corner he turned left again; a siren was whining harshly in the distance, coming closer. He slowed down and tried to walk casually; the police would not overlook a running man after reports of a gunshot.

He reached the Triumph and climbed inside. Through the rear window he could see that a small, excited crowd had gathered on Ramirez's lawn. The flashing lights of a patrol car accompanied the approaching siren.

He heard the sound of another motor, this from the opposite direction. He turned; it was the military police vehicle. It stopped by the side of the Triumph. Brown got out, taking his keys from one of the soldiers.

They saluted the major; he did not return their salutes. The army car started up.

"Good. You're back," said Brown, opening the door.

"We've got to get out of here! Right away!"

"What's the matter? What's the crowd——?"

"Ramirez is dead."

Brown said nothing. He climbed behind the wheel and started the Triumph's engine. They sped off down the block, when suddenly coming toward them was a limousine, its headlights blinding, its outlines those of a giant killer shark slicing through dark waters. Peter could not help himself; he stared into the windows as the automobile raced past.

The driver was intent only on reaching his destination. Through the rear window, Chancellor saw what that destination was: Ramirez's house.

The driver was black. Peter closed his eyes, trying to think.

"What happened?" asked Brown, turning the Triumph west toward the highway. "Did you kill him?"

"No. I might have, but I didn't. You were right; he shot himself. He couldn't face Chasŏng. He was responsible for the massacre. It was engineered to keep the wraps on what they'd done to MacAndrew's wife."

Brown was silent for a moment. When he spoke, it was with loathing as well as disbelief. "*Bastards!*"

"If the story of MacAndrew's wife had been broken," Peter continued, "it would have led to the exposure of dozens of other such operations. Other experiments. They knew what they were doing."

"Ramirez admitted it?"

Peter looked at Brown. "Let's say it came out. What's mind-blowing is the rest. I'm not sure I can even say the words. It's that crazy."

"Hoover's files?"

"No. Hoover. He was killed. He was assassinated! It was true all along! It was never a lie!"

"Take it easy. I thought you said Varak told you it was a lie."

"*He* was lying! He was protecting——" Peter stopped. *Varak*. The *specialist*. The man of a hundred weapons, a dozen faces . . . assorted names. Good God! It had been there all the time, and he hadn't seen it! *Longworth*. Varak *had* assumed the name of an agent named Longworth on the night of May first. It *wasn't* someone else. Varak masquerading as Longworth had been one of the three men, without accountability, who had entered the bureau the night before Hoover died—which meant they *knew* that death was certain! They found half the files missing; that part was true. And Varak had given his life to trace them, then protected Bravo, protected with his life the extraordinary diplomat known to the world as Munro St. Claire.

Varak had been Hoover's assassin! What had Frederick Wells said? *Varak was the killer, not Inver Brass . . . I can and will raise disturbing questions . . . from the tenth of April through the night of May first . . . Varak has those files!*

Which meant Munro St. Claire had the files. Varak *himself* had been lied to, manipulated!

By his mentor Bravo.

And now the cult of Chasŏng had zeroed in on Ramirez. The cult given influence and power by Munro St. Claire, who had used Varak as he had used everyone else. Including one Peter Chancellor.

It was all coming to an end. The forces were closing in, colliding, as Carlos Montelán had said they would collie. It would be finished this night, one way or the other.

"I'm going to tell you everything I know," he said. "Drive to Arundel; they can't follow us. I'll tell you on the way. I want you to stay with Alison. When we get there, I want to take your car. I want you to wait awhile, then call Munro St. Claire in Washington. Tell him I'll be waiting for him at Genesis's house on the bay. He's to come alone. I'll be watching; he won't find me if he's not alone."

41

The sound of waves slapping against rocks drifted up from the water's edge. Peter lay in the wet grass. The air was cold as the ground was cold, the wind from the bay carried in gusts, whistling through the tall trees that bordered the white lawn. A man who had betrayed him, a man he had believed was his friend, had taught him things in the midst of that betrayal. That was why he was where he was, his eyes on the stone gates of the entrance fifty yards away and on the road beyond.

When making a contact, position was everything. Protect yourself by being able to observe all approaching vehicles; keep rapid, undetectable escape available.

Friends were enemies, and enemies taught one strategies with which to fight them. It was part of the insanity that was all too real.

He saw headlights in the distance, about a half mile away. Peter could not be sure, but the lights seemed to sway back and forth. Every now and then they appeared to be stationary, as if the car had stopped, only to start swaying again. Had the circumstances been different, Chancellor thought, he might have been watching a drunken driver trying to find his way home. Was it possible this powerful manipulator of men and governments had been drinking? Ramirez had blown his own head off because he could not face Chasŏng. Were the revelations about Inver Brass more than St. Claire wanted to hear in a stable frame of mind?

The automobile came haltingly through the gates. Peter momentarily suspended his breath, his eyes riveted on the terrible sight. It was the silver Mark IV Continental! That St. Claire would drive it to their confrontation was confirmation that the man, like the vehicle, was a monster.

He watched as the silver obscenity rolled around the circular drive to the wide steps of the front entrance; then he focused his eyes back on the road beyond the gateposts. He peered into the darkness, his concentration total. There were no headlights on the road, nor any black shapes against gray darkness that would be a vehicle traveling with its headlights off.

He remained in the grass for nearly five minutes, alternately watching St. Claire. The diplomat had gotten out of the car, climbed the steps, and walked to the end of the porch. He was standing by the railing, staring out at the water.

Another man, a compassionate man, had stood on a fisherman's dock staring out at another stretch of water twelve hours before. At dawn. That man was dead, led into a trap by an enemy, cut down by fanatics who obeyed the instructions of a monster.

Chancellor was satisfied: Munro St. Claire had come alone.

Peter rose from the grass and walked across the lawn toward the Victorian porch. St. Claire remained at the railing; Chancellor approached him from behind. He reached into his pockets with both hands and pulled out Brown's automatic in his right, the flashlight in his left. When he was within eight feet, he leveled both up at St. Claire and snapped on the light.

"Keep your right arm above you," he ordered. "With your left reach into your pocket and throw me the keys to your car."

It took the ambassador several seconds to answer. He seemed shaken. The suddenness of Chancellor's appearance, the blinding beam of light, the curt instructions barked from the darkness momentarily paralyzed him. Peter was grateful for an enemy's training.

"I don't have the keys, young man. They're in the car."

"I don't believe you," said Chancellor angrily. "Give me those keys!"

"I suggest we return to the car, and you can see for yourself. I'll keep both hands above me if you wish."

"I wish."

The keys were in the ignition of the Mark IV. Chancellor held the old man against the hood as he checked the diplomat's pockets and chest. St. Claire carried no weapon. The realization was bewildering, as bewildering as the keys left in the Mark IV. An automobile was an escape; the leader of Inver Brass would know that.

The flashlight off, Peter shoved the automatic into St. Claire's back. They walked up the steps and out to the front of the porch. He spun the old man around against the railing and stood facing him.

"If I was late, forgive me," said the ambassador. "I haven't driven in nearly twelve years. I tried to explain that to your unidentified friend on the telephone, but he wouldn't listen."

St. Claire's statement made sense. It explained the swaying headlights. It also proved that St. Claire was frightened. He would never have taken such risks at night on the highways and back roads if he had been anything else. "But you came anyway, didn't you?"

"You knew I couldn't refuse. You found my man. You discovered the transmitters. I imagine they could be traced to me."

"Could they?"

"I'm not an expert at such things. Varak was, but I'm not. I'm not even sure how they were obtained."

"I can't accept that. The man who runs Inver Brass is much more resourceful."

St. Claire drew himself up in the darkness. The sound of the name seemed to pain him. "You've been told, then."

"Does it surprise you? I told you I knew the identities of Venice, Christopher, Paris, and Banner. And Bravo. Why not Inver Brass?"

"How much have you learned since?"

"Enough to frighten me to death. Forty years, countless millions. Unknown men who ran the country."

"You're exaggerating. We came to the aid of the country during periods of crisis. That's far more accurate."

"Who determined what a crisis was? You?"

"Crises have a way of being apparent."

"Not always. Not to everybody."

"We had access to information not available to 'everybody.'"

"And you acted on it rather than making the information public."

"They were essentially acts of charity. Ultimately for the good of that 'everybody' you refer to. We never acted for ourselves." St. Claire's voice rose, his defense of Inver Brass deeply felt.

"There are ways to provide charity openly. Why didn't you use them?"

"That sort of charity is always temporary. It doesn't attack root causes."

"And root causes can't be left to the judgments of those elected to understand them, is that it?"

"You're oversimplifying our viewpoint, and you know it, Mr. Chancellor."

"I know I'd rather take my chances with an imperfect system I can follow than one I can't see."

"That's sophistry. It's quite easy for you to argue civics, but while you're arguing, a thousand pockets of frustration are inexorably spreading. If they touch, there'll be an eruption of violence beyond your imagination. When that happens, freedom of choice will be eliminated in the cause of adequate diet. It's as simple as that. Over the years we've tried to control that spread. Would you want to stop us?"

Peter conceded the logic of St. Claire's reasoning, knowing that this brilliant, devious man, masked in such goodness, was forcing him on the defensive, veering him away from the point of their confrontation. He had to remind himself that St. Claire was a monster; there was blood on his hands.

"There are other ways," he said. "Other solutions."

"There may be, but I'm not sure we'll find them in our lifetimes. Certainly not mine. Perhaps in the act of seeking solutions there's the prevention of violence we hope for."

Peter attacked suddenly. "You found one solution that was rooted in violence, though, didn't you? The bait was the truth, after all."

"What?"

"You killed Hoover! Inver Brass ordered his assassination!"

At the words St. Claire stiffened; a short stifled cry came from his throat. His confidence vanished. He was suddenly an old man accused of a terrible crime.

"Where did—? . . . Who—?" He could not articulate the question.

"For the moment it doesn't matter. What matters is that the order was given and carried out. You executed a man without a trial, without the judgment of an open court. That's what's supposed to separate us from a large part of this world, Mr. Ambassador. From that violence you hate so."

"There were reasons!"

"Because you believed he was a killer? Because you'd heard he had his assassination teams, his 'dispatch units'?"

"In large measure, yes!"

"Not good enough. If you knew it, you should have said it! All of you."

"It couldn't have been done that way! I told you, there were reasons."

"*Other* reasons, you mean?"

"Yes!"

"The files?"

"For God's sake, yes! The files!"

"*You can't do it! You have everything you need. Bring him to trial! Let him face the judgment of the courts! Of the country! There are laws!*"

"*There are the files. . . . People would be reached . . . by others who have to survive.*" . . .

"*Then, you're no better than he is.*"

"You're better than he was," said Chancellor quietly.

"We believed with all our hearts and souls that we were." St. Claire was passing through the first shock waves; he was finding part of the control he had lost. "I can't believe this. I misread Varak so completely."

"Don't try that," replied Peter coldly. "I despise everything he was, but Varak gave his life for you. The truth is you misled him."

"Wrong! Never!"

"The whole time! Varak was 'Longworth,' and 'Longworth' got into the bureau the night Hoover was killed. Varak got those files! He gave them to *you!*"

"*A* through *L*, yes! We've never denied it. They were destroyed. Not *M* through *Z!* They were missing. They *are* missing!"

"*No!* Varak thought they were missing because that's what you wanted him to think!"

"You're insane!" St. Claire whispered.

"There were two other men with Varak that night! One of them—maybe both working together—emptied and switched the folders, or combined them, or just lied. I don't know how, but that's where it was done. You knew Varak wouldn't be compromised about the files, so you went around him."

St. Claire shook his head, his expression tortured. "No. You're wrong. The theory is plausible, even ingenious, I admit that. But it simply *is not true!*"

"Those two men disappeared! Their names were covers, their identities impossible to trace!"

"For a different purpose! Hoover had to be eliminated. The country couldn't stand even the hint of another assassination. There would have been chaos; it would have fueled the fanatics who want to run this government in violation of every constitutional principle! We couldn't allow any traces. You must believe that!"

"You've lied and lied and lied! There's no way you can make me believe anything."

St. Claire paused, reflective. "Perhaps there is. By explaining why, then going one step further: putting my life and everything I've stood for for over fifty years of service in your hands."

"The purpose first," said Peter harshly. "Why was Hoover murdered?"

"He was the absolute ruler of a government unto itself. There was no clear-cut chain of command. His government was amorphous, without structure; he kept it that way. He had gone way beyond the severest illegalities. No one really knew how far, but there was sufficient evidence pointing to the killings you spoke of; we knew about the blackmail. It reached into the Oval Office. All this might, in itself, have justified the decision, but there was a further consideration that made it irrevocable. An amorphous chain of command was organizing; both within and outside the bureau. Viciously unprincipled men were circling around Hoover, flattering, cajoling, pretending to worship. They had only one objective: his private files. With them they could rule the country. He had to be eliminated before any pacts were made."

St. Claire stopped. He was becoming tired; his own doubts showed on his face.

"I don't agree with you," said Peter, "but things are clearer. How are you going to put fifty years of service in my hands?"

St. Claire took a deep breath. "I believe in man's instinct at certain moments to perceive the truth no matter what. I think this is one of those moments. Only two men on the face of the earth knew every step of Hoover's assassination. The man who created the plan and myself. That man is dead; he died in front of you. I'm left. That plan is your final proof, for no strategy conceived by

human beings is perfect; something is always left undone
if others know where to look. By telling you I not only
place my life in your hands, but far more important, I
place the work of a lifetime at your disposal. What you do
with it means more to me than whatever time I have left.
Will you accept this moment? Will you let me *try* to convince you?"

"Go ahead."

As St. Claire spoke, Peter understood the devastating
nature of what was being given him. The ambassador was
right on two points. Chancellor knew instinctively that he
was hearing the truth, and beyond that certainty, he
realized that Hoover's murder was within reach of being
confirmed. St. Claire would not use names—other than
Varak's—but it was reasonable to assume that identities
could be uncovered.

An actress whose husband had been destroyed during
the McCarthy madness; two former Marine communications specialists, both experienced in electronics and telephone interceptions, one an expert marksman; an operative
from Britain's M16, known to have worked closely with the
National Security Council during the Berlin crisis; an
American surgeon living in Paris, an expatriate socialist
whose wife and son had been killed in an accident with
an FBI vehicle that had been involved in illegal, unwar-
ranted surveillance. These had been the team. The threads
were uncut; they could be followed to their sources. The
plan itself was the work of an intelligence genius, even to
the subtle inclusion of a White House advisor's name.

It accounted for Ramirez's judgment: *There was no
autopsy. . . . Orders from Sixteen hundred. . . . The White
House . . . killed him. If they didn't, they think they did.
They think someone over there did it. Or had it done.*

What an incredible mind Varak had possessed!

St. Claire finished, exhausted. "Have I told you the
truth? Do you believe me now?"

"As far as we've gone, yes. There's one step further.
If I sense a lie, it's all a lie. Is that fair?"

"There are no more lies. Not where you are concerned. It's fair."

"What's the meaning of Chasŏng?"

"I don't know."

"It's not significant?"

"Quite the contrary. Varak called it a 'decoy.' He believed it was the key to the identity of the man of Inver Brass who betrayed us."

"Explain that."

Once again St. Claire breathed deeply, his exhaustion even more apparent. "It concerned MacAndrew. Something happened at Chasŏng to discredit his command. Thus the phrase 'Mac the Knife, killer of Chasŏng.' There was an enormous loss of life; MacAndrew was held responsible. Once his guilt was established, it was expected to stop there. Varak thought that it shouldn't. He felt there was something else, something that involved MacAndrew's wife."

"Did you ever learn the composition of the troops at Chasŏng?"

"The composition?"

"The racial composition." Chancellor watched the old man closely.

"No. I wasn't aware that there was any such thing as a 'racial composition.'"

"Suppose I told you that the casualty records of Chasŏng are among the most closely guarded secrets in the Army archives; hundreds were killed and listed as missing. Only thirty-seven survived, six of whom are incapable of communicating. That the thirty-one remaining survivors are in thirty-one separate hospitals across the country. Would all this mean anything to you?"

"It would be further confirmation of the paranoia that exists in the Pentagon. Not unlike the Hoover regime at the bureau."

"That's all?"

"We're speaking of wasted lives. Perhaps *paranoia* is too vague a term."

"I'd say so. Because it wasn't an unnecessary loss of life due to MacAndrew. It was a trap set by our own Army. It was a conspiracy of command. Those troops—to the last soldier—were black. It was racial murder."

St. Claire held his position by the railing, his expression frozen. Seconds passed; the only sounds were the waves against the rocks and the gusts of wind off the water. The ambassador found his voice.

"In the name of God, *why?*"

Peter stared at the diplomat, feeling both relief and bewilderment. The old man was not lying; his shock was genuine. St. Claire was many things that were unforgivable, but he was not the betrayer of Inver Brass. He did not have the files. Peter returned the gun to his pocket.

"To cover an intelligence operation that involved MacAndrew's wife. To stop MacAndrew from asking questions. If it had been unearthed, it would have led to the exposure of dozens of similar operations. Men and women placed on drugs, on hallucinogens. Experiments that would have blown up in the faces of those who conceived them, destroyed their careers, and probably gotten several of them killed by the man they had led into the trap: Mac-Andrew."

"And for *those* reasons they *sacrificed*— Oh, my *God*!"

"That's what Chasŏng means," said Peter quietly. "Everything else was Varak's decoy."

St. Claire stepped forward, his legs unsteady, his features contorted. "Do you realize what you're saying? Inver Brass— Only one member of Inver Brass is——"

"He's dead."

The breath left St. Claire's lungs. For an instant his whole body was contorted. Chancellor continued softly.

"Sutherland's dead. So is Jacob Dreyfus. And you don't have the files. That leaves two men. Wells and Montelán."

The news of Dreyfus's death was almost more than St. Claire could absorb. His eyes seemed to float in their sockets. He held the railing, gripping it awkwardly in his hands.

"Gone. They're gone." The words were whispered in sorrow.

Peter approached the old man, feeling compassion and relief. At last there was an ally! A powerful man who could end the nightmare.

"Mr. Ambassador?"

At the sound of the title, St. Claire looked up at Peter. There was an unmistakable flash of gratitude in his eyes. "Yes?"

"I should leave you alone for a while, but I can't do that. People have traced me. I think they've found out what I've learned. MacAndrew's daughter is in hiding; two people are with her, but that's no guarantee she's safe. I can't go to the police, I can't get protection. I need your help."

The diplomat was finding what was left of his strength.

"You'll have it, of course," he began. "And you're quite right, there's no time for remorse. Thoughts can come later. Not now."

"What can we do?"

"Cut out the cancer in the full knowledge that the patient may die. And in this case the patient is dead already. Inver Brass is gone."

"May I take you to my friends? To MacAndrew's daughter?"

"Yes, of course." St. Claire pushed away from the railing. "No, it would be a waste of time. The telephone is faster. In spite of what you think, there are people in Washington who can be trusted. The vast majority, in fact. You'll have your protection." St. Claire gestured toward the front entrance; he reached into his pocket for a key.

They had to step in quickly. The diplomat explained: The alarm system was suspended by a key for ten seconds while they entered, reactivated with the closing of the door.

Inside, St. Claire went through the arch into the huge sitting room, turning on the lights. He walked to a telephone, picked it up, stopped, and replaced it in its cradle. He turned to Chancellor.

"The best protection," he said, "is to stop the attackers. Wells or Montelán, either or both."

"My guess would be Wells."

"Why? What did he say to you?"

"That the country needed him."

"He's right. His arrogance in no way vitiates his brilliance."

"The files panicked him. He said he was part of them."

"He was. Is."

"I don't understand."

"Wells is his middle name, his mother's. The files make that clear. It was legally assumed shortly after his parents were divorced. He was an infant. His name at birth was Reisler. It's in the missing files, M through Z. Does the name mean anything to you?"

"Yes." Peter remembered. The name evoked an image of a strutting, vicious figure of thirty-five years ago. "Frederick Reisler. One of the leaders of the German-American Bund. I used him as the basis for a character in *Reichstag!* He was a stockbroker."

"A genius on the Street. He funneled millions to Hitler. Wells has been running from that stigma all his life. More important, he's served his country selflessly to make amends. He's terrified the files will expose a legacy that's tortured him."

"Then, I think it's him. The heritage fits."

"Perhaps, but I doubt it. Unless his cunning is beyond anything I can conceive of, why would he fear exposure if he has the files? What did the *hidalgo* say?"

"What?"

"Montelán. Paris. Far more attractive than Banner, yet infinitely more arrogant. Generations of Castilian wealth, immense family influence, stolen and stripped by the Falangists. Carlos has a hatred in him. He despises all sources of absolute control. I sometimes think he searches the world for deposed aristocrats——"

"What did you just say?" broke in Chancellor. "He despises what?"

"Absolutists. The fascist mentality in all forms."

"No. You said *control. Sources of control!*"

"Yes, I did."

Ramirez! thought Peter. The source control of Chasŏng. Was that it? Was that the connection? Ramirez. Montelán. Two aristocrats of the same blood. Both filled with hatred. Appealing to—using—the same minorities they held in such contempt?

"I haven't got time to explain," Peter said, suddenly sure. "But it's Montelán! Can you reach him?"

"Of course. Each member of Inver Brass can be contacted within minutes. There are codes he can't ignore."

"Montelán might."

The ambassador arched his eyebrows. "He won't know why I'm calling. His own fear of exposure will force him to respond. But, of course, exposure isn't enough, is it?" St. Claire paused; Chancellor did not interrupt. "He must be killed. A final life demanded by Inver Brass. How tragically it's all turned out." St. Claire picked up the telephone. Instantly, he stopped, his ashen face now white. "It's dead."

"It *can't* be!"

"It wasn't a moment ago."

Without warning, the shattering sound of a bell filled the cavernous room.

Chancellor spun toward the archway, his right hand lunging into his pocket, gripping the small automatic, pulling it out.

A gunshot accompanied the smashing of glass from a window on the porch. Quick, iced pain spread throughout Peter's arm and shoulder; blood appeared on his jacket. He dropped the gun to the floor.

There was the crash of wood against wood from the hallway. The front door was slammed back into the wall. Two slender men—black men in tight-fitting trousers and dark shirts—raced into the room with catlike speed and crouched, still standing, gripping weapons leveled at Chancellor.

Behind them an immense figure walked out of the darkness of the hall into the eerie light of the room.

It was Daniel Sutherland.

He stood motionless, staring at Peter, his eyes contemptuous. He held out his huge hand and opened his palm. In it was a capsule. He closed his fist and turned his hand downward; his fingers ground against his palm.

A dark red fluid burst from his fist, covering his skin and dripping to the floor.

"The theater, Mr. Chancellor. The art of deception."

42

Everything happened in rapid, crisp movements that were marks of professionals. Other blacks entered; the house was surrounded. Munro St. Claire was held by the table. Peter was pulled away, a strip of cloth strapped tightly over his shoulder wound. A man was dispatched to the gates to await the local police with the proper explanation of why the alarm went off.

Daniel Sutherland nodded, turned, and walked back into the darkness of the hallway. Again, without warning, the inconceivable happened. The man holding Bravo released him and stepped away; sounds of explosions filled the room.

Munro St. Claire was impaled against the wall, riddled by gunfire, his body host to a fusillade of bullets. He slumped to the floor, his wide eyes dead and unbelieving.

"Oh, my *God*. . . ." Chancellor heard the terrified words, unaware that they were his. Aware only of the horror he had witnessed.

In seconds Sutherland returned from the dark hallway. His eyes were sad, his erect bearing somehow burdened with grief.

He spoke softly as he looked down at the fallen St. Claire. "You would never have understood. Nor would the others. Those files must not be destroyed. They must be used to right a great many wrongs." The judge raised his eyes and looked at Peter. "We gave Jacob a more proper burial than you accorded him. His death will be announced in time. As will the others."

"You've killed them all," whispered Chancellor.

"Yes," replied Sutherland. "Banner two nights ago, and Paris last night."

"You'll be caught."

"Mrs. Montelán believes her husband has been sent to the Far East by the State Department. We have men at State; the proper documents will be recorded, and Montelán will be reported killed by terrorists. It's not so unusual these days. Wells had a fatal automobile accident on a wet country road off the highway. You were of considerable help in his case. His car was found in the morning."

Sutherland spoke matter-of-factly, as if killing and violence were perfectly natural phenomena, neither unusual nor to be dwelt upon.

"You have men at the State Department?" said Peter, bewildered. "Then you were able to trace the sterile house in Saint Michaels."

"We could and did."

"But you didn't have to. You had O'Brien."

"I don't think you should try to deceive us, Mr. Chancellor. We're not in the pages of a book. We're all real here."

"What do you mean?"

"You know precisely what I mean. We never had O'Brien. We had others. Not him."

"Not him. . . ." Chancellor could only repeat Sutherland's words.

"A resourceful man, Mr. O'Brien," continued Sutherland. "A very brave man. He fired into the fuel tanks, setting the boats on fire, then risked his life to lead us away from your car. Courage matching ingenuity, an estimable combination."

Peter could not repress the sound of the sharp intake of breath that escaped from his throat. O'Brien had not betrayed them!

Sutherland was talking, but the words had no meaning. Nothing had meaning any longer.

"What did you say?" asked Peter, looking around at the scrubbed, clean faces of the blacks. There were five men now, each with a weapon in his hand.

"I said as gently as possible that your death can't be avoided."

"Why didn't you kill me before?"

"In the beginning we tried to. Then I reconsidered. You'd begun your manuscript. We had to prove you were mad. People have read what you've written; we have no way of knowing how many. You've come remarkably close to the truth. We couldn't allow that. The country must believe those files were destroyed. You wrote otherwise. Fortunately, your behavior has been questioned, and there are some who think you've gone out of your mind. You sustained head injuries in an accident that nearly killed you. You lost a loved one, and your recovery has been abnormally slow. Your paranoid sense of conspiracy is displayed in each of your books, progressively more acute. The final proof of your instability——"

"Final proof?" interrupted Peter, dazed by Sutherland's argument.

"Yes," continued the judge. "The final proof of your instability would come when you swore I was dead. Needless to say, my reaction would be one of amusement. I had met you once, the memory of that meeting dim. It wasn't particularly memorable. You'd be dismissed as a maniac."

"A maniac," Peter said. "The bureau had 'maniacs.' Hoover's inheritors. They worked with you."

"Three did. They didn't understand it was to be a short-lived association. We had the same objective: Hoover's files. What they did not know was that we had half of them, the half that weren't destroyed. We wanted known fanatics who would be caught and killed, the entire files presumably having disappeared with their deaths.

Their other function was to drive you to the precipice. If they killed you, it was on their heads. You were a harmless meddler, but they took you seriously."

"You *are* going to kill me. You wouldn't tell me these things if you weren't." Peter made the observation calmly, almost clinically.

"I'm not without feeling. I don't wish to take your life; I derive no pleasure from it. But I have to. The least I can do is try to satisfy your curiosity. And I do have an offer to make."

"What offer?"

"The girl's life. There's no reason for Miss Mac-Andrew to die. Whatever she thinks she knows will have been told her by a writer who recognized his own madness and killed himself. The pathology is classic for creative people. Depression sets in when the lines of reality are blurred."

Peter wondered at his own calm. "Thank you. You put me in company I'm not sure I deserve. What's the exchange? I'll do anything you say."

"Where's O'Brien?"

"What? . . ." Chancellor drew out the word, bewildered.

"Where's O'Brien? Did you speak with him while you were with Ramirez? He can't go to the bureau or the police. We'd know about it if he did. Where is he?"

Peter watched Sutherland's eyes closely. *Look to the fiction,* he thought. Something was better than nothing, no matter how remote the possibilities. And there was a possibility.

"If I tell you, what guarantees do I have that you'll let her live?"

"Ultimately, none. Only my word."

"Your *word*? You're the one who's crazy! Accept the word of the man who betrayed his friends, betrayed Inver Brass?"

"There's no inconsistency. Inver Brass was formed to give extraordinary aid to the country in times of desperate need—to *all* the men and women of this country, because this nation was for all its people. What has become apparent is that the country is *not* for all its people. It never will be. It must be *forced* to include those it would prefer to overlook. The nation has betrayed *me,* Mr. Chancellor. And millions like me. That fact does not alter who

I am. It may chango *what* I am, but not my values. My word is one of them. You have it."

Peter's mind raced, remembering, selecting. O'Brien had only one place to go after the Chesapeake marina, one place where they had not been followed. The motel in Ocean City. It would be there he would wait—a day at least for Alison and Peter to make contact. Quinn had nowhere else to go.

Look to the fiction; there is nothing else left.

In *Counterstrike!* a telephone call was made to enlist help in an escape. The method was simple: A false message was given, logical to those who overheard it but virtually meaningless to the receiver. In it was hidden a clue to a specific location. It was up to the receiver to figure out where.

"A trade, then," said Peter. "O'Brien for MacAndrew's daughter."

"That does not include Major Brown. He's not part of the exchange. He's our property."

"You know about him?"

"Of course. From the data-processing center in McLean. Within minutes of the Chasŏng records being pulled, we were aware of it."

"I see. You're going to kill him?"

"That depends. We don't know him. It may well be he'll be assigned to a base hospital thousands of miles away. We do not indiscriminately take life."

You'll kill him, thought Chancellor. *Once you know him, you'll kill him.*

"You're telling me you know where Brown and Alison are," said Peter.

"We do. In Arundel Village. We have a man there, outside the hotel."

"I want her driven into Washington where I can speak with her."

"Demands, Mr. Chancellor?"

"If you want O'Brien."

"She won't be harmed. You have my word."

"Let's call it the initial proof that you'll keep it. For God's sake, don't push me. I don't want to die. I'm frightened." Peter kept his voice low; it was not difficult to be convincing.

"What guarantee do *I* have?" asked the judge. "How will you deliver O'Brien?"

"We'll have to get to a telephone. This one's dead, but you know that. I only have a number and a room. I have no idea where." Chancellor raised his arm to look at his watch. The movement caused a sharp pain in his wounded shoulder. "O'Brien should be there for another twenty to thirty minutes. After that he's to call me."

"What's the telephone number?"

"That won't do you any good; he's fifty miles away. He knows my voice. He worked out a code for me to use and one of several places to meet during specific times." Peter's mind raced as he spoke. Several nights ago O'Brien had used a fictitious pay telephone on Wisconsin Avenue as a cover for a second location, a second phone booth, where Peter was to go to take his call. There was a pay phone at a gas station outside of Salisbury. Quinn and Alison had been there with him when he'd called Morgan in New York. O'Brien would remember that booth.

"It's two fifteen. Where could you meet at this hour?" Sutherland stood motionless, his voice wary.

"A gas station near Salisbury; I'm to confirm it. He'll want me to describe the car I'm driving. And I don't think he'll show himself if he sees people in the car with me. You'll have to conceal yourselves."

"It's not a problem. What are the words of the code?" asked the judge. "The precise words."

"They don't mean anything. He was reading a newspaper."

"What are they?"

" 'The senator called a last-minute quorum on the defense expenditures.' "

Chancellor winced and reached across his chest to hold his wounded shoulder. The gesture diminished any importance Peter might have given to the meaning of the code. They were merely words chosen at random from a newspaper.

"We'll use the ambassador's car," said Sutherland finally. "You'll drive the last few miles. Until then you'll ride in the back with me. Two of my men will accompany us. When you take the wheel, they'll conceal themselves. I'm sure you'll cooperate fully."

"I expect your cooperation, too. I want your man away from Arundel. I want Alison driven to Washington. Brown can do that; you can go after him later. How far's the nearest telephone?"

"On the table, Mr. Chancellor. Or will be in a matter of minutes." The judge turned to the muscular black on his left. He spoke quietly in an unfamiliar language.

It was the language shouted at the Chesapeake marina. Shouted in defiance at the moment of death. The language Varak had not understood.

The slender black man nodded and ran quickly into the hallway and out the front door.

"The telephone will be reconnected," Sutherland explained. "The wires were not severed, only placed on an intermediate circuit that does not break the terminal line." The judge paused, then continued. "I spoke in Ashanti. It was the language of the African Gold Coast in the seventeenth and eighteenth centuries. It's not easy to learn; there's no language like it. We can converse anywhere, among anyone; relay instructions, issue orders without being understood."

Sutherland turned to the two men across the room. Again he spoke in the strange-sounding Ashanti. The two blacks put their weapons in their belts and walked rapidly to St. Claire's dead body. They picked it up and carried it out.

The telephone rang once. "It's fixed," Sutherland said. "Call O'Brien. Our man is listening on the line. If you say anything unacceptable, the connection will be broken, the woman killed."

Peter walked to the telephone. St. Claire's blood formed jagged blots and streaks on the wall next to the table. He could feel it beneath the soles of his shoes. He picked up the phone.

He dialed the number of the motel in Ocean City and asked the switchboard for Upper South Suite. The room phone rang; the wait was unbearable; *O'Brien wasn't there!*

Then he heard the click and a quiet "Yes?"

"Quinn?"

"Peter! My God, where *are* you? I've been——"

"There's no time!" interrupted Chancellor, speaking in uncharacteristic anger in the hope that O'Brien would look for a message in his words. "You asked for a goddamned code, so I'm giving it to you. 'The senator called a last-minute quorum over the defense expenditures.' Wasn't that it? If it isn't, it's close enough."

"What the hell——?"

"I want to meet as soon as possible!" Again the interruption was abrasive, discourteous, on the edge of contempt. *So out of character, so inconsistent.* "It's between two and three in the morning. According to your schedule that's the gas station on the road to Salisbury. I'll be driving a light-colored Continental. A silver Mark IV. Be sure you're alone!"

There was a brief silence on the line. Peter stared at the blood-soaked wallpaper and closed his eyes, his face turned away from Sutherland. When he heard Quinn's words, he felt like crying. Tears of relief. "All *right*," said O'Brien, his voice as hostile as Chancellor's. "A Mark IV. I'll be there. And for your information, a code isn't stupid. By using it I know you're not under pressure. And with you, you son of a bitch, that's rare. See you in an hour."

O'Brien hung up. *He had understood. Quinn's final words confirmed it. They were as out of character as his own. The false message had carried the right meaning.*

Peter faced the judge. "Now it's your turn. Call Arundel."

Sutherland sat beside him in the back seat of the Continental, the two blacks in front. They sped south over country roads, across the Choptank River, past signs that proclaimed the townships of Bethlehem, Preston, and Hurlock. Toward Salisbury. The judge had kept his word. Alison was in Washington; she'd arrive at the Hay-Adams long before they reached Salisbury. Peter would telephone her from a roadside booth once O'Brien was taken. It was to be his good-bye, his death to follow, mercifully quick, at an unexpected moment—that, too, was part of the agreement.

Chancellor turned to the judge. The huge black head reflected racing flashes of light and shadow.

"How did you get the files?" Peter asked.

"*M* through *Z*, Mr. Chancellor," said Sutherland. "That's what we have. *A* through *L* were destroyed by Inver Brass. I could only get half."

"I'm going to die; that's not easy for me to say. I'd like to know how you got them."

The judge looked at Peter, his dark eyes magnified in the dim light. "There's no harm in telling you. It wasn't difficult. As you know, Varak assumed Longworth's name. The real Alan Longworth is exactly what I told you he was in my office several months ago: one of Hoover's

closest associates, persuaded to work against Hoover. His
reward was to spend the rest of his life in the Hawaiian
Islands, his wants supplied, beyond the reach of those who
might try to kill him. Hoover was told he died of natural
causes: a disease. In fact, a memorial service was held for
Longworth. Hoover himself gave the eulogy."

Chancellor thought of the outline for his novel. The
fiction was again the reality.

> *A medical deception is mounted. . . . The
> report is forwarded to Hoover: The agent is
> riddled with duodenal cancer. It has spread be-
> yond surgery; his life expectancy is no more than
> a few months at best. Hoover has no alternative.
> He releases the man, believing the agent is going
> home to die. . . .*

"Hoover never questioned Longworth's death?" asked
Peter.

"There was no reason to," replied Sutherland. "The
surgeon's report was sent to him. It left no doubts."

The fiction. The reality.

The judge continued. "I brought Alan Longworth
back to life. From Hawaii. For one day. It was most dramatic. A man returned from the dead for only a single day,
but it was a day J. Edgar Hoover nearly stopped the wheels
of government; his fury was intense. And his fear." A slow
smile came to Sutherland; it could be seen in the swiftly
moving shadows. He went on, staring straight ahead.
"Longworth told Hoover the truth as far as he knew it,
as much as we told him. He was psychologically ready to
do this, so deep was his own guilt. Hoover had been his
mentor—in a way his god—and he had been forced to
betray him. There was a conspiracy to murder him, Longworth told Hoover. For his private files. The conspirators
were unknown men inside and outside the bureau. Men
with access to every code, every release of a vault in an
emergency. Hoover panicked, as we knew he would panic.
Phone calls were made all over Washington—including
one to Ramirez, incidentally—and Hoover learned nothing.
There was only one person he felt he could trust: his
closest friend, Clyde Tolson. He began systematically removing the files to Tolson's house—to his basement, to be
precise. But he fell behind the schedule we had projected;

not all the files were removed. We couldn't press him; we couldn't take the risk of doing that. We could get inside Tolson's home. We had enough. We *have* enough. Files M through Z will give us the leverage we never had before."

"For what?"

"To shape the concerns of government," said Sutherland emphatically.

"What happened to Longworth?"

"You killed him, Mr. Chancellor. MacAndrew pulled the trigger, but you killed him. You sent MacAndrew after him."

"And your people killed MacAndrew."

"We had no choice. He'd learned too much. He had to die, at any rate. Although he wasn't responsible, he was the symbol of Chasŏng. Hundreds of black soldiers murdered, led to their deaths by their own commanders. The most heinous crime of which man is capable."

"Racial murder," said Peter quietly.

"A form of genocide. The most despicable form," said Sutherland, his eyes filled with hatred. "For *convenience.* To stop one man from learning the truth because that truth would expose a network of crimes—experiments—that civilized men should never have sanctioned but did."

Chancellor let the moment pass. The silence was electric. "The phone calls. The killing. Why? What did Phyllis Maxwell or Bromley or Rawlins have to do with Chasŏng? Or O'Brien, for that matter? Why did you go after them?"

The judge answered rapidly. The victims mentioned were not of consequence. "Chasŏng was not involved. Phyllis Maxwell had uncovered information we wished to use ourselves; it led to the Oval Office. Bromley deserved no less. He had the courage to take on the Pentagon, but he crippled an urban-renewal project in Detroit that would have benefited thousands of destitute slum dwellers. Black people, Mr. Chancellor. He sold out to criminal elements who provided him with information that augmented his headline-gathering crusade against the military. At the expense of black people! Rawlins was the most dangerous example of the false New South. He gave lip service to emerging 'new values' and privately in committee thwarted every congressional attempt to give teeth to the laws. And he abused black women, don't forget that. The parents of those children can't."

Sutherland had finished.

"What about O'Brien?" Peter asked. "Why do you want him now?"

"Once again, you're responsible. He's the only one who pieced together the theft of the remaining files. If that were all, he might have lived. His silence could be counted on; he had no viable proof. However, no longer. He knows Venice's identity. You gave it to him."

Peter looked away. He was surrounded by death; he was the precursor of death.

"Why you?" asked Peter softly. "Of all men, why *you*?"

"Because I can," replied Sutherland, his eyes on the road ahead.

"That's not an answer."

"It's taken me a lifetime to understand what the young see every day of their lives. I was too filled with doubts; it's not complicated at all. This nation has forsaken its black citizens. The black man must no longer interfere. America is bored with his dreams; the black man's attainments are suspect. It was fashionable to support him while he was an achieving oddity, but not when he becomes a challenge and moves into the neighborhood."

"You weren't forsaken."

"The extraordinary man never is. I say that with no sense of false pride. My gifts were from God, and they were extraordinary. But what of the ordinary man? The ordinary woman, the ordinary child, who grow up to be less than ordinary because they're marked at birth? No change of name can alter that stigma; no certificate can lighten the skin. I'm no revolutionary in the accepted sense, Mr. Chancellor. I know very well that such a course would result in a holocaust unknown to the Jews. Quite simply, the numbers and the hardware are against us. I'm merely using the tools of the society in which we live. *Fear*. The most common weapon known to man. It has no prejudice; it respects no racial barriers. That's what those files represent—nothing more, nothing less. We can do so much with them, influence so much legislation, enact so many laws, give teeth to statutes that are violated daily. That's what those files can accomplish. I seek no violence that would certainly ensure our annihilation. I want none of that. I seek only what rightfully belongs to us, what's been withheld from us. And providence has given me the weapon.

I intend to lead the *ordinary* black man out of his sorrow and embarrassment."

"But you do use violence. You kill."

"Only those who would take our lives!" Sutherland's voice thundered; it filled the car. "As our lives were taken! Only those who would interfere!"

Sutherland's explosion caused Peter to react in kind, with his own intensity, his own anger. "An eye for an eye? Is that where you're at? Is that what you came away with after a lifetime of law? For Christ's sake, not *you*! *Why?*"

Sutherland turned in the seat, his eyes furious. "I'll *tell* you why. It wasn't the judgment of a lifetime. It was the result of a brief half hour five years ago. I had rendered a decision that was not particularly popular with the Justice Department. It prohibited further abuses of Miranda and upheld the conviction of a well-known superintendent of police."

"I remember," said Peter, and he did. It had been called the Sutherland decision, an anathema to the law-and-order crowd. Had any other judge but Sutherland rendered it, it would have been appealed to the Supreme Court.

"I received a call from J. Edgar Hoover, requesting me to come to his office. More from curiosity than anything else, I bowed to his arrogance and accepted the invitation. During that meeting I listened to the unbelievable. On the desk of the highest law-enforcement officer in the country were spread the dossiers of every major black civil rights leader: King, Abernathy, Wilkins, Rowan, Farmer. They were volumes of filth—scurrilous rumor, unsubstantiated gossip, transcripts of telephone and electronic taps; words taken out of context made to appear inflammatory—morally, sexually, legally, philosophically! I was enraged, appalled! That it could happen in *that office!* Blackmail! Blatant extortion! But Hoover had been through it many times before. He let me vent my rage, and when I had finished, he viciously said that were I to continue to be an obstruction, those files would be put to use. Men and their families destroyed! The black movement *crippled!* At the very last, he said to me, 'We don't want another Chasŏng, do we, Judge Sutherland?' "

"Chasŏng," said Peter, repeating the name softly. "That's where you heard it first."

"It took me nearly two years to learn what happened at Chasŏng. When I did, I reached the decision. The children had been right all along. In their simplicity they saw what I did not see. As a people we were expendable. But then I saw what the young did not see. The answer was not indiscriminate violence and protests. It was to use the weapon Hoover used; make the system work from within. By *fear*! . . . We'll talk no more. You should have silence. Make peace with your God."

The man beside the driver studied a map with the aid of a pencil flashlight. He turned his head slightly to speak with the judge in Ashanti.

Sutherland nodded and replied in the strange African tongue. He looked at Peter. "We're within a mile and a half of the gas station. We'll stop a quarter of a mile short of it. These men are efficient scouts. They learned the expertise of night patrol in Southeast Asia. Those patrols were usually the province of black soldiers; the casualty rates were the highest. If O'Brien's brought anyone with him, if there's any hint of a trap, they'll come back, and we'll drive away. The girl will die in front of you."

Chancellor's throat went dry. *It's over*. He should have known. Sutherland would never settle for words over a telephone. Peter had sentenced Alison to death. He had loved two women in his life, and he had killed them both.

He thought of overpowering Sutherland when they were alone. It was something to keep him from screaming.

"How could O'Brien do that?" Peter asked. "You said he couldn't go to anyone, that you'd know if he did."

"On the surface it would appear impossible. He's isolated."

"Then, why are we stopping. Why are we wasting time?"

"I saw what O'Brien did at the marina yesterday morning. Courage and ingenuity are to be respected. It's a simple precaution."

The car stopped. Whatever thoughts Peter had of attacking Sutherland were dispelled quickly. The man beside the driver leaped out of the car, opened the door next to Chancellor, and grabbed his arm. A pair of handcuffs were snapped to his wrist and to the metal clasp below the window. The movement put his shoulder in agony. He winced and held his breath.

The judge climbed out of the back seat. "I leave you to your thoughts, Mr. Chancellor."

The two young black men disappeared into the darkness.

It was the longest forty-five minutes Peter could imagine. He tried to think of the various tactics O'Brien might conceive of, but the more he thought about them, the more bleak were his conclusions. If Quinn had managed to get help, as surely he must have done, the additional men would be seen by Sutherland's scouts. Death. If for some reason O'Brien had decided to come alone, then he would die. But at least Alison would live. There was some comfort in that.

The scouts returned, drenched with sweat. They had been running hard; they'd covered a great deal of ground.

The black on the left opened the door and Sutherland climbed in. "It would appear that Mr. O'Brien keeps the rendezvous. He is sitting in an automobile with the motor running, in the center of the road where he can observe all sides. There is no one else within three miles of the station."

Chancellor was too numb and too sick to think clearly. His last amateurish gesture had been to lead Quinn into the trap.

It's over.

The Mark IV started. They approached the intersection; the driver braked the Continental slowly, and they came to a stop. The black on the driver's right got out and opened Chancellor's door. He unlocked the cuffs; Peter shook his wrist trying to restore the circulation. His wounded shoulder began to hurt again. It did not matter.

"Get behind the wheel, Mr. Chancellor. You'll drive now. My two friends will be crouched behind you in the back seat, their guns drawn. The girl dies if you disregard instructions."

Sutherland got out of the car with Peter, and stood by the door, facing him.

"You're wrong. You know that, don't you?" said Chancellor.

"You look for absolutes. As with precedents, they're all too often imperfect, and much of the time they don't apply. There's no right and wrong between us. We're products of a long-standing crisis neither of us is responsible for but both are swept up in."

"Is that a judicial opinion?"

"No, Mr. Chancellor. It's the opinion of a Negro. I was a Negro before I was a judge." Sutherland turned and walked away.

Peter watched him, then climbed in behind the wheel and slammed the door. *It's over. Dear God, if you exist, let it come quickly, furiously. I have no courage.*

Peter turned right at the intersection and drove down the road. The gas station was on the left, a single naked light bulb in a bracket above the pumps.

"Slow down," came the quiet command from the back.

"What's the difference?" said Chancellor.

"Slow *down!*"

The barrel of a gun was shoved into the base of his skull. He pressed the brake of the Mark IV and coasted toward the station. He approached the rear of O'Brien's car; it had to be Quinn's. The vapor from exhaust curled in the night air, the headlights illuminating the distant country road beyond.

Peter was alarmed. The lights from the Mark IV shone directly into the rear window of O'Brien's car. It was empty.

"He's not there," whispered Chancellor.

"He's below the seat," said the low voice on his right.

"Get out and walk to the car," said the other man.

Peter turned off the motor, opened the door, and stepped out on the road. He closed his eyes briefly, wondering if a gun would fire at him the instant Quinn appeared. He was not fooled. Sutherland would spare Alison, but there'd be no conversation over the telephone. The judge would take no such risk.

But O'Brien did not get out of the automobile.

"Quinn," called Chancellor. There was no answer.

What are you doing, O'Brien? It's over!

Nothing.

Peter walked toward the car, his temples throbbing, the pain in his throat agonizing. The sound of the idling engine mingled with the night noises; a breeze swirled dry leaves across the roadway. Any second now, Quinn would show himself; gunshots would follow. Would he hear them as his life ended? He approached the driver's window.

There was no one there.

"Chancellor! Get down!"

The scream came from out of the darkness. The sudden roar of a powerful motor filled the night. Blinding headlights shot out from the left, from the gas station! A car came racing out of the dim light, speeding directly at the silver Mark IV. The driver's door swung open; a figure lunged out, rolling on the pavement.

The impact came, a thunderous collision, the crunching of metal, the shattering of glass, the screams of the two men inside   all came at once, and at once Peter knew the last fury he had hoped for had arrived.

Gunshots followed, as he knew they would. He closed his eyes and gripped the hard surface of the road; the searing, icelike pain would come. The darkness would come.

The firing continued; Chancellor rolled his face to the side. It came from Quinn O'Brien!

Peter raised his head. Smoke and dust billowed in the air. In front of him he saw O'Brien throw himself into the side of the idling car; he was only feet from Chancellor. The agent crouched, both hands extended over the trunk, his pistol leveled.

"Get over here!" he roared to Peter.

Chancellor lunged forward, knees and hands pounding the tar beneath, until he reached the automobile.

He saw O'Brien hesitate, then raise his head and take careful aim.

The explosion came. The gas tank of the Continental erupted. Peter crouched in front of Quinn. Through a blanket of flames one of Sutherland's scouts lurched out of the burning car, firing at the source of O'Brien's gunshots.

But the man could be seen clearly in the light of the spreading fires; flames had ignited his clothes. O'Brien aimed again. There was a scream; the scout fell to the ground behind the burning automobile.

"Quinn!" yelled Peter. *"How?"*

"I understood you! When you used 'senator' in your code, you meant it was our last hope. You meant there was a crisis. You said I had to be alone; that meant you weren't. But you were in one car, *that* car, so I needed two. One a decoy!" O'Brien shouted as he inched forward around Chancellor toward the hood.

"A *decoy?*"

"A diversion! I paid a guy to follow me and leave his

car. If I could hit and run, we had a chance. What the hell, there was nothing left!" He raised his gun over the hood and leveled it.

"Nothing left . . ." Peter echoed the phrase, suddenly aware of its ultimate truth.

Quinn fired three shots in rapid succession. Chancellor's mind went blank for a moment, then was brought back to the madness by a second explosion from the Continental.

O'Brien spun around toward Chancellor. "Get inside!" he yelled. "Let's get out of here!"

Peter rose to his feet; he grabbed O'Brien's jacket, stopping him. "Quinn! Quinn, wait! There are no others! Just *him*! Back in the road. He's *alone*!"

"Who?"

"Sutherland. It's Daniel Sutherland."

O'Brien's wild eyes stared at Peter for a brief instant. "Get in," he commanded. He swung the idling car around in a U-turn and sped toward the intersection.

In the distance the headlights showed the immense figure of Daniel Sutherland, standing in the middle of the road. The black giant had seen what had happened. He raised his hand to his head.

There was a final gunshot.

Sutherland fell.

Venice was dead. Inver Brass was gone.

Epilogue

Morning. Peter stood by the hatch table in his study, holding the telephone, listening to the words spoken in quiet anger from Washington. The sun streamed through the windows. Outside, the snow was deep, pure white; sharp reflections of sunlight bounced continuously up into the glass. Proof of the earth's movement. As the voice on the telephone was proof of one aspect of the human condition; ultimately there was to be found a sense of morality.

The caller was Daniel Sutherland's son, Aaron. Firebrand, brilliant attorney for the black movement, a man Chancellor wanted to call a friend but knew he never could.

"I will *not* fight you that way! I won't lower myself to use your weapons. And I won't let others use them. I found the files. I *burned* them! You'll have to take my word."

"I was willing to take your father's when I thought I was going to die. I believed him. I believe you."

"You don't have a choice." The lawyer hung up.

Chancellor walked back to his couch and sat down. Through the north window he could see Alison, bundled in a coat, laughing, her arms folded, warding off the winter chill. She was between Mrs. Alcott and the taciturn groundskeeper, Burrows, who today seemed positively voluble. Mrs. Alcott was smiling at Alison.

Mrs. Alcott approved. The lady of the house was in residence. The home needed that lady.

The three of them turned toward the barn and started down the shoveled path that was bordered by shrubs, a green and white colonnade. In the distance, beyond the fence, a colt raced freely, then stopped and cocked his head at the threesome. He pranced toward them, his mane flowing.

Peter looked down at the pages of his manuscript. At the fiction. The fantasy that was his reality. He had made his decision.

He would start at the beginning, knowing it would be much better now. The invention would be there: thoughts and words put in the minds of others. But for himself no invention was needed. The experience was whole and never to be forgotten.

The story would be written as a novel.

His reality. Let others find other meanings.

He leaned forward and picked up a pencil from the tankard. He began on a fresh yellow pad.

The dark-haired man stared at the wall in front of him. His chair, like the rest of the furniture, was pleasing to the eye but not made for comfort. The style was Early American, the theme Spartan, as if those about to be granted an audience with the occupant of the inner office should reflect on their awesome opportunity in stern surroundings.

The man was in his late twenties, his face angular, the features sharp, each pronounced and definite as if carved by a craftsman more aware of details than of the whole. It was a face in quiet conflict with itself. . . .

ABOUT THE AUTHOR

ROBERT LUDLUM is the author of *The Scarlatti Inheritance, The Osterman Weekend, The Matlock Paper, The Rhinemann Exchange,* and *The Gemini Contenders.*

RELAX!
SIT DOWN
and Catch Up On Your Reading!

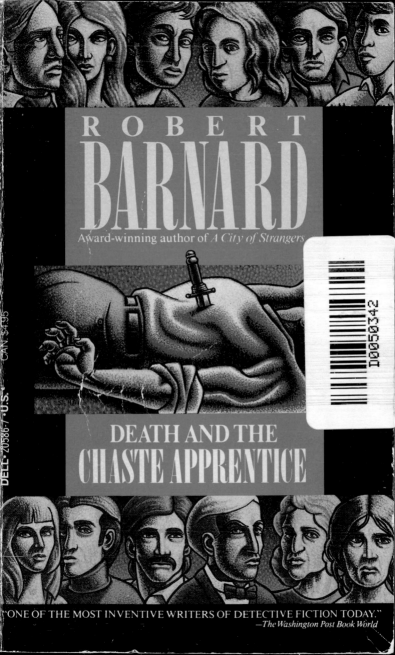

ROBERT
BARNARD

Award-winning author of *A City of Strangers*

DEATH AND THE
CHASTE APPRENTICE

N 0-440-20586-7>>395

9 780440 205869

50395

ROBERT BARNARD

DEATH AND THE CHASTE APPRENTICE

"WITTY, STYLISH, DIVERTING, INGENIOUS, TIDY (THAT IS, NOT BLOOD SOAKED), THE MYSTERIES OF ROBERT BARNARD ARE THE VERY MODEL OF THE ENGLISH FORM."

—*Los Angeles Times*

"TO READ THE BLESSEDLY PROLIFIC ROBERT BARNARD IS TO WONDER WHY ANYONE BOTHERS WITH LIGHT FICTION. MYSTERY NOVELISTS OF HIS KIND PROVIDE THE READER WITH ALL THE AMUSEMENT ONE HOPES IN A PUZZLE BESIDES. . . . HE IS STYLISH, ACERBIC, AND OCCASIONALLY MALICIOUS."

—*The New York Times Book Review*

"IF P. D. JAMES IS THE HEIR TO DOROTHY SAYERS, ROBERT BARNARD IS FAST TAKING ON THE CHRISTIE/MARSH MANTLE. . . . THE MOST APPEALING AND RELIABLE PRACTITIONER OF THE CLASSIC BRITISH MYSTERY TO ARIVE HERE IN THE LAST DECADE."

—*Kirkus Reviews*

"THERE'S NO ONE QUITE LIKE ROBERT BARNARD IN HIS ABILITY TO COMBINE CHILLS AND CHUCKLES AND THEN SPRINKLE THE WHOLE WITH DELICIOUS IRONY."

—*The San Diego Union*

"THE WRYEST WIT AND MOST SCATHING SATIRE IN TODAY'S MYSTERY."

—*Sun-Times* (Chicago)

QUANTITY SALES

Most Dell books are available at special quantity discounts when purchased in bulk by corporations, organizations, and special-interest groups. Custom imprinting or excerpting can also be done to fit special needs. For details write: Dell Publishing, 666 Fifth Avenue, New York, NY 10103. Attn.: Special Sales Department.

INDIVIDUAL SALES

Are there any Dell books you want but cannot find in your local stores? If so, you can order them directly from us. You can get any Dell book in print. Simply include the book's title, author, and ISBN number if you have it, along with a check or money order (no cash can be accepted) for the full retail price plus $2.00 to cover shipping and handling. Mail to: Dell Readers Service, P.O. Box 5057, Des Plaines, IL 60017.

DEATH
AND THE
CHASTE
APPRENTICE

ROBERT BARNARD

A DELL BOOK

Published by
Dell Publishing
a division of
Bantam Doubleday Dell Publishing Group, Inc.
666 Fifth Avenue
New York, New York 10103

The trademark Dell® is registered in the U.S. Patent and Trademark Office.

ISBN: 0-440-20586-7

Reprinted by arrangement with Charles Scribner's Sons

Printed in the United States of America

September 1990

10 9 8 7 6 5 4 3 2

RAD

NOTE

The extracts from the supposed *The Chaste Apprentice of Bowe* are in fact taken from *A Trick to Catch the Old One,* *'Tis Pity She's a Whore,* and other plays of the Elizabethan and Jacobean period.

So don't blame me.

DEATH
AND THE
CHASTE
APPRENTICE

1

THE SARACEN'S HEAD

"Mad as a hatter," said Gillian Soames complacently, striding up the road from the underground towards Ketterick High Street. "Stark raving bonkers. Up the wall. Round the twist to an unprecedented degree."

Peter Fortnum, legging it beside her through the town, was surprised to see on her face an expression of quite sunny anticipation. After all, she was talking about Jason Thark, the producer-director of the play in which they both were to appear. The two had met on the underground, having previously done no more than swap words when they were in different productions at the Sheffield Crucible. Thus they were still in the earliest stages of mutual discovery.

Peter Fortnum was slim, fresh, and twenty-three. Gillian Soames was rather plain, beginning to be dumpy, and was a stage veteran of eight years in small parts. She had had her share of theatrical disasters and had gone on from them to other disasters or to the occasional minor triumph. She knew that this was a festival production, which would run its allotted course of twelve performances and never be heard of again, quite irrespective of the merits or otherwise of the production. Peter Fortnum was a nice lad, she was saying to herself, but you could spot the wetness behind his ears. He still believed that stardom might be just around the corner. Gillian knew that hard work was.

"So be prepared to swallow your artistic conscience," she added darkly.

"He's got a tremendous reputation," Peter ventured.

"Oh—reputation!"

Gillian's tone seemed to contain a limitless scorn for drama critics. Thus did Lady Bracknell dismiss cloakrooms at railway stations. Peter wondered whether Gillian wasn't, perhaps, a Lady Bracknell in waiting. But if she meant that directors' reputations were gained over the bodies of actors who knew better, then Peter could go along with that.

"People do say he does interesting things," he amended.

"The sort of director who gets that said about him," said Gillian, still with the same unruffled composure, "is the kind to run a mile from. What does it usually mean? If the play cries out for a simple, direct approach, he decks it out with moving sets, Wurlitzer organs, and so many spots it looks like the Battle of Britain. And if the play is weak and needs a bit of gingering up, he puts the characters in body stockings and sets it in the Gobi Desert. That sort of director's motto is 'Don't notice the play; notice *me!*' "

"Well, he can't play about much with an Elizabethan stage," Peter pointed out.

"That's true," conceded Gillian with all the reluctance of the born prophet of doom. "At least you wouldn't have *thought* he could. The critics will come down on him if he tries any modern tricksiness, that's for sure. Still—"

She stopped short in her stride as she and Peter noticed simultaneously a poster for the play in an arty little bookshop. They peered into the window, and Peter read out the title with a reverence the play hardly warranted:

THE CHASTE APPRENTICE OF BOWE

The poster was done in the form of a playbill—of the Restoration rather than any conceivable Elizabethan type. Peter's and Gillian's heads slowly dipped down as they read through the list of the players' names. There at the bottom they were: Peter Fortnum and Gillian Soames.

"At least we got on," said Peter.

"Which is more than the author did."

"It was published anonymously."

"Nobody willing to own up," said Gillian cheerily. "It does come rather into the 'justly neglected' category, doesn't it?" They resumed their lithe stride in the direction of the High Street. "Actually, I'd do a walk-on part in the worst play of Robert Greene just for the pleasure of working at the Saracen."

"It must be fabulous," agreed Peter. "Like getting back to one's roots—starting again at the beginnings of drama."

"Something like that," agreed Gillian, who distrusted enthusiasm.

"And actually staying there, too! I thought we'd be shunted off to some crummy bed-and-breakfast dive, with rooms at the Saracen reserved for the stars."

"That's not how they do things at Ketterick. The theory is that there *are* no stars—which is bullshit, but useful bullshit. Of course, a lot of the names have flats or houses in London, anyway. Some of the rest prefer to take theatrical digs. I've got a poky room in north London which I've loaned to a friend for the summer."

"And I'm living out of a suitcase at the moment. I could

have got cheaper digs, but just the idea of staying at the place . . ."

"Precisely. It has an aura. And at the Saracen's Head somebodies and nobodies rub shoulders and swap pints. That's something Arthur has insisted on from— Oh!"

"What?"

"Dear old Arthur. The landlord of the Saracen. I'd forgotten for a moment that he'd died."

"Was he nice?"

"The dearest old man. And one of the masterminds behind the festival. He treated everyone alike, from Hamlet to Second Gent. I suppose the place must have been sold or something. Anyway, we'll soon see."

They turned a corner into a wide but not too busy street, and Gillian pointed histrionically. "There it is," she said.

As if they had but one mind, they set down their cases and gazed.

Even from a distance, viewed through the clutter and bustle of an outer-London suburb, the Saracen's Head looked like something special, something rather out of the run of old English inns. You noticed first its long frontage, which straddled a huge pair of gates. Through these, coaches had once rumbled to disgorge their passengers in the great yard beyond, for Ketterick had been a stopping-place between the north and Dover for fast coaches that had shunned the center of London. As you moved closer, you noticed that, apart from plaster over the half-timbering, it had been neither renovated nor tarted up, but had been left blessedly alone. The Saracen's Head had benefited over the centuries from a family of landlords who were quite remarkably slothful, men who could just about bring themselves to pull a pint but not much more. One of them, it is true, had in the mid-eighteenth century attempted something in the way of modernization, but fortunately he had died, and in his son the family inertia had reasserted itself. In the nineteenth century the railway had removed its principal function, and in the twentieth century hideous shopping precincts and malls had diverted a lot of traffic from Ketterick High Street. The Saracen's Head had slumbered on until it was rediscovered by architectural and theatrical historians in our own century. The sleeping princess had been reawakened by the kiss of the Ketterick Arts Festival.

As Peter and Gillian approached, past the modern facades of video shops and Marks and Spencers, the great gates at the center of the facade were pushed open.

"Half past five," said Gillian, licking her lips with satisfaction. "Opening time."

Peter, seeing it for the first time, took in the details of the frontage as they stood on the other side of the road, waiting to cross. It was an untidy, welcoming facade. To the left of the great gates were the Massinger Bar and the Webster Bar. To the right, Reception and the Shakespeare Bar.

"The Shakespeare Bar's ours," said Gillian authoritatively. "Not that the festival ever does Shakespeare."

"No, we're stuck with *The Chaste Apprentice of Bowe.*"

"Anyway, they were just the Toby Bar, the Snug, and so on until the festival started. Even dear old Arthur wasn't averse to capitalizing."

They crossed the road, and from an unspoken wish they walked straight through the massive gates and into the great courtyard. Here they stopped, and Peter looked around with reverence at the open space within which they would be playing. Here the Lord Admiral's Men and the Lord Chamberlain's Men had played when forced from

London's South bank by the plague or the hostility of City aldermen. The Saracen was, at ground-floor level, the usual array of bars, dining rooms and kitchens, and the other inevitable offices of a large hotel. But at first- and second-floor level, on three of its four sides, it had kept the balconies from which the better class of Ketterick spectators had watched the entertainments provided by the traveling players. On the fourth side, the inn's proprietor of the eighteenth century, in that brief and regrettable spurt of energy, had bricked in the balconies and enlarged the bedrooms behind. Enough remained, with the row upon row of seats in the great courtyard itself, to provide sizable audiences for the Elizabethan and Jacobean revivals that were the staple of the Ketterick Arts Festival.

Even as they stood, silent, antennae a-twitch to get the feel of the place, a couple of late workmen came out with two more sections of the stage. They began fixing them on to the section already set up, which was beginning to project out from the kitchens at the far side of the courtyard to form an apron stage. It was on this bare platform that the festival company had performed *The Devil's an Ass, The Faire Seducer, The Roaring Girls of Cheapside,* and other minor masterpieces of our drama. It was on this platform that Peter and Gillian would perform lesser roles in *The Chaste Apprentice of Bowe.*

"Our stage," said Gillian with satisfaction in her voice, and reverence too. "You're right. It's difficult to see what Jason Thark can do to bugger *that* up."

They watched the workmen and the embryonic stage, silent and companionable, united in some powerful but indefinable respect for their own art and its beginnings. Their mood was brutally shattered by an interruption.

"Would you be the operatic lady and gentleman?"

The voice had an Australian twang, and when they turned, they saw a bulky presence, now running to fat—an ex-rugby football player, perhaps, or the regiment's champion middleweight boxer. He was dressed in a suit of good cloth but baggy proportions, was balding, and his eyes were watery, shifting, and ill focused. But what was most immediately off-putting was his manner, which was unpleasingly ingratiating, yet oddly combined with something cunning, something almost threatening. He oozed up to them, it was true, but his manner had as its subtext something of the bully, as if he were itching to get them under his thumb.

"I'm Des Capper, the landlord," he said.

"Oh." Gillian Soames hardly bothered to keep the layers of meaning out of her voice. After a moment's hesitation she shook his hand because she could hardly avoid it. She did it in a manner that suggested she had already made up her mind he was a lousy replacement for dear old Arthur. "No, we're not the operatic lady and gentleman. We're both in *The Chaste Apprentice.*"

Des Capper's face fell, and his manner lost several degrees of ingratiation.

"Oh. Suppose I should have known. The operatic people tend to come larger, don't they? It's the lung capacity that does it, you know— It's the lung capacity that makes or breaks a singer. You must be Miss Soames and Mr. Fortnum, then?"

"That's right."

"Playing Alison Greatheart and Peter Patterwit."

"Right."

"Most of the principals have been here a week or more."

"The leads always come early. We are not leads."

"Well, I'm sure you'll make something very nice of your

respective roles," said Des Capper, leading the way towards Reception and making no move to help Gillian with her suitcase. "It's not the size of the role that counts, you know. A good actor can make a marvelous thing out of a juicy little part. I've seen it happen."

"We know," muttered Gillian. "We *are* actors."

"Just so long as you speak up and speak out," Des went on, disregarding her. "You can't get away with mumbling on this stage, oh, dear me, no."

"I have appeared in five of the eight productions here," said Gillian, acid-sweetly.

"Then you'll bear me out when I say speak up and speak out. The way some of these young actors produce their voices must have dear old Sir John Gielgud turning in his grave."

"He's still alive."

"That makes it worse. Personally I think it's all part of your mental approach to the part." Des, ensconced behind the reception desk, absently shoved little cards in front of them to sign as he continued to lecture them on their profession. "Have you tried yoga? There's many actors that do. I've got a terrific book of yoga exercises I could loan you. Incredible. They've changed my life, I can tell you. . . . What? Room numbers? Oh, yes. Have you filled in the cards? Fine. You're 227, Miss Soames, and you're 234, Mr. Fortnum. Close without being adjacent." He leered. "Can you find your own way? You should never pick up a heavy case like that, young man. You can do terrible damage to your dorsals that way. I've known people ruined by it, and an actor ought to be specially careful." He came round from behind the desk and put himself in a posture of demonstration. "What you should do is *bend* the knees

slightly, go *down* to it, then lift it smoothly like *this*. . . .
Got it? Don't mind me telling you, do you?"

By now the nature of the new landlord of the Saracen's
Head needed no further defining in either of their minds.
He was that most loathsome of God's creations, the Australian know-all. They both gave him smiles that scarcely
rose to the level of the perfunctory and set off in the direction of their rooms.

Or roughly speaking in the direction of their rooms. The
old inn was a maze of corridors, obscure passageways that
ended in blank walls, inexplicable open areas that must
once have served a purpose but which now seemed merely
to be dumping places for unwanted pieces of furniture. The
inn was innocent of lifts, which in any case would have
been of limited use: The Saracen's sprawl was not vertical
but horizontal. Discreet wooden arrows pointed in the direction of room numbers, which were allocated with the
same beautiful lack of logic or pattern as the general layout
of the place.

"I love it," said Gillian as they toiled back along a passage that had led merely to a laundry cupboard. "Do you
know, I've stayed here five seasons, and I still haven't
fathomed it. And I still expect to hear Tom Jones and one
of his doxies from one of the bedrooms."

But it was not Tom Jones that they heard.

"And if you upstage me again at the end of Act One, by
God I'll have your guts for garters."

They were in one of those inexplicable open spaces, and
the voice came from the bedroom or suite that led off from
it. It was a male voice that was clearly accustomed to making itself heard in large spaces—a traditional theater voice.
Gillian held up a finger and—still holding their cases, fear-

ing they might have to make a hurried exit—they stood listening with the telling stillness of stage actors.

"Carston Galloway," whispered Gillian.

"I did not upstage you. You seem not to want to acknowledge that there *is* anyone else onstage."

"I am perfectly willing to cooperate with real company players. They wouldn't try to ruin each other's performances."

"Oh God, don't talk to me about your performance. Talk to your little backstage drab about that."

"Darling Clarissa," whispered Gillian.

"I suppose that *swoop* to the front was something you arranged with dear Jason in bed?"

"Darling, we have *quite* other things to think about when we are in bed."

"Crap. Sex may be important to you—God knows, I've reason enough to know that it is—but nothing is more important to you than the shoddy little theatrical victories you arrange for yourself. So don't feed me that shit about sex being all in all."

"I love your exquisitely modulated guttersnipe language."

The Galloways were doing their daily exercises. They were famous in theatrical circles for the fearlessly open way in which they conducted their sex lives. The odd thing was that for all their openness and honesty, their emotional lives were just as great a mess as if they had been secret about it.

"I've always been so *sorry* for you," said Clarissa in a lethal purr. "There are so few female directors. And the ones there are direct practically nothing but all-female plays. It does frustrate your instinct to pay back in kind. So you have to content yourself with ingenues and assistant stage managers . . . nobodies. Still, I suppose they renew your youth, which heaven knows has lasted longer than most people's youth."

"My God! Coming from you . . ."

Gillian shook her head at Peter Fortnum, and together they stole down the corridor. A floorboard creaked under them, as floorboards could be relied upon to do at the Saracen when one was trying to be circumspect. It was unlikely that the Galloways in full flood would notice or care.

"Par for the course," said Gillian when they were out of earshot. "We can expect a feast of that in the next week or two. Ever worked with them before?"

"No," admitted Peter. "I've mostly been in pretty experimental stuff. Disused warehouses and upstairs rooms in pubs. That's not really their line, is it?"

"Oh, dear me, no. The thought of Clarissa in a Hackney pub is practically lèse majesté. Revivals of *Lady Windermere* or *The School for Scandal*—all powdered wigs and rustling taffeta—that's the Galloways' line. I believe Rattigan was about to write something for them when he died, and they certainly created some minor roles in late Coward. They're a practically extinct theatrical breed."

"The giant egos?"

"Well, that particular form of giant ego. Nowadays it takes different forms. The day giant egos are extinct in the theater we may as well all shut up shop and go home. . . . Good Lord, we're here. Do you think we'll ever find our way here again—or find our way out, for that matter?"

They put their keys in their doors and swung them open. Each discovered they were in unlovely little boxes clearly furnished with castoffs from other rooms.

"It's all right," said Peter cheerfully. "I never expected anything better."

"It's *not* how dear old Arthur used to organize things. All the actors were given good rooms. Still, at least we've got a view of the courtyard and the stage."

They went to the window of Gillian's room. At the far end of the courtyard the stage was a little further towards completion—that great projecting space that would so cruelly expose any faults in their techniques, any immaturities or imperfections. Peter drew his eyes away, almost in fear. Down in the front part of the courtyard Des Capper was oozing forward again, this time to welcome a woman and two men, who had been disgorged from a taxi, and had come in to view the great space.

"Probably the operatic lady and gentleman," said Peter. "And if so, they're *not* large."

"Have you ever known that sort of blowhard to get things right?" Gillian asked bitterly. "Is that young one Indian? He looks rather plump, an incipient fatty. No doubt Des Capper will put that down to his lung capacity. Actually the woman looks decidedly presentable. I say— just look at Des! Look at the way he's fawning and scraping! It's a fair bet they're the stars of whatever it is, isn't it? Isn't he odious? Stomach-turning! Look, he's even rubbing his hands. He's one of the most ghastly men I've met."

"He doesn't seem much of a replacement for your Arthur," agreed Peter. "I wonder why they appointed him."

"Appointed? I thought he must have bought the place or something."

"Didn't you see the plaque outside? It said the Saracen was one of the Beaumont chain of hotels. He called himself the landlord, but he must be some kind of manager."

"Really? Well, someone who's appointed can be sacked.

The festival committee ought to do something about it. There must be some way he can be got rid of."

She said it casually. Others in the course of the next week or two were to say or think the same thing with more vehement emphasis.

2

THE SHAKESPEARE BAR

Gillian and Peter went out for their meal that evening. There was a little bistro called The Relief of Mafeking, Gillian said, where you could get a wholesome nosh-up for £2.95. In fact, they found the price had gone up way beyond the rate of inflation, as it did with most good things once they caught on, but it was a satisfactory bargain all the same. Even actors in work—and Peter was only intermittently so—had to watch their pennies.

"I never eat at the Saracen before I've got my first paycheck," Gillian explained over the chicken casserole, "and then only every three or four days. It's very pricey, though the food is marvelous." She added darkly: "Mind you, it's probably shark meat and kangaroo steaks nowadays."

She did not actually sing "Change and decay in all around I see," but the dust of mortality was definitely in the air. She had hit on the phrase The Great Australian Blight, G.A.B. for short, and she used it rather frequently in the course of the meal.

Later, with an agreeable sense of wallet and purse hardly at all depleted, they dawdled back to the Saracen's Head. They paused outside the Alhambra, a tiny theater,

Victorian Moorish in design, a thing of many domes and minarets, which had been rescued from the degradation of Bingo when the festival first got under way. Here they inspected the poster for that year's operatic offering at the Ketterick Festival.

"Adelaide di Birckenhead," read Gillian, shaking her head. "Never heard of it. Not that that says anything. Since they did *Anna Bolena* five years ago I haven't heard of any of them. They deliberately go in for the unknown, as we do on the drama side. The critics feel they have to come if it's the first performance for umpteen hundred years."

"Adelaide di Birckenhead has just got to be early Romantic."

"I should think so. It almost always is. You're right. *'Opera semiseria di Gaetano Donizetti.'* I presume that means we only have to take it semiseriously, which is a blessing. Who's in it? Oh—a Russian-sounding lady. She's never been here before. The tenor and baritone are old festival standbys, but they don't usually stay at the Saracen. The American tenor's rather dishy, but the Mexican's a nasty piece of work. God—I'm dying for a drink. Let's get back and see if I can find anyone I know."

The fact that the Shakespeare Bar at the Saracen was the one used by the festival people had nothing to do with any desire to pay tipsy tribute to the Swan of Avon. All the actors and singers who stayed at the inn had rooms on that side, the side where the balconies had been bricked in. The rooms on the other three sides had to be vacated for the duration of the festival, on the orders of the fire chief, so that members of the audience seated on the balconies could have unimpeded exit in the event of fire (in which case they would undoubtedly have been lost and frizzled in the maze of corridors). The Shakespeare was a big, warm, scarlet-velvet bar, with sofas and easy chairs, and its only disadvantage, that particular year, was its closeness to Reception. Des Capper alternated between the desk and the Shakespeare, where he hovered from table to table like an unappetizing headwaiter, determined to give more of his personal attention than anyone actually wanted.

At the bar a gaunt, harassed woman with pulled-back hair was worked off her feet. As she waited to be served, Gillian was delighted to see that there was someone she knew there. Ronnie Wimsett had been in two earlier Ketterick productions with Gillian, and his Theodorus Witgood in *A Trick to Catch the Old One* the previous year had been much admired. He was a rather plain young man by actors' standards, though wholesome and presentable in a middle-class sort of way. One's first instinct on meeting him was to put him down as a bank clerk or a clothes store assistant. It was only after talking to him for some time that one realized this was the chameleon's self-protection. He had a talent for imitation and deadpan comedy that lit up his face and voice and a rubbery looseness of body that made him wonderful in farce. He was well into rehearsals, for he played the chaste apprentice himself.

"I shall say *nothing* of Jason's direction, nothing of his interpretation or of his understanding of my part in the play," he announced solemnly when Gillian and Peter had settled themselves down at his table. "Not because it's dreadful, you understand. But because you should come to your first rehearsal tomorrow with no trace of bias or *parti pris.*" He took a great draught of Saracen ale. "Let us instead while away the hours by ripping to shreds our fellow actors in this little-known masterwork."

Gillian smiled evilly, leaned forward, and the two went

at it. Peter Fortnum, sitting on the edge of this gory arena, was interested and amused for a time, but his short career in the theater had left him with only a small circle of acting acquaintances, and after a time the names, their couplings and uncouplings, their tantrums and their delinquencies, began to pall. He was just beginning to wonder whether an obsessive interest in the marital affairs of the Galloways was not playing their game as they wanted it played, when he heard muttered words of Russian from the table beside him. He pricked up his ears at once.

Peter Fortnum was grateful to his minor public school for two things, and for only those two: These were the opportunities he had been given in the annual school play and the chance to learn Russian. Quite apart from anything else, the latter had given him quite spurious claims on any small parts going whenever anyone decided to do a Chekhov or a Gorki. He swung his chair around, chipping in a few words, and in no time at all he was sitting beside the star of *Adelaide di Birckenhead* and interpreting for her as she made her first real effort to communicate with the agent who had brought her to the West.

Natalya Radilova was slim, dark haired, and beautiful. She was also very much at sea. It was only her second time in the West, and her attempts to discuss financial and other arrangements with her agent had been hindered by the fact that she knew no more than twenty or thirty words of English. She had in all their preliminary communications pretended to a "competent" knowledge of the language, but her letters to him had in fact been written by a friend.

"I've arranged all this with your Ministry of Culture," her agent said somewhat wearily.

"Arrange it with me again," said Natalya.

The agent, Bradford Mallory ("Call me Brad") was, like

the Galloways, something of a theatrical throwback, though in his case, Peter suspected, it was much more of a conscious act, for it had the label "performance" stamped on it, as theirs had not. He wore a cloak, he said, "dear boy," and he occasionally patted the hand of the other singer on his books whom he had brought to Ketterick. This was the young man whom Mallory had apparently rechristened—"rather witty, wouldn't you say, dear boy?" —with the single name of Singh. An incredibly good looking young man, his Indian complexion had lightened from long, perhaps lifelong, residence in Britain. He said little, occasionally pouted, and sometimes smiled abstractedly at Mallory's affectionate advances. But what he did most often was to look at his reflection in the mirror on the wall behind Brad Mallory. When he had a clear, uninterrupted view of himself, he would put his chin up to pose in his most attractive position, pat his immaculately cut hair, adjust his tie, and then smile a catlike smile when the image presented to him was at its most pleasing. He was, Brad Mallory said, *the* coming countertenor, and he was to sing in the concert on the opening night of the festival.

As Peter Fortnum translated between Natalya and her agent—yes, she did know the role, yes, she did realize that, small though the theater was, the festival held a unique position in British musical life and success here could be a springboard for a very promising operatic career—he was conscious of a discordant presence in the vicinity, an intrusive note. The Australian voice has a cutting edge, admirable in the opera house but less well adapted to the social hobnobbing of a saloon bar. Des Capper was giving someone the benefit of his curious store of knowledge and opinions, which meant, in effect, he was giving them to everyone.

"Do you know that in Queensland they've got this new law forbidding hoteliers from serving sexual perverts?" There was a dirty little snicker. "Be a bit of a problem here in festival time, wouldn't it? Couldn't afford to lose half my customers." Peter half-turned his head and saw that it was the Galloways and Jason Thark whom Des was regaling with his muckiness. Peter's glance caught him gesturing in the direction of Brad Mallory and Singh, and he immediately changed his tone. "Mind you, I'm tolerant. Live and let live, that's my motto. I don't know if you've read about it, but it's been proved by scientists that sexual deviancy's purely a matter of brain damage during childbirth. Just like spastics. I know all about what causes spastics. Well, it's just the same with poofs, only more minor. It's like this . . ."

"Dear God!" breathed Mallory, raising his eyebrows to heaven with theatrical eloquence. "What have we done to deserve this antipodean clodhopper clumping all over our private lives and our personal sensibilities?"

He put his hand warmly on Singh's, but Singh's smile did not suggest that he had heard or, if he had, that he had understood. He said in an English that was perfect yet oddly inflected, addressing Mallory alone:

"Can we go up and watch the video? I've got *Little Lord Fauntleroy*. You said we could watch it later tonight."

"And so we shall, dear boy, after one more little drinkie. It's my first chance to have a real talk to lovely, lovely Natalya, and she's full of questions that only I can answer."

Singh pouted but let himself be bought another sweet sherry.

Over at the Galloways' table, the theater's most glamorous couple had been stimulated by the company—though

Des Capper was not in himself stimulating—to stage a public version of their afternoon row. It was a cleaned-up version, much more elegant, suggesting that they carried the idea of rehearsals and trial runs into other areas of their lives.

"We've never had any secrets from each other, nor from anybody else," Clarissa was proclaiming. "We take our pleasures when and where the fancy takes us. Of course it is a tiny bit unfair on Carston that all the people of real *weight* in the theater are men. Hardly any female producers, and the only kind of heterosex most of them are interested in is rape, and they're against it. And though Carston is not *averse* to men, as a variation, even he would hardly find the average impresario or producer attractive. Which leaves the balance of advantage very definitely on my side."

"And puts *me* very much in my place," said Jason Thark with a wide, untrustworthy smile. He was, in fact, a not unattractive man—broad shouldered, commanding. But he was—and he let you know it—a man to keep on the right side of.

"Darling, I'm honest with you, as with everyone else. You're really rather attractive, and I'd have slept with you even if you hadn't been our producer. On the other hand, that does add a sort of spice . . ."

Des Capper, watching them, had assumed an exquisitely misjudged air of being a man of the world.

"I've known plenty of couples in my time who had what they call nowadays an open marriage," he put in, bending forward confidentially. "It's nothing new, oh, my word, no! I was in India just after the war, and what I could tell you about the Mountbattens' goings-on would make your hair curl!"

Clarissa regarded him with the sort of look she might use to wither a bit player who had interrupted her big speech five lines too early.

"Which is why Carston, poor darling," she swooped on," "does *very* much prefer that we get work as a *couple.*"

"Though that's not so easy these days," Carston confided genially. "Playwrights aren't writing bitch parts for women as they used to."

"And why he himself has to make do for his sexual adventures with"—Clarissa's smile widened triumphantly as they were joined at their table by an inconspicuous young woman—*"awfully* promising young stage managers like Susan here. Susan, dear, we were just saying what a *won*derful job you're doing."

In the face of a smile which resembled that on the face of the tiger that had just swallowed the young lady of Riga, Susan Fanshaw sat down and said nothing. She was getting good at doing that with the Galloways. She had bought her own drink—for Carston Galloway was not a generous lover—and she had noted Clarissa eyeing her as she stood at the bar. Knowing Clarissa, she had realized she would be a target as soon as she joined them. She sat down with a mixture of unease and defiance. Jason Thark was more used to the Galloways and their social style, and he sat there, slumped, gazing about him with an easy tolerance. Des Capper, on the other hand, was beginning to feel ignored and made motions of moving on.

"Well, it's been nice having a chinwag," he said with a little wave of his pudgy hand. "Better get along to have a chat with some of the others in my little flock."

"Darlings, I had no idea he was a *cler*gyman!" floated Clarissa's voice after him, exquisitely modulated so that he could not avoid just hearing. "I would have tried to be polite to him if I'd known."

Des Capper, lips tightening, settled himself down at the next table. Nobody made any move to admit him, but somehow he managed to get himself in all the same.

"All settled in nice and cozy?" he inquired to a quartet of frozen faces. "Are the Russian lady and the Indian gentleman finding everything to their liking? They've only to give a shout if not and I'll personally see that something is done."

"Singh is English." Bradford Mallory sighed. "As English as I am—and rather more so than you. Natalya has not, so far, been able to express any discontents she may have accumulated, but she has now acquired an interpreter, so if she feels you don't warm the samovar sufficiently before you pop in the tea bag, she will be able—thanks to our *char*ming young friend here—to expostulate with you on the subject."

Des Capper blinked, as if he had been hit with a dictionary. But he was unputdownable, at the same time giving the impression that he was registering all the snubs.

"Ah—Mother Russia." he said with a sigh.

"Motherfu—? Oh, Mother *Rus*sia."

"Mother Russia. It's an expression . . . sort of a nickname. It's a country that has always held a fatal fascination for me. The Winter Palace, Anastasia, *Battleship Potemkin* . . ."

" 'Lara's Theme,' *Gorky Park*," murmured Brad Mallory.

"Exactly. It's a country of great elemental passions. I think I'd have been able to come to terms with it. The tragedy is, I've never been. I'd like to have told them a thing or two about how to run their agriculture. Ask the little lady"—he turned to Peter Fortnum, but he patted Natalya Radilova on the knee—"if they've ever been lucky enough to hear our great Joan Sutherland at the Bolshoi."

"Tell this stupid peasant to take his fat hand off my knee," said Natalya Radilova in Russian.

"Ah—she understood me. What did she say?"

"She asked you to take your hand off her leg," said Peter diplomatically.

Des Capper burst out into a chilling mine-host laugh.

"Well, well, well. No offense meant and none taken, I hope. I know they're a little puritanical still in these Iron Curtain countries. Me, I believe in being broad-minded. There's more than one kind of partnership, eh, sir?" Des gave a broad and repulsive wink at Brad. "If you ask me, the Russkies could take a few tips from your country, young man," he added, turning to Singh, who was lost in rapturous contemplation of the mirror image of himself sipping sweet sherry.

"Singh is English," breathed Mallory.

"The Indians know a thing or two about sexual tricks, eh? Not that we were in a position to cast the first stone as far as moral habits were concerned. We, the Raj, the ruling class, I mean. As I was saying at the next table, I was there in '46–7, aide-de-camp to the Viceroy—"

"*Aide-de-camp,* now?"

"That's right. And some of the goings-on and permutations and possibilities that I saw while I was with the Mountbattens you wouldn't believe. Still, when you went out among the natives—as I did, because I've got what you might call an inquiring mind, as you may have noticed—you saw things you'd never even *read* about. Even an old soldier like me had his eyes opened, I can tell you. Ever since then India has always exercised—"

"A fatal fascination?"

"It has. It's been calling me back—"

"Please. That chair. Madam—you are my soprano?"

The voice—clipped, exact, icy—seemed to come from a great height. The young man was no more than six feet, but he seemed as high as the Matterhorn, and as daunting. He took Natalya Radilova's hand and, bending over, implanted on it a kiss, much as if he were stamping her passport.

"Gunter Gottlieb," murmured Brad Mallory with a pretense of enthusiasm.

It was a name more often breathed with devotion, even fanaticism, but that was always by people who did not know him, or need to. Orchestral musicians usually crossed themselves as they uttered the name or spat. Gunter Gottlieb had only recently become a name to conjure with in British musical life. He had been appointed conductor of the Midland Symphony Orchestra at the early age of twenty-seven. It was not, then, an orchestra with a great name. Mahler said that tradition is slovenliness; with the Midland Symphony Orchestra slovenliness was a tradition. Not any more. In a matter of months that mediocre band had been transformed by a mixture of sackings, threats, taunts, hectoring, and rehearsals that became torture sessions lasting well beyond the limits of endurance.

Now Gunter Gottlieb's concerts had become the talk of the Midlands and beyond. London critics traveled to Coventry and said that the young Austrian's Mahler was definitive for his generation. Old men wept at his Brahms and Schumann. Young girls waited outside the studios and concert halls for his autograph, undeterred by the open contempt with which he treated them. One or two of them would be selected for brief and violent couplings with the great man by one or other of the two thugs who, in imitation of more established conductors, comprised his embryonic entourage. Already the first records were in the pipeline. He was the talk of the musical world. It was a pity, everybody said, that he was such an unadulterated swine, but his music—!

Gunter Gottlieb had been in Ketterick a week. Des Capper—even Des Capper—knew his man. Without a word he vacated his seat and evaporated. Gunter Gottlieb sat down, knowing the chair would be there. His attendant heavy fetched him a drink and stood behind the chair looking menacing, though no more menacing than his master. Gottlieb sat in his chair, his back straight as a Victorian spinster's, his body seemingly bent by two perfect right angles at the knees and the buttocks. He fixed Natalya Radilova with his glassy, inquisitorial stare.

"You know your part?"

"Yes," said Natalya after translation.

"Perfectly? Including my embellishments for the cabalettas?"

"Yes," said Natalya.

"You are late," accused Gottlieb, tight-lipped and schoolmasterly.

"Natalya, as you know," put in Mallory with an expression of tired courtesy, "was called in to save some performances of *Norma* in Cologne."

"Performances at Köln are no concern of mine. The production of *Adelaide* is. I was not consulted about your late arrival. Next year, when we perform *La Straniera,* I shall be in charge of *ev*erything: schedules, sets, costumes, production—and singers. Especially singers." He smiled his sunset-over-the-gulag smile. "No production can be perfect unless one man has total control. I have made it clear to the committee that I must have that control."

"I have no doubt you will get it," Brad said with a sigh.

"Is that quite understood? Now let us turn to your *aria di sortita* in the first act. . . ."

He bent forward an inch or two, apparently in a gesture of intimacy, and went into lengthy instructions on how to phrase, project, and act during the heroine's opening aria. Any idea that this was hardly the time or place did not seem to occur to him. Peter Fortnum's powers as interpreter were taxed to the limit. Natalya listened with every appearance of attention. She was used to the ways of totalitarianism.

At the bar the gaunt, exhausted woman with the pulled-back hair, who incidentally was Des Capper's wife, was up to her eyes in orders. Des, however, was not in the business of helping behind any bar. He stopped by the table where Gillian Soames and Ronnie Wimsett were still deep in the entrancing business of character assassination. Nowhere, except perhaps the House of Commons, offers more scope for that sport than the theater, and they were set fair to continue until the call for last drinks.

"Everything all right here?" Des asked, clearly intending to muscle in. "Anything I can do for you?"

Gillian Soames raised her head, clearly about to say, "Yes—piss off." But Ronnie Wimsett, a peaceable young man, took her hand in his, gazed adoringly into her eyes in the manner of a second-rate tenor in Act I of *Bohème,* then turned to Des and sighed. "No—everything is just wonderful."

There was nothing Des could do but leave them to themselves. He threw some orders at his drudge of a wife, then pottered off to his little office behind Reception, convinced that that pair were resuming an affair of long standing. It was one of a series of assumptions, some true, some false, that Des Capper made about his artistic guests. These assumptions soon attained in his mind the status of facts, as the many harebrained theories he read about in magazines did. They were stored up and gloated over, for Des was convinced in his mind that knowledge was power. It never occurred to him that knowledge was also danger.

3

OPEN STAGE

The nature of Jason Thark's directorial gloss on that year's
Ketterick Arts Festival play became clear to Gillian the
next day. On the way down to breakfast on that, her first
morning of rehearsals, she stopped to study a large poster
in Reception detailing all the major events and the backup
arrangements. Among these latter was a lunchtime lecture
on *The Chaste Apprentice,* to be given by the lecturer in
Gay Studies at the local polytechnic.

Whether the chaste apprentice of the play was gay in the
modern sense of the word was open to question. That he
was dreary in any sense of the word was incontrovertible.
Gillian mentally reserved her position on whether the gloss
could be made to work.

Behind the grand apron stage, now finally assembled,
lay the magnificent and sprawling kitchens of the Saracen's
Head as well as a couple of private dining rooms. When
the festival began, the actors would take over the dining
rooms as well as a good half of the kitchens. Until then the
actors tended to lounge around in the yard as the play was
being rehearsed or camp in the dining rooms where they
could talk and laugh and quarrel with more freedom. To-

day was the first full stage rehearsal, and Gillian experienced the familiar lift of the heart when Clarissa Galloway, as Lady Melinda Purefoy, came on with Peter Fortnum as Peter Patterwit to begin the play:

MELINDA: A private word, Sir, nothing else.
PETER PATTERWIT: You shall fructify in that which you came for: your pleasure shall be satisfied to your full contention: I will (fairest tree of generation) watch when our young friend is erected (that is to say up) . . .

The authorship of *The Chaste Apprentice of Bowe* was a matter of some lethargic scholarly dispute. It was variously attributed to Dekker and Chapman, to Beaumont and Marston, to Beaumont and Massinger, and to Heywood and Middleton. It was generally agreed that two hands were discernible in it, though only half a brain.

At the lower level of the play the story line concerns the attempts of two apprentices, Peter Patterwit and Matthew Cotter (who is really Sir James Cotterel in disguise), to persuade the third apprentice, Simon Clear, to lose his virginity. At the same time, Sir James is being sought by his true love, Lady Melinda Purefoy, whom a family feud is preventing him from marrying. On the other level, the apprentices' master, Ralph Greatheart, the goldsmith, is resisting his wife's attempts to marry off their daughter, Alison (Gillian's part, and a lousy one), to an elderly aristocratic roué, Sir Pecunius Slackwater. At the end of the play the chaste apprentice loses his virginity to a whore in Deptford, Matthew is unmasked as Sir James (much to the chagrin of Mistress Greatheart, who would have consigned her daughter to him had she known), and Alison is given in marriage to Peter Patterwit, who is thus much too well rewarded for all his dreadful jokes in the course of the play.

Jason Thark's notion of how to ginger up the play was evident from the moment Ronnie Wimsett took to the stage as the chaste apprentice. He had been instructed to deck out his performance with every gesture from the camp repertoire: the fluttering hands, the swooping voice, the wiggled bottom, the mincing walk. It was pure sixties camp, an exercise in behavioral archaeology: Thus are homosexuals *not* played on stage today, and thus do they *not* behave. But Ronnie was a superb comedian, and the performance in itself was a riot. Gillian could see Ronnie making a great effect with it, which he could never have done with the lines as they appeared on the printed page:

SIMON CLEAR: Why sure, Madam, I will do it straight

was no great shakes as a line, yet said with a spaniel wiggle, a lewd gesture unseen by his mistress, and with vocal leaps worthy of a Mozart soprano, it was a surefire laugh getter.

Gillian also saw, of course, that as an interpretation it was open to several objections: The apprentice was supposed to be a dull young man, so that every other line Ronnie spoke and half the things that were said about him by others were contradicted by his physical performance; this young man might be innocent of the knowledge of women, but chaste he could not conceivably be. In Jason Thark's reinterpretation the crowning episode with the whore of Deptford became no more than a brief shift of allegiance. Not that it mattered much; this was no masterwork. But homosexuals were these days as sensitive about their image as other minority groups. They could take against the production, and—remembering the usual makeup of the festival's audience—Gillian could imagine them banding together to form a fair-sized picket.

The idea that there might be some element of exaggeration and stereotyping in this performance got through even to Des Capper. On the second day of stage rehearsals he oozed up behind Gillian and Ronnie, while up onstage Carston Galloway, as Ralph Greatheart, was having a tremendous row with his (stage) wife. Having so much experience with his real one, Carston was making a great thing of it, and Gillian and Ronnie were talking in their normal voices when Des came up behind them and thrust himself uninvited into their conversation.

"That's a real little gem of a performance you're giving there," Des nasaled out, clapping Ronnie on the shoulder. "Got all the mannerisms fit to kill. I was pissing myself laughing back there."

"Thank you," said Ronnie briefly, unwilling to be rude to a man in his own courtyard.

"I wonder—don't mind me saying this, do you?— whether you've quite got at the psychology of the bloke. I wonder whether you're really living inside him yet, understanding what makes him tick. Ever heard of Stanislavski?"

"Didn't he compose *The Rite of Spring?*" said Ronnie brusquely, and marched backstage. Des nodded sagely.

"I think I got through to him," he said with grotesque complacency. "You could see he got my point. Though I think it was a quite different Stanislavski wrote *The Rite of Spring.*"

As the days of rehearsal flew by and the play took shape, both Gillian and Peter saw enough of the Galloways to wonder whether the balance of power—was that the word? of strength? of influence?—was quite as it had seemed to them on the day of their arrival. Gillian had seen the situation then as pretty much the same as when she had acted with them in a Haymarket revival of *The Rivals,* or two years previously here in Ketterick in *The Faire Seducer*; Peter, new to them, had seen it as the classic henpecked husband situation, though with a strong element of fighting back. Now they began to revise their opinions.

The first thing they noted was that Carston Galloway was giving a superb performance as Ralph Greatheart: warm, crusty, independent, salty. This was light-years away from the elegant, youngish man, cigarette holder in one hand, White Lady in the other, which was how the theatergoing public had hitherto seen him. Galloway was making the transition to being a good character actor. And like most actors, he knew his worth. Peter heard him one day when he took Jason Thark aside.

"Oh, Jason, that understudy to little Soames—is that still going begging?"

"Yes, we haven't got anybody."

"Then give it to Susan, will you? Susan Fanshaw. She's not really stretched by all these fiddling stage-management jobs."

Jason paused only for a second. "All right, Carston—gladly. Will you tell her?"

"If you like," said Carston, winking.

Whether Clarissa would ever make the transition to successful character actress could only be a matter for guesswork. What was sure was that she was not willing to make it yet. That really was the trouble: Melinda Purefoy was young love, she was romantic interest, she was dewy-fresh virgin. The actor playing Sir James Cotterel, with whom she was in love, was a public-school smoothie of twenty-six. Whereas Clarissa was—what? The reference books differed, or rather most of them kept silent, having no wish to give currency to Clarissa's blatant untruths. But the record of her career was public knowledge: She had made her West End debut in an H. M. Tennent revival of *Present Laughter* in 1962. Put her beside her supposed lover in the cruel light of day—which, after all, was what they would be acting under, with some blessed softening of evening light and the gulf between them was brutally apparent. Put her, on the other hand, beside Constance Geary, a gin-ridden old bag whom everybody loved, who was giving a great performance as Old Lady Sneer, and you saw at once what Clarissa would become. Both were mature ladies at different stages of maturity. They were sisters under the gin.

Why she wanted to play the part was obvious—to prove she could still convincingly manage young women. It was as unwise an ambition as could be conceived, and how she had got the part was far from obvious. Gillian and Peter never saw any great evidence that her bedding with Jason Thark brought her tangible rewards in the way of added prominence or any shielding from his wrath. Could it be, then, that she had got the part because they wanted Carston for Ralph? Quite the reverse, in fact, of how she wanted people to see the situation.

Clarissa, however, was not to be underestimated, and she retained her unrivaled power of fuss making, which was legendary in theaters the length and breadth of the country. On Gillian's fifth day of rehearsals, during the midmorning break when everybody was in the little private dining room drinking coffee or something stronger, Clarissa burst in on them in a manner that certainly did not suggest she was going to ask whether anyone was for tennis. She used, in fact, her standard stage manner for delivering disastrous news or staggering developments.

"Really! It's too bad! Jason, you'll have to do something."

Jason was going over business with Ronnie Wimsett. He merely turned and raised a coolly inquiring eyebrow.

"It's that appalling Capper person. I've just been up to my bedroom—"

"Which one, darling?" inquired Carston languidly. "Ours or Jason's?"

"Ours, pig. And I found this . . . antipodean monstrosity poking around in my drawers."

"Underwear fetishist, would you say?"

Clarissa drew her hand across her brow. "God! Don't trot out all those ancient jokes, Carston. In the drawers of my dressing table. Actually poking and prying in them."

"Did you catch him in the act?" inquired Jason.

"Well, not quite," admitted Clarissa with a sigh designed to be heard in the dress circle. "One of those damned floorboards creaked just as I was opening the door. He'd got the drawer shut by the time I'd got into the room."

"What did he say?" Carston asked.

"He said he was just checking up on the maid's work." She put on a hideously nasal stage Australian accent. " 'She's new to the job, y'see, and I'd like to be sure she's up to the high standards we set ourselves at the Saracen.' "

Jason shrugged. "Seems a fairly foolproof explanation."

"Oh, does it? Well, let me tell you, the maid who does our room every day, including this morning, was here two years ago when we were in *The Faire Seducer*. I count her as an old friend. She's just thrilled by anything to do with the theater. I gave her a pair of my stockings when we finished here last time—they do so appreciate something personal, these people."

This artless revelation of Clarissa's rather blunted the impact of her indignation. The assembled company was so staggered that the Galloways apparently tipped the hotel staff with items of their castoff clothing that they were unable for a moment to focus their minds on Des Capper's iniquities.

Constance Geary sighed and said privately to Peter Fortnum: "I wonder if I could tip my maid with my castoff gin bottles." Then suddenly a thought struck her, and she spoke up. "Oh—I've just remembered."

"What?" asked several people.

"Yesterday morning, when I was in the bathroom—making the best, darlings, of what never was very much—the maid came in and started doing the room. I sang away like mad, to tell her not to interrupt my mysteries. When I finally emerged, blushing all too artificially, she wasn't to be seen, and the door was open. So I poked my shy, virginal little head out, and there she was with this anthropoid Australian at the far end of the corridor. She had my wastepaper basket in her hand, and as far as I could see, darlings, they were actually *counting* the half bottles of gin in it."

"Really!" said everybody, laughing as they were intended to do.

"Perhaps they were thinking of sending your score to the *Guinness Book of Records,* darling," said Ronnie.

"But isn't it such *fun?*" exclaimed Connie. "What do you think he does with his knowledge?"

"Enjoys it?" suggested Jason.

"Oh, I rather hoped he might feed it into a computer or something so I could become a statistic."

Clarissa was annoyed at losing the limelight and annoyed that Connie had defused any anger she might have generated against their prying Mine Host.

"You call this *fun*?" she demanded with a vocal swoop reminiscent of an eagle picking up a lamb. "Fun? To have this *grubby* little creature scrabbling around in our private lives?"

"Well, it's hardly something we need to take seriously, is it?" Connie said reasonably enough. "It's a bit late in the day for me to go all coy about the fact that I spend much of my time pickled in gin. And you Galloways run much the most public private lives in the business."

"Carston and I have always been quite open about—"

"Yes, darling—spare us the party manifesto. Since you *have* been so open, what's the point in getting upset if this little Australian mole comes sniffing around in your underwear drawer? It's been washed in public often enough, heaven knows."

Clarissa shot her such a look that they resembled nothing so much as two old bags in early Coward. She held her fire only because she knew Connie was a redoubtable opponent.

"What's he doing it for, that's what I want to know?" she asked, looking around. "What does he want?"

"It's for the knowledge," Gillian said. "It's a sort of instinct, and as Jason said, he probably just enjoys it—hugs it to himself, makes good stories of it after we're gone. He is unutterably loathsome, but he can hardly expect to be able to *use* things which none of us is trying to hide."

But Clarissa was far from being placated. "I think something should be done. You, Jason—you're the obvious one to do it. You could go direct to the festival committee. It's your first year here—you don't remember how wonderful it was at the Saracen in previous years. If something's not done quickly, the festival will lose all its spirit, all its old character. That man's got to *go.*"

Jason took that point, at least, seriously. "I think, actually, you may be right. But the time to do something is not *now.* All we would achieve would be bad blood, recrimination, frustration. Not good for the show, for any of the shows. What might work is a collective letter, after this festival is over, from all the artists staying or working at the Saracen—a letter sent both to the festival committee and to the hotel chain that appointed him. Though what on earth possessed them to appoint him in the first place I can't imagine."

"Might one suggest blackmail?" said Clarissa sweetly.

"That's a point." Jason was thoughtful. "If so, we've really got a problem on our hands. . . . Come on, boys and girls. Back to the grindstone. All onstage. We've really got to lick the brothel scene into shape."

Gillian had had to revise her opinion of Jason Thark as director somewhat. There were large areas of the play where he did, in everyone's opinion, excellent things. He worked tirelessly with Carston Galloway on the part of Ralph Greatheart, and together they created a rounded, human, and funny character from the bare bones of the script. He coaxed from Constance Geary, whose technique had been formed in proscenium-arch theaters, a performance that exploited all the potential of the apron stage. All the swirling crowd scenes, including the Deptford brothel one, went with great brio. The chaste apprentice as archgay seemed to Gillian funny but misconceived, and with Clarissa he could do nothing—but Melinda Purefoy was never going to be much of a part in anybody's hands.

But all in all she had no doubt he was going to put together a real performance and probably have a critical success.

Of Jason as director, then, her estimate had risen. Of Jason as a person she felt she could reserve judgment. On Jason's intelligence generally, her opinion took a nosedive one evening. (She was sitting with Peter, Constance, and him at a table for four and telling them how much better the food at the Saracen used to be.) Suddenly Jason came up with one of his "ideas."

"I say, wouldn't it be effective if Singh could introduce each act with a few Elizabethan part songs?"

"With *what*?"

"Elizabethan part songs. I'll suggest it to Brad."

"I didn't know Singh was a ventriloquist," said Gillian. "I suggest you say Elizabethan lute songs."

"That sort of thing," said Jason blithely. "Something suitably bawdy could go down well."

Unfortunately the idea came to nothing. Singh had such songs in his repertoire and had performed them in Balliol College Hall and to other select musical societies. But on the first night of *The Chaste Apprentice* he would be performing Handel arias in an operatic concert in Town Hall.

"The opening concert of the festival," said Bradford Mallory. "A bit of a popular mishmash, to get audiences, but I've persuaded some of the London critics along to hear Singh. I am *not* having the dear boy dashing from one end of town to the other to fit you in. But he could sing on the other nights."

But Jason was only interested in the first night. That, after all, was the night the critics came. As with Brad, it was success with them that really counted with Jason.

"Rather typical," said Gillian. "And what appalling ignorance in somebody directing an Elizabethan play. I think he is essentially brilliant but vulgar."

She might, if she had thought about it, have admitted that this was a pretty good combination of qualities for the director of a minor Jacobean comedy. But Gillian was not disposed to like directors, and her nerves were just a little bit on edge as the first night of the festival drew nearer. So were all their nerves. The matter of Des didn't help to keep them calm. They were all watching him, wondering. More to the point, they felt him watching them. Few of them had any inhibitions about their sexual lives, though few would care to conduct them under the sort of spotlight the Galloways directed on themselves. But it can be that the most lavishly open people in fact have corners in their lives that they reserve from public scrutiny, and the grubby, obsessive nature of Des's interest made them feel threatened. It was a rare person who did not have a few private, personal things to be cherished in solitude, blushed about, cried over in the dark.

Who could be sure that Des, in his snufflings in the undergrowth, would not find some path that would show him the way to those personal walled gardens?

4

THE ALHAMBRA THEATER

Five days before the festival was due to begin, in thin afternoon sunlight, Peter Fortnum made his way through the streets of Ketterick towards the Alhambra Theater. The afternoon session at the Saracen was mainly to be devoted to scenes involving the Greatheart family, and he was not required until later. There were great stretches of the play in which Peter Patterwit did not appear, and contemplating the arid desert of smutty facetiae and labored puns that constituted the dialogue when he did, Peter was inclined to think the audiences might wish those stretches still longer.

On days when he was free he had got into the habit of going along to the Alhambra to see if he could be useful, which meant, in effect, to act as interpreter. Today, however, he had a more specific mission. He no longer looked at the silver-blue-and-maroon Moorish facade, merely nodded to the stage-door keeper, and forged his way unhesitatingly through the maze of cold, painted brick passageways to the backstage area. Today was to be the first full stage rehearsal with orchestra.

As Peter slid into the wings, he signaled to Natalya.

"Ah—Peter," she said in a pause.

"Oh, Peter—great," shouted Terry Potts, the producer. "Sit there at the side in case we need you, will you?"

Glad to be recognized and useful, Peter sat quietly in the wings and peered out into the auditorium. He recognized the director of the festival casting a benevolent eye over the second cornerstone of his two weeks of events. He saw Brad Mallory, with Singh, sitting in the third row and looking out for the interests of his other client performing at Ketterick. Very much his secondary interest, thought Peter rather bitterly.

He turned his glance back to the stage area and took in his first view of the set. The festival organizers had gone back to a designing pair who had served them well two years before for Donizetti's *Il Diluvio Universale.* ("This is less a revival than a resurrection, in the Burke and Hare sense of the word"—*The Observer.*) Now they had constructed a permanent set with fragmentary bits of castle dotted around. It was handsome and serviceable, and splashes of color were provided by tartan wall hangings, for just as Bellini had called his opera set in Portsmouth *I Puritani di Scozia,* so Donizetti had apparently been convinced (or preferred to believe for romantic/commercial reasons) that Birckenhead was north of the border. Indeed, to him or his librettist all England seemed to be an appendage of Scotland, which at least righted a balance, some might think.

"With passion," shouted Gunter Gottlieb, a domineering intensity oozing from every pore. "This man is your lover and your king! Thrill your audience!"

For upstage had entered the handsome figure of the Swedish-American tenor who was to sing Roberto il Bruce ("Broo-chay," as the language coach constantly insisted they all must call him). On stage Adelaide di Birckenhead, her husband Adalberto, and a motley collection of retainers and clansmen were about to launch into an exciting ensemble with choral backing. It was an ensemble that was later to serve for a vengeful heroine who had been abandoned in the catacombs in *Maria di Rudenz* and for conscience-tormented Christians and Romans in *Poliuto,* proving that Donizetti certainly recognized a showstopping tune when he hit on one.

"Now—passion!" shouted Gunter Gottlieb. "Controlled, thrilling passion!"

Adelaide di Birckenhead had had a history even more checkered than most of Donizetti's immense output. Composed originally in 1825 for the soprano Ferron and the castrato Velluti, it had been put aside when the latter deserted the company for meatier pickings in London. Later, at the height of his powers in 1835, Donizetti had unusually found himself without a libretto. "For God's sake write me a libretto," he had gone around frenziedly wailing to all his poet friends, displaying all the withdrawal symptoms of today's druggies. To no avail. He had had to reset almost the entire text of *Adelaide,* recasting Velluti's part for tenor. Unluckily, he had promptly forgotten about it in the excitement of composing *Lucia di Lammermoor.* Part of the manuscript score had lain for years in the Sterling Library in London, while the rest had been discovered only the previous year serving as a doorstop in the Conservatory of Music in Naples. This was to be its first-ever performance.

The story concerned a crucial moment in Scottish history, which it travestied. It was said by one Italian commentator to have *"origine walterscottiana,"* a suitably vague description which obviated the need to ransack the works of the great unread Walter. The noble and patriotic

Adelaide is unfortunate enough to be married to the skulking Adalberto, who supports the English tyrant Edgardo, who is busy suppressing the noble Scots. Adelaide is in love with the true Scottish king Roberto il Bruce, who is in hiding from the ravaging English armies. When he comes to *il castello di Birckenhead* in disguise, seeking succor, he presents her with a crisis of conscience which she solves spectacularly in the last act by hacking off her husband's head, then stabbing herself at the climax of a thrilling cabolotta. The stalwart clansmen of Birckenhead, typically willing to change sides at the drop of a coin, acclaim Roberto as their king.

The American tenor Krister Kroll stood at the Romanesque doorway at the very back of the stage, decked in furs left over from *Attila* ("proving that even Verdi nodded"— *The Observer*) in 1978 and tartan bought in bulk from the local Pricewise chain of discount stores. He was the only one in costume, because he said it was the sort of costume you needed to get the feel of. He was in the mold of so many American tenors: stalwart, clean limbed, and rather small of voice. He had appeared, pleasantly, in Rossini's *Torvaldo e Dorliska* ("a stillborn curiosity"—*The Observer*) the year before. As he stood, dramatically, at the doorway, first Adelaide whispered her apprehensions at the sight of her lover, then her husband expressed his suspicions at the sight (in furs and tartan) of the handsome stranger. And then Krister Kroll launched himself into the great tune:

> *Io son pari ad uom cui scende*
> *Già la scure sulla testa . . .*

Even to Peter, sitting in the wings, it was an anticlimax: It was like being handed lemonade when you had expected champagne. He saw the festival director mask an expression of dismay; he seemed to be wondering what sound, if any, would penetrate to the gods.

Gunter Gottlieb, with an impatient gesture, stopped the orchestra. Silently, pregnantly, he pointed with his baton to the center front of the stage. Krister Kroll looked uncertainly from Gottlieb to Terry Potts, the producer, in the stalls. Terry was already jumping out of his seat in agitation.

"But, Gunter, you can't have him there. He's just arrived, and he's apprehensive and agitated, uncertain of his reception. He can't just barge his way right to the center of things."

Natalya seemed to agree with him. She was expostulating violently in Russian against the improbability of the thing, which Peter was just about, somewhat nervously, to translate when he saw that Brad Mallory, with Singh in tow, had come on to the stage and Brad was expostulating with her and calming her. He seemed to be able to do it without benefit of common language, but that was doubtless a necessary talent of agents.

None of which cut any ice at all with Gunter Gottlieb. He pointed icily once more to center stage. Nervously, Krister Kroll moved forward.

"Now again from the soprano."

The annoying thing was that the man was undoubtedly right. You couldn't have the opera's one big moment, comparable with the Sextet from *Lucia,* go by default because the tenor couldn't be heard. Now Kroll rang out sweet and true, lacking only that dash of kingly swagger and animal excitement that the part seemed to demand. In a conflict between what made musical sense and what made dramatic sense, the music had to win. And yet, and yet . . .

"Now," said Gottlieb, stopping the orchestra at the end of the number and gesturing to the producer as if he were a dog he was sending to retrieve a partridge, "now you rearrange the staging."

And with a sigh the poor man, knowing when he was beaten, did just that.

"All right, if we must, we must. Yes, I know it's improbable, Natalya. I agree with you, darling. But you'll have to go *there*, center left, and . . ."

"I know how he feels, poor bastard" came a voice behind Peter's shoulders. He turned and was astonished to see the figure of Des Capper arriving in the wings. His eyes gleamed brightly with malice as he contemplated the scene. "Been a bit of a brouhaha, has there? Looks like it."

Peter, for some reason that he could not analyze, did not want to swap derogatory opinions of a fellow artist with Des Capper. Gottlieb was a bastard, but a brilliant bastard. He merely said: "They're just having to rearrange the positions a bit."

"Looks like there's been a good old-fashioned blowup to *me*. I know the signs. That swine has got the light of battle in his eyes. I know just how that producer must feel."

"Oh, yes?"

"*Just* how he feels. I've felt his nasty tongue myself. He's got no thought for the feelings of others. I'm sensitive. I don't like being spoken to like I was dirt."

Peter did not comment on Des's sensitivity. "What are you doing here?" he asked.

"Oh, I'm committee. Ex-officio as landlord of the Saracen. I've a right to go anywhere—" He suddenly caught sight of Singh, still onstage with Brad Mallory. "My! I see they had Indians in Birckenhead even then. Running the corner shops, I suppose."

Peter turned away with a grimace of distaste and didn't bother to correct him. He wondered about Des's right to go anywhere. It wasn't a right that any other member of the committee seemed to exercise. Peter turned back to the stage. Gunter Gottlieb, on the podium, was softly tapping his baton on the score. His expression suggested that he was long-suffering but had been pushed near the limits of even his saintly endurance.

"Now," he said when Terry Potts paused for breath, "is all clear? We go from there to the end of scene."

It was only ten minutes of music, but it seemed endless to Peter. The ensemble developed into a big scene of suspicion and suppressed fears, with every character generously sharing his innermost feelings with the audience. The problems of balance were acute, not least because of Krister Kroll's sweet but small tenor, which was swamped by the larger voices around him. Again and again Gottlieb stopped the music, reorganized the singers, hushed the orchestra, subjected Krister Kroll to heavy, biting irony, lashed the other singers, and ridiculed members of his orchestra. Even Peter felt himself sweating with tension. It was at the height of the unpleasant session, when the frayed tempers of singers and players were beginning to conquer their fear of Gottlieb and find open expression, that Peter from the wings saw Gottlieb's "heavy" sitting in the front row of the stalls, a slow, relishing smile on his face. He might not like music, but he certainly did appreciate aggro.

At long, long last Gottlieb called a break, and the tension dissolved. Peter's immediate visual impression was one of sweat. The orchestral musicians, jostling their way out through the door at the back of the pit, were shining with it, and one of the younger men seemed close to tears. The chorus members were bathed in it and wiping their foreheads, and the principals were drenched and close to the breaking point. Backstage everything became a jumble as singers and players made for the Green Room in search of cold drinks or chocolate to revive their strength. Peter was conscious of the Mexican baritone standing by a wall, clenching and unclenching his fists and muttering furiously to himself in the manner of operatic baritones. He was conscious in a far corner of the room of Krister Kroll being collared by Des Capper. Des had been in the Green Room when they arrived, making himself at home and waiting for a victim. The chain-saw voice cut through to Peter:

"You know, physiologically speaking there's no such thing as a small or a large voice. It's all a question of the diaphragm and the way you use it. If you'll take a tip from me . . ."

The American seemed to be a supernaturally nice person, for he was showing only small nervous signs of wanting to get away. Then Natalya Radilova arrived from the stage, and Peter darted away and took her aside.

"The message came through for you," he said in Russian. "It was 'Best wishes for rehearsals and the first night.' "

Natalya smiled, a smile apparently out of all proportion to the banality of the message. She squeezed Peter's hand, and they found themselves a private corner of the Green Room.

Once the chaos there had sorted itself out into groups, Peter and Natalya found themselves joined by Krister Kroll, still wiping the sweat from his open, engaging face.

"Who is that *creep* who got hold of me?" he demanded. "That schmuck? That smart-ass? I have never *heard* such crap as that guy was spouting."

"It's the landlord of the Saracen," said Peter. "A loathsome Australian by the name of Capper."

"I've known plenty of Australian singers," said Kroll, "and they've mostly been great people. But this, this—"

"It's not the nationality, it's the type. As with Gottlieb. Keep away from Capper. He's poison."

"Boy, am I glad I rented an apartment. I nearly went to the Saracen this time, to treat myself. But to have that creep giving me advice about breathing all day would—"

But he stopped, because heads were turning in the direction of the door, and conversation was stilling so that people could hear what was going on there. Gunter Gottlieb, alone of the performers, did not require sustenance or refreshment. His heavy had procured a soft drink for himself and was standing massively behind Gottlieb, doubtless to prevent a stab in the back. But Gottlieb had captured a prize: the director of the festival, who had been sitting in on the rehearsal after checking receipts at the box office. He had been hauled to the Green Room by Gottlieb with an end in view.

"Next year," said Gottlieb in his unattractive clipped tones, "we do *Fidelio*. People are waiting for my *Fidelio.*"

"It's an idea," said the director in a practiced neutral voice. He was a local man, but one with long experience in arts administration. "Though of course we have tended to stick with the Italians. But next year's already tied up. We're doing *La Straniera.*"

"I change my mind," said Gottlieb, putting aside *La Straniera* with a contemptuous sweep of the hand. "We do *Fidelio.*"

"My dear chap, it's not on. Even if the committee were to agree—which I wouldn't bank on—it's still not on. You don't seem to understand the operatic world. All the worthwhile singers are booked up years in advance. All the principals for *Straniera* have been engaged. They'd hardly be suitable for *Fidelio*."

"I have my cast here," said Gottlieb, drawing a sheet of paper out of his pocket. "With alternatives if my first choices are not available. It is clear, yes? If you can get neither of them, you come back to me. Understood?"

"No, I'm sorry, old chap, it is not understood. There's no question of our upsetting our existing arrangements—"

It was at this point that Des bustled up.

"I wonder if I could mediate. As a member of the festival committee I think we ought to try to come to some compro—"

Gunter Gottlieb turned on him with a savage fury and pointed to the door.

"Out! Out! Out!" he bellowed. "I do not take advice from taverners! Get out and do not come near this theater ever again, is understood? You come near one of my rehearsals ever again and I have you removed, thrown out on your fat bottom. Is understood?"

Des had retreated three steps. When the heavy advanced from behind Gottlieb's back, he spluttered back any riposte and turned to slink out.

"No offense," he was heard to mutter.

Gunter Gottlieb turned back to the festival director, iciness reasserting itself.

"Is all your committee fools? They must learn to know their place. Now, as to *Fidelio*, I have a designer in mind . . ."

"Oh, my God," said Peter, pushing back his chair.

"This bear garden makes life with Jason Thark seem a haven of rest. I must be getting back to the Saracen."

"Peter," wailed Natalya in Russian, "you're forsaking me. I have that dreadful finale to get through."

"Sorry, love. Duty calls. I was only given till four. They'll probably all be crying out for some fresh and engaging humor from Peter Patterwit. . . ."

But they weren't, and he spent most of the rest of the afternoon and early evening lounging around, not unhappy to have escaped from the Alhambra. Gunter Gottlieb's plans for the festival were inevitably the topic of conversation in the Shakespeare Bar that evening. Gillian and Peter went out and bought a Chinese takeaway, enduring with sweet smiles the murderous glances from Des as they marched through Reception with the little cardboard boxes. Des, understandably, was looking murderous all evening. When they had eaten their fill in Gillian's room, they went down to the Shakespeare and found Natalya, Ronnie Wimsett, and Krister Kroll at a table together. The last named kept looking round nervously for routes of escape should Des feel impelled to come over and offer further advice on what he should do with his diaphragm. Gillian and Peter joined them, and soon they were well at it.

"It would change the whole character of the festival," Ronnie Wimsett said when he was told of Gottlieb's demands. He was a serious-minded, private young man, but he had come to feel passionately about the festival, to appropriate it in some way as a part of himself, as Gillian had. "The two things go together—Jacobean drama and nineteenth-century Italian opera. People like the music critic of *The Observer* sneer because it's not ear-wrenching stuff, but in fact it's wonderfully direct and passionate, really theatrical. And it's what people expect of Ketterick, what gives it its character. Give Gottlieb his way and it'll become just like any other festival. We'll be doing *The Marriage of Figaro* and *Pallyarse and Smellyhands,* and they'll be *his Figaro* and *his Pallyarse.* When that happens, we'll be just like any other festival. The next thing will be, he'll start dictating what plays are done, to tie in with *his* opera of the year."

"Still, the guy, though scary, has a way with him," said Kristor Kroll ruefully. "What're the odds that Ketterick will *not* be doing *La Straniera* next year?"

"Never having heard it," said Gillian, "I can't weep bitter tears about the *specific* loss."

"Oh, it's great Bellini, and practically unknown. Even Beefy and Scrawny haven't recorded it."

Beefy and Scrawny, it was explained, were the currently highest paid tenor and soprano in the world.

"It's the principle I'm concerned about," said Ronnie.

"It's the personal level that concerns me," said Kroll. "It won't be the death of the festival if I don't come back, and I certainly won't while that monster is in charge. I'm a peaceful guy, but some of the things he said to me . . ."

Natalya Radilova, who was beginning to follow bits of conversation in English, went off into a bitter tirade in Russian. Peter paraphrased for her.

"She's complaining about my not being there when she did her big final scene this afternoon. He was vile to her apparently. It's a difficult scene— It's where she brings her husband's head in on a platter and goes mad over it."

"My God!" said Gillian. "I thought this was supposed to be *'opera semiseria.'* I'd really hate to see a serious one."

"No, that's just another example of the amiable Gunter's influence," explained Kroll. "There are two manuscript endings, and they'd chosen the first. In that, some functionary comes along and explains that for unspecified reasons Adelaide's marriage has been invalid all along. Adelaide goes off to be Roberto il Bruce's queen amid general rejoicing, with only the baritone throwing a fit. That Mexican is awfully good at throwing fits. Anyway, along comes Gottlieb at the first rehearsal and says: 'No, we do the second.' In that one Adelaide hacks her husband's head off and then stabs herself after some fearsome coloratura. That's what Natalya is having to do. The annoying thing is that, as usual, Gottlieb is right. It's a much more effective conclusion."

Natalya went on at length in Russian. Peter explained. "Natalya says it is ridiculously difficult to do because it's so way out—so gory and savage. The audience will reject it at the drop of a hat, because it just seems impossibly savage."

Once again a familiar voice came from behind Peter's shoulder. He was beginning to feel he had a minor devil following him around.

"You wouldn't say it was impossible if you'd seen some of the things I saw in 1947, at the time of independence. Some of those poor bloody Indians had been so hacked about that their own mothers wouldn't have known them."

"Was this when you were viceroy?" Gillian asked sweetly. But Des did not appear to be listening. He was gazing ahead dreamily.

"Oh, yes, I've seen some sights, don't you worry." His eyes were on a far table, where Gunter Gottlieb was pontificating to the Mexican baritone and Brad Mallory. "I learned all you need to know in India about how to even scores."

5

THE ALCOVE

A mist hung over Ketterick and the London suburbs around it as the first day of the festival dawned. During breakfast, though, it began to lift, and by ten the town was bathed in gentle sunshine from a pale blue sky.

The visitors were arriving, that was for sure. By now Ketterick was securely established in the festival catalog, cunningly poised to take advantage of that moment, around May to June, when longen folk to goon on artistic pilgrimages. By car and coach, by late-arriving trains from Newcastle, Bath, and Manchester, even by bicycle they came, changing the character of the complacent suburb. Some of the visitors were regulars, with their diaries already filled in and their seats booked; some came on spec and sat around in parks and squares going through the festival brochure to see what they might take in. There was the *Play of Daniel* in the ruins of Walsey Abbey, three miles out of town; there was Bruno Brazen, the well-known American organist and showman in St. Margaret's Church; there was a wispy French soprano singing wispy French songs; there was Morris dancing in the Queen's Square and a superb black dance group from Leeds in the

Civic Hall. Tonight there was *The Chaste Apprentice* at the Saracen's Head and a popular operatic concert. Both these events were booked solid, but for the disappointed there was a beer race in the Ketterick football stadium. There was—as there was on that other pilgrimage, to Canterbury —something for everybody.

At one time or another during the day most of the new arrivals strolled into the Saracen's Head to look at the wonderful courtyard and stage. One of the hazards of this was that Des Capper was liable to sidle up with a proprietary air and ply them with information, advice, and cures for constipation. One of the American visitors, a lecturer in Renaissance studies at Kent State University, called him "a true English innkeeper" and "a real Harry Bailly after Chaucer's own heart"; but most of the rest sensibly ducked off to one or other of the bars. These were kept very busy, and Mrs. Capper in the Shakespeare was rushed off her feet, though help from her husband got she none.

If they were lucky, these stray visitors saw scraps of last-minute rehearsal. In the true spirit of the Elizabethan troupe, the cast was quite unembarrassed about putting finishing touches to the performance before future members of the audience, who marveled at the contrast between their apparel of jeans and T-shirts and their talk of ruffles and codpieces. The brothel scene had caused particular difficulty, being such a whirl of activity, and the casual dropper-in might see Peter Patterwit open that unedifying scene with Doll, the whore, indulging in some typically sparkling Jacobean wit:

DOLL: You, goodman swineface.
PETER: What—will you murder me?

DOLL: You remember, slave, how you abused me
t'other night in a tavern?
PETER: Not I, by this light.
DOLL: No, but by candlelight you did . . .

Oddly enough, such samples did not put off most of the
visitors. Somehow the setting and atmosphere (or the "am-
bience," as several of them preferred to put it) were so
exactly right for the play that many of them dashed
straight off to the festival box office to see what tickets
were available for later performances.

If Des was a hazard for the occasional visitor, he was an
ever-present danger to the performers and residents. It
was, after all, his first festival, and he naturally wanted to
see everything he could. Unfortunately, he wanted to be
part of everything, too, and there was abundant evidence
that despite his recent rebuff at the Alhambra, the start of
festivities had gone to his head. He was liable to pop up
everywhere, poking his nose in and having his little word
of worthless commendation or erroneous advice to all and
sundry. Few were polite back, but he gave no sign to their
faces of having registered their contempt.

Constance Geary's part as Old Lady Sneer was not a
large one. She played a cousin of Sir Pecunius Slackwater,
dragged into the marriage negotiations. Her performance
was already a matter of well-routined gestures and intona-
tions, and she left it to younger generations to over-
rehearse. She sat around in various parts of the Saracen's
Head, holding court and allowing visitors to buy her
drinks. Sometimes she could be found on her own in the
little alcoves and open spaces that the inn abounded in,
quite happy with her memories and her gin bottle. She also
noticed a lot more than might have been thought, though

she would have been hard put to order it in any way in her mind. It was nearly lunchtime, in one of those alcoves, apparently deep in thought after a copious swig from her bottle, that she saw Des Capper coming.

"All on your own-e-o?" he asked with his horrible brand of jocularity.

"Trying to be," said Connie.

"They can get tiresome, can't they, actors?"

"We can. But then so can most people."

"What I mean is," said Des, leaning closer, Connie thought to catch the smell of her breath, "you can have too much of them. They tend to emote is how I'd put it. Those Galloways, for example. Always at it, aren't they?"

"At it? You mean like Alice?"

"At each other's throats might be a better way of putting it. Morning, noon, and night. And both of them having a bit on the side and talking about it openly. Jeez, I don't know; it's not my idea of a marriage."

"My dear man, I've known more different kinds of marriage than I've had hot dinners. There are as many recipes for a good one as there are for a bad one."

"What makes them stay together, that's what I wonder. Why stick it out?"

"I imagine it must be because they rather like it."

Des looked at her, then shook his head with wonderment. "Then there's young Peter Fortnum. He's up to something, that I do know."

Connie Geary paused, looking at him contemplatively. She took her bottle out of her handbag, had a swig, and replaced it. Then she looked at Des again. "I presume we are now changing the subject, am I right? Because Peter Fortnum hardly comes under the heading of actors who emote. Indeed, he is an exceedingly quiet young man, which is pleasant but unusual. A youthful Alec Guinness, no less. So we are now discussing what he is up to, and I must confess I have no idea. Do you mean to ask if he is sleeping with the charming but impenetrable Russian lady?"

"Oh, as to that, maybe, but I think not," said Des, rubbing his hands together. "But there's something going on, and I think it might be a sight more interesting than them sleeping together."

"I'm glad to hear it. At my age there are a lot of things more interesting than sex, though I'm not sure there ought to be at theirs. Have you any idea what it is?"

"Oh, I've ideas all right. There's no flies on me, you know. I'll get to the bottom of it."

"This is fascinating," said Connie. She sat there hoping she would remember enough of this conversation for it to form a vital piece in the complaint to the committee when the present festival was over. She even decided to stop sipping from her bottle, to keep her head clear. "Is there anyone else at the Saracen in whom you are taking a special interest?"

"Oh, lots," said Des, leering. "A student of the human condition, that's me." He leaned forward. "Know how that Kraut conductor gets his girls?"

"He's Austrian. Not that anyone imagines *that* makes much difference after the Waldheim business."

"Right. Same difference, that's what I say. Well, do you know how he gets his girls?"

"Animal magnetism?"

"His heavy recruits them for him. Just like that. He puts the proposition, then they're taken up to his room for a quick you-know, then they're out. He picks them out from among Krauty's fans. Doesn't pay them, either. I expect they form themselves into a sort of club or have a special tattoo or something."

"I did hear whispers about that," said Connie with a shiver of distaste. "It *is* rather disgusting."

"And I'll tell you this: He likes them young. The younger the better."

" 'His favorite form of sinning is with one who's just beginning,' " sang Connie, from the Catalogue Aria.

"That's it. That's just about it. If I could catch him with one who was below the age of consent . . ."

"Yes?"

"That would do the trick. . . . Trouble is, at that age they're not usually interested in classical music, are they? And the heavy tells me he's very careful."

"You'll have to find something else, then."

"Yes, I will, won't I?"

"And is there anyone else of us that you have your eyes on?"

"Oh, yes. Oh, there definitely is. No question about that. . . ." Connie sat there quiet, but a cunning expression came into Des's eyes. "But that would be telling, wouldn't it? You're not going to draw me out on that."

With a sigh, Connie took out her gin bottle.

"You know what that stuff does to your kidneys, don't you?" asked Des. He went on to describe it in detail before leaving with a wave and his favorite addendum: "Don't mind me telling you, do you?"

Onstage they were rehearsing a quarrel between Sir Pecunius Slackwater, suitor to Alison Greatheart, and the whore of Deptford, who was an old acquaintance.

SIR PECUNIUS: Out, you babliaminy, you unfeathered, cremitoried quean, you cullisance of scabosity!

WHORE: Good words, Master Slackwater, to speak before a maid and a virgin.

SIR PECUNIUS: Hang thy virginity upon the pole of carnality . . .

By the wall of the courtyard, Natalya, in slacks and jumper, was standing in a patch of sunlight near the windows of the Shakespeare Bar. She was beginning to tap her feet and look anxiously at her watch, but then she saw Peter Fortnum coming through the great gates from the High Street.

"Did you get through? Have they arrived?" asked Natalya urgently in Russian.

"No, there's been some confusion about times. The party's not due for another hour at least."

"Oh, my God."

"I think it's a genuine confusion. There doesn't seem to be any doubt they will arrive."

"I've got to go. I'm due at rehearsal in ten minutes."

"I know. I'll stick around and ring them again in an hour or two."

"Will you come and tell me?"

"Yes, if I can. I don't *think* I'll be needed to rehearse here, but you never know what people may take it into their heads to want to go over. But I'll try."

"Please come if you can. *Please*, Peter."

"Of course. You know I will. And it'll be all right."

He took her hand, but they sprang apart as they heard an involuntary cough close to Natalya's ear. Des Capper was standing just inside the open window of the Shakespeare Bar. From the expression of extreme frustration on his face it was clear that the fatal fascination that Mother Russia had always had for him had never induced him to learn her language.

In the street near the Alhambra Theater the big man with the Midlands accent was approached by a girl.

"Excuse me, but you're Gunter Gottlieb's bodyguard, aren't you?"

He looked at her appraisingly. "Something like that."

"It's just that . . . he's always in such a hurry after rehearsals . . . and I wondered if you could . . . get his autograph for me."

She proffered a book. It looked very new. The big man did not take it.

"Maybe I could . . . And maybe I could go even better."

"Really?"

"Maybe I could arrange a . . . meeting."

She smiled up at him, looking all of fifteen. "I wondered if you could."

"At a price, of course."

The operatic offerings of the Ketterick Festival were never premiered until the second or third night. Nothing was allowed to draw attention from that year's play. Maybe in future years Gunter Gottlieb would change all that, but he had not done so yet. By tradition the musical event on the first night was something undemanding: a Viennese night, a Gilbert and Sullivan evening, a nice bit of Tchaikovsky. This year it was a popular operatic concert. Gunter Gottlieb, needless to say, would have nothing to do with it.

Thus, the final rehearsal with the Midlands Orchestra in the Town Hall was under the command of a pleasant young man who had done well in a recent conductors' competition. They'd put together a very nice program, with an overture by Rossini, some ballet music by Verdi, and lots of standard arias. Natalya was singing *"Vissi d'Arte"* and the letter scene from *Eugene Onegin,* the Mexican baritone was spitting out Iago's "Credo," and Krister Kroll was singing an aria from *Faust* that the program, through slovenly proofreading, referred to as *"Slut! Demure, chaste et pure."* Singh's arias had presented more of a problem, since the countertenor repertoire hardly counted as popular opera, but Brad had hit on two surefire Handel arias, and these he was to sing in the first half. Brad had insisted he was to *conclude* the first part of the concert, knowing that the scope for excitement and applause would be the greater if there was nothing coming immediately after.

Natalya was finishing the letter aria in a glorious flood of sound when Peter arrived at the Town Hall. He listened approvingly. He was no expert on music, but he knew a good sound when he heard one. It was a very informal rehearsal, and the Town Hall was dotted with people. Peter was pleased to note approving glances going from person to person. Natalya came off the platform and into the body of the hall, looking around for him. He put up his hand, and she came over to him.

"I got through," said Peter.

"And?"

"They'd just arrived."

Natalya did not allow herself any obvious expression of relief, but Peter could see her tension relax.

"All of them?"

"Yes, all of them. I spoke to him."

"Oh—marvelous."

"He sent his love."

"Only three more days now."

Onstage Singh had launched into Caesar's aria with horn obbligato from *Giulio Cesare*: *"Va tacito e nascosto."* His rich, agile voice was filling the Town Hall effortlessly and weaving brilliant patterns with the horn. Brad Mallory, sitting in the middle of the hall, looked to be purring.

"What an extraordinary voice," said Natalya.

"Quite amazing."

"What else did he say?"

Peter looked around, instinctively cautious.

"It's all right," said Natalya. "I'm sure that dreadful man doesn't speak Russian. I could see it in his face."

"No, I don't think so. Anyway, he's over there."

And as Peter launched into an account of what had been said on the phone, he looked toward the back row of seats where Des had ensconced himself, exercising in the absence of Gunter Gottlieb his right as a member of the committee to go anywhere and see anything. He was gazing ahead of him, almost dreamily, with a smile of pure, luxuriating pleasure playing on his lips.

6

THE HIGH STREET

Performances of *The Chaste Apprentice of Bowe* began at seven o'clock. Everything at the Ketterick Festival began early, for many members of the audience were not staying in Ketterick but came from other suburbs and were nervous about traveling on bus or underground late at night. So at six the great gates of the Saracen's Head were closed, and the small door cut into the right-hand one was opened for the collection of tickets. Everyone, even those seated on the balconies, went through this gate, and the ticket collector stationed himself there from six onward. All the bars were closed to members of the general public until after the performance was over—enough to do to serve the players and the audience. Frank, the hotel's commissionaire, stood by the main entrance to the hotel, to the right of the gates, to stop anyone who might try to get into the play without paying by slipping through Reception and then through the Shakespeare Bar.

Once through the little door in the great gates, the audience, chattering and laughing and sure they were in for a rather special experience, separated up, some going to one or other of the bars, some to sit in their seats and read their programmes, some merely to sit and soak up the atmosphere of the great courtyard. Those who had seats on the balconies had directions on how to get to them on the backs of their tickets—directions which mostly added to their confusion, so indescribable were the complexities of the Saracen's Head.

Behind the stage, in one half of the enormous kitchen, and screened off from the rest, the actors changed. The women had the private dining room next to it, but coming and going between the two was frequent and unrestricted. Costume was important in the Ketterick plays, for splendor and variety of dress provided the feast for the eye that compensated for an otherwise bare stage. No producer—not even Jason Thark—had yet suggested a modern-dress production at Ketterick, and anyone who did would have been firmly rebuffed. The stage demanded ruffs and bodices, buskins and codpieces.

Fish was being served in the dining room that night. The smell penetrated into the dressing rooms and provoked feeble witticisms like "Odds fish!" A limited meal was provided for the few residents not involved in the play and the richer members of the audience. Late-night snacks would also be served after the performance: lasagna, fish pie, or risotto. Most people, though, contented themselves with drinks.

They were pleasantly busy in the Shakespeare Bar. This meant that Win Capper was run off her feet. Hair drawn back, unhealthily sallow, she somehow looked like a woman who had been run off her feet since girlhood.

"Des," she called, unusually daring, when she saw her husband going around the bar doing his Harry Bailly act among the early arrivals for the performance, "do you think you could come behind the bar and help out for a bit?"

Brad Mallory, sitting at the bar, thought this must be an unprecedented request. He had never seen Des giving a hand at anything around the hotel except Reception. Certainly Des received the request gracelessly, casting his eye up to heaven and taking his time in getting behind the bar.

"Des," said his wife, working on an order for three different beers, "you're going to have to come and help at Interval. I'm not going to be able to cope."

"You'll have Dawn from the kitchen to help you," said Des, pouring soda into a whiskey in an infuriatingly leisurely manner. "There are three other bars for people to go to, for Chrissake."

"The Shakespeare's the biggest and most popular. There's only twenty minutes, and people have to have time to drink their drinks. You'll have to come and help."

"All right, little lady," said Des, leering around at a sea of proffered fivers. "Your wish is my command."

"No, I *mean* it, Des. I need you here."

"And I'll be here. Am I in the habit of not meaning what I say? . . . I ask you, Mr. Mallory, don't I usually mean what I say? Now, what can I get you?"

Outside in the main entrance Frank, the commissionaire, was getting bored. There was a steady queue waiting to go through the little door into the courtyard, but nobody was attempting to sneak past him into the body of the hotel to get an illicit view from somewhere or other. This was not surprising, as he was six feet two and built like a barrel. The only residents in the hotel at the moment were the festival people, in the rooms over the Shakespeare. Any other would-be guest who had arrived in Ketterick without a bed was turned away by Frank with a word, courteous but final. In fact, there was nobody manning Reception, because there was no point in it. Des had assigned the girls there to other work for the duration of the festival. Frank thought it very dull, really. Still, soon, when the play started, he could walk along and have a chinwag with Bob, the ticket collector on the gate. They were good friends and usually talked the play away during festival time. Unless, this year, that Australian twerp should take it into his head to put a stop to it.

The poncy Mr. Mallory—Frank had got *his* number—had come mincing out of the Shakespeare and now came through Reception, looking pale but not interesting. He nodded to Frank as he came through the main entrance and headed off in the direction of the Town Hall, clutching his cloak around him. A *cloak,* for God's sake. . . . Des Capper came out almost immediately after.

"I've been helping in the bar," he announced to Frank, as if it were a newsworthy event. "Helping the little lady. Now they're all taking their seats. I think I'll slip in at the back and watch the first few minutes. Mind you, I think I've got *this* play's number, by seeing the rehearsals. It's no literary masterpiece, you take my word for it. Still, as a member of the committee, it's as well to see how the audience is taking it."

And he rambled through the little door into the courtyard. Frank gave a meaningful stare, of skepticism verging on contempt, at Bob, standing in the street by the door and taking tickets. So long a stare was it that he nearly missed seeing a young woman going through the main door of the hotel. He hotfooted it back to the door and into the open area around Reception, but by this time the young woman had crossed it and had gone, not to the Shakespeare Bar but to the stairs leading to the bedrooms.

"Can I help you, miss?" Frank called.

The girl turned round. She was a cool, fresh little thing, in a bright summer frock—and not much else, Frank guessed. Frank was an ex-soldier and experienced in such matters. A tingle stirred his old blood. She looked about fifteen, he thought, but when she spoke her voice was not a schoolgirl's.

"No. No, I don't think so."

It was an attempt—and not a bad one—at upper-class impertinence. Frank bristled.

"The play's about to start, miss, and the bars and dining rooms are shut, and—"

"But I'm not going to the bars or dining rooms, am I?"

"Would you mind telling me, miss, where you are going?"

She left a cool pause before she replied. "No, I don't mind. I'm going to see Gunter Gottlieb. You know, the great conductor."

"Ah." Frank did know. There had been other young ladies. "Mr. Gottlieb's not occupied with festival stuff, then?"

"No, evidently not, I should have thought. I have an appointment with him."

"I see. Very well, miss. Sorry to have troubled you."

She smiled at him, a practiced ingenue smile. Then she turned and went up the stairs. Shaking his head gently, Frank went back to take up his position outside the main door. The evening was clear and sunny, and both Ketterick folk and visitors were strolling along the High Street, window-shopping, eating ice cream, flirting and hoping to be flirted with. The odd car drove past, but no heavy trucks. They were banned from the center of Ketterick during the hours from seven to ten at festival time. Only heavy trucks could have made any impression through the massive gates of the Saracen's courtyard. Cars, Frank knew, made no disturbance at all.

A fragment of the play wafted out to him. That meant the ticket gate had opened:

RALPH GREATHEART: I hope to see thee one o' the monuments of our City, and reckoned among her worthies, when the famous fable of Whittington and his puss shall be forgotten, and thou and thy deeds played i' thy lifetime by the best companies of actors, and be called their get-penny . . .

So the first scene was over, and Carston Galloway was on, inciting the chaste apprentice to City greatness (with Ronnie Wimsett looking and acting about as unlike a City worthy as it was possible to get). Frank had timed things in dress rehearsal, and he knew this meant the play was ten or twelve minutes in. Turning his eyes, he saw that Des Capper had emerged through the little door in the gate and was now closing it.

"Ah, well, it's going very much as I expected," he said judiciously when he came up to Frank. "Quite nicely on the whole. Whether that mob knows what they're laughing at is another matter, but so long as they think they're enjoying themselves, that's the main thing. Make 'em laugh, make 'em cry, eh? I haven't read up much about this opera they're doing yet, but I expect it's the same principle there. That's show biz, the world over. . . . Well, I'll maybe look in during the second half to see how it's going. Meanwhile, I'll be in Reception if I'm wanted, Frank."

"Right you are, sir."

"Or up in the flat. Call up the stairs if I'm wanted. Keep on the door the whole of the first half. We don't want any gate-crashers seeing the play for free."

"Right. Oh, by the way, there was a young girl, sir . . ."

"Oh?"

"But she was a guest of Mr. Gottlieb's. . . ."

They looked at each other, and Des laughed lasciviously. "Someone should have told me that at festival time this place doubles as a brothel."

He winked and chuckled, as if that were a high honor. Then he went in and turned towards the reception desk, apparently in high good humor.

For a few minutes Frank stood just inside the door, looking out, hearing Des fiddling around on and under the desk. Then Des went into the manager's room behind. Frank nonchalantly went through the door into the street and stood for a few minutes there. The characters had changed a bit from a half hour earlier, but the activities were much the same. As a spectacle it lacked variety. So, giving a nod to his friend Bob, who was standing by his little door, they met halfway, towards the end of the hotel wall. From here they could both keep an eye on their respective doors, yet there were no open windows to inhibit them from launching into a fine old discussion. Men, contrary to general belief, are much the best gossips, and the festival and its artists always provided these two with ample manure to spread. Every year it was the same, and they went at it with a will.

The first interruption came when they were just five minutes into their chat and hardly beginning to disentangle the marital and extramarital affairs of the Galloways.

The girl who had gone up to Gunter Gottlieb's room came prancing out again.

"*Good*-bye," she called, waving.

"Well, *she* didn't take long," said Bob.

"They never do," said Frank. "It's in and out."

"Perhaps he pays them by the minute."

"And perhaps he doesn't pay them at all. We'll come to Mr.—I beg his pardon, *Herr*—Gottlieb in a minute. But as I was saying . . ."

In the Town Hall concert the Mexican baritone was giving the audience his Iago. It was a part to which he was suited, if you regarded Iago as a snarling, spitting, teethbaring villain who could never have convinced anyone for two minutes that he was a good chap. But his enunciation of belief in eternal nothingness was getting through to Brad Mallory. At any rate, he was sweating. Sitting there in his aisle seat, he was sweating profusely. What was next? The march from *The Trojans*. Then little Natalya in the letter scene from *Onegin*. After that would be the time to slip out. Anyone who knew him would assume he had gone backstage to congratulate her. Or to spur on Singh, who was on soon after. There was that phone box just outside the Town Hall. Please God it would not be occupied.

Brad Mallory sat on and sweated. Never had the Trojan March seemed so long.

Frank and Bob had a long, uninterrupted chat during which few of the performers staying at the Saracen came off unscathed. It was only at a quarter past eight that Frank looked at his watch and shook his head.

"Blimey. Quarter past eight. Interval in fifteen minutes or so, I should guess. Better get back to my post."

He looked around him, like a diver coming up for air. Approaching along the High Street was Bradford Mallory, clutching his cloak about him, though the evening was still warm.

"Concert over, Mr. Mallory?" Frank asked, back at his post at the entrance. Brad Mallory fluttered.

"The first half. That was all I'm interested in. Singh sang divinely! He had a phenomenal success!"

"I'm glad about that, Mr. Mallory." The romantic figure, having poked his head into the Shakespeare and then come out again, disappeared up the stairs. Frank repeated sardonically under his breath: "I'm *very* glad about that!" Then he went outside again and made a gesture to Bob at the ticket door which said, as plainly as talking, "These artists!"

Behind the stage, in the screened-off part of the kitchen that was the men's dressing room, the members of the cast that were not onstage sat in dim light, listening to the performance.

"It's going well," said Gillian Soames.

"Very well," said Ronnie Wimsett. "They're laughing at the jokes."

"And at a lot of things that aren't jokes at all."

"That's natural," said Jason Thark pedantically. "We get further and further away from the Elizabethan language. I sat through a performance of *Macbeth* last year and realized I understood less than I did when I saw it as a teenager."

"That's because nowadays we play the Bard complete and gabble him," Connie Geary pointed out. "In the past they cut him and spoke him properly."

"At least no one seems to have taken offense at the chaste apprentice," said Ronnie. "That's a relief."

"That's because we made him so far out he was a parody of a parody of a homosexual," said Jason, still with his schoolmasterly manner, which was perhaps a sign of nerves. "That was my intention all along."

"The amazing thing is, they're even laughing at Peter Patterwit," said Connie Geary in her rich, throaty tones. "He's the sort of Elizabethan character who makes me groan and switch off the moment he sets foot onstage."

They were silent, listening to Peter Fortnum, who was doing his stuff onstage.

PETER PATTERWIT: Why, sure my blood gives me I am noble; sure I am of noble kind, for I find myself possessed with all their qualities: love dogs, dice and drabs, scorn wit in stuff-clothes, have beat my shoemaker, knocked my seamstress, cockolded my pothecary, and undone my tailor. Noble? Why not?

"He's doing a good job, that lad," said Carston Galloway. "He's got the projection for it, so he gets the meaning across, however feeble it is."

"Oh, God," said Connie Geary suddenly and loudly.

"Shhh," said Jason.

Connie was rummaging frantically in her bag, which she carried around with her everywhere.

"Darlings, I've never done *that* before. I've run out of gin. Somehow or other I've forgotten to put my second half bottle in my bag. I was sure—"

"Do you want me to get some more for you?" asked Peter Fortnum, who had just come offstage and was beaming with pleasure at the experience of an audience that was with him. "I'm not on again before Interval."

"But *can* you?"

"Of course. I can go through the kitchen and dining room and into the Shakespeare Bar. Or shall I go up to your room and get you a half bottle?"

"Darling, could you? You angel. Because we have *hours* to go yet, and bar measures go very little distance. The halves are all set up on my dressing table like a line of soldiers. Here's my key. It's the first floor."

"I'll find it," said Peter.

But the Saracen has ways of defeating people who say that. At any rate, he seemed to be away an awful long time, and when he returned, Connie was wailing that she felt like the Sahara Desert at the height of the season. Peter was out of breath and explained that he had got utterly and completely lost. By then Carston Galloway was on-stage, with Mistress Greatheart, Alison, and Sir Pecunius Slackwater in a tremendous quarrel scene that concluded the first half. The Interval was upon them, and the audience sounded good-humored and nicely thirsty as they hotfooted it to the bars.

In the Shakespeare Bar tension had been rising as the Interval approached.

"Well, the glasses are all ready," said Win Capper, looking at her watch. "Interval's supposed to be at half past. Fifteen minutes to go, if they stick to their times. *Which* they won't, knowing these artistic people. No consideration, as a general rule. Still, I think you could go and get the snacks from the kitchen. Here, take this tray."

Dawn, roped in as the best of the dining-room staff, trotted off to get the little plates of savory this-and-thats which were to be set out on bar and tables in celebration of *The Chaste Apprentice*'s first night. When she got back, she found that Win had poured out a large number of red and white wines and some gins and whiskeys.

"They're the staples," she said. "You can't go wrong pouring them in advance. And we'll be rushed even with Des here. If they want ice, they'll have to serve themselves with it. Now let's put the snacks out."

In the event, Interval started only three or four minutes late. "I expect Des is watching from the window," Win said, "and he'll dash through when it starts." But when the great mass of the audience from the courtyard began to stream into the Shakespeare, saying things like "It's *awfully* funny, isn't it?" and "I never expected to understand so much," Des still hadn't arrived. Win and Dawn had no option but to begin taking orders and serving them in double quick time, seeming at times to have four hands each, and needing six, and taking the next orders while giving change from the previous one and totting up prices in their heads and being at both ends of the bar at once. And when they collided over the red wines or the whiskeys, Win would mutter to Dawn: "Where is Des? He promised faithfully he'd come. There's much too many of them for the two of us to cope with. Where *is* Des?"

7

RECEPTION

They didn't find Des until long after the play was over. As soon as the audience had been summoned by bell back to the courtyard, Win sent Dawn off with two trays of glasses, to pile them into the dishwasher in the kitchen. There wouldn't be time to do all of them by hand, she said, and she was right. The concert ended at nine-fifteen, and as the Town Hall was only five minutes away, it was not long before some members of the orchestra staying at the Saracen drifted in, and then soloists. Natalya had walked back with Singh. They had not been able to communicate very much, but since Singh was wrapped in a cloud of self-approbation brought on by a gaggle of critics, arts administrators, and early music enthusiasts who had fawned over him at Interval, and since even Natalya was quietly hugging herself at the warmth of her reception, they had been companionably quiet.

Singh had gone straight to the rooms *en suite* that he shared with Brad, but they soon joined Natalya in the Shakespeare. Now they were both positively purring with delight, though Natalya thought she had never seen Brad's hands flap more nervously. Singh had been offered a prestigious engagement for the next Bach Festival and had been urgently pressed to take the role of Idamante in a new Welsh National Opera production of *Idomeneo*. Natalya congratulated them but would have been more interested in offers that would display her own talents. After a time, she left them to their delighted self-absorption and watched the closing stages of the play from the window. The second half of the play was shorter, being mainly Deptford and whores and rollicking fun, but it ended with a great scene of reconciliation and matrimony, which was guaranteed to send audiences out with a warm glow. By five to ten it was all over, and the actors, with Jason, were receiving delighted acclamation from the audience. The great gates were opened, and critics scurried away to telephone in their reviews for the later editions. Then the Shakespeare was bustling once more.

"I suppose we can cope," said Win to Dawn, "since we did at Interval. There's not the same rush now. There's over an hour to closing time."

It was always pleasant at the Saracen after the play was over. Some of the actors, still in costume, usually mingled with the audience, as Peter Fortnum did now, though he confined his attentions to Natalya Radilova, going off with her into a corner and having a long and serious conversation. Constance Geary was in the Shakespeare, too, letting longtime admirers buy her drinks. Before long Krister Kroll arrived—the general public being admitted after the play was over—wanting to talk about the concert. He had changed into casuals and looked very handsome, but after trying to break into the rapt little duo of Mallory and Singh, he gave up and went over to join Peter and Natalya. He was welcome, because he was the sort of person who always was welcome.

In another corner Gillian, Ronnie Wimsett, and Jason Thark were going over the performance blow by blow. Gillian was just deciding that they were doing this mainly as a boost to Jason's ego, rather than with any thought of revising or strengthening the production, when a thought struck her.

"I say, the Great Australian Blight's not here. I'd have expected him to be worming his way around, calling Stanislavski to our attention or telling us to speak up and speak out."

"Probably got other fish to fry," said Ronnie Wimsett. "Some agreeable little piece of blackmail or something."

"I suppose it's too much to hope that he's had a heart attack while executing some particularly problematic yoga exercise?" hazarded Jason Thark.

Gillian suddenly noticed that Win Capper was collecting glasses and ashtrays at the next table, and she kicked the other two. When Win turned around, she smiled and said: "I'd have thought your husband would have been here, Mrs. Capper, to tell us how we'd done."

She had nothing against Win Capper, but the faint spark of malice in the last words was irresistible. It eluded Win Capper.

"I'd have thought he would've myself. I was expecting him at Interval, but he never showed. Rushed off our feet we were. I expect he's got something on."

"I expect *so*," said Gillian.

Win had spotted the great bulk of Frank, the commissionaire, standing proprietorially by the door of the bar.

"Frank, you seen Des?"

Frank's forehead creased. "Saw him during the first half, Mrs. C. He went in and watched the play for a bit."

"Haven't you seen him since then?"

"Only when he came out. He went into Reception, said he'd either be there or up in the flat if he was wanted. He said he might look in on the second half, but he didn't. He's not in Reception now. Want me to call up the stairs?"

Win considered. "No. Better not. He'll have something on. He hates being disturbed when he's got something on."

"I *bet* he does," muttered Ronnie Wimsett as Win moved away.

At eleven o'clock Win called "Time," and at ten past she flicked the light switch two or three times. The townspeople and festival-goers had drifted away, but the performers were reluctant for the evening to end.

"Don't they have any all-night bars in this place?" demanded Krister Kroll.

At the bar Win contemplated the second mountain of dirty glasses and ashtrays.

"It really is too much," she said to Dawn. "I think we should count this as a special night and leave everything till morning. I'll ring Des and tell him."

But when she dialed the flat number on the telephone behind the bar, she got no reply.

"But if he's not in the flat, where *is* he?" she said in bewilderment to Frank, who had just come into the bar again. "I just hope he's not *ill*—but Des is never ill. He's so conscious of health things."

"That sort's sometimes the first to go," said Frank with gloomy tactlessness. "Would you like me to go up and have a look."

"Oh, dear . . . Well, I think *I'd* better go. You know how Des is— But if he's not in the flat, I don't know where to look. . . ."

She bustled off, distractedly poking at a stray strand of hair. Everyone left in the bar had been pushing back their chairs, preparatory to going to bed or continuing the parties in their rooms. Something made them wait. It *was* odd that Des had not been around after the show—*his* show, or so he had often seemed to believe. From his table in the corner with Natalya and Krister Kroll, Peter could see through the glass door of the Shakespeare Bar. He saw Win go out, saw her cross the hotel entrance lobby, saw her go around the reception desk and into the manager's room behind. Then he could see no more, but could only wait. It *was* not a long wait—less than a minute—before he heard clattering footsteps falling over themselves on the stairs and cries, cries that continued as Win stumbled through the manager's room and out into Reception, her face twisted in horror, her hands bloodstained.

"Oh! Oh, my God! He's dead! He's been killed! Frank! Frank! Call the doctor. No. Call the police. Someone's killed my Des!"

8

THE MANAGER'S OFFICE

In the car from the Police Station, coming from the other side of town, Superintendent Iain Dundy gazed gloomily out over the dark, nearly deserted streets of Ketterick. He was a man in his mid-thirties, with a broken marriage behind him, a reputation for fairness, and a long fuse to his temper. He was already possessed by the conviction that on this case he was going to need it.

"I've always thought of myself as an unprejudiced man," he said apropos of nothing to Sergeant Nettles, who was driving. "I've never had any sort of a 'thing' against homosexuals, never hated blacks or Indians. Most of the Japanese I've met seemed perfectly charming, though I've never been able to understand a word they've said. I've had a holiday in Germany and quite like the people, and most of the American tourists we get here seem pleasanter than you're led to expect. I even once had a friend who was a Northern Ireland Protestant. . . . But I do hate arty people. I admit it. I can't stand them. They touch a nerve in me. I've had a feeling ever since this festival started up that one day I was going to get stuck with a case chock-a-block full of arty people. And I wouldn't mind betting this is it!"

His expression became positively dyspeptic as the police car drew up outside the main entrance to the Saracen's Head.

It was difficult, the Saracen residents found, to know what to do after Win's spine-chilling reappearance. Of course, she had to be seen to first. While Frank made an imperative phone call to the police from the reception desk, Gillian helped Dawn, the stand-in barmaid, to get Win into the Shakespeare and settle her onto the sofa. But when Frank came back with a portentous expression on his face, as if the world's cares were now on his shoulders, and when he had announced that the police were on their way and had peremptorily forced on Win a stiff neat brandy, there really seemed nothing left for the rest of them to do. Actors do not commonly feel themselves *de trop,* but that was how they felt now. Win, after all, had never seemed particularly to take to their company, and she obviously would be more at ease with her own kind, whatever that was. She was moaning, "Oh, it was horrible," and crying intermittently, but she was calming down. To leave might seem like copping out, but to stay and gawp would surely be vulgar—since Sir Henry Irving, the British actor, has above all things eschewed vulgarity. They cleared their throats awkwardly and skulked off.

"We'll be in our rooms," said Jason, "if we should be wanted," and Frank nodded importantly.

That wasn't how it worked out, though. Singh certainly went to his room; he said to Brad that he wanted to see the late-night movie, which was *The Texas Chain-Saw Massacre.* Gillian went rather green at that, but Brad Mallory murmured fondly: "Oh—the young! They have such wonderful powers of recuperation." Though in fact Singh had given no sign of having anything to recuperate from. The rest of them seemed instinctively to cling together. The thought of solitary bedrooms was uninviting. They lingered in one of the large, open spaces on the first floor, which had a window looking out onto the High Street. From there, silent, they saw the police arrive—first the detectives, then a uniformed constable, who took up position outside the main entrance, then several more from the uniformed lower ranks. The actors had an odd sense of passing almost imperceptibly from one drama into another. This second one was certainly not going to be amusing.

"If only," said Ronnie Wimsett, "if only we knew exactly *when* he died."

"Why?" asked Gillian.

"Because, dear dumb cluck, if he died during the play and if he's up there in his flat, you must see that no one of us could have done it."

"I never considered for a moment that one of us could have," said Jason Thark. The silence that followed this was one of relief, as if Jason's position as producer gave him some sort of authority in police matters as well. That his statement was untrue, however, he immediately revealed by his next. "I suspect that we can narrow down the time much more closely than merely that of the duration of the play. Because when I was getting my drink after the show, poor old Win was wondering where Des was, and that girl from the dining room—Dawn is her name?—said rather sharply: 'It's no good him showing up now. It was during Interval that he was wanted and when he said he'd be here.' So I rather suspect that the police will find that he's been dead some time."

"Which will let us out," said Ronnie Wimsett.

"We-e-ell," began Gillian, but she was interrupted by footsteps on the stairs. And not just footsteps. The carrying voices of the Galloways were unmistakable.

"It was Des, dreadful Des" came Clarissa's voice.

"Are you quite sure?"

"I heard the commissionaire, or doorman, or whatever you call him, say it to the constable by the main entrance. 'His name is Capper, or was. Des Capper.' Unless he's gone out of his mind, the police are here because somebody's dead, and that somebody is Des Capper."

"Well, I'll be damned" came Carston's impeccably well-bred tones.

They emerged blinking from the stairwell: Clarissa, Carston, and Susan Fanshaw, who characteristically was saying nothing. When they had got their bearings, Clarissa stared triumphantly at the assembled cast of *The Chaste Apprentice of Bowe*.

"There! You see? Everyone's here and discussing it, aren't you, darlings?"

"We are," admitted Connie Geary. "But where have you been that you missed the fun?"

"Oh, my dear, such a miscalculation! I wouldn't have missed being first to hear of dreadful Desmond's death for the world if I'd known! But how could I? We went to the Webster."

"Why on earth did you do that?"

Clarissa had her audience and, as was her wont, immediately began acting a big scene, though it was a little enough matter she had to tell of.

"Well, darlings, after the play and the curtain calls— only there is no curtain, and I *do* find that awkward!— Carston and I changed, because the fact is we do feel it a *tiny* bit unprofessional to mingle with the dear old general public in costume—" She gestured round at Ronnie and Peter, still in their apprentice's costumes. "Call us old-fashioned if you like."

"Old-fashioned," said Gillian, and was rewarded with a dazzling reptilian smile.

"So when we were ready, we collected Susan Fanshaw, my husband's *sweet* little mistress, who had had a heavy evening seeing you'd all got your swords and cudgels with you and that your wimples and codpieces were straight, or whatever codpieces are supposed to be, and we went out into the yard, and there were *fans* waiting for us, still waiting after all that time. . . . Well, we saw you all in the Shakespeare, and we thought we ought to *spread* ourselves around a bit so as to be fair, so we took the fans into the Webster and let them lavish on us the best hospitality their purses could buy. Poor dears, they loved it!"

Susan Fanshaw looked at Clarissa (from behind her) with an expression of the utmost contempt on her face. Clearly she had been embarrassed by their sponging. Carston did not notice the glance and took her hand absent-mindedly.

"Anyway, the consequence was, you missed all the excitement," said Brad Mallory. "Win's announcement was a real Act One curtain, I can tell you."

"Darling, don't tor*ment* me! I would so have enjoyed it. Because the fact that he's been murdered—I take it, with all those police, murder is in question?—"

"Apparently," said Jason.

"—the fact that he's been murdered does seem a singularly apt retribution for his grubby little interference into my private life."

"Don't say that to the police," said Carston, sighing. "They might scent a whiff of megalomania. Or paranoia. It takes an odd kind of mind to find death an appropriate punishment for rummaging around in someone's drawers."

"Carston, of *course* I am not so stupid as to talk like that to the dear policemen. Naturally I shall tell them what an *int*eresting little man he was, with his homely medical advice and his en*tranc*ing accent and his *fas*cinating memories of the last days of the Raj. I shall say that in the short time we have been here I had come to number him amongst my dearest friends."

"Don't overdo it the other way either, Clarissa," said Jason in a tired voice. "The police are trained to smell rats." He added, rather insultingly: "And the last thing I need at this stage is to lose one of my leads."

"Fortunately I've always found the police to be charming and *most* respectful," said Clarissa, hardly hearing. "I've always got on famously with them."

"Don't I remember," said Carston.

"This is all getting way off the point," said Gillian. "When you came, we were trying to establish when he'd been murdered. We rather think it must have been before Interval."

"Before about eight-thirty, then?" asked Carston.

"That's it. Or a few minutes after. We were running ever so slightly late."

"And it must have been after—oh—seven-ten, seven-fifteen," contributed Carston.

"Oh?"

"Because he was standing at the back during the first scene and into my bit in the second scene. I've got good long sight, and there's a moment when I peer into the audience, trying to see Sir Pecunius arriving from the Palace of Westminster. I saw him at the back then, and I saw him leave, which almost put me off my stride. So it was after that."

"Brilliant!" said Ronnie, rubbing his hands. "So we have a *terminus post quem* and a *terminus ante quem.* And they let all the actors out entirely. Because we'd have had to go through the kitchens, which had a card game going on in them, then through the dining room, which had most of the staff there, judging from their faces at the windows, then through the Shakespeare into the foyer. No way anyone could do that and then murder Des without being seen. Anyway, we were all behind the stage when we were not on it."

His words fell on an embarrassed silence. Gillian looked down at her hands and then dared to look up at Peter Fortnum. She found that Jason and Connie were looking at him too, and Natalya was looking at them and frowning in puzzlement.

"Well, not quite *all* the time," said Peter, brazening it out.

"Come along, let's go to bed," said Connie briskly. "They're going to want to question us in the morning. Let's leave the question of my gin till then. We'll go to bed and think things through."

And that was exactly what they did. Some of them had a great many things to think through.

While the actors and musicians had been chewing over things in the alcove, Superintendent Dundy had been sweating his way through some preliminary questioning of Mrs. Capper in the little manager's office behind the reception desk.

No, Mrs. Capper had said, she didn't mind talking. Would rather, really. Would rather go to bed knowing she'd got it over. And if she talked it through with him, perhaps the memory of poor Des lying there with the dagger between his shoulder blades would become less horribly vivid.

So talk she did, with Iain Dundy keeping her, at the start, on fairly neutral background topics.

"When did we come to Britain? Let's see, it was the time of the miners' strike—not the last one, the one before that. Seventy-four, was it? I remember because there was no electricity most of the time, and lots of the industries were shut down, and the shops, and I wanted to go home after I'd been here a couple of days, I can tell you."

"Home?"

"New South Wales. Des was manager of a very nice hotel in Dubbo. I wish we'd never left. People don't go sticking knives into each other in Dubbo."

Dundy let pass this romanticization of her past. "Why did you leave?" he asked.

"Just chance, really. There was this English hotelier stayed with us, got pally with Des—everyone got on well with Des—and offered us a job. Des thought if we didn't go then, we never would, though it wouldn't have broken my heart if we never had. This was back in—oh, seventy-three, it must have been. So eventually we came over, and Des became bar manager of this big hotel in Bournemouth. Then it was manager of the Excelsior in Carlisle, then here. All of them hotels in the Beaumont chain. Des was very pleased to get Ketterick. It's what he called a prestige hotel in the group, and it gave him a bit of a stake in this festival that's going on now."

"You weren't so pleased?"

Win Capper shrugged. "Drinkers are pretty much alike wherever you are, that's what I say. And the people who go on about what a lovely hotel it is don't think of the amount of walking that's involved!"

"But what about your husband? Had he enjoyed his time since you both came here?"

"Oh, yes. Happy as a lamb with two tails. All this airy-fairy arty stuff was meat and drink to him. But of course Des was a very well-read man."

"And he got on well with people?"

"Oh, yes! Des was always good chums with people right from the word go."

"Why was that?"

"Well, he never put on airs. He was always chatty and always had an appropriate word for everybody. As I say, he knew an awful lot. He had an inquiring mind."

Iain Dundy wondered whether an inquiring mind was really likely to make a hotel manager popular. Des Capper was dead, after all. Perhaps he had pursued his inquiries in foolish or dangerous directions. He said: "You mean he was interested in everyone?"

"Well, I meant more that he knew what everybody was interested in, so he was on their wavelength and could talk with them. Like about acting and singing with this lot now. He could give them tips, little bits of advice. And I think he was very useful on the festival committee. He'd really wised himself up on the play they're doing, and he was starting to read up about this opera with the silly title. He said he had to be clued up, so he could discuss with the people staying here. He was very thorough, was Des. And a walking encyclopedia sometimes!"

More like a barroom philosopher, Dundy guessed, and a know-all to boot. Des sounded quite unbearable.

"So what exactly happened tonight?" he asked.

"Oh, Lord . . . I wish I could forget it. . . . We

opened at six, but just for members of the audience, because we don't open to members of the public until after the play's over. We were quite busy. I was behind the bar, and Des was going around talking to people in the Shakespeare, as he usually did. I had to call him over to help me, and I told him we wouldn't be able to cope at Interval time without him. He said he'd come. Then of course the audience started drifting out into the yard to take their seats, and Des knocked off. That was the last I saw of him until—"

"Did he say where he was going?"

"He said he might go and watch the play for a bit from the back. Frank—that's the doorman—says that's what he did. Dawn and I were busy in the bar, so I didn't think about him until he didn't turn up at Interval."

"You and this other barmaid—Dawn is it?"

"Yes. She's one of the waitresses, and very capable."

"You were together in the Shakespeare Bar the whole time until Interval?"

If Win Capper understood why he was asking this, she gave no sign. She just answered obediently, as if she were a child in class answering by rote.

"Dawn went to fetch the snacks from the kitchen. That took three or four minutes, I should think. Otherwise we were together the whole time."

"And you had to cope together at Interval?"

"That's right. We were so rushed that I didn't have time to ring around for Des."

"And after the Interval you didn't get worried?"

"I knew he would have come if he could." She dabbed at her eyes, which were very full. "I didn't *think*. How could I? And I knew we could cope after the show, because most people go straight off home. Dawn told me that; she'd helped out previous years. Anyway, after the Interval we got everything shipshape again and got the glasses washed, and then, when the concert finished, people started coming in again."

"When was that?"

"Twenty, twenty-five past nine. The Town Hall's only five minutes away, and some of the residents came straight back here. Our Interval had finished a bit before nine—ten or five to. Then, of course, when the play ended, towards ten, we filled up quite considerably."

"Tell me about finding him."

"Oh, my God, do I have to? You've seen—" She swallowed at the memory.

"Try to do it quite objectively, as if it were someone else involved, someone else's body."

She looked up at him as if hardly understanding, but then she swallowed again and tried.

"We were quite busy until just after eleven, but after I'd called 'Time' I realized I hadn't seen Des since before seven. And that wasn't right. He'd have wanted to go round the Shakespeare and talk to people after the play, see how they thought it had gone. I wasn't exactly *worried*, because he could have been in the Webster or the Massinger, but the Shakespeare is very much *his* bar and the easiest to get to from Reception and the flat. And then Frank said he hadn't seen him since soon after the play started. That didn't seem right, either. So I rang the flat, and there was no reply, and then I *did* start to wonder."

"Did your husband have any history of illness?"

"No, always fit as a fiddle. Like I said, he had this thing about health and lots of little tips about how to keep in shape. He read up on it you know. . . . Still, he is over sixty. . . . *Was* . . . So you do think about heart attacks.

. . . Anyway, I went to the manager's office, and he wasn't there, and I opened the door that leads up to the flat and called—"

"Was the door unlocked?"

"Yes. It usually was, except at night. So I went up the stairs and opened the door into our lounge, and—well, there he was. You couldn't not see him."

"Was the body exactly as it is now? Did you disturb it in any way?"

"No. Or not much. You see, I screamed, and then I knelt down and looked at his face, so I maybe touched his shoulders. But I know a dead body when I see one. And there was the knife between his shoulders—"

"You recognized the knife?"

"Oh, yes, it was a knife that Des brought back from India years ago. Had it before we were married. It was always on the little table by the sofa."

"Had you or your husband ever entertained any of the present festival guests at the hotel in your private flat?"

"Not that I know of. Why would we?"

Why indeed? Dundy thought.

"Did you notice whether anything else had been disturbed in the flat?"

"No, I just got up and . . . ran downstairs. Screaming. It was so horrible."

Iain Dundy looked at his watch. "I think that's all we need from you tonight, Mrs. Capper. Have you got anything to make you sleep?"

"Not personal. Des didn't approve of things like that. But there'll be something around somewhere in case one of the hotel guests asked for it."

"Then I suggest you take it. You'll be able to use one of the hotel rooms to sleep in, won't you? Oh—one last question: Did your husband, to your knowledge, have any enemies?"

She looked at him, wide-eyed.

"Oh, no. Des didn't have an enemy in the world. Anyone'll tell you the same."

He jumped up and opened the door for her, and she walked across the foyer to where Dawn was waiting for her by the door into the Shakespeare. At the sight of a friend and female sympathy, Win tottered a little as she walked and then crumpled into her arms, to be led inside.

"Excuse me, sir."

Dundy swung round and saw that there was a young man standing talking to the constable at the main entrance. He had an air of fledgling copper about him, but he wasn't a policeman Dundy knew. This he was sure of because he was black, and black policemen were rare enough to notice. When he raised his eyebrows, the young man came over.

"They sent me from the station, sir. I'm Metropolitan CID, but I was there visiting a mate from training days. They thought I might be useful because I was in the audience tonight."

"Here, for the play?"

"That's right, sir."

"You might well be useful. Are you free at the moment?"

"Free for the next forty-eight hours." He held out his hand. "I'm Peace, sir. Charlie Peace."

9

THE HOTEL STAFF

"I don't know how much help I can be," said Charlie Peace as Dundy gestured him to the vacant armchair in the small office. "The bloke on the door says he was killed in the hotel here."

"That's right."

"I can't say I registered much from inside the hotel while the play was going on. Women collecting up glasses in the bar, staff watching the play from the dining room—not much more than that."

"Why were you at the play?"

"Came with a girlfr— Well, a girl. Student at London University. She asked me along, and I came to see if she was really interested or whether it was the okay thing these days for girl students to have a black boyfriend."

"And which was it?"

"We said polite farewells at the gate." Charlie's mouth expanded suddenly into a great, generous grin. "Plenty more where that came from."

"But you've got a clear idea of the play itself?"

"Oh, yes. It wasn't half bad, really, and one or two good laughs. Oh, I remember what went on onstage. It's what went on behind the stage that you'll be interested in, won't it, sir?"

Dundy sighed. "It will. Most of that will have to wait till tomorrow, though. Shall we contact the Yard and see if we can use you for a couple of days? Then you might get days off in lieu."

"If you could," said Charlie. "Days off have been pretty scarce as long as the football season's lasted. Are you going to be doing anything more tonight, sir?"

"Well, there was one thing. . . . Did you notice that doorman chappie, Nettles?"

"Oh, yes, sir. Know him by sight. Probably even exchanged a few words, back in the days when I was on the beat."

"My guess from the look of him is that beneath that old-soldier exterior there lurks a leaky-mouthed individual who'd tell you his life story for the price of a pint."

"I think that's probably true, sir. The bloke on the door says he's already had his war memoirs."

"He didn't give him his boss's life story as well, did he?"

"Afraid not. But he did say the place had gone to the dogs since he took over."

"Right. That sounds like an antidote to Mrs. Capper's 'not an enemy in the world' delusions. Let's have him in now."

"Is that what she said?" asked Frank, the doorman, shooting a cynical smile across the manager's desk at Iain Dundy and taking in Nettles and Charlie as he licked his lips in anticipation. "Life and soul of the Shakespeare, popular with all and sundry?"

"That's pretty much what she told me," said Dundy, looking straight at him.

"Balls," said Frank succinctly. His mouth was still working with relish at the prospect of character assassination ahead, and there was a glint in his old eyes. "Balls with the best of intentions, I don't doubt. I'm sure she believed every blessed word she spoke. But it's balls nonetheless."

"Not popular?"

"About as welcome as the death-watch beetle."

Frank expanded in his chair in the manager's office. This was the life. This was something to take home to the missus. A murder investigation and him in on the ground floor. Key witness, in fact, by reason of his position outside the main entrance. *And* he could tell them a thing or two about the hotel, the superintendent would find, a thing or two that he wouldn't hear from anyone else. There wasn't much that had escaped him in the last week or two.

Iain Dundy looked at Frank skeptically: his big body expanding with self-importance, his furry mustache twitching with relish at the idea of being part of a murder inquiry. He had been through the events of the evening with him, when he had last seen Des, and so on, and that had been moderately satisfactory. Now he was getting on to the nitty-gritty, which was hearsay and conjecture, and all the more enjoyable to Frank for that. He'll tell me everything, thought Dundy, but will that everything be right? He looks like the sort of man who turns suggestions into conjecture and conjecture into fact in the twinkling of an eye. Basically a stupid man but possibly to be trusted on the things he knows best. And he must have come to know Des Capper pretty well.

"Mind you," Frank resumed, "fair's fair. He came after poor old Arthur Bradley— Know Arthur, did you? Most everyone did hereabouts. Him being so popular and the perfect gent, it would have been difficult for anyone coming after. This one no sooner showed his nose and everyone was asking why the devil he'd been appointed."

"You mean, if he was unpopular in the Saracen, it wasn't altogether his fault?"

Frank scratched his ear in puzzlement. "No, I don't altogether mean that. What I suppose I'm trying to say is that no one could have been really popular, but he sank plumb to the bottom of the charts. And that was because of what he did and the sort of man he was."

"Maybe you'd better explain," suggested Dundy.

And explain Frank did. Explained Des's manner—the oozing, oleaginous manner that hid the desire to dominate. Explained his know-all ways that made him believe he could pronounce and advise on all subjects under the sun. Explained that on his daily rounds as manager of the hotel he made it his business to gain knowledge of his guests rather than to minister to their comfort. And Frank went further. He made it clear that if it struck Des's fancy to use his knowledge, gain a covert pleasure by flaunting it, then that is exactly what he would do.

"To take a case in point," Frank concluded, still expressing the utmost pleasure in his narration by the whole set of his body. "This happened several weeks ago, but I actually saw it, and I can vouch for it. There was this bloke, late middle-aged, who'd been here before with this dolly-bird, who he'd signed in as *Mrs.* Williams, or whatever it was. This time he had a middle-aged lady, one on the sour side, or that was how she looked, and she was also Mrs. Williams, obviously the real one. He was a fool to do it, but there you are—some people *are* fools. Now, dinnertime it was, and I had to deliver a telephone message to the next table, so I saw this as it happened. Des Capper was doing his rounds—the headwaiter does *not* like him doing it in the dining room, but he hadn't a hope in hell of stopping him—and he went up to the Williams table, obviously singling it out, and with his usual dripping-oil manner he said: 'Good evening, Mrs. Williams. Everything to your satisfaction, is it? This is the first time we've had the pleasure of welcoming you to the Saracen, I think?' And after the usual courtesies, he turns to her husband, and he says: '*Mr.* Williams, on the other hand, we have seen before. Though that time, if I remember rightly, you were . . . on your own, weren't you, sir?' And he puts his hand on the man's shoulder and applies a bit of pressure."

"Ouch!" said Iain Dundy.

"It was *daft,* that's what it was. One way to make sure that bloke was never again seen at the Saracen with or without fancy woman. There's hotels where a man like that knows he's safe, and there's others, and Des Capper had put us into the second category with a vengeance. But you see the sort of man he was, don't you? He couldn't resist that little display of—what shall I call it?—intimate knowledge, power over the man."

"And I suppose that at festival time there were plenty of things going on in the hotel that Mr. Capper could feed on?"

"Was there ever! *I* get a kick out of the goings-on at festival time, I can tell you. So you can guess what Des Capper was like. Went poking his nose in everything, giving advice here, a little bit of reminiscence there, and sniffing out intimate secrets all over the shop!"

"Which was not popular with the guests, I imagine?"

"They were getting up a petition, that I *do* know."

"A petition?"

"To get a change of manager by next year. Des unsuitable in view of the central position of the Saracen in the events of the Ketterick festival—that kind of thing."

"Hmmm. Interesting. Have you any idea what kinds of thing Capper had found out in these nosings around?"

"Ah—there you may find Win knows more than I do." He winked. "Pillow talk. Though mostly when he spoke to her it was to give orders. As far as him and me were concerned, we didn't swap information. I like to know what's going on as much as the next man, but with me it's just a case of 'That's the way the world goes.' With him it was something more . . . something nasty. Mind you, as often as not he'd know I knew, and I'd know he knew, if you get me. As in the case of Mr. Gottlieb—I beg his pardon: Herr Gottlieb."

Iain Dundy sighed. At last we must be coming to the arty ones, he thought. "And who is Mr. Gottlieb?"

"Some kind of musician. Conductor, I think. Travels around with a couple of heavies. And this is the grubby bit, which is what Des enjoyed most, because he really had a nose for the grubby: They pimp for him from among his fans. It's almost like them pop stars back in the sixties. He had one of the little groupies visiting him tonight, and Des commented on it when he came back from watching the play."

"So there were visitors to the hotel during the first half of the play?"

"Just the one. Just her. Between her going and Mr. Mallory coming back from the concert, there was nobody."

"Capper was interested in the girl, was he?"

"You bet. He was interested in anything connected with Gottlieb. Probably goes back to the war or something, though he always says he was in India and the Far East.

Mind you, so far as I can see, everybody seems to hate Gottlieb. But with Des it seemed to have a special edge."

"But he never talked it over with you or told you why?"

"No, he just winked when I told him about the girl."

"Anyone else he was interested in?"

"Oh, everyone. His little antennae were always a-twitch. But not everyone gave him the sort of raw material he was interested in. There were the Galloways, of course—"

"Ah, *them* I've heard of," said Dundy. "May even have seen them on tour or on television. Definitely a couple, aren't they? Melissa is her name? And—"

"Clarissa and Carston. Yes, they act as a team, as often as not, and they were here a couple of years ago, when they created the same sort of brouhaha. They *act* as a team, but they don't act like a team, if you get my meaning, sir. Not offstage. She's sleeping with the producer, and he's sleeping with an assistant stage manager, and everyone has to put up with a running commentary on the whole business from dawn to dusk, which is part of some sort of nonstop row they're having."

"A row about that?"

"I don't think so. No, according to the room maid they're completely open about that. But they spend their time sniping at each other nonetheless, and they give the impression that's as much habit as anything else."

"Maybe it is. On the other hand, there could be a specific reason, and Capper could somehow have got wind of it. Anything else?"

"One of the older actresses drinks. Who doesn't these days? A fair bit of A sleeping with B. Not all that interesting. Then there's something interesting happening around the Russian lady."

"Oh?"

"Something hush-hush."

"Do you think she wants to defect?"

"Maybe. I expect that's probably it. But if so, she's a long time about it. What's to stop her defecting now if she wants to? Anyway, there's something going on between her and one of the younger actors. Peter Fortnum, his name is, and he speaks Russki. Of course, it could be just good old-fashioned sex, but it looks like something more, *too*. If she's wanting to defect, I'd have thought Mr. Mallory would be in on it, too, but though this Fortnum is always making hush-hush phone calls and going to and fro with messages, I haven't noticed that Mr. Mallory is involved in any way."

"You mentioned Mallory before. Who exactly is he—and what?"

"A poncy agent. He acts for the Russian lady and for a superponcy Indian boy who apparently sings with that choirboy's voice I can't stand. He was at the concert tonight, of course."

"But did you say he came back at Interval time?"

"That's right. He said he left at the *concert* Interval, and he got back to the Saracen sometime before *our* Interval here. Around eight-fifteen, I'd say. He'd heard Singh—that's the name of his poncy Indian boyfriend, if you'll believe it—do his bit and came away. 'Singh sang divinely,' he said. That was all he was interested in."

"So the only outsider who came into the hotel during the first half of the performance—say, from seven to about eight-thirty—was the girl for this German conductor?"

"That's right. Austrian, I think he is, if you're getting technical."

"Otherwise there was Des Capper coming out to watch

the play from the courtyard and then going back in again?"

"That's right. And going on about how he was going to serve in the bar at Interval, as if it was the height of bloody condescension on his part to serve in his own pub."

"And then just Mr. Mallory?"

"Right again."

"Now, you were talking, I know. Can you really be quite sure that no one could have got past you?"

"Sure and doubly sure. Bob and I talk every year during the play, but both of us keep our eyes open. It's our job to stop gate-crashers, and we do."

"What about the other entrances?"

"Well, obviously there are other entrances on a normal day. Each of the three bars has one, for instance, and there are doors into the kitchens. But naturally, when the play is on, you can only keep open manned entrances, and that means the one in the central gate. All the others are locked, and I watch the one into the hotel and Reception."

"That was the regular procedure each year, was it? Not something Mr. Capper had organized?"

"No, no, I've been doing it for years now. And as I say, generally me and Bob at the ticket gate meet halfway and have a bit of a natter, because we can't watch the play even if we'd wanted to, which we don't. But we keep a sharp eye on our entrances. You couldn't have it getting around that there were ways of slipping into the plays without buying a ticket."

"Well, if that's true, it does narrow the field a bit. And the field could do with some narrowing." Iain Dundy sighed and looked round at Nettles and Charlie, sitting quiet and respectful in the background. That young Peace looked as if he was following well. He was on the ball and was going to be of help. Dundy looked at him as he said: "Anything else, I wonder?"

Charlie cleared his throat. "Just one thing, sir. I was here with a girl for the performance, as you know—"

"That's right," put in Frank. "Saw you going in."

Charlie smiled at him ferociously, as if daring him to voice the thoughts that had gone through his mind at the time. "Well, I thought you should know that we went into the Shakespeare Bar at Interval, and the door out to the street *was* locked, because we thought of going outside to get some air. At the time I wondered about fire risk. As it was, we had to go out into the courtyard again, which was very crowded, what with the seats and all the people."

"Right," said Iain Dundy. "So that confirms what has just been said."

"That's right, sir. There was just a question in my mind about the key. It wasn't in the door, of course, or we could just have turned it and gone out. I wondered who had it."

"It would be Mrs. Capper," said Frank promptly. "And the barmen in the other bars would have had theirs with them, too, while the play was going on. I think it's the headwaiter who sees to the back kitchen door. The drill was that they would open up just as the performance was ending."

"Right."

"The chief fire officer has okayed the arrangement," said Frank self-importantly. "The fact is, we can get the big gates open in a matter of thirty seconds, so the major part of the audience would be out in the twinkling of an eye. The balconies are not high, and there are rope ladders on every one."

Dundy nodded. "Well, I think that's it—for the moment only, of course. I'll want to check up on details later. I wonder if that girl Dawn is still around. If she is, maybe I could just tie up a few loose ends with her before everyone goes off to bed."

"She was getting poor old Win Capper off to sleep," said Frank. "She's a very conscientious girl. She may have waited to see if she was wanted."

And she had. She had started cleaning up the Shakespeare, but one of the constables had said she'd better not do that in case there was anything there that might be important in the way of evidence. So she had sunk down into a chair in the foyer and lit a cigarette. She was a smart girl, with normally dancing eyes and a humorous expression. Now she was tired to the point of exhaustion, but she tried to pull herself together enough to answer Dundy's questions.

"The last time I saw Mr. Capper? Let me see, that would be before the play started. Mrs. Capper had got him to help behind the bar. Not that he was much help, I imagine—all talk and very little action."

"You didn't like him?"

"Nobody did," said Dawn blithely, with the confidence born of a feeling that no one was likely to accuse *her* of murdering her boss. "I don't want to speak ill of the dead, but it doesn't do to tell lies about them, either, does it? He was damn-all use about the place, and that's a fact. Win did all the work, and she was nothing better than his slave."

"Nevertheless, Mrs. Capper got her husband to promise that he'd be there to help at Interval?"

"That's right. I came in just as they were talking about it, so I overheard. He was trying to wriggle out of it: 'You'll have Dawn to help you.' As if two was enough when they're crowded five or six deep waving five-pound notes at you! But he hated *serving.* He liked swanning around—that was all *he* was good for."

"And as it turned out, Mrs. Capper had only you for help, and you were with her all evening?"

"Yes, as it turned out. We coped at Interval. In point of fact, if you've got a third who doesn't do much but get in the way, he's more of a hindrance than a help. And Win had got a lot of glasses poured out in readiness while the first part was going on. So it was hectic, but we managed."

"But you *were* with Mrs. Capper all evening?"

Under Iain Dundy's calm, clear gaze, Dawn faltered as she understood what he was getting at.

"What you're saying," she muttered, "is that in this sort of case it's always the husband or wife who's suspected first. Though in fact Win thought Des was God's gift, poor cow."

"I'm not *saying* anything. I'm just trying to get at times."

"Yes, well— I filled the dishwasher in the kitchens with glasses in the second half. There were just too many to do in clear water in the bar, like Win normally would. That took me—what?—ten minutes."

"And in the first half?"

"I just fetched the snacks. . . . They were something a bit special, a sort of free extra because it was the first night. There was a bit of balancing plates on the tray and that, but it couldn't have taken me more than five minutes. Less, if anything."

Iain Dundy gave a meaningful look at the other policemen that said, Five minutes would be enough. But Dawn, under inquisition, had regained some of her perkiness, and she noticed the look. She said, smiling sweetly: "And when I came back, Win had poured out drinks for Interval, like I said. While I'd been away, she'd done about fifteen white wines, about ten reds, and the same number of whiskeys and gins. You try doing that in five minutes and killing your husband!"

"Couldn't they have been done before you came on the scene?"

"Where would she have kept them? The white wines would have to have been kept in the fridge. I was in and out of the fridge during the first half of the play, getting ice and whatnot. There were no ready-poured glasses of white wine there; that I can tell you for sure."

Charlie cleared his throat. "Excuse me, sir," he said. "My girl had white wine at Interval. First thing she said when she sipped it was 'Lovely and cool!' "

Charlie's imitation of upper-class girlhood was perfect. Superintendent Dundy sat looking gloomily ahead of him. To Sergeant Nettles his expression said as clearly as words: It's the arty types we're going to be stuck with.

Finally he shifted in his chair and turned to Dawn with a smile. "Thank you, love. That'll be all for tonight. I think we ought all to go home and get an hour or two's kip."

10

THE DINING ROOM

The headwaiter supervised breakfast next morning. This was not something that he did very often, but he did it the day after Des's murder. He had heard about the killing the night before, of course, as he and his staff were waiting for the last of the supper-takers to leave. Dawn had been the first to bring the news, and further snippets of information had been gleaned (by guile) from the many policemen infesting the Saracen's Head. The kitchen and dining-room staff had been thunderstruck and hadn't enjoyed anything so much in years. They had quite lost the desire to get rid of the eaters and go home to bed. In fact, they had related the news to favored eaters with varying degrees of subtlety. ("I'm sorry the service has been a bit erratic tonight, but you see, the manager's just been murdered.") The headwaiter participated in all their contradictory emotions, though on a loftier plane, of course, and he had made do with a very few hours' sleep in order to be at the Saracen early, apparently to ensure that the dining room's high standards of food and service were in no way compromised by the untoward little incident of the night before.

Incidentally, he also intended to be the first to inform

the headquarters of the Beaumont hotel chain. It is in the nature of headwaiters that they like to be the first with news, however hushed, regretful, or reverent the tone of voice in which they choose to broadcast it.

Thus, when the various members of the cast and other residents of the hotel came down severally to breakfast, they found eggs scrambled to a nicety, kippers beautifully frizzled, the traditional fry-up traditionally fried up. What was different was the atmosphere. They all dallied over their breakfasts for a start, hoping that someone else would come down with a new theory they had thought up in the long watches. All the play people sat at adjacent tables (not something they normally did) and exchanged intimacies and abrasions across the gaps, while the orchestral players and odds and ends sat as near them as they decently could and listened unashamedly, as did the unusually attentive waitresses, who fussed unconscionably around the tables in the hope of picking up something new.

"The point is," said Jason Thark, still in the magisterial mood of the night before, "that it would be quite impossible for any of us to go through the dining room here without being seen. Let alone the kitchen, let alone the Shakespeare Bar, but the dining room would have been quite impossible. And we would have had to go through all three to get to the stairs that would have taken us up to the first floor. No—Ronnie was quite right: We're out of it."

"There was just one thing," said Ronnie, "something I've been thinking over during the night. When I was playing onstage, I was conscious of faces in the windows of the dining room watching the play. . . . *Were* you?" he asked, swiveling round in his chair and transfixing the waitress, who was dawdling round with a toast rack in her hand as an excuse. She blushed.

"Well, some of us was watching."

"Never all of you?"

"No. Some of us watched some of the time. But you couldn't hear, not through the window, so you couldn't follow what was going on, though it looked a good laugh and you had us splitting our sides, sir."

"But some of you didn't watch at all?"

"No, sir."

"And where were the ones who were not at the window?"

"They were around the table by the door into the kitchen having a bit of a giggle and a gossip, sir."

Ronnie leaned back in his chair, satisfied.

"So I was right. Nobody could have got past."

"There was also some poker playing in the kitchen," volunteered the waitress, unwilling to lose the limelight now that she was used to it.

"Right. Them we could see from our part of the kitchen. I admit that they most probably wouldn't have noticed if anyone from the cast had tried to sneak past. But the gag— Sorry, collection of staff by the door into the kitchen would certainly have noticed anyone, wouldn't you?"

"Well, I expect so, sir. We did see this gentleman"—she gestured at Peter Fortnum—"go through and then go back again. Not that it meant anything, I'm sure."

She retreated rather suddenly from the table, as if she had all but accused Peter of murder. She left some embarrassment behind her as well, though not in Jason Thark, who was impervious to any such human emotion.

"You see? She noticed. *One* of them would certainly have noticed if our murderer had tried to go that way. And apart from Peter, who was not to know that Connie would run out of gin, so I see no significance in his trip, nobody did."

For one moment this made everyone feel better. For only a moment.

"Oh, *come*," said Clarissa Galloway, putting back on her plate a delicate triangle of toast. "I really wouldn't have expected you to be so deficient in logic, Jason, my pet. For a start, Peter could have made sure Connie would run out by nicking a half from her bag. She said, if you remember, that she had never forgotten to have one there in reserve before. Secondly, he could have been intending to use some other excuse but seized on this when he heard Connie's laments. Of course, Peter *dar*ling, I'm not saying that any such thing happened, merely that we must, above all things, remain *log*ical, because we can be sure the police will."

"I quite understand," said Peter, tight-lipped.

As soon as he saw it was nine o'clock, the headwaiter ceased supervising the mundane business of distributing breakfast goodies and slipped into his little office in the corner of the kitchens. Somebody would now be in at the head office.

The Beaumont chain had hotels from Aberdeen to Bodmin and from the sublime to the disgusting. Its headquarters was in Kensington, and when the headwaiter made it clear that this was a matter of the utmost urgency, he was put through without further ado to the managing director's office.

"He'll not be in until ten or so," said the great man's secretary. "He's been at Brighton with his son—he's a spastic and takes a lot of looking after. Where did you say you were speaking from?"

"The Saracen's Head, in Ketterick."

"Ah, yes. One of the jewels in our crown."

"Precisely."

"Haven't you got that festival thing on there at the moment? I hope it's not causing any problems."

"No, or not directly. It's the manager. Mr. Capper . . ."

"Ye-es?" Did the headwaiter detect an note of wariness, or at least of circumspection?

"He's dead. Murdered."

"Good God! Have you called the police?"

The headwaiter raised his eyebrows to heaven. "It happened last night. Of course, the police have been here since then. That's all taken care of."

"I shall inform the managing director the moment he comes in. He'll be most upset. He knew Mr. Capper personally. And he won't like all the publicity there'll be. It will clash horribly with the Saracen Head's image."

It was the headwaiter's opportunity, the reason he had been so keen to relay the news. His voice took on tones of the most magisterial: "If you will allow me to say so, the whole Capper appointment clashed with the Saracen's image."

"Ah . . ." There was silence at the other end, as if the secretary were not used to being taken down a peg or two by employees from the suburbs. "You thought so?"

"I would say the whole hotel thought so."

"As far as this office was aware, he was doing an excellent job. He rang up last night, you know, to say that the play was going well. The duty man left a note for the managing director. He was first-rate like that, at keeping in touch. He must have been murdered after that."

"He must indeed. At what time did Mr. Capper make this phone call to your duty man?"

"The note is dated seven-thirty."

"I shall certainly inform the investigating officer."

"I hardly think— Is that necessary? Do we really want to involve Head office? Well, you must use your discretion. . . ."

"The main thing now is," interrupted the headwaiter, who had every intention of following his conscience and doing his duty as a citizen, "that we get a temporary manager as soon as possible. You do have qualified people who are between assignments, I suppose?"

"Oh, yes. Of course."

"The play isn't on tonight. It's the first night of the opera. After that the play runs every night of the festival except Sunday. It's essential we have somebody here by tomorrow. And preferably someone who could learn the ropes tonight."

"It's a tall order. But I'll list the possibilities and show them to the M.D. as soon as he gets in. I suppose Mrs. Capper isn't in a condition to—"

"Mrs. Capper is not the managing type, and by all accounts she is in no condition at the moment to do anything. It would hardly be seemly in any case even to have her helping behind the bar, whatever her mental state."

"No. No, of course not. Well, I'll try and get a lightning decision and ring you as soon as I have any news. Meanwhile, soldier on, eh?"

The discussion was continuing in the dining room. Breakfast had never taken so long, but the kitchen staff was not complaining. The waitresses were picking up an unending stream of fact, conjecture, innuendo, and downright falsehood, and they were regaling it to the cooks, who were putting their own interpretations on them. ("You mark my words!" the head cook kept saying after each particularly bizarre leap of the imagination.) Before long, they all felt, they would be ready to make an arrest, even if the police were not.

"Right," Ronnie Wimsett was saying. "Peter's absence is not in dispute. He went to get gin for Connie. We all find it pretty impossible to get to our own rooms—*still*, after a fortnight here—so it's not surprising that he found it difficult to get to Connie's."

Peter, and Natalya, too, sat stewing over their tea, looking straight in front of them.

"The question is, could any of the rest of us do it? Now, to my mind, going through on the Webster and Massinger side of the hotel is simply out. For one reason, at some stage you would have to come *out*—either into the courtyard or into the street. In the courtyard you have audience who would see you, including twelve standing-room customers at the back, by the main gates, whose vision you would have to cross. On the other hand, if you go out into the street, you still have to get back in past hawk-eyed Frank on the main entrance. Impossible—right? That leaves the route via the kitchens and the Shakespeare, which is inconceivable for reasons we've already gone into. So all in all—apart from Peter, and sorry about that, old chap—there simply seems no way any of us *could* have done it."

There was silence after this, though one or two, notably Susan Fanshaw, looked unhappy. Indeed, she started to speak but cast a half look in the direction of Carston Galloway and cut the sound short in her throat.

"Well, that settles it," cooed Clarissa. "We'll explain it

to that rather *mel*ancholy-looking policeman, and it will leave him free to direct his attentions elsewhere."

"After all," said Ronnie Wimsett, "we've been here for a couple of weeks or so, but Capper's been manager for months. Who knows what backs he's put up in his time?"

"The main thing is," said Carston, pushing back his chair and making to get up, "that we're all in the clear and can now get on with our business."

Brad Mallory's drawl broke unnervingly into the general euphoria. "Anyone would think," he said, "that the Saracen's Head was a one-story building."

He was sitting slightly apart, at a table for two, which Singh had just left. There was silence for a moment after his words, but then Ronnie Wimsett broke into it confidently:

"No, no, old chap. I've thought of that. To get to the stairs in the foyer outside the Shakespeare you still have to go through the kitchens, dining room, and the bar itself. And on the other side the stairs are between the Massinger and the Webster and you'd have to go through the one and could be seen from the other. No, that doesn't wash."

"Brad doesn't relish his position," said Clarissa in serpentine tones, "of being one of the few actually in the *hotel* part of the Saracen at the time of the killing."

Brad's smile in return revealed that he was hardly to be outdone in the friendly-snake department.

"Quite true if Des was killed after eight-fifteen. Yes, I could in fact have returned from the concert and gone straight upstairs and killed him. In *fact,* I went to my room, but I could just as easily have gone along to his flat. But what if he was already dead by eight-fifteen?"

Clarissa shrugged. "So what? It leaves us exactly where

we were. Apart from young Peter, none of us could have gone through to the front part of the hotel."

Bradford Mallory, no less than Clarissa, could relish a big moment. "I seem to remember," he said, almost dreamily, "from one of my visits to your delightful play in rehearsal, a moment . . . a line—what was it? 'What mean these sudden broils so near my doors?' Something like that!"

" 'Have you not other places but my house, to vent the spleen of your disordered bloods?' " went on Gillian Soames, as if this were something she had been itching to bring up for hours.

"I know what you're going to say," said Clarissa Galloway with all the considerable force at her disposal. She had put her hand over the breakfast table and covered her husband's in a display of solidarity. It was a revealing gesture, which suggested that their instinct was to draw together at moments of crisis. She also revealed that this was something they had discussed overnight. Brad Mallory ignored her and went on in his dreamy fashion.

"It was, if I remember, a speech of Ralph Greatheart, at night, quieting the riotous behavior of the apprentices . . . and appearing to them in his nightshirt . . . appearing— and this is the point—*above,* on what we may call the upper stage. In fact, appearing on that part of the balcony over the center of the stage. Is that not right, Miss Fanshaw?"

"Yes," said Susan, tight-lipped.

"And my impression is that this scene occurs—what?— about an hour into the play?"

"Something like that," agreed Susan.

"And that with Ralph Greatheart on the balcony there is his stage wife and his daughter Alice—dear Gillian."

"Right," agreed Gillian.

"And did you, Miss Fanshaw, accompany them to the first floor to see that all was well?"

"No, I checked costumes and props at the bottom of the staircase as they all went up."

"The staircase," said Brad.

"I went up," said Jason Thark, hurriedly, before anyone else could mention it. "It was a tricky scene, and I went and stood in the bedroom behind."

"That's right," said Carston, "and you—" He shut up suddenly.

"I think, you know," said Brad, "that the police had better look into that scene and that staircase and who was there for that scene and who might have used the staircase before and after."

"There goes your alibi for all of us," said Gillian to Ronnie. "Somehow it always did seem too good to be true."

11

THE MANAGER'S FLAT

The residential quarters of the manager of the Saracen's Head consisted of four rooms immediately above the entrance foyer and reception desk. They could be reached by a small staircase from the manager's office behind Reception or by a door from the maze of corridors and open areas on the first floor—a door that led directly into the sitting room. Des's murderer could have gained or been given access to the flat from either of these.

Superintendent Dundy had sent Nettles off to talk to the kitchen and the cleaning staff. Nettles was an excellent chap, but he did tend to chat, to comment, to make his presence felt. Dundy liked to sniff out a place in silence—walk around, get the feel, sense a personality. Then he would look around and think of what was missing, what was out of place. So he said to Charlie, down in Reception: "Let's go up and quietly get the lie of the land, shall we?" Charlie nodded, and together they ascended the stairs and went to work.

The manager's living quarters—or dying quarters, as they had so soon become for Des Capper—had been inhabited for twenty years by "dear old Arthur," as Gillian

Soames and others always called him, and his impress was still on them. His had been the choice of furniture, his the choice of the pictures on the walls. It was mainly in the extras and inessentials that Des and Win had made their tenure felt. Or that Des had made his tenure felt.

The photo of the hotel in Dubbo, squarely in the center of the sideboard, had Des standing by the wrought-iron pillar of a wonderful nineteenth-century structure, looking loathsomely proprietorial. Win was not to be seen. Perhaps she was behind the camera, but as it seemed a highly professional photograph—you could feel the flies, smell the sheep-dip—this was unlikely. Probably she had been behind the bar as usual. The books all seemed to be Des's, too: *The Homemaker's Medical Enquire Within*, *The Secrets of the Tarot*, Desmond Morris, *Reader's Digest* evaporated books, L. Ron Hubbard, and Arthur Hailey. Even the *Jane Fonda Exercise Book* belonged, Dundy guessed, more to Des than to Win. There were newish paperbacks of several biographies of the Mountbattens, presumably purchased to give corroborative detail to Des's recent incautious claims, which Dundy had heard about from Frank. There was also *Heat and Dust* and a popular book on Indian religions.

Des's research for the festival took in heavier tomes. From the Ketterick Public Library he had borrowed a thick book on Donizetti by William Ashbrook and a volume on Elizabethan and Jacobean comedy. The latter had been much renewed, with dates handwritten in. The former was a new borrowing, with a return date ten days hence. They both sat on a small table by the biggest armchair. Charlie took them up and skimmed through the sections on *Adelaide* and *The Chaste Apprentice*.

Iain Dundy was over by the sideboard, getting whiffs of

Des's personality. There was a pile of old records there—
Mantovani, James Last, and the Beach Boys—but the record player did not look as if it had been touched since
they had moved in. The *Mirror* and the *Sun* of the day
before were beside one of the easy chairs, and some old
Penthouses were stacked under a coffee table. The racing
pages of the newspapers were marked for possible bets. In
one of the papers something was cut out; it seemed to be
the regular medical column. Iain Dundy raised his eyebrows and went on.

Win's influence seemed mainly to consist of dainty linen
and lace mats on the dressing tables, sideboards, and occasional tables, such as the one on which the knife had lain.
Probably also hers were the antimacassars on the backs of
easy chairs and sofa. Leaning against the sofa, Dundy
found that the covering was slightly damp. The furniture
in the room was all solid, capacious, and worn, and had no
doubt served "dear old Arthur" for years, until it had now
gained this light accretion of alien personality from the
new managers. No doubt it was like this when a stately
home was taken over by new stately owners.

The body had by now been taken away, though chalk
marks and tapes marked where it had been, and Iain
Dundy could remember it very well. The sitting room in
the manager's flat was a large one, with the main bedroom
leading off at one end, kitchen and second bedroom leading off from the other. The sofa and the easy chairs were
clustered around a fireplace, with a small dining table and
two chairs positioned by the window that overlooked Ketterick High Street. This left a goodly space at one end,
where the stairs down to the ground floor and the door out
to the corridor were. It was in this open space that Des's

body had been found. It had pitched forward, its head towards the door into the corridor, its back decorated by a knife between the shoulder blades. The table on which had rested the knife had been in that open space too, just behind the sofa. One could still see the imprint left by the handle of the knife on the embroidered table mat it had rested on. Anyone, on an impulse born of overwhelming nausea or provocation, could have taken it up and stabbed the loathly Des with it on the spur of the moment.

Did the position of the body tell one anything? Could Des have been starting towards the door when he was stabbed from behind? Possibly. Equally, he could have been standing in thought, facing in that direction, and propelled sprawling forward by the force of the blow from behind. There was nothing particular to look at on that wall apart from the door and a reproduction of Morris's *Queen Guinevere* beside it. But a man in thought does not need anything to look at, and Des, Dundy suspected, was a man with a variety of projects demanding thought.

Did he, Dundy wondered, keep all these projects in his head, or did he keep some written record, however vestigial?

Dundy and Charlie spent over an hour circling the flat warily, like two animals careful not to invade the other's territory. Then Nettles came up after a not very rewarding session with the domestic staff, and inevitably they all settled down to an interim comparing of notes. Dundy came out at once with the question of Des's projects and his thirst for scraps of knowledge.

"I don't think there can be any doubt," he said, "that he was a man who loved information. First of all, just information. Have you met people like that? Do they still exist in your generation? They'll bring it out anywhere, anytime: the age of the pyramids, the average number of eggs a chicken lays a year, the estimated population of China in the year 3000. Totally out of the blue they'll come out with it—some real conversation stopper. And like as not they'll just think they've floored you and congratulate themselves on their cleverness."

"I know that sort of bloke," agreed Nettles. "The sort who makes you slope off to the saloon bar if you hear his voice coming from the public. But in his case it shades off into something much more nasty, doesn't it?"

"Apparently. But I think it starts off as this sort of desire to accumulate out-of-the-way information. The sort of fact you got in the old Ripley "Believe It or Not" column or as a little paragraph in the *Reader's Digest.* That sort of interest is rather boring but totally innocent. When it spreads itself out and becomes a desire to collect information about living people, that's when it becomes dangerous. And so far as we can see, Des's magpie instincts about information also embraced people—the guests at the hotel and very probably the staff at the hotel as well."

"What I'm trying to get a handle on," said Charlie, "is the point of it all. I mean, with some people it can be just accumulation for the sake of accumulation. I wouldn't think it was that way with Des Capper, would you?"

"No," said Dundy emphatically.

"Then was it for pure, straightforward blackmail? Was it for chuckling over and poking ribs—as in Frank's story about the man who'd brought his bird here? Or was it something more subtle than either?"

"Yes, that is the question, isn't it? I suppose the murder gives us the answer to that, if we're on the right track."

Iain Dundy paused and scratched his ear. "But perhaps it's not completely clear-cut, not as neat as you put it. You say: Did he accumulate grubby bits of information just for the sake of it, did he chuckle over it, or did he use it for blackmail? Perhaps the answer is: All three. It's not necessarily either/or. If the information was not usable, he just enjoyed having it. If it was usable, he had to decide what use to make of it."

"And there was one other possible use for it," said Charlie thoughtfully.

"What's that?"

"Revenge."

Dundy nodded.

"There is also this question of how he got appointed here," said Nettles. "It's something the staff keep bringing up. He wasn't just awful; he was the wrong type."

"We'll have to start looking at that," agreed Dundy. "If he was as unsuitable as Frank and everyone else imply, then the question of blackmail must surely arise there."

"And if it arises there, then the chances are that it has arisen again now," said Nettles.

"Yes, though let's remember one thing: That would be blackmail for personal advancement. It could be done very subtly. Just a whisper and a nod. It could be done so indirectly as hardly to be blackmail at all."

"Though not by this Capper character, surely, sir, if what we've heard of him is to be believed?" objected Charlie. "Hardly a subtle character, by all accounts."

"Probably you're right. But still, it is one further step to blackmail for money. A further and a very dangerous one. But if he was blackmailing one of the festival guests here, what else could it be but blackmail for money?"

Charlie coughed. "What the class newspapers call 'sexual favors,' sir?"

"Well, maybe," said Dundy. "I haven't had a very strong sexual whiff from this case yet. More a matter of sheer black bile, as far as Capper is concerned. But we'll have to talk to people and find out if that was one of his interests. I presume there are some reasonably attractive women around connected with the play in one way or another. His wife would be the last to know—or, on the other hand, she could be leading us on in a big way, don't forget. Still, I would like something just a little more definite than sexual favors."

"There's nothing written down, is there, sir?" asked Nettles. "No kind of record of the little things he found out?"

"That's what I've been wondering. Nothing's been handed over by the technical experts, and we haven't come across anything today. I wonder if he was the sort to write things down. What impression do you get?"

The other two frowned, then shook their heads.

"No impression, sir," said Charlie regretfully. "Could have been a real little Samuel Pepys. Could have kept it all in his head."

"The sheer *amount* he seems to have accumulated might be a hopeful sign," said Nettles.

"Yes, and at least that generation's more likely to write things down than a younger one," said Dundy hopefully. "Youngsters these days need a keyboard connected to a screen if they want to remember anything. I suppose the first thing is to organize a search of all the obvious places —desks, drawers, sideboards, and so on. You take the big bedroom, Peace, you take the small one and the manager's office downstairs, Nettles, and I'll take this room and the kitchen. If we get no results, we'll start thinking of hiding places."

And so they got down to it. But of results in the obvious sense, there were none.

There were just a few things that they thought it worthwhile to collect up and mull over afterward. Des had apparently eaten All-Bran for breakfast and taken Ex-Lax regularly. He had used a mouth spray against bad breath, and an antiperspirant. His teeth were his own, but he used a toothpaste designed to remove heavy stains. There were many used packs of playing cards and a backgammon set. There were road maps with routes laboriously marked out, perhaps by Win. The routes, mostly from Carlisle, had not taken them to well-known beauty spots or places of tourist fame, not to Wordsworth's Cottage or Castle Howard. They had been exclusively to towns. When Dundy compared them to a leaflet downstairs on the reception desk, he found that they were all towns that boasted hotels in the Beaumont chain.

No harm in that, of course. Doubtless the Cappers would have got a reduction on their stays. But the fact that most of the routes were from Carlisle made Dundy wonder if they had been prospecting during Des's previous job, deciding which of the hotels they—or rather *he*, surely— was going to blackmail himself into the managership of.

On a personal level the only haul they got was a few letters and postcards. There was little any of them could make out of the postcards: one of the Alhambra with "Fantastic place—Kevin" on the back; one of Michelangelo's *David* with "Christ what a nancy boy, eh? Jacko." The postmarks were from the fifties, and they were addressed to hotels in Parkes and Coonabarabran, New South Wales.

The only reason the policemen could see for keeping them had to be the pictures.

The letters were marginally more revealing. Three of them were from Des's mother. The latest, very feeble and practically without meaning, was addressed to Des and Win after their move to Britain in 1974. The earliest had also been addressed to Des in Britain—in fact, to a street in Pimlico. The date was December 1945, and it expressed the wish that he had waited until things were more settled before going "home":

> But then you always did what you want, but I hear such dreadful things on the wireless and wonder and with everything so short there are you getting enough to eat?

The other was addressed to Private Capper, of the Second Borderers, serving in India, apparently stationed near Bombay. So Des's army career had begun *after* the Second World War. Not the impression he had given Frank, the doorman. The letter expressed bewilderment as to why he had joined up:

> You always were a mystery to me, but one blessing youll be nearer home so when the three years are up you can come back, this is where you really belong son I hope youve learnt that by now with all love Your Ever Loving Mum.

The only other letter of interest was from India, dated 1947, and addressed to Corporal Capper, stationed in Hong Kong. After jocose preliminaries, it said:

You lucky bastard, getting out before it all turned nasty. My God, the things I've seen, but I expect you've heard from some of the boys, and you can believe it. Don't write and tell me you're living the life of Riley in H.K., Des, because I don't want to know. You always were the kind of crafty bastard who could slip out from under.

Not this time, thought Dundy.

"Well," he said, shaking his head and looking at the meager haul. "This is the sum total of finds of interest, and I can't say it gets us much further. No written notes of discoveries, no written evidence of any blackmail attempts. What does that mean? That he didn't write anything down?"

"Could be," said Nettles. "If he was a serious blackmailer, it would be much the wisest thing."

"Yes . . ." said Dundy. "Somehow the vibes I'm getting from this man don't suggest that he would always do the wisest thing. . . . But maybe I'm getting him entirely wrong."

"I may be wrong, too, sir," said Charlie, "but the vibes I'm getting suggest that he was a very *obvious* man, for all his cunning. As I said before, not subtle at all. Awful in an obvious way . . . obvious minded, somehow."

"Sort of second-rate brain?" suggested Dundy.

"Yes, or third. You know, the sort of person who thinks it's true because he's read it in the papers. Quotes *Reader's Digest* as if it were the *Encyclopaedia Britannica*."

"Oh, God, yes."

"That's how I see him. And I wonder—if he's taken notes of any sort, then it seems to me he's probably hidden them in a very obvious place. I mean the sort of places old ladies hide things, the places that are always the very first ones that the experienced burglar looks in."

"Kept under the geranium pot, do you mean?"

"Yes. Laughable, and a bit pathetic. Where in the house do old people hide their little bits of money, their pension books, their savings certificates?"

"The backs of cushions," said Nettles promptly. "Behind the books in the bookcase. Under the sofa cushions. Under the mattress. In the tea caddy. On top of the kitchen dresser."

"That's the sort of place. I just wondered, sir, whether it might be worthwhile looking there."

In the event, Charlie turned out to be right about the obviousness of Des's mind. Des and Win had gone in for Scandinavian-style beds, with the (hard) mattress laid straight onto a board. Good for the back, as Des would no doubt have told many a bar customer at length in his time. His notebook was pushed under the mattress, on top of the board. Apparently Win Capper had not had the aristocratic sensibilities of the princess who could not sleep on a pea. The notebook was on her side.

But there was no doubt it was Des's. Dundy took it downstairs and compared the handwriting with his entries in the hotel register. It was Des's hand, all right. Or fist, more likely. Because the little notebook, bound in green plastic, was mostly a jumble of jottings in no particular order and dubiously legible in places. These ill-spelled notes were *aides-mémoires* in the strictest sense. They seemed to be scribbled down pretty much anywhere, just as he felt the urge to commit things to memory. So that "Geary—gin?" came two or three pages after another note that read: "Geary—ten half bottles in six days *known*." There was, then, no sequence or continuity, and Dundy and his two assistants had to get from it such isolated nuggets as they could. If they were baffled, it had to be said that Des was frequently, too. His bafflement expressed itself in such diagrams as:

Underneath the diagram there was scrawled the question "What gives???"

Question marks, in fact, were very frequent. There were "Gillian S.—Ronnie Wimsett??" There was "Fortnum—Natalya R.—phone calls—where?—expensive—what's up? Defecting?" Later, presumably connected with this, there was "Why Mallory not involved?" Mallory also appeared in "Mallory—Singh???" Underneath which was written: "Where?"

But there was one page in the book where there seemed to be some sort of organization, where the information seemed grouped around one central figure. There was a note that said: "Girls—young." Then he had added: "Constant supply—recruited by bodyguard. Bodyguard paid by the girls? Age?" This last word had been underlined many times. At the bottom of the page there was an enigmatic "HAD 9." What could that mean? That he'd had nine such assignations with classical music groupies to Des's knowledge? But there was a shaky arrow leading to the side of the page that suggested that this entry related to something on a previous page. In any case, it was overshadowed by an entry in red: Stretching from the bottom left hand corner to the top right, misspelled but sharp in impact, in letters that bit deep into the page as if they had been scrawled in a fury, there was the legend:

GET GOTLIEB

"I think we may have struck gold," said Iain Dundy.

12

PEOPLE TALKING

For the actors it should have been a day of delicious anticlimax. It should have been a day for reading the early
reviews, letting off a bit of steam, of shopping for unneces-
saries. But it wasn't like that at all.

Reviews there were, luckily. Reviews that praised the
"tireless energy" of the *Apprentice* cast, the "mature
warmth and humanity" of Carston Galloway's Ralph
Greatheart, and "the sense of a send-up of a parody" behind Ronnie Wimsett's chaste apprentice. The music critics had done their bit, too. There was acclaim for the "incredible and flamboyant richness" of Singh's voice and for
the "golden opulence and vivid femininity" of Natalya in
the letter scene. All these were lapped up, swapped, discussed, and disputed, though not by Clarissa Galloway,
whose Melinda Purefoy was not mentioned at all.

But it was all, somehow, a bit academic. A bit of a side-
show. Because at half past eleven the superintendent, who
had only been glimpsed hitherto walking purposively
around the hotel, began interviewing people who he
thought might be of help to him. And since the staff of the
hotel had all been together at the crucial time and had

been given a thorough going-over by one of his men, that left the actors and the residents. And of course, it was all quite ridiculous, but . . . but one really had to decide how much to tell him, didn't one? And one had to decide which of one's fellow actors one could talk to about how much to tell him. Probably it would be mostly routine, wouldn't it, and rather dreary, but then there would be those areas . . .

And it *was* mostly routine, this preliminary round of interviews. But there were areas in which Dundy and his men found tiny nuggets of interest.

"But I *can't* see," said Clarissa Galloway, "why we can't be interviewed together. We do everything together. Except sleep together, sometimes, but that goes in waves."

She crossed a shapely black-stockinged leg, doing it *at* Charlie Peace, as being the youngest man in the room. His eye gleamed with a spark of amused appreciation. Iain Dundy's mouth tightened. Of course with these arty people it all came back to sex in the end.

"I'm afraid interviewing you together would be quite against regulations," he said.

"It must be terrible to be so *bound* by regulations," said Clarissa with stage thoughtfulness.

"You say you do everything together, but in fact you weren't playing husband and wife in this play, were you?"

"Good God, no. Ralph Greatheart is an *ancient* character."

"Do your parts link up? Are you together onstage a great deal in the course of the evening?"

"No, we have a scene together at the end of the first act, but then we're hardly onstage at all together until the last act."

"Then were you offstage together a lot?"

"Oh, yes, a fair bit."

"Talking together in the dressing rooms behind the stage?"

"Well, I don't remember talking together," said Clarissa, again with that contrived thoughtfulness. "But of course terribly *aware* of each other. *Al*ways terribly aware. It's what distinguishes us as a partnership."

And that, Dundy suspected, was nothing but the truth, in spite of the stagy manner in which it was delivered.

"I see. While you were backstage, were you aware of anyone leaving the dressing room—the two dressing rooms, rather, in part of the kitchen and the private functions room—to go into the main part of the hotel?"

"No, I can assure you Carston didn't. As to the others— Well, of course there was young Peter Fortnum."

"Ah."

"*Quite* a talented beginning. Plays Peter Patterwit and has some quite *fright*ful jokes, which is almost inevitable in this kind of comedy, but he carries them off rather well. . . ."

"Yes, I'm sure. But it was his trip into the main part of the hotel you were going to tell me about."

"Was I?" She smiled dazzlingly at the three men. "Well, if you *want* to hear about it. It's surely of no importance. Let me see . . . He came offstage—it was towards Interval time, perhaps a quarter of an hour before—and Connie Geary was complaining that she'd run out of gin. She's a dipso, poor old thing, though quite a happy one, which is a blessing when you see the other kind. Where was I? Oh, yes, Peter Fortnum had just come off, and he wasn't due to launch any more of his *leaden* innuendos at the audience until after the Interval, and he said straightaway that he'd go and fetch her a half, which is what he did. Actually, it *did* seem to some of us that he was gone an awfully long time."

"I see," said Iain Dundy. "Well, no doubt it's something I shall be able to follow up. Now, about the dead man himself—what were your impressions?"

She leaned forward. She had decided that honesty would be the best policy and sincerity the best manner. She delivered herself of a great deal of sincerity.

"Quite frightful! A squirt, a pusher, a bore. And of course dreadfully inquisitive! I don't expect *that's* news to you, is it? He made no secret of it. Now, when you've been a *star* for . . . some years, as I have, as Carston and I have, you get used to inquisitiveness—from fans, from the press, and so on. But quite naturally some of the others here aren't *used* to it in the same way and react very badly to prying and snooping. I think you'll discover in the end that that's where the answer lies. His snooping was the death of him."

And a very satisfactory end, too, her dazzling smile to all three men seemed to imply.

"My movements?" said Brad Mallory. "My dear man, they are an open book and vouched for by thousands. I was in the Town Hall. I had a seat in the back row—in case I was needed behind the scenes. I had people beside me who would certainly remember me even though I didn't have any conversation with them. I should think Frank, the doorman, noticed me when I left, and I remember speaking to him when I returned at Interval."

"You actually left the concert at Interval?"

"*Exhaus*ted by the splendor of Singh's performance." His hand flapped, like a vulture's wing.

"And you came straight back to the Saracen?"

"Yes."

"And then?"

"Straight to my room—to recover some degree of equilibrium."

Unvouched for by thousands, thought Dundy.

"Ralph Greatheart is, I suppose, the biggest part in the play," said Carston Galloway judiciously. He made it sound as if he were calculating the number of lines rather than being immodest. "I *think* it's bigger than the apprentice himself. So I'm onstage a great deal of the time. Last night, when I wasn't onstage, I was in the improvised dressing room backstage."

Iain Dundy was conscious of movement behind Galloway in the cramped quarters of the manager's room, which had been put at his disposal to conduct the interviews in. It was Charlie Peace, who had been making signs and who now cleared his throat.

"Yes, Constable?"

"If I may, sir, there's one question I would like to ask the gentleman. I should say that I happened to be in the audience last night. There is one time, isn't there, Mr. Galloway, when you actually appear on the balcony? You and one or two others?"

"That's right. The upper stage. I included that, of course, when I talked of being onstage."

His manner was that of one rebuking an inattentive schoolboy. Nevertheless, he hadn't mentioned it, Dundy noted. If Peace hadn't been in the audience, would it have come up? He shot a grateful glance at Charlie, then took over the questioning again.

"This upper stage, sir—is it part of the regular balcony around the courtyard?"

"That's right. Divided off from the rest of the balcony by a couple of makeshift partitions."

"And reached through a bedroom?"

"That's right."

"And how, sir, did you reach that bedroom?"

"We went up a little service staircase in the corner of the kitchen. Apparently it's one that's used by the cleaning women and sometimes by the maids when they're taking up breakfasts in bed or room orders."

"I see. You say *we* went up, sir. Could you tell me who the other actors were who were on with you?"

"Oh, yes. It's a scene where the Greatheart family have been woken up at night by the horseplay of the apprentices, which of course has been taking place below on the main stage. It's a fairly traditional situation—"

"And your family in the play is—?"

"Joan Carley, who plays my wife—my stage wife—and Gillian Soames, who plays my daughter. Oh, and I think Jason Thark, the producer, followed us upstairs to see how the scene went."

The wonderful casualness of these arty people when they lob their grenades, Dundy thought!

"Ah, he would remain in the bedroom, I suppose?"

"Yes . . . Though now that you mention it . . ."

"Yes?"

"I seem to remember, as we all went into the bedroom, sounds from the corridor—almost like a row." He passed his hand over his forehead in one of those stage gestures that he and his wife specialized in, which set Dundy's teeth on edge. "No, it's too vague. Remember I was about to go out onto the balcony. It's a scene that calls for a lot, vocally and dramatically, so I was only thinking of that. You'll have to ask Jason."

And you've made quite sure that I do, thought Dundy.

"This Jason Thark is the man your wife says, er . . ."

"They've been sleeping together since we got here," said Carston indifferently.

"I see . . . And did you all go back to the kitchens together after the scene was over, sir?"

"Er, no. The ladies, you see, go twittering off quite early in the scene, after a drunken obscenity from Matthew Cotter, one of the apprentices—only it's an obscenity nobody understands any longer, so it rather misfires. After they go, I have several more minutes haranguing the lads; then I go in."

"And last night they'd already gone downstairs?"

"Yes."

"And then did you go down with Mr. Thark?"

"No . . . No, Jason must have gone down by that time. I went down to the kitchen alone."

"I see. About what time was this scene, Mr. Galloway?"

"Oh, good Lord, one doesn't notice times. Well on in the first half but not Interval by a long chalk. I may say that I spoke to little Soames the moment I got down to the bottom of the stairs. Asked her how she thought it'd gone."

"And you couldn't put a time to it, roughly?"

"Oh, say, five to eight, or eight—something like that."

"I see. Thank you."

Iain Dundy did not have to look down at his notes to remind himself of the police doctor's preliminary estimate of the time of death. He thought it had occurred at some time between eight and a quarter past nine.

* * *

"I was in my bedroom," said Gunter Gottlieb. "I plan, I read the score, I *hear* the music to myself. So do I *feel* my way into the performance tomorrow—that is, tonight. Even Donizetti—which is piffle, pure piffle!—even Donizetti has to be *felt*, experienced, heard inside."

"I see," said the superintendent, feeling an intense dislike for the lean, arrogant figure sitting opposite him. "So you were here in the hotel, alone in your room, all evening?"

"Yes. Oh—one moment. A girl came."

"A girl? Her name?"

Gunter Gottlieb shrugged.

"I don't know."

"What did she come for?"

"Sex. We just have sex; then she go."

"I see. Was she a prostitute?"

"Certainly not. I don't use prostitutes."

"How did you meet this young lady, then?"

"Meet? I not meet her. I have sex with her. My bodyguard, Mike, he got her for me."

"I see. He made all the arrangements?"

"Yes."

"When was this? How long did it take?"

"It was, oh, seven something. I suppose altogether it took about twenty minutes. It usually does."

"I see . . ." Iain Dundy sighed internally. He was being very honest, this repulsive man. Was a lack of hypocrisy to be commended in a matter like that? he wondered. "Tell me, Mr. Gottlieb, can you think of any reason why Mr. Capper should feel a particular dislike for you?"

"Who?"

"Des Capper, the dead man."

Again Gottlieb shrugged. "I have no idea."

"You did nothing to him?"

"I was quite unaware of his existence."

Dundy felt quick glances in his direction from both Nettles and Peace. That was a lie, surely. The hatred of that "Get Gottlieb" scrawl could only have come from some incident the man would be sure to remember. Did the lie spring from his prodigious arrogance? Or was it a clumsy attempt to disguise guilt?

"Oh, he was the most *horrible* little man," said Gillian Soames. She had decided that Iain Dundy was just the kind of man she liked and was talking a lot to cover the fact. "Well, not little at all—all too large. You know the type—the sort of man who, the moment he puts out his hand to shake yours, you know you don't want to touch. Shiversome. Yukky. But I'm talking nonsense. You must meet a lot more of that type than most of us."

Iain Dundy had relaxed considerably. This was the sort of witness he liked: nervous, for some reason, but direct, reliable. Not arty at all, he told himself.

"Oh, I don't know," he said expansively. "Most of the people we meet are pretty average individuals. But it's interesting you should say that. When you connect him with the kind of people I meet, do you mean you thought there was something . . . criminal about him, right from the start?"

Gillian considered. "No, that would be going too far. I just took a dislike to him. Later on, when one heard of the man's snooping activities, one did start wondering what was the end in view."

"What snooping activities were these?"

"Oh, it was Clarissa who made the big fuss. He'd been

snooping around in her room, she said, looking in drawers and so on. Occasion for big scene. But I'm sure on this occasion Clarissa was telling the truth. In fact, the more one took notice of him, the more he seemed to be snuffling around after information that might prove useful to him."

"May I test him on something?"

"Go ahead."

"He thought you might be having an affair with someone called Ronnie Wimsett."

Gillian laughed uproariously. Iain Dundy felt obscurely glad that Des Capper had been wrong, which was odd, because he had not yet swapped a word with Ronnie Wimsett. Behind Gillian's back a tiny glance passed from Charlie to Nettles and from Nettles back to Charlie. They recognized a sexual spark when they saw one. They were seeing one now.

"I take it he was wrong?"

"Of course. Want to know how he got the idea?"

"Yes."

"He was going round from table to table in the Shakespeare, pushing himself into all the conversations. That was my first evening here. When he got near our table, Ronnie and I held hands and looked into each other's eyes to keep him away. Somewhat surprisingly, it worked."

"Couldn't see below the appearances, eh?"

"Well, with the performance Ronnie and I put on, that's not surprising. I was just surprised he thought being in love was a sufficient reason for his staying away. But often he got things wrong even when nobody was trying to mislead him. Like when he oozed up to Peter Fortnum and me the day we arrived and assumed we must be 'the operatic lady and gentleman.' The fact that we were gazing reverently at the stage should have told him that we were actors. Still, it doesn't do to assume that everything he thought he'd found out was wrong."

Dundy sighed. "No. The likelihood is that in one case he hit the jackpot. And a lot of good it did him. Now, can we talk a bit about that scene in the play that takes place on the balcony?"

Gillian crinkled her forehead. "Yes, I assumed you'd want to talk about that. It's funny, you know, but we discussed and discussed how we—the actors—*couldn't* have done it, and yet we never thought of that scene or never admitted we realized its significance."

"It seems to me," said Dundy, "that you never thought of the staircase, either."

Gillian smiled at him self-deprecatingly. "You must think us very dim. But in fact there were a number of people sitting around the bottom of that staircase all the time, so it would have been pretty difficult to slip up it without being noticed. That scene, of course, was different; that was legitimate business."

"Can you tell me exactly what happened?"

"I'll try—as I remember it. I think we gathered at the foot of the staircase and all went up together. That was Carston, Joan, myself, and Jason following. I remember Carston being first into the bedroom and then being in there with him and Joan just before going out onto the balcony. . . ."

She became silent.

"You don't remember Mr. Thark being there?"

"No. I have to be honest, don't I? I remember, just before we went on, hearing voices in the corridor. Angry voices."

"And the other voice?"

"Well, it *could* have been Des Capper."

"You can't be more definite than that?"

"No, it wouldn't be fair to."

"And when the scene was over?"

"Joan and I came out first. Joan went down, and I watched a minute or two more of the scene through the window. Then I went down, too."

"Do you remember when Mr. Thark and Mr. Galloway came down?"

"No. I went to talk to Connie Geary. Jason may even have been back in the kitchen already. But I'm afraid I didn't notice at all."

Charlie Peace cleared his throat. "Mr. Galloway remembers coming up to you after he came down, miss. To ask you how you thought it had gone."

Gillian frowned. "Oh, yes. I think you're right. He did come up at some stage. I'm sorry I can't remember exactly when."

"You're a good, careful witness," said Dundy.

Or a clever one, thought Charlie.

"I sang," said Singh.

He looked towards the mirror at the far end of the manager's office and was annoyed to find it angled to reveal whether there was anyone standing at Reception outside. So it was reserved for Iain Dundy to gaze on that smooth light brown skin, those doelike dark eyes, those perfect girlish features, that plump, underexercised body. Singh brought back all his distrust of "arty" people that Gillian Soames had done so much to banish.

"Yes, I realize you sang," he said, his irritation showing through for the first time that day, perhaps because subconsciously he was judging Singh to be as yet a person of little importance in any world. "I gather your arias were towards the end of the first half, is that right?"

"*At* the end. So the applause could go on."

"I see. So that would mean you were singing from just before eight, maybe, till about—what?—ten past?"

Singh shrugged. "Probably."

"What were you doing for the rest of the time?"

"I was sitting in the room for the artists. All the time. They were asking me about my voice, my technique. It is very extraordinary. And at Interval there were impresarios and theater directors talking about possible offers of engagements. I was never alone."

He smiled a catlike smile. The pleasure seemed not in having an alibi but in being so sought after. If what he said was true, and it seemed likely, Dundy thought he would not need to interest himself very much in Singh. It would in any case be impossible to be as interested in him as he was himself.

"Darling, it would be totally irresponsible of me to say *any*thing," said Connie Geary. She smiled at him with the art of one who had once cared if she pleased men. "I am a totally reliable actress: I get on and off the stage when I should, and I never slur my lines. But apart from that I live in a *haze*. If you ask me 'Was he or she around at such and such a time?' I can only give you an impression. *If that.*"

"I see." Dundy sighed.

"And that wouldn't be fair."

"No. It's a pity, because you were around in the kitchen most of the time."

"Yes, I was. I only have three scenes, though *very* meaty

ones. But I can't tell you anything definite about what went on backstage because it wouldn't be right."

"Do you remember sending Mr. Fortnum for more gin?"

"Oh, yes, though I don't remember when."

"Do you remember whether he took a long time?"

"Darling, it *seemed* an age!"

"Sure I took a long time," said Peter Fortnum.

He was firm spoken and fresh faced, and all Iain Dundy's experience told him he was about to tell lies. The same half look that had passed between him and his men when Gunter Gottlieb was talking now passed again.

"Why should it take so long? The maids say you ran through the kitchens and dining room."

"Superintendent, would you like to try an experiment? Send one of your policemen here to find room 146 and see how long he takes."

Dundy smiled. "I may do that. But it wouldn't be quite the same thing, would it? My men have probably never been in the residential part of the hotel. You have been here nearly a fortnight."

"It doesn't help," protested Peter. "You never get used to it. You think you've got it taped, and then it throws down a nifty one and you're lost again. And anyway, my room is on the second floor, and Connie's is on the first. I just got lost looking for it."

"Miss Geary's room is, as you say, on the first floor. It is also not that far from the door into Des Capper's flat. Did you go anywhere near that door?"

"No."

"How can you be so sure if you were lost?"

An expression of irritation crossed Peter's face. "Not knowingly, I mean."

"Did you see anyone while you were searching for room 146?"

Slight but perceptible pause.

"No."

"Well, well." Iain Dundy shifted in his chair. There were lies being told here, but for the moment they were not nailable lies. "Let's get on to something else. I believe you've been helping a bit as translator for the Russian lady."

Another tiny pause.

"That's right."

"Including at rehearsals for the opera—whatever it's called?"

"Adelaide di Birckenhead." Peter pronounced the name with relish. "Yes, I went along there when I could."

"Tell me, can you give me any reason why Des Capper should feel particularly bitter about Herr Gottlieb?"

Peter settled back more easily in his chair. "Oh, yes. Yes, I can. It was just a few days ago, actually. I was in the wings, and there had been one of Gottlieb's scenes. You've talked to Gottlieb?" Dundy nodded. "Then you can probably guess what they're like. Icy, premeditated murder. I don't think Des Capper saw the scene; otherwise he might have been more careful. Most of the cast were onstage, and Mallory and Singh had gone up, too. Capper came up behind me, saw Singh onstage, and made some remark about not realizing there were Indians in medieval Birckenhead. 'Running the corner shops, I suppose.' " Peter's imitation, like Gillian's earlier, brought the dreadful Des momentarily but vividly to life. "Typical barroom joke, and just the sort of thing that Des would think was clever."

"Just one moment. What was Capper doing backstage?"

"Exercising his right as a member of the festival committee to go anywhere and watch anything. I gather this is a right nobody else exercises. Anyway, eventually there was a break—God, we needed it!—and when I got to the Green Room, there was Des already there, irritating the hell out of everyone, particularly the poor American tenor who had been the main victim of Gottlieb's scene. . . . That's when it happened."

"The incident."

"Yes, the row. Gottlieb was having a discussion— No, Gottlieb was *telling* the director of the festival that he intended changing the opera scheduled for the next festival to *Fidelio*. It was typical Gottlieb unreasonableness. The director was beginning to get a bit heated when Des stepped forward. Trying to mediate, so he said."

"Ah, and Gottlieb—?"

"Bawled him out. Sheer barrack-room stuff. Get out, don't come near my rehearsals again, that kind of thing. If it had been anyone else, there'd have been applause."

"And how did Des Capper take it?"

"With Gottlieb you don't have much choice. He slunk out."

"Meditating revenge, do you think?"

"I know so. He practically said so later, said he'd learned all he needed to know about revenge in India in 1947. Des tended to go on about India."

Iain Dundy sat considering. Then he threw a bouncer.

"Tell me, sir, why have you been making so many expensive phone calls since you came here?"

Peter Fortnum blinked at the change of subject but had his answer—Dundy could have sworn to it—prepared.

"My girlfriend is in Germany. She is with a theater company in Stuttgart."

"She must have very good German."

"She is advising on costumes. For a production of *The Merry Wives of Windsor*."

"It's remarkable that you can afford all these calls. You're a young actor, and I believe you have quite a small role."

"Is it so remarkable?" Peter asked. "With a name like Fortnum?"

Superintendent Dundy reminded himself that from one point of view all an actor's performing life is living a lie.

"You're damned right I wasn't going to tell you," said Jason Thark. "And don't, for God's sake, ask why not, because it's bloody obvious, isn't it?"

"Well, let's get the facts clear first, shall we, sir? You went upstairs with the three actors who were about to appear in the balcony scene."

"That's right."

"But you never followed them into the bedroom?"

"No, because I saw Des Capper coming along the corridor. There was something about him—something pushy and self-satisfied—and so I lingered by the door. I'd heard about a set-to between him and Gottlieb at the Alhambra. He had the cheek to say, 'After you,' and make to go into the bedroom as well."

"Which in a way you might say he had a right to do," said Iain Dundy in fairness to the dead Des.

"In a way. With any other manager I might have admitted the right: it was his place, as the Alhambra wasn't. But give Capper an inch and he took a mile. He'd been barging in everywhere pretending he had a right as a member of the festival committee. Next thing would be he'd demand to sit onstage, as the noblemen used to. So I gave him the rounds of the kitchen and told him to stick to his quarters."

"How did he react to that?"

"How do you think? He bridled, muttered, threatened, but in the end he trotted off."

"And you, sir? What did you do?"

"I was rather pleased with the whole affair, quite frankly. It made a good addition to the 'grand remonstrance' that the cast and I were going to address to the festival committee when the festival was over."

"Grand what, sir?"

"A sort of general complaint by the actors and the other people staying here. A letter to the powers that be in the Beaumont hotel chain and to the festival committee as well. So I went away to one of those little alcoves the place abounds in, one where there was a writing desk, and wrote down the threats that Capper had made and the ridiculous rights he claimed."

"I see, sir. Do you still have this memorandum?"

"Yes, as a matter of fact I've got it on me."

As he took it, Dundy was under no illusions. The memorandum could have been written ten minutes ago.

"Any thoughts?" Dundy asked his men when at last they were alone.

They looked at each other.

"On the face of it, Mallory seems the best bet," said Charlie Peace slowly. "Alone in his hotel room from around eight-fifteen till Interval time and after. If we take it Capper was killed by Interval, that gives him a quarter of an hour to do it in."

"Oh, and by the way, he poked his head in at the Shakespeare Bar on the way up," said Nettles. "Dawn told me that. Perhaps he wasn't just *exhausted* by Singh's performance, after all."

"Looking for someone?"

"Dawn couldn't say, of course. He said nothing. But maybe he was looking for Des."

"And maybe he found him," said Dundy.

"I'm not sure, on thinking about it, why I picked on Mallory as the best bet," said Charlie. "After all, there are at least three others who had good opportunities to get at Des as well. Carston Galloway after the balcony scene—and *didn't* the Galloways chuck around innuendos about the other actors? Then there's Fortnum, of course, when he went to get the gin. And Gunter Gottlieb any time after his girl left. He, in a way, had the most opportunity and was the least accounted for."

"Yes, but can you see anyone arranging an assignation like his was just before committing a murder? If, of course, he did intend committing it. The trouble is, we know of no reason for Gottlieb to kill Capper. He'd seen him off. It would make more sense the other way round: Gottlieb as victim."

"A highly popular corpse," commented Nettles.

"One thing, though," said Charlie thoughtfully. "If the key to all this is in Des's determination to 'Get Gottlieb,' then it may be we're paying too much attention to the play and not enough to the opera. Perhaps we should forget the actors for a bit and take a look at the singers."

13

THE DIRECTOR'S OFFICE

"Anyone for the opera?" asked Dundy.

Evening had come, and weariness set in.

"Er, my wife has just had a baby," said Nettles.

"Of course. I'd forgotten."

"It is the fourth, but I'd quite like to see it."

"Oh, Lord. Haven't you seen it yet?"

"Only got the message as I was coming in this morning." Nettles shrugged. "Policeman's lot. Policeman's wife's lot."

"What about you, Peace?"

"Try anything once. But we're not going to get seats, are we?"

"We'll try to get them to slot us in somehow."

Dundy had begun to feel that the line of interviewees would stretch out to the crack of doom. It was all too much. There were others to interview, but they could wait: One of them needed a Russian interpreter. Ronnie Wimsett seemed to have been onstage much of the evening, and never on the upper stage. Gunter Gottlieb's heavy would at least have made a change after all the arty people, a reversion to familiar territory after uncharted shores. But he couldn't see that Gunter's girl was of much significance. She had apparently come and gone well before the earliest time the murder could have been committed. And it hadn't been anything more than a quick dip, for either of them, so far as he could see.

Sitting for a moment in the little manager's office, Nettles having scurried off, Charlie standing waiting for some action, Dundy meditated on the unattractive figure of the world's next "great conductor." He realized that all such figures had two sides, the artist and the private man, and that with Gottlieb the private man trailed badly last. He wondered briefly at such an unadulterated swine being the mediator between great composers and the ordinary man. He seemed to remember that a lot of musicians had behaved very badly in Nazi Germany. Then he shook himself and put aside the thoughts as unprofitable.

"I'll ring the festival office," he said. "See if something can be arranged."

"Well, of course," said the voice on the other end of the line, "the director of the festival is very busy, because it is the first night of the opera. That's what he's doing at the moment. He's down at the Alhambra seeing that the critics get their creature comforts and welcoming distinguished guests: Lord Harewood is coming, and Lord Goodman, and all sorts of people like that. On the other hand, I do know that he's very concerned about this murder, concerned that it shouldn't cast a cloud over the festival. . . ."

"Ha!" said Dundy to Charlie as they collected together their notebooks and got ready to leave the Saracen for the first time that day. "Cast a cloud over the festival! Murder never casts a cloud over anything! As far as the mob coming here is concerned, it'll be a great bonus. Murder is the great British spectator sport, the ultimate in good clean fun."

Walking past the copper on the door and out into the pale evening sunlight, they found they had to cope with cameras and media persons stationed outside. One reporter looked pointedly and hopefully at their wrists ("Black held in Aussie slaying"), while another pursued them along High Street with questions. "Wrong man, sorry," lied Dundy, and they managed the rest of the five-minute walk in peace.

By now it was nearly seven o'clock, and the audience was flocking around and into the blue-and-maroon little theater, splendid, yet slightly dotty. Charlie looked at the audience curiously. It was certainly not like the Covent Garden audience—not dressy and ignorant. Charlie had got the measure of a Covent Garden audience in his younger days, when he had done duty for a ticket tout in Floral Street on a Pavarotti night. This audience was very different. There was the odd sprinkling of black-tie-and-long-skirt couples, but in general this was a young people's festival and a mecca for enthusiasts and cranks. Dress was casual, even colorful. Dundy, too, watched them for a moment; then they both slipped through into the foyer. Here Dundy gave a discreet message to one of the attendants, to be passed on to the director. Then they made for a deserted corner to wait for the rush to subside.

"My mother used to play Bingo in a place like this," said Charlie cheerfully. "This one's gone uphill."

The director Dundy could point out to Charlie, having seen his picture in the *Ketterick Evening Post.* He was a comfortable, candid-looking man, with just a hint of being worried out of his life, which Iain Dundy could quite understand, granted what much of his life must be like. He was standing by the stairs welcoming faces in the audience that he recognized. There were many of these, for the festival thrived on its regulars, and they seemed as pleased to see him as he apparently was to see them. The audience was as comfortable-looking as the director. They were mostly discussing the singers and waxing lyrical about the particular canary they fancied.

"It's a bit like a sports meeting," said Charlie. "People comparing Cram with Coe."

"And going all the way back to Bannister," agreed Dundy. "Some of these people sound like canary fanciers from way back, or gramophone freaks who collect seventy-eights. It wasn't like this in the old days. They've built up these audiences, just as the Saracen has."

For Dundy had been to the festival opera years before, when he had had a wife to buy tickets and the tickets had miraculously coincided with an evening off. The opera had been Donizetti then, too—*Don Sébastien, Roi de Portugal* ("like listening to a mouse trying to roar"—*The Observer*). Dundy had rather enjoyed it, but he remembered the audience's commentary as being more bemused than informed.

Eventually the forward-moving stream thinned, the director's genial greetings became fewer, and the noise of the orchestra's tuning up penetrated through the doors into the auditorium. Last-minute arrivals, scuttling through, managed no more than a smile and a nod at the director. He looked towards Dundy, raised his eyebrows, then nodded up the stairs. Dundy and Charlie went over, and all three went on thick red pile up to the circle, then through a door that led them into a maze of corridors out of bounds to the general public. Eventually they came to a door labeled "Festival Director," and Charlie and Dundy were ushered into a tiny but cozy office with a desk piled with reference books and telephone directories and with room in front of the desk for only a couple of chairs. The walls were decorated, like London Italian restaurants, with publicity photographs of opera singers.

"I have a little office at the Saracen as well," explained the director, making them comfortable and pouring them both neat whiskeys from a bottle in the filing cabinet. "But somehow it's been less pleasant working there since poor old Arthur died."

Dundy was willing to hear just one more verdict on the unlovable Des.

"The new manager?" he asked. "Our popular corpse?"

"Exactly. I'm sure you've got the general idea by now. An appalling know-all, a peddler of folk wisdom and quack remedies, a one-man popular informer."

"And a great collector of inconvenient information about people," added Dundy.

"Yes, I—" The director hesitated, looked at Dundy, and then plunged in. "I suppose you remember the case earlier this year when my daughter was accused of shoplifting?"

"Yes, I was sorry you got all that publicity. I wasn't involved."

"Of course not. I don't blame the police. But she'd just lost a baby, had postnatal depression— Anyway, it made a good story for the local papers, and damn the consequences for her. It was all perfectly public, but what made it worse was Des coming up at the first committee meeting after the magistrates' hearing. 'Terribly sorry to hear about your little family trouble. As a father myself I can sympathize.' All done in a nicely raised voice. I could have— Well, no, I couldn't. But I *felt* like it then."

"I had no idea Capper had children."

"Nor had anyone. Maybe it was just a fiction to justify

the sympathy. If he has, he seems conveniently to have cast them off, or it off, somewhere along the line."

Dundy looked at Charlie. He knew that both of them were toying with the entrancing notion of Des having fathered Singh during his time in India. Dundy shook his head and put the notion from him. Singh was about twenty years too young.

"You have no idea how he came to be appointed?" he asked.

"None. It's something all of us on the committee have discussed, I can tell you. We could only assume some . . . hold on the chairman or managing director of the Beaumont chain."

"Blackmail, you mean?"

The director looked mildly horrified, as if such a thought had at least not been put into words hitherto.

"Oh, come, come," he said. "It didn't have to be anything so dramatic. He could have done somebody some . . . service."

"Saved his son and heir from drowning?" said Dundy cynically.

"That sort of thing. Saved his life in the disturbances at the time of Indian independence. He waxed very eloquent about his experiences at Mountbatten's right hand."

"Hmmm," said Dundy. "Very *Jewel in the Crown.* As a matter of fact, I wouldn't mind betting Capper got his notions of what happened at independence time from that TV series. He wasn't in India at the time; he'd gone on to Hong Kong. You mentioned his characteristic as almighty know-all and crushing bore. But it wasn't those in particular that annoyed the festival committee, was it?"

"No, though it was embarrassing, because he was pig ignorant, and we had to find ways of listening to him pontificating about things he knew bugger-all about. No, it was his pushiness and his prying that touched us on the raw. He took it as his right to go everywhere, poke his nose in everything."

"Did he have such a right?"

The director shrugged. "In theory, maybe. No other member of the committee would have *thought* of exercising it. But Des went everywhere, got to know everything, and *gave his advice.*"

Dundy waved his hand in the direction of the auditorium, whence pale echoes of vocal glory penetrated even to the director's office.

"I gather on occasion he poked his nose into rehearsals of the opera we can hear now."

"Oh, yes. I don't know how often. I was down here one day watching rehearsals and waiting to see that swine Gottlieb afterwards. There was a nasty moment, with Gottlieb humiliating the tenor, who had to be brought to the front of the stage if he was to be heard, and Mallory having to placate the soprano. The producer was rearranging positions, and suddenly I saw Des was there in the wings. I remember my heart sinking and thinking: Des is all we need at this stage."

"We've heard about this little episode," said Dundy. "And about what happened afterwards in the Green Room."

"Do you remember exactly what Gottlieb said to Capper?" asked Charlie.

"Pretty well. 'I do not take advice from taverners'—I remember that. 'You come near one of my rehearsals ever again and I have you . . . thrown out on your fat bottom.' He has the men who could have done it, too."

"Did Capper say anything?"

"Nothing to the purpose. 'Sorry, I'm sure,' or 'No offense'—something like that. He just slunk away."

"But hoping to get his revenge," said Dundy. "We've evidence of that. He didn't like public humiliation."

"Who does? But with Capper it would have been a strong emotion, I'm sure. He nursed grudges."

"Yes." Dundy looked at him straight. "Tell me, if you were out to 'get' Gunter Gottlieb—"

"As, God help me, I may be yet."

"—how would you do it?"

The festival director considered. "I think my first reaction would be to say: hit him professionally."

"Ah! That's what I wondered. Because he is, shall we say, vulnerable, on his personal side, too, isn't he?"

"Girlies," said the director, shaking his head. "I know. It's something I've had to be very aware of. It's the popular press I fear: Royals and vicars and people in the arts world—those are the ones the tabloids have a particular down on. He seems impregnable, but that could be his Achilles heel. That's why I had a word about it with his minder—"

"Ah! You did that?"

"It seemed the sensible thing. I discovered that he was thick as two planks, but he had learned enough about the law to know how to keep on the right side of it when he had a mind. So I made it clear to him: nobody underage. And preferably nobody local. I think he's been recruiting from the groupies who followed him from Coventry and from people here for the festival. Gottlieb's needs are occasional and brief."

"So that's made him pretty near impregnable on the personal side, you think? That's why you'd go for him on the professional side if you had to?"

"Yes, because odd though it may seem, the festival is important to him. It's part of his overall strategy, and he wants to be a success here, make it *his* festival."

"How did you come to appoint him?"

"That's easily explained. It seemed such a coup! He came with the Midlands Orchestra last year and gave a quite wonderful concert. Mahler and Beethoven—the most thrilling Seventh you can imagine. Our regulars were over the moon: It was the sort of glorious music-making they heard in their dreams, one of them said. Our regular opera conductor was off to be resident chief of one of the state orchestras in Australia, so there was a vacancy to be filled. Not expecting him to accept, we approached Gunter Gottlieb."

"And he accepted?"

"Not immediately. He thought for three days, then accepted provided he had charge of all the musical side of the festival. That seemed like a wonderful bonus to all the committee. We couldn't believe our luck."

"I take it you've learned better since?"

The director thought a bit, trying to be fair. "It would be wrong to say that. I think this festival will probably be a great success from a musical point of view. The opera will, too: He makes Donizetti sound as good as mature Verdi. But it will all be a personal success for himself, and to some extent it will be manufactured."

"You mean he brings his own fans, and so on?"

"Well, yes, he does, but I didn't mean that. There are four orchestral concerts, and the third will be given by the Welsh Symphony Orchestra. At the planning stage he insisted that they give *Death and Transfiguration* and insisted, too, that we engage Ernest Petheridge to conduct. Between ourselves, never the brightest conductor, and now, at seventy-five . . . Well, he can be relied on to endow the idea of eternity with new degrees of tedium. They'll be snoring in the aisles. *Then,* two nights later, the final concert, with Gunter Gottlieb conducting *Also Sprach Zarathustra*—surefire popular success, brilliant orchestral showpiece, and of course brilliantly conducted. And don't get me wrong—it will be. But it will *seem* that bit more brilliant by comparison. You get me?"

"Oh, I get you."

"And then, of course, there's the business of next year."

"That was what the row was about in the Green Room, wasn't it?"

"Disagreement . . . Well, yes, row. Except that I did manage not to lose my cool. It would mean changing the whole direction and character of the festival. You probably know what sort of festival Ketterick has had up to now: a festival for families and enthusiasts, with something for everyone. Some of the sillier critics sneer at the operas we do, but they're wonderfully direct and involving—first-rate theater. Gottlieb's is an attempt to change all that and put us in the international league. And, of course, it put us in a cleft stick."

"How?"

"If we say no and lose him, all the arts establishment and all the newspaper people will say we've opted for safeness and provinciality and second-rateness. If we say yes, we hand the festival to him on a plate, the rest of us become ciphers, and we betray our existing audiences."

"Yes, I see. An impossible decision. And I take it an impossible gentleman to work with?"

"Bloody impossible, between you and me. I think we'd be justified in turning him down and letting him go if only because he's obviously using us as a stepping-stone to something else and because it will certainly all end in tears, and pretty soon, too."

"So your view is that he's totally geared to being a success in his professional life and if you hit him there you would really touch him where it hurts? Something along those lines was my conclusion, too. He's a man programmed to succeed. He's to be the next—who's the bee's knees?—Karajan?"

"The comparison has occurred to other people. At the moment, his whole being is intent on two glorious successes: first the opera, then the final concert, where he'll hope to have people standing and cheering, led by his own groupies. Which he almost certainly will. And to be fair to him, which isn't easy, almost all of it will be deserved."

"He is good?"

"He is *very* good. He rides roughshod over everyone, but he is almost always right. And yet there is still . . . somehow—I can't put it simply—a lack. An emptiness. . . . And I wonder whether in the long run music lovers aren't going to find this out. . . . Would you like to see him doing a bit of the opera?"

"There can't be any seats, surely?"

"There's mine. I have to go and see to the Interval jamboree for nobs and critics. You've no idea how we butter up the critics from the big newspapers. You can have my seat until the break." He turned to Charlie. "And you can stand at the back, if you don't mind that. It's not usually allowed, but we can explain to the fire people that you're a policeman."

"I'm used to standing about," said Charlie. "I was in uniformed branch for a year."

"I think we'll say yes," said Dundy. "Though I'm not

sure that I'm musical enough to understand this . . . this lack that you talk of."

They went back to the front of house, down the staircase, and along the corridor that spanned the back of the stalls. The director collected programs for Dundy and Charlie and then, with practiced stealth, opened the door into the stalls. As the music washed over them, he pointed Charlie to a place by the door and then led Dundy down to an aisle seat three rows down. Then he himself evaporated to attend to the wants of the important visitors.

Once settled, Dundy found himself cocooned in a devout attentiveness. This audience was a totally committed one. Onstage, and close to the front of the stage, a very personable tenor was emoting in slow time, sighing his way towards a close. Iain Dundy had only a smattering of holiday Italian, but he had an awful feeling that the tenor was boasting about how much his love had cost him. The cad, he thought. Then the orchestra hotted things up, and an attendant or junior terrorist rushed onstage to deliver an urgent message, of which the words *Inglese* and *Birckenhead* could be distinguished. At which the tenor leapt to his feet and with a skirl of his (unhistorical) kilt began delivering a martial cabaletta that taxed his sweet voice to the uttermost. When it was over, there was polite applause, the curtain came down, and dimmed lights came up while changes were made to the permanent set.

In the half-light at the back of the theater Charlie read the program. He had got a rough idea of the story from the volume in Des's sitting room: The personable hero, he remembered, would be Robert the Bruce, on the run from the English and about to take refuge, disguised, at *il castello di Birckenhead,* the power base of his rival, who was also the husband of the woman he loved. Well, that was all clear, wasn't it? He turned to the history of the opera and immediately found himself gripped in a way he did not quite understand. He read through the account of the first version of the opera, then the story of the recent redis-covery of the later version. Only when he had finished that did he begin to realize that the break had been rather long. Looking up from his program, he found he was not alone in this feeling. In the Victorian intimacy of the Alhambra Theatre everyone could see everything, and even from the back of the stalls Charlie could see the figure of Gunter Gottlieb, his baton steadily beating on the open pages of his score in patent irritation. No doubt Gottlieb had de-creed no more than two minutes for the break, and it had stretched out to four. But then the lights went down, there was a perceptible relaxation of tension in the audience, and Gottlieb raised his baton for the last scene before Interval.

In the previous scene, Charlie, for all his lack of knowl-edge of opera, had been conscious of a shimmering beauty that Gottlieb extracted from the very simple accompani-ment to the tenor aria. Now he began to notice something very different. The curtain had risen on the peasants and retainers of the castle of Birckenhead (all kilted—in defi-ance not only of historical but also of geographical proba-bility). They were celebrating something or other, probably Hogmanay, in song and dance. The stage picture was sup-posed to be one of uninhibited revelry, but what Charlie was most conscious of was the *lack* of real spontaneity. What impressed him most was the drilled nature of the performance—the military precision of the drumbeats, the terrified accuracy of the chorus, which at times affected their acting. It was as if—another historical absurdity—the opera was being performed by the soldiers of Frederick the Great for their commander in chief. One might see

Gottlieb as the Prussian bandmaster writ large. Charlie did not quite see things in those terms, but he did register to himself: Everyone is bloody terrified.

He stood there, drinking it in, thinking that he might be able to make a habit of this kind of music if he ever got the opportunity. There was a scene for a dreadful comic servant, and then the baritone and soprano arrived to join the merrymaking, exuding manorial graciousness. The baritone found time to snarl something about *"gl'Inglesi"* to a retainer out of the corner of his mouth, in the way baritones have. Then suddenly the sound of merrymaking died away. The tenor had arrived. He stood for some moments at the back of the stage, commented on by everyone in hushed tones. Then he advanced to the front in what Charlie recognized as a clumsy but necessary maneuver. Soon he was launching into the great, swaying tune:

> *Io son pari ad uom cui scende*
> *Già la scure sulla testa.*

This was the moment, Charlie felt sure, that Des had come in on in rehearsal. Standing there in the darkness, letting the music lap over him and swaying in time to its irresistible impulse, Charlie thought that he might have had the glimmerings of an idea.

14

THE CORRIDORS

" 'The trivial round, the common task, should furnish all we ought to ask,' " misquoted Dundy under his breath next morning. And in future it bloody well will. Here we go on another load of backstage chitchat, shortly homing in on more accounts of what gives with the Galloways. At least when I rowed with my wife it tore us apart, because we meant it. With these arty people, who knows when they mean *anything*?

And what gives with Peace this morning? His mind isn't on it. And this girl's a perfectly personable little thing. . . . He dragged his mind back to the interview he was conducting.

"As far as the balcony scene is concerned, I inspected them all before they went up the stairs," Susan Fanshaw was saying. "They were all in night gear, so it was quite straightforward. Then I was off hither and yon doing other things. The apprentices were onstage—onstage and off, because it's a very busy scene, and I have to see whether the costumes have suffered in the horseplay, whether they've lost anything, and so on. So though normally I might have noticed when Carston at least came back down the stairs, that night I didn't."

Iain Dundy coughed a dry, diplomatic cough.

"Er, you say normally you might have noticed?"

Susan obviously wanted to get that part of the discussion over with.

"Oh, Carston and I are vaguely sleeping together."

"I see. I had, actually, some idea of this, but perhaps you could put me into the picture. I gather his wife knows?"

"Oh, yes. Everybody knows. It's no great passionate affair. I mean, Carston is nice—" She pulled herself up. "No, not nice exactly, because he's mean as hell, and vain as well. Still, he *is* a wonderful actor, when he's fully stretched, whereas she will never in essence be more than a rep queen, for all her name. So it *is* rather exciting; it is decidedly a pleasant interlude. . . . Not least because of his vast experience."

"Ah . . . You don't mean acting? No. Er, you don't mind being one of a long line?"

"Not at all. It's part of the thrill."

Iain Dundy sighed. He was never going to understand these people, still less like them. His bewilderment was increased when Susan Fanshaw added: "A long, long roster. Both male and female."

He drew his hand along his forehead. "I see. Then Galloway is—?"

"Predominantly hetero, but he takes it as it comes. He covers the waterfront, like Brad Mallory. It's pretty common in the theater."

"Oh, then Mr. Mallory—?"

"Must be the same. He doesn't make much secret of being besotted with young Singh—not even from you, I imagine. But I know an actress who had a pretty serious affair with him five or six years ago." She saw Dundy's face and laughed. "It must make it pretty difficult for you."

"All in a day's work," said Dundy bravely. "So you are sleeping with Mr. Galloway, and I gather Mrs. Galloway is sleeping with the producer, and this is all out in the open and talked about quite unashamedly?"

"Yes. What a lovely word: 'unashamedly'! So you think we should be ashamed? Of course, Clarissa uses the situation to launch lethal little barbs against Carston and me, but that's just her nature."

"I find it difficult," said Dundy, trying not to sound prim, "to get a picture of this marriage. Why do they stay together if they're quarreling all the time?"

"Haven't you ever met a soldier who's only happy in action? Or a policeman who couldn't be happy on the beat in a quiet area but is always itching for a bit of action?"

"Frequently."

"Well, then. 'Pleased with the danger when the waves went high / He sought the storms; but for a calm unfit . . .' Dryden. It's quite impossible to imagine either of the Galloways having a *calm* relationship with anyone."

"I see," said Dundy, sighing. "My point in trying to establish how open all this is, is to make the point that there was very little mileage to be got—by Des Capper, for example—out of threatening to reveal the truth of the situation to any of the people involved."

"None whatsoever. We all knew. The whole hotel, down to the kitchen skivvies, knew. The room maids probably had a running bet on as to who would be sleeping with who each night."

"Right . . . Right . . . So if any of you had a grudge

against Capper, it would have to be on some other grounds."

"Oh, certainly. Like that he was the biggest bore, the biggest ignoramus, and the biggest liar in a fifty-mile radius."

"I doubt whether people get murdered for any of those reasons," said Iain Dundy. "And I suppose if there were anything more substantial, you wouldn't tell me. Now, let me get this clear, finally. Your duties in the play never led you to leave the kitchen?"

"Never once. I was there the whole time, even during the Interval, checking costumes and props. Jason aims to give the sense of Jacobean bourgeois life, so in the absence of sets, props are very important."

"And the balcony scene we've mentioned is the only time in the play when the upper stage is used?"

"Yes, the only one."

"I suppose you checked that the room upstairs that led onto the balcony was in fact unlocked?"

"Oh, yes," said Susan unsuspectingly. "But well before the performance started. In any case, Carston had a room key in case one of the maids had locked it by mistake."

Dundy nodded his head and mentally wiped Susan Fanshaw from his list of suspects.

"Of course, I'm onstage practically the whole evening," said Ronnie Wimsett, clearly not immune to the same little vanities as Carston Galloway. "Or just off, or just about to go on. So quite apart from the fact that it would be difficult for me to have done it, it's also difficult for me to remember anything that went on backstage."

"Why? Because if you weren't on, you were hovering about around one of the doors onto the stage?"

"That's right. Whereas someone with a smaller part could certainly spend an hour or more in the kitchen just sitting around and noticing."

Wimsett was a very different type from most of the actors, Dundy decided. Apparently open, genial, conversational, but with an overriding reticence, particularly about himself. On essentials he presented a bland front to the world. Dundy was willing to bet that his fellow actors knew little about his character, his private life, his sexual preferences. He kept, in popular parlance, himself to himself. Like many policemen, Dundy thought.

"Miss Geary ought to be ideal," he said. "She was sitting around for most of the play. But for obvious reasons that she makes no secret of, she's not much use. Tell me, during the weeks of rehearsal, who reacted most strongly to Des Capper?"

"Well . . ." Ronnie was either plainly reluctant or plainly acting out reluctance. "I suppose you'd have to say Gillian Soames. She'd been *very* fond of Arthur Bradley, the earlier manager, in a father-and-daughter sort of way. I think anyone would have been a letdown. But Capper she thought the absolute pits."

"Yes, she's been quite open about that," said Dundy quickly. The foot of one of his attendant policemen gave a gentle tap on the ankle of the other attendant policeman. "What about the other people staying at the Saracen? How did they react to him?"

"Oh, in various ways. Carston Galloway with a sort of lordly, amused contempt . . . Clarissa taking the opportunity for a scene. . . . Connie Geary rather relished him. She enjoys the chance of plumbing the depths of human awfulness, and she got that with Des. It's something actors often enjoy—watching dreadful people, to use them afterwards." He thought. "I think some of the people whom he most got under the skin of were the ones he gave advice to." He grinned self-depreciatingly. "That includes me, I suppose. He tried to educate me in the method school of acting. He tried to give Krister Kroll a lesson in breathing techniques, and that riled him."

"Krister Kroll? He is—?"

"The lead tenor in *Adelaide.* He's not staying in the hotel, but he's been around a fair bit with Peter and Natalya, having a drink in the Shakespeare, and so on. He's sung here before, so he knew the Saracen in better days. He was around after the concert."

"I see. Yes, I saw Mr. Kroll onstage last night. And what about Gunter Gottlieb?"

"Oh, God! Rather an appropriate exclamation, now I come to think about it. Gottlieb resembles the God of our worst fears. Well, I don't think for much of the time Gottlieb was aware that Des existed. I think that was probably worse than ridicule as far as Des was concerned. I mean, if we laughed at his ideas of correct breathing or his cures for the piles, then we were just *wrong,* because he'd read it in *All You Want To Know About Your Innards,* or some such tome, so he *knew.* But if you just ignored his existence, you undermined his whole basis for living."

"And Gottlieb did that?"

"I tell you, I once saw him come into the Shakespeare, where Natalya and Peter Fortnum had been holed up at a table by Des Capper. Gottlieb wanted to speak to Natalya —the usual urge to make sure that she did *exactly* as he demanded at some moment of the score, because he has this need for *total* control and a terrible mistrust of anyone else's creative powers. Anyway, instead of asking Des to go away, he just walked over, pushed against his shoulder, and pointed. Des was in full flood about something or other as usual, but he was so astonished he got up, whereupon Gottlieb simply sat down and started in on whatever he wanted to talk about. And all this was done without a word, as if Des were some kind of intrusive insect."

"Yes," said Dundy meditatively. "One sometimes feels in this case that the wrong person got murdered."

"Oh, don't get me wrong," said Ronnie, putting up his hand. "I had no sympathy for Des. He was quite loathsome, but perhaps in ways that are more difficult to convey."

Dundy turned to another aspect. "You mentioned Mr. Fortnum and Natalya Radilova—"

"Ye-es."

"What's going on there?"

"Search me." Ronnie Wimsett shrugged. "They're keeping very quiet about it, whatever it is. I don't think even Gillian knows, and she and Peter are quite close."

"But you agree there's something going on?"

"Seems so. I know that Peter makes long phone calls involving speaking Russian, and German as well, and that he immediately afterwards likes to report back to Natalya. Apparently these calls are to Germany. Make of that what you will."

"Why doesn't she make them herself?" wondered Dundy.

"I'd guess because she only speaks Russian. Peter is a great linguist. Also she's very involved with rehearsals. She arrived late and has an immensely demanding part, while Peter has quite a small one. I don't imagine it has anything to do with Des Capper's death."

"Except that Des Capper took an interest in it," said Iain Dundy.

* * *

When Ronnie had gone, Dundy sat in thought for some moments, then looked at his watch.

"I'm expecting a Russian interpreter at ten-thirty. I wonder if we could call on the hotel for some breakfast? Just tea and toast would keep the inner man happy. And we *are* investigating the death of their manager, however glad most of them seem to have been to see the end of him."

"I'll go and rustle something up," said Charlie, getting up. "They've got a new body from the Beaumont head-quarters here today as temporary manager. I'm sure he'll fall over backwards to keep us happy. He'll want us out as soon as possible."

When he had gone, Dundy remained thoughtful.

"The difficulty in this case," he said, "is sorting out the wood from the trees. I *think* whatever Fortnum and this Russian lady have been getting up to is undergrowth, to be cleared away. And yet it could be the most important thing that Capper was on to. More important than the Geary woman's drinking, obviously, or the Galloways' sleeping around. The trouble with dealing with arty people is, it's like dealing with foreigners. You don't know what they think is important."

"You mean like a Neapolitan would kill to revenge his sister's honor, whereas an Englishman wouldn't care tuppence about his?" asked Nettles.

"Aptly put. Though I'm not sure you're entirely up-to-date with Neapolitan mores." Dundy groaned. "I've just thought: This Radilova woman is *both* foreign *and* arty!"

"Right," said Charlie, coming back from the kitchen, a large tray in his hands. "Very sharp, the young man now in charge. Admits he's been sent from the head office to bring things round. Tea, coffee, toast. Something more substantial if we want it; we've only got to ring. *And* a bit of news to go with it."

"News? What's happened?"

"Literally news. On the news headlines at ten, and I happened to hear it in the kitchens. Five musicians have defected from the Moscow Radio Orchestra. They'd just completed the last concert on a short visit to Stuttgart."

"Ah! What happened?" asked Dundy, interested.

"Well, the concert had just ended with a performance of Tchaikovsky's *Wet Dreams* Symphony— Would that be right, do you think?"

"I very much doubt it, but it's a happy thought. Go on."

"Anyway, the conductor and orchestra acknowledged tumultuous applause, and by the time it was over, they found they were five members short: two violins, a cello, and two French horns. Ten minutes later the five were asking for asylum in the nearest police station. There's no doubt they'll get it."

"I suspect," said Dundy, "that this is going to make our task much easier." He looked at Charlie, who was stuffing toast into his mouth. "And now, young Peace, tell us what's on your mind."

"On my mind, sir?"

"On your mind. Come off it. You've been sunk in thought since you got here this morning. Hardly paying attention. Something occurred to you overnight, or maybe at the opera."

"Well . . ." Charlie stopped eating and looked at Dundy. "It's so fantastic. What's that French word? *Outré.* That's what it is, it's *outré.* Or maybe I just mean sick."

"Come on, man!"

"Well, can I just fetch something from upstairs?" Charlie jumped up and headed for the stairs up to the manager's quarters. A moment later he was back, carrying books. "Look, I'll just put it before you—right? Because if I just explain it, you'll probably think I'm out of my mind. See this book? It was by Des's chair when we first went through the room. It's William Ashbrook's *Donizetti and His Operas,* apparently the standard work borrowed from the local library. Des was wising himself up on the opera, having learned all there was to know about the play. The book was published in 1982. Read what it says about the first version of *Adelaide.*"

He laid the book in front of Dundy, who read it, nodded, and handed it on to Nettles.

"Right. Now here's the program the director gave us last night. Did you read it?"

"Skimmed through it."

"Read the account of the *second* version of the opera, which was only discovered, or put together, a year or so ago."

Dundy read it and looked up at Charlie, a light in his eyes that was the beginnings of comprehension.

"Yes?"

"Now look at this. *Heat and Dust.*"

"Why on earth—?"

"Remember the note in Des's little book? HAD 9? With an arrow pointing to the side. The note *both* belonged on the page about getting Gottlieb *and* referred back to earlier speculations. Look at page nine."

He put the book in front of Dundy. Dundy read it and looked up, aghast.

"I don't believe it."

Charlie stood there silent. He knew that the words meant the opposite of what they said.

"You don't mean—?"

"Maybe that's how Des intended to 'Get Gottlieb,' " said Charlie.

For a moment there was silence. Then it was interrupted by a knock on the door. The police interpreter had arrived, but he was not really needed. He had met up with Peter and Natalya in the foyer, and both of them were cock-a-hoop, ready to tell all. Peter's exuberance dominated the small manager's office, now decidedly overcrowded.

"Right," he said, rubbing his hands, when they were somehow settled in. "Now we can come clean."

"I suppose it's no good giving you a lecture about how serious an offense it is, misleading a police officer?" asked Dundy.

"No, because this was a once-in-a-lifetime affair, and there was really nothing else we could do. I promise never to do it again and all the things schoolboys promise, but I'm not going to pretend I'm sorry."

"Who precisely is it who's defected?"

"Natalya's father—one of the violinists. And one of the French horns is a young man she's . . . friendly with. I should say there's no romantic interest between us at all, just so you don't get things wrong."

"Only a very deep friendship," said Natalya in Russian, and in a very Russian way.

"I see. Tell me, was all this cloak-and-dagger stuff necessary? Aren't things much freer, more open, at the moment in Russia?"

Natalya understood that and said something vitriolic in her own language.

"She said, in effect, 'Tell that to the Ministry of Culture,' " put in the interpreter.

"That's it, you see," said Peter. "Glasnost just isn't fil-

tering down. The ministry is run by the same combination
of bureaucrats and secret policemen, and they're not
changing their ways. Now, Natalya has been allowed
abroad before, but there has never been any question of her
father being allowed to go at the same time. Natalya has
always been adamant in her own mind that she would
never defect and leave her father behind. Her mother died
young, and they are very close. Her father is with the Moscow Chamber Orchestra, but he deputizes with the Moscow Radio Orchestra when they need a particularly large
band or when there is illness. Which there was. Just before
coming away on this German tour. Five string players fell
ill. . . . I think I should say there may have been a bit of
skulduggery, because Natalya somehow hoped her father
would be coming before the orchestra even left Moscow."

Peter grinned at Natalya, who smiled mysteriously into
her lap.

"Not my business at all," said Dundy.

"I imagine it was something nasty in their vodka at a
drinking session," resumed Peter. "Anyway, her father
was called on, and for once bureaucracy and the KGB
were caught napping: He was allowed out of the country
while his daughter was already outside. All this phoning
has been to check that he got out, to confirm plans, and so
on—all under the guise of innocent-sounding messages
from daughter to father. It's as simple as that."

"And these five didn't want to defect until the tour was
completed?"

"That's right. The regular members of the orchestra insisted on that. For the honor of the orchestra and so as not
to cast a shadow over the whole trip for the others, who
would practically have been locked in their hotel rooms.
They had a series of concerts in Hamburg, Mannheim, and

Frankfurt, then this final one in Stuttgart before flying back. They just got to the end of the *Winter Dreams* Symphony—"

"What an odd name for a symphony," put in Charlie.

"—and *whoosh* they were away. There's no doubt they will be given asylum in Germany. There's so many orchestras there that certainly one or another will want them."

"And Miss Radilova will be joining her father?"

"She hasn't decided where she will live. She's had lots of offers since the concert and last night's *Adelaide*. She's been parrying them with talk of the Ministry of Culture, who normally arrange all this sort of thing, and with a very heavy hand, too. Now she can talk over with Brad Mallory which to accept. A good soprano is never going to starve."

"Was Mr. Mallory in on all this?"

"No."

"That seems odd. He is her agent, isn't he?"

"Yes, but the explanation is simple: He didn't seem to Natalya to be completely reliable. She didn't feel she could trust him not to let something out, say something indiscreet. And I must say I agree with her. So she used me because I could speak German and Russian."

"Right," said Dundy, stirring in his seat. He felt sure that he had now cleared part of the undergrowth away. Was there anything of more vital growth to be revealed? "Well, as far as it goes, that's clear enough. You had no hint that Des Capper was on to all or any of this?"

"No. The phones in the rooms all go through the hotel switchboard, so presumably he could have listened in. Or he could have listened outside my door; he wasn't above doing that. But it was all in German or Russian, and all in coded language, so really I don't think he could have made anything of it. Not anything specific."

"He could have guessed," said Dundy. "It was a fairly obvious possibility."

"Yes, I expect a lot of people wondered," agreed Peter.

"Which brings us," said Dundy, "to what you did on the night of the murder."

Peter Fortnum seemed to lose several degrees of confidence and looked distinctly uneasy.

"Come, come," said Dundy. "You know, I know, everybody knows, that you didn't spend all that time lost in the corridors."

"No," admitted Peter. "Though one can. It wasn't a bad story, and you couldn't have disproved it. Only in fact Connie Geary's room is very close to the main stairwell, so it was comparatively easy to find. I went through the dining room, through the Shakespeare—"

"And Mrs. Capper was there?"

"Oh, yes. Then I went upstairs and fetched the gin. . . . I'd already decided to phone Stuttgart then rather than after the end of the play. Then I could give the news to Natalya as soon as I came off. . . . They put an appalling extra cost on all the calls you make from your rooms here—"

"English hotels are scandalous at that," agreed Dundy.

"—so I went to the pay phone in one of the little alcoves. I am *not* one of the Piccadilly Fortnums, by the way, if they exist, and money is always scarce. That alcove —you can go and look—is a dark little place, and anyone phoning there is not conspicuous. I dialed and then waited while it rang and rang . . ."

"Yes, go on."

"While I was standing there, someone went past. He

didn't see me. He went on—didn't go down the stairs, but went past. You're familiar with the geography up there, are you?"

"As familiar as a day or two's acquaintance can make me."

"The first door after the stairwell is the first-floor door to the Cappers' flat. I'm sure it was there that he knocked. It was not more than a few steps after the stairwell, though I couldn't actually see the door."

"Knocked—and went in?"

"Yes. There was a call; then I heard the door open. Then they answered in Stuttgart, and I didn't pay any more attention."

"You haven't told me yet," said Dundy, "who it was who went past."

"No, I know. I wish I didn't have to. I've nothing against him. But it was Brad Mallory."

Dundy looked at Charlie, then down at the books, and in the crowded little room there was silence.

15

EN SUITE

When the little office was cleared and the Russian interpreter had gone off to hobnob with Peter and Natalya Radilova in the Shakespeare Bar, the three policemen who were left sat for some moments in thought.

"Brad Mallory is one of the ones I wondered about," said Dundy at last.

"Me, too," said Charlie. "To be honest, there were others, too: I wondered why this American was so often around the Saracen if he loathed Capper's guts. I wondered why Mrs. Capper didn't ring up to the flat to find out what had happened to Des after the Interval . . ."

"But both those oddities were probably explicable in terms of character," said Dundy. "The tenor is naturally gregarious. Mrs. Capper is a natural doormat."

"Right. But you can't say the same for Brad Mallory. His actions make no sense in terms of character or of anything else. First of all, he leaves the concert halfway through to flap his way to the hotel, and then he expects us to believe that he was so affected by dear Singh's performance that he had to come back to his room to recover himself. The man's an agent, after all!"

"Wouldn't seem to be much future for him in his own profession," commented Nettles.

"Right," agreed Dundy. "There is Singh enjoying a fabulous success, apparently, with critics and opera directors there to hear him—pressured to come by Mallory himself. And we know for a fact—Singh told us—that offers were made to him to work, future engagements, during Interval and later. But what had Mallory done? Sloped off and left Singh to receive all the plaudits and offers of engagements on his own, holding court in the backstage rooms in the Town Hall. What's an agent for if not to take care of things like that?"

"And it wasn't only Singh," chipped in Charlie. "He was also agent, at least in the West, for Natalya Whatsername. She was a great success in the first half, and she was singing again in the second. He didn't even bother to stay and hear her but left her in the lurch, without translator or any sort of intermediary. If she was any ordinary singer in the West, surely she'd have given him the old heave-ho and got herself an agent that didn't go down with palpitations every time his pet protégé sang."

"One other thing," put in Nettles. "He looked in at the Shakespeare on the way up to his room. If he was wanting peace and quiet to recover in, why would he do that? He was looking for someone, and it's a fair bet it was Des Capper."

"It is," agreed Dundy. "Because look at the sequence of events earlier in the evening when he left the Saracen. He'd been in the Shakespeare, and he came out of the main entrance to go to the Town Hall, immediately followed by Des Capper. Now, let's conjecture that precisely then, on the way out of the Shakespeare and through the foyer, Des came up to him—timing it purposely, Mallory being on his way to Singh's triumph—and said something that showed him his secret had been guessed."

Nettles looked ahead of him, hoping to hide the fact that he was not too sure he understood what the secret in question was. Charlie nodded vigorously, knowing all too well.

"That all makes sense," he said with an enthusiasm born of a love of the chase. "But did you get why he thought he could use Mallory and Singh to 'Get Gottlieb'?"

"I think so. I *think* I sorted it out," said Dundy. "Let's get it clear in our minds. Let's go back to that rehearsal we've heard about from more than one witness. It was a rehearsal with full cast and orchestra, but it wasn't a dress rehearsal. I checked that this morning, by the way, with the director. The tenor, Krister Kroll, was in stage costume. That was because he has to wear that rather camp number in furs and tartan. The rest were in mufti."

"I don't get the point," said Nettles. "Remember I haven't seen the show."

"But you read the program. Anyway, as far as I can reconstruct it, this is what happened. The tenor entered at the back of the stage and launched into his big tune. He's got quite a nice voice, but small, and it was quite ineffective—wouldn't have penetrated beyond the third row of the stalls, even I could hear that. So Gottlieb made him come to the front of the stage, and that totally upset the production. Natalya Whatsit got upset, and Brad went up onstage to calm her down, accompanied by Singh—Brad Mallory being the solicitous singers' agent at this point, you notice. How much he could do to calm her down without a common language I don't know, but he certainly tried. Now, at this point Des Capper arrived backstage to assert his right to go everywhere and poke his finger in everything."

"Yes," said Nettles, still puzzled. "He spoke to Peter Fortnum."

"That's right. Then the staging was altered, the scene played through to the end, then a break was called. We needn't go into that. But what would someone arriving at that point in the rehearsal think?"

"That the Third World War was about to start and the Germans were on the other side as usual?" suggested Nettles.

Charlie jumped up and down excitedly. "No! He'd see Singh up there onstage, in civvies like the rest, and he'd assume that he had a part in the opera. Remember that he made that endearing little joke to Fortnum about the Indians running the corner shops?"

"And not only that," insisted Dundy. "Remember that when Fortnum and Gillian Soames first arrived at the Saracen, he thought they were 'the operatic lady and gentleman.' He not only got the wrong people, but he was wrong about Singh, too. He wasn't singing in the opera, only in a concert."

"I still don't quite see—" began Nettles.

"It means," said Charlie, bubbling on, "that if he wanted to get even with Gottlieb, the best way to do it was through the opera—prestige affair, second big event of the festival, the stepping-stone for Gottlieb taking over the festival as a whole. And Des, getting it wrong as usual, thought he could get at the opera via Singh, who he thought was in it."

"What he thought, I'm sure," agreed Dundy, "was that he could bring the whole thing down around Gottlieb's head by going to the tabloids with a really grubby little story that they'd love. The fact that he'd also destroy Singh's career—and probably Mallory's, too, in the process—wouldn't have worried him. Why would it? He had no reason to love them." He got up and looked at the other two. "Come on. I think it's time that we talked to him."

They got together their things and went out of the office. As they passed the reception desk in the foyer, Iain Dundy pulled out the guest book and found Mallory's rooms. They constituted the Grand Suite—rooms 116 and 117. As they went up the staircase, they threw a glance into the Shakespeare. The new manager, a fair-haired, efficient looking young man, was coping with the help of Dawn. It was getting on for two, but the bar was very full.

"Ghouls," said Dundy.

Once up on the first floor, the policemen began to have a renewed sympathy with Peter Fortnum's point about the geography of the place. Yes, this *was* a hotel that you wouldn't necessarily get the hang of in a few days. After a few abortive sallies up dead-end corridors and down stunted flights of stairs that led nowhere, they finally came, almost by accident, it seemed, upon room 116. It was next to room 145. Dundy listened outside the door of room 116, then room 117, and finally knocked on the latter door. There was a moment's pause and then a reasonably confident sounding "Come in."

They went in to what was obviously one of the best rooms in the hotel. It was, in fact, a sitting room with bedrooms leading off from either end and a gleaming bathroom visible through a half-open door. In the sitting room there was a large television and radio, a dining table and chairs, and coffee tables dotted here and there. The furniture was either old or new-old, Dundy couldn't decide which. On one of the coffee tables was a tray with plates and glasses on it. Brad and Singh had obviously just lunched on something sent up from the kitchens. Dundy

wondered whether Mallory was becoming embarrassed by
Singh or fearful for his discovery. A half bottle of German
wine stood on the dining table, and beside it a bottle of
Coca-Cola.

Singh was sitting in an armchair on one side of a little
table, reading *Uomo,* or perhaps just studying the fashion
plates. He looked chubby and satisfied, and Dundy
thought there might be a suspicion of makeup on his face.
Brad Mallory was sitting on the other side, a cravat tucked
airily into his open shirt, suede shoes on his feet. In spite of
such old-fashioned dash in his attire, it struck Dundy that
he looked very small. As he put his book down hurriedly
on the table and bustled to welcome them all in, he looked
apprehensive, almost frightened. He was not a good dis-
sembler of fear. Dundy bent down and took up the book.

"Ah, press-cuttings," he said. "I hear you had a great
success at the concert, sir." Singh, who had watched the
bustle as a disinterested observer, allowed his sallow
cheeks to crease into a smile but then let them sink back
into handsome repose. "I haven't had time to read the
reviews myself, but I hear you gave a very remarkable
performance."

"The reviews are *very* good, *very* gratifying," said Brad
with a nervous, jerky intensity. "It's the beginning of a
brilliant career for Singh. But I don't suppose all three of
you will have come to talk about music, Superintendent?"

"No, indeed, sir. I wonder if we could speak to you
alone? No reason for bothering Mr. Singh in this instance."

Brad Mallory seemed both nervous and yet glad. "Of
course, yes. Do you mind, dear boy? The video is in your
bedroom. You seem to have been up half the night with it.

I'm sure you have something you'd like to play over again."

Singh smiled again and got up gracefully. He moved as if he had studied deportment with some very aged teacher, possibly with Mr. Turveydrop himself. As soon as he had shut the door, the policemen heard a click, then the opening music of *Mary Poppins*.

When he heard it, Brad Mallory flinched, as if this were a masterpiece with which he was all too familiar. Then his face dissolved into a smile.

"The dear boy," he said, looking round at them. "So faithful to his old favorites."

He waved Dundy and the other policemen to seats, but Dundy waited before he accepted.

"The dear boy seems to have pleased the critics as much as he affected you," he said, tapping the collection of pasted-in reviews. "It must be a disadvantage to you in your job to be so easily incapacitated emotionally."

Brad Mallory looked disconcerted. "It *is*," he said. "But that's one of the penalties one pays for the artistic temperament."

Iain Dundy sat down and gave him a hard look. "Mr. Mallory," he said. "I'm not going to beat about the bush or get into little sparring bouts with you. And I wish you'd drop this performance."

"Performance?"

"It seems to me you're giving a *performance* as an aesthete, practically a parody of one. You remind me of a character in a not very good detective story from the twenties. You also seem to me to be giving a parody performance of a homosexual."

"Like the chaste apprentice in the play," put in Charlie.

"He's doing a parody of the *Carry On* homosexual, and you're doing the quivering aesthete one."

"I really don't think you understand the *feelings* of someone who—"

Iain Dundy leaned forward in his chair. "Come off it, old cock. You're a bloody singers' agent. If Singh was such a triumph at the concert the other night, your job was to remain there and talk to the important people you'd invited to hear him. Natalya Radilova was something of a hit, too, and she couldn't rub more than two words of English together. Your job was to stay down there, and you'd have to be a bloody bad agent not to do it. I don't believe you're that. Why did you come away?"

Brad's voice came feebly, hardly penetrating the pepped-up jollities of *Mary Poppins* from the next room.

"I've told you: Singh is something very *special* to me. His singing affected me profoundly."

"Codswallop! If you were that knocked all of a heap emotionally, why did you look in at the Shakespeare before you went up to your room? You were looking for someone. And I may as well tell you that you were seen knocking on Des Capper's door at twenty past eight."

Brad Mallory's jaw dropped, and he gave out a little squawk, like a strangled chicken.

"No! No!"

"Oh, yes. I tell you, you were *seen*. And I've thought all along your story wasn't worth a bean. I think you came back because of something Des Capper said to you as you left the Saracen on your way to the Town Hall."

Again there was this little squawk, and Brad Mallory writhed in his chair as if he were sitting on hot coals. Then quite suddenly he went still, sagging down into the chair like a half-empty sack of potatoes—small, pathetic, tired.

He had dropped the mannerisms, but it was as if the mannerisms had become his self and there was nothing remaining. His eyes stared ahead, the most lively things about him. He was calculating how much he could tell.

"Since you know . . ." he said in a low voice, hesitating as he chose his revelations with care. "Yes, he did say something to me as I was leaving to go to the concert. . . . He'd already said something loaded in the bar about always meaning what he said. Then when I left he caught up with me in the foyer. . . . I won't say what he said. It's not relevant. . . . By the time I got to the concert, my mind was in turmoil! Absolute turmoil!" He caught Dundy's eye and dropped the mannerism. "I was greeting everyone I knew, everyone I'd asked there, and I was casting around in my mind what I could do. I tried to phone him before the concert started, but there was no answer. . . . He was in the courtyard, watching the play, I believe. . . . I went in for the first half of the concert. Luckily I had an aisle seat at the back. I couldn't settle, couldn't concentrate on anything. . . . During the letter scene, Natalya's aria, just before Singh's pieces, I slipped out and rang him again. This time he was in. I said I had to see him, and at once. I said there was an interval coming up in the concert and that I'd come up to the Saracen at about a quarter or twenty past eight."

"What was his reaction?"

"Very genial . . . in his dreadful way. . . . Gloating, really. But before he rang off, he said: 'Not that it will do you any good, Mr. Mallory, but I'm quite happy to have a natter about it.'"

"Right," said Dundy, stretching his legs. "Well, that's clear enough so far. Except, of course, that you've skated over the little matter of what Capper was threatening you with."

"It's not rele—"

Dundy held up his hand. There was no reason why Mallory should be allowed to get off this particular hook.

"There's no way this discussion is going to make any sense unless the whole thing is brought into the open. For the moment, this will be among ourselves. What would need to come out at any future trial I can't possibly say as yet. May I suggest that what Des said to you as you were leaving for the Town Hall—"

"*No!* Please, no!"

"—was something like: 'So you're off to see your little castrato performing, are you, Mr. Mallory?' "

Nettles blinked. So that *was* it! The little bundle in the chair, after a brief spasm of life, collapsed again. He looked like Grandmother Smallweed, needing to be shaken up. At last he said:

"Actually what he said was 'Give my best wishes to your pet castrato.' "

"Right," said Dundy, still refusing to let Mallory off the hook. "I'm sure we're all better off for having that out in the open. Now, I think you'd better explain to us all exactly what a castrato was—*is*—don't you?"

Brad Mallory swallowed and thought. When he spoke, it was very low, as if he were reading to himself from a dictionary of music.

"It was a man who had been castrated just before puberty to preserve his high singing voice. They chose boys with beautiful voices, of course, and as it developed, it became something quite unique—full, brilliant, agile. They used the castrati in the papal choir right up to the end of the nineteenth century, but in opera they more or less died out early in the nineteenth century. The practice had become . . . unacceptable. The castrati were very spoiled, demanding, capricious, vain, and people got tired of their whims. They also became very fat, so they became ridiculous in heroic parts. But a lot of operas *need* that kind of voice: Handel, Gluck, early Mozart, early Rossini. Nowadays they use women for the parts, or countertenors, but it's not right."

"A countertenor, as I understand it," said Dundy, "is a choirboy who keeps his voice high by a big effort, right?"

"Something like that. The trouble is, the castrato roles call for brilliance and volume, and a countertenor voice is too weak; it won't fill a modern opera house. And a woman's voice is quite different, too, and she always looks like a woman in men's clothes." He cast them a look of feeble cunning. "It's a problem nobody has been able to solve."

"Until you came along," said Dundy quietly. "Until you decided to fill a long-felt want."

Brad Mallory sparked up a little. "It's not as though there weren't any eunuchs around! People talk as if you couldn't do that today. That's just ignorance. It's being done all over the world—Turkey, India . . ."

"Yes, indeed: India. How did you come to know about the survival of the practice in India?"

Brad Mallory looked down into his lap and again spoke low. "I went there often when we used to arrange a World Theater Festival in London. I was one of the directors. I got to know all the major Indian troupes and some of the lesser—"

"These would have been some of the lesser, wouldn't they?" Dundy shook his head. "This was something that Des Capper also proved to be expert in, wasn't it?"

"Damn the man! Damn the bloody little know-it-all!

. . . Yes, I suppose so. We never talked about *how* he came to know. Part of his Indian experiences, presumably."

"Yes, it must have been. Of course, he'd never done most of the things he claimed to have done, but he had been there. This is what I think happened. Des came along to the rehearsal of *Adelaide,* and he happened to come backstage at the moment when you and Singh had gone onstage to comfort or reassure Natalya Radilova. He'd always assumed that Singh was 'an operatic gentleman,' in his words, and this confirmed him in his mistake."

"I can't think what part he imagined he played."

"Ah, but remember that the version of *Adelaide* that is being played here is Donizetti's rewrite from the 1830s, which was only discovered last year. When he went to the standard work on Donizetti, all he found was an account of the *original* opera of 1825, written for the castrato Velluti. So he assumed that Singh was playing Velluti's part of Robert the Bruce. What was actually going on onstage during the bit of rehearsal he saw meant little to him, because it was in Italian, and he hadn't then done a great deal of homework on the opera. He was looking for some way of getting revenge on Gottlieb, particularly later, after the scene in the Green Room. He didn't have much luck with Gottlieb's taste in young girls, because his minder was being careful. So when he got the idea that you had got hold of a *real* castrato for the Velluti part, he got the notion of getting at Gottlieb by turning his operatic triumph into a scandal and disaster that the popular press would seize on like vultures over carrion."

"That's something I don't quite understand, sir," said Nettles. "Would they have been that interested? Opera's pretty much of a minority interest."

"Oh, but they would, they would." Dundy turned to Mallory. "I'm sure you realized that throughout."

Mallory nodded sadly. "Oh, yes. I always knew the public would never stand for a castrated male if they knew. Imagine what the *Daily Grub* would make of the sick tastes of"—his voice took on an Australian twang— " 'so-called culture vultures.' Think of the great mountain of pretended outrage and vulgar ridicule they would pile up. They would have a field day. If it were known, Singh could never perform in public again. People would be sickened."

"And Gottlieb's opera would be a disaster. He would be buried in sludge. Except, of course, that unknown to Des Capper, Singh had nothing to do with *Adelaide*. It would have been you who was buried."

"So what we think happened," put in Charlie, "is that Capper saw the rehearsal, went away and read about Donizetti writing the opera for a castrato, and something clicked in his mind, something he remembered from his Indian experiences."

"That's it," resumed Dundy. "India has been in everybody's minds recently, what with *Jewel in the Crown, Gandhi, A Passage to India,* and the rest. No doubt Des bored his saloon-bar regulars with his superior knowledge of the place each time one of them was shown on television. But knowledge he did have, and some reading, too, and when he thought of the subject of eunuchs, he remembered the hijras. He not only remembered them. There was a note in his little book of useful bits of information: HAD 9. He'd remembered that they appeared in *Heat and Dust* and had gone away and looked them up."

"I still don't understand who or what the hijras were," said Nettles. "Or *are.*"

"Are, definitely. Perhaps you could tell him, Mr. Mallory," said Dundy. "I presume it was from them, or through them, that you—what shall we say?—acquired Singh?"

Brad Mallory flinched. His voice was still low, as if he were a great distance away. "They are bands of traveling entertainers. They perform on the streets, at stag parties and suchlike occasions. Probably it would have been at a stag party that Capper saw them. They're hermaphrodites and eunuchs, and their act is scabrous, very sexual, really rather horrible. There is a religious basis somewhere—they have a shrine in Gujarat—but it's not very strong. In fact, for the ordinary Indian they're the next thing to outcasts, though they're very often beautiful, weirdly so, and sometimes talented. Sometimes they buy children; sometimes they kidnap them. Then they castrate them."

"As you knew from your visits to India."

"Yes. I saw a troupe of them the very first time I went there. They fascinated me. They planted a seed in the back of my mind. And when early operas became more and more popular, I thought: *That's* what is needed. Only that sort of voice can really do justice to the music."

"And probably you were right. As we can see from these reviews." Dundy tapped the already pasted in collection of reviews. "They all exclaim how *different* Singh's voice is from the usual countertenor—so much more powerful and brilliant. They guess it's something to do with his being Indian. None of them guesses the real reason. It's interesting that Des Capper did. I wonder what gave him the clue."

"I don't know. I always insisted that Singh was English," said Brad Mallory. "I think I overdid it and gave him the first clue."

"Yes, and I suspect that he was puzzled by your homosexual performance. I suppose you did that to give Singh some kind of sexual identity?"

"Yes. I adopted them gradually, as if I was changing my . . . my sexual orientation. It was a preparation for when I would bring Singh forward, launch him on his career."

"But I suspect that Des learned from the room maids here that there didn't seem to be anything going on between you. 'Where do they do it?' he asked in his little book. . . . But you haven't told us how you procured Singh."

"If you're suggesting that I had him . . . *done,* you're mistaken," said Brad with a brief spurt of fire. "He was twelve when I saw him and had already been . . . operated on. I listened to several of the boys, heard their singing voices, chose the one that seemed most beautiful and most Western. Then I arranged for the boy to be adopted by an Indian couple that I knew in this country. He had no obvious parent or protector, so it was quite easy. From the day he came here he has been having music lessons. Everything has been geared towards his debut. . . . The man who will show us how Handel opera should be sung. . . ."

His voice faded into silence, but then he looked wildly round at the other three men. "I mean, *why not?*" he almost cried.

They didn't tell him. They left a pause, and then Dundy said quietly: "I imagine it hasn't been easy."

Brad Mallory smiled sadly. "Oh, no. It hasn't been easy. As you've seen, he's very vain and childish. It's almost as if he stopped growing up when . . . I'm used to artists who view the world as revolving around themselves. That's usual. And they are *artists.* Singh is a baby. At the center there is . . . a hole. Sweet nothing. And he can be cruel, too. To defenseless things. And he eats sweets. . . ."

"Eats sweets?" asked Nettles, mystified.

"I tell him not to. Already he's getting very chubby. If he becomes grossly fat, he will remind people of nothing so much as the old castrati, and then someone will ask questions. I tell him this over and over, but he takes no notice. . . . He has no gratitude."

"Gratitude?"

"You think he shouldn't have? Maybe. Anyway, he has none. I have this fear that in two or three years, when he has made his name, he will throw me over. All the financial gains will go to someone else. And I'll have nothing to threaten him with to keep him faithful. Any revelation about his . . . state would tarnish me much more than it would tarnish him. No, it has not been easy."

"I must say I'm rather glad to hear that," said Iain Dundy briskly. "Now, let's come to the night of the murder, sir. Let's hear exactly what happened?"

"Oh, God." Bradford Mallory went white. "It was a nightmare. It needed all my little . . . queer mannerisms to carry it off. . . . After I'd telephoned, I went back to the Town Hall to hear Singh's arias. He was brilliant, but I could hardly concentrate. What was I going to do? Was I going to offer him money? If so, how much? Was it possible to brazen things out? Because, after all, I didn't see how he could *know.*"

"You left the concert as soon as Singh was finished, did you? When was that?"

"About ten past eight, as I told you before. I was back at the Saracen by a quarter past. I came to this room, put a flannel over my face, lit a cigarette, and put it straight out. It was so *damnable,* after all my work, and just when it was coming to fruition. But I hadn't made up my mind what to do when I went along and knocked at his door.

That was about twenty past eight or so, as you said. If only I'd *decided* to face it out or *decided* to pay up. I put up a front, but I think Capper could see from the moment I walked into the room that I was beaten. He behaved as if I was a mouse he'd brought in and was preparing to torment."

"What was he like?"

"Oh—*horrible*. Rubbing his hands with glee, making barroom jokes, leering . . . He was quite disgusting. I tried to face it out, to say there was nothing to it, but the mere fact that I was there told him that wasn't true. He said a medical examination could prove it one way or another. He said he had a good mate on the *Daily Grub*. I could believe it. It's just the paper Des Capper would know someone from. He said it was the sort of story that paper would love, and he was right there: salacious, voyeuristic, anti-art, and the racial overtones wouldn't have come amiss—they could make something of them. I can just see the headlines. They'd have gloated for days over the sick tastes of opera lovers who could watch a nonman who sang like a woman. . . . All this time he was rubbing his hands and leering and making elephantine innuendos. My God, he deserved to die. I shouldn't say that, but he did."

"What happened next?"

"I offered money, of course. That seemed to delight him even more. It was me wriggling on the hook. His hook. He positively chortled. It wasn't money he was after, he kept saying. It was to get even. I was quite bewildered. I asked him why he wanted to get even with me. What had I done? Or was it Singh he wanted to get even with? He said he had one or two little scores to settle against both of us, but it was neither, and so there was nothing in the world I could do about it. I just didn't understand. How could revealing Singh's secret get him even with anyone other than Singh or me? He was rubbing his hands and chortling to himself. I just didn't know what to do. It was like being in a maze."

"What *did* you do?"

"What could I? I kept thrashing around in my mind: Could I explain why I'd brought Singh over, trained him? Would he understand? Was there anything he wanted besides money? He was positively gleeful that there was nothing I could do: 'It's a very unfortunate position for you, Mr. Mallory,' he kept saying, 'caught up in a quarrel that's not your own. I'm afraid there's just no way you can prevent me making a splash of it.' He was loving it, of course. . . . Normally I'm quite tough. You're quite right about my little mannerisms; they've become a cover. If you deal with singers all the time, you've got to be tough, believe me. But this situation was beyond me. In the end, with his standing there grinning at me as I wriggled, I just turned and walked out."

There was silence in the room. "Are you telling me that you didn't kill him?" asked Dundy.

Mallory's face was suffused by a hopeless, beseeching expression. "Of course I didn't kill him. I knew there was no chance of your believing me; that's why I didn't even try to tell you part of the story. I knew I probably wouldn't believe it myself if I were in your shoes. But it's the truth. I'm not the killing type."

"When you left the room, he was still alive?"

"Yes!"

"What time was this?"

"About a quarter to nine. The Interval was still on— I

remember hearing talking and laughter coming up from the Shakespeare Bar."

"And you never went back to the flat?"

Brad Mallory swallowed. "I went back to the flat. I never went into it."

"What do you mean?"

"I went back to my room. It's just along the corridor, as you know. I lay down on the bed and tried to think. I was desperate for a way out, but there was none. Even in a maze you know there *is* a way out, but now it seemed as though I'd been put down in the middle of one which had had its way out blocked. But—I don't know—perhaps I'm a congenital optimist; perhaps I don't like admitting defeat. I convinced myself I hadn't pushed the money solution hard enough. Perhaps he was just playing with me, I thought, and was really after money all the time. Everyone responds to money, I thought, if you offer enough—and we hadn't even mentioned specific sums. I decided to try again."

"What time was this?"

"Just about nine. I saw the news headlines, downed a quick scotch, and went along that damned corridor again. My hand was just knocking the first knock at Capper's door when it struck me there were low voices inside. And the moment I finished knocking—"

"Yes?"

"I heard a cry—a grunt—and then a heavy thump."

"What did you do?"

"I ran. I knew then that someone had killed him. I ran back to my room and thought over what the hell I should do. For God's sake, I'm not stupid. I knew then that somebody was going to suspect me of murder."

His face was so agonized that it was almost possible to believe him. From Singh's bedroom came the sound of a high soprano voice assuring him that a spoonful of sugar would make the medicine go down.

His face had reported that it was almost possible to believe—and Dundy himself almost gave in to the sound of high strains or remorse . . . possibly of suffering words.

16

THE SHAKESPEARE AGAIN

The last thing Dundy did before he left the suite was caution Brad Mallory not to leave the hotel without getting police permission first. When the three of them were out in the corridor, Charlie noticed a look of dissatisfaction on Dundy's face, a look of niggling doubt. It disappointed him, but he respected the man's greater experience. Dundy walked on but paused at the little dark alcove where the telephone was. There was a sofa there, and an easy chair. Dundy took the latter and sent Nettles to the kitchens for three coffees. Then he took out a cigarette, lit it—the first time Charlie had seen him smoke—and soon began leafing through his notebook. The three of them sipped strong, hot coffee, and all of them kept silent. Charlie was wondering why Dundy was unsatisfied with Mallory as murderer and what were the consequences for the case if his story was believed. Nettles was somehow simultaneously thinking when his wife and new baby would be home and what would be the ideal side for England to field against the West Indies in the first Test. It was a companionable, not a strained, silence. After twenty minutes or so, Dundy's expression of dissatisfaction began to lift.

"You believe him, don't you?" said Charlie.

The disappointment in his voice was palpable. It had been his brilliant deduction that had led them to Mallory, and it should have been crowned by the coup of his arrest.

"I suppose I shouldn't," said Dundy slowly. "We wouldn't have any difficulty in making one hell of a good case against him. All I've got on the other side is instinct."

"Instinct about—?"

"Character, I suppose. I just don't feel he has it in him to commit murder. Oh, I grant you he's tougher than he's been pretending. His job proves that. And the motive is there all right. I believe what he says about Singh's career being ruined is true. It would be destroyed by the popular press. There might be a few recordings, because that's closed-door stuff, but a stage career? I doubt it. I suspect that there is one thing Mallory has lied about. I think it may be that he did "choose" Singh, did pick out the boy with the best voice and the best appearance, and then have him "done." And if that is so, he has a motive whether or not Singh's career would be ruined—because sure as hell *his* would be. The papers would crucify him. So there's no doubt whatever about motive. But guts, courage, bottle, nerve—call it what you will. I don't think he has it to the sort of degree that murder demands. I still think he's basically a gadfly, a dilettante. When he shed all those gay mannerisms, there somehow—how shall I put it?—there wasn't much left. I try to square him with all I've ever learned in my life about killers, and all I've ever read about them, and I can't."

"But where does that leave us, sir?" asked Nettles. "Back at square one?"

"No, of course not," said Dundy crossly. *"Think,* man.

Surely you can see that if we believe him it alters our whole perspective on the case."

"Time," said Charlie.

"Exactly."

They all three sat thinking about that for some moments. Downstairs, time had just been called. Dundy stubbed out his second cigarette and got up.

"We'll go down."

In the Shakespeare there were a few stragglers left. Newspapers were strewn around on the tables, mostly turned to the arts pages, and a collection of singers and orchestral players were laughing over an article in the *Times* in which Bernard Levin confessed that he was unable to take Donizetti seriously. At the sight of the policemen, they drank up and left. How they knew they were policemen was no mystery: In the Saracen at the time, it was a fair bet. Dundy noted that among the disappearing party was Krister Kroll, the tenor. He let him go and surveyed the rapidly emptying room with satisfaction. Then he went to the bar, where Dawn and the new temporary manager were tidying up the lunchtime debris.

"Ah, you would be the superintendent," said the new manager, coming round from behind the bar, his manner somewhere between the friendly and the ingratiating. He seemed a pleasant enough young man, but people in any way connected with the licensing trade never quite knew how to behave with policemen.

"That's right," said Dundy. "You've been got here quickly. Getting things round?"

The manager's face assumed a serious expression. "Oh, officially, there's nothing to get round. *Un*officially we may admit that perhaps the best appointment may not have been made last time, that there may be a few bridges to mend."

"I think I might like a brief word, eventually, on how that appointment came to be made."

"Of course. I was briefed about that before I was sent over. Oh, by the way, this came this morning from headquarters." He drew from his pocket a Saracen's Head envelope and handed it to Dundy. "We didn't think there was any need to bother about fingerprints since it had been through the postal mill. It's Capper's handwriting, isn't it? Sent the day he died, but by second-class mail."

There was no letter. What Dundy drew out of the envelope was a newspaper clipping. It was the medical column of one of the newspapers they had found in Capper's flat. It dealt, in laymen's terms, with a newly developed treatment for spastics.

"I think you'll find the appointment quite understandable when you know the facts," the temporary manager was nervously saying. "It's far from suspicious. In fact, redounding to the credit—"

"Right," said Dundy, cutting him short. "But before we go into that—"

"Yes? Anything we can do to help, of course."

"—I'd like to try a little experiment with Dawn here."

Dawn looked up, surprised. She was much more alert today, rested and in almost sparkling form. She had, of course, been very much the center of attention both at home and in the hotel. Now she looked puzzled but intrigued.

"I don't see—"

"You don't have to. It's quite simple, and something you're used to doing. Now, I want you to fill a tray with dirty glasses—or clean ones, if you haven't got enough—just as you did on the night of the murder."

"We do generally prefer to wash them by hand, Superintendent," said the fair-haired manager, then seemed to realize the fatuity of this remark.

"I'm sure you do, sir. You can do them later by hand if you like. Did you load up the tray on your own on the murder night, miss?"

"No, Mrs. Capper helped a bit."

"If you could help her, then, sir?"

As he watched them filling a large tray, which it seemed would be all Dawn could manage to lift or encompass the breadth of in her arms, Dundy was conscious that behind him, at the door into the foyer, there was a movement, a presence. He wondered if it were possible . . .

"Now it's full, isn't it? It's now exactly two-fifty. I want you to take it up, go through with the tray to the kitchens, stack the glasses into the dishwasher just as you did on Thursday, at the same sort of rate you did it then, and then set the machine going, do anything else that you—"

"Oh, my God, you know!"

Win Capper, standing at the doorway, seemed turned to stone, her usually sallow complexion turned to an unhealthy white. Dundy held Dawn back from rushing over to her, and after a minute she tottered forward and sat down on a chair. Dundy released Dawn, who swiftly poured a neat scotch at the bar and hurried over with it. She put it to Win's mouth, then sat beside her at the table and put her arm around her shoulders. Win stared down at the table, then took another gulp at the whiskey.

When she spoke, it was in a dull, flat voice. "I overdid it, didn't I? About how wonderful Des was and how he hadn't an enemy in the world."

"It did occur to me," said Dundy carefully, "that the wife of someone like Des Capper might think he was wonderful, but she couldn't remain unaware that other people didn't share the same view. Not in a pub, where she could see people's reactions to him and would probably overhear opinions of him."

Win nodded. She looked up now, and faint traces of color had begun to come back into her cheeks.

"I'm ready to come along with you. It's almost a relief. I was always afraid someone else was going to be charged. Dawn will help me pack one or two things, won't you, dear? I'd just like to say why I did it"—she patted Dawn's hand— "so you won't think so badly of me."

"I don't," said Dawn, only with an effort refraining from saying that she thought Win had done a public service.

"I expect by now you know what Des was really like. He was mean, cunning, and a slave driver. I should have left him years ago, but perhaps I'm a natural slave. Or I'd become one over the years. I was a nurse when I married him. Guess I just went from slavery to matron to slavery in a bar for Des. Seven years ago I got pregnant. I was over the moon. Des was pretty pleased, too. Me not getting pregnant was one of the things he used to throw in my face the ten years we'd been married. Then Kevin was born, and a few days later they told us he was a spastic. . . . It didn't make any difference to me. I only loved him the more. But that was the end for Des. If he wasn't a healthy, normal child, he just didn't want to know about him. He said you couldn't have an idiot child—that's what he called him—growing up in a pub. The customers wouldn't like it. He had to go into a home. So we put him in one in Lancashire, and I went from Carlisle to see him every Sunday. I didn't think I could ever forgive Des for that, but there was more." She put her handkerchief to her mouth and swallowed.

"The director," murmured the new manager.

"That's right. The director of Beaumont Hotels. He's got a spastic son, too. He brought him to our hotel in Carlisle, on his way to the lake district. He's a wonderful father, devoted, always taking the boy places, bringing him out, arousing his interest. Like I would do if I could see Kevin more than once a week. . . . Of course Des was all over his boy. You'd have thought he was Prince William the way he fawned. And he kept saying it made a *bond*—us having a spastic boy as well. The director was the only person I ever remember Des mentioning him to. And Des said if only we had a bigger hotel to run, with room to bring up a family and to get a bit of privacy—"

"The place in Carlisle is not one of our better hotels," put in the manager. "It's very small and inconvenient, with very little residential trade out of the summer season."

"That's right. Des desperately wanted to get somewhere with a bit of prestige. So he went on and on to the director about how he longed to get Kevin out of the home if only he could get somewhere with a bit of space for him to play, somewhere with a good staff, so I could be freer. After the director went, he used to send him anything he read on cerebral palsy and its treatment. Used to cut things out of papers and the like. Said it was so I shouldn't see them. 'Only set you off again,' he'd say. But he always sent them to the director. When Arthur Bradley died, Des heard about it through the grapevine, of course, and bombarded the director with hints of how he'd like the job and what a difference it would make for Kevin's life. . . ."

"That's true," said the manager. "That's how he got

appointed. The director told several people at Head office after we began to get hints that the appointment was not turning out well. Naturally he felt responsible."

"I won't say I ever believed Des," Win went on, dabbing at her eyes. "But I thought—hoped—that if we got it he'd have to keep his word. I should have known better. We'd been here a month when he wrote to the director and told him Kevin had had a setback and was hospitalized and it would be dangerous to move him. . . . The lying bastard! Kevin was just as he'd always been. But what could I do about it? That's when I decided he had to die. From then on I was just waiting for an opportunity." She got up, now quite steady, and turned to Dawn. "I'll get my things together now, dear, if you'll come with me. It won't take long. Then I'll be quite ready to come with you." She paused at the doorway. "They won't separate me entirely from my boy, will they, sir?"

Dundy hoped he was speaking the truth when he murmured: "No, I'm sure they won't."

As Win and Dawn went up the stairs, Dundy slipped out into the foyer and detailed a police constable to follow them and station himself outside the room. When he got back to the Shakespeare, the new manager had tactfully taken himself off. The others, inevitably, were wanting a bit of a natter.

"I *think* I can see why Brad Mallory's story changed everything," said Nettles, his forehead creased. "We've been going badly wrong over the times, haven't we?"

"Of course we have. Gently led astray by Win Capper. We put so much weight on Des Capper's promise to help at Interval and the fact that he didn't turn up that we began to assume that he was dead by then. But there was nothing in the medical evidence to suggest that he need have been.

It was slipshod thinking on my part. Once I'd established that Win must have spent the *first* period when Dawn was away pouring nice cold white wine, I began almost without noticing to exclude her—fool that I was! Because the first person you pay attention to when a husband has been murdered is the wife—and *vice,* of course, *versa.*"

Dundy sat for a moment in thought. "Actually, there were two things of importance in Brad Mallory's story, if we decided to believe it. The first was that Brad rang Des up from the Town Hall to make the appointment for twenty past eight. That meant Des knew well in advance that he wasn't likely to be able to help in the Interval. The second, if we believed him, was that he was *not* dead by Interval—probably not for some time *after* it. That didn't really alter things as far as the play people were concerned, though it let Peter Fortnum off the hook. But it did alter it for others."

"And for Win Capper in particular," said Charlie.

"Yes. I began making an alternative scenario in my mind. You know, people tend to divide murders into premeditated ones and ones done on the spur of the moment. But there is another kind: killings that are *intended* over a long period, the killer merely waiting for a convenient opportunity and then seizing it. That was what we had in this case."

"I think I'm there now," said Charlie. "I think I've got the opportunity Win seized on. Capper rang Win in the bar while Dawn was fetching the snacks."

"That's it, I'm sure. Knowing Des, he might do it, or he might not. But let's assume he did, at about a quarter past eight, when Dawn was in the kitchen getting the nuts and the cheese dainties. I suspect he did it because he wanted to gloat. He told Win she'd have to cope or get someone else from the kitchen, because he'd be holding someone over a slow fire. He may even have named him. We don't know how much he told Win about his activities and the people he wanted to 'get.' Anyway, she decided then and there that now was the time. As she said, she'd intended doing it for some months, and while the festival people were here was obviously a good time, since Des had put up so many backs. The fact that there was now going to be an interview of murderous potential made this an irresistible opportunity. She was getting ready the drinks for the Interval, which gave her a marvelous alibi for *this* period on her own. As she poured them out, her mind must have been working furiously."

"And she decided not to mention Des's phone call to Dawn when she returned," suggested Nettles.

"That's right. So that when he failed to turn up at Interval, the presumption would be later that he was dead by then. And even if the plan misfired—say, Des came down after his interview with Mallory—well, forgetting a phone call was no great matter. The plan could be put on ice."

"I did wonder," said Charlie, "why she didn't ring up to the flat after the Interval. I thought it must be because she knew he was dead."

"No, it was because she knew that he was alive. So, during the Interval she commented on Des's nonappearance to Dawn, and doubtless within the hearing of customers as well. Then, when Interval was finished, she had to make herself an opportunity. She packed Dawn off with glasses for the big kitchen dishwasher—an unusual procedure but easy to justify. Then she was off through the manager's office, up to the flat. She was just talking to Des —*making* conversation, by the table with the knife on it, perhaps about the problems at Interval—when there was

Brad Mallory's knock on the door. Des turned, she took up the knife she'd all along intended as the implement, and she shoved it in his back."

"Come to think of it," said Charlie, "that knife was always a pretty unlikely murder weapon for Brad Mallory."

"Right. It was Indian. It directed too much attention to Singh."

"Another thing," said Charlie. "That damp patch on the cover of the sofa in their flat. It probably came off her apron; she'd been washing up pretty well nonstop all evening."

"Yes. I think she leaned against the sofa to give herself purchase as she stabbed. When I thought about it, there was nobody else, other than Dawn, likely to leave that sort of wet patch."

"And provided she was back in time, she could wash off any blood in the sink in the bar."

"That's it. She went back into the bar, and she acted as usual for the rest of the evening. She wanted the body found as late as possible, of course, so that the *time* of the murder would be reasonably open. So she expressed no great worry about Des's nonappearance, and Dawn, and all the regulars in the bar, knew that Des was just the sort of person who would say he'd turn up and then not do so."

"He hated working in the bar," said Charlie.

"Yes, and it was only his wife who was inconvenienced. He treated her like a skivvy, and he didn't care who knew it. By closing time she thought it would be all right for the body to be found, so she talked to Frank and began to express worry. For a plan that was largely improvised at short notice, it was extremely cunning. It could very well have worked—except that I rather think that if we had charged anybody else, Win would have come forward and confessed. I can't see her letting Brad Mallory take the rap for her."

"Interesting question," said Charlie: "Would we have believed her confession?"

"That's rather a frightening thought," agreed Dundy.

The fair-haired head of the new manager appeared at the dining room door.

"Sorry to intrude. I've just been on the phone to head office. They're glad it's all cleared up, though the fact that it's Mrs. Capper does tie it in rather unpleasantly with the chain. But they've told me to make it plain that they'll do everything in their power in the matter of legal advice, defense, and so on. The director was very insistent on this. Blames himself a lot, as I said before. Feels that if he hadn't pushed for Capper's appointment none of this would have happened. And of course he feels very cut-up about the boy. . . ."

"I can't see the police pushing very strongly for a heavy sentence," said Dundy. "It would be hard to argue that she'd be a danger to anyone else in the future. The courts take a surprisingly lenient view, sometimes, these days, especially in cases of domestic murder."

They heard a sound from the stairs, and the policemen went out into the foyer. Win was coming down the stairs. Dawn was following, carrying a small suitcase. Win needed no help now. She was quite composed. As Charlie and Nettles went out to usher her from the door to the waiting police car, Dundy went forward to take her arm. She smiled at him, a smile he had not seen before, with some faded prettiness in it.

"I feel much happier now," she said.

17

THE WEBSTER

Much later that day, after a long interrogation of Win Capper, the policemen came back to the Saracen. The play was just over, and the audience was streaming out of the great gates or into the three bars. It had been full, of course. If it had not been booked solid before, the murder would have seen to it that it would be now. Rumors that an arrest had been made had rather disappointed most playgoers as they arrived. Secretly many of them had cherished the unlikely hope that at some point in the evening a uniformed cop would stride onstage and arrest somebody, preferably one of the Galloways. Now *that* would be something to tell one's grandchildren!

The policemen collected up their papers and anything they thought might conceivably be used as evidence at the trial. They told the temporary manager that the flat would be available to him in a few days, but he said he didn't fancy it and would use one of the hotel bedrooms. Then there was really nothing more to be done. Yet Charlie and Nettles felt that Dundy was oddly reluctant to be gone. He surely wasn't getting a taste for arty people, was he? Awkwardly they made conversation.

"You'd better be booking your ticket sharpish, hadn't you, sir?" asked Nettles.

"Ticket?"

"For *The Chaste Apprentice*. You'll want to see a performance, won't you, after all we've heard about it?"

"I suppose it might be an idea. I expect they'll let me in if I say I need it to set the seal on my case. As a Ketterick man I can't think why I've never seen a play here before."

"Personally I wish Singh was giving another performance," said Charlie. "Someone might guess the truth at any time, and that will be the end of his career. It would be something to boast about to the sort of girl from London University who fancies a black boyfriend: 'I'm one of the few people in the world who's heard a real castrato.' "

"You have a twisted sense of humor." Dundy's head jerked round. "Oh, I say, excuse me for a moment. Or actually you two can push off home."

But they didn't push off home. They made themselves discreetly scarce and watched while Iain Dundy walked up to Gillian Soames, who had appeared down the stairs from the upper rooms, having changed into civvy clothes. If the superintendent had been a younger man, they would have said that he was chatting her up. It must be said that Dundy got somewhere in a remarkably short time. Indeed, it was almost as if she had been waiting for him to make a move.

"I did wonder if you'd care for a drink," they heard him say after two or three minutes.

Charlie's foot moved for the last time to tap Nettles's ankle.

"I'd love one." Gillian glanced toward the Shakespeare.

"Or even a late supper?" said Dundy, moving towards

the street door. "There's a place I know—little Indian place—where they'll still be happy to serve us."

"That would be lovely," said Gillian, following him out into the High Street. "After a performance I always feel I could eat a horse."

Charlie and Nettles looked at each other.

"It has been known," said Nettles. "Policemen marrying actresses."

"Hope for me yet," said Charlie cheerfully.

"Drink?"

"What else?"

"The Shakespeare?"

Charlie looked towards the Shakespeare Bar and seemed to see the ghost of Des Capper leaning familiarly over the shoulders of his guests with his quack remedies, false information, and real threats.

"The Webster," he said firmly.

FREE FROM DELL

with purchase plus postage and handling

Congratulations! You have just purchased one or more
titles featured in Dell's Mystery 1990 Promotion. Our goal
is to provide you with quality reading and entertainment, so
we are pleased to extend to you a limited offer to receive a
selected Dell mystery title(s) *free* (plus $1.00 postage and
handling per title) for each mystery title purchased. Please
read and follow all instructions carefully to avoid delays in
your order.

1) Fill in your name and address on the coupon printed below. No facsimiles or
copies of the coupon allowed.

2) The Dell Mystery books are the only books featured in Dell's Mystery 1990
Promotion. No other Dell titles are eligible for this offer.

3) Enclose your original cash register receipt with the price of the book(s)
circled plus $1.00 **per book** for postage and handling, payable in check or
money order to: Dell Mystery 1990 Offer. Please do not send cash in the
mail.
Canadian customers: Enclose your original cash register receipt with the
price of the book(s) circled plus $1.00 **per book** for postage and handling in
U.S. funds.

4) This offer is only in effect until April 29, 1991. Free Dell Mystery requests
postmarked after April 22, 1991 will not be honored, but your check for
postage and handling will be returned.

5) Please allow 6-8 weeks for processing. Void where taxed or prohibited.

Mail to: Dell Mystery 1990 Offer
P.O. Box 2081
Young America, MN 55399-2081

Dell

NAME_____

ADDRESS_____

CITY_____STATE_____ZIP_____

BOOKS PURCHASED AT_____

AGE_____

(Continued)

Book(s) purchased:_____

_____

_____

I understand I may choose one free book for each Dell Mystery book purchased (plus applicable postage and handling). Please send me the following:

(Write the number of copies of each title selected next to that title.)

☐ **BLOOD SHOT**
Sara Paretsky
V.I. Warshawski is back—this time a missing person assignment turns into a murder investigation that puts her more than knee-deep in a deadly mixture of big business corruption and chemical waste.

☐ **FIRE LAKE**
Jonathan Valin
In this Harry Stoner mystery, the Cincinnati private eye enters the seamy and dangerous world of drugs when a figure from his past involves him in a plot that forces him to come to terms with himself.

☐ **THE HIT MAN COMETH**
Robert J. Ray
When a professional hit man who has his sights set on a TV evangelist wounds Detective Branko's partner instead, Newport Beach's hottest detective finds himself with a list of suspects that is as bizarre as it is long.

☐ **THE NANTUCKET DIET MURDERS**
Virginia Rich
A handsome new diet doctor has won over Nantucket's richest widows with his weight-loss secrets—and very personal attention. But when murder becomes part of the menu, Mrs. Potter stirs the pot to come up with a clever culinary killer.

☐ **A NOVENA FOR MURDER**
Sister Carol Anne O'Marie
"Move over, Miss Marple, here comes supersleuth Sister Mary Helen, a nun with an unusual habit of solving murders."
—San Francisco Sunday Examiner & Chronicle

☐ **SHATTERED MOON**
Kate Green
When a young woman gets involved with the L.A.P.D. and a missing person case, her most precious gift—her healing vision—becomes her most dangerous enemy, filling every moment with mounting menace. . . and turning the secrets of her past murderously against her.

☐ **TOO CLOSE TO THE EDGE**
Susan Dunlap
Jill Smith, a street-smart, savvy detective, finds herself trapped within a murder victim's intricate network of perilous connections.

☐ **A NICE CLASS OF CORPSE**
Simon Brett
When the sixty-seven-year-old Mrs. Pargeter checks into a seaside hotel for some peace and quiet, what she finds instead is a corpse in the lobby and a murder to snoop into on the dark side of the upper crust.

☐ **POLITICAL SUICIDE**
Robert Barnard
A member of Parliament meets an untimely—and suspicious—demise.

☐ **THE OLD FOX DECEIV'D**
Martha Grimes
When the body of a mysterious woman is found murdered, Inspector Richard Jury of Scotland Yard finds himself tracking a very foxy killer.

☐ **DEATH OF A PERFECT MOTHER**
Robert Barnard
Everyone had a motive to kill her. . . so Chief Inspector Dominic McHale finds himself stumped on his very first homicide case—puzzled by a lengthy list of suspects and a very clever killer.

☐ **THE DIRTY DUCK**
Martha Grimes
In addition to the murders being staged nightly at the Royal Shakespeare Theatre, a real one has been committed not too far away, and the killer has left a fragment of Elizabethan verse behind as a clue.

Dell

**TOTAL NUMBER OF FREE BOOKS SELECTED ___ X $1.00
= $_____ (Amount Enclosed)**

Dell has other great books in print by these authors. If you enjoy them, check your local book outlets for other titles.